KT-119-392

ANNA JACOBS

A Valley Wedding

Backshaw Moss Saga Book Three

HODDER

First published in Great Britain in 2022 by Hodder & Stoughton
An Hachette UK company

This paperback edition published in 2022

1

Copyright © Anna Jacobs 2022

The right of Anna Jacobs to be identified as
the Author of the Work has been asserted by her in accordance
with the Copyright, Designs and Patents Act 1988.

All rights reserved. No part of this publication may be reproduced, stored
in a retrieval system, or transmitted, in any form or by any means without the
prior written permission of the publisher, nor be otherwise circulated in any
form of binding or cover other than that in which it is published and without
a similar condition being imposed on the subsequent purchaser.

All characters in this publication are fictitious and any resemblance
to real persons, living or dead, is purely coincidental.

A CIP catalogue record for this title is available from the British Library

Paperback ISBN 978 1 52935 359 4
eBook ISBN 978 1 52935 357 0

Typeset in Plantin Light by Manipal Technologies Limited

Printed and bound in Great Britain by Clays Ltd, Elcograf S.p.A.

Hodder & Stoughton policy is to use papers that are natural, renewable
and recyclable products and made from wood grown in sustainable forests.
The logging and manufacturing processes are expected to conform
to the environmental regulations of the country of origin.

Hodder & Stoughton Ltd
Carmelite House
50 Victoria Embankment
London EC4Y 0DZ

www.hodder.co.uk

Also by Anna Jacobs

THE BACKSHAW MOSS SAGA
A Valley Dream
A Valley Secret

THE BIRCH END SAGA
A Daughter's Journey
A Widow's Courage
A Woman's Promise

THE ELLINDALE SAGA
One Quiet Woman
One Kind Man
One Special Village
One Perfect Family

THE RIVENSHAW SAGA
A Time to Remember
A Time for Renewal
A Time to Rejoice
Gifts For Our Time

THE TRADERS
The Trader's Wife
The Trader's Sister
The Trader's Dream
The Trader's Gift
The Trader's Reward

THE SWAN RIVER SAGA
Farewell to Lancashire
Beyond the Sunset
Destiny's Path

THE GIBSON FAMILY
Salem Street
High Street
Ridge Hill
Hallam Square
Spinners Lake

THE IRISH SISTERS
A Pennyworth of Sunshine
Twopenny Rainbows
Threepenny Dreams

THE STALEYS
Down Weavers Lane
Calico Road

THE KERSHAW SISTERS
Our Lizzie
Our Polly
Our Eva
Our Mary Ann

THE SETTLERS
Lancashire Lass
Lancashire Legacy

THE PRESTON FAMILY
Pride of Lancashire
Star of the North
Bright Day Dawning
Heart of the Town

LADY BINGRAM'S AIDES
Tomorrow's Promises
Yesterday's Girl

STANDALONE NOVELS
Jessie
Like No Other
Freedom's Land

Praise for Anna Jacobs

'[Anna Jacobs' books have an] impressive grasp
of human emotions'
The Sunday Times

'A powerful and absorbing saga – a fine example of
family strife and struggle set in a bygone age'
Hartlepool Mail

'Anna Jacobs' books are deservedly popular. She is one
of the best writers of Lancashire sagas around'
Historical Novels Review

'A compelling read'
Sun

'This is a rare thing, a pacy page-turner with a
ripping plot and characters you care about . . .
[Anna Jacobs is] especially big on resourceful,
admirable women. Great stuff!'
Daily Mail

'Catherine Cookson fans will cheer!'
Peterborough Evening Telegraph

Dear Readers,

I hope you enjoy reading this last story set in the Ellin Valley. I have very much enjoyed writing the four series. *A Valley Wedding* is the 14th book set in my imaginary valley – which sometimes feels a very real place to me.

When I first started writing seriously, I was also working full-time and we were raising teenagers, so it took a while to polish my skills to a professional level. I had just turned fifty when I heard the news that one of my books had been accepted after years of trying.

The first novel published was *Persons of Rank,* which won a $10,000 prize in Australia – and that paid off our mortgage. I was thrilled to be published and literally didn't sleep all night, just lay there feeling joyful. My economist husband was thrilled for me, and just as thrilled that this lump sum paid off our mortgage. He keeps my feet on the ground, thank goodness.

I remember thinking that if I wrote steadily, I might get as many as 10 novels published before I made my final exit. Shows how good I am at foretelling the future, eh? *A Valley Wedding* will be my 100th book published.

I still love telling stories as much as I always have and I'm not considering giving up writing or even slowing down. It's my favourite activity. I'm already planning my new series, but I shan't give you any details about it yet. I'll just let you know that my publisher was so pleased by the basic idea that they accepted my suggestion for the new setting after a two-sentence description of it. As a consequence, they have contracted me to write three more historical novels and set them there.

As for the characters who will be involved, they are lively enough now to have woken me several times in the middle of the night to 'show' me scenes. Well, that's what it always feels as if they do. I usually think about a series long before I start working on the stories which take place there.

And finally, on a personal level, I'll share with you my joy that this September will mark our 60th wedding anniversary. Something to celebrate big time. Dave and I have had a wonderful life together. In addition, he deals with the business side of my writing, so he's an integral part of the writing team. And it does take a team to turn a story into a book and sell it to the world.

Thank you for reading my story. I hope you enjoy it as much as I enjoyed writing it! I'll now go back to working on the next one.

All the best
Anna

A Valley Wedding

I

Lancashire, 1936

As Gwynneth Harte was getting her basket and purse ready to go shopping in town, the post arrived. She picked up the letter that had dropped through her door. It was addressed to her youngest son. Well, letters usually were. She turned it over and let out a muffled groan at the sight of the sender's name stamped on the back.

Lucas had already been to a week-long course at this workers' college and had come home thrilled to pieces. Apparently he'd done so well they'd found a private benefactor who would pay for him to go to Manchester University and become a doctor. It was something he'd wanted since he was a small child, caring for an old teddy bear and 'mending' its broken limbs.

She wished he was at home to open the letter and put her out of her misery about when he'd be leaving. She shouldn't begrudge him this chance and she didn't, but these people would take him away from her, she knew they would, and things would never be the same.

Three sons she had, all of them over thirty, and none of them had produced grandchildren for her to love. Well, during the past ten years when times were at their worst and little steady work available, how could they have married? As a widow, she'd often depended on their support.

Then, as life improved slightly and they were getting on their feet again, she'd fallen ill and nearly died, costing them a lot of money for an operation. Now, however, her two eldest sons were in employment and married, so surely there was hope that they'd start families?

She'd tried to introduce Lucas to suitable young women, but he'd told her bluntly that he didn't intend to get trapped in marriage because he was determined to become a doctor. That would take him years, so he wasn't likely to marry till he was at least forty, if then.

She'd known her youngest lad was clever, but no one she knew had ever had a son go to a university. What would happen to him there? Would it change him, make him look down on the rest of the family? She paused, head on one side. No, not their Lucas.

She was working as a part-time housekeeper and lived in the flat at the rear of her employers' house, but she hated the thought of living there on her own.

She mopped her eyes and blew her nose, telling herself to pluck up. She caught sight of the clock, snatched up the basket and hurried off to take the bus down the valley into Rivenshaw. What couldn't be cured must be endured, and best do that with a smile or you'd drive folk away.

Biff Higgins walked into the seedy pub in the poorer part of Rivenshaw, keeping a careful eye on the men sitting there, some of whom looked ready to cut your throat for twopence. He doubted anyone drinking in the middle of the day had any sort of job.

He walked up to the bar and asked the chap behind it for a half pint because in his experience as a private investigator, people who worked in pubs were usually more willing to talk to you if you bought something. He'd decided to lose the slight Irish accent he'd pretended to have last time he visited this town.

He paid for the drink and put a further shilling down on the counter, keeping his forefinger on it. 'I'm looking for Arthur Chapman. I was told he comes in here regularly.'

'What do you want him for?'

'I have some good news for him.'

After a searching gaze, the man said, 'The poor sod definitely needs some good news, for a change. He's the one in the corner by the fire.'

Biff turned to stare in that direction and saw a scrawny, sad-looking man of about the right age, who looked chilled through and was holding his hands out to the fire. Nodding thanks to the barman, he pushed the shilling across the counter, not surprised at how swiftly it vanished.

As a private detective, he'd found the heirs to the other two properties left by Miss Jane Chapman and her nephew, and now, hopefully, he was about to find the heir to the final house.

He sat down in a chair across the tiny table from the man, who seemed to be drinking lemonade, or was it water? If so, the barman must have taken pity on him and given him a drink so that he would have an excuse to stay and warm himself.

'Are you Arthur Chapman?' he asked quietly.

He got a suspicious glance in response. 'Who wants to know?'

'Biff Higgins.' He extended a business card.

After a slight hesitation the man took it, read it and dropped it on the table. 'Has she set a detective on me now?'

'She?'

'Don't pretend. That Mrs Hicks will do anything to keep me from my granddaughter.'

'I've never met or communicated with anyone of that name. I've been sent by Mr Albert Neven, a London lawyer, to find Arthur Chapman who has been left a bequest by a distant relative.'

That was greeted by a frown. 'That's my name, but who'd leave me anything? I've got no close relatives left.'

'It was a Miss Sarah Jane Chapman.'

After a moment's thought, he snapped his fingers. 'Ah. Dad's second cousin on his father's side. He allus spoke well of her. I didn't think she knew I existed, though.'

'She must have done, because she's definitely left you something.'

Arthur shook his head, clearly baffled.

Biff realised that the men sitting nearby had fallen silent and were trying to listen to their conversation. 'How about we go somewhere more private to discuss it, Mr Chapman? I could buy you a meal at the Star hotel. They're open for luncheon and I'm hungry, even if you aren't.'

'Well, I could certainly do with a good meal, so I'll thank you kindly for that offer.' He stood up, leaving the rest of his drink, so Biff left his beer. It had served its purpose and he didn't enjoy drinking in the daytime anyway.

At the hotel, the waiter glanced at Arthur and showed them to a table in the corner, away from the better-dressed folk.

Biff's companion seemed to relax a little once they were seated. 'Eh, it's a long time since I've been in a posh place like this.'

'They do excellent food. Let's order, then we can talk.'

When he nodded across the room, a waitress came to their table, smiling at him. 'Nice to see you here again, Mr Higgins.'

After she'd taken their order, Arthur asked abruptly, 'What has the old lady left me, then?'

'A house and its contents.'

Arthur gasped, then spoke in a shocked, croaky whisper, '*A house?*' Then he scowled. 'You're mocking me.'

'I'm not. It's the simple truth. She left houses to three of her distant relatives who'd fallen on hard times, people she thought deserved a helping hand.'

Tears came into Arthur's eyes and he blinked furiously. 'I don't deserve anything. I've made a mess of my life in the past two years. Yes, a right old mess, and all my own fault.'

'Well, now you've got a chance to sort things out.'

'As long as it's not too late.'

'What do you mean?'

'My wife died two years ago, an' I started drinking. I let myself get cheated out of what savings I didn't spend on beer. I'd talk to anyone, buy them a drink rather than go home to an empty house. I missed my Susan that badly I could hardly think straight for the first few months. We'd been wed since we were eighteen, you see, courting since we were fourteen.'

'Grief can do strange things to people.'

'Aye. I turned into such a drunken sot my son wouldn't speak to me an' I don't blame him.'

He was speaking in such a bleak monotone, Biff's heart went out to him.

'Then my daughter and her husband were killed in that big railway accident down south a few months ago. Her husband's widowed mother, who is a mean old devil, took my granddaughter in and got the minister of her church to speak for her as being a proper guardian. As if he knows her, he's a new man to this town, that one is!'

He stared into space for a few seconds, then said in a husky voice, 'She's not let me speak to my little Beatie since, not once, and has threatened to bring down the law on me if I go near them, even though I've give up the booze.'

'Could you not have hired a lawyer to help you?'

'I might have if I'd any money left. Or a job. Only I haven't got either.'

'Ah. I see.'

'What upsets me most is that my granddaughter looks unhappy since she's gone to live with Ruby Hicks. Beatie may be warmly dressed and live in a comfortable house, but she's downright miserable there if you ask me. It fair breaks my heart to see her in the street. She used to be such a happy little lass, skipping along an' chattering away.'

'How old is she?'

'Just turned nine.'

Their meal was served and Arthur proved how hungry he'd been by clearing his plate rapidly. He looked across the table apologetically as he laid down his knife and fork, because Biff's plate was still half full. 'Sorry for my poor table manners. I were famished.'

'Have a piece of apple pie for afters, then. They do a good one here.'

His companion gave him another of those wry, twisted smiles. 'I've not been eating well for a while, so I couldn't fit anything else in. Thank you for the offer, though. That were extra kind of you.'

Biff finished his own meal then pushed away his plate. 'Can you prove who you are?'

'Aye, easy. I've lived in the valley all my life. There's a dozen folk in Rivenshaw who've known me since we were childer together.'

'We'll go and see Henry Lloyd straight away then. Do you know him?'

'I'd recognise him by sight. Folk speak well of him.' Arthur closed his eyes, murmuring, 'I hope I don't wake up and find this is all a dream.'

Henry Lloyd studied the man Biff Higgins had brought to see him. 'You don't need to prove who you are, Mr Chapman. I used to see you around town when you worked for Sam Redfern. After you lost your wife, you seemed to vanish, and when I wanted to find you, I couldn't.'

'Well, it's good that you can identify him yourself,' Biff said. 'That'll save me one job. What do we need to do next, Mr Lloyd?'

'I'll contact Mr Neven and we'll get him to send us the key to the third house.' Henry turned back to Arthur, and added,

'Miss Chapman said those houses weren't to be opened up again until the heirs had been found, just kept weatherproof. So I'm no wiser about the contents than you are.'

'It's a strange business altogether,' Biff said.

'But kindly meant. Both Miss Chapman and her nephew were very pleasant people to deal with. Now, where can I contact you, Mr Chapman?'

Arthur flushed, looking embarrassed. 'I don't have proper lodgings. You could leave a message for me at the church hostel in East Rivenshaw. I earn my night's shelter there by doing some cleaning, and they let me leave my spare clothes in the cellar, but no one can stay there during the day so I never know where I'll be then.'

Biff had seen unemployed men both here and in London walking the streets in the daytime come rain or shine, some carrying bundles, some without any possessions.

Mr Lloyd nodded. 'I'll do that.' He glanced at the clock. 'Now, if you two will wait in reception, I'll telephone Mr Neven and see if we're in time for him to send the house key here by the overnight express service.'

He came out to join them again a few minutes later. 'They've just got time to catch today's post, so the key will arrive in Rivenshaw late tomorrow morning. Perhaps you'd like to check tomorrow that it's arrived, then bring Mr Chapman to meet me at the house at one o'clock in the afternoon, Mr Higgins, then we can hand everything over?'

Both men nodded, then Biff turned to Arthur. 'There's something else I need to tell you, Mr Chapman. Because of the difficulties the heirs had last time, with Higgerson trying to bully them to sell him the properties at a knock-down price, Mr Neven has hired me to keep an eye on you for a week or two and help you settle in. Will that be all right with you?'

Arthur looked from one to the other in puzzlement. 'Higgerson wants my house?'

Mr Lloyd nodded. 'Yes, and you know what he's like. You'll definitely need to be on your guard, Mr Chapman.'

Biff knew what he still had to tell the heir would give him further difficulties, so he tried to think how to cheer the poor fellow up. As they left the lawyer's rooms, he asked, 'Would you like to see your house from the outside today?'

'I'd like to, of course I would, but it depends where it is. I can't afford bus fares, and my shoes have holes in the soles, so I can't walk very far. I put fresh cardboard in them every morning, but it soon wears through, especially on rainy days.'

He saw Biff's pitying expression at this admission and added, 'I made a vow after I stopped boozing to tell the truth – when it doesn't hurt anyone but me, that is – so I'm not pretending about how broke I am.'

'Well, I have my car and was expecting to drive you there and back. I'll need to give you some more information after you've seen the house. You'll understand better then why I'm here.'

He shrugged. 'I'll do whatever you and the lawyers think best. Where is this house exactly?'

'Backshaw Moss.'

Arthur looked disappointed. 'If it's in that slum, it can't be up to much – though anything's welcome, of course.'

'It's quite a nice house, actually, the end one on Daisy Street, so not in the bad part of Backshaw Moss. What's more, the council knocked down the row of slum dwellings that was on the other side of the street at that end, and they've built a row of new houses in their place. They've worked quickly, and the new places are almost finished. So where your house is situated is being transformed into a respectable area.'

'Eh, that's a relief. I've had enough of living in slums this past year, I can tell you. Thank you for that offer to drive me there, Mr Higgins. Once again I'm grateful to you, an' I won't forget your kindness. I can't wait to see the house. Maybe even that Hicks woman will let me see my granddaughter now.'

And maybe, Biff thought, he could help him with that as well. He could try, anyway. Not being from the valley, he didn't know who this Ruby Hicks was, but he'd make it his business to find out and get a look at her and the child, who clearly meant so much to her grandfather.

Arthur sat in the car as he was driven slowly up the hill to Birch End, enjoying the comfort of this means of transport. He wondered what he had to be warned about. Whatever it was, he'd cope. Life wasn't always easy, but if the house was even halfway decent, he'd do it up gradually. He was good with his hands.

Surely he could find a job of some sort to earn the money for that? Especially if he didn't have to pay rent. Maybe he could take in a lodger or two as well? No, they'd need someone to prepare meals for them, and he wasn't a cook.

As they slowed down to go through the village centre of Birch End, they passed a couple of women standing chatting. Biff had to slow down just then to let an old man cross the road, and waved to one of them. She waved back, smiling.

'Nice woman, Gwynneth Harte. Do you know her?'

'I don't think I've ever met her, but she looks friendly.'

'You'll be bound to meet her now because as well as visiting her son, who lives two doors away from your new home, she lives just down the road in Birch End.'

Arthur turned his head to take another look at her. She was about his own age, he'd guess, and had a lovely warm smile. Comely was the word that came into his mind to describe her. It was old-fashioned, but it suited her, some- how. He always judged people by their smiles. His wife had had a lovely one.

He forgot the stranger as the car drew up at the very end of Daisy Street. He hadn't been up to this part of the valley since before his wife died. If he remembered correctly, a huddle of tumbledown old houses had once stood on the other side of the street, as if signalling the entrance to a slum. They were gone now, and a row of brand new terraced houses were standing there, giving a completely different impression to those who passed by.

As he opened the car door, he could hear the sound of hammering coming from inside one of them, and there was a lovely smell of freshly sawn wood. He turned his head slowly, hardly daring to look at his inheritance in case it was a tumbledown place. But it wasn't! On this side of Daisy Street there were three larger houses. He'd passed them a few times, but hadn't taken much notice of them until now. He sucked in a sharp breath. His inheritance couldn't be one of those, surely?

As Biff got out of the car, he pointed to the end house. 'That one is yours. Number 25.'

It felt to Arthur as if the world had stopped turning and he with it. When he did manage to put a few words together, all he could say was, 'But it's a big house!'

'Bigger than the average dwelling, yes.'

'It can't be mine!'

Biff smiled at him. 'Well, it is, thanks to Miss Chapman and her nephew.'

'I don't deserve it, 'deed I don't!'

'She thought her bequests might help her descendants to pull their lives together, and it has done with the other two. She would be so pleased about that. I'm sure this one will do the same for you.'

Biff waited, but Arthur still said nothing, so he continued to offer information in a gentle flow to give him time to get used to his inheritance. 'These houses are very soundly built, but you'll probably find that yours needs modernising inside, as the others did. They've been empty for over a decade, you see, and all that's been done in that time is maintenance of the exteriors.'

Arthur put one hand on the roof of the car, as if to steady himself, and said harshly, 'I have only a few shillings in the world. How would I do any modernising at all?'

'Miss Chapman will probably have left you a way to do it, with a bit of effort. She was a great believer in working hard if you wanted something. We'll find out more tomorrow when we see the interior.'

'What were the other houses like inside?'

'Number 23 had been divided into flats, with some very badly behaved tenants needing throwing out. The owners have done a lot of modernising, and they have a couple of good tenants living there now, so maybe you can do that too. The whole of Number 21 was crammed so full of larger furniture, you could hardly walk through it.'

'Why would anyone leave it like that?'

'Miss Chapman had inherited two other houses when she was old and failing in health, so she had just had the furniture from them dumped inside to be dealt with later. I gather she had expected to recover and live to a ripe old age like most of the Chapmans. Sadly, she didn't.'

He waited, but Arthur just nodded.

'I have no idea what we'll find inside yours, but probably some things to help you set yourself up.'

'Anything would be a help, but I'll sleep on the bare boards and use sacks for blankets if I have to.'

Biff nodded acceptance of this. He'd have been the same. Owning your own house was an impossible dream for most people. 'Shall we walk around the outside and peep over the wall into the backyard?'

Arthur nodded, following him past the side of the house along which ran a side street where the better village of Birch

End began. They could just see into the backyard if they stood on tiptoe. It contained the usual outhouses and was paved with big square flagstones.

They studied it in silence, then continued.

When they finished their circuit, Arthur stared at the house again from the front, muttering, 'Eh, it's a fine building. I don't deserve it, 'deed I don't.'

'Then you'll have to make sure you do deserve it by the time you get things sorted out.'

Arthur stared at Biff and nodded slowly, as if that remark had hit home.

Biff gave him a little more time to stare, then said quietly, 'I'll drive you back down the valley to Rivenshaw now. Can you meet me at half past twelve outside the town hall tomorrow and we'll drive up to meet Mr Lloyd?'

'Yes, of course. I'll be grateful for the lift. Thank you.'

As they got out of the car, Biff slipped a ten-shilling note into his hand. 'To help you smarten up a bit.'

Arthur stared down at it then nodded thanks. This was no time to stand on his dignity.

He watched the car drive away and walked slowly along the street to the hostel to do the cleaning job that would earn him a night's shelter. On the way there he bought a second-hand pair of shoes from the pawn shop. The uppers were a bit scuffed, but the soles were sound, which was the main thing.

He also spent sixpence at the public baths that evening, taking his one spare set of underclothes in with him to wear afterwards so that he could wash the others in the bath water. He could dry them overnight at the hostel.

Sitting in the warm water, he bent his head forward and wept for both joy at the prospect of owning a house and sorrow that Susan hadn't lived to move there with him.

★

When he raised his head, he felt cleansed in more ways than one, and utterly determined to make full amends for his recent mistakes and stupidity. He didn't know how he'd do that, but he'd find a way.

He didn't tell anyone at the hostel what had happened, though. Time enough for that later.

2

Gwynneth was glad to be going into Rivenshaw. It'd take her mind off her worries to do some shopping and maybe meet a few people she knew and chat to them. The village shop in Birch End supplied everyone's basic needs, but it didn't stock much beyond essential groceries.

She had a quarter of an hour to wait for the bus, but there was a bench behind the bus stop and she enjoyed watching people. Today she saw a little lass she'd noticed before walking sedately along the street, accompanied by a harsh-faced old woman.

Other children of her age skipped along and chatted to their companions, but this one always walked sedately. She'd have been bonny had she not been dressed in funereal black, with her hair dragged back into a tight single plait.

The stern-looking woman seemed to be scolding the child. Why was she not at school? Ah, that was a bandage on her wrist. Perhaps she'd been to see the doctor.

The child's face bore an expression of what looked like the stoic calm of utter despair to Gwynneth, a way to hide her real feelings. Such a young creature to be so guarded and unhappy. She couldn't have been more than about nine or ten.

It tore at Gwynneth's heart to see her. She'd have given anything for a grandchild of that age to take for walks, chat to and make clothes for.

The old woman's expression remained grim. Once, when the lass started to move in a pattern of steps to avoid stepping on the cracks between the paving slabs, she cast a quick, furtive glance around and slapped her young companion good and hard on the back of the head. From her expression, she enjoyed doing it.

The blow was so hard it sent the child tumbling to the ground, and when the poor little thing got up, she was cradling the arm with the bandage on it. That didn't stop her getting scolded for not walking properly. The bandage was now trickling blood.

The woman's shrill voice carried clearly in the damp air. 'You stupid fool. Look what you've done to yourself now!'

Gwynneth knew better than to intervene, but she wanted to. Oh, she wanted to very badly! It was heartbreaking how some folk treated those weaker than themselves.

That particular day, the woman must have got a stone in her shoe, because she stopped suddenly, pointed to one end of a park bench, and snapped out a command. Sitting down at the other end, she pulled her shoe off and shook something out.

The child didn't attempt to sit down, just stood motionless next to the bench while the woman bent to put on her shoe again. Gwynneth winked at the little girl as they started moving again and walked past the bus shelter, giving her a tiny wave with her hand lowered so that the woman didn't see it.

After a quick look of shock and a glance to check that the old woman wasn't watching her, the lass gave a tiny nod and a flicker of her fingers in response.

Gwynneth jerked in shock when someone spoke to her. 'Did you see that, Mrs Harte?'

She recognised the voice and looked up to smile at Sergeant Deemer, who was standing nearby, half-concealed behind an evergreen bush. Had the policeman been watching the woman too?

'Yes. And it's not the first time I've seen her hit that poor child, sergeant. I think she's the grandmother.'

'Yes, she is. The child's parents are dead, and she looks after her, but I'm starting to worry about what's going on. My constable's seen the woman hitting poor Beatie several times when they're out in the back garden because his beat takes him past it. Mrs Hicks must think she can't be seen there.'

They both sighed at the same time.

'It's one thing to slap a child for being naughty, another to beat them regularly,' the sergeant said. 'I wonder how Beatie got that injury?'

'Who knows? There's nothing we can do, though, is there? People are allowed to chastise their children.'

Deemer scowled. 'That doesn't mean beating them black and blue.'

As the bus came into view in the distance, a thought occurred to Gwynneth. 'If something really bad happens and you need a place for the child to stay in an emergency, Sergeant Deemer, I'd be happy to take her in and look after her.'

He studied her face. 'Are you sure about that, Mrs Harte?'

'Yes. Definitely. I love children, and I don't have any grandchildren yet.'

'I'll bear it in mind.' He nodded and moved on.

Gwynneth sighed as she got on the bus. She couldn't get the memory of that poor child being knocked to the ground out of her mind.

And here she was with all that love to spare. Life could be so unfair.

In London, Albert Neven called his clerk into his room. 'Good news!' he said by way of a greeting. 'That phone call was from the lawyer in Rivenshaw. Mr Higgins has found Arthur Chapman.'

'Oh, jolly good, sir.'

'Yes, Penscombe. But the poor fellow is apparently in a sorry state. He lost his wife, then his daughter and son-in-law within the space of a year, and fell to pieces.'

'Those were some hard blows.'

'He's pulled himself together during the past year and stopped drinking, but is living in poverty. *Respectable* poverty, Biff says, so he will be allowed to inherit.'

'Good to know, sir.'

'Can you please send the key to Number 25 up to Mr Lloyd by overnight express? He'll take Higgins and Chapman to the house and hand it over. It'll be interesting to find out what it's like inside, won't it? Miss Chapman and her nephew had some very devious plans for their heirs, if you ask me, and they knew how to keep their plans secret.'

'Their ideas worked well for the first two houses, did they not? Jerked both of their relatives out of ruts and into happier lives. Let's hope this final heir can also benefit from their generous if eccentric actions.'

3

Arthur arrived outside the town hall ten minutes early the following day, so eager was he to go inside the house. *His* house! He had to keep reminding himself that he owned a house now, it seemed so impossible. He came from a poorer branch of the Chapman family and no one on his side had ever *owned* a house before.

He'd spruced himself up as much as possible for this first visit, but that wasn't much. These might be his best clothes, but they were threadbare, only used for going to church – and he hadn't done much of that since Ruby Hicks had taken his granddaughter away from him and joined that strange little church in Birch End. No one looked happy as they came out of it, certainly not the subdued group of children.

He looked down and brushed away a speck of lint. At least his clothes were clean now. Maybe he'd be able to find a full-time job too. He still had the necessary skills and was gradually living down his bad reputation as a boozer.

He was one of the fortunate ones. There were still some chaps who'd never be fit enough to hold down a job after being injured in the Great War. He'd been lucky; he'd come out of the fighting whole, physically at least.

It seemed a long time till Mr Higgins drove up, so Arthur went to read the public notices. They were still showing the tribute to the old king, who'd died and been buried in January. The new king was the eighth to be called Edward.

Arthur sniffed in disapproval at the official photo of the
latter. This one sounded to be a bit of a playboy, if you
believed the newspapers, and he didn't like the snooty
expression on the fellow's face.

Arthur read a lot of newspapers, usually ones a few days
old that he acquired for free after they'd been discarded. Once
he'd become sober again, he'd taken up his old habit of trying
to understand what was going on in the wider world.

Then he forgot about kings as Biff stopped his car beside
him, smiling and beckoning to him to get into the front passenger seat.

'Excited?'

'I don't know how I feel to tell you the truth, Mr Higgins.
I'm all of a tozz-wozz, as my mother would have said.'

'That's very understandable.'

As he set off again Biff looked in the rear-view mirror and
frowned. A couple of minutes later he pulled in by the side of
the road and looked once more, muttering under his breath,
beginning to worry. He set off again.

'Is something wrong, Mr Higgins?'

'That car seems to be following us. Do you recognise it? Or
its driver?'

Arthur twisted around. 'Yes. It's Jem Stanley driving Mr
Higgerson's new car. He's been working for him since he
came out of prison.'

He let out an involuntary chuckle. 'Everyone's still laughing
at the way that Dobbs fellow, who used to arrange for Higgerson's dirty work, ran off with his boss's car.'

Biff smiled too. 'Sergeant Deemer told me the police hav-
en't found any sign of Dobbs or the car, but I'd guess he hasn't
tried all that hard, knowing how he feels about Higgerson.'

'He's a wicked man, that one is. Done near as much harm
to folk in this valley as the war did. We've had villains before,

every place does, but not usually as bad as him. Why, even his own wife ran away from him.'

They both fell silent for a few moments, thinking of poor, pale Lallie Higgerson.

'I hope she stays safe,' Arthur murmured. 'She gave me six-pence once when she was out shopping, said I looked hungry. I was. I'd not eaten for two days.'

As they left the town, the other car stayed behind them. 'I can guess why Jem Stanley is following us,' Biff admitted.

Arthur twisted his head round again. 'Because of the house.'

'I don't understand how Higgerson could have found out so quickly that you're the heir to Number 25.'

'Someone will have reported seeing you and me together looking round the outside of the house yesterday. He'll have put two and two together.'

'Why would he be interested enough to be keeping watch on you, though?'

Arthur scowled. 'Higgerson likes to think he's king of the valley. I refused to do a job for him last year because I *don't* steal or hurt people, and ever since then he's been trying to get at me. He's lost me a few temporary jobs that I know of.'

'If he bears a grudge against you, you'd better be more careful than ever before from now on. He tried to get hold of the other two houses Miss Chapman had left, and not by honest means, either. Mr Neven is worried he might go after your house too, though why the man's so keen to get hold of any of these houses is more than either of us has been able to work out. Most of his properties are in the slums, bought cheaply and nearly falling down because he skimps on maintenance.'

'He's even had extra cellar rooms dug out on a few of them,' Arthur said. 'You should have seen the mess it made.'

'But that's dangerous! How the hell does he get away with it?'

Arthur couldn't hold back a sigh. 'Eh, who knows? I just hope I can keep out of his way from now on.'

'Don't forget that I'm available to help you. I could stay with you for a while to help you settle in.' He saw the regret on his companion's face and added quickly, 'Don't worry! Mr Neven is paying me to do that as part of his duty to ensure that the final bequest is passed on smoothly. It won't cost you a penny.'

'Oh. Well, I'll appreciate any help you can give me, Mr Higgins, I definitely will.'

'Since we'll be working together, why don't you call me Biff from now on?'

'Biff it is. And you should call me Arthur.'

They turned right off the main road that continued to the top of the valley, and drove through Birch End, stopping where it ended at Daisy Street.

Jem Stanley drove slowly past them, hooting the car horn and making a rude sign. After stopping about a hundred yards further along the street, he got out and leaned against his car, watching them openly. He was a big, lumpy man with an ugly face, whose nose had been badly broken at some time.

'He's only been out of prison for a few months,' Biff said. 'We'll stay in the car until Mr Lloyd arrives. I'm not afraid of Stanley or his master. I can look after myself in a fight, believe me. But I always prefer to avoid trouble, if possible.'

'So do I. I used to be able to stand up for myself when I was younger. Well, you had to where I lived as a kid. What I'm worried about now is being outnumbered and then beaten up. Mr Higgerson has no scruples about hurting folk if they've upset him. He might not do the beating himself these days, but he knows others who'll do it for him.'

'Well, there are two of us at the moment, which makes it a bit more difficult for them.'

Arthur was grateful, but couldn't help wondering what he'd do after Biff left the valley and he was on his own again. Then he got angry at himself for being so timid. Use your brain, Susan would have told him.

He stared at the house, thinking hard. If he made a will as soon as the house was his, leaving it to someone honest and with a bit of power like . . . like Mr Lloyd, Higgerson would have no way of getting hold of the house.

That idea made him feel a bit better. He still had a brain. It was just a bit rusty.

The lawyer arrived at Daisy Street five minutes later and got out of his car straight away, smiling at them till he noticed Jem Stanley, who was lurking next to a car further up the street. It was all too obvious that he was there to watch what they were doing.

Mr Lloyd's smile vanished and he led the way towards the front door at a brisk pace, asking in a low voice, 'Has that fellow been causing any trouble?'

'Not so far. But Higgerson must have sent him to report on what happens here today. How did he even find out enough to think us worth following?'

'Sergeant Deemer told me a while ago that our so-called builder sends out word asking for information about people he's interested in and pays sixpence for anything useful. But we can ignore Stanley today because he won't be able to follow us inside. He won't find out anything about what's in the house from me afterwards, I promise you.'

'Don't you have any idea about what's there?' Biff asked.

Mr Lloyd hesitated, then admitted, 'Not much. I've been given some guidance, since I have a part to play in what happens next, but there's nothing else I can tell you at the moment.'

He stopped at the front door and pulled a large, old-fashioned key from his pocket, holding it out to Arthur.

'Perhaps you'd like to open the door of your new home and go in first, Mr Chapman?'

Arthur took the key, staring down at it, then tried to put it into the lock. He had trouble getting it in at first because his hand was shaking. They must think him a fool.

Then the key slid in suddenly and he unlocked the door. Taking a deep breath, he turned the tarnished brass knob and pushed the door open, staring inside.

The hall was dusty and bigger than the main room in the terraced house where he'd lived with his wife and two children for many years.

He forgot the others and walked to the centre of the space, turning round slowly on the spot and marvelling at the huge window that took up most of the upper part of one side wall, shedding multi-coloured light on the staircase, which led up to the next floor. He noticed the exquisitely carved bannisters and also that they needed a good polish. He'd like to get his hands on them, bring that wood to life again.

The glowing jewel colours in the stained-glass patterns brightened the whole space, even on a late winter's day. The tinted light was reflected across the hand he stretched out towards the nearest shaft of sunlight that angled across the space. It felt as if the house was greeting him.

It was so beautiful! So elegant! Or it would be, if properly cared for.

A thought came from nowhere, taking him by surprise. He'd need a wife to help him look after his new home. Even Susan would tell him to find one. That was partly why people got married, she'd always said, to help one another through life, and if either of them died, the other should marry again.

For the first time since his loss he felt the need to move on with his life, though he would never stop feeling glad for the wonderful years he'd had with Susan.

Was it possible for a house to do that to you when you owned it? Make you see its needs as well as your own?

Time enough to think about that later. For the moment, there were several closed doors waiting for him, and he was eager to see what lay behind them. He walked across the hall to the right and opened the nearest one.

Biff was still standing at the front door, watching Arthur, when he heard footsteps crunch on the gravel of the path behind him. He spun round to see who it was, anger rising in him when he saw that Stanley had moved through the gate and was part way down the path, craning his neck, trying to see into the house.

'Get out, you!' He walked quickly along the path, fists clenching instinctively. He wasn't as tall or as muscular as Stanley, but he was furiously angry. After one look at his expression and the lawyer frowning at him from the doorway, Stanley took a hasty few steps back on to the footpath.

Biff slammed the gate shut on him and said slowly and clearly, 'Do not set even one foot on my client's property again or I'll report you to the police for trespassing! Your sort are not welcome here.'

Stanley squared his shoulders and shook himself, looking as if he was debating whether to fight.

Biff watched him steadily. He didn't feel nervous or hesitant about defending Arthur and the house.

After a couple of moments, Stanley shook his head, like a dog shaking off water. 'You're going to find out differently soon whether I'm welcome here or not, Mr Bloody Higgins, so you'd better make the most of the house while you can.' He jabbed his forefinger towards the building. 'That drunken sot won't be staying there for long, that's for sure. Mr Higgerson will make certain of that.'

Biff didn't respond, merely turned and followed Mr Lloyd back into the house, removing the door key from where Arthur had left it on the outside. He closed the front door behind him and used the key to lock it from the inside.

He was thoughtful as he moved across the hall. Clearly Higgerson was planning something. He must really want these houses. What the hell could he do to get hold of this last one? Even he couldn't just take it off Arthur.

Ugh! He had only to think of Higgerson to feel disgust roil inside him. The man claimed to be a respectable businessman and he had even managed to get elected to the town council, but he was an out-and-out villain and should be locked away instead of let run loose to harm those weaker than him.

Mr Lloyd was now standing at the open door of the sitting room, watching the heir, who had lingered a couple of paces inside to stare round. Biff joined the lawyer and gave him a quick, whispered summary of what Jem had taunted him with.

'We may have to hire more guards, as we did with the other houses. Don't say anything to Chapman yet. Let him have his first tour of the house in peace. He's looking so happy.'

Arthur began to walk slowly round the room, but the others stayed where they were, letting the new owner touch pieces of furniture and pause to stare up at the paintings on the walls. He was fairly glowing with joy. It was lovely to see.

After a circuit of the room Arthur went to stand by the fireplace, bafflement slowly replacing the initial joy as he stared round again.

Biff looked round too, giving the room more than a cursory glance this time as he tried to work out what was puzzling the heir.

The room contained several substantial pieces of furniture and some smaller tables and stools. He suddenly realised that though every single piece was of good quality, most of them were damaged in some way. Chairs stood lopsidedly, a small side table was propped up by a pile of books, with the missing leg lying on the floor beside it. Some of the stuffing was coming out of the seat cushions of a sofa.

He watched the heir move across to the small table and run gentle fingers over the dusty carving at the curved tops of the three intact legs, then pick up the fourth one from the floor to examine it.

'This was beautifully made,' Arthur said suddenly. 'It could be repaired, and so could the other pieces. I don't understand why everything has been left in such a sad state. There isn't a single piece of furniture in this room that doesn't need some attention. If I had my tools, I could do a lot of the work myself, but I pawned them when I was at my lowest point with the drinking. The tools will have been sold by now, because I've never had enough money to retrieve them.'

'Are you sure you're skilled enough to do any necessary repairs?'

'Oh, yes. Most of the ones needed by the furniture anyway. I'm not good enough at French polishing to do justice to pieces this good, and if there's plumbing needing doing elsewhere in the house, I've no experience of that. It's wood I like working with. I'm not trained, because my parents couldn't afford to pay for an apprenticeship. They needed my wages as soon as I could leave school, but Mr Redfern used to say I had an instinct for it and I learned a lot from working with him.'

Well, if Redfern said it that boded well, Biff thought. He ran a respected cabinet making business in the valley.

Arthur stroked another piece as he spoke, not even seeming aware that he was doing it. 'Eh, I've never handled such fine work in my life.'

4

Biff found it touching to watch Arthur's reaction to his inheritance, but he saw Mr Lloyd surreptitiously pull out his watch and peek at it, so he knew they'd have to get through this preliminary tour more quickly.

He moved across to Arthur. 'Let's go and look in the other rooms now. We can study the details later, but it'll be better to get a sense of the whole house first, don't you think? You can look your fill after you move in.'

Arthur nodded happily. 'Aye, I mustn't keep a busy man like Mr Lloyd for too long, must I? I'll have plenty of time to look at everything later.'

'Maybe somewhere we'll find a clue as to exactly what Miss Chapman's nephew wanted you to do with the house. You'll not only need to repair the pieces of furniture but bring the whole place up to date and install modern amenities.'

It upset him to see the bright smile fade.

'I don't have any money at all. I couldn't make even a start on that.'

'There may be provisions for helping you in the will itself.' He glanced at Mr Lloyd, who gave a slight nod.

'Do you think so?' Arthur asked.

'I doubt she'd leave you without some means of looking after your inheritance. Come on.' Biff led the way across the hall into what turned out to be a dining room. There was a big table there, but it lay in several pieces. The beautifully polished mahogany top leaning against the wall showed it had been a good table in its day.

Arthur bent to examine the other pieces. 'These don't look damaged. Someone's just pulled it apart and left it. Why would they do that?'

'To move it from one house to another, perhaps?'

The heir didn't look convinced and the lawyer was deliberately staring out of the window.

After that Biff only gave Arthur time to peer into the other two nearest rooms and work out what they'd been used for: a small sitting room and what looked like a cosy study behind the dining room. It was immediately clear that they too contained several broken pieces of furniture, so he chivvied the heir along.

'Let's find out what's at the back of the house on the other side.'

Mr Lloyd gave Biff another slight nod of approval when Arthur wasn't looking.

The last door at the rear of the hall led to the kitchen and related work areas. There was more damaged furniture there, but the cooking equipment didn't appear to be harmed and was of a high quality, even though it was as dusty as everything else.

Arthur stopped suddenly in front of several sets of crockery set out neatly on shelves. 'Why would anyone need all these dishes?'

'When these houses were built, there would probably be a housekeeper and at least one maid, as well as the family,' Biff told him. 'The servants would use the cheaper crockery and cutlery.'

'Well, I can't even support myself properly, let alone hire a maid, so no one except me will be using any of these pieces.'

He took the initiative again, making his way across to the scullery, which led off the rear of the kitchen, and relaxing visibly at what he found. 'Eh, look! My grandma had an old-fashioned slopstone made of sand-coloured stone exactly like this one, with a cold water tap over it.'

'So did mine.' Biff smiled at the fond memories it brought up.

'The modern white ceramic sinks are a similar shape to this one, but they're much easier to keep clean. Why, there's not even a gas geyser here to heat the water. Didn't my relatives have enough money to keep up to date?'

He was about to move on when he noticed an envelope propped against the lower corner of the window addressed to 'Arthur Chapman, Esq.' in large black handwriting.

He did nothing, staring at the envelope as if expecting it to bite him.

Mr Lloyd gave him an impatient glance. 'It's addressed to you, Mr Chapman. Why don't you pick it up and find out what it says?'

Arthur stretched out his hand, but still hesitated to touch the envelope. It was such a posh one, and the handwriting was really fancy. But it was definitely addressed to him so he picked it up, blew the dust off, then tore open the top as carefully as he could.

He found two sheets of paper inside, covered with the same black handwriting. It took him a while to work his way through it, given the fancy, unfamiliar style of writing. He was uncertain of the exact meaning of a few of the words, too, but didn't like to ask for help and show his ignorance. Anyway, he was pretty sure he could understand the main points being made, and the letter was very friendly.

Dear Arthur

Welcome to your new home. I hope you'll be happy here.

I know about your lapse into drunkenness and the sad reasons for it. The fact that you have stopped drinking and are trying to remake your life in a better mode has prompted me to give you this chance to do something with your future.

This house originally belonged to my aunt, Sarah Jane Chapman, a distant cousin of yours. I know she would approve of you inheriting it. She wanted all three properties to go to relatives who needed a helping hand, you see.

It will take a lot of sheer hard work to turn this house into a real home again. And I'm told that you have good practical skills, especially with woodworking.

I know you don't have any money, so once you've moved in, a set of basic tools will be supplied by the hardware store. You must collect these in person, and there will be £5 credited to you there as well to spend on screws and the like.

There is also £100 in an account at the bank which will be transferred to your name as soon as Mr Lloyd gives them the word. I hope you will use this to start modernising the house.

There isn't enough money to bring it fully up to scratch, what with the need for a sewage connection, electricity, and a bathroom, but there's enough to make a good start. It'll be up to you to work out how to finish the job.

Please hire Mr Tyler to do any building work for you. He can be trusted. Others in the valley can't.

With warmest wishes for your success.
Your distant cousin.

James Barker

Arthur gaped at the pieces of paper and laboriously squinted his way through the letter again, after which he held them out to Biff with one shaking hand, tears welling in his eyes. 'It's as if my family has reached out from beyond the grave to help me, as if I'm not alone any longer.'

The detective read the pages quickly, then asked, 'Are you skilled enough to work on the furniture and house?'

'I can do some of it, aye, now that I'm sober again.' He held his hands out in front of him, palms upward. 'These seem to know how to make or mend wooden objects, but I might as well tell you now that I have a bit of trouble with reading and writing, especially when I'm tired. My teacher said I needed glasses but my family couldn't afford them. And even if I'd had some, we lived in a rough area and the other lads would have enjoyed breaking them. Glasses wouldn't have lasted a week. And I've been too busy scraping a living to bother about reading and spectacles lately.'

The lawyer spoke, changing the subject slightly. 'Well, Mr Higgins will make sure you get some glasses. How did you manage to acquire your woodworking skills, Mr Chapman?'

'Bit by bit. On the job I'd watch the men who'd hired me to run errands and do whatever else they needed, and I'd try to copy them on throwaway scraps of wood. I made my mum a few platters and such.' He sighed. 'I had to leave school at eleven, half time, you see, to help put bread on the table. Kids could do that in them days, work half a day and attend school the other half. Mornings one week, afternoons the next. You have to stay on full-time till you're fourteen nowadays.'

Biff couldn't stop himself from reaching out and putting one hand on Arthur's shoulder in a gesture of unspoken comfort. 'Doing this house up should suit you down to the ground, then.'

'Yes, if—' He broke off, staring blindly into the distance.

'What is it? Tell me.'

'If Higgerson doesn't find a way to prevent me. He's got a lot of power in the valley.'

'I keep telling you: we won't let him do that. I won't leave you on your own until it's safe, I promise you, and there's money been left to hire watchmen as well, till things settle down.' He hated to see the happiness fade still further, and had been dreading telling him Higgerson's interference had been expected.

It was at that moment that Biff realised something about himself. He liked this valley and, against all the odds, he felt he'd found a home here. He liked the plain-spoken northern people, and there was no one waiting for him in London now, after all. He was tired of travelling all over the country, hunting for missing relatives or spouses, many of whom didn't want to be found again.

He even had an idea about how he might be able to earn a living in a different way here: by setting up an employment agency. His former employer had sent him on an investigation for one a few years ago, and he'd found it interesting seeing how they did that sort of work. He'd dealt with other agencies since then, after opening his own private investigation business. He had a fair idea of how to organise an employment agency, yes, and do that more efficiently than most of the ones he'd seen.

In the modern world there were better ways to find workers than at the labour sections of markets or fairs that they'd used in the old days, or by asking around at the pub, as still happened. If you advertised in a newspaper, you had to wait for replies, and interview people to see if they were suitable. An agency could often provide a worker more quickly, sometimes within an hour or so.

Here in the valley they were not quite as forward-thinking as they were in the south and he felt that would be an advantage for him. He suspected it was partly because of a lack of jobs since the Great War. You don't need an agency when there's little or no work to be had. But the work situation here was improving all the time.

It surprised him when he looked back over his life and thought how the world had changed. More affluent people now had all sorts of labour-saving devices in their offices, as well as their homes. Telephones were so useful and saved a lot of running around, especially as towns were growing larger. And offices could be equipped with typewriters, adding machines, Gestetner copying equipment, all sorts of gadgets, and more being invented all the time.

He should be able to sell his little detective agency on the outskirts of London to give himself some start-up money, but he was tired of the work and ready to move on.

He jerked to attention, realising he'd been ignoring his client, but Arthur too had been lost in thought.

He looked at the third member of their trio, who was being very patient with him and Arthur. 'What do we need to do next, Mr Lloyd?'

'Go to my office and complete the paperwork, after which I shall send it by express post to Mr Neven in London. Only he has the power to hand over the inheritance officially. We can't take you to the bank and introduce you till we hear from him. Anyway, it's past three o'clock now, so the bank will be closed for the day, but if we bustle, we can still put the envelope on the train to catch the evening express post from Manchester to London.'

'The money will be very important to our client, given his circumstances,' Biff said quietly.

'Of course.' Mr Lloyd started moving towards the front door, talking to Arthur now. 'It'll be up to you to sort out how you go on after I've handed things over, Mr Chapman, with Mr Higgins' help at first, of course, but don't hesitate to contact me if I can assist you in any further way.'

As they went outside, Biff saw Jem Stanley standing near his car further down the street, still looking at them with that sneering, confident smile on his ugly face.

He was quite sure Higgerson would have some nasty tricks brewing, but he'd do his best to prevent trouble.

He'd taken a liking to the heir, who seemed a gentle, honest soul, and he also liked the idea that his final job as a private investigator should consist of helping a man climb out from the pit of despair to make a respectable place for himself in the world.

Biff kept a careful watch on the other vehicles as he drove into Rivenshaw. As he'd expected, Stanley followed them into town. He drove past them when they stopped near the lawyer's rooms, slowing down to give them another of those rude signs with his forefinger before driving off down the street.

And good riddance to bad rubbish, as the saying went, Biff thought as he followed Mr Lloyd into the building and watched him guide Arthur through the necessary paperwork.

They also made a quick, simple will – only a few lines long – in case anything happened to Arthur, but the lawyer insisted on Biff being the beneficiary not himself. He hoped it'd never be needed.

After that Biff took Arthur to the upper storey of Charlie Willcox's bigger pawn shop, where they sold better quality second-hand garments. They found some surprisingly cheap but decent clothes there.

Biff paid for them himself, but pretended he'd been given some money by Mr Neven before he left London to cover necessary expenses like these. And if he was being soft doing that, too bad. You should help decent people who were in trouble when you could.

As they came out of the shop, he asked, 'Where are you sleeping tonight, Arthur?'

'Ah. Well, I hadn't thought. The hostel, I suppose, but I'll have to get back there quickly and do some cleaning to earn a bed.'

'Hmm. I'd rather you don't move around town alone from now on, not till I'm sure you're safe. Let's go to the hostel to pick up your things, and then I suggest we set ourselves up with somewhere to sleep in your new house. Would that be all right? It'll be easier for me to make sure that you're safe there than at the hostel, where anyone can come in for a night's lodgings.'

'There were mattresses at the house, but the bed frames need sorting out, and I didn't see any blankets,' Arthur said dubiously.

'Well, it won't matter to me if we have to sleep on mattresses on the floor, and I'm sure I saw some blankets in that big cupboard next to the scullery. We can light a fire in the sitting room and give everything a good airing, then sleep on the floor in front of it.'

He'd got it all worked out, because Arthur seemed too bemused by his good fortune to plan anything. 'On the way back to Daisy Street, I'll have to pop into my lodgings to let my landlady know I'm leaving, and collect my possessions. It'll be all right if I stay with you for a week or two, won't it?'

'Of course it will. I'd welcome the company, actually. I'm really grateful for what you're doing for me.'

Biff shrugged and changed the subject. 'We'll get some fish and chips and have an early tea before we leave town, then buy some basic food and tea-making stuff from the shop in Birch End.' He grinned as he added. 'We can sit in the car and eat our tea with our fingers while it's still hot. Fish and chips always taste better hot from the shop, wrapped in greaseproof paper and newspaper, and slathered in salt and vinegar.'

'Ooh, yes. It's ages since I've had any.'

'Tomorrow we'll come back into Rivenshaw and let Mr Lloyd introduce you to the bank manager, if the paperwork has been sorted out.'

But before then Biff had one more job he intended to do now he'd seen Higgerson's henchman following Arthur around: hire a couple of men to help keep watch over the house and its new owner at all times from tomorrow onwards. He'd had to do the same for Maisie when she inherited Number 23 next door to Arthur. Mr Neven really had supplied him with the money for further protection.

If Rob and Phil Becksley were free, he'd hire them again, because they hated Higgerson, who'd tried to make their lives difficult after they had also refused to do his dirty work. Biff had found them decent and reliable, and they lived in a nearby part of Birch End.

Luck was with him. When they were leaving the village shop with the tea-making materials, plus a loaf, a pat of butter and a jar of jam for breakfast, they ran into Rob's wife just coming in. Biff stopped her to ask if her husband was working at the moment, explaining his need.

She beamed at him. 'That'll suit my Rob down to the ground, it's so close to home. And I happen to know Phil has just finished a little job for Mr Tyler. Shall I send them both to see you? They'll enjoy stopping that horrible man causing more trouble.'

'Yes, please. Tomorrow morning will do. No one will know we're there tonight. Thank you.'

'It's me as should be thanking you, Mr Higgins.' She frowned at him. 'Didn't you have a bit of an Irish accent last time we met?'

He beamed at her. 'I did indeed. I put on that accent as a sort of disguise, but I don't need to do that any longer.'

She looked a bit surprised but didn't question what he'd said.

All in all, things were going as well as could be expected at this stage. He'd do his very best to see that they stayed that way.

When they got back to the house, they used Biff's torch to light their way to the kitchen, where they lit two of the candles they'd bought and fixed them into old-fashioned portable holders, then searched the house for suitable beds. Unfortunately there were no bed frames that were intact and Arthur said he'd rather do the repairs by daylight.

They did find mattresses, so lit a fire in the kitchen and hauled them downstairs, putting everything to air in front of the fire. Then they made themselves cups of cocoa.

Biff thought regretfully about his comfortable lodgings as he snuggled down among the chaos. At least he was warm enough, but this was a lumpy old mattress. Tomorrow they'd sort out proper sleeping accommodation and get some oil lamps set up for the evenings.

On the other mattress, Arthur heard his companion sigh into sleep, but couldn't follow his example for a while.

He didn't mind lying awake and mulling over the day. He was still coming to terms with his good fortune, and working out what to make a start on repairing as soon as it was light. Chairs to sit on and bed frames, he decided.

He'd been given this chance to improve his life, and he wasn't going to waste even a second.

There was hope singing through him now, and that felt so good.

5

After he saw the two fools going into the lawyer's office, Jem Stanley drove back to see Mr Higgerson. His employer had been staying later at his office since his wife left him. Jem loved driving and wished he didn't have to go back to him. It'd been good to drive around the valley in the new motor car today without a sharp voice criticising him or yelling orders from the rear seat.

He knew why Mr Higgerson had been in such a bad mood lately. Well, the whole town knew that, which only added to his boss's fury. His wife had run away, and he hadn't been able to get her back, and everyone knew it.

Even worse, Lallie Higgerson was staying with the son who'd also run away a year or two previously, and Higgerson hadn't been able to get him back either. No one wanted to live with such a cruel, bad-tempered sod, it seemed to Jem.

He didn't really like working for Higgerson, but he enjoyed the money, enough of it for his wife to build up some savings for the first time in their lives. She wasn't letting him waste it on booze, said she'd leave him if he did.

Well, it was Higgerson's own fault. He shouldn't have bashed his wife. It stood to reason that if you thumped your wife she'd not be on your side. And Mrs Higgerson had been a frail-looking little thing, too. It'd have been like bashing a baby.

Jem always made sure his wife had nothing like that to complain about. He might not be the best provider, but he'd never thumped her, and he'd looked after her as much as he could, just as she looked after their two sons. She'd even stood by him while he was in prison, sending him a couple of food parcels. Good lass, his Callie.

'How could you have missed the chance to see inside the house?' Higgerson yelled at him suddenly.

Jem continued doggedly between such interruptions to report what had actually happened.

Thump went a fist on the desk. 'You were just along the street from it. You could have *pushed* your way in.'

'I didn't see inside it because that detective chap was guarding the gate.'

'He's smaller than you are.'

'He's a good fighter.'

'How do you know? You didn't even try.'

'I don't have to fight him to know just by watching him, and by the way he holds himself as he looks round. And anyway, it was broad daylight and people were nearby. They'd have called in Deemer if I'd attacked him, and I'd have got arrested.'

That stopped the complaining. Higgerson always trod carefully around their police sergeant, Jem had noticed.

'We'll have to break into the place one night, Mr Higgerson. If I do anything openly, I'll get sent back to prison. How would you manage without me now? I'm in the middle of sorting out quite a few things for you.'

Higgerson looked at him in surprise, opened his mouth, then snapped it shut again and scowled down at his clenched fists as Jem continued talking.

'With that house next door, the so-called detective hired men to keep watch night and day. I bet he does the same with this one. I'll go and check tomorrow, if that's all right with you.'

Higgerson stared into the distance, as he often did when thinking, so Jem waited in silence for him to give permission.

'Yes, do that. We'll have to work out how to get rid of the heir, or discredit him.'

'I could set a fire in one of the outhouses. That'd upset them.'

'Don't be stupid. I want to use that house, not turn it into a wreck. There has to be a way to get hold of it, yes, and the two others as well eventually. I'll sort it out. I always get what I want in the end, one way or the other. Those houses are perfect for my purpose.'

Jem had worked out what that purpose was even though his employer hadn't been specific. It baffled him as to why setting up a fancy brothel had become so important to a respectable man, then abruptly, he remembered that Higgerson's wife had left him, and smothered a desire to grin. He wanted a woman at his service, but not any old woman from the streets, and he wanted to provide the same service for other gentlemen, and charge highly for it.

But why did he want to keep making more and more money? You'd think he had enough now to sit back and enjoy the rest of his life.

Still, not for him to quibble at his master's orders, as long as they didn't put him in danger. Jem had been lucky to get this job, and he knew it. He didn't intend to lose it, whatever it took.

'You can drive me home now. Come round to the back of my house after you've put the car away. You've given me an idea. There's something else I've been waiting to do. People have to be reminded that they don't get away with messing me about. I've been waiting to pay back Wilf and Stella Pollard for refusing to sell to me. And don't forget to bring me the keys to the car and the garage.'

Jem didn't smile at that till he was out of sight. Dobbs had kept the keys all the time, and been able to drive away when the time was ripe.

He went to see Mr Higgerson in his fancy room at the back, but was shocked at what he was told to do. It seemed so stupid for Higgerson to hold grudges against people and take risks to pay them back for going against his wishes. No one could win all the time, not even this man.

He opened his mouth to protest, then shut it again. He couldn't keep refusing to do the things his master wanted. He had to tread carefully with this job. Best to do this himself so that no one could betray him, though it was a waste of time and effort.

Higgerson jabbed a finger at him to emphasise his next instructions. 'And tomorrow morning you'd better check on the new basement room that's being dug out in Clover Lane. Tell those lazy sods to hurry up with it.'

'Yes, Mr Higgerson.'

That made two jobs that Jem would rather not have done.

He frowned as he walked home. It seemed to him that Higgerson was getting rash and careless, far too sure of getting away with anything he decided to do. All he wanted was money, more and more of it, the way a drunkard went after booze.

And as for digging out an extra basement room in two of the worst houses in Backshaw Moss, it was asking for trouble. Those houses hadn't been built on good foundations in the first place, and to dig out an extra underground room with only the scantiest bracing around it was just plain daft. All for a few more shillings a week that the man didn't need.

Jem wouldn't like to live in one of those new rooms, by heck he wouldn't. He hated the shut-in, airless feeling that any cellar gave him, and these were going to be bad places. He'd never feel safe in them, never.

But some folk were so desperate for a roof over their heads, somewhere cheap and out of the rain and cold, they'd live anywhere they could afford.

That night Gwynneth went to bed early. Lucas had left for Manchester that morning, suddenly called to start his new work early. Only it wasn't like real work, being a student, was it? Fancy getting paid for reading books!

She was proud of him for being supported by a benefactor, of course she was, but she'd shed a few tears after waving him goodbye. She shed more after she went to bed, sad at spending a whole evening all alone.

She had trouble falling asleep, even though she was worn out by all the rush of getting her son packed and off. She tossed and turned, then suddenly realised she could smell smoke. She sat bolt upright in bed. Lucas usually put the fire out last thing at night and checked that everything was safe.

Could she have left a live coal that might have rolled out of the grate and set the rug alight? She had to check.

She switched on the light and ran into the living area, but there was nothing wrong there. The smell of smoke was still strong, however.

She followed her nose, which led her outside at the back of the house. Not only was the smell coming from the main house, there was a glow at the far corner of the building. A flame shot out, licking the air hungrily, and she squeaked in shock, freezing for a moment before starting to shout for help at the top of her voice.

She didn't wait to put her dressing gown on, but switched on the outside light and went to get the hosepipe they used to water the small garden at this side. Only, the hosepipe was missing, nowhere to be seen. How was that possible? She knew it had been there earlier because she'd tripped over one of the coils that had come loose.

Oh, no! Someone must have taken it, and that meant the fire had been lit on purpose. She shouted even more loudly, calling on the neighbours for help, and screaming the dreaded words, 'Fire! Help, fire!' at the top of her voice.

Lights came on in the main house and Wilf burst out of the back door in his pyjamas, stopping dead when he saw the fire.

He went looking for the hosepipe at his end of the building. Only that one wasn't there either.

'Have you taken the hosepipe?' he called.

'Someone's took them both!' she yelled back.

'Fill some buckets.' He too began to roar for help at the top of his voice, alternately shouting to his wife to get the kids out of the house.

Gwynneth ran into her flat for her buckets, filling the biggest one at the outside tap where the hosepipe should have been. Still yelling for help, Wilf snatched it from her and went to hurl it on the flames, by which time she'd started filling the other one.

She saw Stella bring the two children out to stand at the far end of the garden, then go back inside their house. She appeared at the window filling a bucket at the kitchen sink. Flames were now licking further up the corner of the house, but the walls were thick, and if Stella was still working to put the fire out from the inside, it couldn't have spread far into the house yet.

To Gwynneth's relief, neighbours had now come running out of nearby houses in their nightclothes, some also bearing buckets. When Wilf told them what had happened, one man ran back home for his hosepipe, panting back a couple of minutes later with it looped around his arms. He connected it to the tap outside Gwynneth's flat and started dousing the flames.

She continued to fill buckets at the outside tap and the kitchen sink, the full ones being snatched and replaced immediately by empty ones brought back by neighbours.

'Where's your hosepipe gone?' the neighbour who'd brought his asked.

'Someone's took it,' Gwynneth told him. 'Mark my words, that fire was set deliberately.'

'No! What's the world coming to?'

They all knew what each other's houses and gardens were like. Hosepipes didn't vanish into thin air. He cursed fluently, something he'd never normally do in front of a woman, and she couldn't help wishing that the dire retribution he was calling down on the villains really would happen to whoever had set the fire.

Buckets filled at the houses next door and across the street were now being passed along lines of willing helpers, and didn't stop coming till the fire was out. Thanks to their ability to work together, they'd caught it in time to save the main house, though the back corner and scullery had been badly damaged by smoke and water.

Sergeant Deemer had been called, and arrived just before the last flames were being extinguished.

The helpers left several full buckets of water 'just in case', then stopped filling more. Stella went to bring her children to stand with her as she joined the people gathered around the sergeant.

He listened to their tale. 'I'll find whoever did this,' he said in a harsh voice, unlike his usual quiet tone. 'But I need to know every detail you can remember. Everything. Starting with you, Mrs Harte. I gather you're the one who found the fire, and thank goodness you did.'

Gwynneth went through it, stopping to answer questions, though she didn't feel she knew anything that might indicate who had done it. She'd not heard any strange noises. It had been the smell that caught her attention after the fire had been set.

'Hosepipes can't just vanish,' he said. 'And there was a distinct smell of paraffin near that end of the house. I've got a good sense of smell.'

There was a gasp and a ripple of shocked murmurs as this confirmed their fears.

'Why?' someone asked. 'Why would anyone do such a thing? They could have killed Wilf and his family but for Gwynneth sounding the alarm.'

'I don't know why ... yet.' Deemer let that sink in for a moment or two, then said, 'We can't do much in the dark, but can some of you keep watch for the rest of the night? And please try not to trample on the soft earth of the garden. The intruder might have left footprints in it.'

'The children went down to stand at the far end, so they'll have left prints,' Stella said. 'And so would I when I fetched them back.'

'Their footprints will look different from a grown man's.' He glanced down at her feet. 'And you're barefoot.'

She looked down in surprise at her muddy feet. 'I never even noticed.'

'Well, you should try to rest a little, but you won't want to go into that end of the house. It stinks of smoke. Besides, we'll need to make sure it's safe. We don't want you encountering any other nasty surprises. Can you and the children stay with Mrs Harte, perhaps?'

One of the neighbours from across the road said, 'Mrs Harte's flat is only small. Shall I take the children back with me, Stella love? They can sleep with my two. And you won't need to worry about them. You know I'll look after them like my own.'

Stella's voice wobbled. 'Thanks. Yes, please.'

Sergeant Deemer nodded approval and turned to Gwynneth. 'Perhaps you could make her a cup of tea, Mrs Harte? I'd like to have a word with Wilf and the other men.'

'Yes, of course.' She could see shock setting in with Stella. Well, she was feeling a bit shaky herself, and was also embarrassed to have been seen in her nightdress, not even her best nightie, either. Thank goodness it was made of nice thick flannel with long sleeves and a high neck, and didn't show any of the body inside it!

'Come through into my part of the house, Stella love. It's escaped the worst of the smoke. I'll make us both a cup of tea, shall I?'

When they got into the flat, Stella began shivering and suddenly burst into tears. 'S-sorry. It's just that I lost my first husband in a house fire. It's brought it all back – such terrible memories. And – someone has tried to burn this house down before, only they didn't even get started then. They more than got started this time, didn't they? Who can hate us so much?'

Gwynneth was certain she could guess who'd done this, or at least arranged it. There was only one person in the valley wicked enough. She didn't say anything though. They'd work it out for themselves. She guided Stella to a chair and put the kettle on, grateful that the gas was still working.

She found clean dishcloths for the two of them to wash their smoke-blackened faces with, then she got out a large man's handkerchief left behind by one of her sons for Stella to continue mopping her tears.

It had to be Higgerson's doing. Had to be! How could even he do such a thing with two small children in the house?

★★★

Sergeant Deemer was asking himself the same question and coming to the same conclusion about who'd caused the fire as he drove home. Why had Higgerson done this now, out of the blue? He'd been quiet for a while, but had started to cause trouble again, and in bigger ways than before. And if that man didn't realise that people would guess who was behind it, he was getting stupid as well as careless as he grew older. Or perhaps he thought he was powerful enough to be untouchable.

It was strange, because he was usually extremely cunning.

Deemer sighed. Whatever the reason, wasn't there enough trouble in the world without causing more? One wicked man was creating wholescale mayhem in Germany, and those in the know were worrying about him starting another war. Now another evil man was causing upsets in the valley, just as times were at long last getting better.

The sergeant had a strong sense of impending trouble. He'd applied several times for an extra constable to be appointed, given the increase in population in his valley. He'd apply again, of course he would, but would the authorities give him another man even now?

It had been hinted to him that someone with influence was preventing such an appointment. Did Higgerson have a way of pressuring someone with power in the county?

Deemer was worried sick, definitely couldn't do any more with only himself and one young constable to look after the whole valley. He had to find a way to get more help, not just the special constables you could call on in an emergency, but full-time help.

6

In the morning, just before dawn according to her little bed-side clock, Gwynneth woke with a start. Well, she hadn't slept soundly, had she? It was not only the fire, but the fact that she had guests. Stella and Wilf were sharing Lucas's bed-room, but they could only have got an hour or two's sleep, so probably wouldn't get up for a while yet.

However, when she tiptoed into the kitchen area, she found the fire burning brightly in the grate, and Wilf sitting at the table hugging a mug of tea.

He gave her a faint smile and a nod. 'Stella was upset last night and it took her a while to drop off. I couldn't sleep at all for worrying, so when it started to get light, I came up here to let her have a bit more time in bed.' He gestured to the tea-pot. 'I hope you don't mind me making myself a cup. It's only a few minutes old, so the tea won't be stewed yet, just a bit stronger than usual.'

'I don't mind at all. Do you want a piece of toast?'

He looked faintly surprised. 'I do actually.'

She poured herself a cup and got out the loaf and bread knife. She could guess what was coming. As she was getting dressed, she'd reached the conclusion that she'd have to move out of the flat and let the four of them use it while the main house was being repaired. They were the owners, after all, and there were four of them. Their kitchen and living area must have been badly damaged by smoke, and there was only one of her to re-house.

He was looking uncomfortable, and that'd be why. Well, he was a kind man, wouldn't turn her out lightly, so she said it for him. 'It makes sense for me to move out. Let alone, you own this place, you'll want somewhere to live while you do the repairs.' She cut a slice of bread and reached for the toasting fork.

'I hate to turn you out of your home, Gwynneth.'

'It was already feeling empty without Lucas. Anyway Gabriel and Maisie will have room for me in their house. I shan't want to stay there permanently, but it'll give us all breathing space.'

She hesitated, then threaded the bread on the toasting fork. 'It'll be Higgerson's doing, don't you think? He hates you, and he always tries to hurt people who have upset him, even if he has to wait to do it. He's a bad man.'

'He's more than bad. I think he's crazy. But surely he wasn't always this bad?'

She held the bread out to the heat of the fire. 'I don't think he was. He's grown a lot worse since his wife left. It's as if her escaping made him feel he has to prove himself to the world – as if he's showing he's still a force to be reckoned with. I'd not like to be in her shoes. He'll go after her and catch her one day, for sure.'

'She's in another town. It's harder to get at people from a distance. And Sergeant Deemer told me that the man about to become her son's father-in-law is very clever, and has people working for him who'll keep her safe.'

'Let's hope that's true.' She turned the toasted side and held the other side out to the fire. 'I'll walk round to Daisy Street to see our Gabriel in an hour or so about moving in with them. I'll give him and Maisie time to get up first. I can be out of this flat by teatime, probably earlier. I'll have to find someone to cart my things, and—'

'I'll see to that. You just do the packing, Gwynneth.'

'Thank you. I'm so sorry this has happened to your lovely house.'

'So am I.'

She buttered the toast and handed it to him without bothering with a plate, then started toasting another piece of bread. He gobbled the first one down and stood up.

'I'll have something else later. I want to look round the outside of the house now that it's light, and start assessing the damage. The sergeant had said not to touch anything till he's checked it all, but I can see how bad it is.'

Gwynneth watched him leave, then wept into her apron briefly. She didn't let herself dwell on feeling vulnerable for long, and forced herself to stop. It hurt to think of losing her home, but it was no use crying. She was old enough to know that life hit you with nasty surprises every now and then. You just had to find a way to carry on. At least she was sure her son would welcome her into his house.

The trouble was, she'd much rather have her own home and run it her way. She *liked* housework and keeping things nice, had taken a pride in this flat, small as it was, and in the housework she did for Wilf and Stella to pay for living there.

She helped out other people from time to time too, for free if someone was sick or had a crisis, for payment otherwise. She was sure she'd pick up more cleaning jobs once it was known she'd lost her main job. She didn't intend to be a burden on Gabriel, or on anyone else if she could help it.

How lucky that his wife had inherited that lovely big house in Daisy Street. The new man who'd been left the end one was lucky too: Arthur Chapman. She'd heard that he'd had some bad things happen, but she only had a vague idea of what they were because he'd lived down the valley at the other side of the town.

No doubt she'd find out when she moved in with Gabriel and Maisie. She just hoped Mr Chapman inheriting a house hadn't upset Higgerson because she'd be living two doors away from that house from now on, and didn't want to get caught up in anything else involving *that horrible man*.

Now, enough of that. She had to go and catch her son before he started work. She put the bread and other things neatly out at one side of the table. She wasn't hungry, but Stella might want some breakfast and Wilf would definitely want more later.

Gabriel answered the door, looked at his mother, and held his arms out. 'Whatever's upsetting you, we'll find a way to sort it out.'

She hugged him and managed not to burst into tears. 'You heard about Wilf and Stella's house being set on fire?'

'Yes.'

'They're going to need somewhere to live while they're repairing the damage, and the flat is the obvious place, with only me living there now. So . . . I have to find somewhere else to live.'

'And you're coming here, naturally.'

'Will Maisie mind?'

Her daughter-in-law joined them, giving her a quick hug. 'Will Maisie mind what?'

Gwynneth explained, and Maisie said, 'Of course you must come here. We've got rid of a lot of the excess furniture that had been left in the house when we moved in, thanks to Charlie Willcox, so we can fit yours in easily.'

'Thanks, love. Wilf said he'd get it brought over today.'

Maisie nodded. 'It's the least he can do if he's turning you out. Come and have a cup of tea with us and we'll decide which room you should use and where to put any spare pieces.'

'Anywhere will do. I won't stay for tea now, if you don't mind. I need to start packing my things.'

Gabriel exchanged glances with his wife but didn't say anything. 'We've got a few empty cardboard boxes, Mum. I'll drive you back and you can use them to make a start, then I'll check that Wilf can come for everything with Mr Tyler's van later this afternoon.'

Gwynneth had expected her son and his wife to take her in, and she knew they'd be kind to her, but she still didn't like the idea of living with them. That might be ungrateful, but she couldn't help it. She valued her independence. It had been hard earned.

Trouble was, she knew only too well that older women on their own had trouble finding decent places where they could live independently, so she had no choice. It'd probably be months before Wilf and Stella got their house repaired, and would they even want her to move back? They'd said they'd ask her to do some cleaning for them once the house was repaired and cleared up a bit. In the meantime, she'd have to try to find some other work because she didn't want to be a burden on her son.

Oh, who knew anything? she thought, as Gabriel drove her the short distance to her flat.

She waved goodbye to him, forcing a smile. Well, she hoped it looked like a smile. It didn't feel like one.

Ah, just get on with it, you fool, and stop worrying about the future, she told herself as she walked inside.

It took her until mid-afternoon to pack all her things, and some had to be stuffed into pillowcases. There were also the items Lucas had left behind. He wouldn't want to lose his precious collection of books, she knew.

While she was waiting for Wilf she wrote a quick postcard to Lucas telling him not to try to come home yet. His things would be safe in his brother's house. It was a good thing she always kept postcards and stamps handy. She gave a neighour's child a penny to drop it in the post box near the village shop.

Wilf turned up later in the afternoon with another man sent by Mr Tyler to help out. They wouldn't let her help carry the heavier articles, like her bed, table and chairs, so Gwynneth had nothing to do but stand and watch them.

When they got to Gabriel's house she took the men upstairs and showed them where to put her bed. The other larger items went into the fancy dining room, which Maisie and Gabriel weren't using.

While he went off to pick up the rest of his mother's furniture and possessions, she chatted briefly to Maisie, then went to stand by the front door enjoying the early spring sunshine.

While she was there, two men drove up and went towards the end house, the nearest one to Birch End. Biff must be bringing the new owner of Number 25 to see his inheritance. Eh, imagine inheriting your own house like her son's wife and this man had done. Wouldn't that be wonderful? No one could throw you out, then.

The stranger would be quite good-looking for an older man – well, he would if he weren't so thin – and he had a nice, if rather shy smile. You could usually judge people by their smiles.

Gabriel came back just then with Wilf, and the two of them went across to say hello to the new owner and beckoned Gwynneth across to be introduced properly. 'My mother has come to live with us because of the fire at Wilf's house.'

'My family need to use the flat till the main house can be repaired. The downstairs isn't liveable, and the whole place reeks of smoke. We'd not have turned her out if we didn't know she could come here,' Wilf said.

'Any idea yet who set the fire?'

'We can guess. But there's no proof.'

Mr Chapman was standing next to Gwynneth. 'Hard to lose your home like that,' he said quietly. 'I hope you'll settle in comfortably here.'

She didn't intend to appear weak, so she said as firmly as she could manage, 'Thanks. I'm only staying for the time being till

I can find another job as housekeeper somewhere. I know Wilf will give me good references.'

He nodded. 'I certainly will.'

Gabriel put his arm round her shoulders. 'No rush to do that. We're happy to have you here with us, Mum.'

Mr Chapman shot a quick glance at her and she thought from his understanding expression that he must have guessed how badly she wanted her own home again.

She gave them another nod and followed her son into the house, forcing a smile to her face.

'Do you think they'll find out who set that fire?' Arthur asked Biff as they went inside Number 25.

'From what I heard in the shop, everyone's sure it's Higgerson, but of course they won't be able to prove it.'

'He's a wicked man, that one. Causes a lot of harm and unhappiness.'

'I won't let him hurt you,' Biff said, not for the first time.

'I won't just cower in a corner if someone attacks me – or you.'

It pleased Biff that Arthur was already sounding as if he was pulling himself together.

Arthur hesitated, looking as if he wanted to say something but was unsure about it.

'Just say it,' Biff told him.

'All right. No offence, but I'd like to walk round the house on my own, if you don't mind. Get to know it a bit. You sometimes get feelings when you go into new places, don't you?'

'Yes. Shall we make a shopping list before you do that, then I can nip out and buy some food for today?'

'No need for a list. I don't mind what you get. I'm not fussy.'

'All right. You'd better lock the door while I'm out. Don't let anyone inside, and don't go outside on your own. That Stanley brute might still be lurking nearby.'

'Yes. I'll be careful.'

When he was on his own, Arthur walked slowly round the ground floor, mentally working out which pieces of furniture would be easy to repair. They'd need a kitchen table and chairs first, he decided, and set the chosen pieces out. He could easily put these right once he had some tools. After Biff had brought back the groceries, he'd suggest going to collect the set of tools waiting for him at the hardware store.

He smiled at the kitchen. He didn't want to waste another minute in getting started. In fact, he'd not go and look round the upstairs yet, but sort out the things down here which he could easily repair for their daily needs. He'd seen several comfortable chairs scattered here and there.

He looked round and soon found two that'd be simple to repair.

'Thank you Sarah Jane Chapman,' he whispered as he took them into the kitchen. He stared towards the ceiling as you seemed to do when talking to those dead before you. 'I won't waste this opportunity, I promise you.' They could make this room their headquarters, and keep nice and warm.

He glanced out of the kitchen window, and it occurred to him that they hadn't gone outside into the yard. Once Biff got back, he'd suggest taking a quick look at the outhouses. Who knew what was in them?

He hadn't needed Biff's warning. He wasn't stupid enough to go out of the house on his own yet, not with that Jem Stanley turning up everywhere.

It was half an hour before Biff got back, judging by the crooked little kitchen clock, which had one foot missing but still managed to produce a happy-sounding tick. Arthur made sure who it was before he opened the door, and put the idea of buying a chain lock for the door on his mental list, so that he could partly open it and have a chance of shutting it quickly if he didn't like the looks of someone.

Biff was accompanied by a lad with a home-made trolley full of brimming paper carrier bags. When they'd unloaded them all, Arthur saw him slip the lad sixpence, a generous payment when threepence would have brought the same service.

It took the two men a while to put the food away, because they had to work out where they were going to keep each item, then wipe down the shelves.

When that was done, Biff suggested going to collect the tools from the hardware shop in Rivenshaw. Arthur nearly agreed, but then suddenly wondered if there were any tools in the house. There might be some in the cellar. It'd be worth checking.

His stomach let out a growling sound and he realised he was ravenous. He'd got his former appetite back with a vengeance, was feeling better than he had for ages. It'd have to wait, though.

When they got down into the cellar he gasped in both surprise and pleasure.

'This is set up as a workshop, a really good one too, and there are a few tools left. Look at that workbench. Lovely wood it's made from. And there are even wooden offcuts piled up over there ready to use.'

He stared at the bench and how it fitted against the wall, then frowned and bent closer.

'Something wrong?' Biff asked.

'I'm not sure.' He ran his fingers over the rough wooden panel behind the workbench. 'This isn't quite— Look, the grain of the wood doesn't match. Why put in a new piece at the bottom corner?'

He ran his hands over that area again, stopping at one edge, which seemed slightly raised, and pressing it. The wood moved slightly and when he pressed harder there was a loud click, and the whole back panel and bench top moved, just a little.

'Why would they build a workbench that comes loose?' He tugged at it and exclaimed in surprise as the whole workbench then slid to the left, giving a space just big enough for one person to squeeze through. Below the space were steps leading down into utter darkness.

Arthur ran his fingers over the edge of the panel. 'This is very skilfully done! It takes two movements to open it. I reckon it's the work of a master craftsman.'

Biff whistled softly. 'What next? This whole house is puzzling. Let's find out where it leads.'

He was about to start down the steps, but Arthur put one arm across the gap. 'Have you got a torch?'

'No. Why?'

'We don't know what's down there – or who – or even if the panel will stay open. No use going down there without getting a torch and finding something to prevent the panel closing behind us.'

Biff looked at him with new respect. 'You're right. I think there was a torch in the scullery, but I don't know whether it had any batteries in it.'

'Probably not, after all this time.'

Biff's stomach rumbled suddenly. 'Let's get something to eat first. I'm famished.'

'So am I.' Arthur turned to leave, then swung back. 'I think we should close this again and put a few pieces of wood on the surface.' He bent to check the lock more closely. 'I'd guess when this piece is fitted into place at the side, it'll prevent anyone coming in from below. I'm not sure, though. I'll need to check the other side more closely, but it's very dark down there so I won't be able to make out the details.'

Biff was still peering into the hole. 'There's not a sign of light coming in from anywhere else down there.'

'None at all. I wonder what's beyond the bottom of those stairs.'

'Let's go and find that torch.'

They shut the panel and went back up to the scullery. There was indeed a torch standing on the windowsill, but it had no batteries in it.

'This is the most frustrating house I've ever been in,' Biff said. 'Nothing's ready to use. And most of the stuff is broken.'

Arthur's voice was soft. 'It could be such a lovely house. If I can keep it, I'll bring it up to scratch again, however long it takes.'

'You do that. Let's grab some food quickly, then go to the hardware store in Rivenshaw. We can buy some torch batteries at the same time.'

'Yes, let's. It used to be one of my favourite shops.'

Arthur felt disappointed not to have found where the stairs led straight away. But that was only one of the many things he needed to investigate in his new home. He still had trouble believing this house and its contents belonged to him.

Eh, he wished Susan were still alive. She'd have loved this house. And it'd need a woman's touch as well as his to bring it up to scratch. Women seemed to notice and deal with the details of daily life much better than men.

He remembered again how Susan had several times said if she died, he should marry again, because he'd need a wife. He'd got angry at that, but when he'd told her he'd never be able to replace her, she'd said gently that no one could replace another. It'd simply be a different type of partnership, and nothing wrong with that.

Maybe she'd been right. She'd been such a wise person, even as a child.

Of course he'd need to meet a woman he at least *liked*. You couldn't marry someone if you didn't find them easy to get on with. But he could see already that he'd need a wife to manage a big house like this.

And why was he thinking about that now? He and Biff needed something to eat.

Besides, what decent woman would want to marry someone who'd been one of the town drunks only a few months ago?

After they'd eaten some thick slices of buttered bread and a piece of soft, crumbly Lancashire cheese, they drove into town and called in at the hardware store.

Arthur checked out the set of tools that had been paid for and compared them mentally to the few tools in the cellar. He asked diffidently whether he could swap one or two for others that he preferred to work with, and explained that he had a few tools already.

'Of course, Mr Chapman. You can have anything you like as long as it comes to the same value in total.'

It was the first time anyone had called him 'Mr' for a couple of years. The term of respect made him straighten up and square his shoulders.

He'd make Susan proud of him, he vowed. And maybe one day his son would start speaking to him again.

He didn't let himself dwell on that sadness, concentrated instead on checking out each tool he was offered, changing a couple of them for better quality pieces, and adding a few smaller tools. He also chose a basic collection of screws, nails and a glue pot, enough to start him off.

'You enjoyed doing that, didn't you?' Biff said with a grin as they carried the two full boxes out to the car. 'You were very impressive, clearly knew your stuff.'

'It'll be good to get tools in my hands again. I won't lose this lot, I can tell you.'

Back at the house, Arthur repaired a couple of kitchen chairs and the table, by which time the short February day was coming to a close, but at least they had somewhere to sit and eat.

Biff said quietly, 'Well done. That was a good day's work.'

'Thanks for your help.'

The two Becksley brothers turned up just then.

'Are you sure it's necessary to hire them?' Arthur was worrying now about how much it was going to cost to have two men keeping guard.

'It was necessary with Maisie's house, believe me. One of them will do days, and one nights for a week or two, but they'll both sleep here. They'll keep a very careful watch, believe me. Once Higgerson sets his mind on acquiring something, he'll play any nasty trick there is to get it. You and I need our sleep if we're to stay alert as we settle in.'

When his companion still looked dubious, he realised why. 'Don't worry. You won't be paying for this.'

But Arthur did worry. How could he not?

7

Sergeant Deemer strolled along the street, still worrying about the fire at Wilf's house a couple of days ago. He could guess who had arranged for it and why? Did Higgerson think he was fooled? What worried him was what that fellow would try next.

But he hid his feelings, nodding and smiling as usual to people he knew. He took note of more than most of them realised, though, as he walked along. He always kept an eye on the various goings-on in his town.

He saw Judge Peters strolling towards him and slowed down. The judge was a capable man, a decade or more younger than Deemer, and folk reckoned he was going to rise high in the county's legal circles one day. He'd been working in London for a while and hadn't been back in the valley for long.

Peters also slowed down, smiling a greeting but waiting to speak until there was no one nearby. 'Can you make it to an extraordinary meeting this Sunday, Gilbert?'

The sergeant nodded, not needing to be told what sort of meeting, let alone who would be involved or where it would be held. 'Happy to.'

'About nine o'clock in the morning?'

'Fine by me.'

'We'll drive there together.' The judge raised his voice as a woman came towards them, 'And do please give my regards to Mrs Deemer.'

The passer-by gave the sergeant a half-smile and hurried past them, her shopping basket bobbing about on her arm, her mind clearly on her imminent purchases. The two men waited till she was out of hearing, however, before carrying on their conversation.

'On another topic, I found out that you've made several applications for another constable to be appointed in the valley and they've all been turned down. I was surprised at that. If a man of your experience says you need more help, Gilbert, then I'm quite sure you genuinely do need it. I can see two reasons for it myself even after only a short time back, one being the increase in population round here, but the other is Higgerson. It hasn't escaped my notice that he seems to be growing more active again.'

'Unfortunately he is, and yet he's as slippery as ever. I haven't been able to pin anything on him.'

'He had the nerve to invite me to lunch with him at the inn yesterday.'

'I'd as soon lunch with the devil in hell.'

Peters smiled. 'I made it very plain that I wasn't interested in ever spending any time with him socially, and said it loudly enough to be overheard by several people. I don't think he'll risk asking me again. Anyway, re your request, I had a word with a couple of chaps I know who have some influence in this region, and they've been making sure the new officer you've asked for will be assigned. The people who'd been blocking the appointment were, I think, also warned about making decisions without consulting others.'

A sigh of relief escaped the sergeant. 'I can't tell you how grateful I am, my friend. I've been finding it . . . well, rather disheartening to be under-manned, and to tell you the truth, I've been feeling over-tired lately. I'm not getting any younger. My wife says I've been doing too much for a man of my age.'

'Thinking of retiring?'

'I'm not quite old enough yet. And I certainly won't go until I've put an end to Higgerson's criminal antics.'

'The valley's lucky to have a man of your calibre in charge of policing it. You should have been promoted years ago.'

'They did offer me a promotion, and more than once, but I prefer to be involved with people. I don't enjoy paperwork and meetings, not to mention political to-ing and fro-ing, which seems more like childish bickering to me half the time.'

'That doesn't surprise me. Anyway, someone will be phoning you to say your new man will be starting work here next Tuesday. It's a promotion to senior constable for him, and well deserved. He's a capable chap, should go far: Mike Grafton. Do you know him?'

Sergeant Deemer beamed. 'I've not worked with him, but I've heard good things about him from a couple of chaps who have. Did he want to come here? We're a bit out of the way for those who are likely to climb high in the service.'

'He got married recently and his wife grew up round here. She wants to move closer to her family for a while because she's expecting their first child.'

'Even better. I'm sure Grafton will fit in.'

'Yes. And I'm sure you're the right person to help him on his way up the ladder of promotion by polishing his skills at managing situations and people. At the same time he'll supply you with some younger legs to run around the valley as needed. Oh, and he's also a very good driver if you need to get anywhere fast.'

Gilbert nodded and suppressed a sigh. He resented the limitations of growing old, and simple things galled him these days, such as not being able to run as fast as he used to. Only you didn't get much choice: slowing down as you got older came to everyone. He felt he still had a lot to offer, though. The age of retirement for police officers in his local force was sixty, lower than for the average citizen, who had to wait till sixty-five to retire under general government rules.

He remembered when old age pensions were first introduced in 1908. It had been a measly five shillings a week after age seventy, means tested, yet his grandfather had blessed the government for even that small amount. Eh, how times had changed! The sergeant would receive half his salary as a pension, and he'd already saved hard and bought a cottage for when he and his wife had to leave the police house they currently occupied.

He could apply to retire later than sixty, and he might do that, because he was still in good health and enjoyed his job. Besides, if it was humanly possible, he was determined to catch Higgerson before he left the police force.

'Will your present constable resent someone being brought in over his head?' Peters asked.

'Bless you, no. Cliff is well aware that he still has a lot to learn. He'll probably enjoy having someone younger to work with instead of an old fogey like me though.'

'The police could do with more old fogeys like you, Gilbert. Experience is a valuable commodity. Anyway, I can't stand here all day chatting. See you on Sunday.' He offered his hand and they shook warmly before parting.

That was done deliberately to show anyone watching how highly the judge regarded their police sergeant, Deemer guessed. Well, the respect was reciprocated.

As he went on his way he noticed Jem Stanley on the other side of the street haranguing a chap who looked terrified. The thug poked him in the chest so hard he staggered backwards and thumped against a wall.

The sergeant changed direction abruptly and started to cross the road. Unfortunately, by the time he'd waited for a slow-moving lorry to pass, Stanley was striding away so fast he was almost running, and his victim was making a hasty escape down a nearby alley.

The sergeant didn't call the fellow back, but he knew the man and didn't have to wonder why he was being bullied. He lived in one of Higgerson's run-down houses, and had most likely fallen behind on the rent.

Deemer had been surprised when Higgerson employed Stanley, who wasn't nearly as clever as the previous henchman had been at this sort of thing. Dobbs had known how to hide what he was doing most of the time; Stanley went after people like a bull at a gate.

Most of his victims declined to lodge a complaint against him, even after he'd given them a thumping. But Stanley would make a mistake soon, Deemer was sure. And he'd be watching out for it, ready to pounce.

He let out a happy sigh. Only this morning he had been feeling down in the dumps because he simply didn't have the manpower to keep a proper watch on Higgerson. There were, after all, only twenty-four hours in a day, however cleverly you used them.

Now, after his conversation with Peters, he was feeling much more optimistic. Things were going to improve, he was sure of it.

And he'd be waiting to seize the moment where Higgerson was concerned.

Sergeant Deemer set off early on the Sunday morning, leaving the young constable to hold the fort in the valley. Even his wife didn't know exactly whom he was meeting or where, it was so hush-hush. He'd told Cliff he was visiting a sick acquaintance who lived outside the valley, so the constable was to stay on duty at the police station and answer any calls for assistance.

Deemer considered the meeting extremely important. When the Great War had broken out, the country had been caught napping, with outdated equipment and horse-based approaches to fighting in a world where vehicles were taking over transport at an increasingly rapid rate.

Sadly, it looked as if war was brewing once more, however much the authorities denied it. Mr Churchill had gone against the current government's pacifist approach, calling publicly in newspaper articles and at meetings for better preparations to be made in Britain this time.

The present government consisted of a bunch of short-sighted weaklings in Deemer's opinion, but he and many other people who'd lived through the Great War had a lot of respect for Mr Churchill and took that man's warnings seriously. The articles were well written, with cogent arguments for being better prepared.

It was partly as a consequence that some people had formed groups to make sure unofficial preparations were made in their area of the country for resistance, even allowing for the worst that could happen and Britain be invaded – 'just in case'. You were a fool if you didn't recognise that Hitler was gathering together a much cleverer group of men than had been in command in 1914. It seemed obvious that he had his eye on the parts of Europe near Germany, but dictators rarely stopped their rampages once they got going, and who knew where he'd turn after that?

The people in the local group were making preparations even while hoping that they'd never have to put these measures into operation. Fortunately there was an abandoned quarry just outside Rivenshaw, to the south-east of Birch End. The workings had been extended over a century ago by those labouring in it, to connect the natural caves and tunnels nearby with the town and villages in the valley. This had been done on purely selfish grounds, to give themselves a safe and dry journey to and from work in inclement weather.

Only a few of the older generation knew exactly where these tunnels were these days. The group Deemer was working with had renovated and extended them, while at the same time spreading rumours that they were being blocked off because they were dangerous.

Given that there were natural tunnels, the work had not been arduous. It meant that people could leave or enter the valley secretly by various routes. This would in turn allow them to access a national system of concealed routes and refuges. No one in the country knew the details of the whole system, only their own part of it and how to get in contact with nearby groups.

If there were another war and, heaven forbid, an invasion of the country really did take place, the government might be caught napping again, but others, deeply loyal, would be able to lead a loosely organised resistance.

No true patriot believed the country would ever allow itself to stay occupied for long. 'Rule Britannia' was more than just a song; it was a deeply held belief for most inhabitants of the country.

The sergeant felt honoured to have been invited to join the local group, but prayed that another generation of their best and bravest lads – yes, and lasses too these days – would not again have to give their lives to keep their country safe.

When he and Peters arrived at the quarry, they found the usual man on guard. Its so-called caretaker was a genial fellow who was reputed to make a good living selling chunks of rock for the owner, a gentleman in London, and also selling a few on the side for his own benefit.

That had given him the excuse to set up a stout gate across the entrance and keep it locked except during opening hours when he would be there to deal with bona fide customers. There was another way into the tunnel system on foot, again not known to many except a select and trusted few.

The gate was open at the moment, though with a wheel-barrow parked sideways to block the entrance. The caretaker moved it to the side so that the sergeant could drive through and park his car out of sight of the road, then the wheelbarrow was put back across the space.

The two men got out of the car and walked round to the far side of the quarry in silence, going along a narrow tunnel to the large cave a little further inside. The entrance was so low they had to bend uncomfortably to get inside, but as they turned the first corner out of sight of the road the ceiling quickly became higher.

Lanterns guided them into a larger cave where most of the people in the group were already assembled. Nodding to the others, the two men found places to sit on rocky ledges or on large chunks of fallen rock and chatted quietly with the nearby people they rarely met other than here.

The leader of the group waited for the last few to arrive, then stood up and everyone fell silent. He was an imposing figure, tall and still handsome in spite of his silver hair, as well as highly respected by everyone who knew him.

'Thank you for coming today, ladies and gentlemen. I'll get straight to the point: I have some bad news for you. There is a traitor in Rivenshaw, who has been making overtures to a certain minor political party whose members would support a fascist invasion and takeover of our country. This man has told them about our group's existence, though he doesn't know any details yet. He guarantees to stop us taking action against them *when* the invasion happens—'

There were involuntary gasps of shock and anger at this.

'—but he wants their guarantee in return that he'll be appointed as the local officer in charge of this part of Lancashire after Hitler takes over our country.'

This was followed by dead silence as all those present considered the information. It was the last thing they'd have expected to hear today or any other day.

'How did anyone else even know about us, Your Lordship?'

'That's what I want to know,' he said grimly. 'Fortunately, this chap doesn't seem aware of the full details or wider connections our group has, and thinks it consists of only a few men, myself included.'

'Do you know who the traitor is?'

'Not yet. I heard of this from a man who is in a position elsewhere in the country to pass us further information – when he can do so safely. The initial contact has been made by the traitor very tentatively, it seems, and he's taking great care to conceal his identity. I brought you here today as soon as I heard about this. I felt it was important to make you aware of the situation and ask you to keep your eyes and ears open.'

'We'll find him,' someone muttered.

'And eliminate him,' someone else added and no one disagreed.

'I didn't want to put anything in writing or even mention it on the telephone in case an operator was listening in. If you hear anything, even if you're not sure whether it's true, please take the same precautions and let me or one of our two deputies know in person.' He inclined his head to another man and a woman as he said this.

He waited until the ongoing buzz of speculation and anger had died down, not surprised to hear the name Higgerson mentioned several times.

When someone said bluntly, 'It has to be Higgerson. Who else would betray our country?'

'I don't think that fellow is clever enough to do this, or interested enough in politics. Higgerson's personal god has always seemed to be to make money, not gain political power.'

'Nonetheless we'll keep an eye on him. How the hell did anyone find out about us?'

'My guess is that the information has probably come in the first place from one of the workmen we employed to extend the tunnels. I know those of you involved in that vouched for the men you gave the work to, but pressure can be brought to bear on even the most loyal people, especially if they fear for the safety of their loved ones. Or someone could simply have spoken carelessly.'

He shook his head sadly, gave them a little longer to murmur to one another, then continued in his usual quiet tone, 'I think it might be best for you to form pairs, or at the most, trios, chosen according to location. You should share every single piece of information about your area, however minor, so that if one person is attacked the other can spread the word about where to look for the traitor or traitors. Perhaps you'd like to decide now whom you could best work closely with?'

There was a quiet buzz as they sorted out their partnerships and contact arrangements.

It was clear that Sergeant Deemer and Judge Peters would be able to form a suitable alliance, but the two of them also chatted to the people who lived closest to Rivenshaw and the Ellin Valley. Peters knew them all, had done for years, but Deemer had not moved in the more elevated social circles, so didn't know nearly as much about them, except as a police officer.

There had been no snobbish treatment offered to him when he joined this group. Their leader was one of the shrewdest men in Lancashire, and His Lordship had chosen his working partners very carefully indeed. They'd been told to use his title and not the rest of his name when working on this venture. If a man of his calibre valued people enough to choose them, the others felt they could rely on his judgement.

As Sergeant Deemer drove back, the two men were mainly silent.

'It's worrying to have a leak,' Peters said after a while.

'I know who my first suspect is and some of the others seemed to feel the same.'

'If you're thinking of Higgerson, Gilbert, I'm in agreement with His Lordship. I doubt it's Higgerson. I checked and he got out of fighting in the Great War for genuine health reasons, some heart problem or other. No, it must be someone else, a newcomer to the valley perhaps.'

'I shall certainly keep my eyes open.'

'You're probably in a better position than me to do that. No one knows our valley folk as well as you do. But don't hesitate to call on me if I can help in any way, and I shall, of course, keep my own eyes open and share any information with you.'

'I shan't hesitate to ask for your help if needed, Dennison. And if you don't mind, I'll tell my wife the broad details and say that if I'm not available and she feels suspicious, she can call on you for help and trust you implicitly.'

'Of course. I've heard nothing but good of her.'

That pleased Deemer greatly. 'I've not told my wife any details so far, but she's not stupid, and has no doubt guessed that we're involved in some secret work for our country. I would trust her with my life any time.'

'You're a lucky man. I lost the woman I loved in the Great War. She was a nurse, working in France.'

'I'm sorry to hear that. And you're right: I am indeed lucky in my wife.'

He didn't say anything else, was a bit embarrassed at having confided so much to Dennison, but he hadn't met many men he liked and trust as he did this one.

In fact, after a slight hesitation, he confided another worry to Peters.

The judge was shocked. 'Are you sure?'

'Yes. But I don't have any proof.'

'I can't act without it.'

'I know. I'm getting rather worried about the safety of the child, though.'

8

That same week Ester Goodsal found herself a job in another town. She'd been looking around for a while because she couldn't stand to work as Mrs Hicks's general maid any longer. Having to stand by helplessly while that poor, orphaned child was beaten and harangued tore her apart.

She didn't give her notice because she didn't trust her mistress not to do something terrible, like accusing her of theft. She felt it'd be safer simply to vanish and forfeit the pay owing. She didn't want to leave Beatie without anyone to keep an eye on her, though, so on what she'd decided would be her last day at that unhappy house, she got permission from the housekeeper to slip out in her midday meal break supposedly to do some urgent personal shopping for Kotex sanitary towels.

The housekeeper was old-fashioned, and grimaced at the thought of buying such items publicly. She had several times told the maid she could save money and make do with rags that she soaked and washed, as women had done for centuries. But in the end she gave in and let her go out.

Instead of shopping, Ester went searching for Sergeant Deemer. Her grandparents knew him and, when she'd confided in them, they'd assured her that he'd believe her. They had been shocked at the tales she'd told them over the past few months.

She was lucky enough to catch him at the police station and, after a hasty glance around to make sure none of her mistress's acquaintances was walking along the street, she slipped through the door.

He was behind the counter and looked up in mild surprise at the sight of her coming in so furtively. 'What can I do for you, Ester lass?'

'It's what you can do for that poor child I look after sometimes, sergeant. If Mrs Hicks goes on beating her like this, she'll kill her. I can't stand by and watch helplessly any more.'

He stiffened. 'Beatie Hicks, you mean?'

'Yes. Are you aware of what's going on?'

'I'm aware of what I *think* is going on, but I can't do anything to stop the woman officially till I can prove it. People are allowed to chastise their children, after all.'

'But not beat them till they bleed. If you take a doctor to examine the child today, you'll find evidence of her being severely beaten – the poor little thing can hardly sit down. And it was for nothing, as usual. She was supposed to have been looking at her grandmother "cheekily". Just looking!'

'Tell me the details.'

He listened carefully, then said, 'Will you sign a statement to say what you saw happen?'

'Yes. But I'll have to do it today and quickly, because I've found myself another job and I'm leaving tonight without giving notice.'

'Come through to my office and I'll take your statement down, then young Cliff can witness it.'

'You won't do anything till after I leave?'

'We'll see how it goes.'

When she'd finished, he looked at her regretfully. 'Eh, lass, I have to act straight away on something as bad as this. We can't let that child be killed or maimed!'

She stared at him in mute dismay.

'Can you get your possessions out quickly? If you leave them in the laneway behind the house, young Cliff will pick them up and fetch them here.'

'I have them packed already. I deliberately broke the lock on my trunk and said I was sending it to be repaired last week, but I sent it to my grandparents instead. It was full of my possessions and my summer clothing. I think I can get the rest out without being seen.'

'I can bring you here for questioning if she tries to stop you leaving, then let you slip away with your luggage, since you've already signed a statement. Have you got somewhere to go?'

'Yes, straight to my new job, and my grandparents have got a friend who's going to drive me there. The minister at their church knows my new employers and gave me a reference. They've already sent me a train ticket. I can't go to my grandparents because it's the first place Mrs Hicks will look. They're giving my trunk to their friend today.'

'You've got it well organised. I'd appreciate knowing your new address, just in case I need to ask you something else.'

'I'd rather not. I don't want *her* to have any way of finding me again.'

'Will you be able to live with your conscience if that child dies? I may need you to act as a witness to keep her from being sent back to her grandmother.'

Ester couldn't hold back a sob. 'No, I couldn't bear that. She's such a loving little lass given half a chance. I wish there was somewhere for her to run away to as well.'

The sergeant hesitated, then said, 'There's another person worrying about her. Do you know Mrs Harte?'

'The one who lives in Birch End?'

'Yes. Turns out she's seen that woman thump Beatie more than once when they were out in the park. She's already told me she'd take in the child if she needed a refuge.'

'Really?'

'Yes. She's just moved into 23 Daisy Street, in Backshaw Moss. You could tell Beatie to go there if she ever needs to escape.'

'I'll do that, and make sure Beatie knows where it is. She really isn't safe at Mrs Hicks's, Sergeant.' Ester whispered her new address, vowing to tell Beatie to run away as soon as she could.

'Thank you. I'll call in to the doctor's and we'll go and check the child's injuries out together later today. I'll try my hardest to get her away from that woman, believe me.'

Ester worried all the way back about whether Mrs Harte had meant it, and decided that if the sergeant believed in her offer, she must have done. She'd definitely tell Beatie to run away and go to her as soon as she could. Who else was there for the child to turn to? She didn't trust the grandfather to stay sober.

Beatie lay on her bed, her body aching and sore where she'd been beaten with a cane. She wasn't going to stay here, whatever the minister at her grandmother's new church said about it being her duty to obey her grandmother. He'd also said these beatings were for her own good, to teach her right from wrong. Only, she knew she hadn't done anything wrong, couldn't understand why her grandmother hated her so much.

She had somewhere to run away to now, though, because Ester had sneaked in to see her while her grandmother was having her afternoon nap. The nice lady who'd smiled at her in the park had offered to look after her. She knew exactly where Mrs Harte lived now, because Ester had made her memorise how to get there in case she ever saw a chance to escape.

She wasn't going to wait for a chance to happen. She was going to find her own way of escaping and do it straight away to take them by surprise.

It was a risk to expect a complete stranger to hide her till she could find out how to contact her grandfather, but she had no one else to turn to. And surely a lady with such a nice smile wouldn't lie about helping her? Ester said the sergeant seemed sure Mrs Harte meant it. He had a nice smile too.

Her grandmother had told her that her mother's father had died, but Beatie had immediately recognised that as a lie because her grandmother's face got a certain look on it when she was fibbing. Her nose wrinkled and her eyes stared at you even harder than usual.

Her grandmother always said when she thumped her that she wasn't having Beatie giving in to the bad blood on her side and behaving as wickedly as him, and that was why she hit her. That was so unfair. Beatie knew her grandfather wasn't wicked, and nor was she, but she'd decided that her grandmother was a horrible woman.

She lay in bed till the house was quiet after the evening meal, then put a pillow under the bedcovers to look as if she was still there. She was wearing two layers of clothing to keep warm, and had crammed some underwear and a change of clothes in her school bag so that she'd have some spare clothes.

As she crept downstairs, she stopped just before she got to the bottom. Yes, she'd timed it right: Ester wasn't in the kitchen. The maid often had a sit-down in her bedroom with one of her magazines at this time of day, and Mrs Garton went into her own little room just off the kitchen to eat a second piece of cake.

Beatie crept across to the back door, feeling her back prickle with fear of being spotted, but no one came into the kitchen. She closed the door gently behind her, then slipped across and through the backyard gate, closing that carefully too, but of necessity leaving it unbolted. She hoped no one would notice that till it was too late to fetch her back.

It was dark now, and since she had no money of her own, she couldn't catch the last bus but had to walk up the hill to Birch End. Anyway, if she'd got on a bus, someone would have seen her.

It took her a long time to get there. Whenever a car passed her she continued to walk steadily, and no one stopped to ask what she was doing out at this time of night. With a scarf over her head, she thought she looked like a maid going home after a day's work, because she was quite tall for nine years old.

Sergeant Deemer phoned Dr Mitchell as soon as Ester left and found to his dismay that he was out attending a difficult home birth and wouldn't be back for a while.

He left a message with the doctor's wife for her husband to contact him urgently as soon as he returned, and sat in the police station to wait. The time seemed to pass very slowly.

It'd be no use going to see the child till he had a witness whose word would be believed in court about her injuries.

It was late when Beatie reached Birch End, but Ester had told her exactly where to go, so she continued to plod along through the village. It hurt to walk, though. It hurt so much.

She couldn't help letting out a low groan of relief when she found the three big houses in a row, all alike, just as she'd been told.

She had a moment's panic when she reached the one furthest away from Birch End and raised her hand to the knocker. Did she dare do this? She had to.

Taking a deep breath she banged the brass knocker good and hard.

When a man answered the door, she nearly ran away, but he spoke gently and had a kind expression on his face, so she gathered her courage together. Anyway, she had nowhere else to go, had she, and she was exhausted.

'Is Mrs Harte here, please? I need to see her. It's really urgent.'

He turned his head and yelled, 'Mum, it's for you.'

There was the sound of footsteps and the lady from the park came to join him.

For a moment, Beatie couldn't form a word, then she managed to say what Ester had told her: 'Sergeant Deemer said to come to you if I needed help.'

She couldn't stop herself from bursting into tears. What if they sent her back to her grandmother?

Before she knew what was happening, the lady had pulled her inside and was holding her close, patting her back. 'It's all right, love. It's all right. *Shh* now. I told the sergeant I'd look after you if you ever needed help, and I meant it. I'm really glad you came to me.'

As Beatie let go of the mountain of anxiety and terror that had been weighing her down, everything seemed to spin around her.

'Eh, the poor little thing's fainted. Pick her up quick, Gabriel love, and I'll shut the door.'

He did as she told him, but asked, 'What are you doing this for, Mum? You'll get yourself into trouble if she's run away from home.'

She led the way to the kitchen. 'I'm doing it because that child's grandmother's been beating her for no reason. The sergeant and I have been really worried about her safety. You'll let her stay, won't you? I'll show you why.'

Maisie came towards them.

When they saw the side of the child's face in the brighter light of the kitchen, they all exclaimed in shock. She had a huge bruise on one cheek and, as Gwynneth pushed up her sleeve, more bruises showed on her arm. Not a time for modesty, so she lifted the child's skirt, guessing there would be other marks. She hadn't realised how bad it would be, though. All three of them gasped at the mass of old and new weals near the child's bottom, and the streaks of blood.

Gwynneth let out a sob. 'She's been caned even more viciously than I'd expected. Who would do that to a child this young?'

Maisie stared in horror. 'Only a very wicked person. Look how thin she is. Has she been half starved too? Well, we've plenty of space here, and she's welcome to stay. She can have a nice room of her own till we can work out what to do with her to keep her safe.'

'I think she'd probably rather sleep in my bedroom. She's bound to be frightened of her grandmother finding her.' Gwynneth looked at them fiercely. 'I can't bear to see children beaten and hurt. I'll run away with her if anyone tries to force her back to *that woman*.'

'No need. If we have to hide her while they search the house, we can take her down into the tunnels,' Gabriel said.

Gwynneth looked at him and Maisie, tears welling in her eyes. 'Thank you.' Then she looked at them in puzzlement. 'What tunnels?'

Gabriel looked at Beatie. 'I just have to show my mother something. You'll be safe here.'

She nodded, huddling under the blanket they'd given her.

He took Gwynneth down to the cellar and showed her how to get in and out in case anyone came looking for Beatie. That warmed her heart. She'd expected her son to offer help, but hadn't been as certain of her daughter-in-law, because the two of them hadn't been married long enough for her to know Maisie well.

When she came back she sat down on the sofa and couldn't help planting a kiss on Beatie's cheek. 'You're safe with me, my little love.' Another kiss landed haphazardly.

The child clutched Gwynneth's sleeve. 'I'll be good. I'll help in the house. I won't be a burden.'

'Children are never a burden to me. They're a pleasure. And I especially like cuddles.'

Beatie nestled closer and shut her eyes, sighing softly.

Gwynneth turned to her daughter-in-lw. 'Could you heat up some milk, please, Maisie love? I bet she hasn't been fed properly today. And I'll need some warm water to wash her injuries.'

She didn't wait for an answer but continued to hold the child, trying to make her feel she was not only safe but wanted.

She wasn't even going to tell Sergeant Deemer about the poor child being here yet because he had to follow what the law dictated, and that would probably force him to take her back to her grandmother.

Over my dead body, Gwynneth vowed.

Just after midnight, the phone at the police station rang and Sergeant Deemer was relieved to hear Dr Mitchell's voice.

'My wife says you need to see me urgently.'

The sergeant explained what he'd been told and ended, 'Can I pick you up and take you to examine the child straight away? I think it's a case of the sooner the better.'

A sigh was his answer.

'I'd not ask you to do this, but I've seen the woman at the park hitting the child for no reason I could tell. We don't want a child's death on our hands.'

'Is it that bad?'

'Could be. I'm not risking it.'

'Very well. But I'll come in my own car and meet you there.'

They met outside the comfortable house near the park where Beatie lived with her grandmother. There were no lights showing, but the sergeant didn't hesitate to hammer on the door.

Lights came on in the upstairs and attic windows, but it took a while for someone to open the front door. Were they hiding something? he wondered.

It was the elderly housekeeper not the young maid who'd spoken to him earlier, whose job it should surely be to answer the door. Had Ester left already?

'We need to see young Beatie.' He used his sternest tone.

'Beatie? But she—'

A harsh voice interrupted from inside the house, 'What on earth do you need to see her for?'

He looked up to see Mrs Hicks standing part way up the stairs, wearing a fancy velvet dressing gown. The woman was plump, clearly didn't stint on her own needs, but even he had noticed that the child's clothes were too small for her and she was thin and hungry looking. 'I'll tell you after I've seen her.'

She glared at him, then called to the housekeeper, 'Where's Ester? It's her job to answer the door.'

'I don't know, madam. She wasn't in her bedroom, so I thought it more important for me to answer the door than go looking for her.'

That maid has definitely left, Deemer thought.

'Well, she must have slipped out to meet a man. I shall dismiss her for poor morals.'

'And Beatie?' the sergeant prompted.

'If you insist. This way, Sergeant. Who's that with you?'

'Dr Mitchell.'

'There's no one ill in this house.'

'We've been told there is, and we need to check.' He moved up the stairs and was past her before she could stop him. 'Which is Beatie's room?'

She looked puzzled, but pointed. 'At the end of the landing.'

He opened the door she'd indicated. It looked as if someone was asleep in the bed, but if so, why hadn't they been woken by the noise? When he went across and tugged the bedcovers away, it showed him only a couple of pillows – and something else. 'Dr Mitchell, could you please come and look at this?'

The doctor walked along to the room and this time Mrs Hicks came too.

'That looks like blood to me,' the doctor said.

'The child cut herself today,' she said quickly.

Dr Mitchell shook his head. 'That's not the way a single cut bleeds. Those smears are spread out, come from a much wider set of injuries, I'd guess.'

Sergeant Deemer turned to the housekeeper. 'Come and look at these, please, so you can bear witness to what we've found.'

She hesitated, casting an anxious glance at her mistress, then came across, gasping at what she saw.

He waited for her to study the bloodstains, then said, 'Can you come round the house with me and help me look for Beatie? I'm really worried about her safety. And we'll check for Ester while we're at it.'

The housekeeper shot another glance at her mistress, but Mrs Hicks folded her arms. 'Do as he says, you fool.'

The housekeeper stiffened, looking angry now.

Neither the child nor the maid were anywhere to be found, and they searched every room, including the cellar. Ester's things were all missing from her attic bedroom, but most of Beatie's things were still there. He was surprised at how few there were, and no toys at all.

When he came back downstairs, he found that Mrs Hicks had gone to sit in the breakfast room and got the fire blazing again.

'Neither Beatie nor Ester are there. Do you have any idea where they could be, Mrs Hicks?'

'Of course I don't. The maid must have run away, but she'd not have taken Beatie with her. The child is probably hiding somewhere. She'll reappear when she's hungry enough.'

'Your housekeeper and I have searched the whole house very carefully and there's no sign of her. I'll tell you now that your maid came to see me earlier today and said she was intending to run away because she couldn't bear to see you ill-treating your granddaughter any longer. She said you'd beaten her severely today.'

'Rubbish. No one's been ill-treating that child.'

'Then why did we find blood on her sheets?'

She shrugged. 'How should I know? She must have fallen over and grazed her knee.'

He exchanged worried glances with Dr Mitchell, then turned back to Mrs Hicks. 'I am giving you warning now, madam, that since you can't tell me where that child is, I shall have to take her disappearance seriously and report it officially.'

'Rubbish. I'm sure it's just a child's naughtiness.'

The housekeeper looked from one to the other, then said abruptly. 'I'm giving notice too, Mrs Hicks. I've seen you beat that poor little girl more than once, and I've had enough of it.'

'You'll sign a statement saying that?' Deemer asked quickly

'Yes, Sergeant.'

He got out his notebook and scribbled in it, holding it out to the housekeeper. 'Is that correct? If so, please sign it.'

After she'd read it, nodded, and scribbled her name, he held it out to the doctor. 'Will you please sign this to say that she signed of her own free will?'

'Happy to.'

Deemer put the notebook away. 'Do you have a telephone, Mrs Hicks?'

'No. Why would I want to be annoyed at all hours of the day and night?'

He turned back to the doctor. 'I shall have to stay here in case Beatie returns, but I'll let you get back to your bed now. I'd be grateful if you could please phone my wife when you get back and ask her to contact my constable to tell him to join me here as soon as it's light?'

'Certainly.'

Deemer caught Mrs Hicks's eye and watched her open her mouth to protest, then shrug and say, 'Well, I'm going up to bed. You're making far too much fuss over a naughty child.

And you can be sure I'll complain about this intrusion to your superiors.'

She didn't wait for an answer, but walked out of the room and could be heard going slowly up the stairs.

The housekeeper waited till they'd heard a door close overhead to ask, 'Would you like a cup of tea while you wait, Sergeant?'

'I'd be very grateful for one.'

'I'll make you one, after which I shall pack my things, ready to leave once I'm sure the child is safe.' She hesitated, then added, 'I'm a light sleeper and I'll leave my bedroom door open so that I can hear if Mrs Hicks comes out of her room. If she does, I'll call you. She may have got poor Beatie locked in a cupboard somewhere, though I didn't think we'd missed any.'

'Does she do that as well?'

She nodded and left the room.

He held his hands out to warm them at the fire, which was now blazing nicely. What on earth had happened to that child?

Could she have gone to find Mrs Harte? He hoped so.

In the early morning Cliff turned up at Mrs Hicks's house just before it got light, and he helped the sergeant search the house again from attics to cellar. No sign of the child, and this time they checked every cupboard thoroughly.

Where on earth could she have gone? Surely her grandmother hadn't killed her? There had been blood on the sheets, but not enough to indicate a mortal injury. In the end, he sent Cliff off to the police station and gave the mistress of the house strict instructions to let him know if Beatie turned up.

'Why?'

'Because otherwise I might think you'd killed her,' he said bluntly. That shocked her, at least.

When he left the house, the housekeeper left with him, which was a surprise. 'Do you not want to wait for your wages?' he asked.

'No, Sergeant. Truth to tell, the mistress has been getting very strange lately, ever since she started going to that new church. I'd not like to be left alone in the house with her. I've seen her eavesdropping outside the kitchen, and I even saw her coming out of my bedroom one morning. My drawers had been rifled. I know how I leave my clothes, and it wasn't like that.'

'And you've really no idea where the child could have gone?'

'No. But I hope it's somewhere a lot kinder than here.' She hailed a shabby man passing by and asked him if he had time to fetch her a taxi, holding a sixpence at the ready.

'Happy to, missus.' He ran off at once.

After she'd left, Sergeant Deemer drove home and lingered over a hearty breakfast, telling his wife what had happened and hoping that Ester had passed on his message about Mrs Harte being willing to take in the child.

He wasn't going there to find out during the daytime, in case he gave away her hiding place, nor did he intend to telephone. There were too many people in Rivenshaw at the moment poking their noses in where they shouldn't.

9

The next morning Arthur took the tools he'd bought down into the cellar and set them carefully on the hooks and shelves. It felt good to be putting order back into his life.

What he would do to protect his property once the money from the London lawyer ran out he didn't know, but he'd worry about that when it happened. One step at a time.

After he'd finished he stood back and looked round in satisfaction, then turned to Biff, who'd been watching from the top of the cellar stairs with a slight smile on his face.

'That looks good, Arthur. Now, shall we find out what's down that hole?'

'Definitely. If you get the torch ready, I'll slide open that secret door.'

When he'd done that, Biff held the torch out to him. 'Take it. It's your house, so you should lead the way.'

It felt strange to be the leader, but he moved down into the space at the bottom of the steps. It looked dark and forbidding till he shone the torch down and around the area at the bottom. The open space there was bigger than he'd expected. Well, such solidly built steps didn't usually lead nowhere, did they?

He took a few cautious steps, leaving Biff to position the two pieces of wood he'd nailed together so that they prevented the opening from closing up behind them. 'There's quite a wide tunnel leading off to the right.'

When he took a step towards it, Biff grabbed his jacket and pulled him back. 'Don't go any further yet. I know we've got the wood preventing the panel from closing, but anyone could remove that. I'm going to fetch one of the Becksleys to guard it and then we'll explore a bit further together.'

'You're always very careful.'

'It's my job to make sure you're safe. And I must admit, I'm rather fond of staying safe myself.'

It felt strange to stand in a tiny island of torchlight surrounded by shadows. Arthur shivered and decided to follow Biff to the top of the stairs. *Coward!* he told himself. Or was he just being sensible?

When Phil joined them, they showed him the steps leading to the lower cellar and promised to let him go down and explore later, then left him to guard the entrance.

'Let's check first that there's no concealed tunnel or opening to the left.' Arthur didn't wait for an answer, but moved in that direction.

They found nothing except a dead end, so set off to the right, moving slowly, checking every step of the way.

After a few steps Arthur stopped. 'I don't know where this tunnel comes out at, but we're heading past the other houses. Do you think they have secret entrances too?'

'How can you tell where we're heading? The darkness makes me feel disoriented.'

'I've always had a good sense of direction.'

After about twenty yards he stopped again. 'Look, there are some more steps leading up and they're exactly like ours. I bet they lead to Maisie's house. We've come too far along for the middle house. So two of the houses lead down here. I wonder why?'

'We won't try to go up the other steps today. We'll count our paces going back, then pace it out above ground in the street after we close the tunnel entrance. That'll show us roughly where the other steps lead. For the moment, let's carry on a bit further and see where we get to.'

They moved slowly and carefully, stopping every few paces to shine the torch up and down at each side. They didn't want any nasty surprises.

'I think the section near our house must have been dug out fairly recently,' Arthur said suddenly.

'How can you tell?'

'The walls in this part look . . . I don't know, slightly different from the ones near our house, older and dried out.'

'Do you know about the existence of tunnels? I never had anything to do with them till I came to the valley. I've spent most of my life in cities.'

'I used to play in some tunnels which led out of the old quarry when I was a lad. I should think these are an extension of them. My granddad told me about the tunnels from the quarry and showed me how to get into them once I was old enough to have a bit of sense. They were my secret hiding place. Not many people knew about them then, and even fewer know they're there these days.'

'Well, I think we should go back now and try to find out more about the old tunnels before we go any further in our explorations. There must be some reason for extending the passages if you're right about our part being recent. I reckon Sergeant Deemer would be the best person to ask. If anyone knows what's going on here in the valley, it's him.'

'Why would anyone want to make new ones?' Arthur wondered. 'They can only lead to the old quarry and no one uses it any longer.'

'I don't know. Let's go back now.' Biff shivered. 'I don't like it down here, to tell you the truth. If anything goes wrong with our torch, we'll be in real trouble. Anyway, sorting out the house is more important at the moment, don't you think?'

'I suppose so, but we can still ask the sergeant. There's so much to do to set the house to rights, I hardly know where to start.'

'Now you've got some proper tools you can start by mending some of the furniture properly. There's enough of that to keep you busy for a while.'

'I shall enjoy doing it.'

He stopped walking, head on one side. 'I've had a more careful look at the stuff in the dining room and I think some of the pieces are quite expensive, even though they need putting together again. Maybe if I can mend them properly, I can sell them. I'm going to need money to pay the council rates, not to mention the household electricity and gas bills once it's been modernised, aren't I, however frugally I live? The money I've been left will give me a start, but it won't last for ever.'

'How about we ask Charlie Willcox to come and take a look at the furniture? He'll be able to give us some idea of what the better pieces might be worth if they could be repaired,' Biff suggested.

'Good idea. He's a kind chap. He bought me a loaf more than once when I was at my worst. Eh, I was such a fool.'

'Well, you've come out of that patch now and you're sounding more alert all the time.'

'Good food helps, but most of all it's hope that's buoying me up. I didn't have hope for anything good after Susan died, especially when my daughter was killed and I was kept away from my little granddaughter. My son hasn't spoken to me since then. Perhaps, if I continue to pull myself together, he'll forgive me. I doubt that horrible woman will ever grant me permission to see Beatie though. She always was a spiteful old devil, and how she got such a pleasant son, I don't know. He really loved my daughter, made her happy in their marriage till the accident.'

'You might have to ask Judge Peters to make an order allowing you to see Beatie.'

'I'll need to prove myself sober and respectable again first, so I can't do it yet. I'm worried about my little lass, though.

I'd not give a dog to that woman to look after, let alone a griev-
ing child. I've only seen Beatie in the distance, but she looked
so unhappy.'

'I've not actually met this Mrs Hicks.'

'You don't want to. She's like the wicked witches in the
storybooks I used to read to Beatie.' After a moment of
scowling into the distance Arthur turned and led the way back,
surreptitiously brushing away a tear or two.

Biff didn't say anything but he was glad to hear Arthur
making sensible plans for the future. 'We're agreed to bring
in Charlie Willcox, then? Apart from anything else, he loves
to be the first to find something out, so I reckon he'll jump at
the chance of seeing inside this house. He'll be able to tell you
if anything's worth selling. He came to look round Maisie's
house and gave her some good prices for the best pieces of
furniture.'

'Well, if he can sell some of the stuff for me, it'll be a big
help, and I won't waste the money, I promise you. But I'll still
have to find a way of earning a living in the future, won't I?
It costs a lot of money to run a big house like this one, more
than I can earn as a carpenter's assistant – always supposing
anyone would give me a job now.'

'You don't want to sell the house and buy a smaller one?'

Arthur gazed round, shaking his head. 'It'd break my heart
to do that. I love the place already. Besides, Miss Chapman
wanted me to have it.'

'I bet Higgerson tries to buy it. He did with Bella, though
he offered a ridiculously low price. Don't sell to him, whatever
you do. He'd make the other heirs' lives a misery.'

'I hate to think of him even coming inside here. He's . . . evil,
spreads misery. Even his own wife and older son ran away
from him. He went after me when I refused to work for him.
I had to hide at night for weeks till his men stopped trying to
beat me up.'

'What did he want you to do?'

'Bully folk who fell behind with their rent, hurt them to remind them to pay their debts. But I couldn't have done that to folk down on their luck, not even at my worst.'

Biff didn't let himself smile. He couldn't imagine Arthur doing anything nasty. The man was a bit of a softy, really, but it was good to see him starting to pull himself together.

That was what Sarah Jane Chapman had wanted her bequests to do.

The man who'd been sheltering from the cold wind in the gateway of a yard across at the other side of the back alley managed to hear some of what they were saying when they walked round the yard, because sounds seemed to carry further in damp air.

What he'd heard surprised him. Fancy an old drunk like Arthur Chapman inheriting such a big house!

If he went and told Mr Higgerson about what he'd overheard, like there being valuable furniture in it, there might be a chance of getting sixpence or even a shilling as a reward.

He knew Mr Higgerson collected information and put it together to make money. The man was clever about things like that.

The listener tried not to let anyone see him leave the alley, then made his way to the rear of Higgerson's house. He found Jem Stanley cleaning the car in the garage, whose doors were open, whistling cheerfully as he dipped a cloth in a bucket of soapy warm water and rubbed off the mud splashes.

He explained why he was there.

'I'll go and ask Mr Higgerson if he's free to see you. Wait there and do not touch a single thing.'

He didn't touch anything, but he did hold his cold hands out over the warm air rising from the bucket of hot water.

Jem came back a couple of minutes later and beckoned. 'He'll see you. Make sure you remember all the details.'

'Yes, Mr Stanley.'

As he led the way, Jem hid his satisfaction at how cringingly polite the man had been. Working for Mr Higgerson was a big step up in the world. He watched his master as he listened to what the man told him, asking questions and frowning in thought.

Then Higgerson fumbled in his pocket and brought out a little coin purse. 'I'll give you a shilling for that information. Do not tell anyone else what you heard or that you spoke to me about it. If you find out anything else about Arthur Chapman, there could be another little bonus for you.'

The man went away beaming.

Jem waited, but his master didn't share his thoughts.

He'd noticed that Higgerson had brightened considerably at the news the chap had brought. Something was brewing and it was to do with those houses. Jem was sure he'd find out what was going on sooner or later, and benefit from it.

It puzzled him why there would be a lower cellar hidden under that end house. No place he knew had been built with those, and he thought his master was mad having extra cellars dug out under the Clover Lane houses. Even going there to check on the progress of the new cellar gave him the heebie-jeebies.

He smiled at that word, which exactly described how he felt. He'd first heard it at the cinema. People were thinking up some comical new ways of saying things these days. Heebie-jeebies was one of his own favourite words now.

'Go and finish cleaning the car!' Higgerson shouted suddenly. 'Are you asleep? I've told you twice.'

'Oh, sorry, sir. Just thinking about the new cellar in Clover Lane. It's going to need more bracing on the walls.'

'Then get some, but only the smallest amount you need. I'm not made of money.'

Jem shook his head as he went back to finish off the car. Higgerson said that regularly, acting as if he had to be careful with every penny, yet by most folk's standards, he was rich.

Now that Jem had started to follow his example and let his wife watch where their money went, every single farthing, it felt good to have some coins put by in case of bad times. He was surprised at how it was mounting up. They'd never managed to save money before, and it put her in a very good mood.

Biff left Arthur mending a beautiful little corner wall cupboard with Rob Becksley patrolling the house, keeping watch. He strolled along to the end house to ask if he could use their phone to call Charlie Willcox because there were no buses down the valley at this time of day.

To his surprise, when Maisie opened the door, he caught a glimpse of a little lass running up the stairs and tripping up.

Maisie said quickly, 'I'd be grateful if you don't mention my young guest to anyone.'

'Of course not.'

He waited for her to explain, but she didn't, so he decided to mind his own business. She showed him the phone on the hall table, and when he tried to give her twopence for the call, as folk did at the village shop, she waved his outstretched hand away.

'It's a poor world if neighbours can't help one another. How's Mr Chapman going on?'

'Enjoying his new home, busy mending some broken furniture at the moment.'

She smiled. 'I remember how I felt when I first found I'd inherited this house, so wonderfully happy.'

'He wants Charlie Willcox to come and value a few things, as he did for you.'

'Mr Willcox is very knowledgeable. He's sold quite a lot of things for me already. He's a very nice man, too. Someone was telling me he's the favourite to become mayor next time there are local elections.'

'He'd make a good mayor.'

'An honest one, too, unlike Higgerson's friend, who's also going to stand.'

'I'm a bit out of touch with local gossip. Folk around here regard me as an outsider and are a bit wary about what they say to me.'

She chuckled. 'They did me at first, though they started to soften a little when I married Gabriel.'

Maybe he should find a local lass to marry once everything settled down. Why not? He had been getting on very well with his landlady before he moved in with Arthur. She was a very cosy armful and an excellent cook, fun to chat to as well.

He jerked himself back to the present and made the phone call, not surprised when Charlie said he'd be there in about an hour.

Maisie had told Beatie to run up to her bedroom and stay out of sight whenever someone came to the house, but she was feeling very lethargic today after her long walk up the hill last night, and she tripped on the stairs.

She realised the man had seen her when she looked back and caught him staring. But Maisie waved to her to carry on, and Beatie heard her ask him not to tell anyone. Maisie had smiled when she saw who was at the door, so he must be a nice person.

Hardly anyone ever came to her grandmother's house, and they certainly weren't greeted with smiles. Her grandmother didn't visit other ladies, either, and when she passed them in the street, they just nodded to her and walked on quickly, never stopping to chat. Her mother had had lots of friends and often chatted to neighbours.

Beatie went into the bedroom, which was at the back of the house, and decided to watch what was going on outside.

Out of habit she sat concealed by the edge of the curtain and when she saw a man creeping along the back alley, she stiffened. He looked sneaky, kept glancing over his shoulder as if to make sure no one was following him. What was he doing? Was he a burglar? Or had he come looking for her?

He didn't try to go into any of the backyards, but stood in the alley mostly concealed by the sagging edge of a shed near the end house, the one her Auntie Gwynneth said a new man had just inherited.

The stranger looked dirty, as if he never washed himself, and his clothes were ragged. What was he doing there? She'd better tell someone about him, just in case.

She ran down the stairs without thinking, calling for Auntie Gwynneth, but stopped dead when she saw the visitor just putting the phone down in the hall. She'd forgotten about him. Would they be mad at her for not staying hidden?

Maisie came out of the front room. 'Your auntie has nipped out to the shops. What's the matter, dear? Can I help you?'

'There's a man staring into the backyards from near the end house. He looks as if he doesn't want to be seen. Has he come after me, do you think?'

'I don't think so. You're quite safe. No one can possibly know you're here and I'm sure Mr Higgins won't tell anyone.'

The stranger stepped forward. 'I certainly won't. But I'm living in the end house, and he may be spying on me and my friends. Can you show him to me without him seeing us, do you think?' He looked at Maisie. 'Would that be all right?'

'Of course it would.'

'You can see him best from my bedroom.' Beatie led the way back upstairs and gestured to the window. 'If you walk round the sides of the bedroom and stand behind the curtain, he won't see you.'

The visitor did that and stayed perfectly still, watching.

She looked at Maisie and got another of those lovely reassuring smiles. No one in this house seemed to get annoyed at her, let alone smack her suddenly for no reason. She loved being here.

'It's all right, love. Mr Higgins is pleased that you noticed that man. Shall we sit on the end of the bed and wait? We'll be out of sight there.'

Biff frowned as he watched. 'I don't know that chap's name, but I've seen him at a pub where ne'er-do-wells hang around. I wonder what he's looking for.'

He watched for a few more minutes then said abruptly, 'I think I'll creep up on him from behind and find out what he's doing here. Thank you so much for coming to tell us, Beatie.'

When he left the bedroom, Maisie said, 'I'll see you out, Biff. I won't be a minute, dear. Wait for me here.'

At the front door she said in a low voice, 'You won't tell anyone that the child is here, will you? She's been badly beaten and run away to Gwynneth. Her parents are dead, you see.' She deliberately didn't tell him Beatie's name.

'Of course I won't. Thank you for letting me look.'

She called up the stairs after he'd gone, 'Do you want to finish eating your scone now, Beatie?'

The child came down, still looking hesitant. 'I didn't do anything wrong, did I?'

'Good heavens, no.'

She let out a huge sigh of relief. 'So I'm not in trouble?'

'Not at all. In fact, you did a good thing coming to tell us about that sneaky man. If you see anyone else sneaking around, come and tell someone straight away.'

Beatie took the hand Maisie was offering, walking with her into the kitchen, feeling so safe here. She could have as much food as she wanted, second helpings of anything. The others ate second helpings too, so her grandmother was wrong saying only people with no manners ate like pigs.

★

Biff crept around the houses and managed to take the watcher by surprise. 'Looking for someone?'

The man tried to shake the hand off his jacket and failed. 'Just sheltering. It's a cold day.'

'Go and shelter somewhere else. If I see you around here again, I'll report you to Sergeant Deemer and ask if there have been any burglaries.'

'I'm not a thief!'

Biff let go of him and called, 'Give my regards to Higgerson!' after him as he ran away.

The man slowed down for a moment and turned a startled look in his direction, so he knew he'd hit the nail on the head with that guess.

What the hell did Higgerson want? He'd not managed to buy the other two houses, and he wouldn't get his hands on this one, either, if Biff could help it. This area was coming out of being a slum. Higgerson would only push it back towards crime and misery.

10

Half an hour later someone knocked on the front door and Biff went to answer it, relaxing and opening the door fully when he saw who it was.

'Is it like the other end house, full of furniture?' Charlie Willcox asked before he'd even stepped inside.

'No. It's different again. There's a reasonable amount of furniture, but nearly every piece is broken and it turns out mending furniture is a job Arthur's skilled at.'

He looked over his shoulder, then whispered to Charlie. 'It's obviously been done on purpose to stir him up. He turned to booze after his wife died.'

'Yes, I remember him, poor chap. He might have gone to pieces, but he never stole from anyone that I heard, or committed any acts of violence either.'

Biff nodded, glad to know that others also found Arthur a basically decent chap. He took Charlie through the house to the kitchen, where the man in question was busy screwing a couple of chair legs back on. They stood quietly in the doorway, watching him work so intently that he didn't notice them till he'd finished dealing with the chair legs and stood up to stretch.

'Why, it's Mr Willcox! Sorry I didn't see you standing there. How kind of you to come so quickly.'

'My pleasure. I'm dying to see what this house is like inside.'

'Why don't you show Charlie round and point out the pieces of furniture you think are more valuable?' Biff suggested. 'You know far more about that sort of thing than I do.'

'Happy to, but I don't know as much about the expensive furniture as about the everyday stuff. Just a tick.' He set the chair upright, made sure it didn't wobble, and sat on it, patting the chair back as he stood up again. 'That's better. Please come this way, Mr Willcox.'

Biff tiptoed after them, standing at the back of the hall to check that Arthur didn't need his help and smiling as a few exclamations floated across to him from both men. They were soon deep in discussion as they examined the pieces in the dining room.

Arthur, in a shocked whisper, 'Is it really worth that much?'

Charlie, voice booming as usual, 'Easily. If you can mend it, that is?'

'Oh yes. That won't be hard. There's not a lot wrong, actually. It's a lovely piece, isn't it? Look at that patina.'

More exchanges followed, with a few more shocked exclamations from Arthur as the two men continued to look around.

Pleased with how it was going, Biff went back into the kitchen and filled the kettle. Arthur definitely didn't need his help when it came to furniture.

About an hour later, after he'd heard them go into and out of all the downstairs rooms, he poked his head into the hall to catch them before they went upstairs. 'Anyone for a cup of tea?'

'That'd be champion,' Charlie said at once.

Arthur nodded. 'I'm always ready for one.'

When they came into the kitchen Biff waved their visitor to a seat, and Arthur to one next to him. 'While I finish making the tea you two can carry on with your conversation.' He winked at Charlie, who took over.

'If you repair the small table and the carved hall chair first, Mr Chapman, so that I can see you know what you're doing, I'll sell them for you at around the price I suggested, more if I can get it. I take ten per cent of what I get for the better furniture, plus whatever it costs me to do that, mind.'

'That's very fair. I wouldn't know how to begin selling things. I shall enjoy doing the repairs, though.'

'Can I see the rest of the house after we've had our cuppa?'

'Happy to show you round if you can spare the time.' He turned to Biff. 'Some of those pieces are worth more than I'd expected, a lot more. Isn't that marvellous?'

Charlie beamed at Biff, clearly enjoying his visit. 'Why don't you come with us?'

'I'd like that. I'll just tell Phil to keep an eye on the front door.'

Their visitor stopped dead for a moment. 'You're having the house watched even in the daytime?'

'Better safe than sorry.'

Charlie shook his head sadly. 'I don't know what the world's coming to, but I know one of the causes.'

When the three of them went round the upstairs bedrooms, taking the time to look in every corner, these provided more surprises, beautiful antiques standing cheek by jowl with everyday furnishings.

Then they went up to the attics where there was a similar jumble of smaller pieces.

Charlie moved towards one of the windows. 'I bet you get a good view over this part of the valley from here.' He jerked back and his smug look vanished. 'What's that sod doing watching your house?'

'Who are you talking about?' Arthur went across to peep out. 'I recognise his face but I don't know his name. I couldn't prove it, but I'm sure he picked my pocket one night and took all the money I had left that day. It was my own stupid fault for getting drunk, but still – he preyed on me after I'd treated him to a drink. What sort of person does that?'

'Harry Caxton wouldn't hesitate to do it. He's a real lay-about and one of the most skilled pickpockets in the valley.

Take a look at him for future reference, Biff lad, but be careful he doesn't see you.'

'I've only just sent away another chap who was watching the house,' he said indignantly. 'Why has this one taken his place?'

'Higgerson must have sent him.'

Arthur let out an angry snort. 'I suppose Caxton thinks he can benefit from my stupidity again. Well, he's got another think coming. I haven't had a drink for months.'

Charlie sighed. 'You might have frightened the other chap away, Biff lad, but Caxton doesn't frighten easily. If he saw me arrive, he'll be reporting that to Higgerson, who will guess that there's some valuable stuff here.' He stared into space for a minute or two, then added, 'I'll mention it to Sergeant Deemer next time I see him. He has no time for Caxton. It'd make his day to get that sod put behind bars.'

He studied his fancy modern wristwatch. 'I'd better get going now. Let me know when those two pieces are ready, Mr Chapman, and I'll send someone to pick them up.'

Biff saw Charlie out, and then went to find Arthur, who was standing near the kitchen window, staring blindly into space.

'Will you be able to repair those two pieces for Charlie?'

He jumped in shock but nodded. 'Eh, I was miles away then. Seeing Caxton reminded me how bad I got for a while. I'm deeply ashamed of it.'

'If it helps, you're not on your own this time.' That won him a faint smile.

'No, I'm not, am I? I'm very lucky to have you helping me, Biff lad. Don't think I don't appreciate what you're doing, more than you were hired to do sometimes, I reckon.'

Biff gave an embarrassed shrug. He had more money than they realised, thanks to a nice little inheritance recently.

'But I have to learn to stand up for myself, don't I, can't rely on you for ever? I need to be more self-reliant and alert than ever before. Thieves and other villains didn't pay me much attention when I was just a rough working chap, but they will now I own this lovely house. They'll think I must have come into a lot of money as well as the building.'

'I'm sure you'll find a way to earn a decent living and look after this house.'

'I have to, if I'm to see that little lass of mine again, and win back my son's trust.'

Sergeant Deemer heard that his new constable had arrived in Rivenshaw the day before he was due to start work, and wasn't surprised when Mike called into the police station to introduce himself in the late afternoon.

The sergeant beamed at him. 'You're extremely welcome, lad. We have an interesting situation going on here, but I won't bother you with that till tomorrow, when I'll tell you and my other constable about it at the same time. More important for the moment, do you and your wife have somewhere to live?'

'Yes, thank you. We're staying with her parents for a few days till a nearby house they found for us becomes vacant, then they'll help us move in. Our own furniture is in storage till then.'

'It's not one of Higgerson's houses?'

'Definitely not. I know the name already. My in-laws once rented a house from that man and found him to be a terrible landlord. They haven't a good word to say for him.'

'Neither do I. Anyway, that's for tomorrow. Good of you to call in.'

'I've come out partly to stretch my legs and partly to let my Delia and her mother have a good old natter about people I've never heard of. I thought I'd take a stroll round Rivenshaw to renew my acquaintance with the town centre and start getting my bearings.'

'Why don't I come with you? There's nothing like a stroll for keeping you up to date with what's really going on around you. I try to get out and about regularly. Since you've heard of him already, I'll tell you that Higgerson is our main problem. These days he's gone far beyond what he used to get up to. I shall catch him out if it's the last thing I ever do. Anyway, let's not spoil a fine day by talking about him.'

As they walked the sergeant introduced Mike to some of the people they met. He was pleased to see the younger man act automatically to stop a young boy from running into the road chasing after his ball, and saw that he knew exactly how to tease a group of little girls about their skipping skills and set them giggling and blushing at the attention. A policeman was there to serve his community and needed their willing help to keep order.

Mike also spotted the fact that some people turned off the street in order to avoid meeting the sergeant, and commented on it quietly.

'You've got sharp eyes, lad. There are minor villains everywhere, and I suppose there always will be. You'll gradually get to know our home-grown ones.'

'Just a minute, Sarge.' Mike moved quickly to help an old lady who was having trouble crossing the road, making her laugh by giving her a sweeping bow as they reached the footpath on the other side.

When he came back, the sergeant said, 'Nicely done, lad. That old lady has just turned ninety. She still manages to look after herself and get around the town centre, but she isn't very good with modern motor vehicles, doesn't seem to understand how fast they can go.'

A little further on, he asked, 'Have you ever been up the hill to Birch End and Ellindale during your visits, lad?'

'No, Sarge. When we're here, we usually spend the time with Delia's parents, and they prefer to stay at home and chat, or stick to a gentle amble around the town centre. She's their only child and they miss her greatly.'

'I'll take you for a drive up and down the valley tomorrow, then, so that you can see the framework for what's going on. We have our own fizzy drinks factory at the top, and I'll treat you to a glass of the best ginger beer you've ever tasted. At the other end of the scale, I'll show you our worst slum on the way down, Backshaw Moss, which is just beyond Birch End.'

'How bad is it?'

'Parts of it are about as bad as a slum can get, but the council is making a start on clearing it. Trouble is, Higgerson is trying to prevent that, via the council and by any other means.'

'Have you got any police vehicles?'

'Just one police car, a nice little Morris. Hasn't let me down yet.'

'Must be hard for both of you to get around the valley quickly sometimes, with only one car. It's the coming thing to have more police vehicles.'

'Yes, I know. I doubt local finances can stretch to that, but I've been wondering whether to get a motorbike now you've joined us. I've been tipped the wink that money could be found to fund and run one. We have a shy chap living in a big house near Ellindale who donates to good causes occasionally. Have you had any experience of riding motorbikes?'

Mike chuckled. 'I own one and brought it with me. It's just a small Triumph and—' He noticed the lack of comprehension on the sergeant's face and broke off without going into further details. 'Do you know anything about motorbikes, sir?'

'Not really, and I reckon I'm too old to learn to ride one. But having one might help you and Cliff in your work. And in fact, I might be able to pay you a bit extra if you use yours on the job, as well as our little team having one of our own.'

'It can certainly come in useful being able to get to the site of a problem quickly.'

'Well, now we have someone who understands motorbikes I'll make a bit more effort to get one. We're quite isolated here in the valley, so we have a better case for needing our own transport than places with plenty of regular bus and tram services.'

All in all, Deemer liked his new senior constable even more than he'd expected to. There was a steadiness to this young man, an inner strength, but a kindness too. You needed kindness to deal with some of the situations the police had to face. Well, you did if you cared about people, some of whom had had very hard lives.

Deemer would brief him in more detail about Higgerson tomorrow before they started driving about. Then another day, he'd send the two constables out to patrol the town together. He felt it important to make sure his officers knew one another well, and the two younger men would probably learn to pull together better without their sergeant overhearing every word they said.

He intended to brief them both about the possibility of a traitor making plans in the valley, but would have to get permission before he could do that.

He wondered how Mike felt about the political situation in the country. Many people, especially the younger ones, believed that war wasn't really going to happen again, but Deemer was sure it was inevitable, sadly. During the last war, he'd had to kill ordinary chaps who spoke a different language but weren't all that different from himself in order to save his own life, and hadn't enjoyed doing it.

He recognised the telltale signs of another damned war looming, by hell he did.

He hadn't understood such signs before the Great War began, few people had, but if you couldn't learn from what had happened in the past, you were pig stupid or wearing blinkers.

11

Sergeant Deemer pointed his new constable in the right direction to get back to his relatives' house and called in on Judge Peters, pleased to find his friend at home.

'I've just been making the acquaintance of my new senior constable. Nice young chap, Mike Grafton, and unless I'm much mistaken, as shrewd as they come. He's a motorbike enthusiast, and I feel we won't be able to make the most of him unless we police officers become more mobile and, well . . . ' He hesitated.

'And you're wondering whether there is any way I can help you get funding to buy a motorbike for your police force.'

'Having one as well as a car could be a good way to provide better communications for our group as well, in an emergency,' he said pointedly.

'It will indeed, and I'm sure that will help get your request funded, Gilbert.'

'And I think I should tell my constables about the group, to prepare them in case they have to take over from me.'

Dennison looked surprised. 'Are you retiring after all?'

'No. But a friend of mine just dropped dead, two years younger than me, he was, and it makes you think.'

'Oh. Well, we can't do without you, so don't you dare follow his example.'

Deemer grinned. 'I'll do my best to stay on the right side of the grass. I could tell my officers the bare details without names to start with, well, maybe just a couple of nearby contacts fully named.'

'I'll check with His Lordship, if you like.'

'Thank you. You know him better than I do. There's also Mike's own bike. He'd be happy to use it for work if we refund him for petrol and any damage incurred. It's a cheap way for us to get more transport.'

Dennison looked thoughtful. 'Finn has kindly offered to fund any areas the council isn't covering. Maybe I could ask him. It'll sound better coming from me.'

'Good idea. We have to move forward and use modern equipment. The smarter criminals do, that's for sure.' Deemer felt relieved that he hadn't needed to beg for this sort of help. 'The world is changing quickly, isn't it, Dennison? Modern inventions are transforming life, even here in the wilds of Lancashire.'

'It needs to be transformed in some ways.' He paused, then asked, 'Any progress with finding out if Higgerson is our traitor?'

'Not yet. I'll take my two lads into my confidence about what he may be up to, as well as what I know for certain he is up to already.'

'We'll catch him one day,' Dennison said.

Gilbert scowled. He'd expected to catch him by now, but it was taking longer than he'd hoped. He'd never give up while there was breath in his body.

But you didn't always win your battles in this life, however hard you tried.

Deemer walked home enjoying the exercise after spending so many hours sitting in a car or his office. He had always loved being out in the fresh air.

Suddenly, two men rushed out of the darkness caused by a broken street lamp, and attacked him from in front and behind, taking him by surprise. He fought back, of course he did, roaring at the top of his voice for help. But they were younger than he was, and much bigger, and he'd have no chance of holding his own against them for long, he knew.

Then two lads ran out of an alley and chucked cobblestones at his attackers, knocking one of them sideways and distracting them from the attack. The lads must have had the wit to scrabble at the edges of the alley for loose stones, and they were smart enough to run away almost immediately.

This distraction gave Deemer time to get his whistle and blow it for help, hoping desperately that there would be someone within earshot who understood what that particularly shrill call meant. He tried to grab his truncheon too, but failed because the attackers were on him again.

Only, once again stones were hurled at them by the lads, and he managed to land a couple of return blows.

Then a punch sent him to the ground and the nearest man kicked out at him. He rolled away and was only struck a glancing blow, but that was enough to make him double up with pain.

Before either of them could get in another blow, there was the sound of yelling coming closer, and footsteps pounding along the street. A woman was screeching for help at the top of a very loud voice.

When voices yelled out from the other directions as well, one of his assailants called, 'Leave it now!' and they ran off.

Surrounded by his rescuers, Sergeant Deemer lay back and watched two men chase after his attackers.

He had to leave it to others to keep him safe while he fought for breath, wincing with pain when he moved his upper body where they'd got him in the ribs.

'You all right, Sergeant?' a woman whispered.

It was Gwynneth Harte. 'More – or – less.' If he wasn't mistaken they'd not only bruised his ribs but made his forehead bleed, and his right eye was blurring as blood ran down into it. 'Can you – help me – to stand up?'

As she bent to offer her arm, a man came to his other side, her son Gabriel. With their help Deemer managed to heave himself to his feet. It was a struggle not to moan, so painful was it, and he had to lean on them.

'The sergeant needs to be taken to the doctor,' she called out.

He recognised some of the other helpers too by the light from a street lamp further along, good folk all of them.

The two men who'd chased after his attackers came back, shaking their heads.

'Sorry, Sarge. They were fast runners,' one said regretfully.

'What's the world coming to when a policeman gets attacked on a public street, and in one of the better parts of Rivenshaw too?' another asked.

The sergeant was thinking the same thing. This was usually a quiet, law-abiding area, or he'd not have walked through it alone at this hour.

He hadn't been able to see his assailants clearly because they'd had knitted hats pulled down over the tops of their heads. They hadn't sounded local, though, had spoken with a markedly different accent. Where had they come from and why had they attacked him?

He could only think they'd been brought into town for that very purpose. He shook his head sadly. It must have been Higgerson's doing, because who else would want to put him out of action? Was he getting paranoid about the fellow? Or was the sod growing steadily more dangerous?

He let Gabriel help him into a van and drive him to seek medical help.

Dr Mitchell was as horrified as everyone else at the attack. He strapped the sergeant up and told him to take a few days off work to recover.

Sergeant Deemer didn't argue, but he wasn't going to do that, because it'd show whoever it was that they'd come out from the encounter victorious. He reckoned he'd need his new constable to drive him round for a while, though, because it hurt to move too suddenly – hurt a lot, damn those sods to high hell.

He accepted an offer from Gabriel to drive him home, and was told that someone had already let his wife know he'd been attacked.

The pain was enough to make him say, 'Drive as smoothly as you can, lad.'

'Of course.'

Deemer closed his eyes and leaned back, trying to think of other things to take his thoughts off the sudden jolts of pain, which set his mind losing its focus.

On his visit to Dennison earlier in the evening, they'd been talking about the dark forces gathering in their world, in Europe particularly. What had Shakespeare called those forces? *The dogs of war*, that was it. Which play was that from? *Julius Caesar* perhaps? He couldn't remember for sure, but he would once his head had stopped aching. It was an apt phrase not only for the wider troubles brewing over in Germany and the nearby nations, but here in the valley.

'You'll need to rest for a few days to give your body time to recover, Sergeant.' Gwynneth's soft, musical voice from the rear of the van jerked him out of his thoughts.

'I'm not going to take time off work, because I won't give the one who organised this attack the satisfaction of putting me out of action. He's not getting the better of me.'

Gabriel joined in. 'You sound sure of who planned this, Sergeant.'

'I can guess. I bet you can too.'

'He's a blight on our valley, that one,' Gwynneth agreed.

The sergeant sat as still as he could. The doctor had given him some aspirin tablets, which seemed to be gradually taking the edge off the pain. He'd take more later when these wore off, as the doctor had suggested, because his whole body was protesting at being ill-treated.

'We've arrived, Sergeant.' Gabriel's voice made him realise they'd stopped in front of his house.

He accepted help getting out of the van and into the house, then his kind helpers left him to his wife's ministrations.

She helped him undress and put his pyjamas on, then brought him a hot-water bottle, trying not to let him see the tears she was shedding over his injuries.

'I'm all right, bonny lass,' he told her. 'It's only bruising.'

'What if they come back and kill you next time?' She clasped his hand for a moment.

'I won't let them take me by surprise again, believe me.'

'Let's get you up to bed and I'll fill our other hot-water bottle.'

As he lay in bed his pain subsided a little, but his mind still wandered.

'I'll sleep in the spare bedroom,' she said. 'I've put some aspirins beside the bed and some water. You'll need some more later. You've only to call out if you need anything.'

'Thanks, love. But I'd rather have you beside me.'

'Are you sure?'

'Yes. I daren't cuddle you, but I prefer to know you're there beside me, safe, and you could hold my hand at least.'

'I'll get ready for bed then.'

As he waited for her to come back from the bathroom, he stared at the white shapes of the pills on top of the chest of drawers next to the bed and they set his mind off leaping around again. He'd needed aspirin tablets during the Great War, when they'd first come into common use, and a real godsend they'd been. But he'd never needed them as badly as he did tonight.

His wife came back and got into bed beside him.

'Wake me in the morning at my usual time, love.'

'What? You're surely not going to work! Gilbert, no! You need to take a few days off. I'm sure the doctor didn't say you could go straight back to work.'

'I need to show whoever it is that I'm not going to be easy to stop. But I shall leave Cliff and Mike to do the running around for a few days, I promise, and they can take it in turns to drive me here and there. Will you phone Cliff first thing in the morning and ask him to hand the car keys over to Mike? I'll walk about indoors under my own steam, but I'll definitely need to be driven around whenever I go outside, for a day or two anyway.'

'You're a stubborn man and I don't know why I love you so much.'

'I love you too.' He smiled and closed his eyes, comforted by her love. Then, as she drifted into sleep, he distracted himself by trying to think who the two lads had been who'd come to his assistance. He'd recommend them for a commendation by the mayor. He'd need to . . . need to think out how he could . . . organise the next day or two. He'd just close his eyes for a minute or two to gather his strength.

He didn't wake till morning and his wife had already got up. She must have been listening and the minute he stirred, she refilled the two hot-water bottles to comfort his poor aching body and followed up with the treat of a cup of tea in bed, plus two of his favourite chocolate biscuits and then two more aspirins.

And he took the day off, couldn't summon up the strength to go to work. Eh, he felt his age sometimes these days.

When Gwynneth and her son got home, he went round to ask Biff and Arthur to join them, then told everyone what had happened.

Maisie clutched her husband's arm. 'Who were the attackers, Gabriel love? Did either of you recognise them?'

'I only caught a glimpse of them. They're not from the valley by their accents,' Gwynneth said.

Her son's indignation spilled over again. 'Two against one, it was, the cowards! Actually, I think someone brought them here deliberately to attack our sergeant.'

Dead silence greeted this, then Gwynneth said, 'And there's only one person wicked enough to have done that, as well as having enough money to pay them. Two attackers wouldn't come cheap.'

'Higgerson will have been somewhere public at the time it happened and will pretend to be shocked. It's what that man always does whenever he arranges an incident,' Arthur said.

'Who does he think he's fooling?' Gwynneth let out a little growl of irritation.

'I doubt he cares about fooling us, just about not giving anyone proof that he was involved,' Biff said.

'Well, we need to protect Gilbert Deemer. You couldn't get a better police sergeant than him. I'm going to speak to a few people tomorrow about setting up an informal watch over him for a few days,' Gabriel said. 'He's a good man, but he's not young.'

Arthur gaped at him. 'You don't think they'll try to attack him *again*, surely?'

'They shouldn't have dared do it once, but they did, and if it hadn't been for the people nearby rallying round, who knows what they might have done to him?'

'Deemer said there were a couple of lads who helped hold them at bay by throwing stones and rubbish at them till others could come to his aid,' Gwynneth said. 'I'm going to speak to some women friends. We can keep our eyes open too, especially us older women. We might as well be invisible half the time. Some people just push past us in the street.'

'If there's another attack, don't you even think of fighting back, Mum, just run away! If they can hurt Sergeant Deemer so badly, I don't think they'd hesitate to bash a woman.'

'I'd never try to tackle them on my own,' she said quietly. 'I'm not stupid. But they aren't all as tough as they pretend. Some are slower to hit women.'

'Even if you have several friends with you, please don't get involved. These men are ruthless. And for goodness' sake, don't let Higgerson know you're watching him.'

She smiled slightly, which left him worrying. His mother could be very determined when she felt something was the right action to take. She was a very special woman, who'd worked hard all her life, brought her three sons up with loving kindness, if not always enough to eat, and he was proud of her.

And now, she was caring for another child, one who desperately needed love and feeding up.

12

When Mike and Cliff went into the police station the second day after the attack, they found Sergeant Deemer already there.

'Should you be at work yet, Sarge?' Mike blurted out. 'Your face is really badly bruised.'

'I took one day off and that's it. I'm not giving in to such villains. The ones who attacked me were foreigners, must have been. I'd have recognised such big, strapping chaps if they'd lived in our valley. And they had a different accent to our folk here. Which means a certain person brought them in purely to attack me.'

He scowled at the memory, then nodded more happily. 'I did recognise the young lads who saved me from worse injuries, and I've sent a message asking them to come to the station today because I want to thank them in person. In the meantime, I hear you coped well yesterday.'

There was a tap at the station door shortly afterwards, and Cliff shouted, 'Come in. It's open.'

Two lanky young lads peeped in, looking rather uneasy. 'Sergeant Deemer sent for us.'

Cliff beamed at them from behind the counter. 'He'll be delighted to see you. Come this way.'

Deemer took over as soon as they entered his office. 'Come over here and let me shake your hands, lads. I can't thank you enough for coming to my aid.' He pumped their hands up and down, then looked at them very earnestly. 'You may even have saved my life, and I won't forget that.'

They both flushed slightly and wriggled uncomfortably, then one nudged the other to speak.

'Those men spoke funny so we reckoned they come from somewhere else, Sergeant, and they'd have to leave town by the main road. We kept watch on it overnight.'

'Did you now? Go on.'

'We saw them leave this morning just as it started getting light,' the other added. 'They were still wearing them knitted hats pulled down, so you couldn't mistake 'em. We could see the big black car clearly by then. It didn't have any lights on, but I've got good eyesight an' here's its registration number.' He passed over a piece of crumpled paper with the number written on it in pencil.

'Eh, you're a smart pair of lads!' he said warmly. 'There's not many clever enough to work that out. I think you two should join the police force when you grow up. You're exactly the sort of young chaps we need.'

They gaped at him, smiled shyly, but shook their heads, looking sad.

'I'm not good enough at reading,' one said.

'An' you have to be good at sums too,' the other added. 'I can't seem to get the hang of that long division stuff, an' the master says I'm stupid.'

'We'll find help for you with that once we've sorted out the present troubles,' the sergeant said gently. 'Reading isn't hard. It's just practice. The master is probably too busy to help you, but I'm not. Sums are the same, lots of practice and it suddenly clicks.'

They still shook their heads. 'I'd like to, I really would, Sergeant Deemer, but my mam wants me to leave school an' start earning as soon as I can. She says I'm eating her out of house and home.'

'My mam says the same. She's heard that new church gives lads clothing, for a uniform, like, so she's making us go there. We don't like that minister, though.'

'But you'd like to be policemen if you could?'

They both nodded vigorously.

'Then leave it to me and I'll sort that out for you with your mams once I'm better. Now, I want you to continue helping me. Keep your eyes open, and if you ever see anyone who looks like causing trouble, especially someone from outside the valley, you're to come to the police house in the evening and report it. Do not try to do anything except report it to me because we'll need to watch them first, to see what they do and where they go. You'll be special assistants to the police from now on.'

'Like in the *Boy's Own* comic?' one of them asked in a breathless, excited voice.

'I haven't read it lately, but that sounds about right,' Deemer said gravely. 'Now, I have to get on with my day, so give Cliff here your names and addresses, then any of us can find you again if we need your help. And tell your mams I'm coming to see them once I'm better to say how much you've helped me and how proud they should be of you. I'm a bit sore to move around much at the moment, but not as sore as I'd have been without your help.'

They exchanged quick grins. 'Yessir.'

'And in the meantime, buy yourselves a treat.' He slipped them a florin each and they smiled even more broadly.

Their clothes were ragged and they could have done with a wash, but they walked out of his office with heads held high and beaming smiles on their faces as if they felt like kings.

'Salt of the earth, lads like that,' he muttered and blew his nose to hide his emotions.

The two youngsters followed Cliff into the reception area and, when he'd taken their particulars, he saw them peering round, taking everything in, so gave them a treat by taking them to see the cells and locking them in one for a few moments, then showing them how handcuffs worked.

Once the two had left the police station, Sergeant Deemer called his two constables into his office. 'They give you hope for the future, lads like that do. Well done for showing them the cells, Cliff. Now, I promised to show you our valley, Mike. Cliff here can look after the station for us. He knows the ropes and I trust him absolutely.'

'I shall enjoy getting a good look round, sir.'

'You'll have to drive, I'm afraid. Who knows what rumours are spreading about the attack on me, so I want people to see that I'm all right. I shan't even try to get out of the car if I can help it, though, because I'm stiff as an icicle at midnight, to tell you the truth.'

'The bruises on your face are showing,' Cliff said hesitantly.

'I can't do much about that, so we'll ignore them. This isn't one of those seaside beauty pageants, after all.'

He left behind a beaming constable because the sergeant didn't give praise or express such absolute trust lightly.

And Deemer was driven by a man already won over by his new sergeant's kindness and integrity, not to mention his personal courage.

On the night of the attack on Deemer, Higgerson had been feeling happy. He'd been expecting the men he'd hired at considerable expense with the help of an acquaintance in Manchester to report to him that they'd got rid of Deemer.

He got so bored with his own company as he waited that he fell asleep on the comfortable armchair in his home office, waking suddenly when someone tapped on the window.

He beckoned the men to come in, asking eagerly, 'Did you manage to put him out of commission?'

'We did our best and got in a few good thumps, might even have broken a rib or two. He'll be sore tomorrow, I promise you.' He paused.

'Well, go on!'

'Unfortunately some damned passers-by rescued your sergeant before we could belt him to kingdom come.'

Higgerson felt furious. They might have got in a few good knocks, but he'd ordered them to do as much damage as possible to the old fool, and preferably put him out of action once and for all.

That meant his big scheme to get rid of Deemer had failed, which was bad enough, given how much it had cost him. But these were big men and he didn't quite dare shout at them. Truth to tell, he didn't dare do anything but pay them what had been agreed.

When they'd gone, the silence seemed to weigh heavily on him. He was fed up of having only an ignorant subordinate to chat to. Jem Stanley might obey his every command, but he was stupid.

The sight of Deemer being driven past two days later, with a badly bruised face, cheered him a little, but not much.

To his surprise, he was still missing his wife, damn her, especially in the evenings. It had been amusing to torment Lallie, and he'd found it a relief to thump her when things went wrong.

After fretting about it for a day or two, he decided to bring his younger son home from boarding school and start him in the family business. He'd teach him how to make money, which you didn't do by learning Latin.

It was doing the lad no good to keep his nose in his books and, as far as Higgerson could tell, Kit hadn't even used his schooldays to make worthwhile connections with lads from the better families. So the fancy school was a total waste of money.

Anyway Kit would be company if he were living here at home.

What the lad needed was to taste life, real life, and to start learning how to manage renting out houses so that they brought in steady money. You didn't get rich without some effort, and Kit could start at the bottom, by actually collecting rents, as Higgerson had.

He didn't want to give his son a chance to run away from school as his older brother had done, so he decided simply to turn up there and tell them Kit was needed at home.

When he gave orders for the car to be prepared for a longer journey, Stanley stared at him in shock.

'Where do you want to go to, Mr Higgerson?'

'To my son's boarding school in Cheshire.'

'Oh. Right. Um, have you got a map book, sir? I've never driven so far away from the valley before and I don't know the roads.'

'Isn't there a map book in the garage? I know I bought one a few years ago.'

'Not that I've ever seen, sir.'

'That sod who took my car probably stole it as well.' He thumped his clenched fist on the table.

Jem kept quiet. It was the best thing to do when his master fell into a rage.

After a short time Higgerson let out his breath. 'Well, go out and buy another map book, then. I shall want you to be ready to set off tomorrow morning early.' He fumbled in his pocket and handed over a five-pound note.

'Can I take the car, sir? It'll make it quicker to buy the map book, and I'll need to fill it up with petrol if we're going on a long journey.'

Silence, then, 'Yes. Put the petrol on my account. And don't forget that I check every entry!'

Jem smiled as he drove away. Higgerson always said that, but Jem had a little arrangement with the owner of the garage which added a few pence to every bill and his share was handed over after each purchase. He'd learned from watching and listening to Higgerson that even tiny amounts of money mounted up if you didn't spend them. He now had a Post Office savings bank account and so did his wife.

He wasn't looking forward to going into the bookshop, though. He'd never been in one in his life, but he knew where the one in Rivenshaw was. He didn't dare ask for more information from his master about exactly what to buy because that would show his ignorance. Surely the man at the bookshop would know what he needed?

He drove into town and parked the car, then walked towards the bookshop, stopping before he went in to stare in the window, which was chock full of books for those stupid enough to waste their time staring at squiggly lines on little squares of paper.

He stared inside, wanting to see what it was like before he went in. He wasn't pleased by what he saw, not at all.

There were two elegantly dressed old ladies chatting to an equally old man behind the counter. What was the fellow called? He checked the sign above the door. Oh yes, Mr Twomer.

Jem hesitated for a moment, then decided to stroll along to the end of the street and back, hoping the ladies would be gone by then. Posh old females who were fancily dressed like these two terrified him with their mincy-pincy way of speaking and their habit of looking down their noses at chaps like him.

He walked up and back, then came to a halt outside again, sagging in disappointment. Oh, hell! They were still there, and Mr Higgerson would get furiously angry if Jem took too long. Should he go inside now or take another walk?

He looked at the clock hanging over the entrance to a nearby shop and sighed. He'd have to do it now. Taking a deep breath, he pushed open the door.

The three people inside stopped chatting to stare at him, then Mr Twomer asked, 'May I help you, sir?'

'Yes please. I need a book of road maps.'

'For where?'

'Huh?'

One of the ladies tittered and Jem could feel himself flushing.

'For which part of the country, sir?'

'We need to get from here to Cheshire.'

'Ah. North of England. This way, sir. I have just the thing.' Mr Twomer set off for the back of the shop and Jem followed.

'Here you are, sir. Just check that it's what you want, and if it's suitable, come and pay for it at the counter.'

Jem opened the big floppy book and fumbled through a few pages, trying to look as if he knew what he was doing. None of it made sense to him. He'd never been out of the valley till he went to prison, and they didn't teach you map reading in there. He wasn't good at normal reading, let alone understanding this set of chicken tracks.

He'd just have to hope it was the right map book and that Mr Higgerson could understand it and explain which roads to take as they went along.

He was halfway home before he remembered the petrol, so he had to turn round and drive back into the town centre to fill up the car.

When he got back, he went to find Mr Higgerson and held out the parcel. 'Mr Twomer says this is the one you need, sir.'

'It's you who needs it if you're going to drive me there.'

What would be worse, confessing his ignorance now or tomorrow? Better get it over with now, then his master might be calmer tomorrow. Jem took a deep breath. 'I ain't never used a map book before, sir, and anyway, I'll be keeping my eyes on the road while I'm driving. It's important to keep you safe. It'll take longer to get there if I have to keep stopping to look at that book.' He held his breath and waited.

He thought Mr Higgerson was going to explode and got ready to leg it, but the high colour in his master's face gradually faded and a grumpy expression took its place.

'You're an ill-educated fool, but we don't want to crash or take for ever to get there, so I'll do the map reading. Go and get the car ready for an early start tomorrow. And make sure there's a rope in the car in case we have to tie my son up. I'm not having him run away as well. And I'm going to make sure he learns to do as he's told and also how to look after himself. I want you to teach him how to fight once we get him started.'

Jem's heart sank. This was sounding worse by the minute. If someone who was nearly a grown man didn't know how to defend himself by now, he'd probably have grown up too soft to learn.

He was getting more and more worried at Higgerson's increasingly strange behaviour, and it was getting worse. Tie up his son? Who ever heard of such a thing?

However, Jem had learned from what Dobbs had done. He had a bag packed so that he could take off and head somewhere else to live at the drop of a hat. His wife had helped him pack it and he'd promised that if the worst happened, he'd send for her when he found somewhere else to live. He'd meant it too. She was a capable lass, and why buy another mare when you had a good one to ride already?

He had a better understanding now of why his predecessor had run off. Dobbs had had enough of being treated like dirt. Jem smiled as he always did when he thought of Dobbs not only stealing Higgerson's car to make his escape, but getting away with it.

Pity he didn't have connections with people who sold cars, or he'd do the same one day down the track as well. In the meantime making money was the main thing he and his wife cared about.

★

Since Higgerson wanted to set off early the following morning, he told Jem to be there by seven o'clock sharp and not to turn up with a hangover, thank you very much. He'd need to be alert. Also, he should make sure he was wearing clean clothes that didn't smell of sweat if they were going to be shut up in a car together for a few hours.

Jem put on his Sunday best and got there just before seven. He soon had the car ready to leave, with the spare can of petrol in the boot. He then had to wait half an hour for his master to be ready to set off.

He didn't whistle as he'd like to while he did a bit of pretend tidying because his master might arrive at any minute and he said the noise of someone whistling hurt his ears. He got angry if he caught any servant idling around, so Jem tidied up the same things twice, moving them about, trying to look busy.

Never mind, it was worth putting up with the fussing about because Jem loved driving even when, as today, he didn't know where the hell he was going.

He enjoyed the driving except when his master read the map wrongly and directed him to turn down a narrow lane anyone could see wasn't a main road, yelling at him to do as he was bloody told. When the road came to a dead end in a muddy little village, his master blamed him, naturally.

Jem got out of the car and asked directions, finding it hard to understand the way the locals spoke, but to his enormous relief, the pointing fingers did the trick and he got them back on the main road.

Once there Higgerson took over giving directions again and they managed to get to the fancy school without any more detours and only a little later than he'd wanted to arrive.

They stopped in a wide open space in front of a huge building. There were two big doors up a flight of steps. Higgerson snapped, 'Get out and open the car door for me, you fool. What would it look like, me opening it myself?'

Jem did as he was told and to his relief, his master vanished into the building. First thing he did was go and find a wall and have a nice long pee behind it.

Kit Higgerson was standing by the window of the class-room, ignoring the other boys and wishing he were outside, wandering through some woods. They were waiting for the teacher to arrive for this lesson, and this particular master was always a little late.

When he saw a car draw up and his father get out of it, his heart sank. What on earth did *he* want?

Soon after that, the teacher came in and the lesson began. It was interrupted almost immediately. One of the junior boys knocked on the classroom door, came in, and handed a folded note to the teacher.

He dismissed the child, read the message and crooked one finger. 'Higgerson!'

Feeling dread in every fibre of his being, Kit went out to the front of the class. 'Yes, sir.'

'You're wanted in the headmaster's study. Your father's come to take you away from school permanently, it seems. Any idea why?'

'No, sir. It's the first I've heard of it.' And he didn't want to leave, let alone go and live at home again permanently.

'Better go and find out, then. Don't keep them waiting. See if you can persuade him to let you stay on. You're bright enough to go to university.'

As he walked slowly along the corridor, the thought of being taken home to live with his father, without his mother to help him stay out of trouble, made Kit feel sick. He'd been dreading the next holidays, absolutely dreading them after the horrors of spending Christmas alone with a drunken father who'd lashed out at him with a heavy fist several times.

He perfectly understood why Felix had run away, and was planning to do the same before he had to leave school at the end of next year. Had the time come to do that?

He slowed down still more, then stopped at the end of the corridor and took a few deep, shaky breaths. Before he could have second thoughts, he turned towards the sleeping quarters instead of towards the headmaster's study.

He rushed up the stairs and into his sleeping cubicle, relieved that there was no one around. He threw a couple of changes of clothing into his sports bag, including some old clothes they used for painting classes so as not to get paint on their uniforms. Grabbing the last of the Christmas money that he'd hidden among his underwear, he shoved it into his pocket and crept down the servants' stairs.

His heart was pounding and he felt literally nauseous with fear. If anyone caught him and realised what he was attempting, he'd be in more trouble than at any time in his whole life. But he had to try to escape, had to at least try.

Luck was with him and he managed to get out of the school the back way and slip along the narrow muddy space behind the lavatories, getting to a nearby copse without being seen. There he quickly shed his uniform and put on the old clothes.

He'd better get off the school grounds before he did anything else.

He walked quietly through the copse, with an anxious moment when he nearly bumped into one of the gardeners. Luckily the man was smoking a forbidden cigarette and had his back to the school, wasn't paying attention to anything but the pleasure of puffing away. He didn't even notice the noise Kit made darting behind a bush.

Once the man had finished his cigarette and moved away, Kit ran to the back fence, hurled his sports bag over the top, and clambered after it.

He snatched up the bag and started running then, not stopping until he reached the quiet lane that led past the village towards the main road. He knew where his mother was living now because his brother had written to him. If it was at all possible, he was going to seek refuge with her.

But first he had to get to her. He'd walk all the way to Wiltshire if he had to, even though it'd take him days. He wasn't going back to his father, whatever anyone said or did.

He was in luck again, had only walked a mile or two, heading south, when a truck carrying some large cardboard boxes stopped and a man leaned out of it to shout, 'You look weary, lad. Where are you going?'

'Swindon.'

'Long way, that. I'm going in the same direction. Want a lift down the road a bit?'

'Yes, please. Thank you very much.'

'Hop on board then.'

When Kit was settled in the cab the man set off again. 'I hope you're an interesting talker. I get bored on long journeys. Tell me about yourself.'

No way was he going to tell the truth, so Kit made up a story about a sick grandparent. It must have been good enough to keep the man entertained, because he not only bought Kit a pie and a cup of tea at a café, but said he could take him as far as Reading if he didn't mind sleeping in the cab for a while when the driver got tired and took a nap.

'Who are you running away from, then?' he asked as they set off again. 'The truth this time, mind, though you do make up entertaining stories, I must admit.'

Kit stared at him in terror and nearly flung himself out of the lorry.

'Don't try it,' his companion warned. 'Now, let's start again. My name is Monty Norton. And your real name is?'

*

Higgerson sat in the principal's office, in a damned uncomfortable chair which stood with two others in a draughty bay window.

The principal made polite conversation about the weather and the fine display of crocuses for a few minutes, then frowned as a clock struck the quarter hour. 'It's taking your son longer than I'd have expected to get here. Let me just go and check that he knows where to come.'

He vanished, leaving Higgerson alone and rapidly running out of patience, even though he usually kept his temper under control when he was with the nobs.

The principal's secretary came in, a fat older woman who seemed to be suffering from a head cold.

'Would you like a cup of tea while you're waiting, Mr Higgerson?'

He held back his anger. 'Yes, please, but could you hurry up with it. I have a long drive home after I leave here.'

She forced a smile and nodded.

It was ten minutes before she brought in a tea trolley, followed shortly afterwards by the principal.

'I'm afraid your son can't be found. We don't understand it. He did get my message. I've sent people out to search the grounds.'

Alarm bells rang in Higgerson's mind. Surely Kit couldn't have run away? How could he have known what was intended today? There was only one way. These idiots must have told him his father had come to take him away.

It was a full hour later that the principal was forced to confess that Kit couldn't be found and they'd looked everywhere in the school and its grounds.

'We'll have to call in the police,' he said.

Higgerson rose to his feet. 'I'm not hanging around while you dither with them. If my son isn't returned to me by tomorrow teatime at the latest, you'll be hearing from my lawyer and I'll be suing the school for every penny I can get out of you. You're not paid annual fees as high as that to *lose* people's sons.'

'But sir—'

He pushed the man out of the way and strode out of the building, finding his chauffeur leaning against a wall chatting to a gardener. 'Stanley! Get over here, you lazy sod!'

'Yes, sir.' He ran across the gravel and stopped by the car, glancing towards the school. 'Has Master Kit been found?'

'No, he damned well hasn't and I'm not hanging around here waiting. They're a bunch of effeminate fools. Drive me home as quickly as you can.'

'I'd appreciate it if you'd remind me which roads to take as we go, sir.'

'Heaven help me! I live in a world full of morons!'

Jem set off, not speaking in case he said the wrong thing. He wondered if Kit had run away like his brother Felix. A voice boomed out suddenly from the back seat, making him jump in shock.

'I've told those lazy sods that if they don't find my son and return him to my care by tomorrow teatime, I'll put the matter in the hands of my lawyer and sue them for a large amount of money.'

'Yes, sir. Quite right, sir.'

Higgerson continued to talk angrily about ungrateful sons and stupid women, then went on to give his views on how lads ought to be educated. But he didn't forget to yell out directions and curse other motorists as they went.

Jem could see in the rear-view mirror that his master was nearly purple in the face with anger and he worried that Higgerson might have a seizure. What the hell would he do then?

It was a huge relief to get back to Rivenshaw, and since his master didn't tell him to stay and do anything else, he locked the car away, sent the key in to his master, and hurried home.

He changed out of his best clothes, told his wife what had happened, then grabbed a cheese sandwich and went off to drown his sorrows in the company of his friends at the pub.

13

Arthur telephoned Charlie Willcox from Maisie's house to say that the pieces of furniture were finished. He thought he saw a little girl vanish up the stairs, just the back of her skirt and skinny little legs still showing. That made him feel sad, reminding him of how long it was since he'd spent time with Beatie.

'I can't come round till tomorrow to check that the repairs are all right,' Charlie said. 'I expect they will be. You sound as if you know about wood. And there's another piece I remember seeing in the dining room that might suit a client of mine, that small bookcase over by the window, so we'll look at what needs doing to that while we're at it.'

Arthur thanked Maisie for letting him use the phone and went to re-join Biff, who was waiting for him outside. As the two men went back to Number 25 he told his companion what Charlie had said.

'If he likes what you've done, and I must say the pieces look perfect again to me, I think we should nip into town and buy you some better clothes,' Biff said.

'I don't have the money to spare, so I'll manage with these. They've still got plenty of wear in them if I'm careful.'

'Those clothes are worn out, suitable only for wearing when you're at home working on mending stuff, not for going outside the house and looking decent. Trust me, what you're wearing will matter a lot more to other people now you're living here.

If you're short of money, I can lend you some till Charlie sells some of your better furniture.'

Arthur went to look at himself in the nearest mirror and pulled a face at what he saw. Biff was right, the clothes wouldn't have attracted attention in a slum area, but he had to look better, not only because of inheriting the house, but also to keep showing people that he was respectable again.

Only, he was so worried about the money needed to run this big house he'd already grown to love that he hated to spend a penny if it wasn't absolutely necessary.

'We can go to Charlie's other shop, the one where they sell better quality second-hand clothes,' Biff said quietly. 'You won't have to spend as much money there.'

'Good idea. Just one or two things, eh?'

Biff went to tell Phil they were going out and remind him to keep his eyes open for any attempts to break in.

'Do you think they'll try that?' Phil asked. 'They know by now that we keep a careful watch here. And people don't usually break into houses in the daytime anyway, not if someone's inside them.'

'Word is that Higgerson is in a tearing rage about something, and even I know that he's famous for lashing out blindly at people when he's angry.'

'I'll be careful who I open the door to. I always am,' Phil assured them.

Biff and Arthur drove off and Phil went round the house, making sure as he went that all the doors and windows were indeed locked.

Ten minutes later he heard the sound of glass breaking in the kitchen, and went pounding down the stairs to find out what the hell was going on.

Gwynneth was in the bedroom she shared with Beatie when they heard the sound of glass smashing somewhere nearby. She rushed to the window that looked out over the backyards. 'Oh, no! There are two men breaking into Number Twenty-five.'

Beatie came to stand beside her just as one man looked up and Gwynneth shielded her from view. Surely the burglar had been too far away to see the child clearly?

She hesitated about going to help, but she couldn't leave these men free to steal things. She was alone in the house with Beatie, so yelled, 'You stay in our bedroom. Bolt the door till I get back, and don't stand near the window where you can be seen.'

She ran downstairs and grabbed the telephone, calling the police number and telling them what she'd seen, asking for immediate help. Then she went into the backyard and stood on a stepladder, trying to get a glimpse into Number 25. Only, she couldn't see the men now. Had they got inside already?

Bella had also come out of the middle house, and called across. 'What's going on? I heard glass breaking.'

'Two men looked to be forcing their way into Number Twenty-five by breaking a window, and there's only one of the Becksleys there at the moment. I've rung the police.'

'If they think they can break into these houses in the day-time, it won't be long before they're coming after us all.'

Gwynneth stared at her for a moment, then said, 'Are you game to go and intervene. There would be two of us, plus one of the Becksleys, and surely they'll run away if someone else turns up.'

'I suppose we could always run away again ourselves if they don't, and look like they're going to turn violent.'

'I'll go in if you will. But get something to defend your-self with. It always makes me furious when burglars get into houses and steal things decent people have worked hard for.'

Bella still hesitated. 'Dare we?'

'Dare we let whoever it is think it's easy to break into these houses? We'll go in the back way.'

She clambered down the ladder and grabbed the big mallet from the yard, one that her son used for breaking up pieces of coal as he loaded the scuttle from the coal shed. Hefting it in her hand, she nodded. As she hurried out of the back gate, Bella came out of the next yard, carrying a poker.

'We should hide our weapons in our skirts,' she called. 'Surprise them if necessary.'

As they opened the end gate cautiously, they heard yelling and shouting coming from inside.

'Sounds like Phil's in trouble. We can't leave him on his own. Let's scream for help before we go in, though.'

They spent a minute proving there was nothing wrong with their lungs, and to their relief someone yelled from down the back alley. 'What's wrong?'

'Burglars in Number Twenty-five!' Gwynneth yelled back.

A man called, 'I'll bring help!'

'That makes me feel better about going in,' Bella said.

'Come on, then. Let's give 'em what for.'

As Gwynneth led the way into the kitchen they saw Phil rolling about on the floor fighting with a stranger. Then there was a crash from the hall. No one seemed to have noticed them.

Bella whispered, 'You stay here. I'll find out what's happening in the hall.'

She found one of the intruders raising a short metal bar as if to smash the hall mirror, and let out an involuntary cry of protest. He must have already smashed a chair lying in pieces to one side.

'Put that down!' she yelled at the top of her voice.

He swung round, lowering the bar briefly, then laughing confidently. 'Ooh, I'm scared,' he mocked. 'A woman is so frightening.'

She backed into the kitchen, still hiding her makeshift weapon in the folds of her skirt. As he followed her and reached out to grab her, she caught him by surprise, walloping him across the lower arm with her poker.

He yelled out hoarsely in pain.

'You'll regret that, you bitch.'

As she backed away again, Gwynneth saw who the man was and stepped forward. 'Let me deal with this one, Bella. You see if you can thump the other one.'

She smiled at the man. 'Haven't you learned your lesson yet, Fred Shorter?'

He stared across at her, looking shocked at hearing his own name.

Phil and his assailant were still tussling on the floor. Bella kept an eye on them, but watched the man who'd just followed Gwynneth in from the hall. He looked frightening to her, but her neighbour suddenly seemed to have lost her fear of him.

She pulled out the mallet and stopped moving. 'I hit you where it hurt most last time you tried to grab me, Fred, and I've a fancy to do it again.'

'Shut up, you bitch!'

'Idiots like you can't make me.'

The man didn't seem to have noticed Bella and was watching Gwynneth as if he really was nervous about tackling her, so she darted forward and used the poker on his nearest leg, taking him by surprise and causing him to stumble backwards.

Gwynneth immediately carried out her threat and managed to kick Fred in his most vulnerable place. He yowled in anguish and clutched himself, bending over protectively.

She stepped back, smiling. 'I learned to do that when I was living in the worst part of Backshaw Moss.' She held her mallet ready, but he was in too much pain to continue the fight.

Phil was still holding his own, but with Fred disabled, his opponent rolled nimbly away and ran towards the back door.

He ran straight into another man coming into the kitchen from the yard, and jumped back again, trying to grab

Gwynneth who was nearest to him. But she wielded her mallet again, and then a second neighbour came into the house, looking furiously angry.

The intruder looked round, as if trying to see another way out, but before he could move the newcomers jumped on him.

Gwynneth smiled down at Fred, who was clearly in agony, raising her mallet again. 'Stay where you are.'

A car screeched to a halt outside the back gate, and a minute later two young policemen rushed into the house.

'Nice to see you, gentlemen,' Bella said with a smile, letting her poker hang down by her side.

The injured intruder winced as he moved incautiously, trying to get up, and one of the constables said, 'Stay where you are.'

The other intruder spread out his hands in a gesture of surrender.

Deemer followed his constables through the back door, moving more slowly than usual. He paused to study the people in the kitchen. 'Having a bit of trouble, Gwynneth love?'

'We were, but I know where to hit a man. I was just wondering whether to kick this one again. What do you think?'

'Don't let her touch me, Sergeant,' Fred begged, edging across the floor away from her, still looking as if it hurt to move. 'She's a wild one, she is. I won't give you any trouble.'

Deemer chuckled openly. 'Beaten by a woman, eh?' He turned to his constables. 'Handcuff them, lads. If they give you any trouble, just ask Gwynneth to help you deal with them.'

The one called Fred shrank back visibly, shuddering and putting one hand protectively in front of his vital parts.

'Fasten their handcuffs to the rails in the car and take them to the lock-up, then one of you come back and collect me.'

He watched them handcuff the two men inside the car before turning back to the group now standing in the kitchen, all of them laughing.

'Folk aren't usually so amused about catching intruders,' he said mildly.

One of the neighbours chuckled. 'It was the daftest fight I've ever seen. Heaven help me if ladies as fierce as these two ever come after me.'

Gwynneth shrugged. 'I'd met that Fred before, yes, and bested him the same way. He looks fierce, but he's never keen to fight unless his opponent is much weaker, the coward.'

Biff and Arthur arrived back just then, and had to be told what was amusing everyone. Soon they too were smiling broadly, though Arthur's smile faded quickly as he assessed the damage.

'What's it going to cost to have those windows repaired?'

'The lawyer will pay for it and I know a glazier who'll fix the windows as quickly as possible,' Biff whispered to him, guessing what he was worrying about.

Deemer was still smiling. 'The best of it is that when the details get out about how you two ladies dealt with them, that sort of chap will keep out of your way for a while, so your houses should be safe.'

'I'll still keep something to defend myself handy,' Bella said.

'I expect these two will get a couple of months in prison. And a certain person will be furious about their failure.' He hoped Higgerson would hold back on causing trouble for a while till the general amusement died down, but it was hard to guess about that lately, the way the man had been behaving.

What upset him most about this incident was that when he questioned the men at the police station, no threats would persuade them to tell him why they'd chosen to try to burgle a house full of broken furniture, or why they'd deliberately smashed several panes of glass.

He could guess they'd been told to make a mess, and was quite sure who had hired them, but as usual he had no proof.

His biggest regret was that he'd not seen Gwynneth vanquish Fred Shorter. What a redoubtable woman she was.

While they were waiting for Mike to come back, Arthur offered the visitors a cup of tea.

'Thanks, but I've got a stew simmering on the stove, so I'd better get back to give it a stir,' Bella said.

'And I've left Beatie locked in the bedroom,' Gwynneth said. 'Another time perhaps.'

As she turned to leave, Arthur grabbed her arm. 'Did you say Beatie?'

'Oh dear! I didn't mean to say her name. Please don't tell anyone she's staying with me.'

'Beatie Hicks?'

'Yes.'

'She's my granddaughter.'

It was a few seconds before this sank in fully. 'I hadn't realised – well, I haven't had much to do with your family. You can't know the family details of everyone in the valley, can you?'

'Is Beatie all right?'

He was still clutching Gwynneth's arm and looked so anguished she patted his hand to comfort him. 'I'm afraid not. She's been badly beaten and ran away from that Hicks woman. I'm hiding the child, trying to give her time to recover, and then, well, I haven't worked out what to do afterwards. She can't go back to that life.'

Arthur closed his eyes, still not letting go of her arm. 'The law will send her back to that harridan if they find out where she is. I have – a bad reputation, so they won't give her to me. I used to drink, you see.'

'I did hear something like that. But you haven't done it for a while, if I remember correctly, have you?'

'It'll still count against me and Mrs Hicks not only has the money to hire a fancy lawyer, she has the support of the minister of her church, who deals with the world as harshly as she does. Please tell me, how is the child?'

'Badly bruised with a few lacerations, all from a vicious caning, I'd guess.'

He sucked in a breath. 'Dear heaven, I'd like to cane that woman and give her a taste of her own medicine, except I've never hit a woman or child in my life. Sergeant Deemer was going to ask the doctor to check Beatie's injuries, but she'd run away and they couldn't find her. The law would probably force him to take her away from you. Can you keep her safe till we can work out what to do? Or even, find a way to let the doctor see her before the wounds heal?'

'I don't know. Let me think about it.'

'You'll go on hiding her?'

'Oh, yes. We even have somewhere clever to hide her if they come searching.'

Arthur looked thoughtful. 'I don't think Sergeant Deemer would search very hard. Everyone knows he can't abide children being hurt.' Then he sighed and added, 'That woman would keep searching, though, and the minister at her church would help her. Even if we kept Beatie safe from them, she'd never dare go out again, and what sort of life is that?'

They were still standing close together, looking at one another, and he suddenly went a bit red and let go of her arm. 'Eh, I'm sorry. I didn't mean to manhandle you.'

'You didn't hurt me.'

'Can I come and see her? I've sometimes been able to watch her from a distance, but haven't been able to speak to her since her parents were killed.'

Biff had been watching and listening with interest, and now judged it time to join in. 'You'd better not go next door till after dark, Arthur lad.'

Both of them seemed startled when he spoke, as if they'd forgotten he was even there.

'He's right. Come around tonight, Mr Chapman. About eight o'clock. It'll be fully dark by then and most people will be indoors. Come the back way and I'll leave the gate unlocked.'

Arthur smiled in relief. 'Thank you, Mrs Harte.'

There was a pause, then she said, 'Call me Gwynneth.'

'And I'm Arthur.'

'I'll tell Beatie to expect you.'

After staring at one another for a moment longer, they both stepped back at the same time.

Arthur spoke bitterly, looking at Biff this time, 'My daughter would have thrown a fit at the mere thought of her mother-in-law taking the child. She fell in love with Peter and they married quickly, but she wouldn't have anything to do with her mother-in-law once she got to know her because Mrs Hicks tried to come between her and her husband. Peter only went round to see his mother once in a while, out of duty.'

'I've heard Mrs Hicks can't keep maids for long and doesn't have any real friends.'

'That'd be right.'

Gwynneth took a step towards the back door. 'I'd better go and tell Beatie what's happened. She'll be anxious.'

'I'll see you to your house,' Biff said.

'My son's wife's house, actually. I've had to move out of the place where I worked because of the fire at Wilf's. I'm going to try and find a new job, as well as somewhere to live, though. I miss my independence, even though Gabriel and his wife couldn't have made me more welcome.'

When Biff came back he found Arthur brushing away tears.

'Sorry. I'm being a fool. But it was so good to hear that Beatie got away. I can't wait to see her again.'

'You love that child. I knew that the first time I heard you speak about her.'

'I might not have gone on the drink if I'd been allowed to look after her. I'd lost nearly everyone I cared about, and my daughter was dead. The drink didn't help, on the contrary, and because of it my son has stopped speaking to me. Ah, who knows anything? I can't blame others for my own weakness.'

'You've got over it now, looks like.'

'I have that! I shall never touch another drop of alcohol as long as I live. In the meantime how are we going to keep Beatie safe from that woman? I'd emigrate to Australia with her to do that if necessary.'

'I don't think you'll need to go that far away. And we also have to keep you safe from Higgerson too, don't forget. Eh, your life's in a right old muddle, isn't it?'

'In one way. In another there's hope crept into it again, what with this house and Beatie. Real hope.' He caught sight of himself in a mirror. 'But if I'm going to see her tonight, I'd better change into my new clothes. You were right about these being on their last legs. I don't want to look like a rag-and-bone man, do I?'

Biff watched Arthur stride up the stairs briskly. It seemed to him that every day the other man was growing stronger, more determined to make a new life. It was good to see, exactly what Jane Chapman had intended the bequest to do.

But how they were going to sort out the problem with that child long-term was more than Biff could see. Surely they'd find a way?

The trouble was, Mrs Hicks had a powerful supporter in the minister from her church. Biff suspected that was because she donated generously to the church. And Arthur had blotted his copybook badly after his wife died. Plus, everyone would say a girl needed a woman to look after her properly.

The first step they could take would be to let the doctor see Beatie before the wounds healed. He'd accompany Arthur next door tonight, and tell Gwynneth that, then suggest she pretend the doctor was coming to see her.

14

Kit sat in the cab of the lorry, gave the driver his real name, and explained what had been going on in his family and why he'd run away. This time he told the absolute truth.

Monty let out a long, low whistle when he stopped. 'You sound so sure your father's that bad.'

'I am. He's probably worse, for all we know. He used to beat my mother, so I was glad for her sake when she managed to run away. I knew I'd have to escape from him too eventually, but I wanted to continue my education for as long as I could. I'd really like to become a doctor, you see, only I don't suppose there's any hope of that now. I've been reading books from our school library about first aid and anything else medical, and of course we've studied the human body in science classes. It's fascinating.'

'Good for you, lad. Just a minute!'

Kit stopped talking to allow Monty to put his full attention on driving carefully through a busy junction.

'There are some idiots driving around,' Monty muttered once the traffic had thinned out a little. 'That sort of family must make life very difficult for you.'

'You believe me, then?'

'This time, yes. There's something about the way people talk about what's happened that shows whether it's the truth or not. Well, it does to me, and I've not often been wrong.'

'Please don't hand me over to the police, then. I'm sure they'll have started looking for me by now. My father and the headmaster will have made sure of that.'

'No, of course I won't. I will have to speak to your mother when we find her, though, just to be absolutely sure I'm doing the right thing helping you, and perhaps her as well.'

'We're going to find her?'

'If we can. Who else would you turn to?'

'I know where she's gone, well, I think I do. My brother said something in a letter, not openly, but I knew what he was talking about. My father never thought to tell the school that Felix wasn't to be allowed to write to me, you see.'

'Go on.'

'So I'm trying to go to them.'

They drove on, and after a while, Monty said, 'It's getting late so if it's all right with you, I'll take you home with me tonight and we'll go and look for your mother and brother tomorrow.'

'Will your wife not mind me turning up without warning?'

'Bless you, no. She'll be quite happy to give you shelter. I've taken in a few waifs and strays in my time.'

'I'd be very grateful for your help.' Kit had to concentrate and dig his fingernails into the palms of his hands to stop tears of sheer relief escaping his control.

They drove on for a while and were nearly at Monty's home when an accident happened so quickly that Kit was never afterwards sure how it could have come about. Another lorry suddenly drove out of a side road and hit their lorry at speed. They spun around so rapidly that Kit was thrown from one side of the cab to the other.

Monty was flung about too, but the window of his door was smashed by a pole outside. To Kit's horror, shards of glass whirled around everywhere in the cab of the lorry. One of the larger pieces sliced into his companion's arm and blood immediately began to pump out through the torn clothing.

The trucks had both stopped moving, but the blood didn't stop pouring out, and Kit guessed that an artery had been hit. He pulled away the shreds of cloth around the huge gash, dragging off his tie and fastening it tightly around the arm in a makeshift tourniquet. He'd never even seen this done before, but he'd read about it and could only hope he'd got it right.

As people came running to help them get out of the twisted wreckage he yelled, 'An artery in the driver's arm has been cut open. Don't loosen the tie.'

The bystanders got Monty out and then helped Kit.

'I've got to help him.' He pushed his way through the group, shouting to let him take over the tourniquet again till they could get help.

Another man came across, calling, 'Someone's gone for a doctor. He says there's one lives nearby.'

Kit continued to keep an eye on Monty, who was still losing blood, but at a much slower rate thanks to the tourniquet.

'That lad seems to know what he's doing,' one woman commented.

He so hoped she was right.

The crowd around them parted suddenly and a man carrying a small leather bag elbowed his way through, calling, 'I'm a doctor. Is anyone hurt?'

'The driver's got a big cut!' Kit yelled back.

The doctor quickly checked the tourniquet and said as he worked, 'The person who did this has probably saved this man's life.'

'It was the lad here who did it.' A man clapped Kit on the back.

'I phoned for an ambulance and it's on its way,' someone called out from a nearby garden.

When it arrived, Kit was told to go in it as well to have his own cuts tended. He hadn't even noticed them, and looked down in surprise at the bloody gashes made on his hands by flying glass, feeling blood trickling down his face as well. He'd read about a new sort of safety glass for car windows that didn't splinter and had thought it a good idea at the time. Pity the lorry hadn't had that sort of glass fitted.

'I'll take over the tourniquet now,' the nurse in the ambulance said gently. 'You've done really well. Just sit in that corner and hold tight to the strap.'

At the hospital Kit told them he was Monty's nephew because he was terrified of being taken away from him. To his relief someone had found the driver's home address in his wallet, so Kit wasn't asked for it.

They took Monty away, tended to his so-called nephew, and left him sitting to one side of the reception area. He felt sick with worry about that kind man.

Half an hour later a lady arrived and she turned out to be Monty's wife. The people at the reception desk were so eager to tell her that her clever nephew had saved her husband's life that they didn't notice the puzzled look she gave Kit.

The hospital doctor came back and took the two of them into a small room further inside the building.

'Your husband will have to stay in overnight, but your nephew can go home with you now, Mrs Norton. You should be extremely proud of him. He definitely saved his uncle's life today.'

Kit had been watching her warily. She didn't say anything to him, but she put one finger briefly to her lips when the doctor wasn't looking, which he took to mean he should be quiet, so he nodded and said nothing more.

Once they got out of the hospital, she led the way across to a car where a neighbour was sitting behind the wheel waiting. 'Say nothing till we get home,' she whispered to Kit as they walked.

'Yes, ma'am.'

Once they were in the car, she explained the situation to her neighbour, and the man marvelled at what had happened, then drove them to her home, which was outside a village along a winding road, with him the only person living nearby.

'Thanks, Tim.' She left the neighbour to put his car away, assuring him that she'd be all right. Then she led the way into the house via the kitchen.

'What's your name, lad?'

'Kit.'

'Sit down and tell me all about it while we wait for the kettle to boil.'

He tried to do so, but suddenly began weeping. 'S-sorry.'

'Shock.' She put her arms round him and gave him a long hug till the sobbing tailed off, then handed him a big handkerchief when he couldn't find his own.

'Right. We both need a nice, sweet cup of cocoa. Are you able to talk now?'

'Yes. And thank you for bringing me back here, ma'am.' He then managed a jerky explanation.

'Ah. That's all right, then. You've told me enough for me to be happy to take you in, because that's what Monty would have wanted.' She chuckled suddenly. 'He's a great one for gathering waifs and strays and sorting out their problems. And you've already more than paid him back for his help, so I'm very happy to give you a bed for the night.'

'I can't tell you how grateful I am, ma'am.'

'Then drink your cup of cocoa and we'll sit quietly for a while. My name's Chrissie, by the way. It'd better be Auntie Chrissie to you from now on, and you can call my husband Uncle Monty when he comes home. We'll work out what to do with you once he's better. He'll figure something out. He's a clever chap, my Monty.'

It was her turn to brush away a tear or two, and she suddenly plonked a kiss on Kit's cheek. 'Eh, if you hadn't been there, I could have lost him. What would I have done then?'

He let her persuade him to go to bed early. He didn't expect to sleep much, comfortable as the bed and hot-water bottle were, but to his surprise he didn't wake till morning.

He found the bathroom as a matter of urgency, then made his way downstairs.

Chrissie smiled across the kitchen at him and gestured to the teapot. 'I heard you moving about and brewed a fresh pot of tea. Would you like a cup?'

'Yes, please.'

As she poured it, she asked, 'Did you sleep well?'

'Like a log.'

'Get that down you and I'll make you some breakfast. Are you hungry?'

To his further surprise he was.

They had a telephone, so she was able to phone the hospital at the time they'd told her to, to check how her husband was, and to her relief they said that Monty could come home as long as he took things easy for a few days.

'You won't run away while I'm gone?' she said to Kit as she got ready to leave with Tim, the neighbour.

'No, ma'am. I have nowhere to go and very little money. And anyway, I've never had an aunt or uncle before. It feels nice, even if it is only pretend.'

'Bless you, we can carry on pretending afterwards, if you like. You've earned a place in our family by what you did yesterday.'

He smiled shyly, not having expected that. 'Thank you.'

'And remember, whatever the rights and wrongs of what your father's been doing, as far as I'm concerned you can come here any time you feel you need shelter, and I know Monty will say the same.'

Kit watched the car drive away and went to sit and read the newspaper. But soon he felt sleepy again so let himself slip into a doze.

Safe. He was safe for a while. How marvellous that felt!

★

Arthur sat and watched the clock until it was five to eight, then stood up and looked pleadingly at Biff. 'I can't wait another minute.'

'Let's go, then.'

'They only live two houses away, so I don't need to trouble you. I can find my own way over that short distance, even in the dark, and surely there won't be anyone else hanging around?'

'Sadly, anyone might be waiting nearby in the darkness, and we'd not like you to get murdered or to lead someone to Beatie, would we? Two good reasons for putting up with my company.'

A shrug was his only answer.

They crept out the back way, putting the lights out before they opened the door, and leaving both Becksley brothers on watch. Biff insisted they stand quietly near the gate and listen for a couple of minutes before going out into the alley. By the time he opened it, Arthur was literally twitching with impatience.

It took only a couple of minutes to slip into Number 21, and when Biff tried the back door, he found it unlocked. Their eyes were used to the darkness by now, and there was enough moonlight filtering in for them to see a man standing inside with a knob-topped walking stick upside down in his hand, ready to defend himself if necessary.

When he saw them he gave a nod of recognition, set the stick down on the kitchen table, and gestured to them to come inside. He locked the back door again before taking them through the house into the sitting room.

Beatie was sitting on the sofa next to Gwynneth.

She and Arthur stared at one another for a moment or two, then he held out his arms and she ran across to fling herself into them, sobbing, 'Grandpa! Grandpa! Where have you *been*?'

He didn't know what to answer, but shame ran through him as it had so many times during the last few months. 'I've been lost,' he managed at last. 'But I've found myself again now, and I've found you, too.'

No one interrupted as they gave one another a long hug, rocking to and fro. He showered kisses on her, and the joy on her face was lovely to see.

After they'd all sat down, Arthur introduced Biff to the child and was about to speak when someone hammered at the front door.

A voice called from outside, 'Open up! Police!'

'Damnation!' Biff muttered. 'They must have found out that Beatie's here.'

Gabriel slipped out of the room and came back almost immediately. 'There's someone knocking at the back door as well. We've got a hidden cellar, though, and you can all three hide down there if you hurry. Follow me!'

He took them down to the normal cellar, fiddled with something, and an opening appeared to one side, showing stone steps leading down. He grabbed a box of candles and a box of matches from a nearby shelf and thrust them into Biff's hands, then the three of them clambered down the steps into the darkness.

The door they'd come through started shutting immediately.

'Stand still,' Biff whispered. 'I need to light a candle.'

When he'd done that he held it up and they stared around.

Arthur's voice was equally hushed. 'I was right about these tunnels. The underground passage from our cellar does lead past all three houses.' He pointed to the left. 'Our house is that way.'

'I don't know how you can tell that in the darkness,' Biff said.

'I'm fairly sure of it, but if you give me another candle I'll go and check, in case we need an escape route. Stay with Biff, Beatie love, and keep very quiet. We don't want them to find you and take you back to your grandmother.'

She nodded, shuddering visibly at that thought.

He was annoyed at himself for upsetting her further. 'Don't worry. We'll keep you safe, love. I'll be back in a minute.' He lit another candle and held it up as he moved to the left.

The other two watched the bobbing light, saw it stop, and then start moving back towards them.

'We can go into my house if we need to. I've worked out how to open it from this side. Eh, it's chilly down here, isn't it?' he said as he joined them again. 'We'll leave some blankets at the top of our steps from now on, Biff, in case anyone has to hide again. There are plenty of spares in the linen cupboard.'

When he put his arm round his granddaughter and gave her a quick hug, she hugged him back.

'I didn't think there'd be secret passages in real life, just in books,' she said. 'I hope no one finds this one.'

Biff smiled across at her. 'I don't think they will. The entrances are very carefully hidden.'

'I'd better not waste candles. We don't know how long we'll be here.' Arthur extinguished his and sat down on the steps. 'Why don't you sit on my knee, love. It'll be warmer than stone steps. Eh, you've grown a lot taller since last time I held you like this.'

But she had never been so thin, and he was quite sure she was undernourished because she had that starveling look to her face. He'd learned to recognise it in other children whose families couldn't afford to feed them properly. Why hadn't she been given enough to eat, though? Mrs Hicks wasn't short of money. Was that woman trying to kill her?

'We should stay quiet in case they come down into the cellar of the house,' Biff murmured. 'Even a faint sound could start them searching.'

The other two nodded and, as they waited, the silence seemed to hug them tightly. They listened very carefully, but didn't hear any sounds from inside the house, so could only hope any noises they'd made earlier had been muffled as well.

Sergeant Deemer was annoyed at being dragged out so late in the evening, because he was still aching all over and he didn't believe what he'd been told anyway by Vanner, the minister from Mrs Hicks's church. He took his senior constable along to drive, and in case there was any physical effort needed.

When they got there, it seemed to take a long time for them to be let into the house. He left it to the younger man to search the place, but Vanner and the two young men whom he'd brought to help search insisted on being involved.

Deemer sincerely hoped they'd find no one hiding. He didn't like or respect Vanner, but unfortunately he couldn't always avoid the man, even though he tried to have as little to do with him as possible. Truly religious people, whatever place of worship they attended, weren't like this arrogant fellow; they were kind and helpful to other people. Vanner was always complaining or scolding or looking for faults in others.

However, there had been no choice about the police being involved because there was a child missing, and it was Sergeant Deemer's duty to look for her.

The minister had sworn very dramatically on a Bible that there had been a sighting of the little girl at one of the bedroom windows in this house by one of the young men from his congregation.

Sadly, the law was on Mrs Hicks's side about who had custody of Beatie. Deemer was worried about the child's safety now, but would be even more worried if he had to return her to her grandmother after what he'd seen in the park several times.

When they were allowed inside, the three occupants of the house denied that anyone had come to visit them that night.

'It was probably someone taking a shortcut along the back alley,' Maisie said.

The minister pointed his forefinger at her. 'You're lying, woman! The child was seen at a bedroom window. Put your hand on the Bible and deny her presence again if you dare.'

She smiled sweetly at him. 'No.' Then she turned back to the sergeant. 'I'm not speaking to him. I prefer to deal with you.'

Vanner actually choked with anger, coughing and spluttering.

Deemer found it hard to keep a straight face as they waited for him to calm down, serious as the situation was. 'Shall we make a start? I'll stand at the rear of the hall, from where I'll be able to keep an eye on both the kitchen area and the back door as well as the front door and the entrances to the various downstairs rooms.'

He could only give Gabriel and the two women a swift, regretful glance as he went to stand there and hope they'd realise that he hadn't wanted to do this to them.

It seemed to take a long time to search the house, and there was so much banging of what sounded like cupboard doors and drawers from upstairs that Maisie went over to Deemer and said angrily, 'I'm going up to find out what they're doing. This is my house and I don't see why they need to search the drawers and cupboards with my underclothes and other personal property in.'

'I'll come with you,' Gwynneth said at once, looking even angrier than her daughter-in-law. 'It sounds as if they're searching my room at the moment.'

Gabriel was about to say he'd go with them, but Deemer grabbed his sleeve and held him back. 'Leave it to your mother, lad. She won't take any nonsense from them. I've seen her get furious at people before.'

He smiled. 'Yes. I have too. Has Vanner had her confront him, do you think?'

'When he arrived, and he's about to feel her anger again. Let's go and stand at the foot of the stairs and listen, in case she needs help.'

'I doubt she will.'

While they were speaking, Maisie had led the way upstairs with Gwynneth close behind. They found the two young men in Gwynneth's room going through her drawers.

'Stop that at once!' she yelled in a very loud voice.

They turned round and stared at the furiously angry woman in shock.

Footsteps sounded behind her on the landing, but she didn't turn, only stepped sideways so that she was completely blocking the doorway.

'What do you think you're doing, going through my under-clothing?' she demanded.

'They're looking for children's clothing, on my orders,' the minister said from behind her.

'In my drawers? Are you mad? Do I look like a child?'

'We found some children's clothes in the top drawer. Where have you hidden that little imp of Satan, and what have you done with the rest of her things?'

Jabbing her elbow hard into him when he tried to push past her into the room, she looked across at the small pile of clothes on the bed and laughed. This clearly took all three men by surprise.

'Those belong to Maddy next door, who sometimes stays with me.'

Vanner looked down his nose at her. 'I don't believe you, woman.'

'I don't care what you believe, *man*. You said you were searching for a missing child, not coming here to fumble through an old woman's underwear. Does it titillate you, make you feel shivery here?' She patted herself on a roughly appropriate part of her body.

The two younger men flushed and stepped hastily away from the drawers.

The minister gaped at her open-mouthed.

She raised her voice and called loudly, 'Sergeant, can you please come up here?'

Deemer sighed and made his way with painful slowness up the stairs. He smiled as he heard Vanner start to say something and Gwynneth tell him sharply to be quiet and wait for the man in authority here to join them.

When he got to the landing, he gave Maisie a quick glance full of suppressed laughter, but it was Gwynneth he addressed. 'Is there some problem, Mrs Harte?'

'These young men have been pawing through my drawers. Do they think I've got a child hidden in them? Of course not. Even they can't be that stupid. You couldn't even fit a baby in there. They're just being nosey. Or they like fiddling with women's underwear, or—'

Vanner tried to speak over her, but she just carried on speaking even more loudly than him. '—or else they're stealing things. If there's anything missing, I'll know, and I'll be reporting the theft to you, believe me.'

The minister once again tried to push her away, and she shoved him back even more forcefully with both hands, so that he stumbled a couple of steps backwards. 'Stay out of my room, you dirty old man!'

It was a couple of moments before he righted himself, then his voice was shrill and loud. 'You know very well there's no theft going on, woman! But I still can't see why you'd have a little girl's clothing here if she lives next door.'

'Well, you're even more stupid than I'd thought, old man, and it shows how much you know about real life. Neighbours, actually help one another; they don't just talk about it from a pulpit like you seem to do. Maddy from next door stays the night with me now and then to give her mother a rest. She stayed with me in my former home, too. Now that I'm living here, it's even easier for me to help them that way.'

'Is there a little girl next door?' the minister demanded of Sergeant Deemer.

'There are two little girls, actually, and a boy. I know from my own experience that Mrs Harte is friendly with the whole family and is a good neighbour to everyone.'

The minister scowled at the sergeant as if he didn't like this information. 'That's as maybe, but we must be free to search everywhere.'

'I'm afraid not,' the sergeant said. 'I agreed to let you search for a child, but as Mrs Harte says, a child couldn't fit into those drawers, so you have no reason whatsoever to go through them. And since you've had more than enough time to search the whole house, I'm calling a stop to this farce straight away. You were, as I suggested when you came to see me, mistaken, and that's been proven. I'd be obliged it you didn't waste my time again. It's obvious that there is no child hiding here or you'd have found her by now.'

'But we—'

'What's more, I've been called from my sickbed to accompany you tonight, or I'd have taken a more active part in this search, believe me, and it'd have been over and done with in half the time. Nor would you have been allowed to intrude on this lady's privacy in that disgusting way.'

He turned and limped back to the top of the stairs and pointed, 'Go downstairs immediately, if you please. This has been a wild goose chase. Mrs Harte is a law-abiding lady, a regular attender at her own church, and I have the utmost respect for her.'

'But I know she—'

'A recent arrival in Rivenshaw, like yourself, can't know as much as I do after years serving here. You should ask advice before accusing decent folk and behaving indecently with their possessions.'

As this speech progressed the two young men turned scarlet with embarrassment, edged their way to the top of the stairs, and ran down them.

The minister stopped at the top, next to Deemer, to say, 'I shall complain to the local JP about this lack of cooperation on your part.'

'And I'm going to be complaining to him about your false accusations and your damned intrusive way of searching. If those young men are the sort who mess around with women's underwear, perhaps you are too.'

The minister gasped in outrage, gobbling like a turkey as he sought in vain to control his anger and speak calmly. 'You can't! I won't let you—!'

Deemer again jabbed one forefinger towards the stairs. '*Downstairs, sir! Now.*'

The minister glared at him. 'You haven't heard the last of this.'

'Nor have you.'

Sergeant Deemer made his way painfully down the stairs after him and gestured to the constable to open the front door. 'Leave this house at once. There's no little girl here.'

The two young men went out quickly, but the minister moved with exaggerated slowness, turning to have a final word with Deemer from just outside.

The sergeant slammed the door in his face before he could speak, muttering, 'And good riddance to bad rubbish!' loudly enough to be heard by those outside.

Gwynneth came down to join him in the hall, but when she would have spoken to him, he held up one hand to stop her. 'I'm sorry, but it's the other Mrs Harte I need to speak to.'

She stepped back and waited as Maisie moved forward.

'Since you're the owner of this house, I shall report my findings to you. As far as I'm concerned a search has been carried out of your premises with no sign of the child they're looking for being found. I apologise for any inconvenience caused.'

When he finished, Gwynneth would again have spoken to him, but he said firmly, 'And that's all I need to know about your situation here, ladies.'

He stared at each woman in turn, and there was no mistaking the meaning behind what he'd said, so each nodded.

'We'll leave you in peace now.'

The constable led the way out, and Deemer followed, shutting the front door quietly behind him.

He looked along the street. 'Damn me! They're still there.'

'I don't like that man, Sarge. He's . . . nasty.'

'Neither do I. But it's a free country, and we can't stop him parking in public areas and watching this house without a very good reason. Now let's get home.'

'My goodness, I'd not like to get on the wrong side of Mrs Harte,' Mike said as he got into the driving seat of the police car.

'Neither would I. But she makes a very good friend, and has helped a lot of people during these hard times.'

Gabriel had been peeping out of the window and wondering what the sergeant and his new constable were talking about. They sat in the car for a few moments, but eventually he heard the sound of the engine starting up. He waited for the other car to drive away too, but it didn't move.

In the end he let the edge of the curtain fall. 'The police have gone now, but the others are still there.'

Maisie blew out a long, shaky breath. 'That was . . . worrying. Thank goodness for the secret cellar.'

'Yes. And for our sergeant. He'd have done more to help us if he could,' Gabriel said quietly.

'That minister is a nasty creature,' Gwynneth said. 'I'd never go to his church. No wonder his congregation is growing smaller. I know of a family that left them last month and then came to worship at our church instead. Nice people they are, too.'

They went to sit in the living room to wait, continuing their conversation in low voices.

After a while, Gabriel went to peep out of the window again. 'That other car is still there. I wonder if they're going to stay all night. I think we'd better wait a while before we open up the lower cellar.'

'The poor things will be chilled to the marrow down there,' Maisie protested.

'Better chilled than have to go back to Mrs Hicks,' Gwynneth said. 'I warn you now: I'll run away with Beatie if anyone tries to return her to that torture.'

'And I'll help you,' her son said.

'Don't worry. I'm completely on your side,' Maisie said.

15

Arthur was almost sorry when the secret cellar door opened. He looked up to see Gabriel beckoning to them from the top of the stairs. But when he looked down again, he saw that Beatie had fallen asleep and didn't want to give her up. He could have sat there all night with his precious grandchild nestling in his arms if it hadn't been so chilly down here.

Biff went up to the exit and whispered to Gabriel, pointing to the sleeping child.

'Do you want me to carry her up to her room for you, Arthur?' their host called down.

He couldn't deny what Biff had noticed. 'Yes, please. I'm rather stiff and cold. May I suggest that you leave a couple of blankets down here in future, in case anyone has to take refuge in the tunnels again?'

'Good idea. We weren't expecting them to find out so quickly where the child was, but Gwynneth told me it was Beatie's own fault. She'd peeped out of the bedroom window earlier and must have been seen by someone from that church of theirs. They're getting a reputation as a nosey lot since this new minister was appointed.'

'Damn them for interfering in what's not their business!' Arthur said with feeling. 'Is it safe to put her to bed, do you think?'

'I hope so.' Gabriel told them about his mother's confrontation with the unwelcome visitors after their intrusive search.

'It's not really safe here then,' Arthur said in a flat, unhappy voice. 'Why don't you keep her downstairs for the rest of the night in case they come back, then you can whip her down into the hidden cellar if necessary?'

Biff looked at Gabriel. 'I think Arthur's right. Why don't we all sit near the fire with her for a while and warm ourselves. I need to explain about our entrance to the tunnels.'

After they'd rested by the fire for a while, Biff took Gabriel and the two women down to show them how their tunnel entrance led to another one under Arthur's house, pointing to the left from the bottom of the steps.

When they rejoined Arthur in the sitting room, Gwynneth looked at the sleeping child and grew angry all over again. 'If I need to get her away, can I come to your house, Arthur?'

'Of course you can. She's my grandchild, and I love her to pieces.'

'I love her too. I hope you don't mind, but I feel as if she were mine.'

'Why should I mind? You can't have too much love. If it starts to feel even slightly unsafe here, don't hesitate to come and stay with me. Even if they're watching all the houses, they won't know how she gets into my place.'

'Thank you. I shall feel better for having an escape route and another possible hiding place. Just let that horrible minister come near me again while I'm out and about, and I'll give him what for. I won't put up with him interfering in my life in any way, and he can keep his stupid opinions to himself.'

Gabriel gave her a worried look. 'Be careful what you say and do, Mum. You don't want to get into trouble with the law.'

'I'll do what I have to if that child needs help. I feel furiously angry every time I bathe her wounds.'

'Are you sure you can manage to get out of this hidden door on your own?' Arthur asked.

'Oh, yes. I'm sure of it now that I've practised doing it myself.'

'Then let me take you along the tunnel to show you where to go once you're down there and how to open our door from the outside.'

'Good idea. Put Beatie on the sofa. We'll keep an eye on her,' Maisie said.

Arthur watched Gwynneth in admiration. He didn't think he'd ever met a woman as determined as this one. She was magnificent when she was angry. His granddaughter couldn't have found a more caring protector.

He took her downstairs, and they went along to the very end of the tunnel system. He showed her the entrance to his house. She practised opening and shutting it several times, her expression intent.

They did no more than peep into the cellar of Arthur's house, and even that brought Phil rushing down to see what was going on, which was good to see. He knew Gwynneth, but Arthur told him about the child and said the two of them could come and take refuge here if it were ever necessary.

'If they do, it'll be more important to look after them than the house,' he added.

Phil nodded. 'I'll make sure my brother knows.'

Afterwards, as the two of them walked back, Arthur said quietly, 'Thanks for what you're doing, Gwynneth, protecting that child.'

'She's a little love. I wish I had grandchildren. None of my sons have produced any, and they're all over thirty.'

'I'm sure Gabriel and Maisie will give you some one day.'

'I'm hoping so. But I can't see Lucas ever marrying. He's more interested in books and studying than he is in women.'

'You can't tell them how to live their lives. My son won't even speak to me. I didn't blame him when I was drinking, but

I wish he'd give me a second chance now.' He added in a softer voice, 'And I daren't even approach him.'

She patted his hand. 'I'm sure he will come round to it. Do you ever drink these days?'

'No. I'm never going to touch a drop of alcohol again as long as I live.'

'I'm glad to hear it.'

He got another pat for that, which pleased him. Some women were like that, touched other people often. His Susan had been the same.

When they rejoined the others, Biff stared at them, then turned to smile slyly at Gabriel, who had also, from the thoughtful way he was gazing at them, realised how strongly his mother and Arthur were attracted to one another.

The two people in question didn't seem to have realised it yet, or perhaps hadn't dared admit it to themselves. Well, they'd both had some hard years, from what people had told Biff.

He wondered what they'd do about it when they did work it all out. Get married, he hoped. People weren't made to live alone, and from the sadness in her face when she talked about Lucas going off to university, he reckoned she'd miss her son greatly. All things considered, these two seemed well suited to one another, as well as linked by their love for the little girl.

After a while, the two women said they'd better put Beatie to bed now. Gwynneth let her son carry her upstairs, and the child didn't wake up.

When Gabriel came back, Biff said, 'Arthur, we should follow the women's example and get some sleep now.'

He went to the window and peered out. 'Their car is still there, Biff. We'll have to use the cellar route.'

Gabriel peeped out as well. 'Do you think any of them will dare try to come inside here again tonight? Our good sergeant was very stern with them.'

'Trouble is, Vanner has those two young men as obedient as a pair of well-trained sheepdogs. What I don't understand is why he's so antagonistic towards your mother.'

'That's easy to work out,' Gabriel said with a grin. 'She dares to answer him back and argue with him. I'd guess he thinks a wife should act like a mouse and not open her mouth, and believes firmly that all men are superior to all women.'

'None of my family or friends believes that these days,' Gabriel said. 'Yet even Mrs Hicks seems to do as that man tells her.'

Biff sighed. 'There are still plenty of men around with that bossy attitude, unfortunately. When you think what women did during the Great War, it's ridiculous.' He glanced at the clock on the mantelpiece. 'Look at the time. We'd better leave you in peace.'

'I'll come to the cellar exit and make sure you get through all right.'

'Thanks.'

When they got back into Number 25, Phil came to check who it was, smiling when he saw them. 'You're going to and fro between the houses like yo-yos tonight. No need to worry. Everything's peaceful here.'

'Good. The minister and his tame sheep are still out in the street, so we came back via the cellars.'

They'd agreed to explain to their watchmen how the cellars of two of the houses were connected. But they didn't know where all these tunnels led and why they'd been dug out further than the older ones that had led to the quarry. It must have cost someone a fortune.

'I prefer to stay above ground, personally,' Phil said.

'It gives us some extra storage space, if nothing else.'

Rob Becksley rolled his eyes. 'I don't own enough to need extra storage space and I'd not like people to be able to creep into my cellar. Anyway, you go and get some sleep now, Arthur. We'll keep a careful watch, I promise you.'

'I've noticed. Well done, lads. We're grateful.'

The following morning Maisie phoned the doctor and when his wife answered the phone, as usual, asked if he could come to the house to see her mother-in-law, who had a problem that made it embarrassing for her to go out.

When he arrived later that day, Gwynneth greeted him, looking the picture of health, and took him up to her bedroom. She followed him inside, shutting the door behind her.

He smiled knowingly. 'Our good sergeant told me about the situation here. Where's the child?'

'Hiding till we're sure you're willing to help us. She's utterly terrified of being sent back to her grandmother, and you'll see why when you examine her. If you'll wait here a moment, I'll fetch her.'

She brought Beatie back, helped her undress, and he stared at the partially healed wounds in shock. 'Mrs Hicks did this to a child?'

Gwynneth nodded, keeping Beatie's hand clasped tightly in both of hers.

'The child is rather thin. Don't you get hungry, dear?'

Beatie nodded vigorously but seemed nervous of opening her mouth.

Gwynneth said it for her. 'She loves to eat, but she's been half-starved.'

After another astonished look, he asked, 'Why? Mrs Hicks is not short of money.'

'Tell him why, dear,' Gwynneth coaxed.

'My grandmother didn't let me have any tea when she said I'd been naughty, which was most days.' Tears welled in the child's eyes. 'But I wasn't naughty. I didn't dare be naughty in case she hit me again.'

'Dear God, the woman must have gone mad!' The doctor's exclamation was barely above a whisper.

Gwynneth looked across at him, feeling close to tears as she did every time she saw the child's injuries and thin body. 'Well, thank goodness Beatie is eating well now, aren't you, love? She's even asking for seconds, and I love to see her clear her plate.'

Beatie nodded vigorously.

'I'm not letting Mrs Hicks get her hands on Beatie again, Doctor. I'll do whatever it takes to keep her safe.'

'I'm glad you sent for me.' He smiled down at the still-anxious child. 'I won't tell her where you are, dear, I promise.' He made the sign of crossing his heart to emphasise this and saw her relax and sigh in relief.

'I'm prescribing plenty of good food, and keep asking for seconds if you're still hungry.' He turned to Gwynneth. 'Don't just give her bread and butter, but fruit and vegetables, eggs, and cheese.'

'Why did my grandmother say I was greedy and ate too much?' Beatie asked suddenly.

'I don't know. She seems to have forgotten that children need good food so that they can grow bigger and stronger adult bodies.'

The child nodded, as if that made sense to her. But what Mrs Hicks had done didn't make sense to the doctor or Gwynneth.

When he got ready to leave, Beatie snuggled down in bed, and Gwynneth gave her a loving kiss before escorting him down to the sitting room to speak to Maisie and Gabriel.

'She's taking a nap because of her disturbed night, Doctor.'

'My main prescription is for love and good food. And if you ever need me to bear witness that she'd been kept dangerously short of food and beaten savagely by Mrs Hicks, then you have only to call on me.'

'That's what we hoped when we sent for you today. We shan't hesitate to ask for your help.'

'I'll speak to our good sergeant and tell him what I found but pretend officially that you brought her to see me so we don't have to talk about where she is.'

'Thank you.'

When he'd left, Gwynneth went back to check on the child, relieved to find her fast asleep.

'I'm still worried about what that woman will do next,' Maisie admitted to her husband.

'And I'm worried about how deeply my mother will get involved,' Gabriel said. 'She can't bear cruelty, especially when children are involved, and she has a bit of a temper when she thinks something is wrong or immoral.'

'She and Arthur both love Beatie.'

He smiled. 'And they're getting on very well with each other, don't you think?'

'Are you thinking what I'm thinking?'

'Yes.'

'And good luck to the pair of them. I feel so lucky to have you, my darling.'

So he had to kiss her. He couldn't seem to get enough of loving her.

Later that afternoon Charlie Willcox arrived to check Arthur's furniture repairs. 'Sorry to have had to postpone my visit,' he said cheerfully as he came in.

He examined the two pieces carefully and nodded in satisfaction. 'You did a beautiful job on these. I knew you would, somehow. You handle furniture like a lover.'

Arthur shot a delighted glance at Biff.

'Can I look at that little bookcase near the window now, see if it's as good as I remembered?'

'Of course.'

Arthur had set it out on the dining-room rug, but it was clear it needed mending. 'I was going to fix it before you came, but we've had some other problems to solve.'

'Oh?' Charlie looked at him inquiringly.

'We should tell him about what's been going on, since he's a town councillor,' Biff said. 'Don't worry, Arthur lad. He can keep a secret.'

Charlie nodded vigorously at that.

So they went through the incident again, though every time they talked about it, Arthur felt anger rise at the minister.

When they'd finished the tale their visitor looked thoughtful. 'I'm surprised Vanner's even got involved.'

'We all were. He's very arrogant, isn't he? Looks down his nose at everyone.'

'You're not the first person I've heard complain about that. Yet he's only the minister at a small chapel that was set up recently. What has he to be arrogant about? As everyone knows, the congregation there has gone down in numbers since they got to know what he's like. I'm surprised anyone donated the money to him to set up a chapel, and that he chose an out-of-the-way place like Rivenshaw to do it in, especially as he seems to hate the area and people.'

Arthur sighed. 'The trouble is, I now have a bad reputation, so even if we could do something legally about Beatie, I doubt the authorities would let me look after the child.'

'I'm afraid you're right. They prefer a married couple when they're placing orphans, and if that's not possible, an older woman. So even without your, er, troubled patch, you'd still have difficulty getting custody of her.'

'My utterly stupid patch, you mean!' Arthur said bitterly.

'Well, you're over that now. I'll keep my eyes and ears open about that Vanner fellow. I don't want newcomers to our valley causing trouble. We have enough of that with a certain local person.' After a brief pause he said, 'Anyway, let's get back to the furniture. How much do you want for the bookcase once you've repaired it, Arthur?'

'Whatever you think fair. I have no idea what it'll be worth. And I trust you.'

Charlie beamed at that, then tapped the side of his nose slowly as he had a think. 'You do the repairs then leave it to me to get the best price I can. It'll bring at least five pounds, I should think, minus my commission, probably more if your repairs are as good as those you've done on the other two, because this one is an eighteenth-century piece. Is that all right financially?'

'Fine by me.'

'Can you lend a hand getting the other two pieces out to the van?'

'Of course.' Arthur stepped forward.

Biff put out his arm to bar the way. 'I'll do that. For the moment, it'd be better if you stayed out of sight.' He didn't say it, but he wouldn't put it past Higgerson to arrange an attack on Arthur – as he had on Sergeant Deemer.

'I can't hide away for ever.'

'Just for a week or two longer. Let me sort the problems out first,' Biff coaxed. 'We need to know exactly who is doing what. Someone has set out to harm you, that's for sure. And we have other folk to think of. I may be able to help them as well.'

Charlie looked from one to the other in puzzlement.

'The Hartes at Number Twenty-one are being annoyed and targeted too.' Biff told him about that house still being watched, this time by Vanner's followers.

Charlie gaped at him for a moment, then said firmly, 'Nice people, all of the Hartes. They can't have done anything wrong. I've bought a lot of pieces from Maisie, good ones too. Her house was so full of furniture when she inherited it, you could hardly get into some of the rooms. There were some really good pieces, and yet others were clumsy cheap rubbish. But even they had a value, and it's better to earn a few shillings than nothing.'

When his visitor had gone, Arthur settled down to do some more repair work. He felt he was marking time till solutions could be found to the problems darkening his life, and that was annoying. But if he could use the time productively and earn some extra money, it'd not be so bad. He was certainly going to need it to look after his house and pay his way in future.

Besides, he always found working with wood soothing. It seemed to set his mind free, and he had a lot to think about. His granddaughter's well-being was the first problem that needed solving. He smiled, as thinking of her immediately brought to mind the way Gwynneth had cuddled her. Lovely woman, Gwynneth. She'd look after his grandchild, he was sure.

He sat very still as it slowly sank in that he was growing rather fond of Gabriel's mother. Too fond? He didn't know.

He'd thought he'd never find another woman who was as 'special' as Susan had been, but maybe he had.

He didn't dare use any other word about the situation yet, so 'special' would do for starters. No use thinking beyond that till he found out what she thought of him, and they sorted out Beatie's problems.

After that he proceeded to think about Gwynneth and Beatie in about equal amounts, as a result of which, his work was slower than usual.

He couldn't help wondering what Susan would have said about all this. She'd have liked Gwynneth, he was quite sure, because he and his wife had always liked or disliked the same people.

He shook his head ruefully. In the past year he'd gone from despair and living mainly on the streets to making his life decent again, then he'd inherited a big house, and hope for the future had blossomed brightly. What a turn-up for the books that was.

You couldn't know what was going to happen to you next in this life, but if he had to choose what he wanted most, it would be to save Beatie from that wicked woman. That child was the most important factor of all to him.

But maybe there was one solution that could help solve two problems at once? He gulped and swallowed hard, feeling his cheeks go so warm he was thankful there was no one nearby to see him.

Did he dare hope for that solution to happen? He didn't deserve it, oh no – but a man could dream, couldn't he? And she didn't have a home, had just lost hers so maybe she wouldn't reject the idea.

As if fate intended to prove it hadn't done with giving Arthur a series of shocks, he had another visitor that afternoon. When the door knocker sounded, Biff called out that he'd answer it, which was good, because Arthur was in the middle of smoothing down and blending in a scratched spot on the bookcase and had to judge very carefully indeed how far to go.

When the door to the small room he'd taken as a workshop opened, he didn't look up at first, thinking it was Biff coming back. Then when no one spoke he did lift his head, only able to stare in shock because his son was standing in the doorway. His son, who had refused to speak to his father for most of the past two years!

Lewis was studying him carefully.

Even after he stopped drinking, Arthur hadn't dared try to see his son and risk another rebuff, not even now that he was getting his life in order.

Their last encounter had sent Arthur hunting frantically for a bottle of something to drown his sorrows, Lewis had been so scathing about his way of life.

'How are you, Dad?'

'Much better than last time you saw me.'

'So I hear. And you look a lot better too. I'd not have come here else.'

'I'm glad you did. Would you like to sit down?'

When his son did so, relief ran through him. He gestured to the bookcase and looked back at the spot he was dealing with. 'I can't leave this even for a few moments because I'm in the middle of doing my preparations for re-polishing it, and it's a valuable piece. I don't want to lose track of even the tiniest detail of how the grain runs, but after I've finished I could make you a cup of tea. If you have time?'

'I do, and I'd like that.' He looked around. 'This is a lovely room.'

'You must have heard about me inheriting this house.' He was hoping desperately that Lewis wasn't here only because of that.

'Several people told me. You're a bit of a nine-day wonder in the town. But I also heard that you'd not have inherited it unless you'd stopped boozing and settled down to live decently, which was far more important to me. I hope you don't mind, but I checked that with your lawyer.'

'I don't mind at all because it's the simple truth.'

'Let's get one thing straight, Dad: I'm doing quite well in my job, so I'm not after your money. But it's sad when family fall out, and if the cause of our quarrel has been mended, well then . . . ' His voice tailed away.

'I behaved shockingly, I know, but my world fell to pieces after your mother died. I'd known her since I was a little lad kicking a football around the streets. I didn't feel alive at first without her. And she died so suddenly.'

'Yes, I understood that. And then we lost my sister on top of it all. People who drive cars dangerously fast should be shot! I still miss Dulcie, and I lost my niece completely as well, because Mrs Hicks won't let me see her and sent me a lawyer's letter when I persisted in trying to.' He hesitated, then added gently, 'I also saw for myself that my niece looked unhappy, and then heard that she'd run away from that horrible woman. I've been hoping you've given Beatie refuge. It's another reason for me coming here today. Did you? Is she safe?'

'No. I wouldn't dare do that, much as I'd love to. I'm the first person they'd come to see about it. Sergeant Deemer asked Biff about it. But I don't want anyone dragging her back to her grandmother, so if I had to snatch her and run far away from here to keep her safe, I would have to try.'

'Haven't you even seen her?'

'I'd rather not talk about that.'

Lewis frowned and opened his mouth to speak.

'Leave it till another time, eh?' Arthur said gently.

'Can you just tell me Beatie's safe, at least?'

'No. I can't tell you anything. You must be able to swear in court that you haven't heard anything about her from me, except that I denied she ran away to me.'

After a long, thoughtful look, Lewis nodded. 'I suppose you're right. If you're involved, it's better for others not to know about it. And if you're not involved, then I don't want to rub a sore spot in your life.'

'Thank you.' Arthur bent over to inspect the bookcase, nodded and put down his sandpaper. 'It's ready for the glue now. I'll do that tomorrow. Would you like a quick look round the downstairs of the house before I make your tea?'

'I'd like that very much. And you must come outside and see my van. I've got my own sales territory now, selling haberdashery into shops all over south Lancashire.'

Arthur shook his head. 'I wish I could, but Biff, the man who opened the door to you, doesn't want me to go outside. Mrs Hicks's minister has men waiting to get at me, you see. They've been sitting in a car just down the street all day.'

'What in heaven's name has it got to do with him?'

'He claims he's helping Mrs Hicks because she's a pillar of the church, apparently, and he wants to save the child from a wicked man like me. I think it's because she gives the church a lot of money.' He paused, then added, 'Biff is acting as a sort of bodyguard. Jane Chapman's lawyer hired him to keep an eye on me for a while. And I'm very grateful for that.'

His son looked puzzled. 'Do you really need a bodyguard to protect you from churchgoers?'

'Not only from them, but because all the people who've inherited these houses from her have had trouble from Higgerson, who wants to buy the houses for far less than their value and is prepared to hire bullies to persuade us all to sell.'

His son nodded with an instant understanding of the explanation. 'That man is a disgrace! How he gets away with things in the valley is disgusting.' He shook his head in bafflement, then followed his father round the house in near silence.

Holding a conversation was like treading on eggshells, with awkward silences in between what they said, but Arthur consoled himself with the thought that they were both trying to communicate.

After they'd shared a pot of tea Lewis said abruptly, 'I've met a lass, Dad. She's called Edith and I've asked her to marry me. We're hoping to do that next year.'

'Eh, I'm glad for you, very glad indeed. I hope you'll be as happy in your marriage as your mother and I were. No one could have asked for a better wife than I had.'

His son's expression softened and he touched his father briefly on the shoulder in a gesture of comfort. 'I know. It was so obvious how you two felt. If things continue to go well between you and me, I'll bring Edith to meet you. I'm not in Rivenshaw all the time, though, because I have to go out taking orders from shops in my area.'

'I'd like to meet Edith very much. A good marriage makes for a rich and satisfying life and is more important than money.'

When his son said he must be going, Arthur walked with him to the front door and looked at the new van from the safety of that position, admiring it and bringing a proud little smile to Lewis's face.

Biff stayed with him, then hurried Arthur inside and locked the door again even before Lewis had driven away.

What a way to live! And all because of one greedy man and a chapel minister who seemed to Arthur to be a big bully, which was not what you'd expect of a person in his position.

He had to be patient, till everything could be sorted out. But it was hard.

17

When a message was sent to confirm the 'tea party' with His Lordship, though it would actually be a regular meeting in the rocky cavern, Sergeant Deemer asked Dennison Peters to drive him there because his ribs were still sore, and changing gears was particularly painful.

'You're still moving stiffly,' his friend said as they set off, this time late in the afternoon.

'I'm lucky to be moving at all, but it's a lot easier than it was.'

'Well, I've got a bit of good news to share with you today, not group business, a local police matter. I've managed to plant a spy in Higgerson's household: a gardener. That should help us keep an eye on him.'

'Who is it?'

'Jack Webster. He's moved back to the valley to look after his widowed father.'

Sergeant Deemer looked at him in surprise. 'Webster's a good chap. I'm surprised he agreed to do it.'

'He'd be delighted to help trap Higgerson, who drove a cousin of his away by violent means.'

'Will Webster be working for him full-time?'

'Just three days a week. He's working for that new minister to keep the grounds at his chapel tidy for the other two days.'

'Rather him than me, with both of them.'

'You're not kidding. You wouldn't believe what a tight-fisted devil Vanner is when it comes to payment, though. He tried to fine Webster the very first week and take money from his wages for some imaginary fault.' He chuckled. 'Vanner backed off when Webster threatened to quit that very minute if he wasn't paid the full amount agreed, and then sue him for non-payment of wages.'

'He would have done it, too,' Peters said. 'If he'd been born to an upper-class family, Webster would have become a member of parliament or a successful lawyer by now. As it is, he's just bought that small but thriving corner shop in Castrill Street, which his wife and her sister are going to run. That'll bring them an income, in addition to his work as a gardener. And he's going to buy a field and set it up as a market garden. I admire him greatly.'

'He sounds a clever chap. I can't stand that Vanner, though. He's mean spirited in every way.'

'Neither can I. As a JP, I've grown used to liars and thieves claiming that they're honest citizens and have done nothing wrong. I'm not used to feeling suspicious of a church minister who clearly isn't true to his calling. I mistrusted this chap from the start, for no reason except gut instinct.'

'Me, too. Though there's nothing happened to *prove* him a bad 'un, and most people wouldn't even consider that a possibility for a man in his role.'

'Well, I'll continue to trust my instincts and we'll both keep an eye on him. I'll tell Webster to keep his eyes on both his employers, just on principle, but I'm more interested in him providing us with some useful information on Higgerson.'

'Don't count on it. Higgerson has broken the law and escaped retribution for many years now. He's only too adept at doing it, damn him, and still has friends in useful places!'

They fell silent. It was a major frustration to both of them what that man had got away with.

They were among the last to arrive at the cave where the meetings were held, so didn't manage to do much chatting to their fellow conspirators, as the final two members arrived soon afterwards. His Lordship immediately cleared his throat and the group fell silent.

'I'll go straight to what I consider to be the most important item: our local traitor is, it seems from certain correspondence, still happy to welcome a German invasion of our country, but is demanding payment for his services as well as a high position afterwards before he reveals who he is.'

'Hasn't there been any clue to his identity?'

'Unfortunately he has continued to conceal it. I don't know what he's said or done to convince them that he has enough influence to be worth listening to.'

'How do we know about his ongoing efforts?'

His Lordship spread out his hands in a gesture of help-lessness. 'I can't reveal my exact source without destroying another project we're keeping an eye on. I'd been hoping one of you might have heard something about who the fellow is.'

He looked around, but people shook their heads.

'Well, I'd be obliged if you could continue making efforts to discover this traitor. It's one way we can serve our country.'

His Lordship let them nod and continue murmuring for a moment or two, then said loudly, 'We come now to the other important item on the agenda: we need to decide whether to push the tunnels further out in case of any future need to accommodate larger groups who might have to live in hiding for a while.'

Peters raised his hand. 'If you do that, you'll have to take into account Higgerson's latest project.'

'What do you mean?' His Lordship asked.

'He's digging out new cellars under some of his rental prop-erties in Backshaw Moss.'

'Is that allowed? It wouldn't be in our local area.'

'It shouldn't be allowed anywhere, but he got three more cel-lars given special approval when we had two of our group on the council fall ill at the same time with severe food poisoning.'

There was dead silence, then a woman asked, 'Do you think someone poisoned their food on purpose?'

'Highly likely. I'd advise you all to be careful what you eat, and to warn whoever does your cooking not to leave any visitor delivering food in your kitchen on their own from now on.'

The woman who'd asked the question looked horrified.

A man said slowly, 'It can't be safe to dig out cellars if preparations weren't made and foundations laid when the houses were originally built, surely?'

Peters let out a scornful sound. 'When they were built, there were very few regulations, and some people employed rather haphazard building practices.'

'I remember my grandfather telling me about a house collapsing on his street when he was a lad,' one man commented.

'I heard about a similar problem in Backshaw Moss from my grandmother,' a woman said.

'We may have got rid of Higgerson's majority on the council, but regrettably we can't change all the regulations at once or remedy lacks from the past, especially the distant past. Some of those houses have stood there for a hundred years or more, even if they are badly built and maintained. Our group of councillors would lose a serious amount of support in the valley if we tried to have them demolished, even on safety grounds.'

'What about new tunnels, then?'

'I think we should leave things as they are unless we come to a time when war is imminent and the government is still skimping on its preparations.'

'Do you think we'll ever need the present set of tunnels, let alone more of them?' one of the female members asked. 'I just can't see Britain being successfully invaded, not by anyone.'

Others murmured agreement with this patriotic sentiment.

His Lordship raised his voice. 'And yet you come here and help plan for that very possibility, Mrs Farson-Greene.'

She shrugged. 'Better prepared and not needed than not prepared at all, after the last war. And I like to keep busy, do my bit for the valley. If *you* feel it's worth doing, Your Lordship, I'm certainly not going to disagree with you.'

Sergeant Deemer didn't allow himself to smile when His Lordship winced at this fulsome flattery. This woman was known as someone who liked to be in on anything that was being organised by someone important, if only out of sheer curiosity. How she fitted all the various activities into her life amazed him. But she had a good heart in spite of being a snob, and had helped a lot of people during the bad times since the Great War.

He was glad when the meeting ended. It hadn't been an important one, His Lordship's main purpose being to remind people to keep watching out for the traitor, he'd guess, and rightly so. They had to put a stop to that potential betrayal, however, in case the chap infected others. Deemer felt fairly sure that the villain would turn out to be Higgerson. Who else was there with both adequate money and consistently evil intent?

His body was still aching and stiff, but he managed to keep a smile on his face till he got back to the car, then he let himself sag, leaning back in his seat, eyes closed. He was grateful that Peters didn't comment on this or try to make conversation.

There were some jolly decent people in this area of the county. He hoped the services of their group would never be needed, but was glad they were standing ready.

On the way home he had a thought, and asked Peters suddenly, 'Why haven't we asked Charlie Willcox to join our group?'

'If I remember correctly, Mrs Farson-Greene protested against it.'

'Well, she can damned well unprotest. It's wrong to leave him out. He can be a very useful chappie.'

Peters sat frowning, clearly lost in thought, so Deemer left him to it and was rewarded eventually by a sly smile on his friend's face.

'If she were made aware that he's likely to be our next mayor, perhaps she might change her mind. What's more, I think I know how to approach her.'

'How?'

'Through my sister.'

'She is another person who ought to have been invited to join our group. Very capable woman.'

'I agree. I've been wondering whether to . . . Look, leave it to me. I'll have a quiet word with Veronica and with His Lordship. We definitely need more women in our group. And those who've been running Women's Institute groups, as my sister has, have developed some excellent skills at organising people and activities. The country has owed the WIs a lot from when they were first founded during the Great War, and they've quietly gathered strength all across the country since then.'

Kit felt rather shy when Monty returned from hospital, but he was given a beaming smile and invited to join him and his wife in the sitting room.

He watched anxiously as Monty sat down carefully, easing his arm a little in its sling. When he found a soft cushion to set under the injured arm, his host smiled at him.

'Thank you. Do sit down with us. I'm not used to being out of commission. I gather I owe you thanks for saving my life, Kit.'

He could feel himself flushing. 'I just happened to know how to make a tourniquet.'

'I'm very glad you did, lad, believe me. Some would have panicked and messed things up, however much they knew in theory. I'm supposed to spend a few days resting, and I shan't be able to drive for a while, so I can't take you to find your mother yet, I'm afraid. I must admit to feeling rather weak.'

Kit dared say, 'If you could lend me some money, I could take the train, sir. And I promise I'd pay you back.'

'I think we should look into your mother's situation first. We don't want you leaping from the frying pan into the fire. Do you know the name of the people she and your brother are staying with in Swindon?'

'Yes. Tillett. He's a merchant of some sort.'

'I wonder if he's the Tillett who sells rugs and carpets both to the public and to shops. They sell other things too. I've delivered all sorts of items for a company run by a gentleman of that name over the years. Eh, we should all be so successful!'

'I don't know any details, just that my brother works for someone of that name and because of his protection my father hasn't been able to get at Felix, which makes him absolutely furious.'

'If he's the Tillett I think, he'll have the money to protect them both, and he's well thought of as an honest trader. But the more you tell me about your father, the less I like the sound of him.'

Kit couldn't help shuddering. 'I'll be happy if I never see him again as long as I live. I think if he managed to capture me and take me back to Rivenshaw, I'd be in serious trouble, not to say in danger of losing my life. He can be vicious when crossed.'

'To the extent that he'd kill his own son? Surely not?'

'Oh, yes. If he got into one of his blind rages he'd do anything. And he'd hurt his own wife too, for running away from him. I know Mum was in fear of her life towards the end. Only desperation would have given her the courage to leave.'

'Shame on him. Well, I'll not be able to do anything to help you today, because I'm a bit tired. I don't know how any patient ever manages to get a good night's sleep in a hospital, because people are making noises around you all night long, not to mention nurses waking you up to check on you.'

Monty fell asleep a few minutes later and his wife put her forefinger to her lips, so Kit sat there quietly, enjoying the peace.

His host didn't wake up until his junior partner in the haulage business came to the door and refused to go away, insisting loudly that he knew Monty was home, and he absolutely had to speak to him today about the damaged lorry if they were not to lose money hand over fist by it being out of commission.

Fortunately Monty had woken feeling a little better, and was able to deal with the matter of repairs and hiring a stand-in driver to keep deliveries going until he was better.

When his wife quarrelled cheerfuly with him afterwards about what he was and was not fit to do, Kit watched in amazement. He had never seen people arguing and smiling like this because of wanting the best for each other.

It ended when Monty grabbed his wife and gave her a smacking big kiss, agreeing reluctantly to take a day or two off work, adding, 'If only to stop you nagging me, woman!' in such a teasing voice that it made the lad smile.

It also made him wish yet again that he'd had a decent father, and his mother the loving husband such a kind and caring person deserved.

When Monty fell asleep again, Kit asked in a whisper whether he could do anything to help his new 'Auntie Chrissie'. She set him to filling the coal scuttles in the downstairs rooms, then doing a few other small jobs around the house. She had to show him how to do some of the tasks because his father had always refused to let his boys do any 'women's work'.

They all went to bed early, and to his surprise Kit had no trouble falling asleep. In fact, he could hardly keep his eyes open.

It was such a lovely, comfy home, seeming full of love and he felt so safe there.

18

A few nights after Vanner had insisted on Deemer searching Maisie and Gabriel's house, a small group of men gathered just after midnight in the laneway behind the three houses on Daisy Street. They couldn't get inside Number 21 the back way because the gate was padlocked, but their minister had told them he would hire someone to help them gain entrance to the house, all in the name of justice. Finding the child would prove the people inside guilty.

So they waited, as rain poured down and the minutes ticked slowly past.

After a while a couple of men slipped away to the comfort of their own homes. 'Justice be damned!' one of them said to the other. 'I don't intend to catch my death of cold.'

'Me neither. We don't know for certain the child is there, whatever he claims.'

Grumbling about the weather, the rest tried in vain to find more sheltered spots nearby as they waited for the locksmith.

'Why isn't Vanner here braving the weather with us?' one man whispered to another.

'He damned well ought to be. This was his idea in the first place.'

'My wife said I shouldn't have listened to him.'

'So did mine.'

Before they could talk themselves into leaving, the locksmith turned up, escorted by a church elder, who indicated the gate he needed to unlock.

The men all moved closer and waited, shoulders hunched against the downpour.

Seeming oblivious to the weather, the man clambered up on to the top of the gate to look over it and check how it was locked.

'It's only an old padlock. Useless, that one is.' With a soft chuckle he leaned over and began to fiddle with it.

The street lamp at the end of the back alley shone on him and one man nudged another. 'Who the hell is he? There's no locksmith like him in Rivenshaw.'

'Look how far he's leaning over it. He'll fall head first into the yard if he doesn't watch out.'

The elder turned around and said in a low voice, 'Shut up! Do you want someone to hear us?'

'I just want to get out of the damned rain.'

As the men shuffled to and fro in a vain effort to warm their feet, the grumbler moved back to stand near the gate of the next house, which was at least out of the worst of the wind. He bumped into it, setting it rattling slightly.

'Stand still, you fool.'

'You're even more of a fool. I don't know why I let you persuade me to come here.'

'*Shut – up!*'

Inside Number 21, Gwynneth was having trouble getting to sleep. She hadn't done more than doze, jerk awake, then doze again, because she couldn't stop worrying about what Mrs Hicks and her horrible minister might try next.

The sudden rattle of a gate caught her attention and that alerted her to other faint sounds. She sat up in bed, trying to work out what was going on. That sort of noise hadn't been made by cats or the wind.

She slid out of bed and went across to peep through the window in time to see the back gate of their house open slowly and several men shuffle through it into the yard.

Letting out a small, muffled whimper she ran along the landing to wake Gabriel, whose room was at the front of the house, going up to the bed and shaking him.

'Come quickly and look through my bedroom window. Some men just came into our backyard. They must be intending to break into the house.'

He ran to look, shocked at what he saw, 'Oh, hell! You stay upstairs with Beatie.'

He pulled trousers on over his pyjamas and went downstairs.

Maisie shrugged into her dressing gown and followed him.

Gwynneth hesitated for a moment, then took a decision. This incident showed that Mrs Hicks and the minister were not going to give up trying to get Beatie back, so she wasn't waiting any longer to move the child across to Arthur's house. He'd want to save his granddaughter, she was sure, and he had such a kind face, she trusted him absolutely.

She shook the child awake and told her to get dressed quickly and quietly, explaining that some men were trying to break into the house. 'We'll have to escape through the cellar to your grandfather's.'

'But—'

'No noise or lights. Hurry!'

She slung on her coat over her nightie and picked up the bag of Beatie's clothes that she had set ready 'in case'. Beatie didn't have many garments, poor lamb, so Gwynneth was able to stuff some of her own clothes in from the top drawer as well, and bundle the few remaining items into a pillow case.

Another peep out of the window made her thank her lucky stars that she'd planned ahead. There were half a dozen men down there, but only Gabriel and two women to protect the house.

'Come on, love. They've not got in yet, so you and I have time to move to your granddad's house. We'll be safe there.' She pulled on a skirt over her nightie as she was speaking.

'Has my grandma sent them after me?'

'I think so. Hurry up.'

'I'm frightened of her.'

'I won't let her take you again.'

While the child finished dressing, Gwynneth made the bed, then looked around. The moon was dipping in and out of the clouds, letting her check that nothing showed anyone had been sleeping there.

'Come on, love. Move as quietly as you can and don't try to switch on any lights.'

Gabriel heard someone try to open the locked back door and peered out through the pantry window, shocked at how many men there were. Too many for him to fight. He'd have to fetch his mother and Beatie, then help them down into the hidden cellar.

He turned to go upstairs, praying he'd have time to hide them before the would-be intruders forced the door. Men coming out in the middle of the night in the pouring rain wouldn't knock and stand around trying to negotiate. They'd do whatever it took to break down the door and get at the child, he was sure.

Thunder rolled loudly across the sky. Would the neighbours hear any calls for help if the storm continued?

To his relief, his mother had already come down.

'I'm going to stay with Arthur. Can you help me get the hidden door open, then close it after me, Gabriel love?'

'Yes, Mam. I'll get you away first, then I'll phone Sergeant Deemer.'

Maisie moved forward, barefoot and wearing her warm woollen dressing gown. 'I'll phone the police, love. You help your mother and Beatie to get away.'

Gwynneth blew her daughter-in-law a quick kiss, then she and the child followed her son down into the cellar. Once they'd shut the door to the hall behind them, he switched on the light.

He was in the middle of getting the secret door open when they heard a big thump from the kitchen area. He glanced upwards, frantic with worry for his wife. 'Hurry up, Mum. Take this torch.'

As he thrust it into her hand, the two fugitives crept out on to the stone steps that led to the hidden tunnel. The door closed above them, leaving them in utter darkness.

As Beatie whimpered and clutched her with a hand that trembled, Gwynneth fumbled with the torch and managed to switch it on. 'There, that's better.'

'I don't like it so dark.'

'Neither do I. Good thing we've got this torch.'

'It's not very bright.' Beatie flung her arms around Gwynneth's waist. 'I'm frightened.'

'Don't be. It's bright enough to show us the way, and it won't take long to get to your granddad's house.'

She dropped a kiss on the child's forehead and gave her a quick hug. 'There's nothing to be afraid of now we're down here, love. Come on. Let go of me and start walking.'

She thrust the pillowcase at her. 'You carry this bundle and I'll take the big bag.'

'You won't walk too fast and leave me behind?'

'Of course not. I'd as soon leave my own head behind as leave you.'

That brought a faint giggle from Beatie, and they began moving carefully down the steps.

Gabriel ran back up to the kitchen, relieved that Maisie was safe in the hall, speaking into the phone. The back door was a heavy one and the windows not only had bars across them but consisted of small panes set in solid wooden frames, making it difficult to break into the house that way.

These people seemed to be hurling themselves against the door now, grunting with the effort. Were they trying to batter it down? They'd have trouble getting it open. It had huge, old-fashioned hinges, with big bolts top and bottom, as well as the lock in the middle.

He disliked fighting and violence, but tonight he'd do whatever he could to protect his family. He heard his wife speaking to the sergeant as he went through to the kitchen.

Furiously angry now, he yelled at the would-be intruders more loudly than he'd ever shouted in his whole life, 'What the hell do you want? There's nothing worth stealing here.'

The banging on the door stopped.

Someone yelled back, 'We're not trying to steal; we're honest folk and we're here for that poor little lass that's been stolen away. She should be in her grandmother's care, not a stranger's.'

Another man called, 'Be a sensible chap and open this door, then you won't get hurt!'

He didn't recognise either voice and he didn't believe they wouldn't get hurt. These men had already damaged his property, and he bet they'd do the same to the rest of his house. Besides, he wasn't stupid enough to open the door to any group of strangers in the middle of the night.

He looked around and picked up the poker to defend himself, then yelled, 'We've called the police and reported burglars trying to get in.'

'We're not burglars, damn you, we've come to free the little girl.'

'What little girl? There's no child here.'

'Liar!'

They rattled the door again, and Gabriel was glad for the iron bars on the windows.

'You're a liar, Harte. We know she's there. *Open – this – damned – door.*'

It rattled several times but held fast, then someone shouted, 'Move back. I've found an axe.'

His heart sank. 'I'll thump anyone who tries to come inside.'

Maisie came into the kitchen. 'The sergeant will be on his way after he's called his senior constable, but neither of them will be able to get here for a few minutes.'

'Go and lock yourself in our bedroom, love.'

'No. I'll fight beside you, if necessary. This is my home.' She brandished a big meat hammer.

The noise the group of men made as they continued to yell and hammer on the back door of Number 21 woke everyone in the other two houses, in spite of the thunder.

In the middle one, Ryan got up and stumbled into the back bedroom to look out of the window. His wife joined him.

'What's going on?'

He put an arm round her. 'I don't know. Some men seem to be trying to break into next door. I'd better get some clothes on in case, then go and help Gabriel. You keep an eye on them while I do that.'

In Number 25 Arthur yanked some clothes on over his pyjamas and joined Phil Becksley, who was keeping watch that night, to peer out of the landing window.

'There are people outside at the back. I can't see very clearly but I think they're trying to get into Maisie and Gabriel's house.'

'We'll see better from Biff's bedroom at the back. Sounds like he's up.' They found him looking cautiously out of his bedroom window, half hidden by the curtain.

He gave them a quick glance, then turned back to watch. 'A group of men have got into Maisie's yard and are trying to force their way into the house.'

Lightning lit up the scene. 'Looks like they've got an axe now.' Phil frowned.

Arthur went to stand behind the other curtain. 'They must be after Beatie. I reckon Gwynneth will bring her to hide with us here as we arranged.'

'She's bound to. Let's go down to the cellar, open the secret door and check whether she's on her way.' Biff began moving towards the door. 'Phil, if you think they've got inside and Gabriel needs help, run down and let us know, then be ready to go to his aid. I'm sure other neighbours will help them too. But you stay here in case they come after Arthur.'

'I'd rather go outside straight away and punch them good and hard. Have they run mad?'

'Hold on a bit. See what happens.'

Biff followed Arthur downstairs. In the cellar they switched on the light, then fell silent and listened intently at the panel that led to the tunnels.

'We won't be able to hear any sounds from here,' Arthur said impatiently.

Biff pulled him back. 'Other intruders might be waiting in the tunnels, for all we know.'

Arthur shook off his hand. 'I doubt it. The sergeant said no one in town knows about the passages and I'm not to tell anyone. It's Beatie and Gwynneth I'm worried about, not myself. I can fight if I have to.' He began to open the secret cellar door.

Looking at his determined expression, Biff nodded, pleased to see the man he was guarding find the courage to deal with whatever life threw at him.

Arthur got the door open and saw only darkness. 'I still can't hear anything. I hope they're on their way here.'

'Let's hope those men don't come to your house next. They might remember that you're the child's grandfather.'

'If someone tries to break in here, they'll meet my fists,' Arthur said sharply, then added slowly, 'This can't be burglars, surely. People who break into houses do it quietly.'

'Well, even if they do get into Number Twenty-one they won't find that child.'

'*Shh.*' Arthur nudged his companion and pointed to the right where there was now a faint gleam of light in the distance. 'Look! Someone's coming.'

'Be careful. Don't rush into danger.'

'To hell with careful! It can only be Gwynneth bringing my Beatie here.' He didn't wait, but went down to stand a few steps lower to get a better view.

Gwynneth and Beatie started making their way along the dark passage, moving slowly and carefully, shining the faint beam of the small torch to and fro across the ground in front of them. Beatie was still clinging to Gwynneth's arm, which further slowed them down. Eh, it hurt to see a child so terrified.

The middle house didn't have a hidden cellar, so there was no flight of stone steps to mark its existence, but it seemed to be taking longer than Gwynneth had expected to get to the third house. Surely she hadn't turned the wrong way?

Then she stopped dead because a light shone suddenly in the dimness ahead. It took her a moment or two to make out two men standing part way up the stone steps. One man was shining a torch down the steps and the other was shining his light on his companion as if trying to show them who he was.

Beatie let out a little squeak and suddenly ran ahead, leaving Gwynneth standing alone in the near darkness.

'Granddad!' The child hurled herself at him, and Arthur picked her up for a quick hug before shining his torch back down towards the solitary figure.

'Let Biff take you into the house, love. I have to wait for Gwynneth.' He nudged Beatie gently towards the other man. 'Look after her, lad.'

Then he hurried down the steps calling, 'Well done, Gwynneth!'

As they met, he took the bag off her and put one arm round her shoulders. 'Are you all right, lass?'

'I will be if we can stay with you.'

'Of course you can. I'm glad you brought her to me.'

She looked back into the darkness.

'Is someone else coming?'

'No, I'm worried about my Gabriel. He closed the entrance to the tunnels behind us, but now he and his wife will be facing those men on their own. Maisie had just phoned the police when we left, but it'll take them a few minutes to get here.'

'Who was trying to break in? Could you tell?'

'It was too dark to see their faces. They were shouting that they'd come to rescue Beatie. *Ha!* Taking her back to her grandma would put her in danger again.'

'They must be from that nasty little so-called church. Careful up these steps.'

Once they were safely inside the cellar of the house, he said to Phil, 'Can you keep watch over our yard? I don't want them coming here and taking us by surprise.'

'Yes, of course.'

Biff smiled down at the child in his arms. 'Let's all go up to the bedroom your granddad got ready for you. It's got lovely comfy beds.'

She leaned her head against him with a tired sigh.

He waited to say to Arthur, 'You'd better check that all the downstairs doors and windows are locked before you follow us. You can never be too careful about such details.'

He started up the stairs without waiting for an answer, smiling slightly even at a time like this at how close Arthur and Gwynneth had been standing to one another. They looked like a couple already.

When Biff had gone ahead, Arthur saw how anxious Gwynneth was looking and said gently, 'Let's check all the doors and windows, then we'll go and join Beatie.'

When they'd done a quick check, she stopped at the bottom of the stairs. 'I've not heard any cars arriving, Arthur.'

'There hasn't been time yet for the sergeant to get here. But he'll have a clear road at this time of night, and his new constable is in Birch End, so he'll get here even sooner.'

He saw tears shining on her cheeks and pulled her into his arms, holding her close. 'We'll look after you and Beatie, lass.'

'I don't know why I'm crying. We're safe now. Only, I was so afraid we'd lose our way or they'd find the cellar and snatch Beatie from me before I could get her to you.'

He kept hold of her, rocking her slightly, and couldn't resist dropping a kiss on her forehead.

She looked up at him, startled, and for a moment they didn't move or speak, then they pulled apart self-consciously.

She gave him an uncertain smile, but a smile nonetheless, and somehow he found the courage to say, 'It's not the time for you and me to get to know one another better *yet*.'

'No. I hope we can do it later, though.'

'Be sure of it. Let's join Beatie for now.' Still smiling, he picked up her bag and took her hand. Eh, it felt so right in his! She'd said 'later', and she wasn't trying to pull her hand away! He felt hopeful.

They went to join the others upstairs. The only light came from moonlight shining through the various windows because the thunder and lightning seemed to be fading away now, but their eyes were used to the dimness.

They could see Biff sitting on the bed next to Beatie, but as Arthur and Gwynneth came into the room, the child ran to fit herself between them, taking hold of a hand from each.

'We'll be all right here, won't we, Granddad?'

'Of course you will, love. I don't think they'll even try to get into this house. Why should they? There are no lights showing, and they don't know about the tunnels.'

'Are you sure they don't?'

'Very sure of it, love.'

'Good.' She yawned suddenly and sagged against him.

'I think the best thing we can do is get you into this nice warm bed. Will this room be all right for you two, Gwynneth lass?'

'It'll be perfect. We'll each be snug as a bug in a rug with such lovely thick quilts.'

Beatie sighed out her breath in a big whoosh, but when he turned back the covers, she looked around with a frown. 'I can't see very clearly what the bedroom's like, Granddad. If we drew the curtains first, we could put the light on.'

'Better not. The curtains wouldn't be enough to hide the light completely. We don't want to show even a tiny glow. You'll be able to see every last detail in the morning.'

Gwynneth pulled the covers back. 'Never mind getting undressed. Get into bed as you are, and your granddad will pull the covers up. You'll soon be as warm as toast.'

'Oh, lovely.'

'Here you go.' As she lay down, Arthur tucked the covers right up to her chin. 'Can I give you a goodnight kiss?'

She held up her face instantly and he kissed first one soft little cheek then the other.

Gwynneth added kisses of her own. 'I'll wait with you till you get to sleep, Beatie love, but then I might need to talk to your granddad. If you wake up later and there's no one here, don't panic and don't put the light on. We'll only be downstairs.'

She sat on the end of the bed, while he stayed by the door, watching them both. It didn't take long for the exhausted child to fall asleep, then he said quietly, 'You'll be all right in this house, lass. I'll make sure of it.'

'I know. I feel safe with you already.' She couldn't hold back a yawn, she hadn't been sleeping well lately.

'Do you need a drink or anything?'

'No. I thought I did, but it's mainly sleep I'm short of.'

'There isn't a bathroom, I'm afraid, but there's a chamber pot under the bed and a jug of water on the stand.'

'Thank you.' She was a bit embarrassed to be discussing the presence of what she'd always called a 'po', though she'd had to use one for much of her life rather than stumble across dark yards to outdoor lavatories in rain and snow.

'I'll leave you to it, then. There'll be at least one of us three men on watch at all times.'

'Good. And Arthur? I'm glad you're here.'

'I'm glad you are too.'

He felt ten foot tall as he walked down the stairs to think how she trusted him. He wouldn't let her and Beatie down, not in any way. He seemed to have found his old self again.

Biff and Phil were waiting for him in the entrance hall.

'We should take it in turns to keep watch till the police have sorted out that lot of idiots along the road. Trying to break into houses, indeed! What is the world coming to?'

'You two could get some sleep,' Phil said. 'Believe me, I'll notice it if anyone tries to get into this house.'

'I doubt they'll even try,' Biff said. 'Why should they? There are no lights switched on. But until the police have got rid of those pests, I'll keep watch from my bedroom at the back as well, and you can watch the street at the front from your window, Arthur. Better be sure they're not coming to get us as well because of you being the child's grandfather.'

'I'd expected the police to be here by now.'

'They won't be long, I'm sure.'

19

When Mike Grafton arrived in Daisy Street, the storm was starting to abate. He took a brief detour and parked his motorbike further along from the house in question. As he walked slowly along the street, he wiped rainwater from his face with his forearm. There didn't seem to be anyone around except for whoever was making a noise at the rear of Number 21.

His sergeant's instructions were to wait for him before confronting the men, unless there was an emergency, in which case he'd have to use his own judgement on what to do.

A man stepped out of a gateway and said, 'Glad to see you, Constable.'

He jumped in shock and moved back a step, annoyed at himself for being taken by surprise, but with the wind rattling anything movable it was all too easy to creep up on someone.

'Don't worry. I live on this street and I'm on your side. So is my friend.' He pointed to another man peeping out of a gateway further along his side of the street.

'What are you doing out here?'

'We were just going to find out who's making that racket and if our neighbours need help, Constable. The noise must have woken the whole street up.'

'The lady from Number Twenty-one called the police to say that a group of men is trying to break into her house at the back.'

'A *group* of men? Why?'

'I don't know yet. I'm waiting for the sergeant to arrive.'

'I never heard of such a thing. Have these chaps run mad? This is England not the wild west!'

'I'd like to go round the back to have a peep at the situation. Will you wait here, in case I need help?'

The man nodded and beckoned to the other one to join them.

'Tell him what's going on, then you two wait here!' Mike ordered.

As they both nodded, he crept along the side wall of Number 21, moving carefully from shadow to shadow. But though there was still a group of men at the rear, they didn't seem to have got inside, and two of them at least were arguing about how best to proceed. They weren't even attempting to keep watch.

A regular thumping sound began suddenly and he hesitated, wondering what exactly it was and whether or not to intervene.

Then he heard a cry of '*ouch!*' and the noise stopped.

'What the hell are you playing at?' someone called out.

'The damned axe slipped an' I banged into the door frame.'

'Can't you do better than that?'

'This is the hardest wood I've ever tried to chop,' the axeman complained.

The thumping began again, but more slowly this time. Mike wondered if he should intervene to protect the property, when he heard a sound in the distance. He strained his ears. It sounded like a car engine and was coming closer, so he went back to the front of the house. It could only be the sergeant.

He kept an eye out for any of the would-be intruders following him, but the men stayed at the rear. Not only were they making a lot of noise, but thunder was rumbling from time to time. They might not have even heard the car. He was puzzled. They didn't seem to be at all experienced at breaking in. And why were there so many of them?

Headlights played along the street, showing up every bump and puddle-filled hollow as the police car rolled slowly to a halt in front of Number 21.

As Mike moved towards it, Sergeant Deemer eased himself out stiffly. 'What the hell is going on here?'

He explained what he'd seen so far, then indicated the two neighbours.

They moved forward to join them. 'Need some help, Sergeant?'

He turned and squinted at them. 'Indeed we do, Fred. And Sam. Thank you for offering.'

'We live here, Sergeant. This end of the street is respectable, and we're not letting anyone from the other end start damaging our homes and putting our families at risk.'

His companion nodded agreement.

'Thanks, lads.' He turned and listened, frowning. 'Eh, it sounds like amateur night at the opera back there, doesn't it?'

Another quarrel seemed to have broken out.

'They're not your usual burglars,' the sergeant said. 'They'll probably run away when they realise I'm here, but if you lads can catch any of them it'll be a big help.'

He turned to Mike. 'Let's go round the back. I will not have riotous behaviour taking place in my town. Who do these people think they are?'

Their two helpers nodded agreement to that.

The intruders did indeed try to run away when he got to the back and roared, 'Police! Stop that at once!'

Three of them were caught, one because he tripped and obligingly fell over Fred's outstretched foot. With his help, Mike managed to handcuff two of them together while Sam kept hold of the wildly struggling third.

'What the hell did you think you were doing?' Sergeant Deemer asked loudly.

After a pause, during which two of them looked at the third, who was older, the man said, 'We were trying to rescue that little lass that's gone missing. You police should have been here doing that job.'

'Are you talking about Beatie Hicks?'

'Who else has been kidnapped by that wicked Harte woman?'

The sergeant grabbed a fistful of the man's jacket and anger gave him the strength to shake him like a rat. 'I'll have more respect when you talk about that lady.'

The man glared at him, but didn't say anything else.

Deemer turned to their two helpers. 'Don't I remember that you've got a van, Fred?'

'Yes, Sergeant.'

'Can I have the use of it to take these criminals to the police station?'

'Definitely. I want them punished so that they won't do this sort of thing again.'

'We're *not* criminals,' one muttered.

Sergeant Deemer poked him good and hard in the chest. 'You are when you break the law.' He turned to his helpers. 'Let's take them round to the street. We'll wait there while you fetch your van, Fred.'

'Won't take me a tick.'

He got his handcuffs out of the police car as they waited. 'I think we'll handcuff the third one to the others, Mike, so that they'd find it hard to run away.'

'What about the child?' the man yelled as he was dragged off to join his companions and the handcuffs clicked on. 'Surely you're going to rescue her?'

A voice came from the front door of the house. '*There's no child here,*' Gabriel said.

'There must be. You can't have got her away because we've been watching the house.'

So Gabriel said it again, 'I didn't need to get anyone away. *There is no child here.*'

The prisoner scowled at him. 'I don't believe you.'

Fred came back with the van just then and they shoved their three protesting captives roughly into the back, then Mike set off for the police station squashed up with their two helpers in the front.

Sergeant Deemer joined Gabriel at the front door and asked if he would take Mike's motorbike into his backyard and keep it safe till he came for it.

'Happy to do that, Sergeant. Thanks for coming to our aid. Do you have to leave straight away or would you like a cup of tea or cocoa? It's a chilly night.'

'A cup of cocoa would go down well,' Deemer admitted as thunder rumbled again, but much further away this time. 'It'll do that lot good to wait for me to charge them.'

'I'll look after the bike. You come inside. Maisie will you lock the front door after you.'

When they were all three settled at the kitchen table, Sergeant Deemer asked quietly, 'Is Beatie here?'

'No. I swear she isn't.'

'Then what the hell has got into those men?'

'Their minister seems to have decided that she is here and also that she has to be returned to her grandmother. Though why he thinks he has the right to send people to break into my house, I do not understand.'

'And he didn't join in the attempt to find her, did he, the coward?'

Deemer didn't pursue the matter of where the child was any further. His Lordship had impressed it upon the members of their group that the existence of the tunnels should not be revealed to anyone except the people who owned the properties the tunnels led to – *not under any circumstances, as a matter of national security.*

Besides, the sergeant had seen for himself how badly Mrs Hicks had treated her granddaughter, and the doctor had told him how dangerously thin the child was, definitely not fed properly. He'd not be responsible for taking her back to that harridan if he could help it.

He didn't mention Beatie again, but enjoyed his cup of cocoa and a gentle chat about how the improvements to the house were going and who would have to pay for this night's damage.

When he got back to the station, he found that Mike had locked up the men they'd captured and left them still hand-cuffed to one another. He'd made cups of tea for his two helpers, who deserved them, but not for the prisoners.

Mike and the other two were grinning at Sergeant Deemer expectantly.

'I'm not charging them till I've spoken to Mr Peters, and I'm too tired to interview them till the morning. Let them stew.'

He went and told the men that. They seemed to have lost most of their defiance now and were standing in a miserable huddle.

'Can we have the handcuffs off, please?' one asked.

He jerked his head to Mike, who undid the cuffs, then locked the cell door again, saying, 'See you in the morning.'

'There's nowhere to lie down,' one complained.

'Then you'll have to sit up, won't you? That's what you get for breaking the law.'

The sergeant didn't wait for an answer, but walked back out to the reception area.

'We'd better be going,' Fred said. 'My wife will be worrying.'

'Just a minute. Bear with me, Sergeant.' Sam went to the door that led to the cells and raised his voice. 'Those villains had better not come disturbing me again, let alone damaging property in my street or I'll really give them what for.'

There was not even a rustle of clothing from the cell after he'd finished.

Deemer winked at him, then asked his constable, 'Can you stay the night, Mike, and keep an eye on them? Gabriel's put your bike into his backyard. I'll drive you up to Backshaw Moss tomorrow morning to retrieve it.'

'Yes, of course I can stay. I doubt that lot will give me any bother, though, from their miserable expressions. I think being locked up is already making them realise how much trouble they're in.'

'I hope they're absolutely panicking,' Deemer said with relish. 'I'll question them tomorrow about what's going on at that chapel of theirs, and ask for the names of the others who took part in tonight's fiasco. Then I'll discuss charges with Mr Peters, not to mention payment for repairs.'

He smiled at Fred and Sam, and walked with them to the door. 'Thanks again, lads. I'll make sure you get a letter of commendation from the senior police officer for this district, and if you ever need a character reference to get a job, don't hesitate to come to me. I can't thank you enough for your help.'

Sam grinned. 'It made a change. Nothing like a bit of excitement for stirring the blood.'

In the morning, Sergeant Deemer gave the prisoners some bread and water, then left Cliff in charge and went to have a chat with Peters, who then came back with him to speak to them in his capacity as a Justice of the Peace.

He asked them why they had tried to break into Gabriel and Maisie's home.

'We told the sergeant that already,' one protested.

'And now you can tell me,' Dennison said sternly. 'I'm probably going to be the one who has to decide whether to send you to jail or not.'

One of them gasped and turned white, another said earnestly, 'It was to save the little girl, your honour. She'll be brought up godless if we don't get her away from that woman.'

'What makes you say that?'

'Because that Harte female used to live in the worst part of Backshaw Moss. That shows you what her morals are like.'

Peters held up one hand to prevent Sergeant Deemer from reacting angrily. 'Who told you that?'

'Our minister.'

'Well, he hasn't been here long enough to get his facts right. A couple of years ago her three sons had to sell nearly everything the family owned to pay for an operation to save her life, and that's why they had to live in one room in Backshaw Moss for a while.'

'Serve her right. Women in that line of work do get certain diseases,' one man said darkly.

Peters stared at him in shock. 'And did your minister tell you that, as well?'

'Yes.'

'Why is he telling such lies? She's an honest, hard-working woman who has raised three sons, all decent young men. And her illness needed an operation due to complications with her appendix, as you can check for yourselves. It was *not* due to an immoral way of life. Only, people need money to pay for some of the fancy modern operations, and then there's recuperation time needed afterwards.'

They looked at him as if they didn't believe a word he said, so he went into the sergeant's office and phoned Dr Mitchell, explaining the problem of persuading the men what had really happened to Gwynneth Harte. 'And you'd better check them out too while you're here. I don't want any complaints being made about ill treatment.'

'I'll call in shortly on my way to do my rounds.'

'No hurry. They'll be here for most of the day, believe me, if not longer.'

Deemer went back and told the prisoners that the doctor was coming to see them.

'I am still undecided whether to charge you formally or not with breaking and entering. It might be better to send you to prison and protect honest citizens if you're going to act wildly just because someone else tells you lies. Maybe a few weeks in prison would make you realise what criminals are really like.'

They stared at him in obvious terror at that remark.

'And there will be the question of repairs to Mr Harte's house. You've damaged the place, so you'll be responsible for paying for the repairs.'

When the doctor arrived, bringing his wife with him to corroborate what he said, the men listened in utter silence and didn't protest.

The doctor then checked them quickly, asking if they'd been injured. 'What's this bruise.'

'That's where the axe slipped.'

'And your hand was grazed recently. How did that happen?'

'I tripped up trying to run away,' another admitted. He shot a quick glance at Deemer and added, 'My own fault.'

After the doctor had left, Dennison gave the trio another severe talking-to, then said, 'This is what I'll do. I'll bind you over to keep the peace, but you must make good the damage to Gabriel and Maisie's house at your own expense. If you break the peace *in any way* during the next twelve months you will be sent straight to jail. Do you understand?'

They stared at him, then nodded slowly.

When he dismissed them, they walked out in silence, not speaking till they were well away from the police station.

'We were too eager, rushed in without there being any proof,' one said when they got outside.

'The minister himself suggested we do it. He wouldn't lie to his congregation.'

'Not knowingly. He must have been misinformed by someone he trusted. I'm sure he'll change his attitude towards Mrs Harte from now on, and help us get the rest of the congregation to chip in for repairs to that back door.'

They went straight to the minister's house, but his housekeeper told them he was busy and couldn't see them at the moment. She didn't meet their eyes as she said this, and tried to close the door on them straight away.

'But this is important,' one of them protested. 'He'll want to know what happened.'

'He says he's very disappointed that you've got yourselves in trouble with the police, and he'll see you at the Sunday service as usual.'

They walked away together and stopped at a public garden nearby. It wasn't raining now, thank goodness, but everything was too wet to sit down, so they stood under a tree to discuss their problem.

'I don't know what to think,' one said.

'It's clear the minister is avoiding us, and yet it was he who sent us to rescue the child. That's not fair. And why is he so interested in that child, anyway?'

'I reckon he wants to keep in with Mrs Hicks. She gives a lot of money to his chapel.'

Silence, then the third one said, 'I don't think my wife will want me to go back there. She didn't want to change our place of worship in the first place, and she's already told me she's going back to our old church where people care about one another and help out in times of trouble.'

'Mine feels the same. She gets angry at the way Vanner talks to women, says he treats them as if they're all stupid, unlike our other minister. And what's more, she says she knows why Vanner isn't married.'

'Why?'

'Because no woman would have him.'

In the end two of them went home and meekly agreed to go back to their old church, but the third insisted to his wife that they had to give Vanner a few more days to make things right. It wouldn't be fair otherwise.

'And in the meantime you and your friends will have to pay for a new door, which means dipping into our savings. That's not fair either. How stupid can you get, believing him about Gwynneth Harte? I could have told you she's a decent person.'

'There is a very good reason why: Vanner was trying to get the child back. Don't forget that poor little girl is still missing.'

'And if he proves to be a liar about the rest of this affair as well as about her?'

'In that case you and I will go back to our old church. I do miss the music there, I must admit. They have the best organist in the valley.'

'And I miss the true friendship they offered, instead of a minister who berates us for imaginary sins and tries to make us put more money in the offerings plate on Sundays.' She glared at him. 'I'm not going back to that chapel, and you can't make me. What's more, you can look after yourself this week while you think about things. I'm going to stay with my parents.'

When Beatie woke in the morning, she didn't recognise her surroundings and gave a little squeak of shock.

Then she saw the woman sleeping peacefully in the next bed, and would have settled down again only she needed to wee.

She went across to the other bed and shook Gwynneth.

'Oh, my! I slept so soundly.' Then she noticed how the child was wriggling, and smiled. 'I can see what's woken you up.

You'll have to use a po because we daren't go to the outside lavvy in case someone sees us. Have a look under the bed. They said they'd left us one.'

Beatie knelt down and sighed in relief. 'Yes, they have.' But she still hesitated to use it.

'We'll put it behind that screen over in the corner, shall we? And don't worry. I'll empty it.'

Beatie looked undecided about all this, but need drove her to ignore her shyness, and Gwynneth turned over in bed till it was her turn.

'Last night was a real adventure, wasn't it? I'm so glad we're here. Let's tidy ourselves up a bit and see if we can find some breakfast.'

'Yes, please. I'll try not to eat too much.'

'You must eat plenty. I'm sure your grandfather isn't short of food, and the doctor said you were too thin.'

Beatie beamed at that.

Downstairs, Arthur drew the curtains in the kitchen as soon as the two of them came in, saying cheerfully, 'We don't want anyone seeing you, do we?'

It all felt so blessedly normal, Gwynneth thought. What a nice man he was. And what a lovely house this was, too.

20

The attack on Gabriel and Maisie's house was a nine-day wonder in the valley. Jem Stanley, who was good at picking up the latest news early, told Higgerson about it almost as soon as the news broke.

His employer snorted in disgust. 'Stupid fools. Who cares about a child? Unless— there isn't a reward posted for finding her, is there?'

'No, sir.'

'Then why bother to look? Daughters aren't nearly as useful as sons anyway – or as sons *should be*.'

Jem nodded and tried to look interested when the other man started ranting on yet again about ungrateful lads who knew nothing about the real world and who sorely needed teaching a lesson or two.

'What I can't understand,' Higgerson finished up, 'is where Kit has disappeared to. The chap who's observing things for me in Swindon says he hasn't turned up there, though *she* is still living in the same house, damn her to high hell.'

He thumped one meaty fist down hard on the desk. 'I'm just biding my time, waiting for the right opportunity to pay her back. You'll see. They'll all see.'

After a while, Jem decided it was time to change the subject. He was getting better at distracting Higgerson, who might be clever enough to make a lot of money, but wasn't clever enough to keep a wife, unlike Jem.

Fancy thumping a woman and then expecting her to care about you and your interests! Plain stupid, that was. She'd rather see you dead.

He waited till there was a break in the complaining and changed the subject abruptly. 'There's something else to sort out, sir. What do you want me to do about those two cellars?'

'Cellars?'

'The new ones you said you wanted digging out under them two Clover Lane houses on the corner. Ty Baker won't do it, not for anything. I even offered him double, an' he still turned the job down. Says he can't abide closed-in spaces and he's got plenty of work without putting himself through that sort of misery.'

'What? Well, don't use him again for anything else. We'll see how much work he has without my jobs. Find someone else to do the cellar and don't pay him double, either. Any fool can dig a hole.'

'I'm afraid you'll need to pay a bit more than usual for having that sort of hole dug, sir, and buy some big planks to hold the new walls back. Ty says it isn't safe to dig too deep in that part of Backshaw Moss, an' he's got other folk afraid to do that sort of work there.'

Higgerson gaped at him. 'Even if I pay double?'

'Even so. I'm sorry, sir. I did try, but most of the fellows who usually work for you won't touch that sort of job. I was speaking to Calum Baxter, though, and he might be interested.'

'Aha! I knew we'd find someone.'

'He can be a bit careless. Leaves a mess behind him, an' people complain.'

'What does a bit of mess matter when you're digging a hole? Let them complain all they like. It won't make any difference to me.'

'All right. But he'll definitely need to be paid double.'

Higgerson scowled but after a few seconds shrugged. 'We'll make up the difference in a few months' rent, because the first house will give me two extra rooms.'

'Two, sir? I thought there was only going to be one under each house. Is there enough space for two?'

'We'll be making the space, won't we? Why be content with one rent payment when we can squeeze in two rooms under the bigger house and get twice the money?'

Jem hesitated but abandoned the idea of arguing. It'd do no good. Once Higgerson had made up his mind to do something, it got done one way or the other. 'I'll speak to Calum tomorrow, shall I?'

'Yes.' He waved one hand dismissively. 'That's all for today. I've not had time to read anything but the front page of my newspaper yet. See that you speak to Calum first thing tomorrow morning. I want to get those new cellars started before some pea-brained fool on the council manages to change the rules again.'

When Jem had left, Higgerson settled down to his newspaper, chuckling. He'd fettled those stupid fools on the council about their damned rules, hadn't he? Some judicious bad food had given him a majority of votes for once, and he'd seized the opportunity to amend the rules to cover what *he* wanted to do.

He might try getting rid of fellow councillors again when he wanted some new by-law to be passed. He'd save that for something important, and anyway, he'd need to work out a different way to incapacitate some of them. An idea would come to him, it usually did.

Meanwhile, he needed a rest. He was run ragged, had far too much to do. His smile faded as he wondered yet again where the hell Kit was if he wasn't with his mother. Dammit, he had to find someone else to help in the central business. There was a limit to what an uneducated fellow like Stanley could do, however willing. The better sort of person didn't like to deal with rough types like him.

He'd find Kit. Oh, yes. Whatever it took, he'd get his son back and teach him to be obedient and useful. He'd lost one son; he wasn't losing the other.

And if he couldn't get his wife back once he'd lulled that Tillett fellow into a false sense of security, his name wasn't Higgerson.

He was paying a fortune to a local chap down there who was a skilled watcher, so he knew where she was and who was with her.

He'd teach Lallie a few sharp lessons. Or maybe he should just get rid of her once and for all. She'd given him two sons, but had never been much fun in bed. He'd have to think about it.

The new gardener worked very busily on the flower beds, readying them for the better weather and planting some seedlings. Jack Webster was well aware that his new master was keeping a careful watch on him. Well, he did his work properly, whether anyone was watching him or not.

After a day or two, Higgerson stopped bobbing up nearby and left it to Stanley to superintend and pay him, which amused him. A dishonest chap who knew nothing about gardening watching an honest, experienced gardener, that was.

Jack worked steadily and found to his surprise that he really liked this garden. Someone had put a lot of thought and effort into planning it. Gardens like this didn't just happen. But when he asked the cook who'd done it, she looked over her shoulder before answering and spoke nearly in a whisper.

'The mistress did it. Loved her garden, she did. She could grow anything. Nice woman, she was, but too gentle for her own good.'

She didn't have to explain that. A gentle person would have no chance against a bully like Higgerson.

Anna Jacobs

'No one has ever said why she left. Do you know?' He saw the cook close her mouth and start to turn away, so said hastily, 'I'm only asking because I don't want to put my foot in it and lose this job.'

'Well . . . the master used to beat her and she was terrified of him. In the end he hurt her so bad, it gave her the courage to run away, though she couldn't have managed it without the help of her maid.'

'Ah. Some men are like that.'

Her expression grew fierce. 'Well, they shouldn't be. If I had a husband as did that sort of thing, I'd wait till he was asleep and take my rolling pin to him every time he touched me. Oh, yes. If someone started to hit me for no reason, I'd give him one or two good reasons to stop.'

He laughed. 'I bet you would. So would my wife. She's a grand lass, my wife is.'

The cook smiled at that. 'I like to hear men say that. It shows their hearts are in the right place.'

'Isn't the master's heart in the right place? Didn't he care for her at all?'

Another of those checks that no one was nearby, and then she whispered, 'He hasn't got a heart that one, and you shouldn't trust him an inch.'

After that they got on very well together and he managed to wheedle explanations out of her about what was going on, not to mention pieces of cake and extra cups of tea. Well, she was normal enough to enjoy a chat, unlike Jem Stanley and his new master, both of whom were surly devils.

Webster found things very different at the Samson Street chapel. No one talked to him at all there if they could help it, let alone offering him a cup of tea to help him through the day. They didn't chat much to one another, either. Miserable bunch, they were.

He shrugged and got on with the work, using his eyes and ears to gather information. He didn't clear up all the shrubs in the graveyard behind the chapel, instead using them to create places from which he could eavesdrop on conversations without being noticed, with the excuse of kneeling down to do the weeding.

He saw the minister doing things that upset him, browbeating women and weaker parishioners, viciously caning children, taking home food donated for the poor, even. No wonder the minister looked as if he ate well.

Jack was glad he'd stood up to Vanner from the beginning about fines and punishments. Fancy extra hours of work being 'required' for no pay, on the pretence that he hadn't done things as well as the minister wished. He'd do what the plants needed or they'd die, and he wasn't working any extra hours for no pay, not for anyone.

He also continued to refuse point blank to attend this chapel.

'No thank you, Mr Vanner. I'll continue to attend the church I was brought up in, which suits me and my wife just fine.'

'But—'

'I've been going there since I was a little lad, and I'm never, ever going anywhere else.' He folded his arms and stared back defiantly.

'Well, you're an ungodly fellow, but you have a way with the grounds and the graveyard, I will admit. Perhaps you'll come to see that what I preach is the right way to worship and live after you've worked here for a while.'

Jack was quite sure he wouldn't change his mind. He was only staying in this pair of jobs to oblige Mr Peters, whom he greatly respected, because he'd quickly come to despise both his new employers.

Once he had found out some information that might trap Higgerson, he'd leave and take a more congenial job. He might even have enough saved by then to buy himself the suitable field he'd noticed, with a stream at one side. It'd make a fine small market garden. He and his wife had been saving for something like that for a while.

Kit enjoyed living with Monty and Chrissie. Monty was teaching him about running a small business. He was rightly proud of his own, which he'd started from scratch.

Chrissie was knitting her guest a sleeveless pullover for the cooler weather later in the year. She also often chatted to him about her grandmother's herbal remedies, a subject he found fascinating.

She looked at him one afternoon and said softly, 'No adult has ever spent time with you chatting and reminiscing, have they? You don't seem to know much at all about what life was like when my generation and that of our parents were young.'

'No, my parents didn't chat to me. I think my mother would have liked to, but she hardly said a word, in case my father was eavesdropping, something he often did or set others to do. I really like to hear your stories. Please don't stop.'

Another time she said abruptly, 'Does your father know you want to become a doctor? I'd have thought he'd have been proud of that.'

'I never talked to him about it. He'd not have let me do it and he'd mock the mere idea, trying to make it sound silly, which it isn't. He wants me to follow in his footsteps and run his business with him. But I won't cheat and ill-treat people like he does, I just won't. He cares more about money than people.'

'Well said. Would your mother let you become a doctor?'

'I think she would, but she's never had any power to allow or not allow things, and she has no money of her own.'

'Well, I think you ought to have a taste of what doctoring is like before you decide for certain. I'm quite friendly with our doctor's wife. Shall I ask her if he'd let you spend a day or two observing what her husband does?' She smiled to see the blaze of joy light up his young face.

'Really?'

'Yes, really. She and her husband like to encourage clever young folk to become doctors, even girls sometimes. Modern medicine is so much more advanced than things used to be, and women can't always talk to male doctors about their troubles.'

'Some men are good listeners, surely?' he protested.

'Yes, but they don't have the same shape of bodies, do they? So they can't truly understand.'

'I never thought of that.'

'You should open your mind to all sorts of modern ways and ideas once you settle on medicine as a career. We'll help you if we can but first we have to get you completely clear of your father.'

Kit didn't say anything, couldn't, because he wasn't at all sure he could ever really get away. His father was so tenacious when he wanted something.

The lad had even thought of emigrating to Australia. It would be so wonderful to be sure you were free. Only then he'd lose his brother, and he and Felix were close.

The next morning Aunt Chrissie came home from her shopping and beamed at Kit. 'I ran into Dr Irving at the market so I seized the moment. When I told him how you'd saved my Monty's life and desperately wanted to become a doctor, he said he'd be happy to let you observe what he does for a day or two. He agrees with me that it's important to see what the life of a doctor is like before you decide.'

Without thinking Kit flung his arms round her, saying in a muffled voice, 'I can't thank you enough.'

She patted his back gently and didn't move till he'd calmed down because young men didn't like to be caught weeping for joy. 'I can't thank you enough, either, Kit, for saving my Monty.'

The following day, she took him to the doctor's house early in the morning and introduced them, then left him to spend the happiest day he could remember for years.

When he came back that evening he couldn't stop talking about what he'd seen and done, not telling them any patients' names or details, of course. And what's more, his new aunt and uncle seemed truly interested.

'It only made me want to become a doctor more than ever, Auntie Chrissie. I can't thank you enough for arranging it. And guess what? Dr Irving knows of scholarships which help pay the university fees for poorer students. I shall have to work extra hard to study for the examinations if I'm to get one of those.'

'Will your mother be able to help at all with the cost of clothes and lodgings?'

'I'm sure she will if she can, only I don't know whether she's got access to money in her new life or not.' Or whether she would manage to stay free of his father. He was quite sure she'd be as worried as he was about that particular danger.

'Well, if she can't do anything for you, we'll see if we can help you find a way.'

He gave her another hug then looked at her sadly. 'I don't know anything about how my mother is living. I do wish I could see her.'

'My Monty is going to phone this Mr Tillett tomorrow. He didn't want to do that till he was well enough to take you to see him, just in case something goes wrong and he needs to bring you back here.'

'That will be wonderful! You're the kindest people I've ever met.'

That got him another lovely hug.

As Kit lay in his bed that night, he felt as if the world was opening up to him like a big, beautiful flower showing off its bloom. He might have a chance, he really might, of achieving his dearest ambition.

How wonderful that would be!

21

Kit's mother was enjoying life with the Tilletts. She particularly liked using her maiden name now that she'd left her husband. Being addressed as Mrs Fennell made her feel more her own person. She never wanted to see her husband again, or her own parents, whom she blamed for her previous unhappy life because they'd forced her to marry him.

Gareth Higgerson was a dreadful person. He was evil through and through, not only in his business dealings, but towards his family too. She had several scars he'd given her over the years, the first one when he'd thrown her down the stairs. Most of the marks were now faint, but still served to remind her to be careful.

Since she'd come here, if she forgot to have a good look around before going outside the house, even if only into the garden, John Joe would remind her gently.

She'd never met a man with dark skin before, and had a lot of time for him. He was kind, clever and a hard worker. Kindness was one of the most important qualities to her and who cared what colour anyone's skin was?

She smiled at the thought of how well he was getting on with Pansy, who had been her maid and who had helped her escape from her husband at some risk to herself. She now counted Pansy as her dearest friend and would love to see her happily married to a good man.

Just before their evening meal there was a tap on the door of her small private sitting room at the rear of the house, and she called out to come in.

Felix joined her, with the solemn expression she saw on his face when he was seriously worried about something. Her heart gave a little skip of fear, because that was usually caused by something his father had done.

She gestured to him to sit beside her on the sofa. 'What's wrong, dear?'

'You can always tell when I'm upset, can't you? It's Kit, I'm afraid. I write to him from time to time, as you know, but the school has just returned my last letter. They'd opened it, though, so I hope they don't tell Father about its contents.'

He paused and took her hand, so she knew it was something really disturbing this time.

'Apparently my brother is no longer a student there and they're surprised that I didn't already know that he'd run away rather than go with Father, who had gone there to take him home permanently, it seems. Here. Read the note they sent.'

She did so, then stared at Felix in dismay. 'What can have happened to him? Surely if he was running away, he'd have come here to join you? And he's had plenty of time to do that.'

'That's what I'd have expected too. I did mention in my letters that "we" are still here, without naming you of course. Kit's very quick-witted and would have picked up on that, I'm sure.'

She reread the note, then looked at him again, not hiding that the information had made her feel seriously worried too. 'Your father will be hunting for him.'

'Yes. That's what I thought. He might even have caught him by now.'

'I pray not.' The mere thought of that made her feel sick.

He took back the letter and stared down at it as if he hadn't read it several times already. 'I think we should tell John Joe, Mr Tillett, and Eleanor about this.'

'I agree. Though we all know that it's likely to be John Joe who works out what's going on and keeps an eye on things.'

'The man's a miracle. I don't think he ever forgets a piece of information. No wonder Mr Tillett thinks so highly of him. Shall I ask them all to join us here as soon as convenient? We don't want to spoil the meal by breaking the news. Perhaps dinner could be a little later this evening?'

'Good idea, Felix. Could you ask cook to delay dinner by half an hour? I need to – pull myself together.'

She'd be shedding a few tears, he guessed.

Would this nightmare caused by his father never end?

Since everyone was home by this time of day, the rest of the family came at once, crowding into the cosy little sitting room.

When Felix told them what had happened, they passed his letter and the headmaster's note from one person to the next, studying them, frowning.

John Joe was last, and held them for longest before handing them back to Felix. 'I don't think there's anything in your letter that will give your father more information about your mother.'

Felix shrugged. 'No. He already knows that she's here and that watcher of his has been seen near here regularly. Does he think we don't notice? But I don't think he knew that I was in touch with Kit regularly, and if the school has told him what I said in my letter, that will make him even angrier.'

'Your brother will be welcome to stay here if he turns up,' Mr Tillett said. 'But I'm sure you all knew that already.'

Lallie smiled at her kind host. 'Yes, Mr Tillett. We did know we could turn to you for help. I can't thank you enough. You're the kindest of men.'

He smiled back at her in a way that made Felix feel sad that she hadn't married a man like him. Even though the two of them always addressed one another formally, you could see the attraction between them.

He frowned down at the letters. 'Where can Kit have got to, though? He won't have had much money to pay for travelling, because my father always kept us short, and it's too far to walk.'

Felix looked across at his mother, worried by how pale she was. Her smile had completely gone now.

'If he can be found, we'll do it, my dear Mrs Fennell,' Mr Tillett said.

'I know. But what if he can't be found? What if Gareth has already captured him and locked him away somewhere?'

'We'll check that out,' John Joe said. 'It isn't easy to make someone vanish completely, not if there are people still keeping an eye on them. There would have to be someone guarding him.'

She stared down at her tightly clasped hands and forced herself to put her worst fears into words, 'Unless he's dead and buried.'

'Even *he* wouldn't do that to his own son, surely?' Mr Tillett protested.

'I think he'd do anything he decided would benefit him financially. He has no morals. His god is money.'

She didn't join them for the evening meal, sent Pansy to tell them that she was indisposed.

When Mr Tillett and Felix sat chatting after Eleanor had gone to bed, the older man said, 'I don't like to see your mother so pale and anxious.'

'Neither do I. I think she'll cry herself to sleep tonight.' Felix stole a glance at the man who was going to become his father-in-law and saw how tightly his hands clenched on the arms of his chair.

'I hope we can find your brother, Felix lad. Your mother has had far more than her share of sadness and trouble in her life. She deserves something better.'

Felix thought again how unfair it was that his mother was legally tied to his horrible father, who would never stop trying to punish her for leaving him.

★

As the three of them gathered for breakfast the following morning in the Nortons' dining room overlooking the garden, Monty declared himself fit to take Kit to his mother as soon as it could be arranged.

'You couldn't wait another day?' his wife asked.

'I think it needs doing now I'm much better. They'll be so worried about him.'

'We could phone to say he's all right.'

'And they'd come for him straight away. No, I'd like to finish what we started and take Kit to his mother myself, just to make sure he's all right. I'll contact Mr Tillett straight away, and then, if he's happy about me taking you to him, lad, I'll drive you there.'

'*We* will take you there,' she corrected. 'If you get over-tired, I can take over the driving.'

Kit couldn't hold back a deep breath of relief. He'd not only been worrying about his own safety, but that his father might trace him before he could get to his mother and then harm his kind hosts for helping him.

It seemed a miracle to him that his mother had managed to stay out of his father's hands for this long. It was thanks to Mr Tillett, and he was almost certain that he would be allowed to join her in that safe refuge until he could work out what to do with his life.

He'd talked with the Nortons about getting a scholarship to study medicine, and it was his most treasured dream, but you had to face facts: it was unlikely to happen, because if he came out of hiding to study, his father would come after him.

He stood next to Monty while his friend made the important phone call, straining his ears to hear every word.

A woman answered, informing them that Mr Tillett had not yet come into work.

'Can you contact him, do you think, and ask him to telephone me as soon as possible? I have some very important news for him, something he'll want to hear straight away.'

'Certainly, sir.'

He put down the phone and nodded to Kit. They'd agreed not to say more than that.

After ten minutes – which felt more like forty – the phone rang.

Monty picked it up. 'Montague Norton here.'

'Edmund Tillett.'

'Thank goodness! Look, the younger son of your guest is here with me and wishes to join his mother. Is that possible?'

He winced and held the phone away from his ear as the man at the other end let out a loud, bellowing hurrah. That seemed such a positive sign that the three of them exchanged smiles.

'Definitely possible. Tell us where you are and I'll send John Joe to collect him.'

'I can bring Kit to you. I'd have done so before now, but I was in a road accident and had to wait to recover.'

'Are you aware of the possible dangers from his father?'

'Unfortunately yes.'

'My deputy, John Joe, is a very clever chap, and it might be safer for him to come to you.'

'Very well.' Monty gave him the address.

'His mother and brother will be very happy to hear that he's all right. My man will set off straight away and he'll be with you in a couple of hours.'

John Joe took one of his employer's faster cars and headed north.

So did another car, whose skilful driver was costing Gareth Higgerson a great deal of money. The driver didn't betray his presence, or that of another man he'd taken with him. The passenger wasn't visible because he was deliberately lying down on the back seat.

John Joe didn't at first notice the car behind him. There were, after all, a lot of Wolseleys on the road.

At one stage he did notice vaguely that one car seemed to have been following him for a while, but it vanished soon afterwards.

The next time he saw another Wolseley, he looked more carefully, but there were two men in the front of this car, so it wasn't the same one. Like most other vehicles today, its number plate was splashed with mud. When he arrived at the turn-off to Mr Norton's house, the other car continued along the main road.

John Joe was surprised at how modest the house was, and he was more than a bit concerned about its isolation. The car standing outside was modest too, a Morris 8, though quite a recent model. He couldn't get the lad away from here quickly enough. He could only see one other house nearby, so if there were trouble, help wouldn't be easily available.

He was glad Kit didn't come running out to greet him. The man who did appear stood at the front door for a moment and waited for a neighbour from the next house to walk across and join him before going across to John Joe.

'Tim will sit in the car and keep an eye on it while you come inside with me, if that's all right.'

'Good idea, sir.'

John Joe recognised Kit at once because he looked so like his brother. 'Your mother sends her love, Kit, and can't wait to see you. She'd have come with me, but we didn't think it safe.'

'Is she still in danger?'

'We fear so. There are men watching our house from time to time. Do you think your father will ever give up trying to get her back?'

'I'm sure he won't. He boasts about always paying back any-one who crosses him, even if it takes him years to do it. He is utterly vicious.'

'So we'll continue taking care of her.'

They heard the sound of a car driving past and fell silent, but it continued into the distance, so they relaxed again.

Mrs Norton came to stand by the lad, her hand on his shoulder. 'We think a great deal of Kit. You will take care of him, Mr— um?'

'Just call me John Joe. Everyone does.' He grinned. 'I don't like my surname, so I keep it to myself.'

'You can change it legally,' she said in surprise.

'Or simply not use it. Anyway, we'll take great care of Kit, I promise.' He glanced towards the window. 'I think we should set off straight away, if you don't mind, so that we can get back before dark. Good idea to ask your neighbour to keep an eye on my car.'

'Can't be too careful. We look after ourselves and our neigh-bours here in the country, more than townies do, I think.'

Monty gave Kit a cracking hug, then stepped back to allow Chrissie to do the same. 'Let us know how you get on, lad.'

'Of course. And thank you for everything.'

Monty smiled. 'Thank you for saving my life.' He turned to John Joe. 'Which road will you be taking?'

'The most direct one I can find. I wish the government would hurry up and finish sorting out the road numbering system. They keep changing it, and it's hard to keep up, even when local authorities bother to put up road signs. I had to wind along a few minor unnumbered roads for the final stretch on the way here, missed my way once and had to ask for directions.'

'In my job, properly numbered roads would be a godsend,' Monty said.

'Well, at least there won't be many vehicles on the country stretches for the first part of our journey. There were very few coming here.'

'Thank goodness. I read somewhere that there will soon be two million vehicles on Britain's roads. Amazing, isn't it?'

They both shook their heads at the thought of that much traffic as they walked towards the front door.

'Let me check first.' John Joe stood at the threshold on his own and listened carefully as well as looking around. But he couldn't see any cars parked nearby, nor was there any sound of cars in the distance, so he told Kit to get into the vehicle quickly.

Monty and the neighbour waited for them to drive off before going back into their own houses.

Another man, who had been hiding nearby watching the group, cursed under his breath as the two men stayed outside until the Ford drove away.

The watcher then moved quickly back to his own vehicle, which was parked off the road in among some trees.

'I thought we were going to get hold of him here once he got outside,' the other man said.

The driver started the car and set off before he answered. 'It wasn't worth risking it. There were two other chaps there as well as that sod John Joe, and the lad's big enough to join in a fight, too. Pity.'

'Aye, it's nice and quiet round here. We could have got hold of the lad without much likelihood of interference if there had only been John Joe. I'd have enjoyed giving him a good thumping in return for the one he once gave me a few years ago.'

'We'll have to push their car off the road at a quiet spot. They won't be able to go fast along these narrow lanes.'

'We'll need to continue taking precautions to stop them noticing us following them though.'

The driver smiled. 'I brought some bits and pieces. You don't need to change much to disguise yourself, as we've learned.'

They exchanged smug grins at that.

They set off and soon caught up with the Ford, but stayed well back from it.

Monty watched John Joe drive away. His neighbour went home, but Monty didn't move for a few moments, because he thought he'd heard another car start up nearby.

Yes, he had! A large black Wolseley drove past his gate almost immediately. He thought it was the local police car for a moment, because they had one of the same model, but he quickly realised his mistake.

Where the hell had that car come from?

A feeling of unease crawled up his spine. Something was wrong. He knew it. And his gut instinct was usually right.

There wasn't a minute to waste.

22

Arthur and Gwynneth introduced Beatie to Biff and assured her that she could trust him completely. She listened solemnly as he explained exactly what a private detective was. Then she was introduced to the two Becksley brothers, who were taking it in turns to keep watch on the house.

Even so, she asked hesitantly afterwards, 'And my grandmother definitely can't get inside this house?'

Gwynneth gave her hand a squeeze. 'Not easily. Even if she did, we'd have taken you down to the hidden tunnels, so she still wouldn't find you.'

'Good. How long will we be staying here?'

'I don't know, dear. As long as is needed to work out how best to help you make a better life with your grandfather, I suppose.'

'And with you, too?'

'Would you like that?'

Beatie nodded vigorously. 'I feel safest of all with you.' She'd been staring longingly at the fire and now moved towards it, holding out her hands to the warmth. 'Is it all right if I warm my hands?'

'Of course it is. Fires are there to keep us warm.'

A happy sigh greeted that, then, 'It's a lot better here than at my grandmother's house. She only has a fire lit in her sitting room and the kitchen, and I used to get very cold.'

Gwynneth could feel her hands clenching into fists at this further evidence of deliberate cruelty to the child.

When they'd set out food for breakfast there was another moment of hesitation and doubt, then Beatie whispered, 'How much is it polite to eat?'

'Good heavens, we're not short of food. You should eat as much as you wish, till you're not hungry any more. The doctor said you needed to eat more, remember? That's why we all serve ourselves at breakfast. We all need different amounts of food.'

The child's eyes went wide with astonishment at this, and she licked her lips involuntarily.

'I don't think you've been eating enough for a while, so dig in. Your body is trying to grow from a girl into a woman, and for that it needs plenty of food to build good bones.'

Arthur had been listening to this conversation with pain in his heart for the child's miserable life. 'Personally, I always start my day with a hearty breakfast. How about we all have two boiled eggs each and soldiers today?'

She looked at him in puzzlement. 'Soldiers?'

'We butter some toast then cut it into narrow strips so that we can dip them into the egg yolk. I don't know why they're called "soldiers", but they make a very nice breakfast, I promise you.'

'I'd forgotten about them. Mum used to make them.'

'You can make the toast for us all. See. There's a nice toasting fork, and the fire's hot.'

'I'd like that.'

He cut some slices of bread, handed them to her, and turned to Gwynneth. 'I'll cook breakfast today. You don't know your way round my kitchen yet, and anyway you look tired.'

'Aren't you tired as well?'

'I'm too excited at having my granddaughter here with me to feel tired today.' He winked at Beatie and she gave him a shy smile in return.

'What do you like to do to pass the time?' Gwynneth asked her as the child carefully watched till the bread was golden, then turned it and threaded it back on the toasting fork to cook the other side. They waited for the eggs to boil and Arthur showed his expertise with the kitchen range.

'My grandmother told me to read the Bible whenever I had nothing else to do, but I couldn't—'

She broke off, looking as if she expected them to be angry.

'You couldn't what?'

'There were so many long words, I couldn't understand a lot of it. I can read other books, but that one was too hard.'

'We'll have to see whether there are any children's story-books in the house. Do you have any favourites?'

'There's a book called *Anne of Green Gables*, and my mother used to read poetry to me. She had a lovely voice. But my grandmother said I was too old to be read to now.'

'Well, I don't think I shall ever be too old to enjoy stories and poetry, however old I get, so if we can find some books, I'll be able to help you read the longer words and read to you sometimes.'

Then the food was ready and they all enjoyed a hearty meal.

A short time after they'd cleared away the breakfast things, Beatie fell asleep in a big armchair. Arthur beckoned to Gwynneth. 'Come over here and sit next to me. We can chat quietly without waking her, and still keep an eye on her.'

She sat down beside him, feeling at ease, as always.

His hand twitched, moved slightly towards hers, then stilled again. She didn't let herself smile. She preferred a man who didn't grab her like a greedy child.

Since he seemed to have difficulty starting a conversation, she took over. 'What a bleak life the poor child must have led in the past year or two.'

He grimaced. 'I agree. That grandmother was always a kill-joy. She wasn't this bad when my daughter married her son, though. As for that new minister of hers, he's worse, somehow. I can't work out what there is about him.'

'He's a wicked creature who takes pleasure in wielding the power he has to make other people's lives a misery. He's not as bad as Higgerson, but he's not a good man, for all his religious platitudes. And he seems to bring out the worst in people like Mrs Hicks. She sounds to like bullying people.'

She let the silence continue and waited, seeing him take a sudden deep breath and watching him screw up his courage visibly before taking hold of her hand. He held his breath as he waited for her reaction, so she gave his hand a squeeze.

'About time, too, Arthur Chapman.'

He relaxed visibly. 'You don't mind?'

'No. I've missed having a hand to hold and someone to share my life with. Besides, I'm too old to waste time pretending, and I never was a flirt. I enjoy your company and would like to get to know you better, Arthur Chapman.'

'I don't want to waste time either. Eh, I've missed having a wife and family around me, missed it sorely. I nearly went mad at first when I lost them. Only you can't marry any woman you happen to meet. You're the first woman I've met in my whole life with whom I'm as comfortable as I was with Susan.'

When he raised her hand to his lips and gave it a lingering kiss, it made her catch her breath.

It was his turn to smile knowingly.

'She sounds to have been a lovely woman, from the way you talk about her.'

'She was. And I'm quite sure she'd have liked you.'

'There have only been me and my sons for a long time, because I haven't met a man I felt attracted to. You know my son Gabriel.'

'And like him.'

'You'll like the other two as well, I'm sure.'

She sighed and let go of his hand. 'That was nice, but for the time being the child has to come first.'

'Yes, but you'll come a very close second for me if I have my way.'

She didn't hesitate. 'So will you for me.'

His smile after she'd said that warmed her to the core, filling an aching space that had been empty for too long.

Monty turned to his wife who was standing in the doorway watching him. 'I'm going to follow them, Chrissie love, just to be sure they get there safely. I've got one of my feelings that something's not right.'

'What made you think that?'

'A car drove past just after they'd left. Where did it come from? It appeared suddenly, didn't approach slowly from a distance'.

'I wondered about that too. And since you're not usually wrong when you sense trouble brewing, I'm coming with you.'

He didn't try to dissuade her. She was a capable woman, stronger than many men. She'd had to learn to defend herself as a girl growing up in a rough area, and she'd never given in to threats or bullying that he'd seen – which had been invaluable in their early struggles to make a living. She'd been his wife and partner in every way possible.

They hurried to and fro, putting on warm hats and coats, and picking up a few other items. In less than five minutes, they were out of the house and he was driving as fast as was safe along the narrow lanes. There was only one route John Joe could possibly have taken from here to start heading south towards Wiltshire.

Monty didn't have to tell his wife that he'd put a small cosh in his pocket, any more than she needed to tell him that in her handbag she now had the small, weighted weapon that looked at first glance like a torch. This was something he knew she took with her when he was away overnight if she wanted to go out after dark to visit a friend.

He didn't let himself think of what might happen if the other man had taken a wrong turn. No, surely a chap as capable as John Joe wouldn't have done that? Surely they had a good chance of catching up with them?

Monty and his wife didn't chat, but watched the road carefully, both of them alert for the slightest sign of trouble.

After a few miles, driving as quickly as was safe, they crested a rise and he sighed in relief as he saw John Joe's car a couple of hundred yards ahead of them, going up another shallow rise. He caught up a little before slowing down and staying two or three cars behind him. To his annoyance, as one small Austin turned off the road, a larger van turned on to it before he got there, which made it harder to see clearly what was happening ahead.

However, he knew this road well, so he didn't worry too much. John Joe wouldn't come to a suitable main road for quite a while, and he was hardly likely to turn down a narrow farm track, so it was safe to stay a good way behind them.

After a while he said, 'Is it my imagination, or has that black car that passed our house been behind them all this time?'

'Yes. And it's a powerful car, so could have overtaken them in a couple of places.'

'That proves I was right to worry.'

'I never doubted you.'

They watched for a while, and at a bend they saw the driver put a hat on without even slowing down. When they were held up by a few cows, a passenger who must have been lying down out of sight on the rear seat got quickly out and moved into the front of the vehicle.

'Whoever is in that car is trying to change his appearance so that he doesn't appear to be following them,' she said. 'Can you overtake them and signal to John Joe to stop?'

'I'm not sure that'd be a good thing to do, Chrissie love. Anyway, I wouldn't risk overtaking anything on such narrow roads.'

'We have to do something.'

'Not till those following them make a move. If we got John Joe to stop now, it might leave us all vulnerable to attack. There are two chaps in that car, and the one who changed seats looked to be a big fellow. I bet they'll be carrying weapons of some sort, bound to be when you think about it. No, it'd be better for us to stay behind so that they don't realise we're following them until we're ready to act. It's my guess that if something happens, it'll be on a quiet stretch of road without houses or farms nearby.'

Ten minutes later they were driving along a winding road from which they could only get occasional glimpses of the cars ahead. There were still a couple of vehicles between the Wolseley which they suspected of going after their friends, and John Joe's car, thank goodness.

Then one of those cars turned off to the left down a farm lane, and a few hundred yards further on the van turned off as well. That left the Wolseley directly behind John Joe's vehicle, and their own car quite a way behind the two of them.

At a particularly sharp bend further up a hill, the Wolseley speeded up suddenly and vanished from sight.

'Oh, hell! Here we go.' Monty put his foot down on the accelerator and began to catch up as quickly as his smaller car would allow.

Before they even got to the bend they heard the sound of metal crashing into metal, so he slowed right down as they came to the corner, stopping where their car was half hidden by some trees to get an idea of what they would be getting into.

They could see that the two men had left the second vehicle, which was only slightly damaged. John Joe's car was smaller and in a much worse state. The men went to try to get its doors open.

Monty drove forward openly and as he stopped, one of the men ran over to him. 'I'm glad to see you, sir. The folk in that car aren't hurt, but after this accident it won't be fit to drive. Could you please stop at the next garage and ask them to send someone back to tow it in for repairs? We'll stay here and see they're all right till then, and afterwards we can take them somewhere to catch a train.'

The man tried to stand between Monty and the two cars as he was speaking, but he couldn't hide all that was going on. Did he think they were stupid?

Kit was now yelling for help and struggling with the other man, who had managed to get the passenger door open. The man who'd been speaking to them said, 'Please fetch help quickly! That lad must be injured to yell like that.'

Monty nodded as if agreeing to do what was asked, but he had no intention of leaving the scene of the accident. To his relief another car came along the road just then, and he flagged it down, shouting, 'Stop! Stop!'

But the driver of that vehicle was a woman on her own, and when he shouted to tell her what was happening and asked her to go for help, she looked at him in alarm and drove off rapidly.

He couldn't tell whether the sound she made was a 'yes' or simply a grunt of shock.

'Damn!' he said, and turned back to study the crash scene.

23

Cursing under his breath, Monty saw both men from the car that had knocked John Joe's vehicle off the road coming towards them, smiling confidently, not attempting to hide the knives they were now holding openly in their hands.

They stopped for a moment, and the one who was closer said loudly and slowly, 'As you've just seen, no one's going to stop and help you, so if you want your lady to stay safe, sir, you'll get back into your car and drive off quick smart.'

Monty shot a rapid glance at his wife, who was holding one hand close to her pocket. 'We mustn't anger these men, dear, so we'd better take care.' He tried to sound as if he was intending to leave but by this time he'd slipped his hand into his own pocket in a way she couldn't fail to notice.

He could see Kit on his knees by the car. He'd put up a good fight, but had been outweighed by his opponent and looked half stunned.

Why had John Joe not joined in to help the lad?

Monty's wife let out a brief, high-pitched scream, as if terrified. It was a signal they'd agreed upon in their early years of driving together on long-distance trips.

They waited for the usual count of ten after it, during which time he prayed she'd have retained her old skills, then they each attacked the nearest man.

He didn't like having to let her face the other one, didn't like it at all, but he hoped the man would be so shocked at being attacked by a woman, he'd hesitate to hit out at her. As he'd expected, the man going after her let out a yell of shock when she hit him. She was always very quick to seize any opportunity to best an opponent.

And as they'd often found, men like these didn't expect women to be able to defend themselves, let alone even try to go on the attack.

And he had no trouble whatsoever in dealing with his own opponent.

The woman who'd driven past the scene of the crash didn't have to go far before she saw a van she recognised coming along the road towards her. She flashed her headlights, stopped, and leaned out of her car to speak to the driver.

'Something wrong with your car, Mrs Peak?'

'No, Gordon. There's a fight going on just down the road. Two men in a big car have run another vehicle off the road. I think they must have been going to rob its occupants, only another car stopped to assist them. It looks like the rescuers need a bit of help now as well.'

He gaped at her. 'Good heavens!'

'They need help quickly.' She stepped back and made a shooing movement with one arm.

He waited to say, 'You go and fetch Mr Warth. I've only just left him. He was planning to drive into the village.'

She nodded. She'd been going to fetch Mr Warth anyway because his farm was the next one down the road.

Gordon didn't wait for her answer but drove off, quickly gathering speed.

When he got to the scene of the crash he saw a woman standing over a semi-conscious man holding what looked like a weapon in her hand, which made him blink in surprise.

Two other men were struggling, and a lad with blood on his face was hovering nearby, looking for an opportunity to help one of them, though which one Gordon couldn't at first tell.

He got out of his van, removing the ignition keys and picking up the knobbly walking stick he carried for defence. He was still trying to work out who was the villain in the fighting pair, when the woman yelled, 'The man in the black overcoat is my husband and he's not long out of hospital. He needs help. Be careful, though. That chap he's fighting has a knife and he's already tried to use it on my Monty.'

Gordon moved forward purposefully just as the man she'd indicated as the villain punched his opponent, sending him staggering backwards. He then turned abruptly away from the fight trying to run across to the Wolseley.

It looked as if the chap was attempting to escape, but the lad managed to drag him away from it until his former opponent could get to him. The woman stayed where she was, standing over the man who was lying on the ground groaning.

When the latter tried to crawl away from her, she threatened to hit him again. As he flinched back, Gordon smiled. She had a very determined expression and must have already used her weapon. He didn't think he'd challenge her either if he were lying on the ground half-stunned by a blow and she was still holding a weapon.

By hell, she was a handsome woman! Sturdy and rosy-cheeked. Reminded him of his sister. Dolly would have fought back, too.

Seeing that she was all right, he turned his attention back to the man who'd been trying to get away.

Just then another van pulled up, boxing in the two crashed cars. The driver got out and looked across at Gordon. 'What the hell is going on? Mrs Peak said you needed help. I was just about to go down to the pub.'

'I think this is an attempted robbery, Warth. You're in time to help us secure these two, then after the police have taken them away, I'll buy you a drink.'

The newcomer, a muscular man more than six foot tall, said loudly, 'I hate thieves. I'd enjoy a chance to teach you two a lesson. My wife will have phoned the police by now. If either of you tries to resist arrest, I shall get very angry indeed.'

Gordon watched with a confident smile. He'd seen before the effect Warth's size had on people who were trying to cause trouble. 'You wouldn't want to make my friend angry, believe me,' he called out as they hesitated. 'He put the last chap who tried to rob his farm in hospital.'

Which was a lie, because Warth was a gentle giant, relying mainly on his size to prevent trouble rather than getting into fights.

The two scowling attackers hesitated, then allowed themselves to be tied up with some ropes Warth produced.

Chrissie was attending to John Joe, who was only now coming fully to his senses. 'He must have been thrown forward and knocked unconscious when he hit the windscreen,' she called to the others.

'Kit,' John Joe muttered.

'It's all right. Kit is safe,' she said soothingly.

'I let myself get caught out,' he groaned. 'I knew by then that the car was following me, but I couldn't do much about it on these narrow lanes.'

'We watched him drop back and change hats, and when they were held up, the second man, who'd been hidden in the back, moved into the front seat. You probably weren't looking at the number plate but checking the people in the car.'

'You're right. You're sure Kit's not hurt?'

'He's fine.'

'Good thing you two came after us. Come to think of it, why did you?' He rubbed his head as if it was aching, and he was still speaking slowly and jerkily.

'Just after you set off from our place, my Monty had one of his feelings that something wasn't right.'

He looked at her suspiciously. 'I don't believe in that sort of thing.'

'Well, you'd better change your mind because his intuition saved you and the boy today. My Monty doesn't get such feelings often, but he has never been wrong about trouble brewing that I've seen, so I came with him to help. Now, sit still and rest. I think you must be concussed. Your eyes aren't focusing properly. We'll speak to the police when they arrive and get your car taken to a garage, then we'll drive you both to Mr Tillett's house.'

'Thank you.' He moved his head involuntarily to look as another car drew up, and groaned as pain jabbed him.

'It's the police. Do as I told you: sit quietly and leave everything to them and us.'

'I should phone Mr Tillett.'

'All in good time. You can't call him till we get to a phone.'

With a sigh he leaned back and closed his eyes.

They were allowed to make a brief phone call to Mr Tillett from the small country police station to which everyone was directed or taken. However, it was dark by the time they'd finished answering questions and proving who they were.

Monty insisted he was going to drive them to the Tilletts' house, though truth to tell, he was feeling exhausted now.

His wife looked at him, rolled her eyes, and barred the way to the driving seat before he could get into it. 'You've been driving for hours, and you're still recovering from injuries, Monty. Be sensible, love.'

'I can manage,' he said.

'Only if you have to, and you don't. I can manage better than you at the moment. I believe I'm the only one of us three adults who isn't recovering from an injury.' She opened the rear door of the car and pushed him gently towards it, taking his ignition key out of his hand, then getting into the driving seat.

The two men exchanged resigned glances, and John Joe got into the front of the car so that he could give her directions.

Kit was watching all this, fascinated. He took a seat in the back with Monty and whispered, 'I've never been driven by a lady driver before. My father didn't believe in women getting behind the wheel.'

His companion gave him a wry smile. 'You've never met a lady like my wife, either. Wonderful woman, she is.'

'I couldn't believe it when she knocked that man down. You're both wonderful!'

He patted the lad's hand and leaned back with a weary murmur. 'I'm not fully up to scratch yet. She was right to take over.'

No one was in a mood to chat, so the rest of the journey passed in near silence, with occasional instructions as to which road to take from John Joe.

When they reached Mr Tillett's house they found the gates open and a man standing outside the house like a sentry on duty. They parked on the drive and he nodded when he saw John Joe, then closed the gates behind them.

'He'll just have to open them again when we drive off,' Chrissie muttered.

'Better safe than sorry,' John Joe said. 'We have to take care at night since we became a target for Higgerson's malice. He's had a few goes at getting his wife back.'

Inside, the house was a haven of light and warmth.

Lallie and Felix were peeping into the hall to see who'd arrived, and with a shriek, she rushed to hug Kit. It was a while before she let go of him, by which time they'd been shepherded willy-nilly into a big sitting room with everyone else, and she could introduce her younger son properly to the Tilletts.

'You all look exhausted,' their host said. 'We've got plenty of spare beds. You will stay, won't you?'

Chrissie said, 'Yes! We'd be most grateful,' before her husband could speak.

'I think we all need to freshen up before we eat anything,' John Joe said.

Lallie stood up and moved back towards the door. 'I should have thought of that. Let me show them up to their bedrooms before we settle down, Mr Tillett.'

As she led the way up the stairs, she added, 'I'll get hot-water bottles put into the beds and find you some clothes to sleep in, Mr and Mrs Norton. We have all sorts of odd-ments in the linen store, because Mr Tillett seems to collect waifs and strays. Kit can borrow some pyjamas from his brother.'

By the time they'd used the bathrooms and had a quick wash, the meal was ready. After sandwiches and pieces of pork pie, they ate bowls of rhubarb crumble with custard.

Once the food had been cleared away, Mr Tillett said abruptly, 'It'll be Higgerson yet again who arranged the car and men to follow you. These attempts to get hold of Kit must be costing him a fortune.'

'He's not short of money,' Lallie said bitterly. 'And he doesn't mind spending it on his own wishes.'

'Well, this can't be allowed to continue. Now that Kit's free, we can do something to stop him once and for all without worrying too much about him taking out his anger on the lad. I'm going to discuss it with one or two friends. There has to be a way to stop the man, even if we need to bend the law a little. This is England, and we don't usually tolerate bandits.'

'If there is a way to do something, the police sergeant in Rivenshaw will be delighted to help you as much as he legally can,' Lallie said. 'He hates my husband too.'

'I'll bear that in mind. Now, you're all looking exhausted, so bed seems to be called for.'

No one protested.

In the morning, Tillett insisted on ordering a car to escort them and make sure no one was trying to follow them, let alone attack them on the way home.

He then discussed with John Joe and the family how best to proceed, because until Kit was over twenty-one, Tillett was fairly certain the lad would be legally subject to his father's authority, not his mother's.

Everyone began to look glum as that sank in.

'How can I stay out of his way for all those years?' Kit wondered aloud. 'He won't stop trying to get me back, you know.'

'It won't be easy, which is why I'm going to propose sending you to live with a friend of mine in Scotland. If the authorities come looking for you here, I'll claim you ran away.'

'That's a long way from here,' Lallie said with a catch in her voice.

'Which is a big advantage. And also, it's a small village, and any strangers coming after him would stand out a mile. I own a farm there, which I usually visit in the summer. It's a beautiful part of the world.'

After a pause to let that sink in, he added, 'Moreover, my friend there is a doctor, and Kit could act as a sort of apprentice and learn a lot from him. It's important to find out whether he's truly suited to what can be a rather demanding profession. My friend has tutored lads interested in becoming doctors before, so his arrival won't look at all strange to the locals.'

As Kit brightened up a little, Mr Tillett watched Lallie force a smile, and his heart went out to her.

She seemed to feel his eyes on her and looked across at him as she said, 'He'd be safe, which is the main thing.'

'And you'd be able to phone him regularly, and write to one another. There would be far more freedom for you to stay in touch with him than you've had in the past few months. I'll phone my friend tomorrow.'

Tillett could see that Lallie was upset by that suggestion, but there was no choice if Kit was to be kept safe.

24

When the phone rang the next afternoon, Sergeant Deemer was on his own while his constables were out on small jobs up in Birch End and Ellindale. 'Rivenshaw Police Station.'

'Are you alone, Gilbert?'

'Hello Dennison. Yes, I am, will be for an hour or two.' He didn't ask if something was wrong, because you could never be quite sure the operator or someone on a party line wasn't able to overhear. Anyway, he didn't need to ask. His friend wouldn't phone him during working hours for a mere chat.

'I'll see you shortly.'

Dennison arrived a few minutes later and joined Deemer in his office at the rear of the building.

He didn't waste time on greetings. 'I've two important things to tell you, Gilbert, and I don't want anyone else hearing them, which is why I've come in person instead of telling you on the phone.'

Deemer nodded. He'd have done the same.

'Firstly, I heard from a friend of mine who's also a JP that the police in his part of the Midlands arrested some villains yesterday who were operating a long way out of their normal territory.'

'Oh? How is that of interest to us?'

'The two men they apprehended refused to admit anything, but the people they'd attacked and who helped capture them, did volunteer some information. One of these people was Higgerson's younger son, and he was quite sure the chaps had done this on the orders of his father. One of them had even taunted him with it apparently.

'The other people backed up the lad's story, saying the men had deliberately caused the accident by pushing a car off the road suddenly. They too were sure it could only have been arranged by Higgerson. Which is why I'm letting you know about it. But this is off the record.'

'Do go on. It sounds interesting. I'd give a lot to trap that sod.'

'It seems the younger son ran away from school a week or so ago to avoid being taken back to live with his father. He headed south, trying to get to his mother and brother. Higgerson has been hunting for him and seems to have spent a surprising amount of money on it, too.'

'If the lad is under age, shouldn't the police have returned him to his father?'

'He, um, slipped away while they were busy with the two attackers.'

Deemer grinned. He'd have let the lad 'escape' too, if it was that or handing him over to Higgerson.

His friend returned the smile. 'Of course, no one can prove who's behind the attack, but it sounds highly likely to me that it's Higgerson.'

'It's definitely the sort of thing that fellow would do, especially as his older son ran away from him a couple of years ago. He'll be desperate to save face about the other lad doing the same. Hardly anyone in Rivenshaw includes him socially these days, for all his money. Go on.'

'The best of it is that the man who has given refuge to Mrs Higgerson and her older son is one of those chaps who live comfortably but modestly, yet are rolling in money and have very widespread influence. Not many people know about that.

Higgerson certainly won't. Tillett has friends and acquaint-ances in upper circles all over the country, including around here. In fact, the man we refer to only as "His Lordship" is one of them. It seems the two of them have had enough of Higgerson, and are intending to do something unofficial but permanent about him.'

Sergeant Deemer was startled. 'Kill him, you mean?'

'No, of course not. They aren't murderers!'

'He probably is though.'

'They haven't decided exactly what to do yet, because there's a complication come up. They said to ask you whether it's all right to contact you if they need your help to bring him to justice.'

'I'd sell my grandmother to do that!'

'I hadn't realised till I came back to live in Rivenshaw how much Higgerson's power has grown over the past few years. I'd just about sell my own grandmother as well to put a stop to his antics. I do believe in the rule of law.'

Deemer waited, but Dennison didn't continue. 'What's the complication?'

'It's to do with the second piece of news, and it's a matter that must remain strictly between you and me for the time being.'

'Of course.'

'An acquaintance has contacted His Lordship because they've been having trouble in their area with a minor group of fascists who are trying to follow the example of Mosley and his damned Blackshirts. During their investigations they dis-covered a connection to an even smaller group that has started up recently in our area.'

'*What?* Now that *is* news to me. I thought organised fascism had declined everywhere since the violence connected with that Olympia Rally of theirs a couple of years ago.'

'It has mainly, but there are some patches of support still here and there, as you no doubt know, hence this group's willingness to give some minimal financial support to the odd "affiliated" group, like this local one, to build up their numbers.'

'How did I miss that happening in Rivenshaw?'

'It's only started recently, and it's not going well apparently. Unfortunately the man leading it has managed to keep his identity secret until recently. Now they suspect who it is, but they're holding back on taking action until they obtain rock solid proof.'

Deemer let out his breath in a whoosh of angry air. 'Well, thank goodness it's not going well for him! How do these people get away with it at all in a country like ours? I blame Hitler partly, for setting a bad example to lunatics like them, and unfortunately he's a lot more successful than Mosley.'

'I gather the new group's main success in gaining members comes because they're providing lads who join up with uniforms – well, part uniforms. It's only dark shirts, leather belts and neckerchiefs, but you know how some fools love to put on a uniform.'

'And there are folk so short of clothes for growing lads that they'll say or do anything to obtain garments without paying for them. I wonder, sometimes, where the world is heading, I do indeed.' The sergeant frowned, trying to remember where he'd seen lads dressed like that. Somewhere in the valley, for sure, and only recently. It'd come to him.

'There's more information, but remember this needs to be hush-hush till we have incontrovertible proof.' Even though they were alone, Dennison lowered his voice to give further details.

Deemer listened in amazement, and when his friend stopped, whistled softly. 'Are you sure?'

'The chap who's infiltrated the main national group of fascists is sure, but he can't prove to the satisfaction of the law that the person in question is doing anything wrong legally.

And the members of the top group might even kill this chap if they find out he's spying on them.'

There was silence as both men contemplated the situation, then Deemer sighed. 'Well, you can be sure I'll do my very best to help catch the traitor.'

'I never doubted that. Remember, no word to anyone else yet, Gilbert. This is just between you and me till we have proof.'

'I shall be keeping my eyes open. I know who my main suspect would be, only he's never been into politics before.'

'You do that. Good thing I've got my chap working for Higgerson, eh? You can rely on Webster absolutely, I promise you, if you need help. He's a smart bloke, not easily fooled. If there's anything to find, he'll find it.'

'I'll remember that.'

When Dennison Peters left, the sergeant sat thinking for a while. Was this going to be a breakthrough with the struggle against Higgerson? He fervently hoped so. But that doubt still lingered. It was so unlike the man to get involved in something that didn't bring him a good financial reward.

His constables came back soon afterwards, and Cliff was scowling. 'That group of lads in Backshaw Moss who've been causing trouble is bigger than we thought, Sarge.'

Deemer stared at him. 'Is it, now? Were they wearing anything that looked a bit like a uniform?'

'Could have been, if you count dark shirts and neckerchiefs as a uniform. Could also have been just a batch of cheap shirts for sale at the markets that got snapped up by all the mothers. I've seen that before.'

'Who's been supplying them? Do you know?'

'I'm not sure.' Cliff went on to tell him what he'd overheard one saying, and the situation got even more confused.

Deemer would bear everything in mind. It was all needles and haystacks at this stage, nothing proven. As he got older, he sometimes dreamed of gathering together all the villains in his valley and dumping them on an island far out to sea, with only bread and water supplied. And he'd leave them to build their own shelters, too.

Sadly, he had to play by the rules, and the villains didn't. And a major villain like Higgerson was even more free to act than Deemer was because the chap had money behind him. It could make dealing with some situations very difficult, as the sergeant had discovered over the past couple of years.

He'd been getting very upset and frustrated about it till Dennison came back to Rivenshaw as their local JP. He felt he'd turned a corner once he'd found himself a clever ally like his friend.

He'd discuss the latest piece of information he'd acquired with Dennison the next time they got together, and in the meantime, he'd keep his eyes open.

Jack Webster had been kneeling down for too long. He was about to stand up and stretch when he heard the minister approaching, talking loudly, as usual. The fellow was either going deaf or was in love with the sound of his own voice.

'We'll arrange a meeting for tomorrow evening, out near the reservoir might be best.'

'Are you going to be there?'

'Yes. But I shall wear my mask. I don't want to reveal who I am yet.'

'You do realise that some of them have guessed, sir.'

'Guessing is one thing, proving it in a court of law is quite another. Make sure you don't say anything, not even to your wife.'

'No, sir.'

Webster waited until they'd passed by to stand up and stretch, nearly jumping out of his skin when a voice nearby said, 'I'm glad you heard that too.'

He turned to see Judge Peters, of all people, standing behind a large bush that had just come into leaf.

'I didn't hear you approaching, sir.'

'I'm rediscovering skills I learned as a lad, one of which was to move around unnoticed. It was a game then, but it can be deadly serious sometimes. What was all that about, do you think?'

Webster frowned. 'Vanner seems to have got a group of lads together to act like a gang, or like the military, he'd say. But I call it a gang. Some of them have already started attacking anyone who says anything bad about the minister or that so-called church.' He jerked his head towards the ugly red-brick building behind them, which had been a bakery before it had been purchased by a religious group. They might have put a big cross on the roof, but it still looked more like a bakery to him.

'I'm very interested in what this group of lads does. Any chance of you watching that meeting tomorrow without them knowing, Webster? I'll pay for your extra time.'

'I thought it was Higgerson you wanted watching, sir.'

'Oh, I still do. But I'm starting to get interested in Vanner too. How do you find him as an employer?'

'He's an out and out bully, especially towards women. I had to make it plain that if he tried to bully me I'd leave. Can't abide that sort of chap. I'd normally have found other work, but I only need the two extra days till we've finished with Higgerson, so it's not worth bothering to change.'

'Bear with both your employers for a while, if you can. I'm hoping the situation with Higgerson won't continue for too long. Got enough saved yet to buy that field?'

'Not quite, sir.'

'How much are you short?'

'About ten pounds, sir.'

'Buy the field now, while you can. I'll lend the money to you and you can pay me back in vegetables over the next year or two. I'm very very fond of fresh vegetables and fruit, especially strawberries in summer.'

Webster's face lit up. 'Are you sure, sir?'

'Very sure. Go and buy it straight away.' It was a pleasure to see such joy on a man's face.

'And if you can report back to me tomorrow after their meeting, Webster, no matter how late it is, I'd be most grateful. You should come to my back door, though.'

They shook hands on that.

The following evening various lads slipped out of Backshaw Moss and Birch End in ones and twos and gathered behind the reservoir, unaware that a hideout had been created nearby and an observer was already in place.

A rather short man wearing a mask strutted to and fro, giving them commands to march tidily.

The observer smiled. Did Vanner really think no one had recognised him? Even his voice gave him away, rather shrill for a man, with an edge to it when he got angry. But why was he doing this? It seemed a lot of fuss that was leading nowhere.

When he reported what had happened, Mr Peters seemed similarly puzzled as to the reason for all this pseudo-military prancing around.

'Perhaps he has a fantasy about being a military commander.'

'Or perhaps he admires that Hitler chap in Germany and wants to imitate his strutting around.'

'That's more likely.'

They knew why the lads did this, for the uniform and the mild excitement, but where was Vanner leading them? Into trouble, Webster feared. And he'd seen a neighbour's son among them. She'd throw a fit if she found out about this.

25

Jem Stanley had never seen his master as furious, or as unreasonable, about a situation. He counted himself lucky that he'd managed to avoid being the target of Higgerson's bad humour for the past few days. One man was now sporting a broken arm because he'd upset their master.

'Are you deaf? I asked if you'd got those basement rooms sorted out yet.'

Thank goodness he'd got Calum Baxter working on the new cellars. 'We've made a start, sir, but I'm afraid we're going to need stronger supports to hold the walls in place than we'd anticipated. Calum went back the second day to find part of one wall had collapsed. He said we were lucky it hadn't brought the others down with it.'

Higgerson breathed deeply, containing his anger with difficulty.

'No use spoiling the ship for a ha'porth of tar, is it, sir? After all, you'll make up for it long term with the rents you'll collect.'

'I suppose you're right. Part of a wall collapsed, you said?'

'Yes, sir.'

'Well, see what he needs and get it for him. But make sure you find the best price.'

'Yes, sir. I always do.'

He went back to Calum, and together they worked out what was needed and went out to order it.

It cost more than Jem had expected, but he was assured by the owner of the new building supplies yard that had opened up recently in Rivenshaw that these materials might be second-hand but they were sound and would do the trick. He knew from his own checking that the prices at this new yard were the best in town, so he bought them.

He told Calum to start work and to get as much done as he could. 'Make it look like more's been done, if necessary, if you want to keep the job.'

Calum sighed. 'I wish I'd not taken it on, and that's the truth, but I daren't leave now.'

'Why do you wish that?'

'It's fiddly work and it's hard to find men who can stand being shut up underground. Oh well, I expect it'll feel better down there when we get the new rooms fully dug out and proper supporting walls made.'

Jem didn't tell his master that, of course, just said Baxter had made a good start and was a hard worker.

'He'd better be. I want those cellars completed as soon as possible.'

'Yes, sir. Definitely.'

But his master remained grumpy, and nothing was right today. Jem was glad when it was time to go home. He'd thought himself in heaven when he got this job. He now considered it more like in hell, the way Higgerson blamed him if anything went wrong.

He hadn't sacked him, though. Well, who would take his place? Jem knew most of the petty crooks in the valley, men who'd do anything if you paid them enough. He was more efficient than them by far and his employer knew it.

Higgerson watched his foreman walk off down the street, then moved away from the sitting-room window, wondering how to pass the evening.

When the maid served his evening meal, which he ate in the small breakfast parlour now he was on his own, he looked at it without much interest. He looked at her the same way too. Old and ugly, she was nothing to tempt a man. It was beginning to worry him that since Lallie left he wasn't getting the urge for a woman very often. Probably because he'd been too busy.

Damn Lallie! She'd had a comfortable life, hadn't she? Always plenty to eat, warm clothing, and a big house. And he'd not hit her very often. All men hit their wives, for heaven's sake.

And damn his sons as well. Ungrateful brats.

He read the evening paper from cover to cover, whether the articles were worth reading or not, then saw that it was eleven o'clock. Time for bed.

But once again he found it hard to get to sleep.

He didn't like living alone, he admitted to himself. He had to work out a way to bring his family back. Trouble was, that Tillett fellow seemed to have some very good chaps protecting them. And the two men Higgerson had hired, who'd given him the most hope of success and who'd cost him a fortune, were now behind bars, the stupid sods. Good thing the police didn't know who had hired them.

At least Jem Stanley was proving his worth. He was a bit rough, but would do anything and was a fast learner.

Higgerson turned over again, trying to get comfortable.

He'd give that new fellow a few days to work on the cellar, then go and check how it was going. It paid to keep an eye on the details and let those working for him know it.

Gwynneth settled happily into Arthur's house – well, she would be happy here if she could live a normal life. But as things stood, she couldn't risk going out at all. She had to leave the purchasing of food to Biff, Arthur, or her daughter-in-law.

Maisie and Gabriel came to see them a couple of times in the evenings, using the tunnel route because they didn't want anyone to wonder why they kept going to visit a man they hardly knew. They didn't want to bring anyone here to investigate that anomaly.

She spent a lot of time playing with Beatie, gentle games at first as they built up her strength with good food. Gradually she started to teach her the things she should be studying at school: the more advanced reading, writing and arithmetic. She was surprised how much she enjoyed that.

Beatie seemed to love learning anything and everything, especially when her efforts won her praise. She devoured any children's storybooks they could find for her, rereading them several times for lack of new ones.

Gwynneth grew as fond of the child as if she were her own, taking particular pride in her rosy cheeks, now that Beatie was eating properly.

Arthur continued to repair the furniture, and encouraged her and Beatie to spend time with him as he worked, explaining what he was doing and why, and smiling at them frequently. Ah, she loved that smile of his!

He might not be formally qualified, but he seemed to have a feel for wood, and when you watched the way he stroked a piece with gentle fingertips you could see his love for it. And the finished pieces were truly beautiful.

She sat with him and Biff in the evenings once Beatie was asleep, and enjoyed their company, the three of them discussing everything under the sun.

But she had to admit to herself that she enjoyed the evenings most of all when it was just Arthur. Biff seemed to have grown rather fond of his former landlady, and called in to see her occasionally. He was also looking for premises to start a business once this situation was resolved, so he sometimes went out in the early evenings now that the days were getting longer. Of course either Rob or Phil Becksley would still be on duty, just in case of trouble, but they didn't intrude.

'Will poor Beatie ever be really free of that woman?' she wondered aloud one evening.

'We'll make sure of it, one way or the other,' Arthur said firmly. 'And if we have to leave the country to do that, I'm willing to emigrate.' He hesitated, then added, 'Would you go that far away with me to help her?'

'Definitely, though I'd rather not, because it'd mean leaving my sons.' She smiled at him, had known he'd say that, then saw Biff look from her to Arthur and open his mouth as if to speak, then close it again.

She guessed he'd been going to comment on their growing closeness and was glad he hadn't done so. Arthur was a rather shy person and it might have upset him. Anyway, they didn't need interference. They were getting to know one another quite nicely, thank you very much, and were old enough to manage their growing friendship in their own way.

She smiled and corrected herself: it was a courtship, really, even if it was a quiet one. No flowers, no fancy words and pro-testations, just a lovely feeling of growing closeness as they got to know the smaller details about each other's lives and hopes for the future.

Well, life was mostly made up of small things, wasn't it?

After some consideration, Vanner went to call on Mrs Hicks in his role as minister of her church. She was one of his most important parishioners and was generous in her contributions to the Sunday collections, and he knew she was fretting about not having found her granddaughter.

'My dear lady, is there any news of that poor child?'

'None at all, Mr Vanner.'

'I was thinking about your situation. She hasn't been seen with her grandfather, I know, but I noticed in the village shop that he was buying more food than I consider necessary for one man, even though he has Mr Higgins living with him.

And there was a Fry's chocolate bar too. Who was that for? The shopkeeper sounded surprised when he bought it, asked if he'd developed a sweet tooth lately.'

She looked at him in puzzlement and he realised he'd have to be more specific. She was not the cleverest of women, though actually he preferred that. Clever women were an abomination as far as he was concerned.

'Do you suppose Arthur Chapman has somehow managed to get the child into his house without our watchers noticing?'

'Even if he has, I can do nothing about it. Mr Peters won't authorise a search of his house or any other without good reason, and no one has actually seen Beatie there.' She sighed.

He wasn't going to let her drop her search because it had occurred to him that the child would likely be Mrs Hicks's heir. Beatie might also inherit a share in Chapman's house if anything happened to him and his son. Money was the one thing Vanner had never managed to accumulate, he couldn't understand why. He had to turn to the church in desperation for financial security.

Maybe he should arrange something else to deal with Chapman. It'd make a useful diversion, taking some of the attention away from his corps of young men. Training them to act in a more military manner was something which gladdened his soul. That was what young men should be doing with their lives. Look at how things were being organised in Germany.

'My dear Mrs Hicks, I think you should get another JP to authorise that instead of the Peters fellow, who is far too friendly with Chapman. Perhaps Mr Forester?'

'I've heard the name, but don't know him.'

'He lives in the country just south of Rivenshaw and they tell me he's strict in his application of the law.'

'Do you think Mr Peters would allow this to happen?'

Vanner took a deep, happy breath. This was exactly the opening he'd been hoping for. 'I don't think he can prevent it, especially as I am a little acquainted with Mr Forester and can explain the situation to him. If you'd like me to help you, that is?'

Her expression brightened considerably. 'Would you do that? I'd be so grateful.'

'You don't have a telephone at home, do you? We can telephone Mr Forester from my house tomorrow, if you like, and find out when he'll be free, then I could drive you over to see him.'

'You are most truly the shepherd of your flock.'

He smiled at her. She was almost literally correct. He had attracted a group of sheep who liked to be told exactly what to do, how to run their lives, and these included men who deplored the modern way of women working outside the home and not obeying their husbands as was only proper. He might not be married, but he sympathised with them. The Great War had led to a sorry situation in this country if you asked him.

If only there was a man of Herr Hitler's calibre to lead them here in England.

Still, if things turned out as he expected in Germany, and some of the covert activities of the remaining English fascist groups paid off, there might be hope that England would be forcibly brought to heel when the inevitable happened, even if it all took longer than they'd hoped.

And in his small way he, Osbert Vanner, intended to contribute to this necessary change, and of course, to benefit from it afterwards.

But at the moment, he wished to reveal Arthur Chapman for what he was, a drunk, an incompetent, and a child abductor.

It was abominable that such a person would inherit a big house like that while a godlly man like himself could so lack money. Chapman didn't deserve it. Most definitely not.

But if something happened to that fellow, and the child inherited under the grandmother's guardianship, well, that might be a very lucrative situation for Osbert to step into.

26

Higgerson had told Jem he intended to visit the new cellars to check that they were being dug out properly, so Jem in turn went to see Calum while he was out on an errand for his master.

'You need to push ahead with the work,' he warned. 'It doesn't look at all near to being finished.'

'We're at a crucial stage,' Calum said. 'You can't hurry this sort of job. You have to dig the foundations properly and put in strong supports for the walls.'

'Can't you just make it look good, then go back and do things properly afterwards? You know what *he's* like. He wants to see progress.'

'He must be a right old sod to work for. Don't know how you stand it.'

Jem shrugged. 'He doesn't bother me too much. He knows there isn't anyone else in the valley who can get things done the way he wants.'

'How does someone who spent a good part of last year in prison know that?'

'Before I slipped up, I worked for Dobbs, and watched how he did things. Smart fellow, Dobbs.'

They both chuckled at the thought of him stealing Higgerson's car. It was still talked about and laughed over.

Calum rolled his eyes. 'I suppose you're planning to get away with his new car, too.'

'I'd rather stay here and make money.'

But his friend's joking words lingered in Jem's mind as he walked home after he'd put the car in the garage and handed the keys to his employer. He didn't know anyone in the valley who dealt in stolen cars, but he'd shared a cell with a chap who had been a used-car salesman in Bury. Cortonby hadn't spent all his working life on so-called honest selling, but had confided in him that he'd also dealt in stolen cars, which brought in a lot more money.

And to tell the truth, Jem was finding it very tiring kowtowing to Higgerson day-in day-out. He would love to get the better of him.

Could he do the same thing as Dobbs, run off in his master's car? He'd have to think about it. No harm in working out how to do something if an opportunity arose, was there?

When he got home that night, he said abruptly to his wife, 'I think you should have our bags packed, ready to take off suddenly. In fact, we should live out of them from now on.'

She clutched his arm tightly and gave him a little shake. 'You haven't lost your job?'

'No, of course not, but you can never be sure of anything with Higgerson, and if I see a chance to do what Dobbs did, pinch his car and run off in it, well, we could make a nice chunk of money. You've always wanted us to set ourselves up in a little business like a shop somewhere, haven't you? Maybe it might be worthwhile keeping our eyes open for an opportunity.'

She let go of his arm but didn't say anything. He cocked his head and waited. You couldn't push her into doing something, only hope she'd agree.

'All right,' she said at last. 'We'll think about it and keep our eyes open. But we'll make sure we work out properly how to do it this time. I don't want the police catching us and putting us both in prison.'

He shuddered at the mere thought of that. 'I don't want to be locked away ever again. I couldn't seem to breathe properly in that place.'

'How are you coping with going down them new cellars, love?'

He shuddered and said nothing. He hated it, absolutely hated it. Which was another reason to get away.

Could he really do it?

Higgerson had told him to be ready at ten o'clock sharp the following morning, to go and look at how the cellars were coming on, so Jem got to work a bit early. When his employer came in, a quarter of an hour later than he'd said, he was yawning.

'If you're tired, sir, we could go another day,' Jem ventured.

Higgerson stared at him. 'Well, it's nice to have someone to notice how I feel.'

'Yes, sir.' He waited.

'I said we'd go today and that's what we'll do. Bring the car round and we'll be off.' He handed over the keys.

It was such a nuisance to have to wait till he handed them over each day, Jem thought as he drove carefully up the hill from Rivenshaw. That was going to be one of the big problems about finding a way to run off with the car.

When they were driving through Birch End and approaching Backshaw Moss, Higgerson said suddenly, 'Stop!'

Jem did as he was told, and waited. What now?

'Look at the damned place! I'd been forgetting what a slum it is. I'd hoped to be out of this sort of business by now if I'd got those three houses, but at least there's money to be made in slums if one is careful. As you'll see today.'

'Yes, sir.'

More silent staring, then, 'Drive on.'

Jem stopped the car opposite the houses with the pile of dug-out muck outside them. 'I'll not arrange for that to be taken away until after all the digging is finished.'

'Yes. Hmm. I think I'll get out here and you can park the car further back in Daisy Street. There seem to be fewer urchins around back there. Find a strong lad and offer him sixpence to keep an eye on the car.'

'Yes, sir.'

Jem chose to pay a hungry-looking man to watch the car rather than a lad. Grown men were more reliable, he'd found, and more grateful if you needed a favour from them one day.

He rejoined his master, who was standing staring round, his eyes darting here and there. He did this sometimes when he was considering how to make money from a place.

After a few moments Higgerson nodded to him. 'Right, then. We'll go inside now. No, wait a minute. I'll take my jacket off. It's a new one and I don't want to get it messed up. Here, you can run back down the street and lock it in the car for me. Look sharp!'

Jem took it, surprised at this order, even more surprised to feel the wallet still in it. His master was in a strange mood this morning, that was sure. He hurried back to the car, then returned to find Higgerson staring round again. He sighed and waited. You did a lot of waiting when you worked for Higgerson, and you did it in silence if you had any sense.

'What are you standing there like a fool for, Stanley?'

Waiting for another fool, he thought, but of course he couldn't say that. 'I was wondering if I should go inside and tell Baxter you're here, sir.'

'No, don't. We'll just walk in on him. You learn more when you take people by surprise.'

Jem prayed that Calum had had someone watching out for their arrival, or at least looked to be working hard.

To his relief, Calum was there in the cellar, digging busily, together with a man he'd employed throughout this job to share the heavy work.

Higgerson walked slowly and stiffly down the new cellar steps that were formed temporarily of wooden planks. He stopped almost at the bottom to look at the progress.

The two men stopped digging to watch him.

For some unknown reason, a shiver ran down Jem's spine and he stayed at the top of the steps. At least there was more space down here, now that the rooms were just about finished. It had been hell forcing himself down the narrow hole formed when Baxter first started.

'I thought the work would be further on. How much longer do you expect it to take?' Higgerson asked Baxter.

'Another two weeks at least, probably more like three, Mr Higgerson. This isn't sand, you know, so it's not simple to dig through it. Luckily it's soil from the original swamp Backshaw Moss was built on. That's how it got its name. But we do have to shore up them walls properly.'

'They look all right to me.'

'If you want to risk them caving in, sir . . .?' He waited, a questioning look on his face.

'Of course I don't, you fool. I suppose you'd better shore them up.'

'That's why I found a man with some bricks for sale, second-hand, which are cheaper but just as strong. I'm going to use them as piers to support the walls. They'll last longer than wooden panels would.'

Jem watched Higgerson open his mouth to protest. He knew that expression and sighed. Why did the man always want the impossible?

Calum held up one hand. 'If you want years of rental money from these cellars, *sir*, you'll need to make sure the walls are held firmly in place and stay that way. I thought you agreed about that when you gave me the money for the materials.'

'Well, do your best to keep the costs down.'

'I always do.'

The other man stopped digging to listen intently as if he could hear something outside, then left the cellar. He came back a few seconds later to call down, 'The bricks are here, Calum. They won't unload them till they've been paid.'

Calum moved forward. 'Excuse me a moment, sir. I need to see the bricks are unloaded into the backyard, so that no one can pinch them.' He paused at the top of the steps to add, 'I'd be obliged if you'd not touch anything down there, sir. Some of the panels are only put up temporarily.'

Higgerson watched him leave, then turned to Jem. 'Go back outside and wait till I call you. I want to pace these cellars out, see if I can get three rooms out of it.'

Jem did as he was told, glad to get back into the fresh air. It always seemed harder to breathe down in that cellar. He couldn't understand why Higgerson would want to spend more time down there than he needed.

He hurried outside, sucking in big mouthfuls of air. Wonderful, that felt. You could almost taste the difference.

In front of the house, Jem found Calum helping a man unload some second-hand bricks into wheelbarrows and then taking them along a narrow path at the side of the house to the backyard. They were all sorts of colours, but they'd not be on view if the walls were going to be plastered over, so that didn't matter.

Calum came to stand beside Jem and left the man delivering the bricks to carry on. 'What's *he* doing down there?'

'Mr Higgerson is pacing it out, trying to work out whether he can fit three rooms in. He wants us to wait outside till he calls.'

Calum scowled. 'Well, I'm not going to extend that space, not for anything. It'd be asking for trouble. He's already had me go further than I wanted.'

'Ah, never mind him. Fancy a fag?' Jem asked.

'Yes, please.'

'He usually takes a while when he's figuring something out, so we might as well enjoy a break. It's no wonder he's made a lot of money. He certainly thinks hard about what he's doing. I sat waiting in the car for two hours once when he was planning something. Only that idea didn't come off. Here.' He held out the packet and they both got a cigarette out and lit up.

'What did he want that didn't work out?'

'To buy them three big houses at the end of Daisy Street. He's still furious about not getting them.'

'He gets angry easily.'

'Yes. Used to treat his poor wife badly when something happened that he didn't like.'

'Well, she escaped, poor woman. Even I heard about him thumping her.'

'He's still sending men to try to get her back.'

'Stupid waste of money, that. He's rich enough to find another woman, one who's more willing like.'

'Ah, but his wife is *respectable* and another woman wouldn't be. He likes to pretend he's respectable, but the other business owners aren't fooled, and they don't have much to do with him outside work.'

They puffed contentedly for a while, then Jem reverted back to today's job. 'Who'd have thought you could get two more rooms under the house?'

'He'd have been better leaving it at one.'

'I'm telling you straight: if he says he wants two, or even three new cellars, don't argue with him.'

'Well, he'll have to find someone else to make more space if he does decide he wants more, because I won't do it. The ground there isn't right for it.'

Left alone in the cellar, Higgerson slowly paced it out. He couldn't see any reason why there shouldn't be another cellar space dug out. It had gone all right so far, hadn't it?

Mind, it was a bit damp and stuffy down here, but that'd be the tenants' problem, not his.

He poked his walking stick into a gap between the temporary wall panels opposite the wooden steps and it slid into it with no problem.

'See!' he said aloud. 'It could easily be dug out further.'

After he pulled the stick out, a trickle of soil ran down from the narrow hole it had made, and only gradually stopped. 'Piece of cake to dig that,' he said scornfully.

He moved along a couple of yards and tried the wall there. Once again, his walking stick could be pushed in easily. '*Ha! ha!*' he said triumphantly as he began to walk up and down the dimly lit space, poking holes here and there, and thumping one of the panels, wondering why he was bothering to pay for bricks.

He calculated how much rent three cellars would bring in as opposed to two over the course of a year, pleased with the amount, and started to work out what use he would put the money to. Another house to rent rooms in or a better house to rent out the whole?

Another trickle of soil ran down the wall, but he was too engrossed in his calculations to bother with that. When one hole started to get bigger he stared at it and thought again how easy it would be to dig out further.

'I'm going to be the richest man in the valley before I'm through, and I'm well on my way,' he added in a loud voice, thumping one clenched fist on the wall panel next to him for emphasis. 'And I'm going to get Lallie back and—'

There was a sudden loud brushing noise, followed by a low rumbling, not like anything he'd ever heard before. He swung round to find out what had caused it, only to see the wall next to the steps bulge outwards.

He moved towards the steps, but it all happened so quickly the way was blocked before he could start to go up them, and he had to jump back out of the way of the tide of muck.

One of the lamps had been tipped over by the movement of the earth, leaving only one still burning, and the cellar had become darker, feeling threatening. He didn't like it, not a bit.

'Help! Stanley! Help! Get me out of here!'

Then the wall behind him turned into a stream of soil and minor rubble, burying his feet to his ankles. As he began to kick his way out of it, more of the wall caved in, and suddenly he was buried up to the waist and couldn't move.

He yelled again for help at the top of his voice.

Then he couldn't seem to find the breath to yell, was having trouble breathing as the soil continued to grip more tightly and the pile moved up his body.

When the earth shook beneath them, Calum tossed his second cigarette aside. The solid wall they'd been leaning against suddenly seemed to be pushing them forward and with a shout of 'Get away!' he dragged Jem forward into the road and they turned to stare as the wall of the house began to collapse slowly, spreading outwards like a flood, pouring some of the house's contents with it.

'What the hell's happening?' Jem demanded.

'It's all caving in, the whole sodding house. An' it's pulling down the next house with it. I told him it wasn't safe to dig that cellar out, but he insisted, didn't he? It's not my fault. You'll tell them that, won't you?'

'Why should I tell anyone anything about this cave-in?'

Calum pointed towards the front door, or where the front door had been. 'Because it'll have collapsed on him and killed him, so the authorities will have to look into it. You surely don't think he's going to come out of that cellar alive, do you?'

Jem could only goggle at him.

'Look at it. Everything has collapsed, and he hasn't run out, has he?'

'We have to get him out, then.'

'I'm not going in there. I like having air to breathe. Anyway, he'll have been crushed to death by now, and serve him right.'

'You mean—' Jem couldn't finish his question because the rest of the house was subsiding as they watched, and they had to move backwards again.

People were running along the street now, calling out, asking what was happening.

'Stay back!' Calum yelled. 'It's a cave-in.'

The man who'd been helping with the digging appeared from one side. 'It's giving way at the back too! We had to jump over the wall to save ourselves. People have run out of the other two houses. I think they all got out.'

The whole world seemed full of dust and strange noises. Jem couldn't form a single word, couldn't move, only watch in horror. He could have been down there, under all that.

Higgerson was down there still.

'Any chance at all that he could be alive?' he asked Calum.

'None. Look at it, all piled up on top of whatever's in the cellar. We hadn't strengthened the walls properly down there yet.'

'It'll have crushed him to death?'

'Of course it bloody will. How many times do I have to tell you?'

Even the people who'd come to gawp were staying well back, whispering to one another and pointing.

'The council or somebody will hold a big inquiry after this, and we'll be called as witnesses,' Calum said. 'Happened to me once before. I'm leaving town before they start all that fussation here. They're bound to blame me, even though I was only doing as *he* ordered. I'll find work in the south, change my name.'

It didn't take Jem long to decide that he wasn't going to stay around for any damned inquiries, either.

Then he realised what this was – his big chance. He sought for an excuse to leave Clover Lane. 'I'd, um, better go and fetch Mr Higgerson's lawyer.'

'What can he do?' But Calum was talking to himself, because Jem had set off running down the road towards the car.

If no one could have lived through a bad cave-in like that, Jem thought, Higgerson wasn't going to need his car, was he? And no one else would notice for a while that it was missing. It'd be simple to drive off in it, easiest thing in the world if he did it quickly before anyone realised what he was doing.

This was meant to be.

People were coming out of houses and shops now to look at what had happened.

'Keep back!' he yelled as he passed them. 'More of the ground may cave in yet.'

'Was anyone caught inside?' one man shouted.

'Higgerson.'

That shut them up for a few moments.

Jem fumbled with the car keys.

A man came over to ask, 'Is he really dead?'

'Bound to be. The whole house has fallen down on top of him.' He thumped one clenched fist down on the other to illustrate this, and saw one woman standing nearby smile as if that was good news.

A man shouted, 'Higgerson was in there. He's likely dead!'

Someone at the back of the crowd cheered, and others joined in. They were all smiling.

Jem shook his head. He hoped when his time came people weren't happy to see him go.

He got into the car and started the engine. The sooner he got away from Rivenshaw the better.

This was his big chance, and if his wife wasn't coming with him, he'd go on his own.

27

When the phone rang at the police station, Sergeant Deemer picked it up.

Whoever was on the other end of the line made no sense, so he said loudly and clearly, 'Start again. And speak slowly. You're not making any sense.'

'A house has fallen down. We think a man's been killed. It just . . . collapsed on him.'

'Where is this?'

He took down the particulars, not surprised that it was in Backshaw Moss.

'And who is missing? Do you know?'

'Mr Higgerson.'

It was the sergeant's turn to struggle for words. It couldn't be. His valley couldn't be so lucky as to get rid of their major villain.

'Are you still there, Sergeant?'

'Yes. Sorry. I was just – um, a bit surprised. Have you called the fire brigade?'

'No.'

'I'll do that, then set off. Don't let anyone try to go inside.'

He didn't put the phone down, but cleared the connection and dialled what he knew to be the fire chief's direct number. He explained what he'd been told, ending, 'I'll meet you there.'

'And they said Higgerson had been killed?'

'Yes.'

'Bloody hell!'

Sergeant Deemer put the phone down and yelled for Cliff. 'Where's Mike?'

'On an early lunch break.'

'Where did he go?'

'Round the corner to the café, said he was fed up of sandwiches.'

'Go and fetch him back quick as you can. There's trouble in Backshaw Moss.'

'There usually is.'

Deemer got the emergency kit out of the cupboard, the pack of items designed to rescue people on the moors. It hadn't been used for a long time, and he wasn't sure it'd be any use today, but it was all he could think of.

He stopped dead, standing motionless as he realised how ironic it would be if he used it to rescue Higgerson.

He couldn't seem to believe that the man was really and truly dead.

You shouldn't hope for someone's death, but Higgerson had done such harm to the people of this valley, the poor ordinary people struggling to put bread on the table, watching their children grow up spindly and stunted. He'd done more harm than anyone Deemer had ever known and — He cut that thought short, carried the kit outside and put it into the car boot, just as Mike and Cliff came racing round the corner.

'You can drive us up to Backshaw Moss, Mike. Go as fast as is safe. I'll tell you all I know on the way.'

The news left two more people stunned into silence.

When they got to the place where the houses at the corner of Clover Street usually stood, they all exclaimed in astonishment at what they saw. There weren't any houses left, just piles of rubble with all sorts of building materials and household items poking out. Everything looked higgledy piggledy, as if a child had thrown a tantrum and destroyed its toys in one fell swoop.

'I've never seen anything like it.' Deemer's voice came out scratchy.

'What should we do, Sarge?'

'To tell you the truth, I'm not sure. I've never had to deal with a house collapse before.' To his relief the fire engine came racing along Daisy Street just then, stopping nearby.

The fire chief and three men tumbled out as if ready to grab their hoses, but then froze, staring in shock, like most of the people nearby.

Deemer hurried across to the chief. 'Where do we start, Nigel lad?'

The chief shook his head. He echoed the sergeant's words. 'I don't know. I've never dealt with a collapsed building before.'

'Neither have I.'

So that made two of them treading new ground, Deemer thought. 'Well, we can only do our best. I'll get my constables to move people back, shall I?'

'Yes. I'll, um, examine the scene.'

A man came across to them before they could put this plan into operation. 'I was outside it when this happened. Sergeant. It wasn't my fault. Higgerson had insisted on digging out another cellar. I told him it wasn't safe to touch the walls till they were braced properly, but he went down there on his own and he must have started poking about.'

'Where's Jem Stanley? He usually drives Higgerson round town. Is he trapped down there too?'

'No, he was outside with me when it happened. He drove off to fetch Higgerson's lawyer.'

Deemer frowned. 'Do you know who that is?'

'I think he's gone to that new chap: now, what was his name? Oh yes, Littleproud, that's it. Why do lawyers always have strange names? Anyway, Jem will be bringing him back to look at this, I suppose.'

This puzzled Deemer. Why hadn't Jem Stanley simply phoned the lawyer, who would have his own car to drive here in?

He looked across at the bystanders. 'Can someone make a phone call for me?'

A young woman stepped forward. 'There's a phone at the village shop in Birch End. I can go, if you like. Only take me a couple of minutes if I run through the back alleys.'

'Thanks. Ask them to phone Littleproud, the new lawyer. Tell him his client Higgerson has probably been killed and there aren't any of his family around, so we need him to take any actions necessary legally.'

That made him wonder what provisions if any Higgerson had made for his death, given that his wife and both his sons had left him. 'And just check that Stanley's with him.'

He frowned. He had a strange feeling about this. Had Stanley gone off to see the lawyer, or had he copied his predecessor and run off with Higgerson's car? No, surely not?

In spite of the seriousness of the situation, a smile escaped Deemer's control. He couldn't help hoping Jem Stanley had done that. It'd be poetic justice, and it'd get rid of another nuisance from the valley.

The smile quickly faded and he turned back to the mess, waiting for the fire chief to decide how to start dealing with the wreckage.

His mother had always said, *If in doubt, do nowt.* He had no idea what the correct procedures were for a situation like this, so he would definitely do nothing without a good reason.

Jem drove down into Rivenshaw as fast as he could. He was going to do it. By hell he was! You didn't often get a chance to make a lot of money. Well, it'd seem a lot to him.

He knew the name of the place where his former cell mate had gone back to work because he'd been there when Cortonby got a letter offering him his old job back and started boasting about it. In Bury, it was. Maybe Cortonby would help him sell Higgerson's car on the quiet in return for a share of the profits. Otherwise he'd just have to dump it.

When he got back home, he pulled the wallet out of Higgerson's jacket and told his wife what had happened.

They looked inside it and found over thirty pounds.

'All that money,' she whispered.

'Get the bag. We're leaving.'

She stared at him, looking terrified.

'It's our only chance to make a lot of money. I'm going whether you come with me or not. Make up your mind. We need to act quickly.'

She steadied herself with one hand on the table, as if she were feeling dizzy at the thought, then said, 'I'm coming with you.'

She had gone so pale, he asked, 'You all right, love?'

'Yes. No. Well, I've never broken the law before. It makes me feel strange even to think of it.'

'We won't break it again after this, but it's our big chance,' he said soothingly. 'We'll see my friend, find out how much money we can get for the car, then change our names and head off somewhere to start a new life.'

She ran upstairs to the bedroom and he followed her, watching her stuff a few more things into the battered suitcase, then fill a pillowcase with their best shoes and some other bits and pieces.

He stopped her getting anything else. 'That's it. We have to go straight away if we want to escape.'

'All right. You carry the case down, Jem.'

He did that, then glanced at her. She was looking better now, had got her colour back, was more like her usual brisk self. He loaded the things in the car, she grabbed their hats and coats from the hooks in the hall, and off they set, just like that. Excitement ran though him.

Even before they'd got through the town she said, 'Stop at the next place with a post office and we'll draw our money out. If we're going to change our names, we won't want to give ourselves away by where we draw money out.'

'Eh, I never thought of that.'

'Which is why you need me.' She was smiling now. 'It might work, Jem love. If it does, we'll go and live in Torquay.'

'What? Why there?'

'I've always liked the seaside and I've got an old auntie there. Auntie Mary. We'll go to her. She'll take us in till we can find a place of our own.'

'We can't tell her what we've done,' he warned.

'We can, you know. She's the black sheep of the family. Her husband made money really quickly one year. My dad always said they couldn't have done that honestly. When they moved away in the middle of the night without telling anyone, we were quite sure he was right.'

'We're not telling anyone where we've gone, either.'

She nodded agreement. 'My auntie didn't get in touch with anyone in the family till she sent me a birthday card with a postal order for five shillings in it three years later. It had her address on a bit of paper.'

'She's the one you send Christmas cards to.'

'Yes. And I've always kept the address. I was her favourite, you see, and I got on really well with her. I always wished she was my mother.'

He still didn't like the sound of it. 'That's all very well, but I thought it was going to be just the two of us from now on, with new names. She'll know who we are.'

'She'll not give us away and she'll help us build a new life. And I'm giving you notice now, Jem Stanley: after you've sold the car, I'm going to be the one who handles the money and does the planning. You're useless at it. Don't worry. I'll make us comfortable – and through honest hard work this time, without having to worry about the police knocking on the door. That's the only way I'm staying with you.'

He looked at the expression on her face and realised he might be getting away from Higgerson but he was still going to be ordered around. Maybe she was right, though. Maybe he should have listened to her more. She was a clever woman, he'd give her that. Probably as clever as Higgerson had been.

Had been! It amazed him to think of his employer as dead. Just went to show that you never know what might hit you next.

Well, as long as he got rid of the car without getting caught, he didn't really mind what they did from now on. It couldn't be worse than working for Higgerson. The man had got more and more unreasonable, and look where it'd led him: he'd lost his wife and now his life.

Jem grinned suddenly. He was doing better than his former employer, still had a wife who was a tidy armful in bed and liked her cuddles, so it wouldn't all be bad, would it?

And it'd be wonderful not to see Higgerson again. Jem had earned more money than ever before in his life working for him, but money wasn't everything.

Then a dreadful thought occurred to him. Was Higgerson definitely dead? They'd assumed it, but no one had seen the body.

If he wasn't, he'd come after them.

Oh, he must be dead, surely! The whole house had collapsed on him, hadn't it? It'd have crushed him as if he were a black beetle crawling out of the wall.

The firemen worked hard under Deemer and the fire chief's supervision, first putting up markers to warn people the area was dangerous, then dealing with the problem of whether any of the tenants from the two houses had been trapped and killed.

It was not at first known who exactly had lived there, and who was there to ask now, with Higgerson, the landlord, missing presumed dead? It was all a big muddle.

They heard someone calling for help and found two women and a baby trapped at the rear of one house. They were able to hand them over to a group of women from the local chapel to be cared for, not Vanner's chapel, whose members didn't seem to help anyone unless they belonged to the same congregation.

The other tenants came home one by one as the day passed, from shopping or work, or just simply visiting friends. All were the poorer sort of people, so were shocked and in despair at losing all their possessions.

In the end Sergeant Deemer and the fire chief commandeered the hall at the Birch End chapel. They sent out a call for blankets and clothing for those who no longer had a home by asking people to phone friends and pass on the message in any way they could about what people were now calling a disaster.

There was no chance of anyone retrieving their possessions, and it was completely out of the question to try to retrieve Higgerson's body.

'We need some miners,' the fire chief said thoughtfully as the afternoon wore on. 'They know about shoring up dangerous places and making tunnels.'

'I don't like leaving a dead body in there,' Deemer confessed. 'Even Higgerson's.'

'We don't have any choice.' The chief paused, then asked, 'Do you have any idea where his wife is? We ought to let her know. In fact, she ought to come back. She will presumably be the one who inherits, her or one of the sons?'

'Who knows what that sod has arranged? I have the phone number of a gentleman who's helping her.' He caught the look on the fire chief's face and added firmly, 'A very respectable gentleman, and I gather Mrs Higgerson has been staying with his daughter who is engaged to marry her older son. There's nothing immoral going on there, believe me.'

'Ah. I see. Rumour said otherwise.'

'Rumour is often wrong, especially when Higgerson is—*was!*— involved. Anyway, I'll phone this gentleman when I get back to the police station and he can find out what she wants to do. In the meantime we have people to house and feed, and a guard to be set on the property in case anyone is stupid enough to try to dig out possessions that might still have value. We don't want any more deaths.'

28

It was eight o'clock before the sergeant was able to pick up the phone and get through to the Tillett household. To his relief it was Mr Tillett who answered, so he explained the situation to him, impressed by the way the man quickly recovered from his shock and started being practical. He suggested the family discuss what had happened and get back to the sergeant in the morning to let him know what they wished to do about the situation.

'You'll have to call me quite early, I'm afraid, because there will be a lot to do tomorrow and I'll have to be out and about. Eight o'clock is the latest I dare leave it to get to the site of the disaster.'

'We'll discuss it and have an answer for you by seven o'clock in the morning about what we wish to do.'

'That'll be very helpful. Perhaps that poor lady can have some peace in her life now,' Deemer said gently, wanting to show that he understood the situation between her and Higgerson.

'I certainly hope so. She's suffered a lot. You're sure about him being dead?'

'I don't think there can be any doubt about that, Mr Tillett, even though we haven't seen the body yet. Three storeys of house came down on top of him, and it was a bare cellar without anywhere to shelter and only wooden support walls. No one could have survived that.'

'Thank goodness. All three of them need to feel safe again.'

★

Edmund Tillett went to join his family, who were starting their nightly ritual of a cup of cocoa and piece of cake as a prelude to going to bed.

His face must have betrayed the seriousness of the news he was bringing because they immediately stopped talking, put everything down, and waited for him to explain what the phone call had been about.

'I have to tell you, my dear Mrs Fennell, that there has been a serious accident in Rivenshaw and it is feared that your husband has been killed.' He gave them brief details, then waited.

'Can he really be dead?' Felix asked in a whisper, as if afraid of saying it too loudly.

'It seems highly likely.'

It was Kit who said bluntly what everyone must be thinking. 'We would all be free if he were. We could build decent lives for ourselves without always having to look over our shoulders and worrying about what he might try next.'

'And you won't have to be sent away from us now,' his mother said.

He beamed at her.

'And you can become a doctor.'

'Oh, Mum!' He gulped audibly.

'You have no good feelings whatsoever for him, do you?' Edmund asked gently.

'No, none. All we feel for him is hatred and loathing.' Kit looked across at his brother for confirmation and got an immediate nod, the same reaction from their mother.

'How can we like him?' Felix asked. 'We've both felt his fists times without number, and we've had years of seeing him thump Mum, and been helpless to stop him. I still get nightmares about him.' His voice came out choked as he said the last few words.

Lallie took over. 'We've all seen him lie, cheat, steal, and, we suspect, arrange for people to be killed or else have to flee from their homes and families to escape his wrath. No, we shan't grieve for him at all, Mr Tillett. The only good thing he's ever done for me has been to give me two wonderful sons.'

Both her sons went to sit on the arms of their mother's chair, each wrapping one arm around her shoulders and kissing the nearest cheek gently.

Tillett gave them a minute or two to pull themselves together, then said, 'I promised to phone Sergeant Deemer tomorrow morning at seven to let him know what we wish to do about the situation, so we'll need to decide on our first steps before then. Do you want to work that out now or get up very early in the morning?'

'I'd rather decide now,' Lallie said. 'I doubt I'll sleep well whatever we decide, but I'd like to have something definite to plan for while I'm wakeful. I'll start the discussion by saying I think I ought to go back to Rivenshaw straight away.'

'You're sure?'

'Who else is there to deal with things? I'm still his wife legally, and he doesn't have any other relatives that I know of, and no real friends. I've sometimes wondered if Higgerson is his real name and where he actually comes from.'

'To whom will he have left his property, do you think?'

'I have no idea. To one of the boys, probably. I hope so, anyway.'

They discussed it for an hour, but she remained adamant that it was her duty to return.

Edmund saw the relief on her face and those of her sons when he said that he was going with them. 'And what's more, I'll take John Joe and a couple of his men, just to make sure you three stay safe. If this is a trick, and he is still alive, he'll not get away with harming you.'

When Biff heard the news he hurried straight home to tell the others in Number 25.

'Higgerson's dead?' Arthur stared at him. 'Are you sure?'

'The houses at the corner of Clover Lane collapsed on him and he's buried under the rubble. He can't have survived that.'

'I shan't truly believe it until they find his body,' Gwynneth said bitterly. 'How that man has survived this long is a miracle, he's hurt so many people. It'd be just like him to crawl out alive.'

'Sergeant Deemer says it's not at all likely anyone could have survived.'

'His death would mean I felt safe in this house,' Arthur said. 'Maybe I wouldn't even have to hire guards.'

'We'll still have the problem of keeping Beatie safe from her grandmother,' Gwynneth pointed out.

He sighed. 'Yes. Poor little love.'

'I'll go out first thing tomorrow morning and find out what's happening,' Biff said thoughtfully.

Phil Becksley, who was on guard duty that night, beamed at them when he heard the news. 'I feel as if there is some justice in the world if Higgerson has been removed from it in such a way. Now, if someone would just deal with that horrible Mr Vanner, people round here could get their lives back again, without him haranguing them in the street.'

His eyes went to Beatie as he said this, and the others nodded slightly. Everyone in the household had quickly grown fond of the child and even in the short time she'd been with them she was looking healthier.

Biff waited till the little girl had gone to bed to tell them something else. 'I didn't want to say anything while Beatie was around, but I heard that Vanner had called on Mrs Hicks and come out of her house looking smug. No one seemed to know why, but you have to wonder what mischief he's planning now.'

'No doubt we'll find out. We must remain ready to get Beatie down into the tunnels at a minute's notice.'

★

Jack Webster watched the minister drive away, then went back to weeding at the back of the chapel. Eh, the place had been sadly neglected. He had got as far as a small shed, and then stopped. Mr Vanner had told him it was to be left strictly alone because it was used to store important religious articles.

As usual the arrogance with which he spoke had irritated Jack, and he wondered why the minister had made such a point of threatening him about the loss of his job if he tried to get into the shed. Usually sheds were used to store garden tools, and surely that's what this one had originally been intended for?

He had to keep the tools they'd provided for him in a small lean-to at the other side, with a cheap padlock on the door that a child could have broken apart.

Naturally he wondered what the minister was hiding inside the shed and decided to see if he could find out. Mr Peters might be interested. And what better time than the present? He'd get warning of Vanner's return when he heard the car engine.

The wood at the bottom of one rear corner had rotted, and he'd brought a few worn pieces of wood from home that would match that of the shed, with a vague idea of repairing it out of sheer pride in doing his job properly.

He always picked up pieces of wood if he saw them lying around, because he didn't like to see things rot when they could be saved, if only to use for firewood. If he opened up the corner of the shed and got caught inside, he could claim he'd only been trying to repair it.

And if the minister sacked him, he wouldn't care. He was finding this job tedious because no one at the small chapel talked to him, not even to pass the time of day. That was strange, against human nature as far as he was concerned. He was only staying at this job for Mr Peters' sake, because now that he'd used the judge's money to buy the field, he was itching to work full-time on preparing the ground.

Besides, with Higgerson killed, who would pay his wages for the other half of the working week, that was what he wanted to know? He'd have to sneak in a visit to Mr Peters and have a private discussion about that.

The rotten wood came away easily, and with a little care he managed only to pull away enough to allow him to crawl inside. It was a very tight fit.

To his amazement he found some weapons stored there, a pitiful collection of daggers and rather old-fashioned revolvers just lying in an old chest of drawers.

What on earth did a minister of religion want with those? And why so many?

Inspection of another drawer showed letters received and copies of letters sent in a folder that had been wrapped up in oiled paper, presumably to keep it from rotting in the damp or being nibbled by mice or insects. The package and folder didn't seem to have been touched for a week or two, judging by the lack of recent dates on the letters at the top of the pile.

Why hadn't Vanner kept these at home?

On an impulse he removed a few letters, choosing a selection of different dates and stuffing them into his inside waistcoat pocket where he kept a few coins and a clean handkerchief when he was working out of doors. He didn't have time to read them now and could always put them back if they weren't of interest. But he'd pass them on to Mr Peters and hope they'd show something that was worth following up.

What on earth was that pitiful excuse for a minister of religion up to anyway?

Webster crawled out and replaced the rotted wooden bits with pieces he could pull in and out of that corner as needed, standing back to admire his own handiwork.

29

The following day it seemed as if the main topic of conversation in every corner of the valley was Higgerson, and how to prove that he really was dead. An anxiety to be sure of that was displayed by people from all levels of society, and revealed how much he had been feared.

People strolled past the two adjacent houses that had collapsed, stopping to stare from the other side of the street. However, there was nothing to be seen except a huge pile of rubble and two workmen keeping watch. It didn't take much persuasion for people to stay clear, and the guards themselves stayed out in the middle of the street. No one wanted to be caught in further collapses.

Was Higgerson really under all that? many asked, and the guards simply shrugged. Who knew?

Later in the afternoon interest shifted to his house in Rivenshaw when a large luxurious car and a big van drew up at the front. Neighbours peeped out of windows, passers-by stopped to stare.

A strong-looking man got out of one of the vehicles and began to walk around the house on the garden path.

Those who had seen them arrive later confirmed that the man seemed to be checking that everything was in order and he was definitely not attempting to break in.

The housemaid had also been noticed staring out of the front window, but she made no attempt to open any of the outer doors, let alone ask him what he was doing.

Another car drew up in front of the house a few minutes later, and a man in a dark suit got out, carrying a worn brief-case and looking flustered.

Only then did John Joe get out of the big Ford and start to walk across to him, then sigh and wait as the man stopped and stared. He was used to this reaction from some people when they first saw his dark skin, and he merely waited patiently for the man to finish staring and move closer.

He held out his hand. 'Good afternoon, sir. I'm John Joe. I work for Mr Tillett and deal particularly with the safety of his family.'

The new arrival hesitated, then shook the hand briefly. 'Oh, er, yes. I'm Stanley Littleproud, Mr Higgerson's lawyer.'

John Joe turned and beckoned to Mr Tillett, who got out of the car and also introduced himself. He was accorded a much longer and visibly more enthusiastic handshake, which amused John Joe.

Mr Tillett took over. 'Shall we go inside and discuss the sit-uation, Mr Littleproud? Mrs Higgerson is waiting in the car to do that. I'm helping her at this difficult time because her older son is engaged to marry my daughter.'

John Joe watched the lawyer nod and glance towards the car as if reluctantly accepting the respectability of the lady. He didn't like the looks of the fellow, who was wearing a cheap suit in a rather loud pinstripe and a shirt that had been badly ironed.

When the lawyer rang the doorbell, the front door was opened by the elderly maid, who nodded to him. 'I'm so glad you've come, Mr Littleproud. I haven't known what to do today and that's the truth. I hardly slept a wink last night, with only me and cook in the house in case of trouble, because Mr Higgerson's man has disappeared as well.'

She obviously thought some respect was due to John Joe and Mr Tillett, so gave them an awkward jerk of the head.

However, when Lallie got out of the car, the maid darted forward, beaming. 'Oh, Mrs Higgerson, it's so nice to see you again!'

'Nice to see you too, Dora. Let's take everyone inside, shall we? It's a bit chilly to linger out here.'

Lallie led the way in and John Joe noticed how she braced herself and took a deep breath before she stepped across the threshhold. Her two sons followed the others into the house.

Two other men slipped out of the rear of the van and went across to speak to the chap who had originally done a circuit of the building. After a quick word with them, he went into the house as well, leaving the front door wide open. One of the men stood outside at the front, arms folded, expression watchful, while the other went round the house to the rear.

Inside the hall Lallie paused for a moment, feeling a strong urge to run out again, shuddering at being back here. She had hoped never to return, but felt it was her duty to be with her sons. She didn't know what her husband had done about a will, but was determined to guard her boys' inheritance to the best of her ability, because quite a large amount of the money had come from her family originally. She couldn't imagine that Gareth would have left anything to her, even so.

It took a while to get everyone except John Joe settled in the big sitting room, which had a forlorn air, as if it hadn't been used much lately.

Dora brought in a trolley with tea things on it.

Lallie made no attempt to speak to the sleazy-looking lawyer. She'd leave him to Mr Tillett.

When the maid had finally left them alone, John Joe came back to join them and said quietly, 'I did a quick check of the house and it seems unoccupied except for the two female servants. Definitely no sign of anyone who shouldn't be here. I've got three men on duty, so we should all be quite safe, day and night.'

'Thank you, John Joe. I don't know what we'd do without you.'

When Mr Tillett looked at Lallie to see whether she wanted to say anything, she waved one hand to indicate that he should continue to manage the proceedings.

'Mr Littleproud, perhaps we can start by finding out about Mr Higgerson's will? Since he seems to have been killed, it'll be up to the heir to manage things from now on.'

'He hasn't left a will, not with me at any rate, and he assured me that he had taken all business away from his previous lawyer. He, er, did say once that he wasn't old enough to need a will yet.'

'In which case, would the property go to Mrs Higgerson or to the eldest son?'

'I don't want it,' Lallie said. 'Let's carry on as if he'd left it to Felix.'

The lawyer looked from one to the other, shrugged, and said, 'As you wish, Mrs Higgerson. Actually, I think my client would have preferred that.'

'Has there been any word about retrieving Mr Higgerson's body?' Tillett asked.

'Not that I know of. The police say that since there seems no chance of him being still alive they don't want to risk anyone else's life searching the rubble.'

'I'll go up to the accident site with John Joe after we've finished our meeting with you. I'd like to see the situation for myself. As for your fees, I can guarantee you payment of any reasonable demand, on the family's behalf, if that makes you feel better about continuing to act as their lawyer.'

'Thank you. That would be entirely satisfactory, Mr Tillett.'

'I think we shall all stay in this house for a few days, given that Felix is likely to be the heir, if you see no problem with that, Mr Littleproud?'

'No problem at all, sir.'

There seemed little else to be done until there was confirmation of Higgerson's death, so Mr Tillett got rid of the lawyer, doing it so adroitly that Littleproud went away convinced that he had made a good impression and would be asked to continue working for the family.

Not until the lawyer had left the house and driven away did Mr Tillett turn back to the others. 'John Joe and I will go and see what's happening in Backshaw Moss, if you'll be all right here, Mrs Higgerson?'

'I suppose you have to call me that while we're in Rivenshaw.'

'Unfortunately, it would be prudent.'

She sighed. 'Very well.'

'I'll come with you, Mr Tillett, if Kit will stay with Mother,' Felix said abruptly.

'Two of the men will stay here as well. You'll be carefully guarded at all times, Mrs Higgerson.'

Lallie nodded acceptance of this.

When the others had left, she confessed to Kit how much she hated being here.

'So do I, Mother. I have no happy memories of my father, only of you trying to keep us safe.' He came across and gave her a hug and she clung to him for a moment or two.

She could do it, she told herself, stay here for her sons' sake.

But she wasn't coming back to live here permanently.

That same day, Vanner picked up Mrs Hicks in the early afternoon and drove her to visit Mr Forester, a very elderly gentleman who was a JP in a nearby village.

When Vanner told him why they were there, he looked at them with a disapproving expression. 'It's rather unusual for someone to ask for another JP to intervene. Are you sure that's necessary?'

'The situation is rather unusual, but it's the child's morals we're most concerned about if she lives with her grandfather.'

'You said you didn't know where she was.'

'We don't know for certain, have no proof, but who else can she be with? And to add to the worries, there's an elderly widow who has also been involved with the child, a Mrs Harte. The two of them were seen with this Arthur Chapman, so it's rather worrying, not to say possibly immoral, that they are cohabiting.'

Forester frowned and stared at them. 'Hmm. Well, all I can promise you is to visit my colleague, Mr Peters, and discuss the situation with him. He may know something you don't.'

'Oh dear. We'd hoped you'd help us to rescue the child straight away. Who knows what she's seeing going on in that house? On top of everything else, the grandfather has been a known drunkard for several years.'

When Mr Forester said nothing, he spoke more forcibly, 'Surely you can authorise me to go into the house and search for her? The members of my church would be prepared to come with me to force an entry.'

'I cannot give you the authority to do that without more proof than just your word. And as I told you, I need to discuss the matter with my colleague before I can do anything.'

He stood up. 'Let me show you out.'

That put Vanner in a very bad mood as he drove back. He dropped Mrs Hicks off at her home and went back to his own to have a think about how to proceed. Apart from anything else, it would make a useful little exercise for him in guiding his flock. He needed to get them used to acting forcefully, ready for when the time came to change Britain.

Sadly it seemed likely it'd be years before that happened, because things were not going as well here as in Germany. But Vanner was certain that reason would eventually prevail against these loose modern attitudes, and men like him would be needed to guide people back to proper ways – and especially to deal with women who had grown morally lax and abandoned their rightful place in society since the last war.

★

That evening Dennison Peters received a phone call from a colleague who lived just outside the valley, asking him if he could visit him the following morning to discuss an urgent matter.

'You'd be welcome any time, naturally. May I ask what is so urgent?' And if it was urgent, why was Forester waiting till the following day to deal with it? He asked that too, as tactfully as he could manage.

After some humming and hawing, Forester told him there had been a complaint that he'd been biased in carrying out his duties as defender of the law of the land.

'I beg your pardon?'

'I really don't care to discuss this over the phone. I'll see you about nine o'clock tomorrow morning.'

Dennison put the phone down, grimacing. Not his favourite colleague, Forester. Very old-fashioned in his ways. And who could have complained? He had never let bias skew the way he carried out his duties, never had and never would.

When the phone rang again, it was His Lordship, asking if there was any progress on recovering Higgerson's body.

'Not yet, I'm afraid. We're trying to find someone with mining experience to come and assess how to do it.'

'Well, I can help you there. I know just the chap, the one who was in charge of extending the tunnels. I'll bring him over to see the site tomorrow morning. We'll be at your place just after nine. Got to go! I've a meeting about to start.'

Dennison sighed. Typical of His Lordship. Well, he'd see if he could sort out Forester's business before His Lordship arrived tomorrow.

Trust Higgerson to continue making life difficult even after he'd died. It was going to be hard even to retrieve his body safely.

Dennison had heard that Mrs Higgerson had arrived in town and had meant to call on her first thing in the morning, but that would have to wait till later now.

★

In Derbyshire a small car chugged up a hill and Jem Stanley nodded to his wife. 'Nice little runner, this. We did well to get this and some money for Higgerson's car.'

'*You* did very well.'

He beamed at that compliment. 'We'll make a little holiday of the journey, shall we? Two or three days on the road. Stay at bed and breakfast places.'

'No, we won't.'

'Eh?'

'You're already trying to spend that money, Jem. Well, it's not enough to make us rich, so we have to eke out every penny and make it do the work of two.'

'But—'

'We're still going to Torquay, mind. I've always wanted to live there. It looks so lovely in the photos other people have shown me.'

He tried to take charge. 'Who got this money, eh? Me, that's who. So I'm the one who says what we do with it.'

'You are if you want to sleep alone and cook your own meals.'

She'd threatened this before, yes, and carried out her threat, too. He tried a softer approach. 'I was thinking of making this into the honeymoon we never had.'

'No, you weren't. And we're not doing it. Do you want to go into the poorhouse when you're old?'

'They don't call it the poorhouse these days.'

'I don't care what they call it. That's what it is. And we're going to do better for ourselves. So when you get tired, we'll stop and have a nap in the car. Yes, and when we get settled in Torquay, I'm going to learn to drive.'

'I am *not* going to be driven around by a woman.'

'Oh, yes, you are, Jem Stanley.'

Nothing he said would make her change her mind. She wouldn't even allow him one night in a bed and breakfast place.

He tried sulking. She slid down in the seat and said, 'If you're not talking to me, I think I'll have a nice little nap.'

'Aw, don't be like that.'

'I am like that. I nearly left you when you were locked up. Did you realise that?'

He was shocked rigid. 'You wouldn't do that to me!'

'I still will if you waste our big chance in life.' She patted her handbag. 'And I have the money here. You'll have to fight me to get it back at all because I know you'll only waste it.'

He stole a quick glance at her. She had *that look* on her face, worse than he'd ever seen it before. His heart sank. Not only had he exchanged one boss for another, but she could be every bit as determined as Higgerson. More determined, sometimes.

Only, he needed her to help him if they were going to start up a little business. She'd always been able to make one penny do the work of two. And he'd miss her in bed.

Another glance showed she'd folded her arms and was sitting rigidly in the passenger seat.

She turned to stare at him and he tried a smile, seeing her smile back after a moment or two. He started hoping he'd softened her a little.

'Our future will be good, Jem,' she said in that soft, come-to-bed voice he loved. 'Hard work, but a good life. I promise we'll do well.'

'You're a bossy bitch,' he said, resignation making him speak more softly now.

'But I stuck with you, didn't I? So you stick with me now.'

It took him a while to face the fact that he would have to do things her way. He couldn't bear the thought of losing her, and had never seen her this determined. 'You'd better make us a lot of money, then.'

'I shall do, love!'

She patted his knee and gave his thigh a squeeze that promised more later. He let her have her way. 'Oh, very well.'

Then something made him smile and he shared the joke with her. 'You'll be more fun in bed than my last boss, that's for sure.'

She grinned. 'Count on it.'

30

M r Forester arrived just before nine o'clock the following morning. Dennison answered the door himself and
took his visitor straight into the small sitting room.

'I'm expecting His Lordship to visit me shortly on rather
important business that's cropped up suddenly, so I hope
you'll forgive me for not offering you any refreshments and
getting straight down to your reason for coming here.'

'Of course.'

'Then I shall start by saying how outraged I am that anyone
should claim I have not applied the law properly and equitably
to a case.'

'Well, I must admit I was surprised myself. And I didn't take
to the fellow who made the complaint, only, well, I felt obliged
to investigate.' Forester paused to shake his head sadly.

'Go on.'

'The complaint is about how you dealt with a child who
had been kidnapped from her grandmother's home, a certain
Beatie Hicks, to be precise. It was alleged that you had shown
a bias in favour of the kidnapper and deliberately let him get
away with it.'

'That's ridiculous.'

'The person who spoke to me does not wish to be named,
so—'

'It's Mr Vanner, I suppose?'

'Ah. He was afraid you'd guess who had made the complaint and treat it less than seriously. How did you know?'

'Because I found out he'd been poking his nose into the upbringing of that particular child and been encouraging ill-treatment of her.'

'What? You're sure she was being treated badly when she was living with her grandmother?'

'Oh yes. And I can prove it. Vanner has very harsh rules for bringing up children, like depriving them of food if they displease him, or beating them viciously enough to draw blood.'

Forester looked at him in patent shock, so he nodded and carried on, 'Precisely. Not only is the grandmother totally in that man's thrall but I'll tell you frankly, he isn't like any minister of a church that I've ever met, whatever the so-called religious denomination. What did the grandmother actually say about it?'

His companion frowned. 'Well, now I come to think of it, she hardly said a word. He did nearly all the talking. What made you so certain the child had been ill-treated?'

'The woman who took her in when she ran away is a very decent person, a widow well respected in this town. She was so worried when she found signs of a severe beating, she called in the doctor to check her injuries. He was horrified at both the beating, which had drawn blood quite a few times, and how emaciated the child was. He said she'd been starved to a dangerous extent, and offered to bear witness to that in a court of law, if necessary.'

'*Starved*? But the grandmother was a well-dressed woman and, to put it bluntly, she shows every sign of eating rather too well.'

'Well, the child was not only dangerously thin but had that starveling look I've seen all too often among the children of the poorest families, the ones who haven't been eating properly for a good while. I felt this child must have acquired that look the same way.'

'I know what you mean by that, Dennison. My wife calls it the hunger look. We do our best to help some of the local families who're struggling, but there are so many. We've been living in sad times ever since the Great War, have we not?' He fell silent, then resumed with, 'Even so, I have to ask whether you know where this child is now?'

'No. I authorised one search of a house indicated by Vanner, but she wasn't there, nor was there any sign of her having been there, so I'm not going to allow invasion of every house because he has a grudge against its occupants.'

'Was it the grandfather's house you searched?'

'No. One nearby. While we searched it, however, Vanner's own men kept watch on the outside of the grandfather's place, and the child definitely wasn't sneaked into it. In fact, no one went in or out.'

'I think we ought probably to check that house now. Vanner told me about the man. He has a very bad reputation, for drunkenness among other things. If someone like that has the child, she really does need rescuing.'

'Chapman has mended his ways and been sober for nearly a year now. He only started drinking a couple or so years ago, after his wife and daughter both died tragically within a few months.'

'Ah. That's sad, of course, but a man on his own isn't usually awarded custody of a child of that age, whatever the other circumstances.'

'And I don't deem it safe to return her to the custody of a grandmother who starves and beats her.'

'Hmm. You have a point there. This Beatie must be put into an orphanage, then.'

'There are decent families here in the valley who would take her in.' Dennison hesitated, then said, 'I want your word not to tell anyone about what I'm going to say. It's a matter of national importance.'

Forester looked startled, but murmured a promise.

'This Vanner is one of the subjects of a secret inquiry in which His Lordship is involved, and I am assisting. In short, we have traitors among us, and Vanner is a suspect. Certain matters have to be kept secret for the time being, even from you, including where Beatie could possibly be and how she got there.'

'How on earth can His Lordship or our nation be involved in the disappearance of a child?'

The doorbell rang just then, and Dennison stood up to peep out of the window. 'Here he is, so you can ask him yourself. His main purpose in coming here today is to help us with the problem of retrieving Higgerson's body, but I'm sure he'll spare you some time to discuss the other matter. I'll let him in.'

Sadly, he'd known it wouldn't be easy to sort out what should be done with the child if he did find her, Dennison thought, which was why he hadn't pursued it.

His Lordship stood in the hall, listened to Dennison's whispered explanation of the other JP's presence, and rolled his eyes. 'That old fusspot.'

'You can't doubt his patriotism, though, unlike Vanner's.'

'No. I suppose not. Well, let's send my chap up to Backshaw Moss to make a start on working out how to get to the body. I'll talk to Forester, then we can both join Harris up there. The car can come back for us.'

In the sitting room His Lordship scowled across at the older man. 'Frankly, I wish you'd waited to raise this matter, Forester. Or mentioned it to me before you've been seen to come here. If the child is safe, we can surely leave her be for a few days?'

'She's nine, needs a woman's care.'

'Sounds to me as if a woman is already caring for her.'

'A woman who is living with a man to whom she isn't married is hardly a respectable guardian.'

'Nonetheless, the child is in no danger, which is what really counts, and this can surely wait a day or two?'

Forester frowned and fell silent, then shook his head. 'I'm afraid Vanner made it plain that if I don't intervene, he'll take the matter to a higher authority.'

'Who could be the very person we're trying to catch out. Leave it with me, then. If necessary I'll take the child home with me after I've finished today's tasks. I am surely respectable enough for your purposes?' He glared across at Forester as if daring him to disagree.

'Oh, definitely. Very well. I'll wait a day or two.'

When Forester had left, His Lordship said, 'If only we had proof about Vanner's involvement with these people further south. I'm wondering now whether he is using this alleged concern about the child to probe into our affairs, find out our weaknesses, and report them to his fellow fascists. What do you think?'

'I think it's surprising that he's making such a fuss, so perhaps there is something else behind the way he keeps causing trouble.'

'Hmm. Well, first things first. Let's go up to Backshaw Moss and see what my man Harris says about this house that's collapsed. If anyone can find a way into it, it's him.'

As they sat in the car, he said thoughtfully, 'I think nearly everyone in the valley would be glad to verify that Higgerson is dead. His fame, or rather infamy, has spread further afield too.'

Beatie let out a shriek when she saw a man she knew only too well walking slowly past the back of the house, studying it.

Both Gwynneth and her grandfather went running up to the bedroom and found her hiding under the bedcovers, shaking with terror and sobbing. 'He's found me. I saw him walk past, looking at the house.'

Arthur held her close. 'I won't let him anywhere near you, my little love. Can you check the back alley, Gwynneth?'

After staring out of the window for a few minutes, Gwynneth said quietly, 'Vanner is walking up and down at the back, deliberately making a noise and showing himself. I wonder what he's plotting now.'

Beatie let out another whimper of fear, so Gwynneth went across to sit on the edge of the bed next to them, and put her arm around the child. 'Let's plan for the worst, Arthur.'

'What do you suggest?'

'Beatie dear, try to calm down and listen to me: would you like to spend the day in the tunnels? You and I can make ourselves comfortable, and that horrible man will not be able to find us there, even if he breaks into the house.'

The child clutched Gwynneth tightly. 'Yes, please.'

'Then we need to collect all our clothes and other things and take them with us so that they can't find any sign of us being here if they come to search. Can you put all your toys and books into a pillowcase?'

'Is this necessary?' Arthur asked in a low voice as the child immediately began to gather her things.

'It won't hurt, and will make her feel safer, which is the main thing. And Arthur – I've been feeling anxious today, too, I don't know why. I think that accident has unsettled everyone in the valley. Better safe than sorry with such a precious possession, eh?' She nodded towards Beatie to show her meaning.

'Yes. I'll tell Biff and Phil what you're going to do.'

She walked to the bedroom door with him. 'I'll pack my own things and we'll leave most of them in the tunnels from now on, except for what we need each night. I don't fancy trying to sleep down there, though. It'd be too uncomfortable.'

He leaned closer to whisper, 'I hate to see that poor child so anxious. Is there anything else I can do for her? Or for you?'

'I don't think so. That Mrs Hicks has a lot to answer for. I'd like to starve the stupid woman for a while, see how she feels about going without food, not to mention whipping her bare legs till it draws blood, as she did to Beatie. I'm filled with rage every time I see those bruises and scabs, and the child never complains about the discomfort, though I see her change how she's sitting sometimes to ease it.'

'Well, she's looking a little plumper already, with some good food inside her.'

They took blankets and pillows into the tunnels with them, not to mention two packets of sandwiches wrapped in grease-proof paper and an old Tizer bottle full of water, plus another one of the special ginger beer made in the valley, for a treat later on.

Only after they'd made themselves comfortable on the steps in the tunnel did Beatie start to relax.

Arthur stayed a short time, then said he'd better return to his woodworking in case anyone came to the house.

After he'd gone, Beatie sat quietly, twice asking if Gwynneth was quite sure her grandmother couldn't find them here. Then she fell asleep suddenly with her head on her companion's lap.

Tears she'd held back until now began to trickle down Gwynneth's face at the thought of what had been done to this little girl for the past few months. She couldn't abide cruelty to man or beast. If she had to leave her family and run away to Australia to save Beatie, she would. They were adults and could manage on their own, but this vulnerable child couldn't.

Those dreadful people were not getting their hands on her again, not as long as Gwynneth had breath in her body.

And she knew Arthur felt the same. Eh, he was a gentle, lovely man.

A smile gradually replaced the tears at the thought of him and the easy conversations they'd had.

The chauffeur opened the door of the big limousine, and His Lordship and Dennison got out.

Harris was standing at the front of the collapsed buildings, and turned to call that he'd be with them in a couple of minutes. He and another man were still poking around in the remains of the lower part of the front doorway and the inner wall beyond it, some of which was still left and was helping hold back the tide of debris.

While they waited, the two men studied the rubble where houses had previously stood.

'I've never seen anything like this,' Dennison said. 'It must have been very badly built in the first place. We're lucky it happened at a time when most of the tenants were out at work or shopping, so only one person got killed.'

'And that's a chap no one will miss,' His Lordship added quietly.

Harris clapped the man he was talking to on the back and came across to join them. 'I'll have to come back tomorrow with the proper equipment to dig a tunnel down to the cellar where they think Higgerson was trapped, my lord. You can be sure I'll make everything safe as I do that.'

'But you'll be able to get down there?'

'Oh, yes. It'll be very straightforward, actually, once we have the right equipment and some very solid planking and metal struts that chap is going to provide. We'll go carefully, testing each area as we move forward till we find where the body is. It's my guess he'll be as far as he could get from the stairs. They must have been very poorly constructed stairs or they'd have helped hold back more of the wall.'

'Well, it's a relief that you can do it. Once the body has been retrieved, can you fill it in and make the whole area safe?'

Harris nodded and looked at Dennison. 'I don't suppose you know what the heir wants to do with the site afterwards, sir, whether he'll build again or leave the ground bare? They could do with a few open spaces around here. Terrible place, this Backshaw Moss, isn't it?'

They all stared in disgust at the tumbledown dwellings crammed against one another, and the ragged people who slouched past occasionally.

'The council is trying to get rid of the worst slums little by little,' Dennison said. 'This will give them added impetus and support from the ratepayers, I'm sure.'

'Have you heard officially who the heir is?' His Lordship asked.

'No. It'll be one of Higgerson's sons surely. But it'll take time to work out what to do.'

'So I'll just make it safe for the time being,' Harris said. 'We don't want any urchins daring one another to go inside and getting buried by miniature landslides of debris.'

His companions shuddered at the thought.

'We'd better have an undertaker standing by to remove the body, which might look a mess,' he went on. 'It'll probably be retrieved the day after tomorrow at a guess. This will be quite a short, shallow tunnel, compared to the mine tunnels I've worked on.'

'I'll speak to the family and help them arrange the under-taker,' Dennison offered.

'I'll be ready to leave when you are, then.' Harris left them and got into the big car.

After a pause Dennison asked, 'Are you really taking the child home with you tonight, Your Lordship?'

'Of course not. Neither of us have been able to find her, have we? I only said that to keep Forester at bay for a day or two. I can take her to my place if it's absolutely necessary, but she's with people she knows, who care about her from the sounds of it, so I'd rather leave her with them for the time being. Don't worry, I shan't let her grandmother have her again.'

He winked at Dennison. 'It's my guess that they've hidden her in the tunnels, which gives us a valid excuse for not revealing where she is.'

'That'd be my guess too.'

'If she can bear to stay there, we may have time to get the proof we need and sort out that damned traitor.'

'Amen to that. More than one traitor, if we're lucky.'

'I'll be off, then.' His Lordship joined Harris in the car and it left at once.

Dennison went to see Arthur before he returned home.

'Let's stand at the front door to talk. I gather Vanner has watchers keeping an eye on this place day and night.'

'So my neighbours have told me.'

'Well, we can be seen by anyone who passes, so they'll know I've not spoken to anyone except you, and haven't been inside to see the child. No one will be able to eavesdrop if we stay here.'

'Fine by me.'

'One of the things I want to suggest is that you employ both your guards for the next few nights. Vanner may get desperate.'

'Isn't there any news at all from those people in the Midlands who're hunting for traitors?'

'I'm afraid not.'

Dennison worried all the way home about what they'd do if proof of Vanner's perfidy wasn't found.

When Peters got back he found Jack Webster waiting for him in the kitchen, and sighed. He'd been looking forward to putting his feet up for an hour or so, hoping to indulge in a refreshing nap because he hadn't slept at all well last night.

However, the man had been doing him a favour working as a gardener for two unpleasant people, so it was only fair to find out what he wanted.

Webster stood up as he went into the kitchen.

'Have you been waiting long?'

'A couple of hours, Mr Peters. But your cook has kindly furnished me with cups of tea and something to eat. Best fruit cake I ever tasted it was, too!'

The cook flushed and tried not to look gratified. Dennison managed to hold back a smile till he'd taken Webster up to the morning room. All the good gardeners he'd ever known had made friends with the cook or lady of the house where they were working, and usually displayed hearty appetites.

'Do sit down. I presume there's some news?'

'There may be. I broke into the shed behind that so-called church and found some weapons.'

'*What?*'

'Surprised me too, sir. Rubbishy old stuff, guns mostly from the Great War, if not earlier, but they'd still kill you.'

'What exactly did you find?'

'Daggers, guns, and some letters. I took a few out of the bundle in case they were of interest, but I doubt he'd notice they've gone because there were quite a few. I can't read that fancy handwriting very well, so I brought them to you.'

He pulled them out of his inner pocket. 'Oops! I'm afraid they got a bit crumpled.'

'Never mind that. Would you give me a few minutes to read them?'

'All right if I glance at your newspaper while I wait, sir?'

'Of course.'

Ten minutes later, after scanning them quickly, Dennison looked across at Webster. 'You've more than repaid me with these for helping you buy that field.'

'I have?' Webster tried in vain to hide his pleasure at this compliment.

'Yes. You don't owe me a penny. In fact it's I who owe you my deepest gratitude.' And so did His Lordship and the whole county, but he couldn't tell Webster that.

'Can I ask what's in them, sir?'

'I'd rather keep that to myself. It's important, but you're better off not getting involved.'

Webster shrugged. 'All right. Good to know it's useful, though.'

'You'll be working at Higgerson's house tomorrow, won't you?'

'I would normally, sir, only I wondered if you'd want me to go there any longer, seeing as he's dead? I'm itching to get started on my field.'

'Bear with me a little longer, if you don't mind. Higgerson's wife and sons will probably be staying there, and they'll want the gardens kept up to scratch. I'm more concerned to keep them safe. You can help keep an eye on them.'

Webster looked puzzled. 'Will Vanner be likely to harm them as well? He's been a bit chancy-like lately. Flies off the handle for nothing. Even the folk who worship here seem surprised by his behaviour.'

'I want to make sure he doesn't hurt anyone, so it would still be good to have you there. In my opinion he is unhinged and may lash out at anyone he feels threatened by. You could just carry on as normal in the garden there for the next day or two and leave the rest to me, but keep your eyes open. I'll make sure you're paid for any work you do.'

'Very well, Mr Peters.'

'Good man.'

Once Webster had gone, Dennison picked up the telephone, intending to leave a message for His Lordship to call him as soon as he got home, then put it down again with a sigh. This was too important, so he'd better not use the phone. An operator or someone on a party line could easily eavesdrop and leak information. This discovery needed to be kept very quiet indeed till their allies further south worked out how best to use the information to identify the traitors.

His Lordship had a special phone line set up at his home, one on which the operator was a special government official not likely to share what she heard with anyone except the authorities.

Talk about treading delicately. Dennison put on his outdoor clothes again and set off to see His Lordship, which meant at least an hour's driving each way.

At least His Lordship had returned home by then, so there was no need to hang around waiting. The information pleased him just as much as Dennison had expected, so it had been well worth coming here. He listened as his host immediately phoned his contact in the Midlands.

The man asked to speak to Dennison directly, but he couldn't give him all the details he wanted. Only Webster would be able to do that. But Dennison could guarantee Webster's honesty at least, and the truth of what he had been able to share.

'You've done well and so has your man.'

His Lordship took over the phone again, holding it between them so that Dennison could listen in.

'We'll get back to you within a few hours, once we work out how best to deal with this Vanner fellow. It's clear that he's a traitor. We can do without fanatics of any sort in this country, especially those who're fascists as well. He sounds to me to be – well, almost deranged. Better locked away in prison on all counts, I should think.'

'I hope no one gets hurt sorting this problem out.'

'I hope *he* gets hurt.'

'They wouldn't do anything to Vanner, would they?' Dennison muttered after the call ended.

His Lordship shrugged and gave him a very direct stare. 'They'll do what they have to. We weren't prepared for a big war last time. If that Hitler chap starts another one, some of us will be a lot better prepared this time. And that doesn't mean leaving proven traitors free to do more harm.'

Dennison nodded reluctantly.

Later that afternoon Arthur left Biff in charge and went down into the secret tunnels on the excuse of taking Gwynneth a big, enamel mug of tea. In reality he simply wanted to see her, be with her. Each time they chatted, he felt they were growing closer.

She looked up, her face sharp with anxiety, as the secret door slid open, relaxing visibly when she saw him.

He clambered down and saw that Beatie was asleep beside her, so handed her the mug and went back to close the cellar door again.

There was just enough light from the single candle for him to see her, and barely enough room for him to sit down on the step next to her unless he put his arm round her shoulders. Which he was happy to do – and which didn't meet with any protests.

'I thought you might like some company as well as a drink of nice hot tea, my lovely lass.'

She nestled against him. 'I want some company most of all, especially when it's you, Arthur love. It's seemed a tediously long day down here.'

Her face was so close to his he couldn't resist kissing her cheek, only she turned her head so he kissed her lips instead. Which he didn't mind at all. And she didn't seem to mind it, either, because she gave as good as she got, and it was an extremely satisfying kiss.

In fact, it felt so wonderful that as he caught his breath again, he risked saying what was in his heart. 'I love you, Gwynneth.'

'I love you too, Arthur.'

'I'm glad you're not acting coy, because I can't pretend any longer.'

'We're too old to waste time pretending, don't you think?'

'Yes. And old enough to realise when something is right for us.'

They kissed again, after which they simply sat there, with his arm round her shoulders and her hand in his, chatting intermittently, falling silent just as comfortably, close in every way that mattered.

When he started feeling that his joints were growing a little stiff, as older bodies do, he stretched carefully and slowly, noticing that she did the same.

He quoted one of his favourite pieces of poetry, not remembering where he'd found it or who had written it, or even if he'd quoted the words accurately, only that he'd found its basic idea so very true of this time of life. 'Old age gives no quarter, though spears spare us.'

'I like that. And it's so right. Even if you don't always show your age, you feel it sometimes.'

'You don't show your age, lass. You're as bonny now as you must have been when you were younger.'

She chuckled. 'Your eyesight is failing you.'

'No, it's not. I've heard other men say you're a good-looking woman.'

Her smile was glorious. 'I don't care about what other men think, just you.'

They sat down again and continued to chat quietly. After a while they inevitably discussed the child. 'How has Beatie been?'

'Fretting. She's absolutely terrified of being sent back to her grandmother.'

'Is it any wonder? I'm terrified of what I might do if I ever got my hands on Mrs Hicks. How she produced a son as nice as my daughter's husband, I'll never know.'

'Perhaps him getting killed soured her. It made even you turn to alcohol, losing your wife and daughter did.'

He scowled. 'Aye. I'm ashamed of that, and I promise you I'll never do that again. I don't touch the stuff now, as I told you, and I never shall. But though her loss might have made Mrs Hicks worse, she was always sharp-tongued. I overheard her tell someone once how badly her son had married and that we were a useless family.'

'How disloyal of her! I'm so lucky that my two older sons have married wonderful women. I think my youngest is married to his books. I can't believe Lucas has gone off to university. I thought only rich people did that.'

'He must be very clever.'

'He is.'

'But he still loves you.'

She gave him another of her glorious smiles. 'They all seem to, and I certainly love them. They'll love you and your grand-daughter too, Arthur. Unreservedly. Never doubt that. We don't ration love in our family.'

After a while she began yawning and he found himself joining in, so he took his leave. 'Are you sleeping down here tonight?'

'I didn't want to, but she's so upset maybe I'd better. It'd be a shame to wake her.'

'Instead of which you'll be uncomfortable and won't sleep well.'

'I'll survive.'

'I'll light a fresh candle for you before I leave. That one's got less than an inch to burn. Do you need anything else to eat?'

'No, thank you. But the warm tea was lovely. We brought plenty of sandwiches and cake. I'm not very hungry, actually.

Thanks for sorting out the candle, though. I'm not afraid of the dark, but Beatie is, poor dear.'

'Can I kiss you again before I leave?'

'I've been hoping you would.'

Such loving moments are beautiful, Gwynneth thought as the door to the cellar closed behind him. Knowing you're loved helps see you through the bad times and makes the good ones even happier.

As she remembered the way he'd said he loved her and how tender the expression on his face had been, she smiled all the way into sleep.

31

The phone rang in the middle of the night and Dennison Peters jerked awake. 'I'll answer it,' he called as he heard his sister stir.

He ran downstairs and picked up the telephone receiver from the hall table. 'Yes?'

'I'm sorry to disturb you, but can you come over straight away. And bring our mutual friend.'

'Yes, of course.'

As the receiver was put down at the other end, he grimaced at the thought of another hour's drive to His Lordship's house. It must be important, though.

He got dressed hurriedly and telephoned Sergeant Deemer. It rang a few times, then a sleepy voice said, 'Police station.'

'It's me. I'm coming across to take you to see our mutual friend. Group business.'

'I'll be ready.'

When he got to the house at the rear of the station Sergeant Deemer must have been watching for him because he came straight out and got into the car.

'Something wrong, Dennison?'

'His Lordship wants to see us. But before we set off, I'm wondering if I've been followed here. I'm sure I saw the glow from car headlights above the roofs of some houses further up the hill.'

'We can go to a place I know and get rid of any followers there. I set it up for myself years ago and use it once in a while.

It'd be better if I do the driving, and we'll switch off the head-lights.'

They changed places and Deemer drove them a few streets, then stopped at the rear of a business whose owner he knew. 'I've got a key. He doesn't mind me going through his ware-house. If we go in by this delivery entrance, you'll find the place is bigger than it appears and we can use a different exit into another street. I'm afraid you'll have to hop in and out, opening and shutting doors. I'm not as spry as I used to be. Good thing there's a three-quarter moon tonight and not much cloud, eh?'

As they drove away from the warehouse by an exit in another street without using the headlights, Deemer stayed at the wheel, driving slowly and trying not to let the car engine make more noise than necessary. After a while he stopped and switched the engine off. They sat in the car with the windows down, listening for about ten minutes. At first they could hear a car driving to and fro along the streets lower down the slight slope, presumably looking for them, but the noise gradually faded away into the distance.

Deemer returned the task of driving to Dennison and they continued out of town, still not using the headlights.

'I hope the information you received gets that chap out of my hair for good,' the sergeant said at one stage. 'And soon. Minister of religion indeed! He's nothing like a real clergyman. He's a lunatic who is basing his life on fixed ideas of what he thinks the world should be like. He wants it run by superior folk like himself and is trying to force others towards that way of living, hence the group of lads he's training.'

Dennison murmured his agreement. 'It's not likely he'll suc-ceed, but he's being encouraged by a bunch of more senior traitors, probably fascists who're using him and other similar little groups as a distraction to cause trouble for the author-ities. Well, that's how I see it, anyway. They didn't succeed in their big push for power in this country, so they're trying to edge forward, relying on Hitler to cause more trouble for our country in the future.'

When they arrived, they saw that His Lordship had the lights on in a room at one side of his large, sprawling family home. They took that as a signal to park nearby and as they got out of the car they saw one of the French windows open, so went straight through it into the library.

His Lordship beamed at Dennison. 'You and your man have done very well, Peters, very well indeed. That information couldn't have been more timely. This is how our friends in the Midlands want us to deal with it . . .'

They stayed for half an hour, first discussing the details, then drinking a glass of excellent port each, before setting off back to Rivenshaw.

'Good man, Webster,' Deemer said. 'We could do with more chaps like him in the world, instead of wicked fools like Vanner. If Webster hadn't taken the initiative, you and I would still be fumbling around for evidence.'

The following morning Harris arrived in Backshaw Moss at seven o'clock in a big lorry, and three men got out of the back and began to unload tools. They immediately followed his directions and started work on the remains of the two houses, taking it in turns to dig and tip the debris from one area into the back of the lorry till he said to stop and brace the walls of the narrow tunnel they were making before allowing them to continue.

People came to watch at first, but they didn't linger for long because there wasn't much to see after the first brief push. Most of the digging was being done inside the newly-created opening.

Harris took great care with the panels and carefully braced them with metal struts.

At one stage a child's rag doll emerged whole from the debris and was perched outside further along the pavement as if overseeing the work.

When a child edged towards it, hand outstretched, one of the local men keeping folk away shouted, 'Is it yours?'

'No. It's my cousin Patsy's doll.'

'Then leave it alone for Patsy and her mum or dad to claim.' His voice softened as he added, 'Why don't you go and tell your cousin about the doll?'

She backed away, scowling. 'Why should I? She never lets me play with it.'

'If you don't care about helping others, I don't have the time to speak to you.' He gave the mother a dirty look and she glared at him as she dragged her sobbing daughter away.

When John Joe turned up just before noon with an urn of tea and a tray of meat pies for the diggers, they fell on them hungrily.

'Eh, that's good,' one said, wiping his mucky sleeve across his lips. 'Thanks, lad.'

'I try to help folk when I can.'

'Aye. Decent folk do. That chap whose body they're searching for was a thief and worse, from what I hear.'

'Far worse.'

It was harder going during the afternoon, and progress was slower. At intervals Harris got out a long thin piece of metal and poked it gently into the loosely packed debris before they put up more panels, trying to see whether there was anything softer and more solid that might be a body. But there was nothing.

By teatime the new tunnel had gone down part way into the cellar. They hadn't managed to find the body yet, and Harris wasn't surprised. He'd always reckoned it must be at the far side of the new part. He set guards for the night, and watch lanterns were placed on the street in front of the entrance to keep cars and pedestrians away from the mess of rubble.

Then he and his men got directions to the tip so that they could dump the debris from the back of their lorry, after which they left for the lodgings His Lordship had booked them into.

There, a hearty meal was waiting for them and they followed that with a drink at the pub, just one pint of beer each.

'I reckon we'll find the body tomorrow,' one man said as they strolled back to the lodgings.

'Morning or afternoon?' another asked.

They all guessed what time it'd be found, winner to buy the drinks, then sought their beds.

Harris smiled as he lay down in his room. He was the one who'd be buying the drinks tomorrow, whoever had guessed correctly. Good lads, they were, hard workers, and they'd more than earn a bit of encouragement.

Lallie chose not to use her former bedroom, but she slept badly even in a single bed in another room, and felt restless when she woke.

Since she could do nothing until her husband's body was found, she spent the first morning sorting through the clothes she'd had to leave behind when she ran away. To her surprise they were all still there in what had been her bedroom.

She'd have thought Gareth would have burned them or given them away. Then she realised he'd probably expected to get her back again, one way or the other, and shuddered even to think of that.

Mr Tillett came to find her when luncheon was ready.

She was sitting on the bed, staring into space, and jerked in shock when he spoke to her.

'How are you?'

'A bit upset at the horrible memories this house brings. I know coming back was the right thing to do, but I hate it here.'

'I'm not surprised, Mrs – oh, hell, now that you're a widow, may I call you Lallie when it's just the family?'

'I'd like that . . . Edmund. Only we're not sure yet that I am a widow, are we?'

He saw the traces of tears on her cheeks and stretched out one hand to wipe the moisture away with his fingertips. 'It's been hard.'

'What has?'

'Not saying how fond I've grown of you.'

'Oh.' She blushed a rosy pink.

'Can I say it now? Or are you too upset?'

'I'm not upset at all about Gareth, if that's what you mean. I feel as if his death will take a huge burden from my shoulders. He can't be alive, can he?'

'I doubt anyone could be alive in those circumstances, but if the impossible has happened, I'll get you away, I promise.' He took her hand in his and raised it to his lips.

She gasped but didn't pull away. 'We'd better be careful.'

'I don't want to be careful.'

'Nor do I.'

He sighed. 'But I don't want to destroy your reputation. When he's buried and his heir has taken over the business, will you marry me and come back to Wiltshire with me permanently?'

'Oh, yes. I'd like that very much. As long as Felix is safe here I shan't stay in Rivenshaw. Gareth tainted it for me even more than I'd expected.'

'Well, your Felix has a good head on his shoulders, so you can leave him to look after things. Felix has talked to me about righting some of the wrongs his father inflicted on people. If he and my lass marry quickly, she'll be able to help him do that. She has a good business head on her shoulders, my Eleanor does. I've had her working with me for years and not fiddling around with housework and embroidery.'

'I've noticed how capable and intelligent she is. And it's wonderful to see how much they love one another.'

'And we can make sure that Kit can go to university and become a doctor. I think he'll make a good one.' He gave her one of his lovely smiles. 'You won't make me wait too long to set our own lives in order, will you, Lallie? I'm an impatient chap when I want something.'

'Of course not. I have years of misery to make up for. Only I don't want a fancy wedding, if you don't mind. I had that last time.'

'Just the family will suit me.'

The smile she gave him was brilliant, and the warm feeling and joy it left behind lingered in his heart for the rest of the tediously long day.

The next morning they found Higgerson's body and it was Harris who'd made the closest guess. The men who dug it out shuddered at the expression on the dead man's face.

'He died in a rage, this one did,' one said in a near whisper.

'People hereabouts have nothing good to say about him. You should hear the things they mutter when they come to look at what we're doing. Anyway, that's not really our business. I'd better tell Mr Harris.' He yelled up the narrow tunnel that they'd found the body.

'Bring it out, then. What are you waiting for?'

When they'd hauled it up, he too stared at the dead face and shook his head. 'Nasty chap. You can often see it in their faces after they've died when they've been bad 'uns. Put him over there and cover him with that old tarpaulin. I'll send someone to phone for the undertaker and the police, too, just to check things out.'

'Do we go on digging, or is that all you want done down there, Mr Harris?'

'I think that's all. No one else is missing, and anyway, we're near the end of the recent excavations they stupidly made. The family have already said to fill in the hole once we find him. They're not sure what they want to do with the land, but they definitely don't want that cellar leaving.'

He stretched, glad not to be going down there again. A bad feeling seemed to linger in the excavation. 'I'll go and make the phone calls from the village shop in Birch End.'

'The sooner they take that body away, the happier I'll feel,' one man muttered after he'd left. 'Fair gave me the shivers, it did, the look on his face.'

When the phone rang, Mr Tillett answered it, then went to find the others. 'They've found his body and they've sent for the undertaker and Sergeant Deemer. I think we should let Mr Peters have a look at the body as well, so that he can confirm it was really him if it's ever necessary. Then you can arrange a funeral.'

'We're not having a funeral, just a burial,' Felix said quietly. 'None of us want any fuss made. All we wanted was to be certain he was dead.'

'Are you sure you won't regret that? He was your father, after all.'

His voice was harsh. 'Quite certain, Mr Tillett. He wasn't much of a father.'

His mother laid one hand on his shoulder. 'Don't let him sour the rest of your life, dear.'

'You're more forgiving than I can ever be.'

'I don't forgive him, but I shan't let thoughts of him spoil the rest of my life. You can't change the past, only take advantage of what the future brings.' Her eyes went to Tillett and the way he smiled at her made Felix stare in surprise. Eleanor had said her father was fond of his mother, but he hadn't realised how fond.

'If it's all right with you,' Tillett said, 'I'll set John Joe to make the arrangements for a quiet, speedy burial. He's the best assistant I've ever had. I'm going to give him a share of the company officially when we get back to Wiltshire. He's more than earned it.'

'It'll be good if he can arrange the burial. I don't want anything to do with it. I think I'll go and walk round the garden for a while, if you don't mind. I need some fresh air.'

She held up one hand. 'On my own, please, Edmund. It'll be so wonderful to be outside and not afraid, and it looks like being sunny all day, even if the weather is still cool.'

Tillett waited till she'd gone outside to ask Felix and Kit if she'd be all right.

'She'll be fine. She loves being out of doors. That garden was her main refuge from *him*. She designed it, you know. She's probably saying goodbye to it.'

They watched through the window as she stopped to chat to Jack Webster and let him show her some groups of plants.

Already she was looking younger, more alive, wearing her freedom like a warm cloak.

32

Sergeant Deemer sent a message to the two lads who'd helped him when he'd been attacked and with whom he'd kept in touch. He asked them to come secretly to the back door of his house.

When they arrived, his wife let them in and handed them a big bun each, which brought beaming smiles to their rather gaunt faces. She then went across to the police station to tell her husband that Alan and Griff had arrived.

'Just going home for my tea,' he called out to Mike, who was on duty at the desk, then he strolled across to his house.

The lads were both sporting the shirt and belt that said they were members of Vanner's squad.

'How's it going with that lot?' he asked.

Alan grimaced. 'I'd only do this for you, Sarge. Vanner's a nasty chap. Makes up for being short by shouting loudly, whether it's needed or not, and loves to march us up and down. If it weren't for the shirts and the food he provides each time we meet, not many lads would have stayed in his stupid squad.'

'Well, it's been very useful for me to have you two telling me what's going on and when you'll be holding meetings, so I'm grateful to you for putting up with it.'

They shrugged. 'It's something to do, at least.'

'I want you to tell him you saw two strangers arrive at this house, a younger one with red hair and an older man who's bald with just a bit of grey hair around the edges of his skull.'

They looked surprised but repeated what he'd said.

'And tell him you managed to eavesdrop and hear that I'm meeting them and someone else tonight at the Methodist chapel hall in Birch End around midnight.'

'Will he believe that, Sarge? You've never met anyone before at midnight that I've heard.'

'That's why he'll believe it. It's going to sound like something special. And your tale will be confirmed when he sees someone with red hair during the day coming and going at the police station. Got all that?'

They nodded, accepted his sixpenny bits, and slipped out again.

He went to find his senior constable again and told Mike to drive over to His Lordship's house and tell him everything was being arranged in the way their friends from the Midlands wanted.

'I'll have to be careful how I drive out of town,' Mike said. 'Maybe take a detour or two to lose anyone who's trying to follow me.'

'On the contrary, you are to let them follow you and pretend not to notice.'

'Really?'

'Yes. Be ready to come on duty again later tonight, and you don't want anyone to follow you then. We'll get to the hall well before midnight.'

When Mike had left, Deemer called Cliff in. 'I want you to call on some of our special constables this afternoon.' He named them and got Cliff to repeat the list and the message without writing it down.

'Vanner's men will try to follow you, so once you're part way to the first place, give the followers the slip by going through Mr Willcox's shop. I'll warn him you're coming, and take those old clothes you keep at the station for doing mucky jobs with you. You can change into them there and leave your uniform with him for when you get back.'

'Good chap, Mr Willcox. Folk are saying he'll be the next mayor.'

'I hope so. He'll get things done, especially sorting out those slums in Backshaw Moss. He's got a bee in his bonnet about them now.'

The next people Deemer called on were Higgerson's wife and sons, just to keep in touch and also to look as if he was doing his normal sort of work.

Vanner went to call on Mrs Hicks to see if she'd heard anything more about the child, but she hadn't.

'We'll find a way to get her back for you. She's the only close family you have left now, and you'll want to train her to do things your way, won't you?'

She stared mournfully at him. 'I'm beginning to wonder if it's worth it, Mr Vanner. She was always a naughty, disobedient child, and I'm not as young as I was. I get tired more easily.'

'Oh, it is worth it, Mrs Hicks, believe me it is. You must hold firm to our belief in where the future of our country lies.'

He had a thought. In one sense tonight was do or die for him, and if things went wrong he could at least make sure the child was taken away from those people. Not that he thought anything would go wrong, because he'd made careful plans, but he always liked to be prepared for every possible outcome. It gave him confidence.

'If anything happens to me, you must be sure not to leave that child in Arthur Chapman's keeping, even if he does have a bigger house than you.'

That sparked the ongoing anger in her, that the man she hated and despised should have inherited such a large house.

'I won't let him keep her,' she said. 'Definitely not. I know my duty.'

★

When the men sent from the Midlands arrived in Rivenshaw, Sergeant Deemer met them openly at the station in the town centre and made no attempt to hide their presence, walking back to the police station with them.

Then he got out the revolver he kept in a special locked cabinet in his office at the station, in preparation for tonight's trap. Just in case things went wrong. He didn't like using a gun, but they might be armed, from what Jack Webster had found in the shed.

All of those coming with him tonight were grimly determined to catch Vanner out. They'd already got a name that they thought was his main contact in London from the few letters Webster had stolen, but hoped to get more definite proof tonight.

As dusk fell, they prepared for the visit to Birch End and drove off, pretending to take care not to be followed, but allowing the small, shabby Austin 7 to stay behind them even after the Morris that was also following them turned off the road.

Deemer produced a key to the Methodist hall, and the three men slipped inside, finding Mike already there waiting for them. He didn't say anything, but pointed to the small room where religious equipment was stored.

They all grinned, since Deemer had been informed by telephone that someone had gone into the hall much earlier, and his watchers had later informed him that no one had come out, he'd guessed that Vanner had planted someone there.

Alan and Griff were very good at following people and had been thrilled to be involved in setting this trap.

The men who'd come with him went across to drag the man out of the cupboard in the room Mike had indicated. He struggled in vain against three men well trained in personal combat, and they managed to muffle his attempts to yell for help. They smiled as they tied him up and gagged him.

'We have other plans for tonight,' one of them said to him. 'Let's put you away again. You'll be nice and warm in that cupboard.'

He could only glare back at them as they stuffed him into it again.

'Parcel to be retrieved later,' one of them said, and they all laughed.

Knowing his man was already positioned inside the hall and would have let the others in, Vanner watched with a sneering smile as Deemer and the two newcomers to the town arrived there.

He walked briskly across to the shed near his own church and unlocked the door. Locking it carefully once he was inside, he took out one of the guns and caressed it lovingly. He'd loaded it carefully this afternoon and was now about to put the hours of practice he'd put in over the years to good use.

When he came out again, with the gun inside his overcoat pocket, he went to the Methodist hall where he intended to prove himself fit to play a more senior role in the ongoing preparations for a time when order would prevail, and Britain would be governed by heroic men who knew how to lead people.

The place was in darkness as he crept round the back. He'd asked the most trusted men from the church to meet him here, but there was no one waiting for him.

He found the back door that led into a small kitchen at the hall unlocked, and realised they must have misunderstood his instructions and gone inside without him. The man hidden there shouldn't have let them in, and they'd better not have started anything yet. It was for him to fire the first shot in this operation, literally and symbolically.

That police sergeant was a fool, was so sure of his own safety in this valley that he hadn't even made any attempt to keep the building secure tonight. Eagerly Vanner pushed the door open and crept inside, then stopped again.

There was still no sign of the men he'd expected to find waiting here. Had something gone wrong? Surely not. There would have been some noise if they'd been attacked.

Should he be cautious and not do anything till he'd found out what had happened to his men? No, not now he'd come so far. His time had come and he was relishing the feeling of warm anticipation about killing Deemer.

He peeped into the hall and heard the sound of someone talking quietly from the far end. It just showed how well careful planning paid off that he'd drawn his main enemy here at a time of his own choosing. And he wasn't going to waste this opportunity. After all, he had a man in hiding ready to come to his support, and he would be the only one armed since the British police only carried truncheons.

Holding the gun ready to use, he moved silently forward. He had several bullets, could kill more than one man if necessary. He had to pause for a few seconds as excitement made his heart leap about in his chest.

Calm down! he told it.

It was dim in the hall, but his eyes were used to the darkness and there was enough moonlight for him to see the sergeant's hat poking above a high-backed pew at the far end. There were faint outlines of others, whose boots were showing under their overcoats as they sat near the sergeant.

No, there was no trouble here. He'd been right to continue even without his men. He took out his gun and crept forward so that he could take aim at the sergeant's overcoat. Taking care to stay in the shadows, he raised the gun and fired, feeling jubilant when the sergeant's body jerked as the bullet hit it and toppled slowly sideways.

Suddenly the hall lights came on and someone grabbed him from behind in a stranglehold that made him struggle for breath. He couldn't work out what was happening.

Then someone else twisted his hand backwards into a painful hold that made him drop the gun. As it clattered to the floor, he felt sick with disappointment, but at least he had shot that damned sergeant.

'We have the intruder, Sergeant.' It was a voice he didn't recognise. 'Can you please identify him?'

Deemer stood up on the other side of the hall from the shadows behind which the figure had fallen sideways. Looking grim, the sergeant strode across to stand in front of the prisoner.

Vanner stared at the man he hated. Who had he shot, then? Had he wasted this important opportunity to get rid of the main person blocking his path to his eventual control of the valley?

'Osbert Vanner, I arrest you for attempted murder.' Deemer continued to recite the usual words that accompanied an arrest, then pulled out some handcuffs and clipped one of them on Vanner's wrist.

He struggled again, but in vain. There were three of them and only him, and no man came out of the back room to help him. The other handcuff was quickly clicked into place by the constable.

Someone was feeling in his pockets, pulling out the contents, and of course they found the letter that had arrived today. His heart began to thump irregularly in panic. He should have left it with the others in the drawer in the hut. He'd meant to, but had been so excited about using the gun and disposing of Deemer that he'd forgotten a mere piece of paper.

One of the men read the letter and laughed softly. 'Fine conspirators these are, Sergeant. This time we have the envelope and the fellow who sent it's full name and address. We shan't even have to go and search that shed for the letter. This fool has been carrying it close to his heart.'

'If he has a heart,' the other man said. 'I can't abide murderers.'

'I'm not a murderer,' he croaked. 'I've killed no one.'

'Not for lack of trying,' Deemer said. 'As I said, you've only been arrested for attempted murder, because you failed.'

They all laughed at him, laughed! He couldn't bear it. Rage erupted in him like a red hot geyser, blinded him, set his heart thumping in great jerks of painful fury.

The room spun around him and the floor rushed up to meet him.

'He's fainted, Sarge,' Mike said suddenly.

'Pick him up and sit him on that bench. Shove his head between his knees.'

But when they did that Vanner fell slowly sideways and still didn't stir. Deemer bent over him to feel for a pulse – and found none. He stared down in dismay. 'He's not breathing. Quick, we need to revive him.'

One of the visiting men put out a hand to stop him even trying. 'No. Better to leave him like this. He has no future but jail, and he's a traitor. Let him go. He's died of rage, if you ask me. Must have had a weak heart.'

'As well as a weak and warped brain.'

It went against the grain, but Deemer picked up the letter and the sight of it made him not attempt anything further. In a sad way, it was the most merciful release for this bitter, twisted man.

Mike shot him a questioning look and he shook his head. 'Leave him be, lad. Go and wake the lady at the village shop and tell her it's urgent that you make a phone call for me.'

As his constable set off at a run, Deemer went to the back door and beckoned.

Two lads appeared from the shadows and came to stand in the light flooding out of the hall.

'Has anyone else come out and tried to join him?'

'No, Sarge. Those special constables you sent warned everyone from the church and they all stayed home. Did you catch Vanner?'

'Yes, but he just dropped dead.'

'Really?'

'Yes. He seems to have had a seizure.'

'Can we see him?'

'No, lads. Let him lie in peace. And well done for acting as messengers and observers for us tonight.'

'Does that mean we don't have to go to those silly marching meetings any more?'

'It certainly does.'

'Good. They were driving us mad. But can we still keep our shirts?'

'Yes. And from now on you'd better study a lot harder in your final year at school. You'd be the perfect sort of lads for joining the police force.'

'All right, Sarge.' But their tone was markedly less enthusiastic about that prospect.

'It'll be worth paying attention to your schooling,' he said quietly. 'There's only a year to go now, after all. You'll make good policemen and you'll like wearing the uniform.'

They brightened visibly at that thought. He loved to see young faces like these filled with hope and excitement as their future beckoned.

'Again, thank you.' He slipped them another shilling each, knowing they'd pass it on to their mothers, then went back inside.

The body was now lying to one side, covered by an old curtain. The two men standing there smiled at him. 'Good night's work, eh, Sarge?'

'I suppose so.'

Maybe he was too soft-hearted, or maybe he had seen too much death in the Great War. That had sickened him to the core and only his return to police work had more or less healed the sad memories. Nothing would ever fully erase them, though.

Still, Arthur Chapman could now bring his granddaughter out of hiding and continue to court Gwynneth Harte.

That would be good news for all three of them. They'd make a lovely little family.

For the time being there would be peace in his valley – though a lot of paperwork to deal with before this case, and Higgerson's doings, were laid to rest officially.

33

Three days later, Lallie confessed to Felix that she couldn't bear to stay in this house any longer. 'I can't sleep properly and I still keep expecting to see Gareth coming through the door. Can you manage without me if I go back to Wiltshire?'

He stared at her pale face and the dark circles under her eyes. 'Yes, of course, Mum. I'll see you at our wedding anyway. Only a month to wait. I'm sure Kit will stay and help me here, if that's all right with you, because he's enjoying working with Dr Mitchell part of the time to get some experience.'

Edmund came up to her and put one arm around her waist. 'Let's sort out a few other things while we're chatting. Your mother and I would like to make it a double wedding if that's all right with you, lad.'

Felix beamed at them, his pleasure in that news obvious before he spoke. 'About time you two were able to bring your feelings out into the open. Wait till Eleanor hears. She'll be delighted. And yes, a double wedding will be wonderful.'

'It's not too soon?'

'No. He's dead and gone, thank goodness, and she hasn't lived with him for months anyway. We can all live in safety now and shouldn't waste our time. I'll feel a lot better, though, when I've remedied some of the wrongs he's done to people.'

'Did John Joe tell you what I suggested?'

'Yes, sir. It's very kind of you, and I accept with deep gratitude.'

Lallie looked from one to the other questioningly.

'I offered to let John Joe stay here for a month to help Felix settle into running the business. He'll help him go through any records and check anyone who used to work for your husband. I'm sure some of them will be suitable to stay on once they accept the changes.'

She beamed at them. 'Oh, that's wonderful. John Joe is such a capable man. I shan't worry about my sons if he's here to help them. And if they're going to help those who've been robbed and wronged, well, I can't think of any more suitable way to mark the change to an honest business.'

Felix grinned. 'Well, I'll help all those except Jem Stanley, who seems to have helped himself to my father's car. I can't get over the cheek of that.'

'John Joe told me you're not intending to pursue the matter,' Edmund said.

'No. I like to think of our father being cheated again that way just before he died. He fully deserved it.'

They were all smiling at the thought.

'Stanley doesn't deserve to have the car,' Lallie worried.

'No, but wouldn't it be funny if having that car made an honest man of him from now on?'

Even she couldn't help a quick smile at the thought. 'We can only hope.'

Edmund took over again. 'I think your mother needs to get away from here as soon as possible, so she and I will plan to leave first thing tomorrow morning.'

Four days later, Mr Forester turned up at the police station without warning. 'I've come to ask that you help me take that child to safety.'

Sergeant Deemer looked at him in shock. 'Beatie is safe with her grandfather and Mrs Harte.'

'As I said last time, an unmarried man with a record of drunkenness is not a suitable guardian for the child. And moreover, the man is living in sin.'

'He is not living in sin.'

'He and the woman are not married, and are living together in the house.'

'To look after the child. They're not sharing a bedroom.'

'That isn't good enough, Sergeant. You can't guarantee it to be true. And if you will not help me, then I must go to your superiors.'

Deemer looked at him in dismay. 'Very well, sir. If you insist, I shall help you to do this. Where will you be taking her?'

'Since no one got back to me about the child's current situation, I've had to make enquiries myself. The grandmother has been very helpful. She no longer feels able to look after the child herself, but she's helped me find Beatie a place in an orphanage on the road to Bury.'

'That place!' Why was that woman still making trouble for poor Beatie?

'The people at the orphanage will take care of her moral welfare, which I consider crucially important, and they'll also make sure she eats a good, plain diet, so her health will improve. Also, the place is kept spotlessly clean.'

And they'll chill the poor child's soul with their harsh rules, Deemer thought.

'I'll just get my overcoat and give my constable instructions.' He managed to tell Cliff to call Mr Peters and send him as a matter of urgency to Number 25 Daisy Street. Deemer wasn't sure their local JP could do anything to stop Forester taking the child away, but he had to try.

Then he went back to rejoin the severe-faced old man pacing the reception area impatiently.

*

When they knocked on the door of Number 25, Arthur answered and smiled at the sergeant but looked doubtfully at Mr Forester.

'May we come in?' Forester asked. 'I don't wish to conduct business as important as this on the doorstep.'

Beatie was sitting in the kitchen chatting to Gwynneth, but when Forester followed her grandfather in, she picked up on his solemn expression and huddled closer.

'The child cannot remain here,' he said baldly. 'You two are not married and it is simply not fitting.'

Beatie let out a wail of sheer terror. 'I'm not going back to my grandmother. I'm not!'

'She doesn't want you to. I've found you a place in an orphanage where you'll be with other children, and—'

'I'm not going anywhere!' She began to sob loudly. 'I'm safe here and they love me.'

Someone else knocked on the front door, and with a tut of annoyance Arthur went to answer it while Gwynneth put her arms round Beatie and cuddled her protectively.

Arthur came back with Mr Peters, who addressed Mr Forester. 'Out of sheer professional courtesy you should have informed me of your intentions.'

'You would have diverted me from what I know to be my moral duty, putting that child into a situation of decency. And no, it's not with Mrs Hicks.'

'It's the orphanage,' Arthur said. 'It's a cold harsh place, and everyone knows how unhappy those poor children are.'

'Let's sit down and discuss the best way to deal with the situation,' Peters said.

'She is *not* staying in a household in which two people are living in sin!' Forester roared, making no attempt to sit.

Gwynneth stared at him for a moment, then, as everyone tried to speak at once, she picked up the meat hammer and banged it several times on the table.

'Be quiet!' she yelled.

Everyone fell silent and stared at her in surprise.

She turned to Arthur. 'This is what comes of not telling people that we're engaged to be married till later! I told you it would be better to do it openly, but no, you're too shy.'

'Woman—' Mr Forester began.

'Don't you "woman" me in that odious way, you nasty, suspicious creature!' Bang went the meat hammer. 'Arthur?'

He moved to her side, waiting to follow her lead. But amusement was starting to twitch at his face muscles.

'Tell them now!' she demanded.

'Gwynneth and I are engaged to be married, and if it's so urgent to you, we can do it by special licence.' He looked sideways at her, hoping he'd said it how she wanted.

She took hold of his hand. 'There. It wasn't so hard, was it?' Then she glared across at Mr Forester. 'I presume it'll be all right for her to live here once we're married? We're going to open as a lodging house for single women once we've got the furniture sorted out.'

Arthur stared at her in such obvious surprise at this news that Sergeant Deemer hastily turned a chuckle into a cough.

'I told you I had a solution to earning our living. I've been looking into it and speaking to Mrs Tucker, who has been doing it for years in Rivenshaw, and she's going to help us set it all up. I shall enjoy the company, and you can continue to make money working with wood.'

Arthur gave her a glassy smile, then turned to look enquiringly at Mr Forester. 'So that's all right, isn't it?'

'That is a perfectly respectable way to earn a living,' Dennison said pointedly to his legal colleague.

'The child can't stay here till after they're married,' Forester insisted. 'And *she* should never have come here in the first place.'

'You are being ridiculous.'

'We can go and stay at my son's till after the wedding,' Gwynneth offered.

'Your idea of respectable and mine do not match, Mrs Harte. Your son lives too close to Mr Chapman.' Forester added sarcastically, 'Perhaps you will take them in, Peters?'

'Willingly.'

'Then more fool you, but I suppose it'll do.' Everyone was glaring at Forester, but he just stared coldly back at them, before turning to Gwynneth. 'Please go and pack your things and the child's, Mrs Harte. I shall escort you to your temporary abode.'

He folded his arms and went to stand beside the fireplace, scowling round the room. 'Though what the grandmother will say about this, I dread to think. She may even appeal to the local courts.'

Gwynneth stopped at the door to glare across at him. 'She won't dare. She'll be too afraid of Dr Mitchell standing up in court and offering his testimony about her ill treatment of the child. And you should be ashamed of yourself for causing this fuss, Forester.'

'*Mr* Forester to you.'

'Oh, no it isn't. I don't call people with a nasty, suspicious mind like yours "Mr". I have always been and always will be respectable, whatever you think. You clearly have an unpleasant view of the world, and it's no wonder you're thoroughly disliked.'

He made a gobbling noise, having difficulty finding a sharp enough response to this.

She reached out to pull the sobbing child up from her seat and drew Beatie into a close embrace. 'Come on, love. We're going to live with Mr Peters and his sister till after the wedding. That'll be fun, won't it? Will you be my bridesmaid?'

Beatie had stopped crying and now positively beamed at her, nodding vigorously.

'For your information, Forester, after we've moved our things, I'm going across to the town hall with Arthur to book a wedding by special licence. Feel free to come and breathe down our necks while we do that.'

He was looking thoroughly embarrassed at her sharp comments by now and didn't even try to answer.

The others watched her storm out, then Peters grinned at Arthur. 'She is magnificent, but I bet she rules the roost.'

Arthur was looking both shocked and happy. 'She can rule anything she wants as long as she doesn't change her mind about marrying me.'

He stared across at Mr Forester. 'Please leave my house now, sir. You and your suspicious mind do nothing but taint the atmosphere.'

Forester's mouth dropped open in shock at this further attack.

Dennison hid a smile and took his colleague's arm. 'I agree that it's time for you to go. And in case you're worrying, I promise not to allow them to jump into bed together while Mrs Harte and the child are staying with me.'

Forester stared at their two hostile faces and saw a third man, who looked equally hostile, standing in the hall holding the front door open. He pushed past Biff and went outside, pacing up and down while he waited to see Gwynneth and the child taken to the home of Dennison and his sister Veronica.

He was merely doing his duty, he told himself, as he'd been brought up to do. But he had a sneaking suspicion that he'd gone too far this time. Once he'd seen the woman move out, he'd leave them to it.

He didn't envy Chapman marrying her. She'd lead him by the nose.

When Dennison explained to his sister why he'd brought Gwynneth and Beatie back with him, she too was furious with Forester.

'There's just one good thing about it.'

They all looked at her in surprise.

'We can make sure we prepare for a very good wedding – to which we're not inviting that old fuddy duddy.'

Epilogue

Ten days later, Gwynneth woke later than usual after a restless night, to find Beatie's bed empty.

Her heart did a little leap of nervous fear at the thought of what today would bring. Her wedding day. And her kind friends were insisting on making a big fuss.

When she saw the time, she got up straight away. She didn't want all this song and dance, she just wanted to get the ceremony over with and start her new life. What she cared about was the people who would be most closely involved in it: Arthur and Beatie. She wanted to make a happy home and a family with them.

She hated, absolutely hated, the thought of being the centre of all this carry on.

Why did everyone, even Beatie, seem determined to make sure everything was done in a style that terrified her.

Her new outfit was hanging in the wardrobe, a gift from her sons. The dress and jacket were beautiful, a soft dusky pink that suited her. But they shouldn't have spent so much money on one set of what would be her Sunday clothes afterwards.

The only good thing about this fancy wedding was that it had brought Lucas home from Manchester for two days to take part in the ceremony. It had been lovely to see him again. They'd had a nice chat last night, and it made her feel a lot better to know how much he was loving his new life.

There was to be a fancy meal that was costing heaven knew how much after the ceremony at the town hall. Dennison was insisting on paying for that as his wedding present to them, but it was such a lot of money to spend on one meal. Three courses, they were having. What if she made a fool of herself and used the wrong cutlery?

There was a knock on the bedroom door and Veronica peeped in. 'Oh, you're awake. Thank goodness. I've brought up a cup of tea. I'll go and run your bath while you drink it.'

She set it down by the bed and whisked out of the room. She was like that, nice but always busy, didn't stop to chat till the late evening.

If Arthur had been by her side, Gwynneth would have felt better, but she wasn't allowed to see him today till they got to the town hall for the ceremony. Another stupid wedding custom.

She felt quite angry at it all.

No, not angry, terrified!

As she was getting out of bed, Beatie peeped into the room. 'Miss Peters said you were awake.' She looked over her shoulder, put one finger to her mouth in a shushing sign, and handed over an envelope.

'What's this?'

'From Grandfather. You're to open it when you're alone.'

So Gwynneth hid it in her towel and went along to the bathroom where a lovely warm bath was steaming gently as it waited for her.

Thank goodness she was allowed to do this on her own, at least. As far as she could see, she'd not be able to take a single breath on her own for the rest of the day.

She stared at the envelope: Arthur's handwriting. Carefully she opened it, trying not to tear it. Such a pretty envelope.

It was a very short note but it brought tears to her eyes.

After today, we'll not let them fuss over us, my dear. I know how you hate it, but they only do it because they're so fond of you.

To me, it's worth doing anything to marry you. I love you and I know you feel the same.

Your Arthur

PS I meant what I said. I'm never allowing that Forester into my house, if I have to toss him out of the front door myself. I am still angry at him for insulting you.

She smiled and found a tear tracking down her cheek. But it was a happy tear and it was followed by a chuckle at the last two sentences in the letter. Her shy Arthur threatening to toss a JP out of his house for upsetting her. That was love, coming from such a gentle man.

And the thought of his lovely little note carried her through the fussing over her hair and clothes, and the drive to the town hall.

Beatie's hand clasping hers helped too, as did the way the child stroked her own new clothes every now and then, and the sight of her rosy cheeks and shiny hair.

Gwynneth got out of Dennison's car and took the arm he offered her as he walked with her into the town hall and through to the rear of it and the registry office.

They stopped at the door and he whispered, 'You all right?'

'Yes, thank you.' Arthur's letter crackled in her pocket as she patted it for courage.

Then they were inside and she let Dennison lead her to a seat in the front next to Arthur, who looked so blissfully happy at the sight of her that the last of her nervousness about being the centre of attention fled.

He stood up and waited for her to sit, before taking his place again and grabbing tight hold of her hand beneath the folds of her new skirt.

'I love you,' she said, not caring who heard her.

'I love you too.'

Then someone called out their names and she let Arthur lead her towards the next room where the brief ceremony was to take place.

Beatie took her other hand and walked with them, clutching the box with the wedding ring in it, an honour that had thrilled the child to pieces.

Gwynneth must have acted automatically because she didn't become fully conscious of her surroundings again until 'Mr and Mrs Arthur Chapman' were walking out of the registry office and then into the open air.

Dennison's car now had white ribbons on it.

Some people were standing just outside the building and they tossed confetti over them.

It was a nice thing to do, but the nicest thing of all was holding Arthur's hand on one side and Beatie's hand on the other.

The three of them sat in the back and let Dennison and his sister sit in the front as he drove them all to the town's smartest hotel for a wedding meal.

She'd tried to tell them not to waste their money on such a fancy meal, but now, suddenly, she was glad of it, had found her appetite again.

She blushed a couple of times when it came to the speeches, but Arthur squeezed her hand and she got through it.

And then came the best part of the day.

Beatie went off to stay with Gabriel and Maisie, and Dennison dropped the two newly-weds outside Arthur's house – her house now as well. To her surprise, after Arthur had opened the front door, he scooped her up in his arms and carried her across the threshold.

'You fool!' she whispered.

'A very happy fool.' He set her down and turned to close and lock the door, while their friends and family cheered loudly outside.

'What do you want to do first?' he asked.

'Make a cup of tea, then get out of these fancy clothes and have my wicked way with you.'

He grinned. 'Your wish is my command, o princess.'

And darned if the butterflies didn't start dancing in her stomach.

'Never mind the tea,' she said in a husky voice.

'You're sure?'

She nodded.

'I wish I were strong enough to carry you all the way up the stairs.'

'I'd prefer to walk beside you.'

'In love and in life,' he said, and kissed her so beautifully she felt the warmth of his love run through her from top to toe.

There were flowers in the bedroom, a pretty new nightdress folded on the pillow – only he tossed it aside. So she tossed his pyjamas aside as well, and fell into his arms and life at the same time.

No woman had ever been as happy as she was today, she was quite sure of that.

Secret defences before and during World War II

This thread in the story was inspired by my ongoing reading about the era in which the Backshaw Moss series is set. If you're interested in the topic, you can read more about it in:

History in Hiding by Stewart Ross (Robert Hale, London, 1991) final chapter in particular.

Churchill's Underground Army by John Warwicker (Frontline Books, London, 2008) especially Chapter 18.

We all know about Bletchley Park these days, but I'm quite sure we don't know all the secrets involved in the past and ongoing defence of Britain or any other country.

Summer 1943 – my mother,
her cousin and me at two years old!

My husband and I at our graduation
ceremony in 1962 – we got married later that same year.

CONTACT ANNA

Anna is always delighted to hear from readers and can be contacted via the internet.

Anna has her own web page, with details of her books, some behind-the-scenes information that is available nowhere else and the first chapters of her books to try out, as well as a picture gallery.

Anna can be contacted by email at
anna@annajacobs.com

You can also find Anna on Facebook at
www.facebook.com/AnnaJacobsBooks

If you'd like to receive an email newsletter about Anna and her books every month or two, you are cordially invited to join her announcements list. Just email her and ask to be added to the list, or follow the link from her web page.

www.annajacobs.com

Don't miss the gripping and heartwarming new novel
from Anna Jacobs:

Silver Wishes

The first novel in the brand
new Jubilee Lake series

Lancashire, 1895. When her controlling stepfather suddenly
dies, it seems that Elinor Pendleton finally has a chance of
freedom. But her hopes are soon dashed when she learns that
the thuggish Jason Stafford has inherited every penny, and is
determined to have Elinor too.

Forced to flee with her beloved maid, Maude, Elinor finds
shelter with Maude's distant cousin in the remote village
of Ollerthwaite, on the shore of Jubilee Lake.

But Walter Crossley has troubles of his own. Having lost
his closest family in a tragic accident, he needs one of
his grandsons to return from America to inherit his farm
– and when practical, kindhearted Cameron arrives, he
appears to be the perfect heir.

But is this young man everything he seems?
And will Elinor's secret wish to have a family of
her own ever come true…?

Available from November 2022 in
Hardback and eBook

An invitation from the publisher

Join us at www.hodder.co.uk, or follow us
on Twitter @hodderbooks to be a part of
our community of people who love the very
best in books and reading.

Whether you want to discover more about a book
or an author, watch trailers and interviews, have the
chance to win early limited editions, or simply browse
our expert readers' selection of the very best books,
we think you'll find what you're looking for.

And if you don't, that's the place to tell us what's missing.

We love what we do, and we'd love you to be a part of it.

www.hodder.co.uk

@hodderbooks

HodderBooks

HodderBooks

WITHDRAWN
FROM STOCK

Sea Legs

GUY GRIE

In Great Britain by CPI Group (UK) Ltd, Croydon cr

B L O O M S B U R Y

LONDON · NEW DELHI · NEW YORK · SYDNEY

To Oscar and Luke, for being brave
when it was not all plain sailing.

First published in Great Britain 2013
This paperback edition published in 2014

Copyright © 2013 by Guy Grieve
Maps by Arthur Prior

The moral right of the author has been asserted

No part of this book may be used or reproduced in any manner
whatsoever without written permission from the Publisher except
in the case of brief quotations embodied in critical articles or reviews

Every reasonable effort has been made to trace copyright holders
of material reproduced in this book, but if any have been inadvertently
overlooked the publishers would be glad to hear from them

Bloomsbury Publishing Plc
50 Bedford Square
London WC1B 3DP

www.bloomsbury.com

Bloomsbury is a trademark of Bloomsbury Publishing Plc

Bloomsbury Publishing, London, New Delhi, New York and Sydney

A CIP catalogue record for this book is available from the British Library

ISBN 978 1 4088 4330 7

10 9 8 7 6 5 4 3 2 1

Typeset by seagulls.net

Printed and bound   RO 4YY

FIFE CULTURAL TRUST

FBT29323

WATERSTONES   9.3.15

910.45   £9.99

TRAV   CA

CONTENTS

*There is nothing more enticing, disenchanting,
and enslaving than the life at sea.*

JOSEPH CONRAD

THE CARIBBEAN SEA

SCALE 1 : 1, 087, 000

Cardinals:
N, E, S, W.

Half-Cardinals:
NE, SE, SW, NW.

Intermediates:
NNE, ENE, ESE,
SSE, SSW, WSW
WNW, NNW

0   25   50   75   100   125
NAUTICAL MILES

Ber

PENINSULA DE LA GUAJIRA

BO.

Gulf of Venezuela

COLOMBIA

Lake Maracaibo

NORTH ATLANTIC OCEAN

SCALE 1 : 5, 870, 000

Cardinals:
N, E, S, W.

Half-Cardinals:
NE, SE, SW, NW.

Intermediates:
NNE, ENE, ESE,
SSE, SSW, WSW,
WNW, NNW.

| 0 | 240 | 480 | 720 | 960 | 1200 |

NAUTICAL MILES

NORWAY

SWEDEN

NORTH SEA

THE
UNITED KINGDOM
OF
GREAT BRITAIN
AND
NORTHERN IRELAND

ENGLISH CHANNEL

FRANCE

BAY OF BISCAY

ITALY

SPAIN

MEDITERRANEAN
SEA

O R E S

PORTUGAL

STRAIT OF GIBRALTAR

ALGERIA

PROLOGUE

*A man can stand anything except
a succession of ordinary days.*
JOHANN WOLFGANG VON GOETHE

56.39N: 05.71W

The alarm clock went off and after hitting the snooze button a multitude of times Juliet at last forced herself out of bed. I turned and lay with my face in the pillow, trying to imagine being active and effective for another day. As usual, I was struggling to produce the spark needed.

'C'mon Guy! We're running late!' Juliet muttered as she pulled on a dressing gown and stuck her feet into a pair of slippers to ward off the winter chill. She walked towards the window and pulled back the curtains, hoping to drive me from my bed with an invigorating burst of sunshine. Instead all that was revealed was the uniform grey of another dreary British morning, frigid rain running mournfully down the glass. I saw her shoulders lift for a moment as she uttered a deep sigh. Though she rarely admitted it, I knew she was as fed up as I was.

She went through to the boys' room and I heard the usual protests as she tried to get Oscar up and ready for school. 'No Mum, please, not the curtains!' I heard him begging, articulating my own thoughts from a few minutes earlier, but then his protests died as he too realised that opening the curtains made no difference to the light levels in the room.

I heard Juliet's footsteps returning and hurriedly pulled myself out of bed, staring out of the window as an almost theatrical curtain of rain glided across the tufty lawn. I saw a few dead leaves blow across before a gust of wind beat the rain so hard against the window that the view was totally obscured, and for a moment I had the impression of being underwater. Reluctantly I went downstairs to join in the daily panic of getting Oscar off to school. As the minutes counted down to the school bus's arrival we charged around with increasing urgency, finding trainers for football, lost homework, packed lunch and jacket, scarf and hat. With four minutes to go I found myself pleading with Oscar to put his shoes on faster. 'I'm trying Dad!' he said, frantically fiddling with his laces, which had been tied in an impenetrable knot.

At last he was ready, dressed in enough layers to survive an arctic winter, and after a flurry of hugs and goodbyes ran down the drive. He leant into the wind like a seasoned fisherman, but nevertheless his hat blew off, and he stopped to retrieve it before climbing into the waiting bus. Nothing could be seen inside, as its windows streamed with condensation from the children's fetid breath, many of whom were no doubt nursing heavy colds. I sighed as I thought of the impossibility of remaining healthy through a British winter. At any given time at least one member of our family was either suffering with, recovering from or just about to succumb to some kind of upper respiratory infection. Right on cue, I heard Luke, our younger son, installed in front of the television already at shortly after eight o'clock in the morning, emit a barking cough. I stumped through to the kitchen, where Juliet was pouring tea.

'There's no way I'm going to be doing this for the next ten years!' I announced.

'No?' She passed me a piece of cold, soggy toast. 'So what are you going to be doing?'

'I don't know. But I know I've had enough of this. The weather, the routine, the colds, school, the house . . . Every day is the same, and so drab – it's like *Groundhog Day*!'

As if to confirm it I reached for the butter and began spreading it on my toast, as I did every day. Juliet looked amused.

'I've heard all this before Guy – it's exactly what you said before you went off to Alaska. So what's your suggestion: escape back to the office?'

I had to laugh. 'Well I could certainly do with a manager again . . .' I thought about my sporadic attempts to earn a living through writing tid-bits for magazines and newspapers. 'Let's find a way to somehow buy a boat,' I said. 'Let's buy a boat and go sailing. For a long time. We'd have a chance to learn, and travel, and spend some real time together for once instead of this . . .' I gestured around, 'This half-life we're leading.'

This was not a new idea: spending some time living on a boat was something we'd both dreamed of for a long time. We had a little experience, but not much: Juliet had sailed with her family as a child, and I had recently done a couple of courses. From time to time we would go through a spate of browsing for boats on the internet, dreaming of a life afloat. Not that we could afford it, as Juliet quickly reminded me.

'But how would we pay for it?'

'Sell the house! Come on, let's do it – let's sell everything and go!' I jumped up on the last word like a child at a magic show.

She shook her head firmly. 'No way. We're not selling the house – that would be madness. Forget it.'

'Why not? What's this house ever done for us? We pour everything we have into it and it traps us in square rooms which are bad for the soul.'

'Oh don't start that square rooms stuff again. This is our house, it's all we have and I'm not risking it for anything.'

'But you like the idea, don't you?'

'Of course I do. I love it. But not at any cost.'

'Well, you're the clever one – try to think of a way.'

She said nothing, just wiped the kitchen worktop in silence, but I knew she was with me.

Later that day I was working fruitlessly on a batch of emails in our cubbyhole of an office when Juliet came in and stood behind me.

'I've been thinking, perhaps we could just about do it,' she said thoughtfully, staring out of the window at yet more greyness.

'Do what?' I pivoted round on the plastic Ikea chair, which threatened to topple over as it had never been assembled properly.

'Raise the money to buy a boat. We could probably extend the mortgage by enough to buy something . . . But nothing too expensive,' she said hastily, as I swung back round to open the internet browser.

Thus began a period of frantic organisation, as we somehow persuaded our mortgage lender to lend us more money on the pretext of 'home improvements' in the days before the credit crunch, extending ourselves way beyond what we could afford. Each evening after the boys were in bed we trawled the internet, researching everything that we could find on the subject of boats, families and the sea. We read inspiring stories of star-filled nights, swimming on pristine reefs and idyllic islands that could be reached only by boat. We read some hair-raising tales too, of pitch-poling yachts, near collisions, divorces, madness and even loss of life. But through it all one great character emerged above all others. The sea. It was, surely, the greatest road on earth, and as I drove along the narrow lanes of Mull I would stop and stare out across the great ocean that lapped the rocky shoreline and find myself easily lost in the beautiful, timeless reverie of escape.

Nine months later we found ourselves at the airport, on our way to Bonaire, an island fifty miles north of the Venezuelan coast in the Netherlands Antilles, where our new boat – a 41-foot Hans Christian yacht named *Forever* – lay patiently waiting. Our house had been let, our animals temporarily re-homed and Oscar had been officially withdrawn from school. Yet inside we had begun to falter. As the day of departure drew near, we grew less confident in our abilities, and less sure of the wisdom of abandoning our secure lives for an entirely new life at sea. We had wanted an adventure, but we were stepping into totally unfamiliar territory: would we be able to cope?

TENDERFEET

12.09N: 68.17W

I n the harbour office, Carlos said: 'Here in Venezuela we have a saying . . .' He smiled, revealing an enviable set of teeth. 'We say, persuade your worst enemy to buy a boat.' He chuckled at his own joke, as he processed my credit card in the machine. I looked on, shifting from foot to foot with the usual anxiety as to whether the payment would go through. The machine beeped and buzzed, unreadable words forming against the yellow background. It spat out a piece of paper, which Carlos ripped off with a flourish.

'You see my friend,' he said triumphantly, brandishing the piece of paper in front of me. 'It say refuse. This expensive world, hey?' Clearly I was livening up his morning.

After repeating the performance with a number of cards I managed to pay the bill, buying us a few more days in the safety of the marina. From the back of the office I could see a woman staring over at me. I raised a hand in greeting, but her eyes dropped back to the computer screen. Probably hates rich white people, I reflected, particularly ones that can't pay their bills.

As I stuffed my documents into my bag, Carlos stood to hold the door open for me. Outside, it seemed as if a blast furnace had started up – the mighty heat of the tropics.

'So what are your plans with *Forever*?' he asked. His words were polite, but his expression held a hint of mockery.

'Well, the plan is ...' I tried to muster an air of confidence. 'The plan is to sail her back to Scotland.'

'Scotland?' He tilted his head. 'Scotland, England? You take the wife and the childrens too?'

'Yes, we're all going together.' I tried to make eye contact but failed.

'You a skipper?'

'Yes, in a way. I'm what you would call a day skipper in Britain.'

Into my mind floated a picture of the shabby sea-cadet hall in the town of Maryport, where I had gone to study my day-skipper theory.

'*Day* skipper?' He sounded outraged. 'But what about the nights?'

This was a question that had occurred to me as well. 'Well,' I shrugged my shoulders and sighed. 'I guess the nights are the same as the days, mostly . . . we've got my father-in-law with us for a bit too, to get us started.'

Carlos clearly wasn't convinced. 'You must be careful,' he said, fixing me with a look that left me in no doubt that if anything went wrong he, as well as everyone else, would hold me entirely responsible.

There was nothing more to say. There was no hiding it – I was an idiot. And so was Juliet for that matter. We had sunk everything into a naive dream, taking out an immense loan to buy a sailing boat with the romantic idea that we would live aboard as a family whilst sailing her back to Scotland. What made things infinitely more worrying was the fact that we were not alone: our two young children, Oscar and Luke, were dragged into this too. Who would care if two adults sailed naively into the blue yonder and landed up sinking? But with a four- and seven-year-old in tow the stakes were infinitely higher. At least we had persuaded my father-in-law, James, to come along and help. J, as he was affectionately known, had years of sailing experience behind him and would be a reassuring presence during the early days of our journey.

With a million questions and thoughts hanging over me like a cloud of biting insects, I hitched my bag onto my shoulder and set off into the sweltering heat. The island's main road was drab and scruffy, and cars and motorbikes zoomed past throwing up clouds of dust. On one side of the road a salty lagoon stretched towards scrubby low hills with a few sad-looking flamingoes standing in its midst; on the other lay the marina, where a variety of gleaming yachts floated beside wide pontoons. I passed a group of men working on a shabby collection of homemade fishing boats tied up alongside the quay and smiled in greeting. But no one smiled back. Of course who could blame them? Trying to catch fish for their families from such makeshift vessels must have been tough, made infinitely worse by having to return to a quayside that lay beneath the immense yachts of visiting Americans and Europeans.

It was midday and nothing moved. The tables in the harbour restaurant were laid up, tempting passers-by like baited lines waiting for a fat school of silvery fish. At the empty bar a local girl sat flipping through a glossy magazine. I said hello, but she barely looked up.

Back on the pontoon my spirits lifted when I saw *Forever*, our new floating home. *Forever* was a cutter-rigged sailing boat of the 'Hans Christian' design. She was stoutly built, with a deep keel below the water, a 6-foot-long bowsprit and a rounded 'canoe' stern. Compared to most of the towering yachts around us, her rig was relatively short and hung around a stocky mast and immensely strong-looking boom. Below substantial lifelines, her bulwarks stood a foot above the deck, capped all the way around with a richly varnished teak cap rail. Somehow she managed to look sturdy and delicate all at once.

I stopped for a moment to look at her, torn between pride and disbelief at what we had done.

Although she was small compared to many of the boats in the marina, she felt immense to us. It seemed impossible that she was ours – the culmination of months of dreaming and planning, now rather frighteningly real. As I stood marvelling, a hatch on the deck creaked open and shut, then open and shut again like a clam flexing its muscles. On the third opening it was pushed right back and two strong hands placed themselves on either side of the frame as the figure of my father-in-law emerged onto the coachroof. Although in his seventies, a lifetime of hard physical work had paid off and J was as flexible and strong as many men in their thirties. He sat in the hatch with his feet dangling inside the boat and his back to me. He smoothed back a shock of curly hair and called down: 'Oscar!'

'Yes Papa?' Our older son's voice floated up from inside the boat.

J stretched his hand down through the hatch. 'Hand me that pot of grease.'

He let his half-moon glasses fall on their chain, reached into his shirt pocket for a little brush and began working at the stiff hatch mechanism.

As I watched him I felt a mixture of emotions. I loved him for having the heart and imagination to volunteer to spend some time with us as we learnt the ropes, but he was a genuine eccentric – confusing, inscrutable, uncompromising – and not always easy company.

J was from an academic family, his father a Cambridge Don who had been part of the Enigma programme during the war. He had worked in the City until his love of the sea and yearning for adventure led him to drop it all and, together with his wife Audrey, head to the Isle of Mull. In the early sixties, Mull was a very different place from what it is now, far more remote and cut off. Soon J and Audrey found themselves playing the classic west-coast-island game of inventive survival. From small-scale farming to delivering coal to running a coastal puffer, they did anything and everything to keep their young family going. I was astonished when Juliet told me that they had only got mains electricity when she was sixteen, making do before that with an idiosyncratic generator and tilly lamps. Though the journey had no doubt been rocky, she had had a wonderfully wild and free childhood. J was a true Renaissance man, and despite his academic background was intensely practical, turning his hand to anything from construction to flying light aircraft. He had never lost his love of sailing, which had been a large part of his motivation for moving to the Highlands, and we felt lucky to have him with us to steer us through the early days. A man of few words, those words that he did offer left one in no doubt that he was firmly in control.

'Hi J,' I greeted him from the pontoon. 'How's it going?'

'Rather slowly.' He answered in characteristic terse style, rubbing sweat from his forehead with the back of his hand. 'I suggest that you and Juliet get yourselves sorted out so that we can leave this infernal harbour.'

I stepped over *Forever*'s lifelines onto the hot wooden deck and took a closer look at the hatch. 'Looks a bit stiff, hey?'

'Yes it is. We need to get everything in order and then your job as *skipper* . . .' he emphasised the word sternly, 'will be to keep it that way. Work, Guy.' He pointed the grease-smeared brush at me. 'You must do a daily inspection of the rigging, hatches, sea-cocks, engine, batteries, water reserves and fuel. And once a week you should have a maintenance day. Come here – I want to show you something.' He stepped out onto the bowsprit. 'See that little piece of steel that keeps that pin in place?' He was pointing towards the bottom of the forestay, where it was attached to the deck. 'That cotter pin will cost less than one dollar. If it starts to corrode and you fail to replace it, one day it will break. Then the forestay will come free and the mast will become unstable and could even fall down. In other words, all hell could break loose for the sake of a tiny piece of rigging worth one simple dollar. Now, you're not going to let that happen, are you Guy?'

I shook my head, trying not to feel irritated at the Nelsonian tone he was adopting. I told myself there were years of experience behind his words, and I needed to learn.

Just then Juliet emerged from the companionway. A strand of her fair hair had come loose and she wound it round her fingers in a moment of distraction before briskly pushing it back behind her ear. She had been sorting out the contents of the lockers and I could see that she was feeling under siege from the heat, the mosquitoes and the boys, who had been squabbling all morning. 'I'm taking the boys for a drink,' she said. 'They're going stir crazy down there and I need some air. Boys!' she shouted. 'We're off! Bring your shoes.'

'J, why don't you go with them?' I suggested. 'I'll carry on with the hatches.'

He handed me the rag. 'Use this,' he said, stepping nimbly over the lifelines and onto the pontoon. Oscar and Luke trailed up, pale and sweaty. They were still suffering from leftover British colds, which hadn't been helped by the drastic change in climate and twenty-four hour journey to get here. J bent to lift Luke across and then stood back to watch Oscar, who refused to be helped. 'Be careful Oscar,' he said. 'If you fall between the boat and the pontoon you'll be crushed.'

Worried, Oscar looked over at me. 'Aren't you coming Dad?'

'No Ozzy. You go ahead with Mummy and Papa – I've got stuff to do here.'

He climbed over the lifelines, judging the gap between the boat and pontoon carefully before jumping across. J patted his head and I watched them walk off together.

Ten minutes later I was continuing with J's work on the hatches when I heard a shrill call.

'Ahoy *Forever*! Anyone home?'

The voice was coming from the water. I peered over *Forever*'s port side and was greeted by the sight of a middle-aged woman and a rather threadbare man, looking up from an under-inflated dinghy that was crammed full of shopping, empty bottles, grubby-looking lifejackets, fins and snorkels and a number of greasy coils of rope. Teetering on top of it all was a golden-brown spaniel with sagging eyes and matted hair.

'Hi! Could you take our painter?' The dinghy sagged and puffed as the woman stood to throw me the line. Her accent was English and she had the bossy tone of a nautical version of Barbara Woodhouse.

I tied a round turn and two half hitches round a stanchion, aware that she was watching me. 'Well, at least he can tie his knots – that's something,' she said to her companion. I smiled and prepared to engage in that classic British conversational game of strike and counter-strike, all hidden beneath a veneer of polite joviality. My paranoid mind began to wonder just what *Forever*'s former owners, Mike and Tessa, had said about us. They were stalwarts of the local cruising community and, unlike us, hugely experienced. It seemed our reputation had gone before us.

'My name is Linda Campbell,' the woman announced. 'And this is Henrik, who's just sailed over from the Netherlands.' Henrik smiled shyly and an image flashed into my mind of his leathery body being dragged into a cabin by Linda. 'We're moored opposite the town beach – wonderfully breezy over there, unlike this place. Family around?' She peered around the deck as if they might be hiding somewhere.

'No, they've gone out for a walk. I'm Guy by the way.' I shook both their hands and then sat down on the coachroof, wondering if I was expected to invite them aboard.

'Are you planning to sail her?' Linda asked and I knew the first missile had been fired.

'Yes,' I said, prepared this time and determined to sound confident. 'We're going to take her back to Scotland.'

'Is that so? Of course many people undertake large journeys at sea when they don't have the experience – I think it's irresponsible personally, especially with children on board. Not that I'm saying you don't have the experience of course ...' She fixed me with a steely look. 'Do you?'

Silence fell as I stared down at the deck – she had scored a hit and she knew it. I changed the subject. 'What about you? Have you been here long?'

'Eight years.' She was trying to sound casual, but now it was her turn to feel uncomfortable. Two could play at this game, I thought.

'Wow, that's quite some time. Why, if you don't mind me asking?'

'Well it just sort of happened.' She looked at me directly now, her guard down. 'I sold my house in Devon and bought the boat. Seemed like a good idea at the time, but now I'm stuck with it. The boat is not in the best of shape you see – can't sell it and not safe to sail anywhere until I get it fixed up. So for now ... looks like I'm staying here.' There was little humour in her laugh.

'I'm sorry to hear that,' I replied, liking her more now.

'Oh well, such is life,' she sighed. 'Your boat looks in pretty good order though – do you have much to do?'

I regaled her with a long list of our concerns ending with cockroaches, which we had been warned would invade the boat if we stayed in harbour too long.

'Cockroaches!' She waved a hand dismissively. 'That's nothing – I've got rats on my boat!'

And with that she motioned to me to untie their line. As I watched Linda and the silent Henrik putter off towards the harbour mouth, the sides of their dinghy barely clearing the water, I reflected that to an outside observer Linda's life must have seemed perfect – living on a sailing boat moored up on a Caribbean island, soothed by the trade winds and warmed by a tropical sun. The reality, however, was quite different. Her boat, which was also her home, was falling apart and was probably going to either sink or blow up some day soon. In the meantime all she had for company was her aging spaniel, the odd passing sailor and a hold full of rats.

I paused for a moment, remembering the interrupted hatch greasing job and J's stern words on maintenance, and made a mental note to complete the job another day. Instead I crept rather guiltily below to examine the chart of the Caribbean Sea. I pushed my finger towards the little island of Bonaire. When we had bought *Forever* we had planned on working our way east along the Venezuelan coast and then up the Windward and Leeward Islands, from where we could begin the journey back to Scotland. But we had failed to take account of the prevailing weather – a basic error and the first of many lessons that we would learn the hard way.

I traced a line along the intoxicating arc of the Leewards and Windwards, to the US and British Virgin Islands. This was where we wanted to go, but how? Travelling directly east into wind and weather would make a terrible start to our journey and very likely damage the boat, to say nothing of her crew. It would also mean risking some of the most dangerous waters in the Caribbean, along the impoverished coastline of Venezuela where, understandably, piracy was not uncommon. The alternative was to sail north-east for the Virgin Islands, which would give us a better course, but would also mean over four hundred miles of open water in an untested boat, with no possibility of shelter should any problems arise. Now – too late – we realised that Bonaire had turned out to be a risky place to start. We were trapped in a corner of the Caribbean at the wrong time of year with the wind and weather against us. Whatever course we chose, it was not going to be easy.

The next morning, I was brewing up some coffee when I heard a chirpy voice singing out from the quay. It was Tessa. My heart sank, though I knew we needed advice from her and her husband Mike, who had sold us the boat. Having lived on *Forever* for ten years they knew her systems backwards, and we were grateful to them for passing on their knowledge. It was a painful process however, and on this third day of intensive instruction we felt little wiser than we had at the start.

'Come aboard Tessa!' I called, trying to match her cheeriness. 'Do you want some coffee?'

She came down the companionway steps, looking more glamour model than seasoned sailor with her dazzling teeth, immaculately tanned skin and sun-streaked hair. Although well into her forties Tessa was in outrageously good shape – in fact she was positively vibrating with energy and vitality. Just looking at her made Juliet and I feel tired and grey by comparison.

She looked around as she stood at the bottom of the steps and I knew she was missing nothing. *Forever* now distinctly bore the mark of a family boat – a scene of chaos with toys, books, charts and manuals piled everywhere; no doubt a far cry from Tessa and Mike's serene and uncluttered existence. Juliet was picking up toys and leftover breakfast things, trying to look efficient and failing. She smiled at Tessa.

'OK, where do we start?' Juliet had spent the past two days figuring out the domestic side of life at sea and had taken Tessa's suggestions about stocking up, preserving food, cooking at sea and washing. Now she was clutching a notebook in preparation for more complex lessons.

'Well, how about the SSB radio? We haven't covered that yet.' Tessa bounded over to the chart table and tapped an instrument that might as well have been the Enigma cipher machine for all we understood it.

'The what?' Juliet stood, pencil poised over paper.

A slight pause and a barely concealed sigh as Tessa reminded herself that she was dealing with two very stupid people. 'The single sideband radio. It's another form of radio communication that comes into its own when you're out of VHF range – you'll need it for getting weather reports when you're crossing the Atlantic . . .' her voice tailed off as she seemed to contemplate the ludicrousness of this concept, '. . . but that's some way off. SSB is real easy once you get used to it. The trick is to make sure that you can get a good connection with a frequency that will hold while you send your message. This is the pactor modem,' she pointed at another obscure electronic item. 'It links up to a laptop – must be in here', she rummaged in a leather attaché case. 'Just wait until you get the green lights signalling a connection and then send off your compressed files. We use Sailmail – you're welcome to use our account for a while, it's paid up till the end of December.'

Juliet valiantly made notes as Tessa talked, but as time went on her pencil slowed and eventually froze as Tessa went into more and more detail – what good connections sounded like, which of the 160 potential channels might best suit us and the various names and frequencies of the weather reports. After a while Tessa stopped and touched her shoulder.

'Juliet?'

She shook herself. 'Yes?'

'Shall I stop for a bit?' Tessa pushed her sunglasses up on her head, and I could see real concern in her eyes. 'I know it's a lot to take in at once – we can take as long as you need.'

Juliet bit her lip, and I knew Tessa's kindness was hitting her hard. 'Actually that would be great Tessa – I'll read over the manual tonight and see if I can get the basics. Then hopefully I'll understand it more when we next talk about it.'

Tessa nodded. 'OK. Anyway, it's Guy's turn now, Mike said he'd be here at ten.' She flashed a sadistic smile at me as, right on cue, Mike's voice called out from the quay.

Mike was a big man, some years older than Tessa. They had met ten years ago, married and lived on *Forever* ever since, making several ocean crossings on her. Now they had washed up in Bonaire, unable to continue sailing due to various health issues that made life aboard too difficult for Mike. Giving up sailing had left a wound in his heart that was there for anyone to see, and I sensed he was emotionally adrift as he tried to adjust to the new realities of his life on land. From their stories, it was clear that *Forever* had been a palace to them and I saw the scene through Mike's eyes as he peered down the companionway into her dark interior. When *Forever* was theirs, mornings aboard must have been serene and orderly, whereas now he was confronted by a cluttered space with two half-naked boys squawking and resisting as Juliet tried to persuade them into their clothes. And with each new bit of knowledge that they passed over to us they must have felt yet more threads linking them to *Forever* fray and fall away.

Mike sat heavily in the cockpit, wiping the sweat from his forehead with a big hand as the sun started its inexorable rise towards the leaden heat of midday. 'OK Guy, I'm gonna show you how to use the watermaker. Can you open that hatch down there below the steps?'

He pointed down the companionway and after manhandling armloads of belongings out of the way I managed to reach a hatch that gave access to the inner workings of the boat.

'Now you run that water maker only when the engine is on – it uses too much battery power otherwise. It runs at 800 psi; adjust that nut with your spanner and hold it at that pressure till the system runs well, then use the tester tube to taste the water until it becomes potable. When you're happy turn the Y valve to direct the water into your tanks – make sure you get it right or you'll fill up your fresh water tanks with salt water. Is that clear?'

I heard a little cough behind me and saw J standing halfway up the companionway. 'I'm not sure Guy has followed that Mike, could you just run him through it one more time?'

Mike shot J a look that must have passed eternally between older men as they watched a beginner grappling with the first rung of a tall ladder they had long since climbed. But I was determined not to let pride get in the way of learning. 'Actually that would be useful,' I said. 'If you don't mind Mike, could you run it past me again?'

I heard some sniggering behind me. The boys had witnessed the whole scene. 'Dad, you're so stupid!' Oscar blurted out. I tried to give him a stern stare but only succeeded in sending them both into gales of laughter.

'You're like Homer Simpson,' Luke gasped, and the two of them rolled around with glee, thoroughly enjoying watching me being the pupil for once.

And so it went on. Mike repeated and repeated; I asked dumb question after dumb question; J rolled his eyes and sighed; the children giggled and squabbled; Juliet grew more anxious; the crease in Tessa's brow deepened and the day got hotter and hotter.

By midday we had our heads deep within the bilges, inspecting the interior of what now felt more like a Russian space station than a simple boat. It was so hot that I had stripped down to my boxers, and the boys had long since flaked out and lay comatose on the sweaty seats of the saloon. All around hatches were lifted, engine and tanks were exposed and lockers were open. In order to get access to the workings of the boat it was more or less necessary to dismantle her, turning her beautiful woody interior into a hellhole. Wisely, J had opted for a walk around the harbour.

'Please tell me you have some cold beers here?' Mike asked as he guided me along the wiring with his torch. 'You've got the freezer working, haven't you?'

'Well I was getting around to that Mike. Isn't it very heavy on the battery?'

As he shook his head, large drops of sweat fell on the teak flooring. 'Not when you're in the marina Guy – you're hooked up to shore power. Remember what I told you about switching to shore power on the console over there?' He gestured behind him without looking. 'That's the Xantrex system – it manages the amp flow and shows you the voltage levels of the house bank and starter battery.'

'Right.' I hoped that my face showed nothing but calm comprehension. 'I'll just hook us up to the shore power and then we could possibly enjoy a cold beer a little later?'

'Actually I'll pass on that if you don't mind Guy.' Mike stood up stiffly. 'That freezer takes a long time to get cold and I'm not a fan of warm beer like you Brits. I'm all done for today – we'll catch up tomorrow.'

After we had thanked Mike and Tessa for the hundredth time we slumped back in the wreckage of the saloon. A depressed silence fell upon the boat and I felt like crawling into my bunk and going to sleep, but the boys were now awake and I knew something had to be done to shake us out of our torpor. 'Hey, let's go swimming!' I suggested.

Luke pulled himself up off the bench. 'Can I take my snorkel?' he asked.

'Can we have an ice cream too?' Oscar chimed in and I felt a pang of guilt as I realised how patient they were being. So far this experience was definitely not the big adventure they'd been promised.

Laden with towels, suntan oil and snorkelling gear, we traipsed a mile or so along the dusty road to the beach. All the way there Luke regaled us with his plans for snorkelling, how far he was going to swim and what he was hoping to see. We made non-committal noises in response, suspecting that he might not find it as easy as he thought, but knowing better than to try and tell him so. At the beach, a ramshackle pier jutted out into the water and reggae music drifted from a nearby bar, where relaxed tourists and locals sat around drinking and playing cards. The boys squealed in excitement and ripped off their clothes. Juliet helped them put on their masks and snorkels and then forced Luke into his armbands. They all plunged into the water and I smiled as I watched them, knowing how good the silky water would feel on their skin. J had settled himself with a book and a large rum by a table in the bar and I lay on the sand, grateful for a chance to forget my worries.

I was drifting on the edge of sleep when I felt drips of water falling on me. Could it be raining? I opened my eyes.

'Dad.'

Luke was standing above me, blocking out the sun. I could see he wasn't happy. 'What's wrong Luke?'

'I hate snorkelling and I don't like that water – there's too many fish. The yellow ones keep following me.'

Beyond him I could see Juliet and Oscar standing together in the water, exclaiming over something they had seen. We had read that Bonaire is famous for some of the best snorkelling in the Caribbean and they were clearly loving it.

'Oh go on Luke – it's perfectly safe, the fish won't hurt you.'

Grumpily he turned and trudged back to the water. I drifted off again but a few minutes later I heard him screaming. I shot to my feet to see Luke hurtling out of the water, Juliet close behind him. 'It's all right Luke, it won't hurt you!' I heard her call, but he carried on running until he reached me, stopping in a shower of sand.

'Come quick Dad, I've seen a horrible thing – it was chasing me.' He was panting and I could see he'd had a real shock.

'What?' I squinted out to sea, half expecting to see a dorsal fin.

'A huge stripy thing, a snake,' he said.

'A snake?' I frowned. 'In the water?'

21

'Yes!' he shouted. 'It was black and white and it chased me. I don't like this place – it's dangerous!' He ripped off his mask and threw it on the sand.

'I think it was an eel,' Juliet said, 'I saw it too. But it wasn't chasing you Luke.'

'It was!' He dragged me by the hand towards the sea where he scanned the water's edge from a safe distance. 'There!' he pointed triumphantly. 'See? It's a snake.'

'It's a baby moray eel, Luke.' I stared in fascination at the little creature, which was swimming along the water's edge with an odd twisting motion. 'Completely harmless if you leave it in peace.'

'It's a snake,' Luke said stubbornly. 'And I'm not swimming in there if there's snakes.'

We retreated to the bar, where Luke retold his drama over and over again. A few minutes later I heard muffled crying and turned to see Oscar limping up the beach. What now? I thought. Even a simple trip to the beach was turning into a disaster.

'Something stung me Dad, I don't know what it was.' He lifted his leg and sure enough there was a fiery red patch on the side of his foot that was swelling rapidly.

'OK, we've got to do something about that.' I stood up and made my way to the bar. 'Excuse me . . .' I addressed the girl behind the bar. 'My son has been stung by something in the water, do you have anything . . . ?'

'Vinegar,' she said, her smile as dazzling as the overhead sun and came round the bar to examine Oscar's foot. 'Probably fireworm.' She doused Oscar's foot liberally with vinegar, while he whimpered quietly. 'There. It'll sting for a bit but you be OK now.'

Thanking her, we returned to our table. 'See Dad,' Luke said, with a distinctly smug look on his face. 'I told you this place was dangerous.'

The next morning we prepared ourselves for the first hurdle. We were going to move *Forever* to a mooring off the town beach, away from the mosquitoes and stifling heat of the marina. From there, we would make the final preparations for our journey. After a tense breakfast we started the engine. J stood beside me as I took the wheel.

'She's going to have the most appalling prop walk,' he said. 'She'll do everything she can to go to port when steaming astern.'

I nodded and gazed ahead over what seemed like miles of boat. The bow looked impossibly far away, the space was confined and expensive boats lay on all sides. I could see that J would dearly like to take command, but was forcing himself to hold back. He stood at my side like a lifeguard, ready to jump in any direction to save our ship.

'Let's start off with the wheel hard to starboard as we cast off, and listen to me as we head off.'

Juliet was standing on the bow and I could see she was as nervous as I was. The boys were huddled in excitement in a corner of the cockpit. By now we had an audience: people from neighbouring boats had gathered to see us off, some hovering nervously on the decks of their boats, ready to fend us off; others standing on the pontoon hoping for a bit of sport. There is nothing sailors like more than watching a beginner mess up.

'OK Jules!' I shouted, a sailor's heartiness in my tone, at least. 'Let go!' She pulled the line in as we went astern and I looked over my shoulder at the gleaming yacht that lay close behind us.

'OK, now ease the wheel round to port,' J said. 'Hold it hard as the water will want to flick it away from you.'

With a sweaty hand I did as instructed and gradually *Forever*'s stern swerved out of her berth and into the wider harbour. With a sigh of relief I slipped the engine into neutral and brought the rudder amidships. But she kept moving backwards and was now rapidly approaching the line of boats on the other side.

'Bloody hell – she's still moving.' I hastily put the engine ahead.

'This is a heavy boat and once she gets going she'll take quite a while to stop,' J said. 'Better allow yourself at least six boat lengths from where you plan to stop – depending on wind and current of course.'

As we turned out of the harbour, the fetid calm of the marina was instantly replaced by a new world of energy and light. A fresh breeze set everything clinking and choppy waves bounced *Forever* up and down as we felt the full force of the trade wind. The sea was such a bright blue it was almost painful, and pelicans dive-bombed on all sides. The boys hung over the side in fascination, and we were all smiling with the joy of being free of the marina at last.

Safely tied up to one of the mooring buoys that lay in a neat line along the town beach, we sat for a while in the cockpit, marvelling at the new world in which we found ourselves. A joyful detachment set in as we found ourselves looking onto the island and no longer a part of it. We could hear neither cars nor people – the only sounds were wind and water and the only smell the sea. The boys were rapt, lost in it all as they hung over the high cockpit sides looking down into the water.

'Dad, look: Papa, Mum, Dad!' Luke beckoned furiously, scared and excited at the same time. He pointed down into the water and as we crouched around him the dark blue shape of a manta ray, perhaps eight feet across and stippled with white, drifted serenely out from the shadow of our keel.

Later, we dropped off the side of the boat into the cool, clear sea and sank into its clicking depths before breaking the surface with relaxed shrieks of happiness. At last we were getting a glimpse of the dream that had brought us here, and while the family splashed and played – Luke holding firmly onto the bathing ladder in case the manta ray made a reappearance – and J circled the boat virtuously, I floated with my feet resting against *Forever*'s rounded sides. From the water she looked immense, and I gazed up at her in amazement that this beautiful boat was ours; that we were on the verge of a journey that we hoped would eventually take us back to Tobermory, our home harbour on the Isle of Mull. We had a long way to go, but we had taken the first step, and it felt good.

TWO

ESCAPE FROM BONAIRE

The next day we set off to buy provisions, trudging across the town until we reached a large supermarket. Inside was a strange, dislocating range of food. Bonaire is part of the Netherlands and this store sold a curious blend of Northern European and Caribbean food, salt fish lying cheek by jowl with a strange selection of vegetables and endless varieties of sausage.

I trailed around after Juliet as she crossed items off a provisions list that would have put one of Stanley's expeditions in the shade. At the checkout, I watched the manicured fingernails of the shop assistant tap the counter impatiently as the till printed out our receipt. She tore off the yard of paper and handed it to us. 'That's three hundred Euros and ninety-nine cents,' she said, giving us a challenging stare as if she suspected we wouldn't be able to pay.

While Juliet rummaged around for her credit card, I saw a large cockroach scurrying towards a gap in the ceiling panels. I tapped her arm and pointed. She looked up quickly. 'Yes I know, I noticed them already.' We both knew what this meant: every single item would have to be taken out of its packaging and repacked into plastic bags. Tessa had given us stern warnings about the dangers of taking cardboard on board, which was often laden with cockroach eggs.

Back at *Forever*, as we transferred the provisions from the dinghy, I looked up and saw clouds racing in a darkening sky – the weather was changing and not for the better. We'd planned to head off the next day, but perhaps this wasn't a good idea. On the other hand, none of us relished the prospect of staying in Bonaire any longer than we had to. We were in suspended animation and the longer we stayed here the harder it would be to face up to what lay ahead.

Every available surface was covered with bags and tins and packets and in the midst of it all Juliet stood looking hot and bothered, trying to find a home for everything in the increasingly congested space. One of *Forever*'s shortcomings was that she did not have a lot of room for storage, and what must have been adequate for Mike and Tessa was very limited for a family of five. What's more, the storage was mainly in lockers concealed behind the cushioned backs of the seats in the saloon, so that a simple request to pass the sugar might mean dismantling practically the whole cabin. This is one of the challenges that first-time live-aboard families face and though in time we would refine our system, for the moment it felt like an impossible task. I was wrestling with one of the sofa cushions, trying to squeeze one last packet of pasta into the cubbyhole behind, when I heard a few polite knocks on the hull.

'Ahoy *Forever*! Anyone in?'

Grateful for the distraction, I pulled myself up the companionway and peered over the side. A man in his forties with salt and pepper hair and an unruly beard was looking up.

'Hey there,' he stood unsteadily in his dinghy and reached to shake my hand. 'My name's Ralph – I'm on a mooring a couple of boats along. I hear you guys are heading north?'

'Yes,' I replied. 'We're planning to leave in the next couple of days.'

'Us too. Bit worried about the weather though. It's been blowing hard for the past couple of weeks and it's out of the ordinary – normally only gets this blowy around Christmas time. Where are you headed?'

'Well we were planning to head east for the Islas de Aves and Los Roques,' I replied cautiously. 'From there we can cross over to the Virgin Islands. It's a longer journey than we'd like, but can't see any other options really . . .'

I waited for the obligatory piece of 'advice' that we had come to expect, but Ralph simply nodded and held onto *Forever*'s caprail, looking up at the lowering sky.

'Climate change has set everything on its head. Trades are all screwy and wind seems to be increasing all the time. We've been waiting for weeks for a weather window – if we're not careful we'll be stuck down here till next year. Course this is a real ocean-going boat', he looked over *Forever* admiringly. 'She's up to it, if you are.'

This statement hung in the air for a few moments. 'Tell you what,' he said. 'Why don't you and your family come over in the morning and we can talk about the crossing. Maybe we can figure it out together.' He gave a bright smile, only slightly marred by his many missing teeth, and waved cheerily as he headed off.

That night Juliet and I both lay listening to the wind, which was now positively howling through the boat. Our enjoyment of the cooling breeze had been rapidly superseded by fear of the journey ahead. I knew we were both thinking of the dark ocean, and the prospect of being hundreds of miles from land in an untested boat. 'Do we really want to do this?' Juliet whispered.

'We don't really have a choice Jules – and anyway the wind sounds much worse than it is.' I tried to sound confident, though the thought of our two little boys, their unconditional trust in us, scared me. I was worried that we were in over our heads.

The next morning we climbed into the dinghy to make our way to Ralph's boat, the boys squealing with delight as we were repeatedly soaked by the choppy waves. 'OK boys, calm down,' I said as we neared the boat. 'Remember you're ambassadors for Britain.'

Juliet rolled her eyes. 'Never mind that boys – just be good.'

'We're ambrassers for Britain,' Luke said proudly.

'Ambassadors,' I corrected.

'Ambressers,' he said stubbornly. 'That's what I said.'

Ralph appeared on deck and waved. As we came alongside his boat rolled in the swell, showing undersides that were thick with green weed. Clearly she hadn't sailed anywhere in some time. As we clambered aboard Ralph's wife, Emma, appeared. 'Welcome aboard!' she greeted us. 'Coffee's on and I got some home-made keylime pie!'

We followed them down below, feeling excited to have the chance to see how seasoned live-aboards did things. Yet as we descended into the dark interior the feeling was not good. Far from being orderly and sparse, this boat was filled to the brim with grubby clutter. A smell of damp hung in the air, and books and charts lay everywhere. We perched around the saloon table in amongst the chaos, trying to look relaxed and friendly but feeling distinctly claustrophobic. Through the door of the aft cabin, I could see a bunk piled high with dirty sails, old rope, ancient lifejackets and other rubbish.

I wondered how anyone could live like this. For us, the whole point of living at sea was to leave possessions behind – not to live in, around and under them in an unfeasibly small space. The children were looking around, wide-eyed and I saw Luke tugging at Juliet's arm. To forestall any embarrassing observations I asked Ralph a few questions about our current nemesis, SSB radio, and he was happily engaged on a detailed description of frequencies, call signs and computer software when Emma broke in.

'That's enough of that technical chat,' she trilled. 'Here y'all go, keylime pie!' and she slid pink plastic plates across the table towards us. We thanked her profusely, overcompensating for our instinctive nervousness as we contemplated the grey, gooey slabs that lay before us.

'Goody, do I love this pie!' exclaimed Ralph, as he steered a glob of it under his moustache-hidden lip. Out of the corner of my eye I could see that the boys were still staring at their plates.

'Now Guy, I hope I can be frank with you . . .' Ralph smiled. 'I've been keeping a close eye on the weather and figure you should wait a while before you head off. I don't know what your experience is . . .' He paused and glanced at Emma. 'But it's a big ocean out there and – well, we wouldn't want you taking any chances, specially with the kiddies and all.'

'Besides,' Emma cut in brightly, 'there are so many folks here who would love to meet you and get you involved with things. Most of the families get together for school each morning and there's tons of stuff for the kids to do. And Juliet, I do an arts and crafts workshop on a Wednesday morning for the ladies. We're doing batik this week – d'you think you'd like to come along?'

Emma and Ralph both watched Juliet closely for a response. Clearly we were being assessed as to whether we were worthy of admittance to the inner circle of the Bonaire cruising community. Juliet nodded, though I knew it would be her idea of hell. 'Thank you Emma, you're very kind.'

'You're so welcome,' she replied. 'And I hope you're listening to the cruisers' net. Channel 68, every morning at 7am. You'll hear everything that's going on.'

We had tuned in to the daily VHF radio broadcast that seemed to form a key part of the live-aboard lifestyle. Hosted by stalwarts of the cruising community, the broadcast gave an opportunity to welcome new arrivals, say goodbye to departing yachts and announce social events ranging from 'pot luck suppers' to bingo nights and dinghy 'raft-ups', all of which sounded equally excruciating. It was very friendly, but hardly the adventurous lifestyle we had looked forward to – in fact it was starting to feel as if we had checked into a floating retirement home.

'Oh yes, we are.' I could see Juliet was looking for a way to change the subject before she was press-ganged into pottery or knitting classes. 'Sounds fun, but we probably won't be here for too long . . .' She paused, trying to look regretful. 'When do you guys plan to head off?'

A shadow of panic crossed Emma's face. 'We're waiting for a weather window,' Ralph said. 'See, this old girl ain't designed for speed . . .' he laughed and gestured around the boat. 'Best we can make is 4 knots and with the wind in the wrong direction and an adverse current considerably less. We'd be fighting a losing battle. Just hope the wind dies down soon or we might land up here all winter. Still, better that than taking chances . . .' His voice tailed off and I felt he was somehow making a point.

I glanced down at my slice of pie. There was no getting out of eating it – to leave it would be unforgivably rude. I dug my fork in and noticed a long, greyish hair, which stretched and then sprung clear of the goo. Must have belonged to Emma, I thought miserably, aware of the rolling of the boat anew. A faint yellow feeling descended on me, not helped when I looked up to see Ralph's lips moving wetly over a plug of chewing tobacco.

The boys were having trouble with their pie too and although they'd moved it around a bit I could see they'd eaten nothing. Emma stood up to clear the plates. 'Aren't you gonna finish up your pie boys?' she asked and I saw them both freeze and look first at her then at me, their eyes pleading for help.

'I think maybe they need to take their time eating it Emma,' I said. 'It's so delicious, but a bit too rich for them to eat in one go . . . maybe we could wrap it up and take it back with us?'

Ralph shot me a suspicious look and I knew I had no choice but to finish my piece. I surreptitiously moved the hair to the side of the plate with my fork before wolfing it down in a few deep swallows.

Back on board we held a hasty conference. The prospect of being stuck in Bonaire press-ganged into pot luck suppers and raft-ups had given us the impetus we needed, and we resolved to leave that night. Our first stop-off would be at the Islas de Aves, a group of islands that lay approximately thirty miles to the east. It was crucial that we arrive in daylight, as we would have to eyeball our way through the treacherous coral reefs. We calculated that our journey might take as long as ten hours, allowing for the fact that we would be heading directly into the wind and weather, so we set our departure for midnight. This gave us some time to make final preparations and grab a bit of sleep before we cast off.

Before leaving Bonaire we needed clearance from Customs, so later that afternoon I hopped into the dinghy and headed into town with our passports. At the customs office I was guided to a shabby waiting room which felt like the headquarters for a right-wing junta, with officials dressed in sharp uniforms complete with sunglasses hanging from shirt pockets and polished combat boots.

A door swung open and I was directed into the office of the senior customs officer. He was a swarthy, powerful man, and his seniority was made clear by the size of his desk. Acres of mahogany stretched between us, and as he looked me up and down I knew I wasn't making a good impression. I cursed myself for not making more of an effort: worn khaki shorts, a grease-smudged T-shirt and Crocs were clearly not going to go down well in this bastion of officialdom.

He stood up from behind his desk, and as he did so I took in his pure Noriega chic: epaulettes, shiny buttons and sunglasses; gun in holster hanging from a well-oiled leather belt and a shirt that had been ironed to an astonishing level of complexity.

'What can I do for you?' he asked.

'Well, we're on a boat,' I began. 'We're planning to leave Bonaire tonight and I understand that you have to be informed?'

He raised his eyebrows and brought his fingers together in a thoughtful triangle as if contemplating a complex chess opener. 'What boat do you come from?'

'*Forever*,' I answered. 'We're on a mooring opposite the town beach.'

He looked troubled. 'Was that boat not in Harbour Village Marina?'

'Yes, she was.'

He leant forward looking suspicious. 'But it is owned by another man . . . Michael Bateson, is it not?'

'Ah yes,' I raised a hand and smiled with relief. 'We've just bought the boat from him.'

He sat back on his chair. 'So you buy the boat and you leave tonight?'

'Yes . . .' I said doubtfully.

'But where is proof of this sale?' He looked annoyed and an image of being blindfolded and dropped from a helicopter played out in my mind. 'We have many boats stolen here – I need to see proof.'

'I'm not sure I have that document . . .' I fumbled about in my knapsack as if I was looking for it, but in reality I knew it wasn't there.

There was a heavy silence in the room, broken only by the officer sliding open a drawer in his capacious desk and taking out a cigar. In a scene so clichéd that I felt like a bit-part player in a B-movie, he slowly prepared and lit it and then sat back in his creaking leather chair.

I thought quickly. I had only one option: to appeal to the boundless ego of this man.

'Sir . . .' I leant forward to gain full eye contact. 'I have never owned a boat before. I am young and this is all very new . . .'

He lowered his cigar and blew a plume of blue smoke up towards the ceiling fan. I took a deep breath and threw away the last shreds of my dignity.

'I come to you as a son might to a father. My family rely on me and I need your help and guidance.'

He nodded slowly and placed his cigar into the ashtray. 'You are inexperienced – I see this. And your family are with you?'

I could see he was weakening. 'Yes, two boys. Do you have any children?'

'Yes, two daughters.'

What a shame, I thought: who's going to inherit his handgun collection? But he was smiling now and I knew we'd found some common ground. Time to make the final appeal.

'Sir . . . would you allow me to sign out of Bonaire now and I will return with the sale document before we leave?' I hoped that we would be able to find some kind of proof of sale – if not we could make a run for it.

Another silence and the hands were in prayer mode again. At last he sat back and nodded. 'Go and see my officials and tell them I said to sign you out. And don't bother with the form – you are not a liar, I can see.'

'Thank you sir,' I said, feeling like a courtier who had been spared the block. I stood up to leave before he could change his mind.

'One thing,' he said, tapping the desk with his finger. 'You must not come into customs office dressed like this again, it is not good.'

I nodded dutifully. In brisk, military fashion he stood up and slapped his hand into mine in a classic macho handshake, smiling widely now as he basked in his role as benefactor. I stood to attention and thanked him again, then sidled out of his office, feeling intensely relieved but also just a little bit dirty. There was no denying it: I had just massaged the ego of a megalomaniac. But then again, at that moment I would have done almost anything to escape Bonaire.

THREE

THE GREAT LEAP

12.7N: 68.17W

The atmosphere on the boat was electric with anticipation as we readied ourselves for departure. We had eaten an early supper, cleared up and carefully stowed everything that we imagined might come loose in rough weather. We knew to expect big seas when we came out of the lee of Bonaire and were prepared for the worst. Snacks and drinks had been placed in strategic places, and Juliet had taken extra care over the boys' cabin, their bunk made up with clean linen and diversions in the form of books and games placed close at hand. I saw that she had put a favourite stuffed toy on each pillow, and some pictures of home were pinned up above their bunk. Our hope was that their cabin might become a kind of panic room for them should things become frightening on the boat.

We gathered in the cockpit after dinner, eager for the time to pass now we were committed to leaving. We had worked out a system that meant two people would be on watch at any one time. J and I would do the first watch from midnight till 4 a.m. then Juliet would take over from J, meaning that I would be on watch all night. I lifted the engine cover and stared into its glistening, oily depths. The engine was old and as yet largely untested – we would be relying heavily on it on this first leg as we were heading more or less straight into the wind. We had filled up on fuel and water earlier in the day; still, I was nervous, engines never having been my strong point. I wondered if I'd ever get to grips with its mysteries.

As if reading my mind, J spoke up: 'Have you checked the oil and water Guy? Need to do that before every long passage. And what about the sea cocks?'

'Yup, all OK. The engine's going to have a good long run – just hope it doesn't let us down.'

He shrugged and half smiled. The boys were sitting side by side on the saloon bench, watching me, sensing our unease.

'Are we going to sail in the dark?' asked Luke.

'Yes.' I smiled, trying to look calm, though in fact I was overcome by a startling pang of fear. I had confronted my own fragility in the face of nature before – a year alone in the wilderness of Alaska – but this time I had my children with me and I was painfully aware of my responsibility to keep them safe.

'But Dad, how can we see?' His voice quivered a little and he looked over to Oscar, who might have felt too grown up to ask the question, but clearly also wanted reassurance.

'Don't worry boys,' I said, sitting down beside them. 'When you wake up tomorrow we'll be at some beautiful islands that hardly anyone gets to go to – real desert islands. Don't worry about it being dark – there's a half moon out and you'll soon see that things aren't ever really completely dark. The instruments will tell us which way we are going, so we can't get lost.'

Outside the night was thickening. On either side the line of yachts rose and fell gently on their moorings, lights glowing and cooking smells wafting over as evening meals were prepared and people settled down for the night. Unlike us, I thought, who in just a few hours would be forging out into the unknown. On the next-door yacht a woman was unpegging clothes from the lifelines, where they had been drying in the sun. She glanced our way and saw immediately the familiar pattern of a boat being readied for a passage. She stood and waved, then cupped her hands around her mouth.

'Hey, you guys, be careful,' she called. 'Don't be too proud to turn back if things get tough!'

'Thanks!' I called back. 'We hope to be in the Aves tomorrow morning.'

She crossed her fingers in the air, sat down on the coachroof and began folding her clothes. A car drove along the waterfront and I saw the beam of its lights catch along the tops of the waves as they curved and rolled into the town beach. It felt hard, counter-intuitive, leaving the security of the land and casting off in the middle of the night. I stood on deck for a long time until it was fully dark, drinking in the sounds and smells of the land, my mind spinning with doubt.

Three hours later, hazy after a short and fitful sleep, we were ready to cast off.

'I think there's enough wind to sail off the mooring,' I said to J, who stood at the helm. He looked around, assessing the distance between us and the other yachts.

'Fine with me,' he replied, 'but get the engine on and keep it in neutral just in case we need it.'

I ducked into the companionway and started the engine, then leant over the side to check for the little stream of water that showed the engine cooling system was working. I hoisted *Forever*'s main-sail, putting in one reef for caution, then left it loose and flapping while I came back to the cockpit to unfurl her massive foresail. The sail opened out fluttering like the wings of a giant bird readying itself for flight.

'Stand by!' I called to Juliet, who was at the bow, ready to cast off the mooring. 'And watch out for the jib – I'm going to back it a bit to get us started.'

As the jib filled with air, *Forever*'s bow gradually came round to point away from the land towards the dark sky in the east.

'OK, let go!' I called, taking my place at the helm. A chorus of 'Let go!' echoed from within the boat as the boys joined in from their cabin. Clearly the sounds of our preparations had woken them.

I heard the splash as Juliet dropped the mooring buoy into the water and we began moving surprisingly swiftly. 'Can you pull in the jib?' I asked J and he shook his head. With great understatement he pointed silently towards a sleek grey yacht that lay directly in our path.

'Fuck!' I shouted, just as Juliet called out: 'Guy, we're going to hit that boat!'

Forever had now gained more speed, her considerable weight adding momentum to my mistake. I imagined a sickening crash and crunch as we ploughed into the sleeping yacht that I had failed to spot in the darkness.

'Turn the wheel to port,' J called over his shoulder, loosening the jib sheet. 'Engage reverse gear and put her hard astern!'

I did as instructed, and was quickly relieved as *Forever* began to respond to the power of the engine and slow down. As she came to a stop, I put the engine ahead and with a great rattling and whipping of sails and sheets steered around the stern of the yacht, halting a course that in just a few seconds would have led to mayhem and disaster. On the yacht, a silver-haired man dressed in boxer shorts lifted himself into the cockpit to see us scything past.

I set us on a course parallel to the coastline, watching as J winched the jib and main sheets in tight and then leant down to turn the engine off. *Forever* immediately picked up speed and heeled away from the wind. 'Let's go!' she seemed to say and I heard faint clinking from the galley as everything settled itself into position for our course. Juliet clambered back along the deck and sat down in the cockpit. For a while we all said nothing. The silence felt pointed: nobody needed to tell me that my first job as skipper at sea hadn't gone well. It hurt more than seemed reasonable, but that was because the stakes were so high. A simple mistake could lead to the nullification of everything: our boat, our dreams, our finances and even our lives.

But soon I was won over by the sheer joy of sailing, forgetting the near-collision as I allowed myself to be seduced by this new world. All around us the night air was filled with the euphoric sound of progress and motion at sea, fizzing and sucking at *Forever*'s sides as we cut across its dark surface. Behind us in the darkness we could see our wake glowing white, with the occasional glimpse of flashing green phosphorescence. The sails were taut, like steel, and their sheets and winches groaned with tension as sixteen tons of boat were hauled across the sea. A gust of wind hit us and I bore away a little as J eased the mainsheet to allow some of its force to pass us by. Now we were sailing the sense of freedom was intoxicating: the joy of travelling silently without reliance on engine or fuel, harnessing the energies of the wind alone.

To port, the dark mass of Bonaire was passing by as we headed southeast, an eerie lunar light on the dark surface of the sea. The boys were too excited to sleep so Juliet helped them into their lifejackets and tucked them in beside her on the leeward side of the cockpit. She pointed up at the mast and they all three tilted their heads back to look up at the great sail glowing white against the starry sky. I knew Juliet and I were thinking the same thing: that our adventure had now truly begun, that we had thrown our lot into Neptune's lap and had to be ready for anything. Our lives had come closer to an edge, a zone where our actions and decisions would have a much more dramatic and immediate effect on the passage of our lives. Here we could not ignore death, as we did in our comfortable lives on land and this factor alone would serve to magnify and underline the sheer joy of living. It would also stalk our every move.

Two hours later and it was a very different scene. We had passed out of the protective lee of the island and were now exposed to the full force of the waves, which had built momentum over several hundred miles of open ocean. The wind was markedly stronger and *Forever*'s movement was now violent as she punched into much bigger seas. We were struggling to hold our course, which was – as we had known it would be – more or less directly into the wind. To make progress we had no choice but to put the engine back on, which led to a horrible motion as the boat pushed directly into the waves. Juliet and the boys had been asleep for a couple of hours, or at least I thought they were, until Juliet appeared at the companionway.

'God, it's a bit rough up here,' she said, gripping the edge of the coachroof for support as *Forever* bucked and plunged. 'Feels awful down below. Is everything OK?'

'So far so good,' I replied. 'Look, you should get some more sleep – there's nothing you can do here.'

Although we had agreed a watch system with two people at a time, it was soon apparent that only one was required on deck, so J had also gone for a nap. Before he did so he double-checked our course and pointed out a couple of hazards on the chart. We were fortunate to have a chart plotter, an instrument which told us where we were in relation to the various landforms and hazards that lay all around. Nevertheless, we had made it a rule to regularly mark our position on the paper chart so that we would know where we were should the instruments go wrong. This meant visiting the chart table at least once every hour to make calculations with calculator, pencil and parallel rules and write our position in the log. This was becoming increasingly difficult for me, as I was feeling distinctly queasy.

As my watch neared its end, I stared up at the swinging mast while *Forever* rose, fell, rocked and thudded on. There were no visible landmarks, in fact nothing solid of any kind and my only point of reference was the compass, which lurched from side to side, lit by a sickly, reddish light. I needed to go below to make my final log entry. I scanned about for the lights of any shipping and seeing nothing switched on the auto-helm. Like a free diver about to descend into the murk, I took a deep breath and stepped down the companionway towards the chart table, grabbing its edge before the next wave sent me flying. In the saloon lay books, food and clothing where they had escaped from lockers and shelves and I noticed a couple of smashed glasses lying in the sink. The engine hummed loudly from beneath the cabin sole and a hot smell of oil filled the whole boat. J was sitting on the edge of his bunk, which doubled as one of the settees in the saloon, pulling on his deck shoes. I could see from his expression that he needed no reminding that his watch was about to begin.

The seat at the chart table had a disturbing habit of swinging out when you least expected it and I pressed my knees hard on the underside of the table to keep myself still. I sharpened a pencil and marked our course on the chart, using the GPS co-ordinates that glowed greenly from the chart plotter's screen. Then, using the dividers, I started to work out the distance we had travelled and the number of nautical miles that remained. Depressingly, we were only about a third of the way through the journey. As I wrote in the logbook my knees kept slipping and the chair pivoted from side to side. I knew this was the beginning of the end: like ink spreading through water, the nausea seeped into every part of me, settling like a layer of pollution and turning my entire world yellow.

J now stood by my side, dressed in overalls and jacket, ready for business.

'How far have we got to go?' he asked.

'About twenty nautical miles,' I replied, finding it hard to speak through a mouth that seemed suddenly thick with saliva.

'Have you given any thought to our approach to the island?'

I shook my head. We were both clinging to the edge of the chart table, our sweaty bodies wedged against the ceaseless motion of the boat. I was trying to ignore the tingling sense of doom rising up in me, but knew I was losing the battle. Through my misery I saw that J was watching me with his characteristic sardonic expression.

'Well you'd better think about it,' he said. 'Plenty of time though – at this speed we're going to take at least another six hours. Better get some sleep.'

'Not sure I can stay down here,' I mumbled, contemplating the horror of another six hours of this torture. 'Think I'm better off out on deck.'

He nodded. Though he was blessed with a cast iron stomach and had famously only suffered seasickness once in his life, I knew that in his own way he was sympathetic. 'Best place for you is the leeward side of the cockpit.'

My body felt as heavy as lead as I pulled myself up through the companionway, wedging myself by the winch on the downwind side of the cockpit while J took the wheel. Slowly, inevitably, I succumbed to the nausea and vomited noisily over the side, my face disturbingly close to the foamy water that swirled and gurgled around the stern. Again and again I threw up, until I felt empty and drained. Yet still my body wasn't content and I continued to retch repeatedly, the sensation made even worse by having nothing to bring up.

'Why did I think I could do this?' I groaned between retches, speaking my thoughts aloud. 'How could I have forgotten how bloody awful this feels?'

J glanced down briefly at the pitiful mess that was his son-in-law. 'Well, you're certainly having a bad time just now.' He looked ahead again, holding firmly onto the wheel that was straining from side to side. 'Still, you'll probably get used to it after a few days, most people do.'

I couldn't imagine feeling normal ever again. I stared up at the stars as they flew past the mast. I remembered our excited conversations back home as we traced the route from Bonaire back to Scotland via almost all of the islands of the Caribbean. Now look at me, I thought miserably: ten miles into an insignificant thirty-mile crossing, lying at the feet of my 71-year-old father-in-law, totally incapacitated.

'Nelson suffered from seasickness you know.' I knew J was trying to bolster my spirits, but wondered what was coming. 'They had an odd cure for seasickness in his day.'

'Really? What was it?' I sat up, ready to try any kind of treatment, even if it was from the eighteenth century.

'The malingerer would swallow a piece of bacon fat tied to a line of string. Then they would pull the end of the string and haul the bacon back up again.' He paused as I slumped back down in the cockpit. 'I suppose the logic was that the cure was worse than the sickness.'

'Well, thank you for those highly comforting words,' I said, lurching to my feet for another vomiting session.

Soon it was time for another log entry, and I ventured below unsteadily, this time taking a bucket from the cockpit as a precautionary measure and hanging it around my neck with a length of string.

Down below, I found Oscar lying face down on his bunk, twisting and writhing with misery at this unfamiliar sensation. Juliet was stroking his head with one hand, a bucket at the ready in the other.

His crying turned to a wail of panic and as I watched him, his face grey and sweaty, moaning with agony between bursts of vomiting, I wondered – not for the first or last time – if we had made a huge mistake.

The next morning the sun rose over a fitful and unhappy seascape. I woke having had a few hours' sleep on a sweaty berth in the saloon, but something in me had been damaged, and it was beyond the physical. Juliet was on the helm, her father seated beside her in the cockpit. Luke was playing, having breakfasted on two slices of toast and a glass of orange juice, seemingly none the worse for the night's dramas. Oscar was stretched out on the opposite bunk in the saloon, still looking very pale, though he was no longer being sick. I ruffled his blond hair, now dark with sweat. 'Don't worry big boy. Won't be too long until we anchor and then we can relax for a bit.'

'I don't think I like this at all Dad', he said. On cue *Forever* lurched as a wave caught her broadsides and I sat quickly as Oscar clung to the shelf above him. 'Dad!' he shouted as pots and plates rattled in the sink.

We still didn't know *Forever* very well, I reflected. She was quite an old boat – who was to say what flaws she might be concealing? I looked up at the varnished butterfly hatch overhead, which every now and then pattered with spray as a wave crashed over the deck. It was just made of glass, I thought – inadequate protection from a really big wave. But the nausea had taken away my capacity for fear as well as every other emotion, and at that moment I felt indifferent to my fate.

Several hours later I was called up from the chart table by shrieks of excitement. 'Guy! Come up!' Juliet shouted.

'Land ahoy!' Luke was pointing triumphantly as if he had person-ally discovered the islands, which stretched across the skyline looking no more substantial than a thread of cloud pulled thin along the horizon. This was land unlike any other that we had seen: no solidity or permanence, no mountains, cliffs or miles of coastline. Almost like a mirage, the faint outposts of ground seemed to belong more to the clouds and sky than to anything else. Yet as we grew closer there was no denying that they were real.

'Land! Land!' the boys chanted, dancing with excitement. J sat with them on either side, holding them close, his large hands cupped around each small shoulder. I stared out towards the islands and felt what can only be described as land-love, a feeling no doubt shared by mariners across the centuries who had completed passages many times more arduous than mine.

I took a bearing and then darted down to the chart, which showed two groups of cays about ten miles apart. Fighting off a fresh dose of seasickness, I leafed through the sailing guide that showed possible approaches through the dangerously shallow coral reefs. We decided to pass by the first group of islands, the Aves De Sotovento, where great clouds of birds were visible, wheeling and calling and diving above tall mangroves. We sailed on to the next group – the Aves de Barlovento – made up of an alluring circle of cays and shoals around five miles in diameter.

As we drew near the islands J stood in the cockpit holding the pilot book in one hand. He squinted at it, then ahead at the islands. 'I think we should go in there,' he said, jabbing his finger at a plan in the book and then pointing ahead.

'Um, I don't know J, I don't like the look of it. It's very shallow and look –' I held the book up in front of him. 'It says you need local knowledge to go in there. We can easily go into one of the anchorages further out.'

'Nonsense Guy,' he said briskly, 'we can eyeball our way in. The water is crystal clear and at this time of day the visibility is excellent. Now let's drop sail and I'll stand on the bow and point our way in.'

'OK,' I said, having to overrule the feelings of caution, natural I supposed, in a beginner. It was hard for me, too, as someone who was used to making decisions by myself, to accept the instructions of someone else, even if I had invited them into that role.

A few minutes later J was in position on the bowsprit with pilot book in one hand and the other arm wrapped around the rolled up jib. Every now and then he held an arm out and pointed, indicating that I should steer in that direction to avoid the shallow water. And so we guided *Forever* through the shoals and extremely sharp coral heads drawing, it seemed to me, unreasonably close to the shore. I knew that if we hit it could be catastrophic, and so, as carefully as if we were passing through a minefield, I concentrated on keeping *Forever* on an exact course.

We had now entered the protective circle of the reef and the water was flat calm. Surely we've gone far enough in, I thought, but J still stood immobile as we edged closer and closer to a sand- and grass-covered cay that barely stood above the turquoise water. I watched the gauge, calling out depths as I waited for his signal to stop the boat, but his big hand waved me dismissively on:

'Four fathoms!' I called out.

'Three point five fathoms!' It was falling rapidly. 'Three!' The hand waved again.

'Two point five fathoms! Two point three!' *Forever*'s draught was around one fathom and for me this was uncomfortably shallow, but still he motioned onward. I turned to Juliet. 'Is he trying to run us aground? Maybe he fancies being shipwrecked.' But then, as the depth gauge dropped to just below two fathoms, the hand at last signalled to stop.

'Thank God,' Juliet muttered, and I throttled astern to stop the boat, letting the backward motion continue gently as J dropped the anchor and let the chain pay out. *Forever* stopped abruptly as the anchor dug into the sandy seabed and I leant forward to turn the engine off. We flopped back in the cockpit with what must have been an ancient sense of relief: the simple joy of being safe, with an anchor well set.

Without the engine we were suddenly aware of the silence, yet within moments our ears tuned into the exotic sounds of the land. Being at sea you experience a kind of sensory deprivation, all the natural sounds and scents of the land replaced by the twin symphony of wind and water. Yet now we could hear birds calling and the wind sighing against the backdrop of the distant boom of the swell. Our sense of smell was heightened too: less than twelve hours at sea and we drank in the rich, almost peppery perfume of the thin, humid soil beneath the mangroves and the fresh green of the leaves. Over all this, the air held the tinge of a stirred-up sea, the surf forming into teetering ozoney rafts of foam over the coral.

The horror of the past twelve hours of seasickness slipped away as I contemplated this new and heavenly world. Like a magic carpet, *Forever* had transported us from a desiccated Bonaire to this enchanted coral circle, luminescent white sand on an azure sea. Juliet went below and as the kettle began to sing, I thrilled at the thought that this boat was actually our home. Here, swinging lightly on our anchor beside this dot in the ocean, we would make tea, eat, read and sleep.

Luke wanted to swim, so I threw out a floating line with a large fender attached to the end in case he needed to grab something. Then I lowered the ladder and dropped a lifebuoy in as well to be on the safe side. He lowered himself into the water, setting off on a series of frenzied doggy paddles with his chin held high and his armbands keeping him up. With obvious relief he made it back to the ladder and hung in the clear, brilliant water. Just then Oscar appeared from nowhere, flying over Luke and landing beside him with a giant splash.

'Oscar! Don't do that!' Luke was incensed but Oscar was off. He had his mask and snorkel on and after a little dive he popped up.

'Mum!' he shouted to Juliet, who was standing beside me, ready to swim. 'We're really close to the bottom.'

Climbing down the ladder, she took his mask from him then swam a little way along the side of the boat, peering down into the water. She surfaced and called: 'Er, it does actually look very shallow Guy, come and take a look.'

I glanced over at J, who was seated in the cockpit. 'Do you hear that J?'

'Yes', he answered without taking his eyes off his book. 'But there's no swell in here and unless the wind changes drastically, which is exceedingly unlikely, we'll be fine for the night.'

I sighed, feeling instinctively uncomfortable, but with no choice other than to trust in his experience. I put on my mask and snorkel and plunged into the water and saw at once that the bottom of *Forever*'s keel was indeed just a few feet above the sandy seabed. Alarmed, I climbed back up the ladder. 'There's only about four feet of water beneath the keel and I don't like it.' I stood dripping.

Still he continued reading. 'As I said, there's no swell in here, we'll be fine.'

I glanced out over the water towards the open sea. 'We could go out into deeper water.'

'Can't do that Guy.' He closed the book with a sigh. 'The visibility isn't good enough because the sun is too low in the sky. We would very likely do more damage by heading out now and hitting a coral head than by staying here. I'm sure the wind will hold – it would be very unusual if it came around to the west.'

And so we remained where we were, savouring the privilege of existing in such a hidden, blissful spot, yet with a slight tension hanging over everything. There was a certain silky feel to our predicament:

like an insect we had ambled our way into what could become a trap. We just had to hope the wind didn't change, because if it did, I worried that we would never find our way out again.

It seemed that Sod and his awful allies had decided to play with us, because sure enough, as night settled, the wind swung round from its characteristic easterly direction into the south. Gradually a little swell built up, lifting us gently on our anchor. As Juliet and I lay in our bunk, the vision of *Forever*'s keel and its proximity to the bottom was firmly etched on both our minds. The boat's rolling motion increased as the swell built and every now and then we would hear a scraping sound.

'Are we touching the bottom?' Juliet asked in a worried voice after we had heard the noise two or three times.

'I don't know,' I muttered, sticking my head up through the hatch above our bunk like a nautical prairie dog to have a look around. I couldn't see anything and dropped back down to hear J addressing Juliet from his berth in the saloon.

'Look, if we go aground you'll know all about it,' he was saying, 'the sound is unmistakable.'

We repeated this process many times through the course of the night, with the uncomfortable knowledge that, even if we were touching the bottom, there was very little we could do about it. The only consolation was the soft sandiness of the bottom and the immense strength of *Forever*'s hull: we had to hope that even if it did touch, it wouldn't be much damaged. Each time I went up on deck I stood for a few minutes, staring in awe at the glimmering water lit by moonlight, with the scented cays all around. Every now and then a fish jumped, sending out ripples on the soft, black water, and the cries of the tree frogs were set against the constant sighing of the wind through the mangroves.

Thankfully the night passed without event and despite our sleepless state Juliet and I felt lucky to be leaving unscathed. After breakfast and a quick swim, we weighed anchor and picked our way past the malevolent shallows and coral heads, now clearly visible in the morning sunlight. I looked down at them as we passed, imagining the horror of colliding with one of their hard, immobile forms. J had been right about staying where we were, I reflected – a brush with a coral head was definitely something to avoid. Yet if Juliet and I had been on our own we wouldn't have gone in there in the first place. We had learnt a lesson: don't get into a situation that you can't get out of, and never take the weather for granted.

Out of the shelter of Barlovento we turned once again into the relentless head sea. The same old crashing discomfort continued for another thirty miles until the little stipples of the next group of islands showed on the horizon. We were approaching Los Roques, an area of over one hundred islands, cays and islets, all framed by endless reefs and beaches of every imaginable shape and contortion. This archipelago had been made into a national park in 1972, due to its exceptional range of seabirds and rich aquatic life, and until recently was the biggest marine reserve archipelago in the world. I traced my finger around the islands on the chart, imagining them as shavings and off-cuts from the great sculpture of South America. In a very real sense they are more part of the sea than the land, being constructed from the skeletons of trillions of aquatic organisms that had formed into coral. I flipped open the sailing guide and there, across the large-scale chart, were the words 'Unsurveyed Area'. The excitement of our mission struck me afresh as I contemplated the thrilling fact that we were approaching a group of islands so remote that large parts of it remained unmapped.

My spirits were quickly brought down with a bump, as I read on. 'Winter can sometimes turn the whole place into a kind of tropical roaring forties. While cruising is not a problem at this time of the year, it is not pleasurable.' I sighed – with sailing it seemed nothing was ever straightforward. I calculated a course to steer and went up to the cockpit.

'We need to steer 098 degrees,' I said to J, who was on the helm.

He looked down at the compass, then back at the horizon and shook his head. 'Can't be right,' he said. 'Go back and plot it again.'

I took a deep breath and descended once more into the lurching pit that had become my world.

'Okay alter that 10 to port?' He looked down at the compass, then ahead, and nodded. I felt a schoolboy's thrill at having got it right.

Gradually the islands came into view and the glittering water around us turned shallow and luminescent. We had opted to anchor off one of the most Westerly islands, Cayo de Agua and on the way passed a red and white candy-striped lighthouse on nearby West Cay. It looked incongruously Hopper-esque in its deserted position on the low-lying coast. We edged our way in between sharp-edged reefs, tense as our depth gauge reported an ever-decreasing margin between us and destruction. At last we passed through the gauntlet of coral and an area of deeper water opened up. With sighs of relief we dropped our anchor and then let *Forever* settle serenely on her tether. There was a kind of insubstantiality to it all that was oddly exciting: using nothing besides a dainty-looking anchor, we could hitch up anywhere and float for a while, like tying Pegasus to a cloud.

That night we savoured the tranquillity. The next day we would be journeying on to Gran Roques, the only settlement in the islands, to refuel in preparation for the four-day passage north across the Caribbean Sea, and we were conscious that this would be our last peaceful night for some time to come. In the middle of the night a sound woke me, and I slipped out of our berth. I wanted to check the anchor, and with a mind half-filled with thoughts of sleep and journeys to come I ambled along towards the bow. Half way along I stopped as my mind registered that we were no longer alone. Just a few metres away, a battered fishing boat lay gloomily at anchor, and I could hear voices drifting faintly across the water. With deliberate casualness I returned to the cockpit and descended the companionway steps, and then picked up the binoculars to study our neighbours more closely from behind the cover of the dodger. Four or five men were seated in the cockpit, and I saw beer cans glinting in their hands, and every now and then the light of a cigarette glowing in the darkness. They were talking quietly. To my paranoid mind it seemed they were staring over at us. Small wonder, when a boat like *Forever* represented several years or perhaps even a lifetime's earnings in Venezuela.

A forgotten fear gathered like lead in my limbs. I had spent a period not long before living alone in a remote wilderness full of bears and wolves, yet had quickly learnt that my fellow man presented by far the greatest threat. Men are far less predictable than animals and much more ferocious and cruel. And now, afloat in an uncharted seascape, we found ourselves in unexpected company.

I forced my mind through a nervous drill. The boat was clearly local and we were not. The men probably knew these waters like the backs of their hands and their engine was far more powerful than ours. What if they had followed us and decided to wait until the middle of the night before boarding? What would we do if they tried to board? Alone in the wilderness of Alaska I had been heavily armed and ready to defend myself against man or beast. Yet here I was in another form of wilderness, this time with my family sleeping around me and with nothing to defend us except a box of useless flares.

It felt awful to be so suspicious: they were probably just fishermen taking a break and meant us no harm whatsoever. Yet I was conscious that we were less than one hundred miles from the Venezuelan coast, where piracy and kidnapping were everyday events. It would simply be foolish to be too relaxed, and if they meant us no harm why had they anchored so close when there was an infinite number of other places where they could have stopped? And what would be the best policy if they did attempt to board: to give them everything they wanted without a fight? I remembered a story about a couple that did allow pirates aboard without resisting: he was severely beaten and she was raped. We had heard many frightening tales of boardings and attacks in this region and opinion was mixed as to the best approach. I thought about the possibility of lifting anchor and heading off, but the uncharted coral heads would foil any attempt at escape. The fishing boat would have no problem with draught and so would be able to move about almost at will. In short, we could do nothing and, like a tethered goose close to a den of foxes, we just had to hope they weren't hungry.

Just before sunrise I woke with a start to the sound of an engine firing up and carefully poked my head up just in time to see the men gliding past us, all staring as they did so. One of them pointed at something on our deck and the others nodded. They would have seen Luke's inflatable life-ring covered in garish pictures of shells and seahorses hanging beside the swimming ladder and our towels hung out to dry. What must they think of us: a white family come to swim and play in a part of the world that to them must only have represented hardship and toil. How easy it would have been for them to have killed us and sunk the boat, traces of us not picked up for ages. I fell back into our berth feeling powerless and confused, my mind torn between paranoia, fear and sympathy.

FOUR

THE FIRST
BIG PASSAGE

11.49N: 66.55W

The next morning we weighed anchor, and J raised his arm as it cleared the seabed, pulling up a little puff of sand into the translucent water and scattering the brightly coloured fish. The morning was cloudless and blue, the trade wind blowing with tireless predictability. We picked our way clear of Cayo De Agua threading a baking-soda white path through the myriad low-lying cays of Los Roques. I marked our progress on the chart, ticking off tantalising, glistening islands: Carenero, Yanqui, Sarqui, Crasqui and Espenqui. Above them all, in the distance, lay El Gran Roque, the biggest and most northerly of all the islands, dominated by a single high hill visible for miles around. This was our beacon and we steered towards it like Celts guided by a standing stone.

'Now, what about this fuel?' J was scanning ahead with the binoculars.

'Um, we were told that you can buy it from one of the boats in the harbour.' I frowned, wishing I had paid greater attention to what Carlos had said back at the marina. 'Apparently it's pretty cheap too.'

'I certainly hope it's true, because there's nowhere else. Let's keep our fingers crossed.'

'I guess we could just rely on the sails if the worst comes to the worst? After all, sailors wouldn't have had any choice in days gone by.'

'Yes, but then we would have to go where the wind takes us,' he said, 'and with the wind in this direction we might land up in Haiti. That's something we want to avoid.'

'God yes,' I agreed, thinking of the horrendous stories I had heard recently about the fates of yachts landing at Haiti, the most gruesome of which involved a skipper and his wife being attacked with machetes. I was conscious that there would be at least as many good stories as bad, but still it wasn't something I wanted to risk with the whole family onboard. Clearly we needed to know that we were well stocked with fuel.

We watched as the 380-foot rock came steadily closer. It looked like a scaled-down Gibraltar. A motley selection of shack-like houses lined a road made of sand, their red tin roofs garish against the rock that stood hovering in the heat haze. At the end of the village a makeshift airstrip was fringed by wind-blown palms, and parked on the tarmac there were two Dakota planes.

'It looks like Tintin!' Oscar declared, and indeed the whole scene looked as if it might have been drawn by Hergé.

We edged our way into the harbour and scanned around for any boat that looked as if it might dispense fuel. It was mid-afternoon and a number of sailing, fishing and commercial boats lay at anchor, but we couldn't see any signs of life.

'That must be it!' Oscar shouted, pointing at a large, rusty vessel with a distinct list to port moored towards the outside of the harbor. We steered towards the boat and saw some men fishing with hand-lines over the stern.

'Gasoline?' I shouted, slipping *Forever* into neutral and affecting a Spanish accent in the absence of any knowledge of the language.

They shook their heads. '*No señor, no gasolina aquí.*' They returned to their fishing.

'Is there another place?' I called slowly, holding *Forever* in place behind their stern.

They gestured towards a large fishing vessel moored in the middle of the harbour.

We approached the fishing boat, which though rusty and dilapidated was clearly in service. There were a number of men on board playing cards in the shade of a homemade awning. 'Gasoline?' I called again and a man with immense hairy shoulders smiled and signalled for us to come alongside. I circled *Forever* as Juliet readied warps and fenders, wincing at the sight of the many bits of rusty metal that projected from the vessel's hull.

J stood beside me. 'Be bloody careful how you do this,' he muttered under his breath, adding with ironic emphasis, 'I wouldn't like to have to claim on these guys' insurance.'

'Insurance?' I mumbled. 'Surely they won't have any?'

'No Guy.' He smiled grimly. 'Their insurance cover would be a lot more tangible and immediate.'

Thankfully we came alongside gently, and strong hands expertly took our warps and tied us tightly to their floating planet.

'*Cuidado!*' one of the men shouted and pulled on a huge white dog that had bounded up and stood on its hind legs, growling at us, spit bubbling between its bared teeth.

'Good dog,' Luke said, stretching his hand up towards it. The growls increased, and Juliet grabbed him just before he lost his arm.

'*Cuidado!*' one of the men shouted and pulled the beast back into the boat.

'I think that means beware,' J said drily.

All the men leant over the rail to look down on us and we stood in the cockpit trying to look relaxed and friendly. A large tattooed man pushed his way to the front, opening his hands in the universal sign that means 'let's do business'. Behind him, the others returned to their card game, dealing out the faded pack around a rickety table in the stern of the boat. Occasionally one would emit an expletive in Spanish, and another would laugh darkly, reaching forwards to light a cigarette or raise a smudged glass. The boys were fascinated, staring with unabashed curiosity at the company of men afloat on their island of rusting metal.

Up on deck, a pleasantly overweight man was leaning over the far rail of the boat, looking out towards the sombre rock that rose behind the sleepy village. His T-shirt had pulled up a little, and there, against a band of chubby suntanned skin, the handle of an automatic pistol could be seen peeping up above his belt line. The sooner we get away from here the better, I thought, and then looked over to J and Juliet, who were negotiating with the captain with the help of a calculator, notepad and pen. I saw Juliet nodding and smiling, and then J shook the hand of the captain, who turned and barked instructions at his men. They rose from their seats reluctantly, and began hauling a series of rusty jerry cans over to the rail.

Forty gallons of diesel were loaded and despite my misgivings about the quality of the fuel I couldn't complain when I saw the cost, which was scrawled on a scrap of paper: just forty-five dollars. We paid up and hoisted over a pack of cold beer for good measure, untied and pushed off. The boys stood at the rail waving. 'Adios!' Luke shouted and the men whistled and waved back. They had been good to us and fair in the price that they offered, when they must have known we had no other options for refuelling.

That evening we left the calm shelter of Gran Roques, slipping past little cays and shallow brown stretches where the water lay inches above sharp coral. Over four hundred miles of open sea lay between us and our destination, the Virgin Islands. There would be no rescue services, no safe harbours, and no other boats to speak of. It was a long way for a boat and crew that were virtually untested, and I just hoped that nothing would go wrong. Oscar and Luke had edged their way forwards to sit on the bow and were keeping very still, knowing that if they were too obtrusive during this watchful time they would be sent back to the cockpit. The wind lifted their hair as they sat close together, their legs splayed out across the hot teak deck. J sat in the cockpit reading a pilot book and Juliet was beside me at the helm. There was a thick silence on board, the only sounds the hiss of water and an occasional call from the seabirds that wheeled above isolated coral outcrops or stands of mangrove trees.

The sun had sunk low in the sky and ahead lay a navy-blue desert of water. I turned to watch our wake fizzle and wash away against a backdrop of the evaporating islands. My eyes focused on the Gran Roques, which glowered mournfully, a giant obelisk. As a last sight of land it seemed portentous and for a moment I had to work hard to keep my imagination under control. When I looked at Juliet I saw that she too was fighting a battle: uncertainty had settled amongst us as tangibly as if we had taken on a new crew member. 'I don't want to do this,' she suddenly burst out, and I could see that she was on the edge of tears. 'It's crazy – we don't even know this boat!' She gestured around her. 'Anything could happen. And with the kids . . .' Her voice faltered as she looked at the two boys on the bow. 'I'm really scared!'

'I know,' I said, trying to sound reassuring. 'But we have no other choice, do we? And I'm sure it'll be OK.'

'Well I'm not so sure,' she answered, her voice wavering. 'I think we've been naive idiots.'

I shrugged sadly. It was true, I had grave misgivings about the journey, and indeed the whole venture, which so far had yielded relatively little pleasure in exchange for the worry and risk. Yet we were here, and we had to deal with it. There was no choice but to press on.

J had been listening in on our exchange and now clearly felt it was time to step in. 'Come on Juju', he said to his daughter, his tone registering sympathy tempered with irritation, 'Stop fussing. We'll be absolutely fine.'

'Oh that's easy for you to say,' she countered. 'It's my children's safety we're talking about.'

'They are all of our children,' he said slowly. 'They are my children too, and they will be fine. Now what about some tea?'

And with that he settled himself at the helm in silence, and I felt a surge of love for the man along with gratitude that he had agreed to come with us as another father.

Juliet had headed down the companionway without answering, and I heard her banging the kettle down on the stove. Her fighting spirit was back.

Two hours later we had left the islands completely behind. The compass glowed red and *Forever* sighed on across a sea that had turned inky black. We were steering north-east now. The wind had come up enough to switch the engine off and in the sudden quiet the elements boarded our boat like ghosts, filling every space with the sound of wind and water.

Down below things were warm and snug, *Forever*'s woody insides glowing against the gathering darkness. Juliet was serving up lasagne which she had prepared earlier, knowing it might be the last square meal for some days. She wedged herself into the galley, carefully stacking plates and cutlery on a tray as I waited to ferry things up to the cockpit. I braced myself as *Forever* took a roll and Juliet deftly placed the lasagne in the sink to stop it from falling.

'Are you all right?' I asked.

She sighed and nodded, handing me a bowl of salad.

'Just wish this was over.'

With *Forever* steering on auto helm, we all sat down to eat around the flimsy cockpit table. What a sight this would be, I thought, if only there was anyone to see: a family eating supper around a table on a boat under full sail in the middle of the open ocean, as if everything was perfectly normal. Not for the first time, I looked at Juliet with a sense of awe. She was already showing great reserves of endurance, that slow-burning emotional strength that I so admired in her. After supper as she settled the boys into their cabin I called down to say goodnight. 'Tonight we're all going to be sleeping on the surface of the ocean boys. Just imagine, all the fish will be sleeping too.'

The weather did not stay benign for long. Over the course of my watch I realised that the sea was not going to be on our side: the waves grew bigger as they headed towards us, driven by a growing wind that was backing round to the north-east. Conflicting with this was the prevailing current, which was heading in a westerly direction. The result was a mean, churning sea-state, with short waves that seemed to be coming from all directions. The familiar yellowness began to settle on me again and I knew that another night of sickness was in the offing. Only this time I could not console myself with the thought that we would be sighting land the next day.

'Mummy!' Oscar's voice rang out from the darkness down below. 'I don't feel well!'

I saw Juliet stumble half-asleep towards the boys' cabin and shortly heard the unmistakable moans that preceded a bout of vomiting.

'Mum! I feel sick too!' It was Luke now. Juliet appeared in the companionway. 'Pass me the bucket – quick!'

'Are they OK?'

'No of course they're bloody not.' She clutched the side of the companionway as *Forever* rolled over a big wave. 'The seasickness pills obviously didn't work – they're feeling awful. And so am I.'

I tried to say something supportive but instead leant over the side and was quickly sick myself. In between retches I shouted, 'Don't worry Jules, it'll all get better when we reach the Virgin Islands!'

Some minutes later she reappeared to empty the bucket over the leeward side.

'This is a nightmare. Why are we doing this?' From my sickly vantage point, bent double over the side by the winch, I saw a higher than usual wave coming. 'Watch out, big wave!'

It slapped *Forever*'s side and a shower of salt water engulfed her. 'Oh shit, now I'm soaked!' she shouted, clutching the binnacle.

I steered on through the tumult, flipping the autohelm on whenever I needed to vomit, then returning to my place at the wheel. With each bout of nausea I grew weaker and more demoralised, and as I retched up the last drops of bile from a completely empty stomach I wondered if it would ever end. Meanwhile down below Juliet acted as nurse, running from one child to the other, emptying the bucket, wiping faces and supplying sips of water, all the time struggling to keep herself upright in the heaving, crashing interior of the boat.

Eventually the boys fell asleep, Juliet collapsed on a temporary bunk that we had set up on the port side of the boat. Ten minutes before midnight I saw J sit up and flip on his little berth light. Bracing himself against the incessant rolling and pitching of the boat he pulled on his waterproofs in preparation for his watch. I admired his endurance: he was leaving me standing. He stopped beside the chart table and scanned my scribblings then passed an eye over the instruments before climbing up into the cockpit.

'Filthy night,' he said grabbing the binnacle as a wave slapped hard against *Forever*'s bow. He turned his back to the spray and I ducked to let the worst of it hit my hood.

'Boys have been having a hard time of it. Have you been sick too?'

I nodded piteously, feeling like crying.

He leant over and checked the compass. 'OK, I'll take over. Juliet on next watch?'

'Don't think she can do it,' I mumbled. 'She's hardly had any sleep – too busy with the boys.'

'Right then,' he nodded. 'See you at 4 a.m.'

Down below I pulled off my soaking outer layer and strapped the bucket around my neck. I looked at the chart, desperately seeking an alternative course that could get us out of this hellish situation. Steering to the north west, where the weather wanted to take us, would make everything more comfortable. Yet the islands in that direction had a bad reputation, and having reached them we would then face an even worse journey to reach the Windwards and Leewards where we ultimately wanted to go. No, there was no alternative: we had to cross the Caribbean Sea, and we were following the only possible course.

As I stared at the chart, a new sound joined the existing cacophony. I looked out towards J, who had hunkered down in a corner of the cockpit as vast sheets of rain washed over him with such weight that he looked as if he was made of water. It coursed down over his head and poured off his arms soaking him right through. He sat still, the picture of endurance, leaning forwards occasionally to look at the compass or to adjust a sheet. I slumped back onto the nearest bunk, keeping the bucket close by my side and praying for the eternal night to end.

A hand shook me. 'Your watch Guy.'

'What, already?' I sat up and groped for my wet oilskins. 'What's it like up there?'

'It's raining and gusting pretty hard. Be ready to bear away when it gets too strong. It's all in the wrong direction too.'

I staggered across the saloon on legs that felt like jelly and climbed the ladder towards the cockpit, which had become my crucible of suffering. As I passed the boys' cabin I heard Luke's voice.

'Daddy?' His voice sounded surprisingly clear and calm. 'When is the sun going to come back?'

'It will soon darling, don't worry.' I reached into his cabin and stroked his sweaty head.

'Will we be there in the morning?'

I had been dreading this question. We had explained to the boys that the passage would take at least three days, but at their age they had little concept of time. Where once they had faced their childish night fears in the safe confines of their bedroom, now they had to share a heaving, sweaty bunk in a world full of inexplicable and frightening noises. A few inches from where their heads lay on their pillows, water gurgled, sighed, slapped and fizzed and all around them the boat creaked and groaned with the strain. Before, they had been scared if we forgot to leave their door open, or if a teddy bear for a moment resembled a monster in the half-light of their room. Yet now they both slept over a great dark ocean full of inexplicable depths, peopled by alien sea creatures and set within a framework of dimensions that were inexplicable to their young minds. We adults had hope: we could follow our progress across the chart and knew it would eventually come to an end. Oscar and Luke had no such comfort and existed entirely within the present. For the foreseeable future, this night, this sea, this pitching and yawing and seasickness was their entire world.

I knelt down and wedged myself in the doorway in a vain attempt to gain some kind of stillness. Luke kept his steady wide eyed gaze fixed on me waiting for his dad to make it all better again. I opened my mouth to speak but was at a loss for words as the boat jolted in response to a hard smacking wave.

'Luke, we have got a long, long way to go still.'

'How long?' I thought for a moment, wondering how to describe it all to him.

'Maybe three sleeps away son,' I said quietly, and with that answer he seemed satisfied and rolled over in his berth. Sleeps, I thought to myself. With a small surge of parental pride I noted that I had just discovered a method of describing distance and time that the boys would understand.

FIVE

WATER, WATER, EVERYWHERE

15.12N: 65.50W

The next morning the sun rose in a gritty grey sky streaked with livid red. I lay in the cockpit as Juliet brewed a pot of tea down below. From his position at the helm, J scanned the eastern horizon.

'Looks like the weather's brewing up over there.'

'Coming our way I suppose,' I said staring out across the restless sea, reflecting on the contrast between our dreams of a pristine Caribbean paradise and the tortuous reality we were experiencing. It was becoming searingly obvious that our dreams had propelled us into the midst of an uncomfortable and testing new world.

Throughout the day the rain continued to fall and bleak gusty conditions prevailed. Tracking our course on the chart, we continually had to adjust our course to the east to counter the prevailing current, which was pushing us all the time to the west. We'd heard this described as the 'Caribbean two-step', with wind and current creating a zig-zagging course that made our progress even slower. No one ate much and all we could do was try to ensure that the boys kept drinking and cajole them to eat the odd dry cracker. Juliet and

I couldn't eat either, all food taking on the flavour of nausea. We had long since abandoned the water from *Forever*'s tanks, which though safe to drink tasted distinctly briny, instead relying on our stockpile of bottled water. Not so J, who felt this was wasteful and insisted on drinking water direct from the tanks, despite the fact that rusty residue could often be seen floating within it. He also polished off a great deal of rum and in the absence of any cooking created horrific snacks of Ryvita heaped with sliced pickles spiced up with strong English mustard. He was a mariner of the old school.

As our second day came to an end the weather cleared and the sea turned velvet, reflecting the dusky sky. Grateful for the respite in our discomfort we sat quietly in the cockpit, staring down at shafts of sunlight that showed like spotlights in the deep blue water. The boys had given up asking when the journey would be over, and seemed to have slipped into a trancelike state. And then we heard a sound that brought us all out of our reverie: the unmistakable chirp of a bird.

'There, look!' Juliet pointed at a tiny, exhausted-looking bird that had perched on the guardrail.

The boys came closer, moving very slowly so as not to scare our visitor.

'It's a swallow I think. Swallows are good luck on a boat, aren't they?' Juliet said hopefully. We all stared at the bird as he looked back at us blankly.

'Maybe it needs some food,' Luke suggested.

J shook his head. 'Give it a drink first. Here, Oscar, pour some of this into your father's hand.'

Oscar poured some water into my outstretched hand but in his excitement spilled some onto my leg. The bird shot over and landed on my leg, where its tiny talons gripped my thigh with surprising force. I kept very still, letting it drink, and to my dismay felt its needle-like beak pecking me, occasionally pulling out hairs as it snatched at the silvery pearls of water. I lay my head back and closed my eyes, grimacing with discomfort. It felt as if a sewing machine had been let loose on me. I half opened an eye and saw the boys giggling behind their hands, and Juliet and J were clearly enjoying the show as well. With a great effort of will I smiled too, although most of me wanted to bat the little torturer away. I felt like one of the Argonauts, being forced to endure an obscure test of will meted out by the gods. Clearly my role on the boat was to be chief sufferer, as even the wild-life was out to quite literally gnaw at the edges of my morale.

Once all the water had been pecked from my leg I managed to convince the dainty marauder to perch on my hand to drink, which it did before flapping back to its perch on the rail. We offered it some crumbs, which it rejected, but it stayed with us for a while longer before suddenly lifting and flying off. The little bird's visit had lifted our morale greatly. On land the passing of a bird is hardly noteworthy, but there, in the midst of that great open wilderness, assisting a fellow creature also engaged in a long and arduous journey had given us new hope and strength.

That night the rain returned and the wind increased and on we ploughed into the unforgiving sea. There was a kind of harsh-ness to the world around us, an empty indifference that left me feeling insignificant and small. I had experienced this before, but always alone, never with my family exposed with me. I felt out of my element, and was desperately missing the scents and sounds of land as well as dreaming of the luxury of being still. But then occa-sionally there would be a sign from nature, almost like notes of encouragement to keep going. Once, steering into the bleak dark-ness, I heard some splashes beside me, and looked down to see four or five enormous fish flashing silver in the dark. I later discovered these fish were tarpon, and they solemnly surfed along beside us, not in the playful manner of dolphins, but more seriously, as if they had a job to do. Like silvery ghosts they accompanied us for an hour or so, so close that I could have reached out and touched them.

One morning after her watch Juliet greeted me with a strange question. 'Do you ever hear voices when you're on night watch?'

I shook my head, wondering whether this was the first sign of Juliet weakening mentally. 'No. Do you?'

She shrugged. 'Maybe it's just the water or something ... But it sounds like a woman's voice, high-pitched – kind of a wail.' She shuddered, 'It's pretty creepy.'

Later we were to hear other people describe this same thing – we even heard of someone who had to abandon an Atlantic crossing because it became so persistent. The mind plays strange tricks when one is at sea.

As day gave way to night and night gave way to day we began to seriously worry about Oscar, who was not holding anything down, including seasickness pills. He had stopped taking an interest in the world around him, and was so weak and listless that he barely moved from his berth. I sat on his bunk holding his hand.

'Feeling any better big boy?' I asked gently.

He shook his head, gamely lifting it from the hot dent in his pillow. 'Are we almost there Dad?' he asked and my insides twisted with the agony of not being able to give him the news he wanted.

'Not too long. Hopefully we might get there tomorrow,' I answered, though I knew this was light years away as far as he was concerned. 'Do you think you could eat something? What about a boiled egg?'

'I'll try Daddy. Not long to go now.'

I bent down and kissed him, admiring his stoicism and hating myself at the same time for putting him through this. As I put his egg on to boil, I noticed Luke at the saloon table, drawing intently on a wide sheet of paper.

'What are you drawing Luke?'

He lifted up the paper for me to see.

'Oh. A house.' A red house with a bright blue roof and smoking chimney, solid, on a green hill. Luke placed the picture back down in front of him and for a moment we both said nothing: lost in the memory of home, a world of stillness and safety. A strong gust hit *Forever* and I braced myself in the galley as the boat heeled hard over.

The weather deteriorated. Dark clouds raced across the sky, some of them flashing eerily as lightning lit them from beneath. These were tropical squalls, which often harboured very strong winds that came from every direction at once. It was important to try to avoid them, but not always possible as they seemed to change direction so often that it felt almost personal. Often they caught up with us, and the wind would howl through the shrouds, *Forever* straining on her side as we eased the sheets to deflect the worst of the gusts.

After a particularly strong squall we noticed something was wrong with the mainsail. It was bagging, half-way down, and we soon saw there was a rip in the luff a couple of feet long. This was a potential disaster, and for a moment we were all frozen with indecision.

'Let's get it down quickly,' J said. 'I'll have a go at mending it.'

For the next hour or so he sat busily sewing, fixing a giant patch onto it which we hoped would stay put for the rest of the journey.

We all stayed on watch that night, J and I sailing the boat together while Juliet ministered to the boys. Each hour I would plot our position, adding another cross to the zigzagging pencil line that had tracked our course seemingly interminably from Los Roques. At 4 a.m. I finally came off watch and plotted our position one final time. Despite being frozen, sick and exhausted I fell into my bunk elated. We had less than thirty miles to go, having covered over four hundred.

I woke to the sounds of celebration on deck. 'Land! Land!' I heard the boys shouting, and I leapt out of my bunk dressed in nothing but a pair of boxer shorts.

'Oh my God, it really is,' I breathed, as I saw the high, green outline of St Croix dimly visible on the horizon. The boys were leaping about on deck and J sat smiling behind the wheel.

Several hours later we were abeam of St Croix, the biggest of the US Virgin Islands, and heading for its main harbor of Christiansted on the north coast. The anchoring possibilities were limited: the main anchorage marked on the chart was in the centre of the inauspiciously named Gallows Bay, between the town and a little island named Protestant Cay. It was crowded with boats and as the wind was still strong we were concerned about dragging anchors. Instead we decided to head for the smaller, more optimistically named Welcome Bank, which lay close to a marina in the north-west corner of the bay. As we steered up the channel we took in the European-style harbour frontage – pastel coloured houses with bright red roofs, built by the Danes in the eighteenth century when Christiansted was the capital of the Danish West Indies.

We approached Welcome Bank and circled slowly, looking for a suitable depth for anchoring. J stood on the bow ready to drop the anchor as Juliet and I tensely watched the depth dropping away, aware that we were hemmed in on one side by a busy shipping channel and on the other by treacherously shallow water. The wind was blowing hard and the sea state was choppy, and it was difficult to keep the boat head to wind. Just as I was about to call out to J to drop the anchor the wheel became stiff and unmovable, and then seconds later the engine stopped.

'Oh shit! What's happened?' I shouted. We had lost all steerage and *Forever* was drifting rapidly towards the shallows.

'Guy, we're drifting . . .' Juliet said, her voice unnaturally calm. 'We're drifting quite badly . . .'

'I can't steer,' I said, wrestling with the wheel. 'J! The engine has stopped!'

'What's the depth?' he shouted back.

'Two point five fathoms,' I yelled and heard the reassuring sound of the anchor chain running out. Hopefully we would stay put for the time being.

'Guy, come over here.' Juliet was peering over the side. 'What's all this stuff in the water?'

I looked over and saw bits of rope and fishing net floating around the stern. 'Damn it,' I muttered. 'We've caught in somebody's fishing net. We've fouled the prop,' I said to J, who had arrived back in the cockpit. 'Unmarked net.'

'Hum, lucky we were within anchoring depth,' he said. 'I've let out ten fathoms of chain – won't do for long, but I didn't want to get too close to those shallows.'

Although it wasn't my fault I felt guilty, as if I had robbed everyone of our long dreamt-of arrival. There was only one thing for it – I would have to swim under the boat and cut the prop free from whatever was jamming it. I strapped a sharp diver's knife to my leg and jumped overboard, sinking into the warm silken water. As the silver curtain of bubbles lifted, I looked towards the stern, where an immense ball of discarded fishing net and rope hung from the propeller and drive shaft. I surfaced, took four breaths and then dived down again and gripped at the great tangle, pulling out my diving knife and slicing easily through the tough line. I rose and took another breath and then dived again, repeating the process until at last I was hacking through the last few strands, setting the great bundle free. I hung onto the prop and watched it sink into the aquamarine depths. I surfaced and the boys clapped and cheered.

The engine restarted without protest and we hauled up the anchor, circled and re-anchored in a more suitable spot. Safe in the harbour, I stretched my arms and yawned. 'Right everyone, let's sleep.' I was craving oblivion after the fear and tension of the past few days.

'Sleep?! Are you crazy?' Juliet and the boys were staring at me in disbelief. 'We're going ashore to celebrate!'

'Right,' I sighed, thinking how little things had changed. Whether at home or at sea, I tended to take my time whereas Juliet and the boys were always in a rush to get going. 'I'll go and get the dinghy ready.'

When we had gone through the tremendous palaver of lowering the rubber dinghy and Juliet and I between us had manhandled the huge outboard engine onto its stern, we motored over to the ramshackle, friendly looking marina. It was some considerable distance over choppy water and by the time we arrived we were soaked, but it didn't matter a bit. The joy of standing on dry land was indescribable. Oscar and Luke stood on the dock, weaving in exaggerated fashion from side to side.

'It feels weird, Dad, it feels like we're still moving!' they exclaimed, as they tried out their newfound sea legs on land. They galloped around like newborn colts, looking down at their legs as if appreciating them for the first time. It felt great to let them run about without worrying about them falling over the side or shushing them because someone was asleep. Tired, dirty and salt-encrusted, I was overcome by an enormous surge of happiness.

'Chips! Mum! Dad! Papa! Chips!'

As we followed the smell of fried food to the small outdoor diner we realised that we were ravenous for the first time in days. People seemed to be staring curiously at us, but then we must have looked pretty odd: a shabby family wandering along the dock, clearly disorientated but ecstatic, sniffing and smiling and looking around as if we hadn't seen land for years. We ordered food, and the boys recounted the story of our journey over and over again to the waitresses and anyone else who would listen. Halfway through salad, grilled chops, baked potatoes and an extra-large portion of the boys' long craved-for chips, Juliet leant back in her chair.

'I can't finish it,' she said, staring down at her plate. 'It's delicious but I'm too full.' It wasn't long before we were all in the same position. Our short period at sea had shrunk our stomachs to the point where American-size meals were way beyond us.

That night we puttered back in the sagging dinghy to *Forever* who lay at anchor obediently waiting for us to return. All was blissfully still where once there had been nothing but tumult and chaos. We washed the boys and covered them in a light dusting of talc before lovingly folding them into their cool berth. That night Juliet and I sat for awhile in the cockpit as *Forever* rolled contentedly. We spoke in whispers about the journey and of the toughness that J had displayed, and in the silences between each sentence I wondered if I was up to it all. Down below we heard a gentle snoring emanating from J's berth. Never mind all the classic father- and son-in-law tension, I thought to myself; we already owed J a huge amount for helping us in the tough business of learning to become useful on the water. Of course it was also correct and natural that he was with us. His knowledge and long experience of life became our living library. At sea, on a boat and on great journeys the ancient patterns that are often overlooked or ignored in our busy lives rise up to the surface once more. On that boat J was our elder, and we turned to him for our answers.

BITTERSWEET ISLAND

17.44N: 64.41W

*F*orever's engine needed some work after the rigours of her passage, so the next day we brought her alongside a pontoon in the marina. The problem was the freezer compressor, whose belt was misaligned and continually falling out of place. The freezer was in any case a point of debate, as it used an immense amount of battery power to keep it cold. I wondered why we needed a freezer at all – surely part of being at sea was not having every modern convenience you had at home. But Mike and Tessa had proudly told us how they had feasted on roast lamb and ice cream in the middle of the Atlantic, and I suppose we rather liked the idea of creating a similar contrast at some point; outside blue desert all around whilst inside there is plenty.

Thus began a day of sweating and swearing as J wrestled with the engine. I hovered by his side, trekking backwards and forwards to the yacht chandlery whenever a part was needed, as usual feeling guilty that he was doing such unpleasant work on our behalf. Once again the saloon was taken apart to expose the inner workings of the engine and as the boat grew hotter and sweatier tempers became increasingly frayed. After a couple of hours Juliet and the children set off to the beach at Protestant Cay. Oscar was becoming a capable dinghy operator and I watched proudly as he held the dinghy alongside while the others got in, then started the engine, backed away from *Forever* and motored off, speeding up so the boat rose on to a plane as they left the sheltered water of the marina.

By the next day we had sorted our engine problem but were still tied up in the marina. Thirty miles of open water lay between St Croix and our next destination, St John, and the wind was still blowing hard. Each morning we listened to the weather forecast, broadcast in a computerised voice by the US coastguard from Puerto Rico, and each day the gale warnings continued. We mooched around examining *Forever*'s deck and varnish, which had peeled off like a bad case of sunburn almost immediately after we left Bonaire. On the third day, fed up with hanging round the marina, we hired a car and set off to explore the island.

St Croix had been a major sugar-producing island since the early eighteenth century and at its peak in 1803 had a population of 30,000, of whom over 26,000 were slaves brought from West Africa. Sugar cane was grown on over two hundred plantations on the island and processed in the island's hundred or so mills, which squeezed the juice from the cane before boiling it down to raw muscovado sugar. In fact the first structures we had seen when approaching from the sea had been the ruined chimneys of the sugar refineries; they stood out against the surrounding greenery like the trunks of dead trees.

It was an uncomfortable history, but nevertheless it had to be confronted, and we duly parked in the shade of a tree at one of the island's old plantations in the west of the island. Oscar was curious to know the name of the strange quince-like fruit lying on the ground around the tree, and asked an old man raking the gravel nearby.

'That's called the pain-killer tree,' he said. 'Fruit and leaves make real good pain relief. When your head hurt you just crush them leaves and tie them up against your head.' He nodded and looked past the graceful plantation house towards the great refinery chimney beyond. 'They needed this tree way back.' He looked down at his raking, saying almost to himself, 'Pain-killer trees always to be found growing round these places.'

As we crossed the lawn we passed a small stone-built shelter with a rounded roof. The guidebook told me this was where the slaves' children were kept while their parents worked. I felt the first surge of shame, which would become a familiar feeling over the coming months. Of course we all knew of the history of the Caribbean and slavery but it had been academic, studied from the distance of the classroom. Now it was real. We were there standing on the same ground. The scene of past brutalities had become our landfall; the children slowed and where normally their instinct for fun would have sent them darting out across the closely mown lawns, here they walked close to us, pushed towards the protective safety of their parents by something that was unknown to them, and threatening.

The grounds were serene but there was an undercurrent of unease, a residue of suffering that one couldn't ignore. The contrast between the tight, airless building that housed the slave children and the planter's mansion, designed with windows on every side to allow the cooling breeze to flow through the house, was shocking. I wondered if the planter or his family ever looked out towards those children from the comfort of their gracious home, and how they could possibly have enjoyed their privileges at such a high cost. I tried to explain this to the children, but these thoughts were too grown up for them, and they pulled me back towards the car.

Our venture into the interior of the island had not been the happy experience that we'd expected, and we returned to the marina feeling deflated. As we stepped back onto *Forever* I noticed that something was bubbling up through the teak deck. I pushed down with my toe and more liquid seeped up, leaving a black gooey sludge of caulking on my toe. I leant back and looked around the boat, and a sorry picture began to reveal itself. As well as her peeling varnish, *Forever*'s entire deck was shabby and degraded, and in the near future would need to be replaced. Rust was visible on much of the metalwork, and the rigging looked distinctly dodgy too. In our month afloat we had had a brutal reality check on the cost of maintaining a boat. Already we had spent a small fortune on fuel and engine repairs, and the journey had only just begun.

It was Luke who alerted me to the next problem, exclaiming that *Forever* had 'bitten' him. Pointing at the steel line of the guardrail running along the port side of the boat he said: 'Touch that, Dad.'

A jolt of pain ran up my arm. 'Ouch,' I said, shaking my arm. 'I see what you mean Luke, it's an electric shock.'

I turned to J, who shrugged his shoulders. 'Must be stray current,' he said, looking careworn on our behalf.

'Meaning?'

'Somewhere there must be a loose connection which is allowing electricity to leak into the boat. Hard to find, as you can imagine . . .'

The next morning I paid a visit to the boatyard, where I regaled Jim, a hard-assed American, with *Forever*'s list of problems.

He listened, whistled, and shook his head. 'Gonna be expensive,' he said. 'Let's just say, I know of someone that had their decks done recently on a boat about your size, and as I recall it was somewhere around forty thousand dollars.'

'What?' My eyes widened in horror. 'Forty thousand US dollars?' I had a vague hope that he might be talking Caribbean dollars, which were around four to the pound.

'Uh huh.' He tapped a pencil on his desk and said, not unkindly, 'Guess you haven't got that, huh?' He swung round to look at a map of the Caribbean behind him. 'Well, you ain't gonna get much better unless you head way down south ...' he traced a thick finger down the islands and stopped at a green blob off the coast of Venezuela '... probably as far as here: Trinidad.'

More or less where we've come from, I thought. 'Good prices there?'

'Yes and no. The workmanship can be second to none, but there are a lot of shysters around, you gotta be careful. Can be pretty dangerous down there as well. Still, that might be your best bet. They need work pretty bad and they've got the skills, if you shop around.'

'So ... what do we do about the electric shocks in the meantime? I mean, it's going to take us some time to get down there.'

He shrugged. 'It ain't gonna kill you, just don't touch any metal.'

Pretty impossible, I thought, when one was sailing a boat with metal mast, stanchions, shrouds, wheel. I made my way back to the boat, where I found the family gathered round the breakfast table.

'I think we should leave,' J announced. 'I'm sick of waiting around. Let's get on with it.'

'But what about the weather?' Juliet said, glancing up through the butterfly hatch. 'It's still pretty windy isn't it?'

'This is a sailing boat,' he reminded her. 'It's designed for the wind. Besides, the weather always sounds worse in a marina and the longer we stay here the more nervous we'll get. Men and boats go bad in harbour,' he said, quoting from some obscure piece of literature and looking pointedly at me. 'It's time to move on.'

After a little more discussion we agreed and set about the massively involved preparations for leaving. Juliet went over to the marina office to settle our bill while J tidied up on deck and I plotted our course for St John. Ten minutes later I heard her calling me urgently as she climbed aboard.

'Guy, the people in the office say we shouldn't even consider leaving today. The storm that's passing over has been upgraded to a named tropical storm. It's called Olga, forecast to reach at least 60 knots.'

'Hum. Well let's listen to the forecast,' her father said.

Juliet and I glanced at each other. We'd been here before: though J had the experience to take calculated risks, with our relative lack of experience and our children on board we always wanted to err on the side of caution. A battle of wills might be approaching. I switched on the VHF radio.

'This is the US coastguard small craft advisory service, broadcasting from San Juan, Puerto Rico on Saturday December 15th,' said the robotic voice. 'At 0600 hours a storm warning was issued. Tropical Storm Olga will be moving through the region, moving at 40 knots in an easterly direction. Winds in the region of 60 knots expected, all craft advised to seek immediate shelter, I repeat, immediate shelter . . .'

As we listened to the broadcast I knew exactly what Juliet was thinking – thank God we weren't out there. The thought of being in the middle of the sea in a serious storm was truly terrifying and put all our financial worries into perspective. Of course, it would inevitably happen at some point: nobody who lived aboard a boat for any decent period could avoid bad weather all the time but when you had some control over your circumstances, as we did now, it felt good to be where we were.

SEVEN

ESCAPE FROM
ST CROIX

It seemed that living at sea your emotions run in parallel with the elements, and bad feelings can blow over as suddenly as a tropical storm. The next day I woke with a new sense of purpose, and stepped out on deck to find the sky a clear and delicate shade of blue, and although it was still windy the nasty edge of the previous days had gone.

J was perched on the side of the cockpit, shaving contentedly.

'Looks like the storm has passed,' I said. 'Let's get the hell out of this place.'

'I agree.' He peered into his tiny mirror. 'Can't say I'll be in a hurry to come back.'

A couple of hours later I was backing *Forever* out of the marina and then gently nursing her out into the narrow shipping channel where we threaded our way past the many reefs. The sea was still rough, and even before we left the shelter of the reefs we saw that Olga had left her legacy, and the waves were two or three times higher than when we had come in. As soon as we were safely in open water we switched off the engine, hoisted sail and set our course for St John. As the sails filled, *Forever* heeled over with an energy and decisiveness that we had not seen before. 'Come on, let's go!' she seemed to be saying and surged forward, free at last. The wind was slightly abaft the beam, the best possible wind for *Forever* and she cut through the waves easily, so perfectly in balance that I only needed to use the lightest of fingers on the wheel.

I glanced over to Luke, who lay on the leeward side of the cockpit with one leg dangling over the other as he flipped through a salt-worn copy of Tintin. *Forever* held him in place like a sea mother and he looked completely content in his tilting, watery home. 'OK Luke?' I asked and he nodded, not lifting his head from his book. Oscar sat on the other side of the cockpit, hanging over the windward rail to watch the flying fish scared up by our bow.

'What a perfect wind!' Juliet said, emerging from the companion-way with a cup of tea. 'If it keeps up like this we'll be there in no time.'

I turned to look behind us and saw our red flag, stretched fully out by the breeze. Everything around us seemed to be united in fluid movement, our worn white sails set like the wings of a gliding sea bird, their edges fluttering every now and then as we dodged a wave. *Forever*'s wind-driven weight armed her bow with colossal power as she scythed through the sparkling blue sea. White spray blew up from the wave tops, and brown boobies wheeled and glided overhead, diving down every now and then to snatch flying fish as they skimmed away across the waves.

'Can I steer?' Juliet asked. She threw her head back and looked up at the wind indicator on the mast top. 'Wow, this feels good – 30 knots of wind! At last, we've got the trades on our side!' I eased the foresail a little to catch more wind and we all felt *Forever* start to surge as all sixteen tonnes of her became like a feather on the wind.

It was true. For the first time we were experiencing the joy of the trade winds in the right direction as our hard slog at last paid off.

During the crossing of the Caribbean the trades had been a constant enemy, pushing us back and slowing us down and kicking the sea up into a mean jumble of peaks and troughs. Now the wind had caught us by the hand and we flew with it, feeling as if all our worries and fear were being blown away.

Gradually as we drew further away from the lee of St Croix the sea grew rougher, and we found ourselves surfing a trail that slipped down the sides of increasingly steep waves. A tickle of fear started to mingle with our joyful sense of liberation, as the waves grew to 15 and then 20 feet: the biggest we had yet seen. We clipped the boys into their harnesses and Juliet put on her lifejacket, a sure sign that she was feeling uneasy. But then over time we saw that *Forever* could easily handle it, and as each bright blue monster wave passed impotently beneath her stern we realised we could relax. Although steep, the majority of the waves were coming at us from the stern quarter, and *Forever* seemed to continually slither out of trouble. At times she would gracefully hurtle over the back of a wave, reminding me of a horse jumping a hedge. I sat back and smiled, feeling the hot sun on my face and the wind at my back. This was what it was all about; the dream wasn't lost after all.

But then a sudden yellowness came over me, and just as Juliet asked 'Are you feeling OK Guy?' I leant over the side and was perfectly sick. Even on the most sublime of days seasickness had tracked me down, and like a man with a bad past I resigned myself to the fact that there was no escape, and assumed the torture position at the leeward rail for what felt like the millionth time. Towards the end of the day the dramatic southern coastline of St John came into view. It is a high island, lush and green, with colourful tin roofs peeping out of the dense green of the hillsides. We were heading for Coral Bay on the eastern end of the island, a wide, generous bay with many protected creeks within it. One of these is Hurricane Hole, so-called because it is one of the few places with sufficient shelter for boats to ride out a hurricane. As we entered the bay we spotted numerous secret coves and inlets, bordered by thick fringes of vivid green mangroves standing on ghostly roots that reminded me of the thorny legs of king crabs. We dropped the sails and nosed *Forever* into a tiny inlet named Otter Creek, where we found ourselves completely alone.

There were a number of moorings in the creek, and we picked one up, anchoring being forbidden within the park to protect the seabed. I watched as the wind blew the mooring line taut, and then, with a touch of ceremony, switched the engine off. The wind was still strong, and I could hear it whipping through the scrub on the high hillsides that surrounded our diminutive pool of calm. Thick mangroves surrounded us on three sides, their roots pawing at the water as if trying to merge with their brethren on the other side. I flopped down in the cockpit, enjoying the contrast with the scene a few hours earlier when the cockpit had been a hive of activity. Now the sheets were coiled innocently around their winches, soft and pliable where earlier they had strummed like the cables of a suspension bridge. The sails were stowed, the instruments off, and our ship lay gently pulling against her mooring, like a tethered horse grazing sedately in a sheltered pasture.

Juliet was washing the boys down below, and I could hear them protesting as she forced them one at a time into *Forever*'s tiny shower. 'Not my hair Mum, please not my hair!' Luke begged, his voice full of terror as if he was about to be scalped. Ten minutes later they crossly emerged, dusted down in talcum powder and not amused when we laughed at the comic contrast between their ghostly white bottoms and golden legs and torsos.

After dinner, when Oscar and Luke had been packed away to bed, Juliet and I tiptoed up to the bow. The wind had died down, and the mooring line hung slack as *Forever* floated motionless on the still water. We stood together on the bowsprit, listening as tree frogs and insects chorused together from the fetid hollows of the mangroves and the drier herby heights of the scrub forest above. The warm air carried the exotic scent of vegetation towards us, and patches of warm, woody light from *Forever*'s oval portholes reflected on the black water that licked against the rounded sides of our floating home. A sense of homeliness and completion settled upon us, and we spoke in superstitious whispers about our progress and our hopes for the months ahead.

The next morning Oscar dived into the water and snorkelled across what now felt like our own little bay. Luke watched his brother wistfully.

'Do you want to go over to the mangroves too Luke?' I asked. 'It's like a nursery for little fish, you'll love it. I can swim you over. You just hold my shoulders and I'll pull you along.'

He screwed up his eyes and I could see he was trying to figure out whether or not he could trust me. I dived in and bobbed beside the ladder as Luke lowered himself into the water, having pulled on his armbands and carefully put on his mask. This was a big event for him: his first proper snorkelling session.

I swam slowly at first, feeling him relax into the water as he became distracted by the beauty of the world below. He leant over my shoulder, peered into the blue-green depths and as we reached the shallows ventured out like a little duckling, squawking and pointing, his eyes wide with magnified excitement through the glass of his mask. He forgot to be worried as we swam along the thick curtain of mangroves, watching tiny, brightly coloured fish flash and group between the roots. Mangrove oysters clung thickly to the roots and conch shells left trails on the rippled sand, and when we raised our heads above the water it seemed surprising to see lush greenery just inches away, as if we were caught between two parallel worlds.

Later that afternoon we piled into the dinghy and motored across to the other side of the bay, where a road passed nearby on its way to the main settlement, Coral Harbour. We tied the dinghy to an extra thick root, and then clambered through the mangroves for a gratefully short distance until we reached the steeply undulating single-track road. We set off in a straggling line like a grizzled family of sea gypsies, feeling slightly disorientated. Ranks of mangroves marched from the road down towards the water, and on the other side dense woodland climbed steeply up the hill. We walked for a while in silence, gradually succumbing to the heat as our legs began protesting at the unfamiliar use.

After twenty minutes' walking, Luke slumped against a tamarind tree. 'How far is it Dad?'

I had been wondering that myself. From the sea it looked like a short distance to Coral Harbour, but the road was taking a sinuous, winding route that seemed much longer than was reasonable. Just as I was about to answer, we heard the sound of an engine.

'Get in to the side boys,' I said, pulling them in beside me as a battered old pickup crested the steep hill behind us. It passed us, and then slowed to a gradual clattering stop. We walked towards it, feeling slightly vulnerable until the door opened and a young West Indian man climbed out.

'You all come in from the sea?'

The phrase made me think of a plague of boat rats and I smiled. 'Yes we have. We're heading into town.'

'Climb in now,' he said, 'I'll give you a ride.'

A few miles on the truck puffed to a stop in a village that looked as if it had happened entirely by mistake. 'Coral Harbour,' the man said and waved away our offer of payment as he clattered away with a bang from his exhaust. We stood by the muddy roadside and looked around at the rickety-looking houses on wooden stilts thrown haphazardly around a tiny school and a clapboard church.

We wandered along, enjoying the quirky, laid back feel of Coral Harbour. A straggly line of buildings ran along the waterfront, and there was a distinctly offbeat feel to the place. We passed numerous battered pickups, often seeming to be driven by long-haired men with scraggy dogs in the back, and felt as if we'd slipped back into the seventies. Gradually all paths led to a bar named Skinnylegs, where we sat in the shade sipping rum punch and watching as aged hippies in vests and shorts played a game of horseshoes beneath the shade of a great almond tree. The horseshoes clanged against the post and kicked up puffs of dust while the men laughed and heckled each other. Above our table a fan turned sedately on a wobbly mount, music played and all around people relaxed and enjoyed themselves.

'I suppose we'd better think about going home,' Juliet said when we had extended our stay to include dinner and several more rum punches.

'I was dreading you saying that,' I squinted out into the darkness, where it had started to rain. 'It's a long way – how are we going to find our way back?'

Just as I was thinking about the torch we had left on the boat, a man with a long beard approached us. 'Greetings y'all', he said, leaning heavily on our table and smiling widely. 'Would you be needing a lift home by any chance?'

'How did you know that?' I asked.

'Oh, we know you guys are on a boat,' he said. 'Just got in from St Croix, right?'

'That's right. A lift would be great, if you've got room for all of us.' I glanced over to Juliet, who was glaring at me.

'No problem, I've squeezed in a lot more in the past, believe me!' He cackled in a way that could have been interpreted as sinister.

'Bob's the name,' he said, sticking a cigarette into the corner of his mouth. 'Pleased to meet ye.'

As we followed him out to the car park Juliet tugged my arm. 'How do we know he's not a maniac? He looks like one.'

'Just have to hope for the best. Anyway, he's so drunk that we could probably beat him off, don't worry.'

'How reassuring,' she muttered.

We climbed into his wreck of a car, which skidded a little as we drove out of the muddy car park onto the main road. I wondered how much Bob could see, as only one headlight was working and the geriatric windscreen wipers were making little inroads into the rain.

'How long have you been living here?' Juliet asked. She and I were both in the front seat, with J and the children squashed in the back on either side of Bob's enormous dog.

'Twenty years or so I guess.' He laughed and relit his cigarette, veering gently across the gravel road as he did so. 'Had a real good job back in the States and all, but I wasn't happy. Traded it all in for poverty and a good lifestyle.'

He burbled on gently as we made our wavering course – luckily he drove incredibly slowly, as two or three times we veered danger-ously close to the muddy sides of the road. At last the mothy beam of the headlight showed the little gap in the mangroves where the dinghy was tied up. 'Thanks, this is us!' Juliet said, her hand already on the door handle.

The truck rattled to a stop. 'Have a great time you guys. Keep the dream alive,' Bob said as he drove off.

'Where's the dinghy Daddy?' asked Oscar. We all peered into the mangroves, which seemed to have closed over in the darkness.

'Here it is,' I said, plunging into the gap that I thought we'd come through, but soon found the way blocked by dense vegetation.

'Back up!' I shouted to the others who were stumbling along behind me. 'This isn't it. Stay here.'

I set off along the road, feeling my way, stopping to look into the mangroves from time to time. After ten minutes' searching I realised it could be anywhere – why on earth hadn't we thought to leave some kind of mark? At last I spotted a familiar-looking road sign, glowing dimly in the dark. I pushed into the mangroves and this time they parted to reveal a little track, at the bottom of which sat our dinghy, bobbing patiently where we'd left it. 'Found it!' I yelled and one by one the family emerged through the trees.

'Funny how it's the things that you least expect that get you into trouble,' Juliet said. 'I was worried about taking a lift from that guy, but losing the dinghy was far more of a risk. We could have wandered up and down that road all night.'

'The moral of the story is,' said J, 'always bring a torch.' We turned and looked at him.

'Yes, thank you Dad,' muttered Juliet.

The next day we sailed round to a large, protected bay named Francis on the north coast of St John, fringed by a wide curved beach and dense tropical scrub that stretched up a satisfying line of steep hills. Juliet took the opportunity of a few quiet days to try to launch Oscar's school sessions, which were long overdue. At the age of four Luke wouldn't yet have started at school, but he insisted on taking part anyway. I watched as Juliet laid out Oscar's workbooks, which she had bought after taking advice from his teachers back at home. She had bought a few for Luke, too, and he sat down beside Oscar at the saloon table, proud to be 'doing school' like his big brother, but then continually distracting him by talking, sharpening pencils in a breezy manner and humming noisily as he traced the shapes of huge letters on the pages of his textbook.

'I can't work,' Oscar groaned after half an hour or so, leaning his head on the table. 'It's too hot.' All the hatches were open and the fans were going full blast, but it was still a furnace down below.

'Well, you haven't done much,' Juliet said, glancing at her watch. She was trying to wash up at the same time as supervising what the boys were doing, and she looked hot and harassed. 'But it is hot, and at least you've made a start. OK, off you go for a swim.'

He leapt up from the table, all tiredness forgotten as he shot off up the companionway before she could change her mind. A few seconds later I heard a splash as he divebombed into the water.

Luke wanted to go too, but after a few minutes in the water he emerged screaming.

We hauled him up the ladder, and he stood on the deck, shaking and stuttering as he tried to get his story out. 'It's a big fish,' he gasped. 'It tried to eat me!'

Please not a tiger shark, I said to myself, knowing that it was not impossible, as we were moored in quite deep water.

'Where's Oscar?' Juliet was scanning the water around the boat but he was nowhere to be seen. Terror clutched at my legs.

'Oscar!' I yelled, cupping my hands around my mouth. 'Oscar!'

'Yes Dad?' his voice came from beneath my feet, and I looked down to see him floating at the bottom of the swimming ladder.

'Come up,' I said, 'Luke thinks he's seen . . .'

'There it is Dad!' Luke shouted, 'Oscar, it's behind you!'

Oscar shot up the ladder, and we all stood together on the side of the boat, staring down into the water at an odd-shaped grey fish around three feet long. The creature circled around the bottom of the ladder, looking regretful at Oscar's departure. It looked up at us with a wary eye, and I saw an odd striped pad on the top of its head.

'It's a remora fish, Luke. They attach onto big fish like sharks and eat bits of fish that they drop – see, there's the sucker pad on its head. It didn't want to eat you, it wanted to attach onto your tummy.'

Luke looked down at his torso. 'I don't want a fish on my tummy.'

'No, I can see that,' I said, 'don't worry, it'll soon go away when it discovers there's nothing to eat.'

But the fish didn't go away, and we soon realised that it was living under the boat and feasting on the detritus coming out of the heads, which didn't add to its appeal. Later that day I caught the boys feeding it with leftover morsels from their lunch, which sent it into a one-fish frenzy, circling and darting ferociously like a mini-shark. Pretty soon they'd given it a name – Cedric – and adopted it as their new pet. But it became less amusing as Cedric grew bolder, and took to dashing at us as we were swimming in increasingly desperate bids for snacks.

'I don't like him,' Juliet moaned as she emerged from the water, having had a particularly vigorous session fending Cedric off. 'He gives me the creeps.'

'Don't worry, if he attaches himself to you just push him forwards to break the suction.' I'd checked up in the diving book.

'God,' she shuddered, 'I hope I never have to do that. I don't want to touch him – he's hideous.'

'He won't let me in!' Luke shouted from halfway down the ladder as Cedric swirled ominously beneath him, looking up through the water with a steely eye.

'It's only a matter of time before he takes a snap at one of the boys,' Juliet said. 'Luke! Don't trail your toes in like that, he'll have them off!'

After a time we were all put off swimming, and I could see that despite his protests to the contrary even J was beginning to find Cedric's frankly ill-mannered approach a little disconcerting. We were all quite relieved when it came to time to cast off our mooring.

Our next stop was going to be the nearby island of Tortola in the British Virgin Islands, where we were due to meet Juliet's mother, who was joining us for Christmas. We also needed to buy some parts for the engine, which was overheating now, in addition to the ongoing problems with the freezer compressor.

From Francis Bay we sailed north east, cutting through the narrow Fungi Passage which lies between St Mary's Point and the islet of Whistling Cay. The wind was marginal for making it through the channel, and a strong current was flowing against us. As we approached it the passage seemed to grow smaller and smaller.

'I don't think we're going to make it,' Juliet said, gripping hard onto the binnacle. 'Let's switch the engine on.'

'Stop panicking,' J said, 'If this wind keeps up we'll be fine.'

We watched as waves broke on the jagged shoreline and as I held the wheel the wind died out completely, the sails began to quiver and slacken and *Forever* drifted towards hungry looking rocks.

'J?' I said, trying to sound calm. 'Could you possibly pop the engine on?'

He pursed his lips and nodded slowly. 'Yes, why not.' He lingered a bit longer, looking towards the rocks, which were was fast approaching.

'Now, do you think?' I suggested mildly.

'Yes, yes', he began to move towards the engine panel, but Juliet got there before him.

'Right, the bloody engine's on, now get us out of here!'

As we entered the Narrows, the passage that divides the British and US Virgin Islands, the engine suddenly began making a loud clanking noise. The wind was gusty and unpredictable, and we were relying on the engine to get us out of trouble if need be.

'Now what?' Juliet asked nervously. 'I hope it's not going to break down.'

'Certainly doesn't sound good,' said J. 'I'll take a look.'

Below deck he hefted off the covers and crouched down to inspect the hot, oily workings of the Yanmar engine as we bucked up and down in an increasing sea. I envied him his iron stomach, knowing that inspecting the engine would be near impossible for me in these conditions. A tickle of worry ran through me: how would I deal with this kind of situation when J had gone?

After a tense inspection he came back up and delivered his diagnosis like a doctor speaking to anxious relatives in the hospital waiting room. 'One of the engine mounts is broken,' he said. 'That's what's making that awful noise. We'll need a part welded – better put in somewhere as soon as possible.'

We gathered around the pilot book to look for a place with boat repair facilities, and concluded that we should go into Soper's Hole, just a few miles across the narrows on the western end of Tortola. There was a marina and boatyard there, and my heart sank at the thought of more time tied up at the dock and expensive repairs, but there was no way around it. Juliet went below to radio ahead to the marina, where a gruff voice confirmed that there would be space for us to come alongside for a few days. We progressed towards it, the rattling of the engine growing worse and worse until we could hardly hear each other.

At last we entered the bay, which was surrounded on all sides by lush hills dotted with expensive-looking houses. Blackbeard had made Soper's Hole the base of his operations in the early 1700s, and I could see that it would make a great hiding place, perfectly hidden within its cloak of hills. 'The worst thing would be if the engine died right in there.' I pointed towards the end of the bay, where boats crowded onto the moorings and commercial crafts and ferries kicked up a sharp, choppy sea.

I steered *Forever* into the packed marina, acutely conscious of her shabby appearance amongst the immaculate yachts. It was soon clear that we would have to enter our berth astern – a prospect that immediately drew out beads of sweat on my forehead as *Forever* steered very badly astern and I hadn't had enough time to practise. For a moment, I considered asking J to take the helm, but pride took over. I had to learn sometime, I thought: may as well start now.

Juliet touched my arm reassuringly. 'Don't worry, it'll be fine,' she said. 'Just go in slowly and we'll fend off if you get too close. There are two warps ready on the stern.'

I took a deep breath and manoeuvred *Forever* into position to begin my approach. It didn't help that the whole operation was taking place within a stone's throw of a packed restaurant: in my imagination chairs were being positioned and drinks ordered as people settled down to enjoy the show. 'OK everyone, here we go!' I shouted. I applied some reverse throttle and then slipped into neutral to let her glide astern. She was moving too fast, so I slowed her progress with a strong burst ahead, but she slewed to one side, drifting towards the gleaming edge of a nearby catamaran. It didn't help that a strong wind was blowing, and on board the catamaran the crew were all seated around the cockpit table, watching as our shabby, heavy old boat slid towards them.

'Shit! This is awful!' I pushed the throttle ahead again, this time engulfing our neighbours in black clouds of exhaust. Sweat coursed down my back as I waited for *Forever* to swing back into position so I could begin my approach again. I looked at the dock, where the harbour master now stood waiting to take our lines. In one hand he held his portable radio while he tapped impatiently on his leg, clearly irritated with my slow approach.

After another aborted attempt I was readying myself for the third and – I hoped – final approach. 'About ten metres,' J called from his place on the stern, 'Five, four, three, two . . . Stop!'

I put on full power ahead, clouds of exhaust smoke making us look as if we were being boarded by a special forces unit armed with smoke grenades. The immaculate, tanned and young crew on the cat leant over the side of their boat to watch us explode or batter the dock. Instead *Forever* veered obstinately to port, threatening to hit the boat on the other side.

'Throw the line!' I shouted to Juliet, realising I was losing the battle. 'I can't, it's too far,' she answered. 'You need to get a bit closer!'

'Just throw it now!' I shouted back, and she did so, only for it to fall short of the quay and flop impotently into the water. 'Great Jules, now we'll foul the prop!' I shouted, and she hurriedly pulled it back in. Meanwhile J had managed to get his warp over to the waiting dock-master, who kept looking about as he pulled in the line as if to say, 'Can you believe these jokers?' I could see that we weren't the kind of company he was used to.

My pride was severely dented by our undignified arrival, and I was feeling distinctly unworthy of my skipper's title. Manoeuvring the boat – particularly this boat – was not easy, and I only hoped I would get better at it. I was also aware of both *Forever* and her crew's shabby appearance, which were at odds with the gleaming charter yachts that surrounded us. I couldn't wait to get away. But first we had to fix the engine. By the end of the day we had removed the broken mount, but the boatyard informed me that getting it welded back together was going to take several days.

Meanwhile we had to collect Juliet's mother from the airport, which was at the other end of the island. We walked together across the street to find a taxi, and the boys spotted a jalopy that had been converted into a people carrier by fixing benches and a high roof on the back, with colourful images of fish and flowers hand-painted all over it. The boys jumped up and down, begging to be allowed into the motorised carbuncle. An aging rasta lowered his sunglasses enquiringly as we approached.

'We need to get to the airport to pick up my mother,' said Juliet, 'and we're running a little late. Can you take us there?'

He shot out of the driver's seat surprisingly quickly and helped the boys climb into the back. 'What time you need to pick her up?'

'Ten,' Juliet said.

'You leaving it real late,' he said, looking at his watch. 'Why you not come round earlier?'

'Well, it's not that far away, surely it won't take more than thirty minutes?'

He shook his head and walked quickly back round to his seat. 'You better get in now 'cause otherwise we is going to be proper late for your mother. Is she old?'

'Seventy-two,' Juliet answered a little defensively.

'Seventy-two! And you gonna leave her alone at the airport?' He sucked his teeth, 'This called proper disrespeck for your mother. Get in now.'

Juliet and I climbed into the seat behind the boys, who chirped like little sparrows, excited at the prospect of a car trip with no windows or doors around them. No sooner had we taken our seats than a faux crocodile slip-on complete with shiny gold buckle slammed down hard on the accelerator, and the jalopy shot off with unexpected speed, weaving through the other cabs, which honked in greeting, and around knots of tourists walking towards the harbour.

'We is gonna be late. You left it so late for your mother, I can't believe it,' the driver muttered, shaking his head as he whipped the top-heavy vehicle round torturously tight bends.

'He's driving so fast,' Juliet whispered, grabbing my hand, and I saw that the boys were holding on tightly to the backs of the seats in front of them, their eyes wide with excitement.

'Hold on tight boys,' I muttered, clutching Luke's shoulders. But then mercifully we reached a hill that was so steep that the truck had no choice but to slow to a crawl, crunching its gears as it did so. Juliet looked back at the boys who were still full of smiles, giggling with anticipation as the vehicle edged up higher.

'What's going to happen when we get to the top of this hill I wonder?' J said under his breath.

'Don't worry too much about getting us there on time,' Juliet called out to the driver in a falsely cheerful voice. 'I'm sure she won't mind waiting a bit if we're late.'

But it was the wrong thing to say, and the rasta shook his head. 'You kids are all the same,' he said. 'She done give you her whole life in service and now you ready to leave her alone and waiting!' And with that the crocodile shoe hit the pedal again, and as we crested the hill the jalopy hurtled down into what felt like a zero-gravity dive. Sharp rocks whirred by along the side of the narrow, pot-holed cliff-top road, and we could see the sea glinting with malevolent glee far below.

The boys gripped the handle bar in front and screamed as if they were on a runaway fairground ride, and Juliet held onto their shoulders as we plummeted. 'Slow down please!' she shouted, but the red, gold and green knitted cap shook from side to side. 'We is not gonna be late for no mother!' he called out, and our free dive continued until with stomach-churning lumpiness we bottomed out before slowly beginning to climb the next hill and grating down the gears again.

At the airport we stumbled out of the taxi pale and shaky with fear. We paid the driver, who set off at a run in search of Juliet's mother, whose flight, it turned out, had been delayed. 'Thank God we made it in one piece', Juliet said. 'Let's find another taxi for the way home – I don't think I can take survive another drive like that one.'

'Oh don't worry,' I answered, 'With your mother in the taxi he probably won't go over twenty miles an hour.'

A few days later, with Audrey and a fixed engine on board, we were able to escape Soper's Hole. We had decided to stay in the British Virgin Islands until after Christmas and for the next week or so we drifted about between the islands. Around the big islands of Tortola and Virgin Gorda lie their smaller siblings, Ginger, Norman, Peter, Cooper, Salt, Jost van Dyke and Anegada. Blessed with good winds and sheltered seas, they lie within easy reach of each other with innumerable cays, rocks and islets lying between them like heavenly points of punctuation. This is the standard Caribbean paradise as seen in the tourist brochures: desert islands, palm trées, white sands and crystal-clear waters filled with an abundance of exotic fish. Gone were the cruel vistas of an open and unrelenting sea; now we began to experience the freedom of sailing, and the true beauty of a life afloat.

But I was struggling. My experiences of sailing so far – the seasickness, the engine problems and the humiliating entrance to Soper's Hole, had left my pride badly dented, and I'd begun to lose hope that I would ever be up to the role of skipper. I was also suffering from a bout of cabin fever – three generations confined within the space of a small boat wasn't easy, and I felt irritable and hemmed in.

Juliet's parents are a disciplined duo, and clearly believed that by starting everything very early each morning they would politely shame us into action. Juliet and I now slept in separate and rather mean little berths in the saloon, having given J and Audrey our more spacious berth as befitted their age and station. As the days passed I began to harbour a little glowing ember of irritation at having to accept their very foreign rhythm of life over our own. In their many years of sailing they had evolved a disciplined routine of onboard living, and as I woke each morning to the sound of J's shaver whirring away in the cockpit while Audrey tiptoed past on her way to her wake-up swim, I grew steadily more annoyed. Juliet had grown up with these routines and cosily settled back into the patterns of childhood, but I felt like the sulky teenager, resisting the early rising as an obscure way of making a point.

Juliet was unsympathetic. 'Oh come on,' she said, giving her standard response to a particularly prolonged bout of moaning on my part. 'J's been a huge help and it's great to have Mum here. They won't be here for much longer – we just have to treat this period as a bit of a holiday.'

Yet it wasn't a holiday: I was supposed to be mastering the role of skipper, preparing myself physically and mentally for some long-distance ocean sailing. It was hard for me to be as lighthearted as everyone else seemed to be and I was itching to get on with our journey. And then there were more repairs needed on *Forever*, the urgency growing day by day. Her varnish had practically all been burnt away by the fierce Caribbean sunlight and with all the foot traffic, the decks were increasingly eroding, the caulking coming off on our feet and smearing all over everything. Galling as it was to face more loss of time and money, there was no alternative to spending some of both in a boatyard getting ready for the long haul home. And from everybody we asked, the advice regarding the best place to go for these repairs was always the same: Trinidad.

Luckily going to Trinidad made sense for us, as the journey would take us all the way through the Leeward and Windward Islands, which lie strung out from north to south like an emerald necklace. We would be helped on our way by the trade winds, which at this time of year blew just north of east, giving us a favourable direction for our journey south. And by the time we came back up the islands the winds would have shifted round to the south east, a perfect direction for blowing us back up again.

A few days before Christmas we anchored in the spectacular North Sound, which lies at the eastern end of the beautiful island of Virgin Gorda. Francis Drake is said to have stopped off here on the *Golden Hind* in 1595 and I experienced an acute sense of the past as we dropped our anchor at Drake's Anchorage, close to the treacherous Colquhoun Reef. The strong wind pulled us back on our anchor until it gripped the coral sand with a reassuring tug and I stood at the bow for a few minutes with my foot on the chain to make sure it was well set.

After the family swims were over I set off on a foray to the reef, which lay a few hundred metres away. I powered towards it, enjoying the contrast of the different landscapes I was passing over, from the great fields of sea grass that waved like the grasses of a prairie to the shattered pink and white coral of the leeward side of the reef. Ahead I could see the white, oxygenated line of water where the waves were breaking as they passed over the reef. I wanted to cross over to the windward side, where my chart had shown that the seabed fell away steeply, but first I had to negotiate the breakers as they passed over the jagged shallows.

I hovered close to the coral, timing my approach so that the backwash drew me in towards it and then pulled myself down close to the reef to avoid being dashed against it by the surf. I held my breath and braced myself as the next wave broke over me, water thundering in my ears and a firm hand of water stippled with white rising bubbles pushing down firmly on my back. It sluiced strongly around my body and then fizzed away and I edged forwards a little before searching about quickly for another handhold. Time and time again I did this, taking advantage of the pause between waves to gradually draw myself across the shallow part of the reef.

In this broken zone of constant movement, the fish were just as busy looking out for themselves and they had dropped their guard. Predator fish knew this fact well and with a quickening of the pulse I spotted a large barracuda, showing his silver side as he turned towards a small school of fish that shot away like sparrows over the rooftops. I paused to find a coral hold as another wave rose up and then looked to my right as instinct demanded and saw the barracuda not more than ten feet away, its wide hunter's eye observing me with cold curiosity. I looked back at it, remembering when I was around Oscar's age and used to hunt for preying mantis in my grandmother's garden in South Africa. I often found huge ones on the whitewashed wall of her crumbling Cape Dutch house. Unlike the other insects they would keep very still, turning their heads to look at me with the exact same hunter's coldness that I was seeing now in the fish's stare.

I edged on, unable to help my curiosity about what might lie beyond the wave line, and then as another wave rose up I saw a line of deep blue and knew that I was through. Now I was in a different realm, one of intoxicating beauty. The meanness of the wave-wracked coral zone had been replaced by the lush gardens of a mature reef and all around me fan corals waved luxuriantly, contrasted against the brittle branches of elkhorn coral with the great domes of brain coral rising ponderously in between. I dived repeatedly over baroquely clothed cliffs, descending into deep gleaming sandy patches, holding myself down for as long as possible, my lungs burning. Clouds of fish shifted and waved around me, and below I saw the antennae of crawfish protruding anxiously from shady overhangs. I rose to the surface and breathed slowly and deeply for a while and then after four deep breaths dived down and held myself between two great coral heads, practising what Italian spear-fishermen call *aspeto*, or the art of waiting. Gradually my patience paid off as myriad fish gathered about me, as if holding a council to discuss how to get rid of such a lubberly visitor.

I was so entranced by this miraculous underwater world that I hadn't realised how far I had strayed, and just as I was thinking about heading back I saw a shadow pass overhead. Immediately all the fish shot away and glancing up I saw the unmistakable silhouette of a large shark. I stared up at the ballistic beauty of its perfect white underbelly and, irrelevantly, registered by its two claspers that it was a male. Suddenly I felt completely out of my element and wished that I were wearing diving equipment so I could meet this creature on better terms. The shark saw me and swam off quickly towards the deep water. I rose up as sleekly as possible and took a breath before descending to watch it again, noticing as I did so some faint markings across its back. With a liquid surge of adrenalin I realised that it was a tiger shark, one of the few aggressive species to be found in these waters. I tried to calm myself with the thought that there were very few reported attacks and, when it had melted away into the murk, began swimming firmly towards the wave line, turning my head every few strokes to look behind me. And then with a judder of horror I saw it again, and realised that far from disappearing it had simply circled round to approach me from the side.

Oh please don't let this happen, please don't let this happen I thought to myself as I swam on, struggling to comprehend the cliché of encountering a dangerous shark whilst swimming alone in deep water. It was nightmarish having to move so slowly when all my instincts were telling me to power for the safety of the reef, but I knew that this would be an open invitation for the shark to make an attack. My back prickled as I swam on, expecting any moment to feel the bite of teeth around my ankle as the shark swooped in for a sample.

After what seemed like an eternity I drew close to the reef and with relief abandoned myself to the power of the surf. The wave threw me forwards and spat me out over the broken coral, missing my chest by inches and I ducked down and held on hard as the backwash gushed past me. Then came the pause before another wave helped me on across dangerously shallow water and I used every bit of my strength to shimmy out of the way of the coral heads as I surged ahead. And then at last I was in the lee again, swimming over the peaceful sea grass as if nothing had happened, looking around anxiously though I knew it was almost impossible that anything could follow me into this shallow water. As I swam towards *Forever* it occurred to me that, though unlikely, the shark could have followed me around the outside of the reef and my spine tingled as I passed over the deeper water, dreading the sight of that ominous silhouette lurking beneath the boat. I reached the ladder and pulled myself up onto the safety of the deck, noticing that my skin was covered in goose pimples as I slumped against the coach-roof.

Luke popped his head up. 'Dad's back!' he shouted. Oscar looked at me carefully.

'Are you OK?' he asked.

I couldn't speak yet.

'Did you see a shark?' Luke shouted and as I nodded his eyes grew wide with excitement.

'Dad saw a shark,' Oscar called through the companionway.

'Really?' Juliet came up and looked about. 'Where did you see it? I was planning to have a swim.'

I pointed over to the distant line of surf. 'On the windward side of the reef.'

'You were all the way out there!' She raised a hand to shade her eyes. 'That's so far!'

'I know. It was too far. I think it was a tiger shark.'

'Oh my God,' Juliet put a hand to her mouth. 'You could have been killed!'

Now J came up the companionway. 'If you will insist on swimming such a long way the odds are that something will go wrong sooner or later,' he said. 'It's irresponsible, Guy.'

The rebellious teenager surged up again and I stared down at my feet, refusing to make eye contact. But of course he was right: it had been silly to swim so far alone. I made a mental note to tow the dinghy behind me in future, which would at least have given me a quicker escape route. That night, as the wind whistled over the deck above us and we settled around the saloon table to eat, I thought of the great privilege of swimming over that incredible reef, twinned with the sense of menace and utter vulnerability when I had strayed too far. That lustrous shark had given me a warning, to remember my true place underwater, which was as a privileged visitor in a hostile zone.

EIGHT

CHRISTMAS &
THE GOLF CLUB
BY THE SEA

18.29N: 64.23W

Amidst all this sunshine and swimming it took a leap of imagination to accept that it was Christmas. Back in the dark, windswept Hebrides, Christmas stood out as a beacon of warmth in midwinter, allowing us some days of cosy excess. But here in the Virgin Islands it felt like an irrelevance, and the plastic Santas and ubiquitous strings of tinsel seemed bizarre. Nevertheless we wanted the boys to be able to enjoy the festivities and the day began just as it would have done back home, with squeals of delight as they discovered their stockings packed with little treats that Juliet had accumulated along the way.

'Mum, how did Father Christmas get into the boat?' Luke asked with all the seriousness of a tax inspector.

'Through the companionway of course,' Juliet answered. 'Probably a relief after all those chimneys.'

'But how did he know we were here?'

'Oh, he just knows these things. He probably likes delivering presents here, much nicer than in Scotland.'

'Don't the reindeer get too hot?'

'He doesn't use reindeer in the Caribbean, he uses dolphins.'

Luke's brow creased as he tried to get his head around this. Oscar, who already had his doubts about the whole thing, gave us a sceptical look.

The Virgin Islands had begun to feel overcrowded, and with Christmas over we were eager to get on with our journey. A couple of days after Christmas we set sail for Anguilla, the most northerly of the Leeward Islands, around eighty miles south. To get there we were going to have to tackle the notorious Anegada Passage, which lies across the 'corner' of the Caribbean, where the Atlantic floods into the Caribbean Sea. We were apprehensive; from our reading we knew that a noxious mix of wind direction, current and Atlantic waves combined to make this a particularly nasty crossing. Its local nickname, the Cape Horn of the Caribbean, didn't help calm nerves either.

We sailed out of North Sound and headed east, aiming to clear the end of Virgin Gorda before we turned southeast for Anguilla. On the way we passed Necker Island, an exotic rock owned by Richard Branson and surrounded by beautiful turquoise waters and dainty little islands clad only in delicate palms, like tourists in tiny bikinis. For the first part of the journey we were in the lee of the Horseshoe Reef, a long sinister curve of shipwrecking coral leading south from the island of Anegada. The most northerly of the British Virgin Islands, Anegada or 'drowned island' is virtually flat, barely above the water, and worryingly over three hundred ships lie wrecked in its waters. Despite modern charts and navigational instruments, every year or so another boat joins the graveyard, and we were acutely aware of the need for caution.

We kept a close eye on the depth gauge and when once or twice it began to fall altered course to the south. Every half hour I plotted our position on the chart until we were pretty sure that we'd passed the southern tip of the reef. The wind was blowing steadily at around 25 knots and though the waves were big they weren't any worse than on other journeys. We sat in the cockpit, making cheerful conversation for the boys' sake, though in reality we were steeling ourselves for the onslaught to come. As the sun began to drop, Juliet read to the boys, drawing them in under her arms as they snuggled up to her. The boys were staring out over the darkening sea as they listened to the story, looking somehow even more vulnerable wrapped up in their lifejackets, and I could see that though they were only half-listening they were finding the sound of their mother's voice reassuring. So for that matter were the rest of us and for a while we all allowed ourselves to drift off into the sure world of the children's story.

Apart from the odd bit of spray things weren't too bad, and I was beginning to think that the reports of the passage must have been exaggerated. I opened my mouth to say as much, but then it all changed as we passed the relative shelter of the reef. With the immediacy of a curtain being drawn or a fire being put out, the sky darkened, the wind strengthened and the waves grew dramatically bigger. Now the ocean had unleashed its full temper, yet Juliet staunchly continued reading, as if she could hold off the worsening conditions by refusing to acknowledge them. She stopped at a stifled cry from Audrey.

'Look!' Audrey pointed behind Juliet and the boys, one hand over her mouth. They turned to peer out from behind the dodger, and the boys screamed in unison as the biggest wave we had ever seen rose up beside the cockpit like a giant sea monster.

'Christ!' Juliet shouted, and pulled the boys down onto the floor of the cockpit, covering their bodies protectively with her own.

'Big wave!' I shouted unnecessarily, and I heard the sound of rushing water high above us as the wave tumbled on itself. I spun the wheel and angled *Forever* towards the great wall of water, hoping to deflect its blow. Slowly the wave lifted us and we rose seemingly interminably until we teetered on the giant's back. I spun the wheel the other way now, trying to lie the boat parallel to the wave as we hurtled down the other side. Now we found ourselves in a devil's playground surrounded by a jumbled and turbulent sea, with waves seeming to come in all directions, as if that monster had been the foreteller of doom. Down below I could hear the sound of glass breaking as our stowed belongings fell from shelves and flung from cupboards: we thought we had stowed everything securely but nothing could withstand a sea like this.

The boys were crying, and after picking them up off the floor Juliet shepherded them towards the companionway. 'I want to turn back! Please can we turn back?' Luke cried, and for a moment I considered it, but then realised that that would mean sailing back into the Virgin Islands in darkness, and shuddered at the thought of that lurking, hidden reef. A wave of self-loathing rose in my chest, coupled with the usual guilt about exposing the kids to such dangers. All the good times were negated as our minds and bodies once more found themselves assaulted by the sea. *Forever* careered up and down and waves broke across her decks as her bow plunged repeatedly into the head sea. I saw Juliet brace herself against the doorway as with maternal tenacity she settled the boys in their cabin; books, toys and foodstuffs slid backwards and forwards past her feet as the boat rolled from side to side. As she turned to leave them Luke's screams went up a notch.

'No! Don't go Mummy, I'm scared!' he sobbed and I saw her bend to reassure him, banging her head painfully on the low cabin ceiling as the boat lurched.

'Is *Forever* going to break up Dad?' Oscar called anxiously through their little porthole.

'No darling, she's very strong,' I shouted back, though in reality I wasn't so sure. This was far the worst sea we had experienced, and it seemed as if no boat could possibly withstand the brutality of this assault. 'Now be sure your porthole is closed up tightly,' I shouted. 'Everything's going to be fine!'

Using the autohelm in these conditions was out of the question and we had to alter course constantly to deflect the force of the huge waves. When I went down below to check the chart, J took over on the helm, staring ahead with an expression of grim tenacity while Audrey sat miserably by his side. As I clambered my way down to the chart table and began to plot our position, the yellow waves of nausea filled my limbs. I reached for the pilot book in search of some kind of salvation and read: 'When the Christmas trades begin to pipe up, the passage is difficult for large boats and well nigh impossible for smaller ones.' A lurch of fear blended with the nausea.

'Would you call this a small boat?' I yelled up to J.

'No, I would say medium sized,' he shouted back, and I could see from his expression that he'd read the same entry, and was plainly lying.

As the sun finally sank away we were left in a world of turmoil and hideous discomfort, made worse by our course, which was more or less directly into the wind. We kept a bit of sail up to try to improve *Forever*'s motion, but really it was our engine that was propelling us, all the while fighting against the current so that the best speed we could make was 3 knots – the equivalent of a child dawdling along a country lane. It felt as if nature was punishing us for going against her, as if she was pulling some mean moves to make us admit defeat. Increasingly the darkness made it harder to spot the waves and every few minutes we were caught out with a sickening, boat-shattering thump. By some miracle of endurance Juliet managed to make some soup, which we soon gave up trying to drink as the wind blew the hot liquid into our faces whenever we brought the mugs to our lips. Both boys had succumbed to seasickness and Juliet rushed from one to the other with the bucket, passing it to me to strap around my neck in between times. 'Do you think we might invest in another bucket?' she asked with a show of grim humour, as she clung onto the cabin steps, waiting for me to pass it down.

The seasickness reached a new level, worse than anything we had endured so far. I was simply unable to stop retching and I was sick and sick and sick again, and it was starting to scare me, as I knew that we had many miles of incredibly rough ocean to cross before things got any better. I tried to keep positive as I had managed to do before, but after hours of vomiting, I felt very low, as if I could not go on. J looked closely at me. 'I think you'd better go below Guy, we'll keep her on course.'

He was right – I was unable to continue as a functioning member of the crew, and I was overcome by the worst feeling of shame that I have ever experienced. At the age of thirty-four I was forced to hand over control of our sailing boat to my wife and parents-in-law and it felt awful. Hard and unhappy thoughts crowded around me: my sense of responsibility, my male pride, my duty as a father and skipper, my family made vulnerable. As I collapsed into one of the high-sided berths in the saloon, I listened to the sounds of my little children suffering through the night, nursed by Juliet. With a combined age of one hundred and forty-three, my parents-in-law had turned out to be far tougher than I was and I now seriously doubted that I had either the mental or physical resources needed to skipper the boat. A cupboard above my head flew open and bags of pasta and rice fell out on top of me before joining all the other objects sliding around on the floor. I did nothing about it and just lay there looking like a breaded chicken as the dry food adhered to my sweaty skin. The boat slammed and juddered and everything clunked around me as I lay in a dehydrated trance, hating boats and the sea more than anything on earth and above all hating myself for failing. I thought for a little bit about stories I had heard of people driven crazy by seasickness who had simply jumped from boats, never to be seen again.

In the early hours of the morning I emerged from my stupor to find Juliet making an urgent call on the radio. She was dressed in her bright red overalls and lifejacket and held tightly onto the lurching chart table as she fiddled with the buttons.

'*Securité, Securité . . .*' she said into the handset. 'Calling merchant vessel at approximate position one eight degrees north sixty-five degrees west, please come in.'

'What's going on?' I croaked.

'There's a big boat behind us,' she said. 'It keeps crossing over our stern and it's getting pretty close. I just want to see if I can raise them on the radio – they must be hove to in this weather and I am worried they're on autopilot with no one on watch.'

She repeated her message a couple of times and when there was still no response tried the coastguard. Nothing.

'All we can do is try and make sure they see us,' she said and flipped on the mast and spreader lights.

'Take some flares up with you,' I managed, but it was a sign of how far gone I was that I barely cared if we were mowed down – in fact if it wasn't for everyone else on board I would have welcomed an end to my suffering. Shortly she came back down to hold the bucket while the boys had another round of vomiting, before being briefly sick into it herself. She flopped down for a moment on the berth opposite me and as the boat gave an extra big tilt I heard the bucket roll away across the floor.

'Shit – the bucket,' I heard her moan and we both knew that the family's vomit had now spilt everywhere and would be mingling with all the other detritus on the floor and trickling down into the bilge.

The next morning a mean yellow light spread across the horizon and I lay in the saloon like a helpless invalid, transparent with sickness and still covered in bits and pieces of dried pasta that had slid off the table in the tumult. In the cockpit, J sat behind the wheel looking like granite and Audrey lay prone by his side. She had been sick through the night, bearing her seasickness with a stoicism that put me to shame. The boys were sleeping and Juliet was making tea.

'Are you feeling a bit better Guy?' she asked and I saw that she was very tired too. I nodded my head, utterly ashamed.

'I feel like such a flop Jules, I've really let you all down.'

'Don't be silly Guy, it's not your fault,' she replied briskly, but there was a slight impatience to her voice that told me that a part of her also felt let down. Oscar seemed to sense this as he tucked himself in beside me.

'Don't worry Dad, everyone gets sick sometimes you know.'

I sank my fingers into his thick blond hair and closed my eyes. And then we heard Luke. 'Land! Land ahoy!' he shouted. I opened my eye a chink and saw him peering excitedly through the binoculars, tucked into a safe spot beside his grandfather.

I felt like crying. 'You've got to snap out of it Guy,' Juliet was saying. 'You just got sick – it's not the end of the world.'

I didn't agree. It was the end of the world as far as I was concerned, or at least the end of this world. My seasickness had been so debilitating – what would have happened if my parents-in-law hadn't been there, how would Juliet have coped alone? J and Audrey were going home in a couple of weeks. If the Anegada Passage had left me for dead, how on earth was I going to skipper the boat across the Atlantic?

'Guy! You're needed up here!' J shucked me out of my self-pity and I staggered up on deck. Ahead lay the low-lying shape of Anguilla – the name means 'eel' in Spanish, and there was something slippery in its rather sinuous-looking profile. We were approaching a wide, generously proportioned harbour called Road Bay, and I'd noted on the chart that the place was strewn with wrecks. There was also a warning in the pilot book that one could not be sure of their exact positions, so we proceeded with extreme caution until we found a spot to anchor, letting *Forever* settle gently into a well-deserved rest. As I checked the anchor chain I saw that the little seat on the bowsprit had been ripped clean off in the crossing and some of the metal-work had been bent; it gave me the creeps, thinking of how often Oscar had sat happily perched up there. All was quiet around us – we were sheltered from the relentless wind and there was no swell. Within minutes we were all asleep; Audrey and J in the cockpit, Juliet snuggled up with the boys and me comatose in the saloon. The sense of relief at having reached safe harbour blew through the boat like the scent of cut grass. We'd made it, we were safe.

By mid-morning I had pulled myself together and felt well enough to take the dinghy ashore so that I could present our passports to customs. I walked slowly up the beach, savouring every step on dry land, comforted by the presence of children playing in the sand. It looked like this island was going to be a safe, easy-going kind of place and I stopped and asked for directions in a restaurant so surrounded by beach that it looked as if it was being devoured by it. Making a mental note to come back later, I crossed the sandy road to the customs office.

While our passports were being stamped, I saw a large man standing by his desk, looking closely at a map pinned to the wall. He raised a hand in greeting.

'You doin' all right?'

'Just about.' I grimaced, 'The Anegada Passage nearly killed us.'

He sucked his teeth. 'Yup. That passage pretty bad, enough to make grown men cry.'

'I did cry,' I agreed. 'And I had to hand the boat over to my father-in-law. I couldn't hack it.'

A silence fell and the lady inspecting the passports held up J's picture for the man to see. 'He aged seventy-two!' she said, and I realised I'd been too honest.

I heard a shuffle behind me and with sinking heart saw that two other men who looked like veteran sailors were waiting in line. 'Well don't go rubbing it in,' I said, and the room filled with laughter.

As I left the office I asked if there was anyone with a good knowledge of Anguilla's history that I could speak to. I knew about the events surrounding the island's recolonisation and was hoping to hear a first-hand account. Without stopping to think she replied, 'You want to speak to Sir Emile Gumbs. He was first minister of the island. Just go roun' to his house, it just nearby.' She walked me to the door and pointed the way to the end of the road. The house was dainty with ornate white gingerbread woodwork and a wild, happy-looking garden. There was no answer when I knocked on the front door, but on closer inspection I saw that the tendrils of a passion fruit vine had wrapped themselves around the door handle and it clearly hadn't been opened for some time. I walked around to the back of the house, where the garden ran down towards a salt lagoon and rickety wooden steps made their way up towards a first floor porch. The back door was open and I heard the sound of cricket commentary drifting out from inside. And then, as I stepped onto the stairs, I heard a floorboard creak and a tall and distinguished-looking gentleman stepped out onto the porch. His silver hair showed his age but he possessed a lightness that told of a life once full of movement. He stopped and deftly poured some unshelled seed pods into a bowl, then looked down at me and smiled inquiringly.

Behind the smile I could see an incisive look and although he was barefoot, dressed in shorts and an old shirt decorated with flowers, he had such natural grace that I wished I did not look so rough – heavily bearded and pallid, dressed in the ubiquitous shorts, Crocs and faded T-shirt of a low budget yachtie.

I stood midway up the steps, feeling like a burglar caught in the act. 'I'm so sorry to disturb you . . .'

'Just shelling pigeon peas – a job that bears interruption. You sailing?' I nodded.

'Well, what can I do for you?'

'I'm looking for someone to tell me a bit about the island – the lady at the customs office said you were the best person to talk to, if you're not too busy . . .'

'Oh, I'm always happy to leave peeling peas for another day. Come on up.'

I walked behind him into the beautifully built old wooden house and as he led me into his relaxed sitting room I noticed pictures of family, sailing boats and one of him with the Queen. The test match was flickering on an ancient television and he flicked the sound off. 'Now you don't often get an Anguillan to turn off the cricket!' He fetched a couple of beers and gestured for me to sit in a large comfortable chair, heaven after our night of heaving madness. He seated himself opposite and regarded me with open curiosity.

'So, where have you come from?'

'The Virgin Islands. We crossed the Anegada Passage last night – it was awful.'

He winced in sympathy. 'Not a good time to come across, certainly. Who are you sailing with?'

I told him about my family, and then turned the conversation to what I really wanted to ask him about. 'I hear that you were Anguilla's first minister?' I said.

'Yes I was, three years 1977 to 1980. That was quite a turbulent time. Didn't want to be dominated by Bradshaw and his revolutionaries over in St Kitts, so we asked to come back into the fold.'

He explained how Anguilla had once been lumped together with its neighbours Nevis and St Kitts as part of a post-colonial settlement and how the islanders had then decided they'd had enough of being dominated by their larger neighbours and after a couple of revolutions asked to be brought back into the British orbit.

'For a while the Foreign Office was confused about what to do with us, even sending over warships, an attack force and launching parachute drops.' He smiled ruefully. 'The parachute drop went all wrong: their charts showed land where there was only water and they dropped a huge amount of kit into the sea.'

'What would you have done if you'd been forced to keep on with Bradshaw?'

He paused and thought for a while, as if contemplating how to raise an ugly subject in as tasteful a manner as possible. 'Well, we did have some means of fighting back . . .' He leant forward and I got a sense of the power and energy that must have existed when he was a young man. 'You see, we were not prepared to be part of Bradshaw's master plan and if we had to fight we had to fight.' He took a sip of beer and settled back again. 'Thankfully we found a peaceful way around and the Brits took us back. When things settled down, we even had a couple of Cockney Bobbies come over to keep the peace. They didn't have much crime to be dealing with so they taught us to play football and in return we taught them to sail. Some Anguillans still speak with a little cockney twang now after all these years . . .'

And in a sense that was what it was all about – the Anguillans were and are still Anglophiles who simply did not want to become independent from Britain and to join the ranks of their hard-line neighbours. On a more prosaic level the story of Anguilla is also one of inter island rivalry and the desire amongst many Anguillans to do anything to maintain their individuality even if it meant remaining as a possession of our remote archipelago of islands.

The conversation then meandered onto boats and the sea and I asked Emile if he had sailed much. He smiled gently before modestly stating that he had once had a sailing boat called *Warspite*. Before I could ask him much on the subject he changed tack and quizzed me about our journey, interjecting from time to time. From his nuggets of advice it was clear that he had a deep wellspring of knowledge on the subject of sailing.

As I creaked down the back steps he called out, 'On your way back come around with the family for some supper – we would be happy to see you.'

On my way back to the boat people greeted me with friendly smiles and the atmosphere of the island felt welcoming and relaxed. A memory of a conversation with a mini-cab driver in London came back to me: like Sir Emile, he was part of that generation of older West Indians whose schooling and entire socialisation had revolved around Britain. His father had fought for the British in the Second World War and he told me how in the early sixties he finished his engineering course and moved with his family to Britain in search of better prospects. 'It was the natural thing,' he said. 'We had heard so much good about Britain, but when we came we were simply not welcome. It was hard to get work, so I had to take odd jobs, not what I was trained for. And look at me now, forty years on I'm driving a minicab.'

It was a familiar story and I thought again now of how the British marginalised and excluded that first hopeful tide of black families that travelled from their sun-bathed islands to our cold, mean archipelago. Maybe Sir Emile had found it easier to accept Britain as part of his identity because he had never had to endure life as a racial outsider, trying to match the promise of a better life to the grim, grey reality.

At the beach I found the bay filled with little sailing dinghies, crewed entirely by children, dancing across the gust-strewn water. I recalled reading that the island once had a reputation for producing some of the Caribbean's best sailors and for a long time Anguillan schooners had plied a skilful trade between the islands.

'Dad!' I heard Luke's voice and looked about.

'We're over here,' Oscar's voice joined in and I soon discovered them tied up in a happy scrum of local children, chasing a deflated football around the beach.

'How did you get here?'

'We swam!' they said happily and I turned and looked towards the little restaurant, where Juliet and her parents were sitting in swimming costumes, enjoying some cold drinks.

'How are you feeling?' Juliet asked as we joined them.

'Fine. I've just met a really good man.'

'Who?' J asked.

'Emile Gumbs.'

'You mean Sir Emile Gumbs,' he corrected. 'An impressive man. Read about him in the pilot book – some sailor too.'

'Yes, he mentioned that he once had a boat called . . .'

'*Warspite*,' J interrupted. 'A 75-foot schooner built on this island in 1905. Emile was the master. According to my book he worked that boat for sixteen years without an engine.'

I shook my head in admiration at Emile's modesty as he had summed up his truly impressive past with sailing boats in the same terms that one might have mentioned a stint in a dinghy. I stood up to buy some drinks.

'You might need this,' he said, leaning to one side to extract a note. 'Eastern Caribbean dollars . . .' He straightened the note in his hand and held it up smiling.

I leant forward to take it but he teasingly held it back. 'Notice anything?'

I looked closer to see the image of a majestic schooner, with the words 'the *Warspite*' written underneath.

SUPERYACHT POLLUTION

17.54N: 62.51W

The relaxed sunny atmosphere of Anguilla did wonders for our morale and a couple of days before New Year we hoisted sail again, ready to continue south. *Forever* threw her head into the sea like a horse galloping on a beach and in a steady wind that didn't drop below 20 knots we crackled across a navy blue, white tipped sea.

We were heading for the French island of Saint Barthelemy – St Barts – and stopped off overnight at the island of St Martin to stock up on food and fuel. On arrival we anchored outside the lagoon, waited for the road bridge to be lifted and steamed through the narrow channel amidst the busy boat traffic. Once inside we discovered a large, shallow bay, of dubiously coloured water, stuffed with boats of all shapes and sizes. We had some trouble finding space to anchor as we motored slowly between them, many of them live-aboard yachts with wind generators, solar panels and laundry strung out along their rails. Curious to discover more about St Martin's floating community, we tuned into the local cruisers' net on the VHF radio. At the end of the broadcast, which included the usual weather forecasts and announcements of social activities, there was the 'Treasure of the

Bilge' section, in which boat owners bought, sold or swapped boat-related paraphernalia. Juliet and I had been looking for an opportunity to sell our overly large outboard engine and exchange it for a smaller one and I waited for my turn to announce our item.

We kept the radio on and ten minutes later heard somebody hailing us. '*Forever, Forever*' and I grabbed the handset just in time before Oscar got to it. 'This is Steve, host of the cruisers' net. Look, I might be interested in your outboard – I buy and sell a few of these things. Do you want to bring it over?'

Later that morning we made our way across to Steve's place, a café bar that catered to yachties. We brought *Forever* alongside, taking the opportunity to stock up on groceries. The bottom shoaled worryingly as we approached the wooden jetty and a strong wind was blowing us straight on to it. I badly misjudged the approach and *Forever*'s bowsprit hit the jetty, knocking over a box that housed electrics for the pontoon.

'Please, not again,' I groaned, as Juliet and J leapt ashore and leant on the bowsprit with all their strength to push her away from the quay. J hastily lifted the box up and put it back in place, glancing over his shoulder in case anyone had seen. 'There, good as new,' he said. 'I don't think you're the first person to knock that thing over and you won't be the last either.'

As Juliet went off to buy provisions in the fabulously well-stocked French supermarket, I trekked round to see Steve, struggling as I went under the great weight of the outboard engine. The place was sheltered from the fresh trades by a rash of tin sheds and the air around us hung heavy and hot. I found him at an empty bar that had seen better days, sucking sadly on a cigarette over a cup of coffee. Dressed in shorts and a chirpy flowered shirt that seemed only to highlight his obvious depression he raised a hand in limp greeting. He knew a lot about sailing in the area and we chatted about boats and life in general. After a while we got down to haggling over the outboard.

'Looks a bit corroded,' he said, scraping at a speck of rust with a dirty fingernail. 'I'll give you two hundred dollars for it.'

'Two hundred?' I knew that we wouldn't be able to replace it for less than five hundred and in fact I was already regretting advertising it for so little. 'No.'

'OK, three hundred – that's my limit.'

'Sorry Steve, I can't do that – I've got to get another one to replace it.'

'Well maybe I could help you with that too – I could give you a trade-in.' He took me round to an outbuilding where a range of dysfunctional engines and parts lay around on the floor.

My heart sank – I was rapidly losing confidence in the whole thing. 'You know Steve, thanks for trying but I think maybe I'll hold on to it for now. Better the devil and all that.'

He shrugged. 'Suit yourself.' As we talked a bit more I began to get the distinct impression that Steve was swopping more than just boat parts on the cruisers' net. 'We get together with all sorts of people,' he said, winking. 'Any time you're in St Martin, Guy, we're here if you need anything . . .' He winked again and I made my way hastily back to the boat before he could draw me into his web.

Later that morning we set off on the twenty-mile passage to St Barts. It was new year's eve and we knew that the island had a reputation as a gathering point for celebrities at this time of year. For me this was a good reason to avoid it, but Juliet wanted to see the place in full swing.

I called up our course to J, who was on the helm, then stepped up to see an immense super-yacht overtaking us, banging up and down as it sped through the ocean, burning hundreds of gallons of fuel. At the risk of being smug I couldn't help comparing its crashing motion with our own smooth progress, cutting through the sea at a graceful angle solely powered by the wind. What a sailing boat I could have had for the money that thing cost, I thought, travelling in style at nature's pace. J raised his chin towards the gleaming white beast. 'That's heading for St Barts too, you know.'

'I know. I have a feeling that we're going to see how the other half lives.'

'I already know how they live – and I don't want to see it,' he said. 'Anyway they're not anywhere near half the population – in fact they're less than 1 per cent. That thing,' he pointed towards the great thumping monster, which was now leaving us behind in its wake, 'would set you back several million pounds, never mind the fuel costs.'

'Look at its name,' Juliet said, peering through the binoculars. 'One More Toy!'

Gradually St Barts came in to view, a small, green island with dramatic views over the sea. We headed towards the main harbour of Gustavia, but soon realised the bay was jam-packed with super-yachts and motor cruisers and we wouldn't be able to get near it. We dropped sail and motored between the giants, looking vainly for a place to anchor. I thought of the miles of anchor chain that must be strung out along the seabed, the high chance of dropping one anchor over another and the possibility of entanglements. We only had an hour or so of light left and this ratcheted up the tension as we motored round between the yachts.

'Mum, Dad, that one's got a helicopter on it!' Luke shouted, waving furiously.

'And look, this one's got a submarine!' Oscar called from the other side of the boat. A mini sub had acually just come alongside its gleaming mother ship – some publicity-shy guests liked to reach their boats via underwater hatches.

I was getting increasingly furious about our predicament and laid the blame squarely on Juliet. I could see she was regretting the decision too, but felt compelled to defend it and soon we were embroiled in a badly timed argument that must have added even further to our shabby appearance, especially in contrast to the surrounding order and polished nautical behaviour. Finally we found a reasonable spot and after a few further cross words, dropped the hook. A grumpy silence descended on the boat.

We stood looking round at the immense yachts and their occupants, many of whom were in party mode, laughter and music drifting across the bay. The contrast with the mood of our ship's company couldn't have been greater, and even though I wanted to make peace with Juliet, I couldn't yet find the words. I felt claustrophobic, hemmed in, with too many people's opinions to take account of when I wasn't even sure of my own. Children, parents-in-law and the tense job of learning to run our own boat – I felt overwhelmed. I looked towards the distant outline of Gustavia. 'Hey, shall we take the dinghy over and take a look at the place?'

Leaving Audrey and J onboard to enjoy some serenity, we lowered the dinghy and helped each of the kids to climb in. Seeing their excitement lifted my maudlin spirits and I felt proud to see our two little boys, all puffed up in their life-jackets, holding the sides of the dinghy tightly, pointing and chattering with glee.

We noticed that the boats seemed to grow bigger and more opulent as we approached the harbour, as if some kind of hiearchy existed, the most privileged spots reserved for the biggest fish. And then we gaped at the sight of the harbour frontage, which was lined with the biggest private yachts we had ever seen.

'That one's bigger than the Isle of Mull ferry!' Oscar said.

Nudging our way in between the towering white side of a vast motor yacht and a sleek wooden yacht, newly built on classic lines, we tied up and pulled ourselves up onto the quayside where we stood looking about in fascination. Wide, gleaming gangplanks made of teak and chrome lined the harbour front, with discreet lighting, red carpets and potted palms. At the bottom of the gangplanks uniformed crew stood to attention amidst faux plastic gardens, waiting to welcome guests or help their passengers off the boats. One even had a small piano set out on the quayside complete with carousing singer. Clearly there was a bad case of gang-plank one-upmanship going on and as we walked along the harbour front we marvelled at the lengths each yacht had gone to to outshine its neighbours.

It proved impossible to find a table in any of the restaurants, everything seemingly booked, but as the waiters looked at us I suspected that it had more to do with our down-at-heel attire than being full. Eventually we found ourselves queuing at a crowded pizza restaurant, which had a takeaway section where the overworked local chef was pawing frantically at the dough and slopping on toppings in between stocking the furnace-like oven. Luke watched him for a few minutes before asking loudly, 'Dad, is that a slave?' Several people around us heard the comment and laughed and to his credit the chef laughed too. I hurried to correct Luke, in case we'd hurt his feelings. 'Of course not Luke! Slavery was banned a long time ago. This man is just working very hard at his job.'

'Well little man,' the chef said, reaching across to ruffle Luke's hair, 'in some ways you are right – I am not so far from a slave you know!'

After we'd eaten we wandered into a shore-side bar and sat at a table overlooking the sea. For a moment we did what parents do all over the world: we tried to pretend that we were alone, just us, as it was in the beginning of our relationship. We settled the kids with their pizza and hoped that we could generate some kind of new year's spirit. The atmosphere in the bar was fun, the people friendly and welcoming – clearly it wasn't glitzy enough for the rich and famous and we could see that there were local people about. In an effort to make amends for earlier, I placed a sumptuous rum cocktail in front of Juliet. She smiled at me and I felt that we were heading back towards a happy place when Luke threw his arm out, toppling her drink all over the only half-decent outfit she had. 'Oh Luke!' she said and he immediately clasped his hands together as if he was the child of two ogres and feared a horrific reprisal.

'Sorry Mum! I'm so sorry!'

'Another drink Jules?'

She looked down at her damp and sticky clothing. 'No thanks.' She stood up. 'Let's get back to the boat – the boys are getting tired.'

I sighed and went to pay the bill. Any thought of the romance of life at sea was long gone. The reality was simply that sparkle between a couple cannot exist in a 41-foot boat packed with children and grandparents.

On the way back we wandered along the quayside and the boys stopped to talk with a smart-looking crewman who stood stiffly beside the gleaming gangway that led from the quayside to another great hulk of excess. He looked happy to be diverted and we stopped and listened to his stories of life aboard a super-yacht.

'These things go at some speed,' I said, remembering the boat we'd seen banging up and down earlier. 'How comfortable is it?'

'Pretty bad actually – our owners wanted to get here in an hour from St Martin, but then got pissed off when they felt seasick. As if it's our fault!'

We piled into the dinghy and motored off into the darkness. Ahead the anchor lights of the fleet of boats in the outer harbour hung over the water, as if the night sky had sunk to sea level. Juliet's parents were asleep when we arrived and the boat was quiet. We put the boys to bed and thought about staying up to see in the new year, but I couldn't muster any kind of enthusiasm.

Later, I heard Juliet whisper through the butterfly hatch. 'Guy, can you hear that? It's amazing.'

It was midnight. Outside I heard the strangest commotion as the great armada of the super-rich welcomed the new year, letting off their foghorns. The smaller boats whooped and screeched, making a weird, tuneless symphony. 'Guy, they're setting off fireworks, come up and see!' But I just rolled over, unable to shake the bad feeling that was gathering inside me, and though I hated myself for giving into this unfamiliar and frightening sense of sadness there was nothing I could do about it. To me, the mournful chorus of the ships was the sound of disaster coming from the deep, a further omen of my building depression.

The next morning we motored around the headland to Anse de Colombier, a little bay on the north shore of St Barts, above which stood a large, tasteful house built by the Rockefellers. A few other modest yachts lay at anchor, but the anchorage felt peaceful and mercifully quiet. We pulled the dinghy up on the dainty beach, set below a steep hill that was richly overgrown with greenery. We all climbed the hill to look down on the dramatic windward side of the island and walked along a cactus-strewn path above the top of the sea cliffs, as the Atlantic waves crashed against the rocks far below. When we returned to the beach we relaxed on the sand, enjoying the simple beauty of the place in contrast to the strangeness of Gustavia under Ivy League siege. The boys lost themselves in an intricate game involving sand castles and bits of crab shell and it felt good to see how powerful their imaginations had become. Just as I was starting to unwind, and about to apologise to Juliet for being such bad company the night before, an immense black super-yacht rounded the headland like a sea monster and dropped its great clattering anchor.

'Oh God, here we go again. Is there any hope of getting away from these people?' I said. The boys stopped their game and stared as an intricate system of pulleys and lines lowered a gleaming launch into the sea. Uniformed crew scrambled about, passing endless boxes and bundles down into the boat. 'What now? The D-Day landing?'

Juliet shaded her eyes to look before returning to her book. 'Maybe they're planning to do something on the beach.'

'Yes, they are planning to take over the beach. Probably got plans to build a golf course with the biggest sand-trap in the world or something.' I tried to carry on reading, but was distracted by what they were doing: it felt like being unable to put down a trashy magazine. The launch pulled away from the mother ship and shot over to the beach, where the crew of three rather clumsily raised their engine before climbing out. They then began unpacking enough kit to supply a six-month expedition: two large parasols were stuck into the sand on either side of a teak table, so as to provide complete shade; three deck chairs were arranged around the table and a privacy screen erected. The two female crew members set up a gas barbecue and began cooking and laying the table while the crewman climbed back into the launch. Next a vase of cut flowers was placed on the freshly laid tablecloth.

Ten minutes later the launch returned with a tense-looking couple and their young son, who looked about Luke's age. The couple settled down onto the deck chairs, looking like chieftains waiting to negotiate with Christopher Columbus, staring vacantly through their sunglasses as bountiful platters of food were placed on the table before them. Meanwhile their boy played disconsolately in the sand, every now and then glancing over to Oscar and Luke who were playing together by the water's edge.

Luke ran up to us. 'Dad, can we go and play with that boy?'

I glanced over to the couple and waved. They raised their hands in greeting but their body language read, 'Are we actually waving to . . . them?' Oscar and Luke ran over to the boy who walked out slowly to meet them, looking back nervously to his family sub-consciously aware that he was crossing some kind of invisible barrier. The boys threw him a ball which he caught and hugged to his chest as if he had been thrown some kind of lifeline. He looked back once but his parents were too busy instructing the hired help to notice his social transgression and in a moment the boys were all lost in play. Before long one of the crew rather apologetically ushered the little boy back to his splendid isolation, where he sat in the sand watching Oscar and Luke longingly. Shortly both parents and child were escorted back to the super-yacht and the crew began packing up. The crewman came over. He spoke in a light Australian accent.

'Sorry about that,' he said. 'He looked kinda happy playing about with your lot, but they don't like it . . . they're a bit funny like that.'

Juliet smiled up at him. 'No problem, we just felt a bit sorry for him.'

The crewman opened his mouth as if he was about to spill the beans but then clearly thought better of it. 'Yeah, well I'd rather be your kid than theirs, I can tell you,' he said. 'Anyway, I came to say there's a lot of food left over – do you fancy some? There's barbecued shrimp, lamb chops . . . lots of fruit if you want it. Help yourselves, we're just going to have to trash it otherwise.'

We picked at the food as they finished clearing up, but soon I felt pitiful scavenging from leftovers of the super-rich. We watched as most of it went into black bin bags.

The next morning we stepped back onto the trade-wind conveyor belt, which whipped us on towards the island of St Christopher. St Kitts was visible from far away due to the impressive mountain at its centre which had once been called Mount Misery but now, looking at its sparkling green hillsides we could see why it was named Mount Fertile. At nearly 4,000 feet, this is the highest peak in the Leeward Islands and one of the highest in the Eastern Caribbean. Even from this distance we could see evidence of the many sugar mill ruins dotted over the hillside, testament to the fact that St Kitts had once been entirely given over to sugar cane. In the early 1970s the hard-line premier of St Kitts, Robert Llewellyn Bradshaw took state control of the sugar plantations and this, combined with falling sugar prices, brought private production of sugar on the island to an end.

This was interesting territory. As one of Europe's first colonies in the Caribbean, St Kitts has a long written history, much of it involving violence and division. As we came into the lee of the island, the boys spotted a remarkable looking Napoleonic fort that wound its way up to the top of a hillside, commanding impressive views over the surrounding sea. We read in the pilot book that this was Brimstone Hill, built by the British and known as 'The Gibraltar of the West Indies', in reference to its height and seeming invulnerability, until 1782 when the French managed to take it in a bloody battle.

We were heading for Port Zante Marina in the island's capital of Basseterre, the official point of entry to the country. The marina had been rebuilt after taking a hard hit from hurricanes George and Lenny in 1998 and 1999. As we approached we heard the heavy beat of thudding music out across the water. Juliet scanned the island with the binoculars:

'It looks like some kind of carnival is going on,' she said.

As we got closer we saw that the waterfront road was jam-packed with people, moving in time to the rhythm of music in what seemed to be some kind of hypnotic trance. Armed guards were standing along the roadside and the streets thronged to the mesmeric beat coming from huge sound systems on top of flatbed trucks. These trucks drove slowly through the town, the crowd swirling around them, and the music was so loud that all you could hear was the gargantuan whacking of a booming bass line.

The entrance to the marina was a long, narrow channel, so we couldn't see what it was like inside. We considered stopping outside the marina where one or two other boats lay at anchor, but I felt that this was the cowardly option. I knew my ability to come alongside a quay safely was still in doubt and I was determined to do this right. I needed praise after the horror of the Anegada Passage. There was already an atmosphere of tension onboard as we motored into the horrendously confined marina. The music was so loud by now that we could barely hear each other and had to yell at the top of our voices, or use hand signals. For a moment I wondered if the water itself was rippling in time. Worse still, I was unable to hear the sound of the engine, what kind of strain it was experiencing. J and Juliet stood at the bow, warps in hand, as I circled round trying to find a good spot to berth. A number of other boats were lined up along the dock – most of them considerably smaller than *Forever* – and my heart sank as I saw that they were all stern to.

'Guy, shall we anchor outside?' Juliet called above the thumping of the music, 'I don't think this is a good idea.'

'No, I can do it,' I shouted and she stared anxiously ahead at the dock, a coil of rope in one hand.

I had been dreading this very situation, where space is more confined. The berth lay between two narrowly placed wooden pilings and the idea was to pass between them in reverse, throwing bow lines around the pilings to hold the bow of the boat secure before tying the stern off to the quay. With *Forever*'s severe prop walk, which made her steerage in reverse very unpredictable, we all knew it wasn't going to be easy.

'We could go in forwards.' Juliet pointed to a boat on the other side of the harbour: 'Look – someone's gone in forwards over there.'

'That boat's a lot smaller than us,' J said, 'And besides, how would we get ashore?'

Oscar was saying something, but all I could see was his moving mouth – his voice was too light to compete with the carnival. I motioned for him to go below so that he would be safe and out of the way. Everything about this harbour felt bad and my instincts told me that we should give in gracefully and anchor outside, but pride was overruling my ability to make a good decision. Audrey stood tense and quiet in the cockpit beside me, ready to relay messages to Juliet and her father, who waited on deck as I circled in the confined space once, twice, three times. I picked a berth between two yachts, a compact Island Packet with a Netherlands flag and a French boat, and began my approach. Within ten metres I knew I'd got the angle wrong and *Forever*'s prop walk sent us veering towards one of the pilings. I slipped into neutral and powered forwards then began another slow loop round to reposition myself. I repeated this twice more and aborted both times. A cold bead of sweat gathered between my shoulders and slipped down my back and I saw that some fishermen had stopped to watch, as well as some yachties, who stood waiting beside the empty space I was failing to get anywhere near to. Clearly sensing the strain I was under, Audrey tapped my arm.

'Guy, do you want to ask J to take her in?' she asked as softly as the music allowed, little realising that the depth of my father-in-law insecurity rendered this the worst of all solutions.

'Thank you Audrey, but that won't be necessary,' I shouted grimly. 'I'm going to get it this time.'

She tried again: clearly her well-honed instinct for disaster was telling her something. 'We can come in by dinghy, if you decide to anchor.'

Finally I had got the angle right and *Forever*'s prop walk now helped us as we glided towards the berth. We passed the pilings rather too fast for comfort and I saw Juliet try and fail to throw her warp around the wooden post. Her father had got his round, but couldn't catch the end and it slipped into the water. I put the gear shift lever into neutral, planning to stop the boat with a burst ahead but as I pushed it into gear I felt it stick for a second before becoming completely lifeless and loose within its housing. We were still moving astern, heading for a massive concrete dock at some speed and there was nothing I could do about it.

I pulled at the lever frantically. 'Oh shit! We're stuck in reverse – J! The gear lever's broken!'

I saw J glance around, clearly wondering what I was doing, but he couldn't hear me over the music. The prop walk was sending us straight towards the Dutch yacht.

'Stop the boat!' Juliet screamed.

'I can't! The lever is broken!' I shouted, but nobody could hear me over the hellish soundtrack of the carnival. It was pure, perfect nightmare come to life, and I realised my only option was to switch off the engine and rushed below to do so – but this achieved little as *Forever*'s sixteen tons of momentum needed more than six boat lengths to stop. She began to t-bone in the berthing space and Juliet and J fended off the French yacht as *Forever*'s massive bowsprit swung around, narrowly missing its forestay. People on the dock ran from all directions and one of the owners of the Dutch boat ran out, screaming 'No! No! My fucking boat!'

But then a split second later, with a ghastly inevitability, *Forever* ground into the concrete dockside and slewed sideways into the Dutch boat. I could see the Dutch couple screaming, an immense Munch painting, but nothing could be heard over the carnival. At the exact point of impact, in a moment of adrenalin-induced slow motion I saw J look at Audrey, his resigned expression registering the sum of all the previous disasters he'd ever experienced and witnessed in a long life running farms and quarries and boats and engines. Juliet was on the quayside now, pushing desperately against *Forever* along with everyone else, trying belatedly to fend her huge bulk away from the boat. Fortunately the inflatable dinghy mounted across our stern had taken the worst of the blow, but as we disentangled ourselves from the Dutch boat's lifelines I knew there had to be some damage.

People appeared with warps and fenders to help settle *Forever* and I moved about trying to look efficient, but I knew that nothing whatsoever could undo the scene of incompetence that they had just witnessed. The Dutchman's crewmate, a statuesque woman in her early thirties, was taking photographs of the crime scene from every angle, as she had been doing throughout the whole incident.

'Pride before a fall, pride before a fall, pride before a fall.' The phrase kept running through my head like a mantra, my legs feeling like lead in the nightmare that had become life at sea. Finally we got *Forever* securely tied up and together with the Dutch owners, we carefully inspected the damage to their yacht. Miraculously it proved fairly minor: a small scrape on her hull, some shaved steel off her shrouds, a bent stanchion and broken lifeline. *Forever* had suffered no damage at all, bar some scraping to her name, which was printed in vinyl across her stern. Our dinghy, which now hung sad and deflated on its davits, had acted like a giant fender and saved the day. I felt utterly humiliated and no matter how often I repeated the story of the broken gear lever it didn't take away the fact that I had damaged somebody else's yacht.

The Dutch couple seemed to be taking the whole thing in their stride, acting with astonishing efficiency and restraint almost as if they had rehearsed going through this very situation. They gave Juliet a memory stick with a copy of the photographs and we swapped insurance details. After agreeing to talk to them later, I lay down in the cabin feeling desperate and hopeless, even worse than I had during the Anegada fiasco, which I thought had been the worst moment of my life so far.

I felt a little head nuzzle into the crook of my neck, and knew it was Luke. 'Sorry sweetie for giving you that fright – Daddy got it all wrong,' I said, holding him close. Then Oscar came and clambered on top of me and hugged me tightly. His sensitivity and kindness was so much greater than mine had ever been at that age.

'We still love you Dad,' he said sadly, clearly fully appreciating the shame that I was suffering. I hugged him too and then asked if they wouldn't mind leaving me alone for a while. With great ceremony they took off my shoes and produced a sheet which they tucked around me, despite the immense heat. Busy little hands moved about, arranging things like a pair of undertakers preparing a body to be embalmed.

'Do you need a glass of water Dad?' Oscar asked, and I cracked an eye open to see him regarding me with deep seriousness, while behind him Luke stood gravely to attention.

'I'm fine boys,' I said. 'I'm just feeling really bad right now. Give me a few moments and I'll be back on form.'

They both nodded, looking so solemn that I realised they were thoroughly enjoying themselves. Having been deprived of television and war games in the garden with their friends, this episode had at last given them the chance to sink their teeth into a genuine drama, in which Daddy would be the blameless victim and they would be the saviours. It was ER for kids and I was the hapless patient.

Silence descended. I sought abandon through sleep with a sweaty arm wrapped across my eyes while Juliet played pick-up sticks with the boys and Audrey and J read. Through it all the bloated abandon of the carnival trampled on, battering the humid, mosquito-filled air. At one point the truck carrying the sound systems passed close to us, the sound waves reverberating through me, like a shame-induced heart attack. After a while Audrey called us all for supper.

We ate mostly without talking, partly because we couldn't hear over the music, but also because I realised everyone was finding it hard to find something to say that would make me feel better. I expected someone to say the words 'if only' or 'we told you so', but instead J disarmed me by saying, 'You did well to turn the engine off Guy, that showed great presence of mind.' I nodded mutely and stared down at the table. The depression that had been stalking me had now almost completely taken over. I couldn't even look at him.

'I am so sorry everyone,' I said eventually. 'It wouldn't have happened if the gear lever hadn't given way like that.' There was silence.

'You don't believe me do you?' I rounded on Juliet with pointless, childish aggression.

'I do Guy! Just calm down. We need to sort out what we're going to say to the Dutch couple.'

'That reminds me,' Audrey said apologetically, 'Henrik and Myken came across while you were sleeping. They want to see you.'

'Well, I've inspected the gear mechanism and it has failed, the cotter pin sheared right off,' said J. 'They can have a look themselves if they don't believe it. Anyway,' he pointed a finger at me, 'this is a matter for the insurance company. Leave it to them to sort it out, that's what they're there for.'

'I'll try,' I said and I saw Juliet looking at me doubtfully.

With dread deep in my heart I knocked on the hull and in an instant the Dutch couple appeared in the cockpit and stood together looking at me. I began to mumble something, but the man held up a hand and smiled. 'Wait a minute!' he said. 'Before anything, let's have a drink! And a cigarette – do you smoke?' Normally I didn't, but at that moment I would have smoked crack cocaine if he'd offered it. He stepped up onto the quay, bearing a bottle of rum and three glasses, followed by his wife, who smiled at me with rather less bonhomie.

They both settled comfortably cross-legged on the concrete and with an open hand Henrik invited me to sit opposite them. He regarded me closely for a moment before beginning to recount the disaster as they saw it and what we would have to do about it. Despite his slightly broken English he spoke with immense courtesy though his tone left no doubt that I must see the situation from his point of view. I felt like a tribesman signing my land away to a trader for nothing more than a handful of beans, as he skilfully imposed a kind of moral debt upon me in which I would underwrite whatever the insurance company came up with. I forgot all my defences as he spoke to me; forgot the fact that, as he confidently told me how I should have entered the berth, his boat was much smaller and lighter than ours, could be manoeuvred easily by hand unlike *Forever*, and had the luxury of a bow-thruster. I eagerly acquiesced to his offer of lessons in docking and forgot what a fantastic ocean-going yacht *Forever* had proved herself to be, as he disparagingly dismissed her as the equivalent of a run-down floating English pub. Before I knew it I had agreed to pay for all the damage to their boat, whatever the insurance company might say regarding my culpability.

'I left home when I was very young,' Henrik was saying as he crushed a cigarette into the concrete with two thick brown fingers. 'Not that I didn't like my parents. I just told them thank you for bringing me up and all that but I am ready to get on with my life now.' He smiled at me with intense eyes that frightened and fascinated me all at once. 'I became an entrepreneur, set up my own business and now, as you see, we are free to do whatever we please, while we are still young. What about you?'

I mumbled a bit about myself, feeling my life story was pretty pathetic by comparison and clearly he thought so too because he soon changed the subject. 'So . . .' he said, 'now we will draft a letter stating what happened and you will send us an email confirming it.'

'Yes.' I suddenly remembered about the insurance company. 'We'll need to submit a claim to our insurance company of course.'

'Of course', he smiled. 'Meantime we will take the boat to St Martin – we were going to leave her there anyway while we go travelling. We will have estimates for repairing the damage – of course we will research the cheapest people possible – and send them to you. OK? And now – another drink!'

'I don't know, I'd better go back to the boat, the kids need to be put to bed and . . .'

'Oh come on man', he said, restraining me with a fleshy hand. 'One more drink won't make any difference . . .'

Two hours later I finally extracted myself, feeling drunk and sick from the smoking. As we said goodnight Henrik focused his gaze upon me and looked deeply into my eyes. 'Now you're not going to disappear without telling us are you Guy? We are trusting you to put things right.'

'I know,' I said, feeling guilty all over again. 'I will, you can trust me. I'm a man of honour.' He grinned at my pompous tipsy words and shook my hand.

I was reluctant to return to the banality of domestic life and in a strange way felt that my family had wronged me, as if only Henrik and Myken understood my predicament. They had given me an insight into life onboard as a couple, free to enjoy themselves without responsibilities. They were setting off to join the carnival as I left them and they had tried hard to persuade me to go too. Although it wasn't my kind of thing really I felt stupidly resentful that I wasn't free to do as I pleased. The wild booming music had not let up once as the crowd continued to stamp on in a kind of cataleptic state, working themselves into an alcohol- and drug-induced frenzy, and I knew that Henrik and Myken would abandon themselves to the experience like everyone else melting into the crowd.

Inside *Forever* I found Juliet sitting alone in the saloon, reading quietly, and as she looked up at me I could see hurt in her eyes. But there was also some anger too. 'How did it go?' she asked.

'Well, great,' I said, 'Henrik and Myken are being really understanding. They've completely put me straight about how I should have come in here by the way – they're going to give me some lessons in manoeuvring tomorrow.' I rambled on a bit more and then petered out as I realised Juliet was staring at me frostily.

'What about the boat? Did you sort out what's happening about the damage?'

'I said we'd pay for it. What else could I say?'

She sighed. 'You should have left it to the insurance company to deal with that. What the hell is wrong with you Guy? You haven't been yourself for ages. You've been sitting there drinking with those two for hours. They give me the creeps. Did you really need to take all that time to do it? And by the way, are you out of your mind agreeing to take lessons from them – it'll just put them in a better position to argue that you were incompetent if we come to blows over all this.'

I leant my head back and looked up at the cabin roof, feeling lost in emotional territory that I was unable to navigate in my current state of mind. I was also a little scared about just how out of sync I was feeling.

'Well I'm sorry that I was having fun.' And then my dark mood gathered momentum. 'I don't think this is working.'

She looked steadily at me. 'Meaning?'

'This.' I gestured around the boat. 'I'm having a really bad time here and you clearly don't think I am up to the task, do you?'

She leant back, as if hit by a hot blast from an oven. 'What makes you think that?'

'Oh come on! I fucked up on the Anegada Passage and on countless other occasions and now this. It's a disaster, I'm no good!'

'You've just had a bad day Guy, and now you've had too much to drink with those people. Or do you think it's more than that?'

'I don't know,' I leant on the table. 'I just know I feel very unhappy. I don't know if it's you and me or the boat, but I feel awful. I don't think I can go on with . . .' I waved my arms about and knocked a

frying pan off its hook as I did so. 'Oh shit! I mean everything ...
this whole thing is not working.'

'We can't just give up and go home, Guy. Think of the kids, how
disappointed they would be. We've built this up into the adventure of
a lifetime and then they have to go home with their tails between their
legs. It's not possible.'

'There have been worse things Jules,' I said. 'They'll be OK. If it's
not working, it's not working. I don't know if we can make it work
when your parents go home anyway – and how can I skipper the boat
with this bloody seasickness?' I thumped my hand on the table.

Anger flashed in her eyes. 'Well that's fine, you can quit if you
want but I'm bloody well not going to. I'll carry on with this with or
without you.'

I gave a hollow laugh. 'Oh yeah, how?'

'I'll ask my father to come with me, or someone else – there are
people. I am simply not going to tell the boys that we're going home
after two months.' She stood up and took her cup to the sink. 'There's
no point in talking any more about this right now. I'm going to sleep
– if I can with this bloody music.'

As we lay in our berths, I knew Juliet was crying but I couldn't
say anything. Instead, as I lay sweating in the fetid darkness of the
harbour, as the music pulsed on and on, I wondered where the dream
had gone. This was the worst of times.

TEN

DOUBLE DUTCH & THE SINISTER MONKEYS

17.17N: 62.43W

The next morning Juliet and I moved carefully around each other, keeping our subjects deliberately neutral and not alluding to our conversation the night before. I could see her talking to Audrey, looking washed out and weepy, and as her mother hugged her I felt miserable and guilty. To give them some space I wandered along the dock with the boys and we stopped to watch a group of local free divers coming into the harbour. They were impressively powerful, strong-looking men and the atmosphere was cheerful as they unloaded their catch of brightly coloured reef fish and a small shark which had been expertly shot with their home-made spear guns. As we wandered back along the quay I saw that Myken and Henrik were eating breakfast out in their cockpit. I hesitated; I didn't want to see them at that moment, but there was no way of getting to *Forever* without passing them. Their heads bent together as we approached and I had the uncomfortable feeling that they were exchanging quick tactical plans regarding me. 'When are we going to start our lessons?' Henrik called out.

'Um, well I think we have other plans today,' I flannelled, thinking of Juliet. 'But maybe some other time . . . ?'

'No problem.' He picked something from his teeth and then wagged a finger. 'But don't forget to tell us when you are leaving, yes?'

'Yes I will. We can't go anywhere until we fix the gear lever anyway.'

'Oh sure.' He winked in a way that left me uncertain whether he was being encouraging or sarcastic. Either way I walked on with an uncomfortable feeling that I was being manipulated.

After breakfast we heard a little knock on the side of the boat. I stepped out to see a trim, leathery-looking man on the quay wearing a faded shirt which looked like it must have been at its prime in the seventies. 'Hello, my name is Eric,' he said. 'I was here yesterday when you had your . . . accident.'

I grimaced. 'Oh God, don't remind me, I really messed up . . .'

He hurried to reassure me. 'Well, don't beat yourself up about it. What matters is that no one was hurt. Anyway, I hear from your mother-in-law that it was gear failure – there was nothing you could do about that.'

'Well thank you,' I said, his words like balm to my damaged morale. His accent made me think of my childhood home. 'Are you South African?'

'A long time ago, yes. I teach zoology at the university here.' A woman walked over to Eric and he introduced her as his friend Jenny. Juliet came out onto the quay and while the two women were talking, Eric took me along to see his modest little day boat in which he'd sailed all around the surrounding islands. When I returned to *Forever*, Juliet said, 'Jenny's asking if we'd like to go to her place this afternoon. She can pick us up.'

That afternoon we all piled into Jenny's small car and drove through the shabby back streets of Basseterre until we left the town. Away from the formal buildings of the harbour front, the poverty in the town was evident and several times Jenny had to slow or swerve to avoid groups of street children who stood staring at us as we passed. Out of the town the car huffed its way up a steep, single-track road around the hillside until we arrived at an imposing and somewhat ruinous gateway. Jenny jumped out to open it and at the end of the drive we saw a large former plantation house, heavily overgrown with luxuriant greenery. Around it stood a scattering of buildings in various states of repair, all surrounded by richly flowering shrubs, thick vines and tall trees that swayed in the sea breeze. It was such a novelty being at a house, that I had to blink a few times to re-orientate myself.

The garden was lush and beautiful and overgrown and as we stepped out of the car we were hit by the pungent aroma of tropical growth and warm earth. 'Wow!' Juliet said. 'What an amazing place!'

'Come and sit down,' Jenny gestured towards a table in the shade of the trees. 'I've baked a cake, boys – I thought we'd make it a proper afternoon tea!'

Though it had a kind of faded beauty, the place was semi-ruinous, possessing a strong sense of the other lives that had passed through it in times of greater prosperity. Once, the house would have stood at the head of a great cane plantation and I imagined the cruelties that would have taken place within the high stone walls that surrounded the grounds. Jenny lived in a small part of the property that had been restored to habitable condition, but the majority of it lay empty, deteriorating fast in tropical conditions, the relentless march of nature more than anyone could keep at bay.

Something large rustled in a fig tree overhead and I looked up, feeling slightly jumpy. I thought I saw a glimpse of a long black tail, but I could have been mistaken. I heard Juliet calling and I walked back to the table, trying to reassemble my features into some semblance of happiness. Jenny had laid out a beautiful spread of china on top of a lace tablecloth and the boys sat down happily to tuck into generous slices of carrot cake as she poured the tea.

'Are there monkeys here?' I asked Jenny. 'I caught a glimpse of a tail in a tree.'

'Yes, there are loads of spider monkeys around here,' she said. 'They can be pretty bold at times. Sometimes they come right up to the house and look in the window: it can give you quite a shock if you're not expecting it, I can tell you.'

'Dad, can we take a look at the old house?' Oscar tugged on my arm.

'Would you mind Jenny?' I asked.

'Not at all – but just be careful you don't go through the floor. The termites have done a lot of damage, but I can't afford to do anything about it just now . . .'

The boys and I pushed our way through an overgrown garden, along what must once have been a well-tended path. Carefully we stepped up onto a wide creaking porch that ran around the old house in the classic plantation-house style. We pushed our way through the creaking swing door and gingerly stepped inside.

'Dad! I'm scared!' Luke was holding my hand in a vice-like grip as we moved into the house, entering a large, wood-panelled room covered in bird droppings. Oscar froze:

'Look up Dad!'

I followed his finger and as my eyes adjusted to the darkness I saw that what had looked simply like a dark ceiling was in fact an immense colony of fruit bats, literally hundreds of them nestled together and only giving away their presence by the odd yawn or stretch of wings.

'OK boys, let's get out of here,' I said. 'Go slowly though – we don't want them to all fly off at once.' We crept along a shady passage towards the porch, on the way passing a closed door that cried out to be opened. Luke read my mind:

'Don't open it! Dad, let's go!'

I held his hand tightly. 'It can't be anything that scary Luke, don't worry.'

'Daaaaaad!' Oscar moaned with terror as I turned the handle and the door swung open. There was a commotion inside and the boys screamed as a large spider monkey bounded out of the glassless window.

'Shit!' I shouted. 'God I hate monkeys!' Then I remembered my parental duties as they clung to me: 'It's just a monkey.' My gaze shifted slowly from the open window to the centre of the room, where there was a heap of dark material that looked like garden compost.

I stepped forward and saw the remains of a piano that had been completely devoured by termites. All that remained were the ivory keys that still lay close to each other, the teeth of a decomposed animal.

'Dad, please can we go now!' Luke screamed.

As we walked across the grass, enjoying the fresh scents after the dim, dusty interior, I saw Juliet coming towards us. 'Come and look at this,' she said and led me to a magnificent mango tree, which was littered below with rotting fruit. 'It's the monkeys – they take one bite and then throw the fruit down because it's not ripe yet. What a waste!'

The profligate behaviour of the monkeys and the rotten mangoes seemed to somehow symbolise the whole property: full of potential but ultimately wasted. I took Juliet's hand as a way of beginning to say sorry. 'Look, I've been thinking . . .' she said quietly. 'Maybe we should just call it a day, the boys and I could go home with my parents and I guess you could stay here and try to sell the boat . . .'

'No, please don't do that,' I said quickly, squeezing her hand. 'Look, I think you were right, I've just . . . I don't know, I just haven't been feeling right, I can't really explain why. Let's not talk too much about it just now, take it day by day for now, huh?'

She nodded but I knew she was only half convinced. Somewhere along the way, she'd lost faith in me, and I'd lost faith in myself, and neither of us knew how to restore it.

Later Jenny told us of the dream that had brought her and her husband out to St Kitts and how they had hoped to restore the plantation house and turn it into a hotel.

'What happened?' Juliet asked, though we knew that the answer couldn't be happy.

'Well, he did what a lot of white men of a certain age do out in this part of the world – found himself a local girl.' She gave a bitter cough of laughter. 'Yup, he got himself a nice young thing and she got herself a meal ticket. Story of the world, hey?' She shrugged and looked across at us, bravely managing an ironic half-smile. 'The worst of it is, they live just over there,' she pointed at a little garden cottage nestling beneath some mango trees.

'What, him and his . . . girlfriend?' Juliet asked.

'Actually it's a newer model – he's had two or three girlfriends since then and a couple of kids too. I think they get sick of him after a bit – obviously he hasn't got what it takes. He doesn't take them away to live in New York or Los Angeles; he just stays on in the place they all want to leave. It's quite pathetic really.'

'That is sad,' Juliet said.

'It is rather. But we haven't been able to resolve things – I don't see why I should give up on the house and neither does he, so the situation rumbles on.' She gave another shrug. 'Still, that's life in the tropics.'

Juliet leant over the table and squeezed Jenny's hand and as I watched I felt a little uncomfortable, as if I also might be turning into one of those oddball men who lost his marbles in paradise. We carried the tea things back into her little house and she showed us her simply furnished rooms, which were pretty, but forlorn. Pictures of her grown-up children adorned the walls and her bedroom opened onto a wrought iron balcony draped in sweet-smelling flowering vines. 'Mum! A humming bird!' Luke pointed out excitedly and we watched the tiny bird hovering with such accuracy between flowers. Then a loud chaotic rattling across the tin roof made us all jump.

'It's the monkeys,' Jenny said. 'They sometimes gather up there in the evenings – they can make quite a racket too.'

That night I thought about how dreams so often become traps for people without enough money to escape them when they go wrong, and how Jenny was forced to confront her shattered dreams on a daily basis.

Seamoss Man told us that every cab driver in St Kitts carries a machete, under the front seat, in the glove compartment or in the trunk. He had offered to take us for a tour around the island and was so named for a drink he was famous for preparing, made of milk, spices and local seaweed, which he mixed to a secret recipe. He claimed the drink was incredibly healthy and it probably was, although none of us were particularly keen on the taste of it.

He had brought his son Quincy along with him to tell us about the island, and he was brilliant – insightful, knowledgeable and gentle with the boys. He began by taking us to the great fort, Brimstone Hill, that we had seen as we approached Basseterre. As we wound our way along the coast through endless fields of abandoned sugar cane I asked if we might stop to cut a piece for the boys to chew on. Swerving to an immediate halt, he was out of the car before we could even open our doors, scoping along the edge of the cane, machete in hand, looking for a good specimen.

'That looks like a good blade Quincy,' I said as casually as if I was admiring his shoes and he flashed me a puckish grin.

'We all come from the people that used to wield these blades in earnest,' he said. 'We are well trained.' He deftly cut a piece of cane, whipping off the tough outer layer and cutting back until the off-white, fragrant inner column lay exposed. 'Here now boys – chew and then spit it out. Don't go swallowing it, OK?'

A few miles further on we passed through a village where children were clambering up trees, picking and eating small yellow-green fruit that I recognised. 'Guavas!' I said, and remembered foraging them myself in South Africa as a child. The boys clamoured to be let out of the car and Quincy pulled over, waiting patiently as they rushed over to climb up the trees to gather some. I showed them how to spot the best ones and felt the hair rise on the back of my neck as I was transported back in time at the sight of little fingers reaching for the fragrant fruit.

Later we walked around the impressive battlements of Brimstone Fort. Built almost eight hundred feet above sea level, the place was daunting and dramatic, but like most forts really only summed up the endless amount of effort that the human race is prepared to devote to control, violence and brutal competition. As the boys explored the cannons, Juliet and her mother admired the breathtaking views over the sea and J studied the stonework and design, but all I could think about was the effects of grapeshot on an advancing body of men, what it must have been like being imprisoned there and the brutalised slaves who were forced to lug the stones up the impossibly steep hill for the ninety-odd years it took to build the fort. Inside we looked at an exhibition of the history of slavery and prints showing the inner design of slave vessels which brought the stolen Africans to the Caribbean. They were forced to lie rank upon rank, chained up in hideous confinement for the entire duration of the voyage so as to pack in the maximum number of people. Those that got too sick or caused difficulties were simply tossed overboard and I thought of the heat and seasickness they must have suffered and the terror of not having the language to be able to communicate with their oppressors to even find out where or to what fate they were being delivered. It must have been an alien abduction in every sense.

As we continued our drive around the island, Quincy pointed out more sights of interest, most of which marked yet more ignominious moments in our European ancestors' history. We passed Bloody River, so-called because it supposedly ran with blood for weeks after the bodies of over two thousand native Caribs were dumped there after being slaughtered by the Europeans in 1626. Then he pointed out his grandmother's house, a tin shack on a sparse hillside where she lived all her life, where her own mother, who had been born into slavery, had lived out her life before her. 'It is a hard thing to live with, don't you think?' I asked him, for the first time having sufficient confidence to ask a question that I'd wanted to ask someone for a while. 'The thought that all of your ancestors were slaves?'

He pursed his lips and thought about it. 'Not really. It is my heritage, my history. And what's worse?' he turned to me and smiled teasingly. 'To have the ancestors who were slaves, or slave masters?' Unknowingly, he had put his finger on exactly what I was experiencing. Shame. The weight of hundreds of years of shame.

The next morning I took our passports over to Customs to sign out of the country, leaving J to fit the new part for the gear-shift mechanism that had arrived by express mail from St Martin. Like a teenager tip-toeing past their parents' room late at night I tried to get by unnoticed as I walked past Myken and Henrik's boat, but just as I thought I was home and dry, his voice rang out behind me.

'Guy!'

I stopped in my tracks, childishly trying to hide the passports behind my leg before I turned round to greet him. 'Oh, hi Henrik,' I said lamely.

'Good morning!' I saw his eyes dart immediately to the passports. 'Are you leaving?' I nodded guiltily and he stepped quickly up onto the quay, fixing me with a searching look. 'You're not going to let us down now Guy, are you?' he said as he shook my hand. 'Remember, you are a man of honour!'

'Yes,' I replied uncertainly, feeling that I was being mocked once again and cursing myself for making such a pompous statement. 'Juliet has written to the insurance company, so . . .'

He smiled and clapped me on the back. 'Good! Then we will be in touch, yes? Just email me proof of this letter and we are in business.'

As we sailed away from the island I looked up at its high peak. 'Mount Misery,' I muttered aloud and shook my head like a horse trying to keep a biting insect at bay.

'What's that you said Dad?' Oscar was looking at me curiously.

I smiled reassuringly. 'Nothing Oscar – nothing you need to worry about.' And as if on cue, a gust of wind filled the sails and *Forever* surged ahead.

We were all relieved to leave St Kitts behind, having found it a battering experience on all levels. I was bad tempered and moody, a mystery to myself. I noticed that Juliet had begun to treat me with kid gloves, phrasing her words carefully and shepherding the children away whenever she sensed I needed to be alone. I had always thought of myself as a positive and easygoing person, yet here I was in the classic role of failed man, making everyone wary, creating a tense and unsettling atmosphere.

We were heading towards the island of Montserrat some fifty miles south east of St Kitts. This small island of just thirty-nine square miles was said to be one of the most beautiful before the eruption of Soufrière Hills volcano in 1995 and used to be known as the 'Emerald

Isle' of the Caribbean because of its Irish roots and dense covering of lush green rainforest. In 1633, the island became an English colony when its governor, Anthony Brisket, opened it as a place for Irish Catholics who had come to the West Indies, particularly St Kitts and Nevis, as indentured servants. The Irish soon outnumbered the English and over the next two centuries merged with the African population, who were imported as slaves in large numbers to work the sugar plantations. The result is that Montserratians still consider themselves at least partially Irish today, with Irish names and even a faintly Irish accent still much in evidence.

This intriguing history, as well as the promise of a sight of the volcano, made us all keen to visit the island, so we sailed on past the green slopes of Nevis and the dramatic rock of Redonda that lie roughly halfway between. We soon glimpsed the angry sight of the Soufrière volcano in the distance. Although not considered an immediate danger, it was still belching out smoke and ash on a regular basis and its vapour cloud carried westwards by the trades could be seen from far away.

'Hey everyone, I think that's the smoke from the volcano!' I shouted, gazing ahead at a long vaporous formation that lay along the horizon, looking like a dense bank of fog.

'Is it really?' Juliet said, 'God, how creepy.' Indeed there was some-thing ominous about it, as if we were approaching the gates of Mordor, deep in Middle Earth. 'I think I can smell it', she wrinkled her nose. And sure enough soon we all caught the whiff of rotten eggs.

'That's sulphur,' J said, as the boys fell about holding their noses. 'Better get used to it boys – it'll get stronger the closer we get.'

'Can I see the pilot book?' Juliet asked and I felt a spark of love light and hold for a moment as she leant over the book, her fair hair falling over her face. She squinted at the steering compass and then looked back towards the smoking island. 'Where are we going to anchor?' she asked. 'We can't go into Plymouth – it says here you're not supposed to go within two miles of it.'

'We couldn't anchor there anyway by the looks of things,' J said. 'There's been a lot of shoaling since the volcano erupted and the harbour has more or less filled in. The only other anchorage is Little Bay near the north end of the island – doesn't look brilliant but I think it's the only option at this stage of the day.' He glanced at his watch and I felt a pang of guilt; I knew we should have left earlier, as night fell very suddenly in this part of the world and it would be dangerous and irresponsible to approach these islands in the dark. This was one of J's mantras and he was undoubtedly right, but somehow the more I knew what was expected of me these days the less able I seemed to do it.

Little Bay looked little more than an indentation in the coastline, and we wouldn't get much shelter there. As with all these islands, their leeward or western edges are protected from the huge Atlantic waves that hit their windward (or eastern) shores with great force. On the smaller ones like Montserrat, however, in strong winds the swell surges around the ends of the islands and some way down the leeward coast. It was just one more misfortune of this island that it had lost its protected anchorage at Plymouth, which was located further down the coast well away from the swell.

The closer we came to the bay the more ominous it looked. There were no other yachts anchored, just a couple of fishing boats and a large rusty barge which lay on its side, wrecked on a long reef that stretched out from the beach. The bay was high sided and claustrophobic, with little space to anchor among the reef and the cliffs and the shipping channel, where a ferry would be coming in at unspecified times. The noise of the waves was overwhelming as they boomed continually against the cliffs; a continual reminder of our fate should our anchor drag, like the stricken barge very close to us on the reef.

From time to time the shattered structure let out a tortured cry as its steel decks and hull shifted with the endless torment of the sea which surged greedily around it. Onshore, a scattering of houses ran down the hillside in a hasty approximation of a new capital, with a cluster of official-looking buildings at the head of the pier. A few straggly buildings could be seen over the shoulders of the heavy dumping surf along the desolate beach. Altogether, at first sight it was far from reassuring and having motored round for a bit we finally plumped to anchor on the north side of the bay as close as we dared to the cliffs.

We let out 200 feet of chain, hoping that the extra weight would help us stay in one place, and prepared ourselves for an uncomfortable night. The motion of the boat was almost unbearable as *Forever* rolled virtually from gunwale to gunwale, crockery clattering in the galley and books and toys sliding backwards and forwards across the table. Juliet managed to cook up some supper, wedging herself in the galley determinedly as the boat rolled interminably. She set plates of food on the table with the usual accompaniments of salt, pepper, glasses, drinks and salad, but everything slid around so much that we each had to take control of something and hold it in one hand while we ate with the other. Luckily the plates had rubber-rimmed bottoms so they stayed in one place, but the food (corned-beef hash) didn't and slopped over the sides whenever there was a particularly big roll. The simple act of eating had become an Olympian task and we clung to the table-edge to keep ourselves still, shovelling food into our mouths as fast as possible between lurches. Oscar reached forward to spear a carrot on his plate, but just as he steadied himself to strike the carrot leapt from his plate and rolled over to the other side of the table. We all laughed as we were struck by the ridiculousness of attempting to enjoy a family meal in these crazy conditions.

'I'm beat,' Juliet groaned, holding up her hands in defeat. 'Now for the washing up . . .'

As I stood up to help her I realised that Oscar had gone out in the cockpit and a lurch of fear ran through me. The danger of falling overboard on such a night was very real. 'Oscar!' I yelled, pulling myself up the companionway.

'Here Dad,' his voice floated down faintly over the booming of the surf.

'No going out on deck alone tonight – it's too dangerous.'

'But Dad,' he shouted, 'there's a beautiful big boat out there – it looks like a pirate ship!'

Luke prised himself away from the table and staggered towards the steps. 'I want to see!' he shouted and I followed behind, taking a strong grip on the back of his shorts. Sure enough a large schooner had anchored nearby and was lit up in the darkness, rolling as badly as we were. Now that it was dark the bay looked even more ominous. The dark cliffs loomed above the wreck, which was still dimly visible, eerily lit up by white surf that foamed across it from time to time. The noise was phenomenal from both the waves and the wind, as it buffeted through the halyards, accompanied by the moans from the wreck. The old-fashioned ship only added to the menace of the scene.

'Dad, can we go across to the boat?' Oscar asked and I looked across at Juliet.

'No way boys!' she said. 'It's far too dangerous in the dark.'

They immediately fell into paroxysms of wailing and stamping like members of a self-flagellating religious cult.

'Boys! Your mother is right – it's simply not safe,' J said sternly.

Once again my stubborn resistance came to the fore and I felt tempted to give in to them. The boys had dealt with all of the travelling so well and with so little complaint and now here they were on an exciting night, staring at a glittering and mysterious ship that was calling out to their adventurous instincts. I thought of my own childhood and the fact that it was the risky journeys that still hung in my mind like priceless works of art. I remembered the Zimbabwean fisherman who had pulled me on to the bow of a boat rowed by powerful tribesmen as they pulled a net across a wild lake. I could have fallen off into the crocodile-infested water or cut myself with the knife that he let me wear on my belt, but I didn't – neither was I suffocated by the immense python that they pulled from a hole by its tail. It was the danger that made these experiences so special and I wondered if, without any jeopardy, children would take any memories worth having into their adult lives.

'OK boys . . .' I looked at them sternly and they both immediately halted their protests and stood up straight. 'I'll take you across, but you need to do exactly as I say.'

'I'm not sure it's safe Guy . . .' Juliet was worried, but I could see that she was also torn between weighing up the danger against the joy of such a trip for the kids.

'Don't worry,' I said. 'It's not far. We'll put the lights on their lifejackets and they can both sit right on the bottom of the dinghy. That's one good thing about having a powerful outboard – we can go out on a night like this.'

The boys jumped up and down with glee and I knelt down and held their arms, looking into both their faces very seriously. 'Now you MUST do exactly as I tell you, or else we won't do this ever again, do you understand?' They both nodded gravely. 'Now go down and fetch your lifejackets and put the lights on them while we launch the dinghy.'

'I don't know why you're doing this,' Juliet muttered grimly as she struggled to undo the outboard engine from where it was mounted on *Forever*'s stern. It was enough of a challenge lowering the heavy beast onto the dinghy at the best of times, never mind in these dark, rolling conditions.

'I think it'll be worth it, Jules, don't worry,' I shouted up from the dinghy, where I was bouncing up and down on the waves, battering occasionally against *Forever*'s side. She lowered the engine down to me on its makeshift hoist and I finally managed to fit it on to the bucking transom. I started it up and stood waiting for the boys, holding onto *Forever*'s sides which rose and fell a few feet with each wave. Oscar stepped over the rail and held onto the shrouds, waiting for me. 'Put your arms around my neck and join your fingers,' I said and then lowered him into the dinghy like a paternal crane. 'Now sit there and wait for Luke,' I ordered. 'When he comes you must hold onto him – do not sit up on the side of the dinghy, OK?'

'Yes Dad,' he answered, his voice sounding very small and brave in the tumult.

Next came Luke, who clung to me with his legs as well as his arms like a little blond monkey. Oscar reached up and pulled his brother down to nestle between his legs and I saw the look of contentment that always came across Luke's face whenever his older brother looked after him. I pushed off, relieved to be away from the tumult around *Forever*'s sides and motored steadily towards the schooner. The waves flung us sharply up and down as if to make us pay for our audacity in venturing out, and spray flew across the boat. I looked back and saw Juliet standing in *Forever*'s cockpit watching and I knew that she had given me a huge vote of trust by letting me take our only true wealth out across the dark water. I felt a lurch of responsibility as I looked down at the two boys, locked in a brotherly embrace at my feet. I was beginning to regret the whole venture and speeded up, eager to get it over with. We came alongside the high-sided ship and I knelt and held onto the side while I knocked sharply a few times on the hull. '*Sea Star*!' I called, but my words floated away on the wind. I waited for a moment and then knocked again, louder. Still no response. My heart sank: had we gone through all this only to be unheard? Just as I was considering turning back a bearded man came out and peered over the side of the ship.

'Are you in trouble?' he asked.

'No!' I shouted. 'We just wanted to come and see you.'

He looked surprised, as well he might: social callers weren't what one expected on such a night. 'Wait a moment,' he said and disappeared, before coming back with an older man that I took to be the skipper. 'Come along to the cargo net,' he shouted. 'We'll drop down the bosun's chair to be on the safe side!'

'Good idea!' I shouted back and manoeuvred my way along the side of the boat to the cargo net. They dropped the bosun's chair down for Luke and I fitted him into it and then gave them the thumbs up.

'Dad, I'm scared!' Luke whispered.

'Don't worry Luke, they've got you safe on this line if you slip. Just climb up the net – go on, you can do it!' I hoisted his little bottom halfway up and then sat back and watched with pride mixed with fear as my 4-year-old son scrambled up the net like a monkey. The two men lifted him over the gunwale, untangled him from the chair and then lowered it back down for Oscar. I scrambled up behind them and the skipper and crewman stood smiling at us: it felt oddly wonderful that they had put so much effort and time into bringing the boys up safely and I thanked them profusely.

'Sorry to arrive unannounced, but the boys were desperate to see the boat, if you don't mind . . .'

'Not at all.' The skipper bent down to the boys' level. 'Welcome aboard boys, you must be quite some sailors if you can make it across on a night like this.' He shook their hands solemnly and I saw that his arms were knotted with veins and covered with faded tattoos. He looked weathered and wise and straight out of one of the boys' story books, as indeed did the whole ship. 'My name is George,' he said in an east coast American accent, 'I'm the skipper and John here's my first mate. He'll happily show you about – go wherever you please. Any questions before you begin?'

'Have you ever met Captain Haddock?' Luke asked solemnly.

'No, I can't say I've ever had the privilege,' he replied seriously. 'As I recall he doesn't sail much in these waters.'

'He doesn't sail much anywhere,' Oscar said. 'He's always drunk!'

'Yes, well, that can be a problem with sailors,' the skipper laughed and waved us on our way. There followed an indulgent session as the boys crawled into every nook and cranny, trying out the bunks and hammocks and asking endless questions. We met more crew down below, seated around the table in the saloon playing cards, and they seemed happy to be diverted, insisting that we accept drinks and snacks with the unconditional hospitality that I was coming to learn was the custom of the sea. After a while I stood to go, conscious that Juliet might be worrying. John accompanied us out on deck and the skipper returned to our side as we stood waiting to climb back into the dinghy. 'Is that your boat?' he asked, pointing at *Forever* and I nodded. 'She's a good-looking boat. Make sure you keep anchor watch on a night like this – it pays to be careful.' He knelt down to look at the boys who stood shyly before him, taking each of their small hands in turn into his great paw. 'You're two great boys. Don't forget to be careful and always remember the sea is the boss – that way you'll grow into first class seamen. Isn't that so John?' he asked the first mate.

Once we were all in the dinghy I waved at the two men and then turned towards *Forever*.

'Dad, can I steer?' Oscar asked.

'Um . . .' I thought for a moment if this might be pushing our luck just a little too far. Most accidents in sailing occur not on the mother ship but in the tenders and children driving dinghies are a particular hazard. But I decided to trust him. 'OK Oscar, but be careful – it's lumpy and you'll have to judge the swell. Don't go too fast now – but don't go too slow either, we need to keep moving.'

He took the helm and steered confidently towards *Forever*, swinging deftly round at the last minute to bring the dinghy gently along her stern. As Juliet helped the boys aboard, looking deeply relieved to have them back safely, I turned and saw the men still watching us, making sure no doubt that we got back safely. I raised my arm and they raised theirs in return before turning to go below.

It was a rough night lit only with the light that comes from people at sea. I spent it fitfully getting up at intervals to check the anchor. The next morning we gathered for breakfast, and Juliet braved the galley again to cook up eggs and toast.

'I can't eat,' she groaned as she sat down, a sheen of sweat across her forehead. 'This rolling is just hideous. When can we go ashore?'

'Strictly speaking you should have signed in last night with customs,' J said, 'but I think we'll be forgiven as long as you go straight away. Then I'd like to see something of the island.'

'I saw the number of a taxi driver recommended in the pilot book,' Juliet said, struggling across to fetch the book from the chart table. 'There it is – Otis Sibley.' She showed me a picture of a big-bellied man standing beside a taxi parked at a viewpoint. 'I'll try calling him on the VHF.'

Juliet called the driver on the radio and he replied immediately, his voice ringing out into *Forever*'s saloon. She explained that we had to sign in at customs and he agreed to meet us there afterwards. As we piled into the dinghy, relieved to escape the turgid interior of the boat, I saw that *Sea Star* had gone, as if our night-time visit had been a figment of our imagination. J dropped us at the dock, returning to collect Audrey who was tackling the washing up, and we scrambled up with some difficulty before making our way to customs on shaky legs. The family waited outside as I suffered the usual stress associated with signing into these islands – the fact that we hadn't signed in immediately had to be dealt with, as did the fact that we had no official ship's papers for *Forever*, as she was still going through the process of being accepted onto the UK Ship's Register. Paperwork not being my strong point, I flannelled my way through the questions as usual, pulling random receipts and documents from my file until the official was as confused as I was. Finally he admitted defeat and stamped our passports with the green shamrock of Montserrat. 'Enjoy our island,' he smiled as I left, and I imagined I could detect a slight Irish lilt within the layers of his rich West-Indian accent.

As we walked along the dusty road towards the shack-like beachside developments we saw a large man dressed in a loose, brightly coloured shirt and sandals pacing backwards and forwards along the road. One hand was gesticulating as he talked urgently into a mobile phone and his head snapped up as he saw us.

'Do you think that's him?' Juliet said, but before we could ask he stepped forward and introduced himself.

'Good morning, welcome to Montserrat. I am Otis.'

'Oh hello,' Juliet smiled. 'We talked on the radio. I'm Juliet and this is my husband Guy, and our two boys Oscar and Luke.' The boys smiled shyly and said hello, and Juliet asked if Otis would be able to take us for a drive around the island. 'The boys are keen to see the volcano,' she said, smiling and ruffling Luke's hair.

'Yes, can you take us to see the volcano?' Luke asked excitedly. 'But can you not take us too close, just in case . . .' his words dried up as Otis gave him a severe look.

'Little boy, I have been taking people to see that volcano for many years now – you leave the job to me.'

I could see Juliet was taken aback by the severity of his tone. 'Yes Luke,' I said, giving Luke a wink, 'I'm sure Otis is a very experienced driver so we can trust him to keep us safe.'

'Yes, well . . . my parents want to come too,' Juliet said. 'They should be here in ten minutes or so, they're just coming across in the dinghy. Can you wait for them?'

Otis sucked his teeth and glanced at his watch. 'Well, OK,' he said, 'long as they not too long now – we wait ten minutes.' He began pacing around, glancing at his watch and then out to *Forever* and muttering to himself occasionally.

The way he'd said it made it seem as if we had no choice but to leave in ten minutes, even if it meant leaving J and Audrey behind. Juliet shaded her eyes and looked out to the boat and I could see she was getting anxious. 'If only we could call them,' she said to me, 'they don't know we're in such a hurry.'

What is this? Rush hour in New York? I felt like saying, but I was conscious of Otis's looming presence. 'Otis,' I said, 'if you're in a hurry just now why don't we do this later? We're here for the whole day, so we don't mind waiting.'

'No, no,' he said irritably, looking at his watch again. 'As long as we get going soon we'll be OK.'

At last we saw the figures of Audrey and J appear on deck and knew they were going through the familiar rituals that preceded a shore trip: Audrey went back down below several times as she remembered things she'd forgotten, J went up on the bow to check the anchor and then they both searched for the padlock so they could lock up. All the while Otis huffed and puffed by our side and Juliet muttered 'Hurry up!' irritably several times. At last they climbed into the dinghy and with agonising slowness puttered towards the shore. After what seemed like an eternity they appeared at the end of the dock, smiling with relief to be on dry land after negotiating the surf.

'Mum! Otis is going to give us a tour around the island. Quick!' Juliet shouted.

'Oh, sorry – did we take a long time?' Audrey said innocently.

'Otis, these are my parents, Audrey and James,' Juliet said.

'Yes, yes. Get in.' He slid open the doors of the taxi which was parked at the side of the road and like the brow-beaten citizens of a police state giving in to a brawny member of the security forces the family climbed obediently in.

'Hey! Careful where you put your feet boy!' he said as Luke unwittingly stood on a pile of stuff in the footwell in front of his seat.

'Sorry!' Luke said, looking at us for reassurance and Juliet smiled and ruffled his hair. Otis shook his head as he settled behind the fur-covered wheel, the driver's seat squealing with protest under his great weight. Reluctantly I climbed into the passenger seat beside him and we shot off in a spray of gravel.

We climbed up the steep road out of Little Bay and then drove into an unexpectedly lush interior, enjoying the coastal road that swerved and dipped along tree-lined valleys and hills.

'Your island is beautiful,' I said, and he nodded.

'Yes it is – and I'm not going to be leaving, whatever happens.' He sounded defensive, but we all knew about the rigours that the island had suffered: between Hurricane Hugo which left the island devastated in 1989 and then the eruption of the volcano that began in 1995, the past twenty years had been very hard. 'I used to have a house in Plymouth,' he continued, 'and now I can't go there anymore – the whole southern end of the island is closed off. We lost everything.'

'That's awful,' Juliet said.

'A lot of people moved to Britain after the volcano erupted, didn't they?' I asked, little realising what a can of worms I was opening. 'Did you ever consider that?'

He glanced round at me angrily, almost swerving off the road in his outrage. 'I am not a quitter like those people – and they are not happy living in your country, I can tell you: cold, damp, mean people.' He let out a bitter guffaw. 'They've run from their problems, givin' up on their island. Now Otis,' he patted his chest, 'Otis and his family ain't givin' up – never!' He leant forward and pressed harder on the accelerator.

We sat in silence, admiring the power of his convictions if a little taken aback by his swipe at our country. But then I remembered about Clare Short, Secretary of State at the time when the volcano erupted, whose response on being asked for further help by the Montserratians was; 'They'll be asking for golden elephants next.' Otis was probably justified in being angry and perhaps it takes fanatically determined people like him to bring us through a crisis.

We chugged our way up a steep little road, the taxi's engine screaming with protest at an incline it was not designed for, and then Otis pulled up in a cloud of dust. He climbed out and made his way over to the side of the road. 'Do you recognise this tree?' he asked, and we all shook our heads. He gathered a couple of brownish husks from the tree, dropped them on the road and then hit them sharply with a stone before bringing the exposed nut to us on the palm of his hand. 'Almonds,' he said. 'You want some?' The boys jumped up and down as he gathered a handful. He bypassed Luke's hand, which was sticking out the window, and passed them across to Juliet. 'Patience!' he said sternly. 'You leave them for your Mama to share out,' and Luke's face fell as Juliet obediently passed the nuts around.

With a spin of the wheels we were off, and as we drove past beautifully maintained smallholdings and neatly kept gardens it was easy to forget what had happened a few years ago. But then we rounded a corner and first saw the real island bully for the first time. The Soufrière Hills volcano was a stunningly frightening sight and banished all the bucolic images that we had formed as we weaved our way through the fertile island. Standing grey, burnt out and forbidding at over 3,000 feet, it was pumping sulphurous steam into the blue sky.

'Can you stop the car?' I asked, and Otis pulled over. We got out and stared in silence.

'Look there!' he pointed and we saw boulders that must have been as big as London buses rolling down from the rim of the volcano like crumbs from a giant's mouth.

'My God!' I muttered and Otis spun around.

'No need to use the Lord's name in vain!' he said disapprovingly.

I backed down and raised my hands in apology. 'Sorry Otis – but it's such a sight.'

'I can take you for a closer look,' he said.

'But I thought the southern end of the island was closed off?'

'It is, but I can take you up a track where nobody else will take you, where you'll get the best possible view to take photographs.'

We climbed back in and continued driving until the neat tarmac road ended at what looked like a flat muddy field, but what was in fact a former valley that had been entirely filled in by a river of greyish brown mud. The tops of shattered trees stuck up through it and the roofs of houses that had been buried right up to their upper floors. Otis struck out confidently across it. 'We not really supposed to drive here, but you OK with me,' he said, and then stopped at the other side so we could look. We walked around the eerie landscape, given the perspective of giants as we peered through the upper windows of the houses. One house was still furnished and we entered at what would have been the second floor balcony, walking through rooms that were now covered in mud. We stood at the top of the stairs, looking down to where the mud ended at the top step, imagining the house as it was flooded. A phone dangled from its cord, giving an impression of last moments in a disaster. Dust-covered paperbacks still stood on a bookshelf and a calendar was pinned open on the day of the eruption, for ever frozen on that date. It was horribly moving, and we emerged into the sunlight to stand awhile in silence.

'I don't suppose they had insurance,' Juliet muttered.

'I doubt it,' said her father. 'And if they did, they were the exception.'

Beside the house, growing outside what would have been a top floor window, we spotted a fresh young plant quivering in the breeze.

'Hey Dad, look – a plant,' Oscar pointed.

'Mother Nature always keeps going, even if we don't,' I said, ruffling his mop of sun-bleached hair.

'OK, here we go,' Otis said a bit later, as we turned off the road onto a very rough track. 'You get a very good view of volcano from up here – nobody else go up here but me.' We began to judder and bump our way up the impossibly steep track, the taxi's undercarriage grinding dangerously on the surface from time to time.

'I have driven on some very rough roads before,' J said politely, 'But usually in four-wheel-drive vehicles. This is two-wheel drive, yes?'

'Of course it is!' Otis replied brusquely, pushing his foot down hard on the accelerator as the vehicle stuck momentarily. 'I drive this car all over the island – you watch me now!'

We sat in silence, holding the children down as we bumped our way on, the taxi pushing through scrubby undergrowth and leaning from side to side as we followed the gradient of the track. Then the greenery cleared and we saw a sheer drop falling away to the south.

'Mum! I'm scared!' Luke whispered, but Otis missed nothing and before Juliet could come up with any soothing words he rounded on him:

'Be quiet boy!' he shouted, his face dark with anger. 'What you saying – that I can't drive? You're safe with Otis Sibley I tell you!' Luke's eyes filled with tears and he leant his head on his mother's lap. I looked at Juliet with an expression that read, 'Do I get into a fist-fight?' but she shook her head slowly, signalling calm. We were all feeling uncomfortable now, but we were at the mercy of this bully, who I felt might easily drive off and leave us here if we questioned him. And to do him credit, he was giving us an extraordinary tour – in fact I was beginning to wonder whether his taxi would survive it.

After a bone-shattering half hour we parked at the top of the hill, immediately below the western shoulder of the volcano. Otis was right – we had a superb view, from the volcano itself looming up beside us to a desolate vista of Plymouth, stretching out below like a vision of a post-apocalyptic world. This vibrant town, famed for its markets, yacht club and shops, was now rendered a uniform pumice grey, with everything completely covered in layer upon layer of volcanic lava, ash and rock. The shapes of the buildings and streets were still visible, running neatly down towards the harbour, but a giant, comic-book crack ran jaggedly through the eastern end of the town. We could see the filled-in harbour and the residue of the mud which had slipped down the hillside and continued to do so, altering the profile of the coastline for ever. Turning north, on the other side of the hill we could see beautiful properties running down to the water, seemingly untouched, but still within the dreadful grasp of the volcano. I stood looking at an immaculate plantation style house surrounded by what must have been an exquisite garden, thinking about the sadness of having to abandon one's property and worse still, the more general impact of the death of the tourist industry on the wider population.

'I used to live over there,' Otis said, pointing towards a cluster of abandoned buildings at the foot of the mountain. 'Lost everything I'd worked for all my life. Course we took what we could, although we wasn't supposed to – I wasn't just goin' to give up on everything, some of these things been in my family for generations.'

We looked on in mute, stunned silence, trying to imagine what it must have been like for Otis, who was clearly a hard-working, resilient man. We murmured a few words of sympathy, but he waved our words away impatiently and turned and walked over to a leafy tree which had bulbous jagged green fruit growing on it. 'Now this is soursop,' he said. 'Finest fruit in the West Indies.'

The children gathered round in anticipation of a fruity treat as he cut into the ugly looking fruit with a penknife, revealing its white pulpy flesh, with the consistency of soggy cotton wool, wrapped around shiny dark brown seeds. We didn't tell him we'd already tried it for fear of offending him, but instead politely waited as he handed it round. He had passed a piece to me and was cutting one for Juliet when Oscar burst out, 'Can I have a piece?' clearly unable to resist asking as he saw me enjoying the refreshing, sherbety flesh.

Otis rounded on him inexplicably. 'You remember your manners boy and wait your turn – your Mama not had her piece yet!' Now Oscar looked crestfallen and Juliet took his hand and walked him away, while Luke folded his arms and glared at Otis. 'Nobody talks to my brother like that!' he hissed to me, and again I had to stop myself from reacting, thinking that Otis was touchy and might simply desert us, here at the top of mountain with darkness not far away.

'Don't worry about the boys Otis,' I said mildly, but I'd had enough of the company of this overbearing and irascible man.

He got worse on the way home: 'Am I so boring you go to sleep?' he demanded when I closed my eyes for a second as he ranted on at length about the shortcomings of our country.

'Not at all,' I said hastily, sitting to attention. 'I'm just tired – we had a bit of a rough night.'

'Humph,' he responded, clearly not convinced. A few minutes later he pulled into the private driveway of a beautiful house that lay in a deserted neighbourhood. 'I want you to meet some friends of mine,' he said, stepping out of the car. 'Bill! Bill, you here?' he shouted, tooting the horn a couple of times for good measure.

There was no response, and I leant out of the car window. 'Look Otis it's OK, really – I think we should get back . . .'

'No, no, I'm sure he here,' he said irritably and resumed shouting. After a few minutes an elderly white man appeared around the corner of the house.

'Oh, hello Otis,' he said without much enthusiasm.

'These my new friends, come in from a boat,' he said, 'I am giving them an island tour and brought them in to meet you.' The man smiled politely, but I had the sense that he was wondering what we were doing there. 'Any chance of a drink?' Otis said. 'These people are real hot.'

'No honestly, we don't need anything, in fact we'd better be getting back . . .' I said lamely, but Otis waved my protests aside.

'He don't mind, do you?' He thumped Bill rather too vigorously on the back. 'He likes to have visitors, don't you Bill?'

'Well yes,' Bill said uncertainly, following him into the kitchen.

'Now what you havin'?' Otis asked me, making his way over to the fridge. 'Beer? And coke for the kids?'

He passed out cans and we accepted them reluctantly and with some embarrassment, as it was clear that these people didn't welcome the intrusion. As we made rather awkward conversation his elderly wife appeared and stood by the doorway, looking resigned. I could see from her expression that this wasn't the first time that Otis had arrived unannounced with his 'friends', and as he talked loudly about the parties that they had enjoyed in this house I saw that these people had no chance against the powerful natural force that was Otis. Juliet and I stepped out on the balcony with Bill's wife, admiring her garden and swimming pool, standing like an oasis surrounded by acres of mud. Once it must have been a beautiful property, looking out over an opulent golf course running down to a palm fringed beach, but all that remained was devastation. They seemed determined not to leave the island and I admired them for that, but living there in an unsaleable property must have been grim; their daily lives hung on the whim of a volcano and Otis.

When our drinks were finished Otis lost no time in hurrying us on and stood impatiently as we said our goodbyes. He drove us back to Little Bay, making a diversion on the way to show us the new house that he and his son were building. We sat in the taxi looking at the empty concrete shell wondering if it would ever reach completion. Even if it did, would disaster strike again on this island? I hoped not, for the sake of this beautiful island and its people, especially Otis whom, for all his gruff fierceness, it was impossible not to admire.

ELEVEN

IF THE GARDEN
OF EDEN WERE
AN ISLAND

15.18N: 61.23W

Dominica marked an important point in our journey, as it was the last of the Leeward Islands, or the first of the Windwards, depending on whom you talked to. Things would become more challenging from now on: the Windward Islands were generally considered to be wilder than the Leewards and there had been several reported incidents of robbery and violence against yachtsmen in recent years. There had even been a couple of murders and though such events were rare, we knew we would have to be on our guard. Psychologically this was also an important point in our journey, as it was from here that Audrey and J would fly home, leaving Juliet and me in sole charge of the boat for the first time.

The overwhelming impression of Dominica as you approach it is greenness, and as we surged towards it on a fresh, 30-knot breeze the island looked from a distance as though it might sink beneath the weight of its tangle of lush vegetation. Several times during the passage we had spotted pods of sperm whales, often lying motionless near the surface (a sign they were calving) and had always kept a careful distance from them. About ten miles off the north coast of Dominica, Juliet was on the helm when she shouted. 'Whale! It just sounded and surfaced right beside me. I could have touched it!' By the time we got up on deck to see where she was pointing, we could only just about see it – nothing compared with the drama of Juliet's sighting.

Juliet radioed Martin Carriere, a local guide and fixer who advertised in the pilot book as being able to help with customs, moorings and transport. He sounded relaxed and friendly, agreeing to come and see us once we were anchored. We were heading towards Prince Rupert Bay, a wide, protected bay sheltering the town of Portsmouth. About a mile from the entrance, I noticed a white speck ahead of us and lifted the binoculars for a closer look. A man was approaching in a tiny open boat, rowing furiously towards us.

'Hey Jules, there's a man coming towards us.'

She squinted out to sea. 'Probably a boat boy.' This was the somewhat patronising term for men from these islands who scratched a living by providing services of various degrees of usefulness to visiting yachts. 'Tell him we've got Martin Carriere helping us.'

I slowed down as the man drew near, not enjoying the prospect of having to brush off someone desperate enough to paddle far out to sea to ask for work.

'Hey Skip! I'm Sidney.' He came alongside *Forever* and stood up, holding the cap rail so that he didn't bump the side of the boat. He stretched out a hand and I bent to shake it. The boys were intrigued by our visitor and leant over the side.

'You must be very good at rowing,' Oscar said admiringly.

He laughed. 'Sure am little guy, it gives me real good muscles.' He pulled back the sleeve of his torn T-shirt for Oscar to see. 'You impressed? Show me yours.'

Oscar stretched out his arm and Sidney felt it solemnly. 'That's pretty good, bit more rowing and you'll be one big man.' He threw his head back and laughed, revealing a set of perfectly white teeth. He turned to me, 'Anything you need I can get it for you Skip: bread, fruit, laundry, get rid of your trash . . .'

'Well . . .' I glanced at Juliet. 'I'm really sorry Sidney but we've already been in touch with Martin Carriere – he's going to sort all that out for us.'

'No problem Skip.' He waved a hand. 'Martin one real good guy – he keep you right. Have a good time in Dominica.' He sat back down, threw out a fishing line and picked up his oars.

'Are you going to get back OK? I mean, I'd offer you a tow . . .'

'No, no Skip, I'm OK now – gonna stay out here and bob about a bit. See, some other boats comin'.' He pointed at a couple of other yachts approaching in the distance. 'Don't you worry about Sidney.'

'Wait a minute.' Juliet went down below and reappeared with a bottle of beer and passed it over to him. 'To keep you going till those boats come along.'

'Sure thing sweetheart,' he flashed his fabulous smile again. 'You have a great day now.'

He raised a hand as he rowed off and we all waved back. 'He was nice,' Juliet said.

'Seems to me you could have offered him something more than a bottle of beer,' her father said. 'I think you should really take the first person who comes out to you – that way you're rewarding them for the effort.'

'I know, but you might get stuck with someone you really don't like,' she said. 'If you've already made contact with someone then surely you've got a way of letting them down gently – otherwise it could get nasty.'

Her point was proved as we negotiated our way into the bay and another person approached us, this time paddling on an old surfboard. 'Hey Skip,' I heard the familiar refrain as he bumped clumsily into the side of the boat. I glanced down at where he hung on the cap rail beside the cockpit. 'Name's Vince. Anything you need I can get it for you.'

'Well thanks,' I said, 'but I'm just trying to get in just now, let me get sorted first.'

He stared at me with anger in his eyes. 'Oh come on Skip, things real hard right now.' He continued clinging to *Forever*'s sides. 'You just say Vince has got the job and I'll come back later?'

I began to wonder if I might have to fend off a potential boarding when Juliet appeared from down below. 'Thanks for coming over, but we're with Martin Carriere – he's coming to see us as soon as we're tied up.'

'Oh that Martin gets all the work around here,' he shook his head in frustration. 'Ain't nothin' left for no one else.' He dropped away on his surfboard looking dejected.

We were approaching a collection of yachts now, some anchored and others tied up to mooring balls that ran in a long line opposite the beach. As we motored round looking for a space a homemade wooden motor launch sped towards us.

'What now?' I groaned.

'No it's OK, it's *Providence*,' Juliet said. 'That's the name of Martin's boat.' She raised a hand in greeting. 'Hello!'

He swung neatly alongside, flipping out a little row of fenders to ensure he didn't scrape our sides. 'Hi, I'm Martin.' He held up a bunch of fresh-cut bananas, 'Welcome to Dominica!'

It was instantly obvious that we were in safe hands. 'Do you want a mooring, Skip?' he asked me as he passed over the bananas. 'You can have one of mine – over there.' He pointed to a mooring buoy ahead.

'Yes, thanks,' I said gratefully and he sped off ahead to the buoy, holding it up for Juliet to reach from the bow. When we'd tied up and turned the engine off he came back alongside the cockpit.

'Do you need anything?' he asked. 'Laundry?'

'Oh, God, yes,' Juliet said and disappeared below to collect several weeks' worth of washing. Doing laundry was one of the most unpleasant jobs at sea and almost impossible to do well, so we tended to save it up for shore visits. It helped that we were barely wearing anything, but still we stacked up an extraordinary amount of salty, gritty bed linen, towels and clothes.

Martin and I chatted while he waited for the laundry, and I learnt that he was married with children and doing well with his business, which he'd been running for several years. He told me how the Dominican government was taking a positive approach to what was termed 'the boat boy' problem and was training the men in how to deal with tourists rather than the old approach which was to swamp incoming boats. Yet, understandably, there was still a problem with crime. He reassured me that we would be fine on his mooring. 'We have someone keeping an eye on our boats,' he said. 'And any problems you have with anyone here – you just tell them you're with Providence.'

Juliet reappeared with three giant bin bags and handed them over to Martin apologising for the state of our grimy laundry. 'No problem,' he grinned, 'these ladies seen it all. Now you need to go to Customs, right?'

'Are they open?'

He glanced at his watch and shook his head. 'They closed now. Don't worry. I take you tomorrow morning first thing.'

He backed off carefully from *Forever* and then shot off towards the town and we watched him wave to other boat boys as he passed them. 'Wow, he was great,' Juliet said. 'Looks like we did the right thing calling him, huh?'

'Definitely,' I agreed, 'but I still feel bad about the other guys. How are they meant to earn a living when boats are contacting Martin before they even get in?'

'I know. It's really tough,' she shrugged. 'But he does employ people locally to do his tours, so I'm sure some of the money trickles down.'

We were salty and hot after our long sail, relieved to drop one by one into the cool, turquoise water. Later, as we tidied the boat and settled down with cups of tea, I heard a familiar voice.

'Hey Skip!' My heart sank. It was Vince, back for another try. 'Skip!' his fist thudded the side of the boat insistently. 'Skip, you in there?'

Reluctantly I climbed up the companionway. 'Vince, how's it going?'

'Good man, it goin' real good.' He grabbed the rail. 'You say you have some work for me?'

'I did?' I thought back.

'Yeah, yeah – that Martin takes all the work around here. You got a beer?'

'No, sorry, we're all out.'

He pushed off, grumbling to himself and I felt bad: black guy on piece of flotsam asks white guy on big boat for any kind of work and is refused. Juliet came on deck with an armful of wet towels and began pegging them out on the guardrails. Vince was still floating aimlessly nearby and spotted an opportunity. 'Hey Sweetheart,' he called.

She smiled down at him. 'Hi, you all right?'

'Yeah man, good. You gonna eat out?'

'Yes, probably. Do you know somewhere?'

He paddled over and grabbed the rail again and my heart sank. 'Yeah, I got a thing goin' with that place over there.' He pointed at corrugated iron shack on the beach. 'Real good food and everything. When you gonna come?'

At that moment Oscar and Luke appeared. 'Hey boys!' Vince shouted. 'You like fruit?'

'Yes!' they shouted in unison.

'What your favourite?' He twisted his face in an approximation of a smile.

'Pineapple,' Luke said without hesitation.

'Pawpaw,' Oscar said. 'And mangoes and guava.'

'Well then, Vince is gonna get you real nice fruits, you wait.' Before we could say anything, he set off speedily.

An hour later he re-appeared looking irritable. 'Here are your fruits,' he said and emptied a bag onto the deck. There were a handful of rock hard mangoes and guavas, clearly raided from someone's tree and far from ripe, along with a heavily bruised pawpaw and the smallest pineapple I'd ever seen. 'Been all around the island for this stuff, it a real hassle. That's Forty dollars EC.'

The Eastern Caribbean dollar was around four to the pound – a lot of money for such inedible fruit.

'Come on Vince,' I said, 'half of this fruit isn't edible. I'll give you twenty.'

'Thirty.'

'All right,' I sighed. 'But we don't need anything else, OK?'

Later that evening we motored in darkness over to the long beach, to the bars, restaurants and holiday apartments strung out along the shore. We pulled the dinghy up on the sand and tied the painter to a tree. A couple of hundred metres along the beach was the restaurant that Vince had recommended. 'Not sure I want to go there,' Juliet said. 'It looks dodgy.'

Right beside us was a much smaller, quieter place with tables on a verandah that lay open to the beach. Fairy lights were strung along the verandah and a board stood outside with the day's specials listed on it. 'They've got fresh snapper and mahi mahi,' J said. 'I think this place looks much better.'

As Juliet and I lingered undecided, Vince appeared out of the darkness. He looked even more spaced out than he had earlier and I realised how tall he was as he loomed over us, clutching a bottle of beer in one hand. 'What you guys doin'?' he said. 'You can't go there – you said you were gonna eat at my place!'

'I know, look, we'll come to your place tomorrow,' I said hastily feeling like a character involved in prison-yard politics.

He took a step towards us. 'No way man, I told them you're coming and they are expecting you!'

J stepped in. 'Look I think we should eat at Vince's place, since we promised.' Realising that things might escalate and that peace was always the best option we walked along the beach with Vince at our side – clearly he was reluctant to leave us in case we were diverted. Inside the restaurant Vince introduced us to the owner, a huge man who clearly ran the place with a rod of iron. I was glad we had come after all as I could see this guy had the power to make Vince's life a nightmare and despite Vince's bully-boy tactics I knew he was more pathetic than scary. He shepherded us inside and sat us down. Only when we had ordered our drinks did he seem able to relax and wandered off to intimidate some other hapless tourists.

As I suspected we were served indifferent food that had nothing to do with the incredible wealth of produce that lay all around us but the family were enjoying themselves, the boys playing on the sand, Juliet and her parents chatting over their drinks. In the corner of the restaurant a shifty white man sat staring into a computer with a hand-rolled cigarette dangling from his lips. He looked haggard and jittery, having clearly over-indulged in something and at his feet lay a clutch of newborn kittens, which should have been cute but instead just seemed to contribute to my own sense of squirming unease. Outside I saw Vince hanging around the wooden dock, trying to badger someone into accepting a lift in his dinghy.

Things brightened up the next morning and we saw another side of Dominica when we visited the local market in Portsmouth. After the obligatory visit to customs we wandered through the town to the market – a pleasant confusion of noise and colour. There we saw the evidence of the island's bountiful produce – its home-brewed beer, tobacco, coffee, chocolate, fruit and vegetables of every kind, freshly baked produce, chickens ranging freely and fish being sold straight off the beach. Much to Oscar and Luke's delight they were offered sweet juicy chunks of pineapple, orange and papaya to try and we staggered back to Martin's boat loaded down with produce, much of which we didn't even know the name of, never mind how it should be cooked.

Buoyed up by our visit to the market we asked Martin to take us up the famous Indian River that runs through Portsmouth. At the mouth of the river he switched off the outboard engine, got out his oars and silently rowed us up the flawless ribbon of clear water. Thick vegetation hung over the edges of the river and we had to bend down to pass below the vines and the Bwa Mang trees. The boys stared into the shaded depths, squeaking as they glimpsed large land crabs scuttling in the gloom for their holes along the forest floor. The cries of innumerable exotic birds rang out through the forest and a light wind moved gently in the treetops. Martin clearly loved his island, bringing to life the history and stories of his surroundings that made everything around us seem sharper and clearer. As the riverbed grew gradually stonier and less muddy and eventually too shallow to negotiate the boys stripped to their underwear and dipped their hot bodies in the little pools, enjoying the novelty of swimming in fresh water. We coaxed them back into the boat with a coconut that Martin had split open for them, and as we drifted back downstream I did not want this magical inter-lude to end. Emerging with the river into the bright noise, sunshine and colour of Prince Rupert Bay I felt as though we'd been given a privileged glimpse of a hidden, secret world.

The next day we set out to meet Paul, one of Martin's guides who was going to take us all into the interior of the island. As we motored towards the beach we saw a fit-looking man leaning against a tree and as we did our usual bungled beach landing, which involved one person leaping out with the painter at the last moment and more often than not getting wet to the waist, he came and caught the painter, proceeding to drag the dinghy with all of us in it halfway up the beach.

'Wow! You must be the strongest man on earth!' Luke shouted as we all climbed out. He laughed and shook his head and together he and I carried the dinghy to the top of the beach. Job done he turned to greet us, smiling widely. I searched his eyes wondering what might be in store. I did not want another Otis experience and I was also getting a little bit wary generally. Yet, with relief, I saw nothing but genuine warmth.

'Welcome to my island!' he said, pumping each of our hands in turn. Then he knelt to the boys' height and they silently shook his hand, entranced by his aura, a beacon of light that seemed to shine around him.

'Now Martin tells me you want a proper tour of my island and I am very proud to show you. Dominica is the Garden of Eden in the Caribbean. Fruit, vegetables, fish, chocolate, coffee . . . everything a person needs. Come on now – we have the whole day stretching before us.'

We made our way over to his van and he slid the doors open and gestured for us to climb in. He got into the driver's seat and then turned round. 'Now you got anything in particular you want to see?'

We shook our heads. 'Wherever you suggest,' I said.

He laughed out loud. 'Now forgive me for talking race, but this is just about the first time any white guys have taken my advice about these things. I'm gonna pass by my home village and take you for some real Dominica food!'

With a heady sense of anticipation we rolled down the windows and breathed in the rich scent of greenery as we followed increasingly steep roads that twisted and turned their way up into the high country. Paul parked the van and we walked into the thick jungle, following a coffee-coloured trail that wound through the luxuriant forest. Thick stands of bamboo stood amidst stands of tropical hardwood trees that were hung with vines and orchids. We almost felt the dense chorus of insects vibrating in our chests as Paul beckoned us near:

'When they tried to colonise these islands, the Caribs here – who were really fierce people I can tell you – held out the longest of all the Caribbean islands.' He spoke in hushed tones and we stood around him in an earnest little circle. He widened his eyes and looked at the boys, 'Those Caribs used to catch their enemies and eat them up sometimes too!'

The boys took a step back and Luke put a finger to his chin. 'Were they cannibals?'

Paul nodded. 'Yes and they ate up all of the Arawak people who were no good fighters.'

'Would they have eaten me?' Luke asked.

'Oh sure,' said Paul, giving him a fierce look. 'They would have cooked you up real fast!' He held the pantomime look and Luke edged nervously towards Juliet.

'Do they still live here?' he asked in a small voice.

'Yes they do!' Paul laughed and ruffled his hair. 'But they just eat fish and vegetables now – done given up eating their fellow man.'

He continued driving us around the island, eyes sparkling with excitement as he described, with a librarian's accuracy, the numerous plant and animal species and the extraordinary fertility that was visible all around. He pointed out numerous small farms that crept up improbably steep hillsides, their neat rows of crops barely discernible within the thick tangle of vegetation that surrounded them. Swerving to a halt beside a little track that led down through a valley thickly grown with coconut palms, he invited us to come and meet a farmer he knew. Within his tiny and intensely fertile patch of land this friend grew more crops than we could ever imagine in our cold northern country, ranging from yams to vanilla. Every kind of vegetable carpeted the slopes, and at the bottom of the valley alongside a clear, sweet stream there was a grove of succulent banana trees, which filled the air with a pleasant, curiously astringent aroma. As we leant against a tree, soaking up the dreamlike abundance of his smallholding from heaven, I noticed a familiar scent.

I brought my hand to my face and smelled it and then saw the nutmeg fruits hanging all around. Paul smiled.

'Cinnamon too,' he said. 'Look.' He walked to a nearby tree and carved a piece of bark off the trunk and held it up for us to smell. 'Dominica is heaven on earth.'

When we got back to the car he brought out a bag of oranges. 'Of course, these are Dominican oranges, the best in the world,' he said with a wink, cutting them open with a penknife and passing slices round. They didn't look that great – some of them were partly or mostly green and they looked small and somewhat battered, but they tasted incredible. Paul smiled with satisfaction, 'Now what did I tell you – ain't they the most delicious you ever tasted?'

As we drove on he shared the secret of his incredible mental and physical state of wellbeing. 'For me a healthy mind and healthy body are one and the same,' he said. 'I start every day with a tea I brew myself from the herbs around me, I eat plenty of fresh fruits, I swim plenty, don't smoke and pray to God every day.'

First days on *Forever* in Bonaire – a floating shambles.

Every boat needs a father-in-law. Here, J struggles to reach a hidden part of *Forever*'s mechanical heart. Intense heat and mosquitoes add to his purgatory.

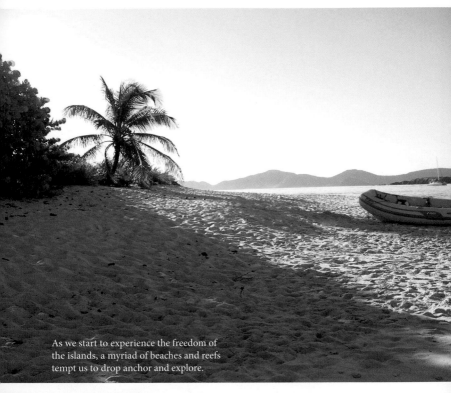

As we start to experience the freedom of the islands, a myriad of beaches and reefs tempt us to drop anchor and explore.

Juliet reads to the boys just minutes before we are hit by the full wrath of the Anegada Passage, known by sailors as the 'Cape Horn of the Caribbean.'

The great bully Soufrière Hills volcano seen presiding over the ruins of Plymouth. If there is a *Paradise Lost* on earth, it is Montserrat.

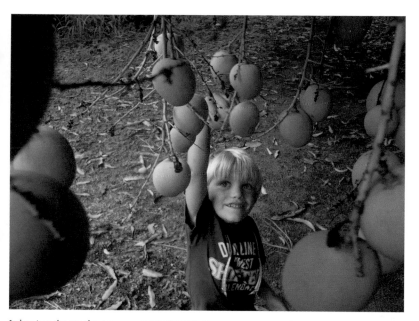

Luke gives the monkeys some competition: picking mangoes in the gardens of a ruined plantation in St Kitts.

The boys cool off in the fresh water of one of Dominica's 365 rivers.

Carnival in Trinidad's Port of Spain – absolutely the wrong time to arrive for boat-work.

Forever arrives at the Powerboats yard in Chaguaramas, the doctor's surgery for boats.

Life on stilts: dust, heat, mosquitoes and the horror of *Forever*'s refit.

A simple, beautiful Windward Island home, shabby but dignified, and typical of the Grenadines.

The wild and treacherous east coast of Carriacou, where many boats have come to grief.

Oscar fishes for our supper – croakers and chips – in the Chesapeake Bay.

Luke puts a brave face on our passage to Cape Fear across the stormy Bermuda Triangle. The passage would last ten days, during which time we would very nearly run out of water.

Luke watches as we approach Manhattan, one of our most dramatic and exciting arrivals.

David Pettigrew – a man with the heart and soul of a lion.

All canvas up as we charge for home. At night we would reduce sail in case the wind increased, but come first light there was no stopping us.

The start of what became a severe storm. The wind was 60 knots before gusts, and the seas reached 'phenomenal' – rising to a height of more than 14 metres. The storm led to the highest waves ever recorded on the west coast of Ireland.

For days a halo of Atlantic common dolphins surfed our bow wave. From my bunk I could hear their chattering clicks; they felt like our guardian angels.

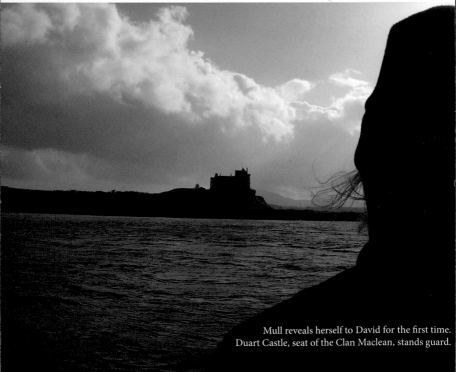

Mull reveals herself to David for the first time. Duart Castle, seat of the Clan Maclean, stands guard.

We crossed the island to its exposed eastern shore where the sea was full of movement and colour, as blue depths gave way to the turquoises of sand patches and the browns and greens of coral outcrops where the water broke and fizzed into white foam. Juliet and I both stared out to sea, no longer able to look at ocean vistas without imagining ourselves out there or considering wave height, wind, dangerous shallows and rocks.

Paul broke into our thoughts. 'Have you seen those?' He pointed up at some trees growing on the hillside that held some strange, yellow fruits. 'Cocoa pods – you ever tried them?' He pulled himself up a steep bank on the other side of the road and returned with one of the pods, which he broke open to reveal a tightly packed mass of brownish seeds wrapped in moist white flesh. He picked out a seed and sucked off the white wrapping and then spat the bitter seed out, passing the pod to the boys, who, with their antennae for chocolate on alert, did the same. 'Mmm, tastes like fizzy cola bottles,' Luke spat out the seed. 'But where's the chocolate?'

'That it down there,' Paul pointed, 'the bit you spat out.'

'I spat out chocolate?' Luke kneeled down and scrabbled around on the ground, not willing to let a chocolate moment pass.

A few miles further on we arrived at a dainty village that stretched along a rocky shoreline protected from the full onslaught of the Atlantic by a long, lime-green reef. 'Now it's lunchtime!' Paul said and we pulled up outside a simple whitewashed building, where men lazed in hammocks beneath orange trees and played draughts at rickety tables. I caught a faint, pleasant hint of marijuana smoke coming from a group of young men who sat chatting in the shade of a vine. They looked up and waved with welcoming smiles. Inside a large woman was wiping down the counter.

'We too late for eating?' Paul asked.

She sucked her teeth, feigned tiredness, then smiled. 'No, we can manage. How many eatin' – all?'

Paul shook a finger. 'Not me sister – I is too fat.'

She looked him up and down. 'You too fat? What you talking about! Enough of your silliness now, go on outside and sit down.'

We sat at a simple metal table, entranced by a man wading slowly along the coral, waist-deep in water with a spear held high, poised to strike. He looked like a human heron, as much a part of that shifting realm of water and coral as the barracuda that hunted beneath. Our food was served, chicken and 'provisions' sourced from the green country around us, and despite Paul's protests he ate heartily, looking around at us all the time to check that we were enjoying our food.

As we finished, Paul beamed magnificently at us: 'Now for the Red Rocks,' he said happily.

Red Rocks was a sort of Caribbean version of Uluru (Ayers Rock) and had a similarly aboriginal and spiritual feel; the sense of many lives having been lived here before. The rounded red sandstone seemed to have been touched and smoothed over by many hands. The place also had the feel of ongoing ceremony as well as history, like a church between services smelling of incense. In a deep gully between the rocks we found a tiny entrance that opened up into a large cave with ancient carvings on the walls. At either end of the gully myriad passageways were cut and their floors were hard packed from the passing of many feet over the years.

'Last stop coming up,' Paul grinned as we got back to the car. 'Want a freshwater swim?' We soon found ourselves trekking through a forest of palm trees for a mile or so to a long, windswept beach where a river entered the sea, forming a large pool where you could have a freshwater swim, if you didn't want to tackle the large breakers that crashed onto the beach. Audrey had a bottle of shampoo in her bag and we all unashamedly soaped up and washed off, aided by a heavy rain shower that added to the experience. A group of local people kicked a ball around, while others lay on the beach talking, sleeping, eating and listening to music. It had a very relaxed, local feel – thanks to Paul we had achieved our aim of getting a glimpse of the 'real' Dominica.

Paul drove us back through his home village, introducing us to family and friends along the way. 'Hey Auntie,' he shouted from the car window to a statuesque lady, 'give us one of them grapefruit.' Obligingly she passed in a grapefruit the size of a football and as we wound our way through the village Paul amassed bags of oranges, passion fruit and pawpaw, a bottle of home-pressed grapefruit juice and a bunch of bananas. He passed it all to us. I felt uncomfortable to be taking all this hard-earned produce, but our protests fell on deaf ears. 'We got plenty,' was their constant refrain and indeed the bounteousness of Dominica seemed to invest its people with a wonderful generosity of spirit.

Audrey and J's stay with us was now at an end and with a sense of sadness, we gathered around the saloon table to eat our last supper. We all felt miserable: J and Audrey because – I suspected – they were worried about leaving their grandchildren in our hands; Juliet and the children because they were going to miss them; me because I felt weighed down by the very real responsibilities I now faced as skipper, plus no small measure of guilt, as I knew I hadn't been good company during their stay. We ate mostly in silence, the boys glancing nervously at us from time to time. Oscar looked at Juliet with a worried expression, 'Mum, are you and Dad going to be sailing the boat alone now?'

'Yes Oscar.' Uncharacteristically, she offered him no reassurance on the subject.

'I don't want you to go Papa,' Luke said. 'Can't you stay?'

'No Luke, we have to go home. And your parents are perfectly up to the job.'

'But do you know how to do the job Dad?' Oscar asked. 'You don't know very much about the sea.'

It was undeniably true. 'Well . . . I've learnt a lot, Oscar, and so has Mummy. Together we'll work things out.'

After supper J unearthed the last of his stash of chocolate and then pulled out his faded copy of *Swallowdale* to read to the boys before bed. Luke lay on his back on the bench, dangling a shell on a string and half-listening, while Oscar sat beside him, listening carefully to the words of the old-fashioned story, which sounded so appropriate read in his grandfather's voice. Outside the sun had sunk away and the saloon glowed in a pocket of warm, woody light, the lamp gently rocking above the table. It already felt intensely nostalgic, as things do when you are on the brink of change.

The next morning Martin sped over in his launch and waited as we passed down Audrey and J's bags. Juliet and the children were going to accompany them to the airport. I hugged Audrey and said goodbye. 'Now you look after everyone and be careful,' she said, holding my arms and looking into my eyes for a moment before stepping into the launch. Now it was J's turn, and as I went to shake his hand he held up a finger. 'Now I want to say something . . .' he cleared his throat and I could see he was finding it difficult to articulate what he was feeling. 'I may not always have been as patient as I should have been and for that I apologise.'

This rather short, formal speech was the height of emotion coming from a man who was usually so reserved. Juliet and I hugged him. 'You're great,' Juliet said, 'we couldn't have got this far without you.'

'You've taught us so much J,' I said. 'And I'm the one that should be saying sorry.'

There was no need to say any more. We stood hugging for a while and then J climbed into Martin's boat, looking away and raising a hand in farewell. I waved until they were out of sight, my mind tracing a red line across a chart all the way back to Scotland. We had such a long way to go before we reached home and I wondered how on earth we were going to make it. Without doubt I had found it tough sharing our small living space, yet J had more than stepped up to his task of being sailing master and I had learnt a huge amount from him. As well as his practical help and experience, we would miss his sense of certainty, his unshakeable belief that we would get to wherever we were going in one piece. Now the duty to bring the family back in one piece lay squarely with Juliet and me, and I hoped we would be up to it.

Juliet and the children returned red-eyed from the airport, exhausted by the emotional parting. We had a pleasant if slightly muted evening: it was actually nice to eat alone as a family, to reclaim our cabin and begin to regain some of the intimacy that we had lost. It was also good to wake up the next morning in our own time, although perversely, I woke up earlier than ever, as if my own motivation had kicked in now that there was nobody to nag me. J would have been proud of us as we made the boat ready and then did our passage plan, checking and rechecking each other's calculations until we were certain they were correct.

We were heading for the French island of Martinique, the next in the chain of islands that would lead us down to Trinidad. It was the middle of January and we were under some pressure to reach Trinidad by the end of the month so that we could have our decks replaced in time to cross the Atlantic before the hurricane season. Replacing our decks had become essential, as we had discovered that water was now leaking through the deck into the interior of the boat – a serious problem. We had no alternative. We had to sail to Trinidad to get the work done on *Forever* that she needed. We had two weeks to get there, seeing what we could as we passed by almost all of the Windward Islands.

Of all the islands thus far Dominica had left the greatest impression on us. Here we had met and connected with real people and had an insight into how people live. Martin and Paul had been inspirational guides and as we sailed south watching its steep, jagged coastline slip away we discussed how it would feel to live in such a place.

We spent the night bobbing on our anchor in Le Marin, in the south of Martinique and the next morning I dashed ashore early to both enter and clear customs. It seemed ridiculous when we'd only stayed one night on the island, but French customs had a reputation for being strict and we had heard of boats being heavily fined or even impounded if they ignored the regulations. I had an odd sense of displacement as I wandered along the dusty road looking for the customs office – other than the palm trees I might have been suddenly transported to the South of France. On the way back to the boat I stopped at a bakery, unable to resist the smell of baking bread that drifted out onto the street. I ordered coffee, a couple of baguettes and croissants, and dusting down my rusty French I thanked the proprietress for the joy these treats would bring my family.

Coming into the lee of St Lucia we sailed on to Marigot Bay, a picture-perfect anchorage, its all-round shelter and dense mangroves making an ideal hurricane hole that offered shelter to pirates and colonial navies alike. We were looking forward to going ashore but this was easier said than done, as there was little space inside the anchorage and after some faffing around, we were eventually ushered to a mooring near the entrance by a wizened old man in a tiny motorboat, who claimed the mooring was his and demanded payment immediately. Relieved at the prospect of being ashore, we paid up and were still securing our mooring line when we heard a knock on the hull and the familiar greeting, 'Hey Skip!'

I leant over the side and saw two Rastas in a red, gold and green painted wooden boat. One was manning the outboard, the other busy talking. 'The name's Derek,' he said, grinning widely and revealing gold teeth. 'You need anything? We got bread, water, fruit, jewellery . . . real nice stuff, have a look.' He gestured to some beaded necklaces and bracelets on a woven mat on the bottom of the boat.

'No thanks, but thanks anyway,' I said firmly, having learnt from our experience.

'Perhaps your lady would like sometin'? Really pretty now.'

'No really, I'm sure it's nice, but we can't buy anything just now.'

'No problem, no problem. Nice boat you got here,' he said, continuing to hang on the gunwale and looking around. Just then Luke appeared. 'Hey brother!' He held up a hand and Luke walked up the side of the boat to do a fist bump.

'You like some of these buddy?' In a time-honoured sales strategy that no doubt had paid dividends for him many times before, he began laying a tantalising line of little trinkets out along the deck, Luke's eyes growing ever-wider as each new knick-knack joined the line. He picked up a tiny turtle carved from soapstone with an iridescent shell back. 'Can I have this Dad? Please?'

He held it up and I felt myself weakening. 'How much does it cost?'

I saw Derek thinking rapidly: if he pitched it too high he might lose the sale. 'Usually these ones are twenty EC,' he said, 'but since I like you guys I give it to you for fifteen'.

'Wait Dad, what about one for Oscar?' Luke asked. 'Oscar! Come and look – Dad's going to buy us something.'

On hearing the word 'buy' Oscar appeared in a flash. Derek smiled indulgently and leant on the deck. He had me now and he knew it. 'Please can I have one of those?' Oscar pointed at a white shell necklace with red, gold and green beads laced in between.

With impeccable timing Juliet appeared.

'Hey, those necklaces look nice – can I see?'

'Sure ting sister. You look as long as you want.' He flashed me a triumphant grin.

'How much is this one?' she asked, pointing.

'Fifteen EC,' I said quickly before Derek could hike up the price.

'There is one matching bracelet too – look. For you only ten EC.'

'It is nice . . .' She glanced across at me, 'What do you think Guy? They're good value.'

'Yeah, whatever. Just go ahead and get them.' And get these guys away from my boat, I felt like saying, or this will never end. These boat boys could show George Foreman a thing or two about how to make a sales pitch, and I couldn't help admiring their chutzpah.

Sure enough, within a couple of hours Luke's turtle fell apart and Juliet's bracelet turned out to have a faulty catch and fell off and got lost. Yet again we resolved to resist these advances in future and as we were issuing dire warnings to the boys not to look at anything without checking with us first, a man came over and demanded payment for the mooring and we realised the first one had been an imposter and we'd been ripped off again. Nevertheless, with some determined chirpiness, after paying up a second time we took a trip ashore where Juliet and I lingered over drinks as we watched the boys swim from a little beach. The original Doctor Dolittle film had been made here and the little bay had a charming childlike quality to it, the swaying palm trees, bright blue sea, cheerfully painted houses and little boats. The sun disappeared with almost comical suddenness and after a simple supper we sank gratefully into our berths, our skins feeling pleasantly tight from the prolonged exposure to the wind, sun and sea spray.

In the early hours of the morning I opened my eyes, aware of a sound that was out of place. Over the months at sea we had become attuned to the many creaking and clanking noises of the boat so any new sounds alerted us to danger. This time it was human. I lay looking up at the cabin roof above our berth, listening hard and hoping I was mistaken. But there it was again – the soft, padded sound of bare feet, moving very carefully so as not to be heard.

I turned and shook Juliet. 'Someone's on the deck,' I whispered as she opened her eyes.

She pulled herself up on her elbows. 'What?'

I put my fingers to my lips. 'I'm going to take a look – get ready to lock the companionway doors if need be.' She nodded. 'Shall I wake the kids?'

'Not yet.'

'OK. Be careful.' And then she actually turned over and went back to sleep. I looked at her for a moment somewhat stunned, wondering when our parameters of normality had shifted so radically that she could sleep while potential marauders roamed above our heads. I might as well have been getting up to let the cat out or close a window for all the attention she was paying. If it hadn't been so sinister it would have been funny.

Very quietly I stood up and raised my head through the hatch above our bed, peering first at the bow, where I saw nothing and then slowly rotating to look towards the stern. At first I saw nothing there either, but as my eyes adjusted to the gloom I saw a sight that made me rigid with fear. A man was standing very still in a pool of moon shadow that slanted out from our mast. He had pushed himself up against the mast and was barely visible, as if the night had shape-shifted to become the outline of a man. It was an awful sight: he looked practised in the art of hiding and had boarded our boat with the stealth of a cat. I thought rapidly of what he might be after: the outboard engine was chained and locked on deck and the dinghy was on the davits. Luckily I had thought to unscrew the expensive chart plotter, from its position on the coach roof. In fact most things of value were down in the saloon and a chill of horror spread through me: might he try and come down below?

We had left the companionway doors open as usual to let the breeze blow through the boat – we only locked them when we felt especially vulnerable – as we had felt safe in Marigot Bay with so many people and boats around. If he went down below, he would come to the boys' cabin first. Abductions weren't unheard of. He might try and grab one of them. I absolutely could not run the risk of that happening – even glimpsing him would traumatise Oscar and Luke. I had to take action now, before he came down below. Moving as quietly as possible, I dropped down from the hatch and tiptoed through the dark boat to the chart table. There I flipped on the spreader lights, which instantly flooded the deck with bright light and then turned the VHF radio on at full volume, squelching it to create a loud buzzing noise. With the aerosol fog-horn in one hand and my diving knife in the other, I charged up to the cockpit, ready to make a noise and fight if necessary. *Forever* stood lit up like a rocket launch site in the desert in the midst of the silent darkness all around. I looked around the deck and saw nothing. I went up to the mast; I peered into the water. But there was nothing – just dark black water reflecting back at me. How could he have got away so quickly? Just as I began to think I must have imagined it I glanced down at the deck beside the mast and saw the outline of a foot picked out in the dew. As I stared down at it I heard a noise behind me and turned to see a powerful launch with the silhouettes of two men on board, moving swiftly away down the fairway towards the open sea.

I stood watching the boat leave, feeling sick with relief and still bemused by the silence and speed with which that man must have operated. What would have happened if I hadn't woken up? What had he planned to do to us? I went below and pulled the companionway doors shut, sacrificing the cool breeze for a sense of safety. I left the spreader lights on, their cold, hard brightness replacing the serene moonlight.

'Everything OK?' Juliet mumbled sleepily as I climbed back into our berth.

'Yes, he's gone.'

'Good. Can you turn the lights out now?'

'Not yet, I feel better with them on.'

'OK. Whatever.' She fell back into sleep. I lay awake worrying, feeling that we had had a very close shave and wondering if we would be so lucky next time. Somehow Juliet seemed less frightened by the human risk than I was: whether it was a result of her laid back childhood on Mull or simply her intrinsic faith in human nature I couldn't tell. But then maybe I was overly paranoid – a hangover from the violent surroundings of my childhood perhaps, or my instinctive defensiveness as a man. Either way the burden of responsibility for our safety seemed to fall on me and I remembered now with a sense of panic the worried looks we had received when we'd said we were heading for Trinidad. Things were different now; we were entering a zone of islands that were rougher, wilder and less predictable. Images came to mind from my paranoid readings about cruising families, alone and vulnerable on their boats, cornered by desperate men, and of brutal assaults and kidnappings. Of course I was exaggerating – yet the kernel of truth remained – we were on our own, we were a family exposed in a watery realm where we were not always welcome.

TWELVE

OSCAR SAVES THE DAY

13.28N: 61.14W

By late afternoon we had cleared St Lucia, sailing past the spectacular peaks of the Pitons, running through strong winds and swell until we reached the shelter of St Vincent, the wildest and least visited of the Windward Islands. It was hard to heed the warnings not to go into any deserted anchorages – there was something powerfully enticing about the mist-shrouded inlet, the promise of seeing the island exactly as the first explorers had seen it.

You could easily imagine stepping back five hundred years as we approached Wallilabou Bay, a wild, impenetrable tangle of jungle running right down to the sea. Wallilabou Bay was the home of 'Port Royal' in the *Pirates of the Caribbean* films, and bizarrely part of the set remained on the shore. As we rounded the headland we saw a number of yachts anchored and in between an armada of boat boys. Perched on surfboards, old dinghies and even planks of wood they soon hung on to our caprail, slamming into *Forever*'s sides and shouting in a growing cacophony.

'Hey Skip, let me take your line ashore!'

'Skip, I'll take your garbage!'

'Want any fruit, vegetables, bread?'

'Skip, Skip, Skip!'

They crowded around us with a complete disregard for the fact that we were still moving and I worried that we might run over someone, or catch one of them with our propeller. We progressed into the bay, pursued by the gaggle of boats, as we looked for a place to anchor.

'Over here Skip!' shouted a man on a surfboard, 'Hey missus, I take your line.'

Juliet was on the bow, joining two ropes to make a line long enough to reach the shore. 'What shall I do?' she called.

'Give it to him I guess,' I answered, but just as she was about to pass it down another man appeared alongside us in a relatively up-market boat with an outboard engine.

'Pass me the line,' he said to Juliet.

'Hey man – this my business,' the first man said, desperately paddling to keep up with us.

'Back off man,' the second man said, barging him out of the way and nearly knocking him into the water. 'Give me the line Skip.' His tone was threatening.

'Jules!' I called lightly. She looked round at me and I jerked my head towards the mouth of the bay.

It was one of our psychic moments. 'Yes – exactly what I was thinking!' and in one fluid motion I turned the boat and headed back out to sea. For a moment the men hung back, thinking we were going to circle back round, but when they realised we were leaving things got ugly. The man who had threatened us sped towards us, grabbing onto our caprail.

'What you doin' man? No way – you not leaving!'

'That's exactly what we're doing. Let go of my boat, or you're going to get hurt,' I shouted, increasing the throttle until he fell away.

I turned round to see him shaking his fist and shouting after us with words that I couldn't hear, though his meaning was clear.

'Where are we headed, Jules?' I asked her and she darted down below.

'Well, there's a place on the south coast of St Vincent,' she said when she re-emerged a few minutes later, 'but the other choice is Bequia.'

I looked back and saw a little sailing yacht being hauled in by the men like a moth caught in a web, the crew standing in silence.

'I'm right off St Vincent,' I said. 'How far is Bequia?'

'About ten miles.' She glanced at her watch. 'It's five o'clock – if we motor-sail we should make it before dark, but we've got to keep the speed up. It's a difficult place to anchor.'

We were overturning one of our golden rules, which was to never leave it too late when entering an unfamiliar anchorage, so using full sail and engine we progressed as fast as we could towards Bequia. We were in a race against the sunset, and it felt as if the elements were conspiring against us as a sudden set of fierce squalls passed over, turning the sea and sky steel grey. We hadn't prepared for such an embattled journey. Juliet eased the mainsheet to deflect the worst of the gusts, while I bore away on the helm. We tried to use the increased wind to our advantage, tightening back up onto our course when the worst of the gusts had died away. 'I hope we're going to make it,' I muttered to Juliet. 'We can't go in after dark – it's too dangerous.'

'If the worst comes to the worst we'll have to stand off overnight,' Juliet said.

'In this weather? God, I hope not.'

We both knew we were potentially in a dangerous situation, with several miles still to go and the tricky job of anchoring in the dark once we got there. We were heading for Admiralty Bay, a wide, beautifully sheltered bay on the western side of Bequia with the island's main town of Port Elizabeth set at its head. Cold, wet and exhausted we eventually drew into the bay just as darkness began to fall. Juliet peered through the binoculars and turned to me with a worried look. 'Doesn't look like there's much space – it's packed with boats. And look at the sky.' She pointed to the northeast where a long bank of steel grey cloud lay out across the horizon.

We lowered sail and approached the anchored yachts that stretched half a mile or so out from the harbour. Further in I could see it was very crowded and we motored slowly around the periphery of the group, Juliet on the helm as I made the anchor ready to drop. A number of huge, expensive-looking yachts lay at anchor, with smaller ones like ours in between. These were live-aboard yachts, with the telltale signs of washing flapping on the lifelines and children dawdling whilst parents tinkered about on deck. A few held out hands and shrugged shoulders as we passed as the brotherhood of the sea kicked in with the universal sympathy for someone arriving late and unprepared.

The wind built as squalls approached and Juliet had to increase the throttle to hold the boat straight on its course. 'Where shall we go?' she shouted. 'There's nowhere!'

We motored round a bit more, weighing up the factors of other boats' anchors and swinging room and where we would have to drop the anchor in order to land up in the right place.

'Over there!' I pointed to a little space in the centre of a circle of yachts.

Juliet approached slowly, steering into the wind and calling out the depth as she went. 'Five fathoms, four point five, four . . . OK, drop the anchor!' she shouted and slipped the gear into neutral, letting the boat fall back on the wind.

I let go of the anchor, watching the chain clatter out noisily as the wind pushed us quickly backwards.

'Guy!' I heard Juliet shouting over the wind and turned round to see her pointing at a large American yacht behind us. The skipper was standing on the bow waving his arms at us and I could see he was worried we might cross over his chain.

'Shit, he thinks we're too close,' I muttered. 'OK, let's haul it up Jules!' I pressed the button on the anchor winch as Juliet moved the boat slowly forward. The man waved gratefully to us.

We began motoring round again, our job made harder by the increasing lack of light. It was raining hard now: large, spiteful drops. All around warm light shone out of the interior of boats as people hunkered down to sit out the storm. In a mood of growing desperation I picked a spot and we dropped the hook again. Juliet pulled the boat astern to test the anchor's grip, but to my dismay I felt the chain jumping and skipping beneath my foot, showing that we were dragging. We lifted it again and as we passed one of the live-aboard yachts a man came out on deck. 'The holding's very poor here,' he shouted, 'took us a couple of hours to get a hold. Maybe try over there?' he pointed across to the other side of the bay.

I ran back to the cockpit for a quick conference with Juliet. 'It's too deep over there,' she said, 'and too dark. I think we should stick with it over here – at least we saw it properly in daylight. Either that or give up and go back out to sea.'

'Bugger that,' I said and we resumed motoring around until we found another spot that looked promising. I dropped the anchor and held my foot on the chain as Juliet pulled back. It jumped and rumbled for a moment and my heart sank, but then I felt it catch. 'It's held!' I shouted to Juliet and she switched off the engine. I looked about to fix our position in relation to some landmarks on the shore. It wasn't perfect but it would do, I decided, and with relief went down below.

It was cozy in the saloon as the wind and rain lashed across the decks. The boys had changed into their pyjamas and were playing contentedly at the table as Juliet set a pan of pasta on to boil. We all felt as though we'd survived a little ordeal and settled down to enjoy the uniquely snug feeling of being safely at anchor in bad weather. As we went through the familiar rituals of an onboard supper – Juliet dishing out the grub, the boys laying the table and me opening a bottle of wine – I had a sudden sense of everything being in the right place. As we tucked into our well-deserved meal, Oscar froze mid-bite. 'Dad! The anchor's dragging!'

I stopping chewing and listened, but could hear nothing. 'No it isn't Oscar, don't worry.'

We carried on talking and eating, but a minute or two later he interrupted again.

'Dad! It is, it really is – it's dragging!'

Irritation fluttered within me. 'It isn't, Oscar. Don't you think we've had enough action for one night? Please, give us a break!' I raised the glass of wine and contemplated its loveliness for a moment.

'Guy, I think you should go and check, just in case.' She winked at me. I sighed heavily and walked a few steps up the companionway to make a pretence of looking around. What I saw filled me with immediate horror. Just a few metres behind us I saw the pointed bow of a huge, immaculate yacht, which definitely hadn't been there before. What was worse, it was growing rapidly closer as we hurtled back towards it on the shoulders of a strong gust. I stared uselessly at it for a few seconds and then sprang into action. 'Jules! We're dragging!' I yelled and turned the engine key. I ran up to the wheel, Juliet close behind me and pushed the throttle ahead to hold us in position against the strong wind. 'Here, you take the wheel!' I shouted. 'I'll go and pull up the anchor.'

Like marines going into action we ran to our stations. Halfway up the anchor chain jolted to a halt and as I pressed the winch button it continued in fits and starts, the windlass straining as if it was pulling some kind of extra weight. I peered over the side as it cleared the water and saw an immense ball of dead coral jammed firmly between the flukes. It swung backwards and forwards like a wrecking ball and I raised it as high as possible to avoid it swinging against *Forever*'s hull, but it was too heavy to lift back on board. I leant down and tried to dislodge it with my hand. I shouted down through the hatch for Oscar to pass up my hammer and he did so, but still no joy. It was stuck fast. With a sinking heart I realised that now even going back out to sea – the only real option available to us – was out of the question as the waves would make it swing backward and forwards until we would have caved in our own hull. Our second anchor, stored in the cockpit locker, wasn't strong enough to hold us in these conditions. It was ten o'clock at night, pitch dark and we were in a strange harbour on a wild night surrounded by obstacles of every kind and myriad pristine yachts peopled by ex-lawyers no doubt itching for some action. It was the stuff of nightmares.

'The only option seems to be to keep motoring,' I shouted to Juliet back in the cockpit.

'We can't!' she shouted back. 'I can't see properly and it's only a matter of time before we foul the prop! Do you think someone might have a mooring?'

'I didn't see any when we came in. I can try radioing to see if anyone can help, but it's pretty late – I don't suppose anyone will answer.'

'Well it's worth a try, but hurry up! I'm scared that the engine might stop and then we'll be truly screwed.'

I rushed down the companionway to find Luke standing anxiously at the bottom of the steps. 'Dad, is everything all right? I'm scared.'

'Don't worry Luke – just a little trouble with the anchor. Everything's going to be fine. Just stay down here with Oscar – he'll look after you.' I turned to Oscar. 'Can you look after your brother Ozzy?' I bent nearer and whispered, 'You're an amazing boy – I'm really proud of you. You saved the day.'

I lifted the radio handset. 'This is sailing vessel *Forever, Forever.*' I spoke slowly, trying to keep the worry out of my voice, but heard nothing but wind and rain. I repeated the call and waited, but again nothing. Third time lucky, I thought grimly and tried again. This time, I explained briefly that we had fouled our anchor and were looking for a mooring. After a pause, the radio crackled back at me and a laconic voice spoke:

'*Forever*, this is Fat Shag . . . Switch over now, channel 68.'

An unlikely name for a saviour I thought as I switched channel, but sometimes help comes from unexpected places. 'Yes *Forever*, what can I do for you?' The rich West Indian accent rolled out into the saloon.

'We've fouled our anchor and are looking for a mooring for the night. Do you know anyone who might have one?'

'Where are you?'

'About half a mile out in the middle of the bay.'

'Switch your spreader lights on, we find you.'

I switched on the lights and ran up to the cockpit, where Juliet was shivering at the helm. Minutes later a small homemade boat appeared bearing two men completely swathed in bright yellow oilskins. The older of the two stretched up and shook my hand. 'The name's Raymond. We gonna get you outta this mess real quick. Keep the boat as still as you can,' he called to Juliet and then steered towards the bow. 'Let the anchor down a bit,' he called and I lowered it on the winch so they could reach it. The younger man held the anchor with a crow-bar as Raymond pounded the monster coral with a sledgehammer until it finally cracked and fell away. He looked up at me and smiled widely from beneath his sou'wester hat. 'Now follow my light – I take you to my mooring.'

Visions of another catastrophe floated through my brain. 'We draw six feet,' I shouted nervously. 'Will it be deep enough . . . ?'

'Jus' follow me.' And they motored slowly off towards the harbour.

We threaded our way through the boats, following the weak beam of their torch and trusting them completely to lead us out of trouble. The depth fell to four fathoms and then three and then just as we were beginning to worry that we were following a couple of skilful wreckers the little boat stopped and I saw Raymond waving his hand. He held up a white mooring ball and when I'd tied it on the bow I leant down, as grateful as I had ever been. 'Thank you so much – we were really in trouble there, I don't know what we would have done. What do we owe you?'

He waved his hand. 'You jus' relax now – we do paying tomorrow.' He disappeared into the gloom.

We awoke the next morning to a world of sunshine and a cheerful breeze, no trace of the menace of the night before. The bay was full of sailing boats, wings folded, bobbing on their moorings. Between them people zipped about in dinghies and local Bequians were busy supplying fuel, water, ice, groceries and laundry services to the boats. Birds landed noisily on our guardrails, taking a look at us before taking off again. A string of cheerfully painted buildings ran along the beach at the head of the bay, where people lounged over breakfast and coffee. There was no sign anywhere of the corporate stamp of tourism: all this had sprung up from local roots. It felt a million miles away from the menace of Wallilabou Bay, or the plastic facades of some of the harbours in the Virgin Islands. It reminded me of *Busy Busy World*, one of the boys' series of Richard Scarry books, with so much to look at that you didn't quite know where to begin.

Despite or perhaps because of our near miss, something seemed to have switched inside me and I felt lighter and less weighed down than I had in months. With relief I could see that Juliet was feeling good too: we had come close to disaster, but in the process had pulled together for the first time and everyone felt stronger as a result.

I looked around and felt blessed and unworthy of such a family – how could I ever have questioned it? I felt as if a mist was clearing that had made everything seem dull and grey; now at last I had a sense that the sun had come out.

Later that morning we strolled along the village street, passing a bank, church, art gallery and various shops. Towards the end of the road there was a large covered market, where tables groaned with fresh-looking fruit and vegetables and kindly-looking Rastas stood about. One of them spotted us and offered the boys slices of watermelon, which they devoured, seemingly oblivious to the rivers of pink juice that dribbled down their chins. 'You boys like that fruit?' he asked, beaming at them indulgently. They nodded wildly. 'You bring your parents inside and they can be picking up all manner of natural goodies, make you real big and strong!' I smiled, still glowing with love for my family which now extended to the whole human race. All my natural guile had evaporated with the rising sun, and soon we found ourselves drawn inside, surrounded by laughing Rastas and happily sampling all manner of delicious fruity samples.

'Hello sista, you have these bags,' a tall Rasta said, shoving a clutch of jute bags into Juliet's hands. 'And you too brother,' he pressed a couple more onto me: 'Don't wanna leave all the carryin' to the lady!'

'No really, we don't need them,' Juliet protested. 'We've got some back on the boat.'

'I not take no for an answer,' he insisted. 'You have these free with my blessing, good for all the shopping,' he smiled with a Cheshire cat's grin.

'You like them orange?' A man beside me asked, full of smiles and bonhomie. I nodded as innocently as one of the children, and before I knew it he had shoved about ten of them into my bag and then seamlessly guided me onward like a top croupier guiding a gambler to bankruptcy. He stopped before a mound of lemons and lime. 'Gotta have some of these,' he said. 'Then you got all the great Caribbean citrus on your boat. Don't want to get scurvy now!' He laughed throatily and I had no choice but to join in as he shovelled them into my bag.

'Hey Dad, look, soursop!' Luke had stopped beside a teetering pile of the fruits tended by a beaming Rasta and a not so naturally beaming woman who was trying to smile nevertheless.

'Great Luke, just let me get there . . .' My words tailed off as I saw Luke proudly accepting his own bag, which the Rasta was smilingly filling with the green spiky fruits.

'How the hell are we going to eat all those soursop?' Juliet muttered. 'Stop him Guy!'

A cunning strategy came to me, and I held up the bags. 'Stop now Luke, we've got no more space, come on guys!'

'That no problem, I got this box,' a kindly voice said, and pressed a cardboard box upon me that seemed to cry out to be filled. Sensitive fingers bedecked in gold gently prodded me on, and like fleshy pinballs we ricocheted from stall to stall, picking up garlic, onions, potatoes, lemon grass, passion fruit, guavas, tomatoes, lettuce and coconuts on the way.

'Where did all that come from?' Juliet asked me, looking a little annoyed.

'Sorry, I just thought we might need some staples.'

'Staples!' She paused and scanned the box, 'You call lemon grass a staple?'

A Rasta was busily writing a running tote on the side of the box and I looked past him at Juliet and saw that she was not entirely innocent either. 'OK, so what have you got?' I asked.

She looked a little sheepish. 'I thought some paw paw would be nice, now we've got all those limes and everything . . .'

Behind her a Rasta nodded warmly. 'That lady of yours – she got real good sense. Paw paw is excellent with limes, and with ginger too.' He shoved in a piece of ginger root for good measure.

At last I reached the stall where Luke was struggling under the immense weight of his bag. 'That's way too many Luke – we can't eat all those.' The Rasta shook his head sadly as I unloaded a few back onto the stall. 'What else you like little guy? You like pineapples?' Luke nodded enthusiastically and a few of them went in as well.

'Right, that really is enough,' I said, trying to be firm.

'Goodbye brother,' the Rasta said to Luke, smiling widely with gold glinting in his teeth. 'Bless.' They touched fists. Luke brought his fist to his heart and said 'bless' in his light Scottish accent.

It was a good sight. But my joyous reflections on race relations and the future of our children were soon overtaken by panic as I spotted Oscar, who was sitting on a Rasta's shoulders reaching up for some cane stored in the rafters.

'Enough now Oscar!' I shouted, 'We've got too much stuff as it is!'

'Hey, give the boy a break,' the Rasta next to me said. 'All kids love to chew that cane – better than sweets and other nonsense.' I looked over at Juliet helplessly and saw that she looked similarly perplexed and confused. Normally I prided myself on my ability to haggle, but it was clear that our time at sea had not honed our commercial acumen – in fact we seemed to have lost it altogether.

Luke and Oscar struggled over to us bearing two 8-foot sugar cane poles. 'That's too much boys, no way. Where are we going to put it?' A Rasta solved that problem for me. 'You can strap them down on the deck man – store 'em up for the journey!'

'Well I suppose we could . . . Jules?' She shook her head. 'Don't be ridiculous – they'll have no teeth left by the time we get to Trinidad!' The Rasta looked indignant. 'But what about the kids? They gonna be real disappointed. This feel like some kind of cruelty! What kind of mother you call youself?'

'I can't believe this,' Juliet held her head in her hands. 'Now I'm being accused of being a bad mother. I give up.'

The two edible punting poles were added to the pile. 'Well at least we can hoist the fruit up on the poles for the walk back,' I said, trying to be funny, but then realising that the joke was definitely on us.

'OK, enough now!' Juliet said firmly. 'Please tell us how much.'

The Rastas recoiled with faux horror, casting sideways glances at me as if in sympathy that I had to live with such a woman. 'Keep your hair on sister, no need to get yourself all het up!'

They turned their backs to us as they toted up our bill, each clutching a scrap of cardboard which held a scrawled record of our purchases during our period of fruitarian hypnosis. We waited with a growing sense of dread until eventually, after much scribbling and muttering the leader of the red, gold and green pack passed her a scrap of paper. 'Two hundred and tirty dollars,' he said triumphantly.

'Two hundred and tirty – I mean thirty – dollars? You've got to be kidding!'

'I no kidding sister,' he said gravely like a judge delivering a sentence. 'Wanna see the bills?'

'Yes I do.'

The atmosphere turned chilly as they gathered in a circle around her while she examined the lists. 'Thirty dollars for a bag of potatoes! That's way too expensive,' she protested.

A woman stepped forward. 'These potatoes flown in from Canada,' she said coldly. 'What you think – we grow them here?'

'Well I don't know, but that's still too expensive.'

'Everything flown in here – this no good place for growing. You people come in yachts and expect everyting to be cheap.' She almost spat the words.

'Not cheap, but . . .' She shrugged, lost for words.

'Well what you want to do – put the stuff back?' the chief

Rasta said coldly. All friendliness was gone now and it was clear that the smiling façade had been purely a sales pitch.

'No.' She sighed and got out her wallet. As we lifted our bags she looked round at the disapproving assembly. 'I'm sorry, but I just feel we've been ripped off.'

A chorus of sucking teeth surrounded us as we did the walk of shame out of the building.

We stood outside in the sunshine, all happiness gone as we lamented our stupidity. 'I can't believe we let that happen,' Juliet said angrily. 'I don't even know what's in these bags – and look,' she showed me one of the paw paw. 'Some of this is really poor quality. I think they put the good stuff on the top to tempt you, but then give you the old stuff from the bottom.'

I shook my head, unsure whether this was the case, but certainly feeling that we'd been stupid in accepting more fruit and vegetables than we could ever hope to eat.

'Look at that!' Juliet was peering inside the building, where the Rastas were dividing up our money like lions at the kill. She pointed at the back wall, 'Read that sign!'

I looked up at a charmingly hand-painted inscription, which read:

Visitors to the market should be allowed to choose whatever they like, without being harassed by the Vendors, e.g. Tugging of people in different directions, pushing of fruits in their mouths for sampling.

'Seems we could have them on trade description,' Juliet said. 'We were totally harassed. And look at that one!'

We the Vendors are committed to provide good service and to offer vegetables of acceptable quality.

We walked on in ashamed silence. 'I could kick myself for being so stupid,' Juliet fumed. 'Boys, don't ever do that to us again – and Guy, I thought you were meant to be the streetwise member of the family!'

It was true, I had often claimed that role. 'I know,' I replied guiltily. 'They sort of mesmerised me.'

It took two runs in the dinghy to ferry all the stuff out to the boat, and then we hoisted bag after bag onto *Forever* in the sweltering heat. As she packed the stuff away Juliet continued raging. 'Half of it's rotten,' she cried in despair, 'and the other half's not ripe!' It seemed her conspiracy theory had been correct, as much of the fruit and veg bore no resemblance to the versions we'd sampled.

'I can't fit it all into the fridge.' She slumped down in the saloon in despair. 'Damn, I hate being ripped off!'

A little later her fury had settled into steely resolve. 'I'm going to come back here one day and go into that place with headphones and dark glasses, and a list of what I want – nothing extra!'

Even she had to laugh at the image these words brought to mind. I hoped fervently that this would never come to pass: Rastas beware, I thought, hell hath no fury like a woman ripped off at market.

THIRTEEN

THE GOOD
GREEN GRENADINES

12.43N: 61.19W

After a few days' joyful relaxation, during which time we ate an immense amount of fruit and vegetables, we sailed from Bequia, vowing to one day come back to this charming island. As we sailed out of Admiralty Bay and passed its south-western tip, I noticed some odd shapes in stone that appeared to cluster along the very steep sides of the headland and a natural arch through which the clear blue sky contrasted with the dark rock. I couldn't figure out what I was seeing – it looked as if giant barnacles had emerged from the sea, motivated by territorial aspirations. I pulled up the binoculars to look more closely and realised to my fascination that these structures were in fact houses built into and around the rocks. I pulled out the pilot book to learn more and read that in the 1970s a sect of innovative architects had grouped together and moved to this very remote spot, where they designed and built homes that completely blended into their environment. No windows, no electricity – nothing besides the simplicity of truly good design. The settlement had been given a magical name too: Moonhole, after the natural rock arch where the first house was built, through which the moon can be glimpsed at certain times of the month.

We continued on our way south, passing Mustique, hangout of the rich and famous, as we headed for the island of Canouan some twenty miles away. These islands are all part of St Vincent and the Grenadines, a nation made up of thirty-two scraps of vegetated coral that stretch from St Vincent in the north to Union Island in the south. This is the Caribbean of the tourist brochures: the shallow seas a perfect aquamarine, the tiny palm-clad islands ringed with delicate white sands, the saturation of the colours so intense that they seem artificial.

'What's that?' Oscar pointed at the rolling swell behind our stern. It was an invigorating day with a fresh 25-knot breeze and we were making swift progress. 'I saw something, like a big fish.'

We all turned and looked and then I saw it too. 'It's a shark,' I said. The brown grey creature rolled up to the surface, staring up at us with a hunter's eye. 'A bull shark, I think.'

'My God!' Juliet was fascinated and alarmed all at once. 'I've never seen one in the wild.'

Luke drew back from the side of the boat. 'Will it jump up Mum?'

'No. But look – there it is again, it almost seems as if it's following us.'

And it was following. It kept pace with us for several minutes, showing glimpses of its rough brown side and predator's familiar sleek shape as it lolled around in our wake. There is a sailors' superstition that being followed by a shark means there'll be a death on board, but I decided against mentioning it.

Juliet shuddered. 'Well that's confirmed it for me – swimming off the boat in deep water is not a good idea with that kind of thing hanging around.'

We were approaching Charlestown Bay on the west coast of Canouan, which looks as if it is sited in the midst of an immense swimming pool thanks to its substantial sandy shallows. We negotiated our way between the channel markers and then dropped our anchor into the sand in the northeast corner of the bay. The wind was blowing hard and causing a large swell and the boat swung around on its anchor causing a dizzying sense of disorientation. We sat around in the cockpit trying to relax, but it was difficult.

'Can we go ashore?' asked Oscar as he looked across at the beach, where umbrellas and unoccupied deck chairs were laid out around a wooden beach bar. It was all part of a large, luxury hotel that looked beautiful, but strangely deserted – like a film set.

I thought about it for a minute. 'No, I'm afraid we can't Oscar. The outboard engine is too difficult to mount on the dinghy in this weather – we simply can't do it.'

He hung his head, crestfallen, and I felt guilty. These were the most difficult times, when nothing was happening and the boys were cooped up. There was a knock on the hull. 'Hey Skip!'

I leant over the side to see a man in a motorboat clinging onto our caprail and bumping up and down in the swell. He squinted up at me in what was supposed to be a grin but came across more as a snarl, his bloodshot eyes hazy and unfocused. 'Name's Lenny. You need anything?'

'No thanks,' I answered. 'We're just fine.'

He muttered and began to push off, but then Juliet came over.

'Wait a minute! Could you take us ashore?'

'Sure ting,' he shrugged.

'But we can't leave the boat Jules,' I said. 'We need to keep anchor watch in this wind.'

'Well you stay – I'll go with the boys.'

'Well, it would do the boys good I suppose . . .' Visions of a little sleep and some contented reading with a glass of rum floated before me. 'Well OK, if you're just going over to the hotel.'

'Can you take us to the hotel?' Juliet asked the man.

'You don' wanna go there missus – it real expensive. Lemme take you to the town over there,' he pointed around a little headland to where a cluster of houses ran down to the sea. 'Real nice bars and such.' He leered and a bolt of worry passed through me.

'No, just to the hotel,' I said firmly and he nodded sulkily.

Juliet rushed around packing a bag with swimming things and the boys leapt about with excitement. 'Be careful Jules,' I said feeling vulnerable as my family ventured into unfamiliar territory without me. I turned to Lenny, 'Will you bring them back when they're ready?'

'Sure ting Skip, I look after you family, don' worry.'

I helped her into the lurching craft. 'Sit in the bottom of the boat, boys!' I shouted, and they obediently crouched down. As Lenny gunned the throttle and turned the boat away I saw that he was, in fact, heading towards the town. I watched for a moment, thinking he might swing round and I saw Juliet remonstrating with him, but he shook his head and maintained his course.

'Hey! I shouted, waving my arms. 'Come back here!' He either couldn't or didn't want to hear me and I whistled loudly several times, ready to go down and radio for help if necessary, but then he began slowing down. Juliet was still arguing with him and I could see the boys peeping nervously over the gunwale. Reluctantly he turned the boat around and swung back towards the hotel. As they passed I shouted, 'To the hotel Lenny – I'm watching you,' and he raised a surly hand. I could still see them as they clambered onto the hotel's smart wooden jetty. Juliet talked to Lenny for a moment before he pushed off and drove towards the town. Juliet and the boys disappeared into the hotel, which still looked eerily deserted and a few minutes later they emerged in their swimming things. The boys ran towards the water and Juliet went across to the little beach bar where I saw her ordering drinks. There were only a few people on the beach, but enough to reassure me that they weren't alone and clearly the beach bar was in business. I settled back under the awning. All was well. I could stand down.

I woke feeling disorientated and confused and glanced at my watch. It was 6 p.m. and almost dark. Where the hell were they? I peered across at the beach: it was deserted. The wind had increased and whistled through the rigging, setting us spinning round the anchor, all the other boats around us moving in unison like a troupe of line-dancers. I began preparing supper, feeling deeply worried and cursing myself for letting them go. My instincts had been against it from the start, I realised: I didn't trust Lenny and now the weather was very wild. Who was to say that he wouldn't turn the boat over? Or the engine could break down – it looked pretty decrepit. I went back up to the cockpit and stared towards the shore. Some lights were on in the hotel, but there was no sign of any people. I looked at my watch again. Six-thirty. Scenes from all the most horrible abduction films began playing through my mind.

I ran through my options and realised they were limited. I couldn't go ashore to look for them because the outboard engine was too heavy for me to launch alone, even in the best of weather, and it was far too windy to row. I had no phone or way of contacting anyone other than the VHF radio, which wasn't monitored by any kind of emergency service. Still, it was my only option: perhaps somebody would be able to relay a message to the police. Just as I was contemplating making a call I heard Juliet's voice crackle out into the saloon.

'*Forever, Forever* . . . this is Juliet.'

'Jules!' I grabbed the handset. 'Switch to channel 68 . . . where are you?' I said.

'I know, sorry. I'm using the radio in the hotel. Lenny hasn't come back for us. We're waiting at the hotel, as we arranged, but he's half an hour late. I can't see any other way of getting back to the boat.'

'Isn't there anyone there who could give you a lift?'

'No, the place is deserted – there's just a skeleton staff here at the hotel. It's really rough at the jetty too.'

There was a pause. 'Well I suppose you'll just have to wait and hope he comes back . . . if not you'll have to stay in the hotel.'

'Not sure that's possible, it doesn't seem to be open. Anyway, hopefully he'll turn up.'

Another half hour passed and I heard nothing. I called the hotel and reached Juliet. The children were hungry and tired now and it was raining hard. Luckily they were able to shelter at the hotel, but they were running out of time as it was starting to close up.

Eventually, around nine o'clock, I heard them arrive. I shot up on deck to find them bumping hard up and down against the hull. 'Hey!' I shouted to Lenny. 'Where the hell were you?'

He looked even more befuddled than before. 'I got tied up in town man, couldn't do nothin' about it. You family all here safe and well.'

'Safe, maybe – I'm not so sure about well.' I lifted Luke to safety, wet and shivering. 'What do I owe you?'

'Well, what do you want to pay?' He held onto the gunwale and waited, the rain streaming down his face.

'Um . . . forty EC?'

'Forty EC! I due at least sixty– I take my life in my hands here!'

'Yes and you took my family's life in your hands too – and you're three hours late! Here – that's the most I'm giving you.' I passed him fifty Caribbean dollars and he counted it, then looked up at me with eyes glittering with dislike.

'You cheatin' me man.'

'No I'm not – you cheated me. It's only a couple of hundred metres to shore and my kids are soaked and freezing. Anything could have happened to them!'

'Oh they OK – just a bit of rain. Not like me man, I have to swim back to shore after I put this boat on the mooring – got a real mean boss and there are sharks in here too you know!' He pushed off, pointing a finger at me threateningly. 'Lenny not gonna forget this.'

'Yeah, well, I won't forget either – and if you want to rip people off, next time fix a price!'

I went down below to find Juliet putting the boys into their pyjamas. 'God, that was so scary Guy – the size of the waves at the pier! They must have been six feet high! I didn't think we were going to make it. And Lenny was totally wasted . . . oh my God, never again.'

The next day dawned blue and breezy and after breakfast Juliet and I looked at the chart. 'Right, where next?' I said, tracing a finger down to Grenada. We need to get to Trinidad within a week and it'll take twenty-four hours to get there from Grenada . . . working backwards I'd say we can only afford two more days in the Grenadines.'

We flipped through the pilot book to the Tobago Cays, an archipelago of five tiny uninhabited islands, four of which are encircled within the spectacular four-kilometer-long Horseshoe Reef. The approach looked tricky and I winced as I saw the plan, which showed mostly yellow, marking the areas of coral. There were complicated directions for the approach, involving leading lines, depth soundings and sketched elevations of the islands. Every instinct within me wanted to give it a wide berth, but I felt it would be defeatist to suggest it, so we lifted our anchor and set off.

It was only about five nautical miles to the Tobago Cays and as we drew near we found ourselves sailing through a zone stippled with sharp peaks of coral, little islands rising from a sea of perfect aquamarine and treacherous shallows where the coral showed green, yellow and brown through the water. Juliet steered whilst I hovered over the chart down below, calling out our course and double-checking our position on an almost constant basis, as even the slightest deviation from our course could lead us into terrible trouble. And yet even as we dreaded the danger that lurked beneath, we were utterly captivated, feasting our eyes on the kind of seascapes that we had only ever seen in our imagination. Following the leading marks, we steered towards a minuscule channel between two cays, Petit Rameau and Petit Bateau, and it took a great leap of faith, as we couldn't see the channel and had simply to steer towards the land. The depths beneath us fell steadily and we checked and rechecked and checked our course again, until at last, miraculously, the channel opened up before us. We inched our way along it, hoping that a boat wouldn't come in the other direction, as we had to stay exactly in the middle to have sufficient depth. The boys sat as still as stone, not uttering a single sound, as they knew now not to distract us when we were sailing close to or even beyond our capabilities. At one point we had three feet of clearance between our world and destruction and no space to turn if it grew shallower still. I began to sweat and willed the depth gauge to show a larger number – eventually it began to creep up again with agonising slowness. After a sharp turn to starboard, we drifted into an exquisite green pool set behind a reef that fizzed white with breaking waves filling the air with the scent of iodine and ozone. The reef provided shelter from the swell and we had an odd feeling of being both protected and exposed, as the ocean crashed and boomed all around us.

We pointed *Forever* into the stiff breeze and dropped the hook into deep, firm sand, watching to make sure it had dug in. Then we switched off the engine and opened all the hatches and as the wind scythed in it blew away the tension of our approach. We were under no illusions that we were experts, but still felt proud to have successfully negotiated such a notoriously difficult passage under sail. A year ago Juliet and I would never even have imagined finding ourselves in such a place: a natural jewel that could only be reached by boat and in this case, enthrallingly, our boat. We allowed ourselves a few minutes of pure joy and silently thanked the gods of life and luck that had brought us here.

'Let's go over there Mum.' Oscar pointed at a tiny desert island with a few palm trees and a tiny beach.

Juliet held up the plan in the pilot book and squinted at it. 'I think that's where the turtles are. OK, shall we do it?' She looked at me.

'I think I should stay with the boat, just in case.' I remembered J's stern advice. 'I don't feel good about leaving her.'

So, I helped Juliet launch the dinghy and outboard and then waved the family off. I lay back in the cockpit with a cold beer in one hand, feeling happy and lazy. A few minutes later, just as I was just dozing off, a large charter boat with about ten people in the cockpit entered the anchorage and began casting about for a spot to anchor. They circled a few times and I walked up to the bow to make sure they kept their distance but before I could do anything they dropped their anchor and began drifting directly over our line of chain. I raised a polite arm, hoping to make them aware of me, but to my horror noticed that *Forever* was beginning to drift backwards. A boat boy surged past and shouted, 'Hey Skip! Them charter people gone lifted your anchor – you gonna hit Jamesby!'

I looked behind me and saw that *Forever* was indeed fast approaching the little island, propelled by the 20-knot wind towards a wave-line that was breaking across its windward side, waiting like a set of hungry teeth. Fear curdled in my stomach and I almost tasted destruction as I looked about in a panic, wondering what to do. I turned the engine on and then rushed up to the bow to winch in the chain, but the watchful boat boy shot over. 'Hey man! Don't go takin' the chain in. Let it all out while he pulls up your anchor and untangles it!'

'Thanks!' I shouted and let the chain out fast – all 200 feet of it – bringing me closer to the cay. I held *Forever* in place with the engine and watched the charter boat, which was in total disarray. Five boat boys had appeared from nowhere and were zipping about like benevolent wasps, shouting instructions to the panicking crew as they winched in their chain in an attempt to free my anchor that soon appeared, ludicrously, on the bow of their boat.

'Quick – drop it!' I shouted and there was a flurry of waving and shouting as they dropped it into the sea. I got *Forever* moving ahead very slowly and then darted forward and began winching up the anchor. When it was up I repositioned her and dropped it once more, darting between wheel and winch as I did so. With relief I felt it bite the sand deeply and hold and *Forever* swung obediently into place. I turned the engine off and thought about waving my fist at the charter boat, but then decided against it, thinking of all the many times that people must have overridden the desire to do the same to me.

I flopped down in the cockpit and lay very still and the boat boy shot over. 'Hey man, you done good getting your anchor down again. I seen many people get in deep trouble in this spot I can tell you.'

'Thanks so much for your help – can I pay you something?' I fumbled about for some money.

He held up his hands. 'Just a beer is all I need today my friend!' I brought him a cold can from the fridge and he held up a fist in thanks.

A few days later we were on our way to Grenada and as we sailed down the coast of that spectacular island, nicknamed the 'island of spice', we wished that we had more time to explore it inland, where it is reputed to be fertile and beautiful with lush rainforest, waterfalls and rivers. Grenada is the last of the Windward Islands, our jumping-off point for Trinidad, the beginning of a completely different phase. We anchored in Prickly Bay on the southern end of the island, a wide, comfortable bay lined with luxurious houses, their highly manicured gardens out of place in this verdant, overgrown setting. Prickly Bay has a number of thriving boat repair businesses and is the home of many live-aboards, as we could see from the ubiquitous laundry and netting fixed along the lifelines to keep pets and children safely out of the water. We stocked up at a little grocery store and treated the boys to pizza at the marina restaurant, getting the usual mixed responses from people when we said we were going to Trinidad. A rich stream of anecdotes had followed us down the islands, leaving us with a confused sense of menace mixed with promise and hope.

'Oh, Trinidad's great,' one man said. 'It's so cheap down there – you won't need to shop for groceries, you'll be eating out every night. People are real friendly too.'

'You're going to Trinidad with the kids?' another exclaimed. 'You heard about the terrible things going on down there? Pirates, robbery, kidnappings . . . you wouldn't get me within a hundred miles of the place!'

We had heard conflicting stories about the workmanship too: Trinidad was well known for its many boatyards in Chaguaramas Harbour in the northwest and some said the work was cheap and good quality, others that it was overpriced and poor, or a mixture of the two. Either way, the only solution was to go and see for ourselves, keeping our wits about us and an eye on everything and everyone. For me, it was exciting to be going to this place that was just a few miles away from the coast of South America yet so different. Long ago I had been deeply moved by the beautiful writing of V. S. and Shiva Naipaul – two native Trinidadians whose prose had brought the place alive to me. It was also the home of steel pan and calypso music and famous for its world-renowned carnival.

The standard practice when sailing the 80-mile passage from Grenada is to leave at dusk and arrive in sight of the island by sun-up so that you can pass through the tricky entrances in good light. A great weight hung over the boat as we made preparations for leaving: this would be our first overnight passage with just Juliet and me in charge and we felt we were going into unfamiliar territory in more ways than one. Also, our prior experiences of overnight passages had been universally bad. We were determined to make this a good crossing and had learnt from past experience that the best way to handle overnight passages with children was to eat our evening meal early whilst there was still plenty of daylight, allowing clearing up to happen in relative comfort when everyone was still feeling perky. Then the children could stay up for as long as they wanted before settling into their sea-berths for the night. This time we had decided to make up two secure berths for the boys in the saloon that meant they could each have their own space within the most stable part of the boat amidships, which we hoped would help with seasickness. It also left their stern cabin free for the person off-watch.

I checked our water, fuel and engine and made sure that the correct charts were laid out, while Juliet repacked the contents of the abandon ship bag and stowed it carefully beneath the companionway steps. We put the flares in easily accessible places, as well as lifejackets, harnesses, waterproofs and – the ultimate piece of safety equipment – the Iridium satellite phone. I hoisted the sails and although old and grubby from plenty of use, they looked ready to serve. After supper, with the wind blowing steadily and from a perfect direction, at *Forever*'s best strength with no forecast of rough weather, we lifted the anchor and turned her bow to aim south for the last time. Once clear of the rocks around the mouth of Prickly Bay we turned the engine off and as the sails filled and the sheets tightened, *Forever* leant confidently into her course, rising and falling steadily like a well-schooled horse breaking into a good slow canter. I checked all the dials and instruments and heard the wind generator whirring behind me, keeping our batteries well fed. The boys came up in their pyjamas to say goodnight, smelling sweetly of talcum powder and toothpaste and I whispered into each of their ears that tomorrow they would wake up to see a different kind of island altogether. They lingered in the companionway for a while, watching the shape of Grenada become a silhouette as the sun sank beneath the horizon.

Juliet and I sat close together as the light died away and the sky settled serenely into deep shades of navy and black over the western horizon. Cold stars pricked out gaps in the spreading blanket of the night sky and for a while I lined up our course with a rising star low on the horizon. *Forever* surged on with enough wind to keep us at a good speed, but not so much that we feared straining her. Confident that all was well, I went below for a nap and left Juliet at the wheel.

By two in the morning we had made good progress. Just after Juliet had gone for a sleep I had spotted the Chacachacare Light, which was flashing out a powerful beam every ten seconds. There was one other boat keeping pace with us a mile or so away on our starboard side, its red navigation light showing that it was going in the same direction that we were. As always when we were underway, the VHF radio was tuned into the emergency and hailing channel, channel 16, and occasionally I heard fishermen making contact with each other. Then a light American accent crackled into the saloon.

'Vessel heading south on the Grenada Passage, on our port bow, this is sailing yacht *Marni*, do you copy?'

Silence – and then I realised the message was for us. I flipped on the autohelm and descended into the red nightglow of the saloon.

'*Marni*, this is *Forever* – switch to channel 13.' I switched channels and waited.

'*Forever*, you bound for Trinidad? Over.'

'Yes we are. Over.'

'Things pretty good out here, huh? Having a good ride?'

'Absolutely, nice and peaceful – no problems so far.'

'Great. Well I'm Dan, here with my wife Jane. We're heading down to be hauled out at Chaguaramas. Just call us if you need anything and we'll do the same.'

It felt reassuring to hear a friendly, capable-sounding voice in the darkness and I was conscious that there was a safety aspect to our conversation that he had no doubt thought of too. Anyone listening in would have heard us make contact and known that we were no longer sailing alone. Juliet and I continued to alternate sleep and watch and just as it was getting light I felt her shaking my shoulder. 'Guy! Come up, I need you.'

I struggled bleary-eyed up to the cockpit. 'Look.' She pointed at the depth gauge, which read four fathoms.

'Christ!' I looked around: the coast of Trinidad was dimly visible on the horizon and there was an oil rig on our starboard side, a good half-mile away – nothing that should have given any cause for alarm. 'But there are no shallows on this passage – I checked the chart.'

'I know, but it's been dropping steadily. At this speed if we hit a shoal we'd be buggered. Perhaps the GPS is playing up and we're not where we think we are. Can you check again?'

I went down to the chart table and checked and rechecked. As I did so Juliet called again.

'Guy! It's two point five fathoms – I'm turning round!'

I rushed up the companionway just as she spun the wheel into a 180-degree turn, sails crashing and the boom swinging across as she did so.

'Bloody hell Jules – you'll break something!' I began resetting the jib on the other tack. I switched on the chart plotter, which we'd turned off to save battery and again there was nothing to indicate any kind of shoal. 'It must be fine Jules – look, there's nothing there.'

She peered at it. 'I know, it doesn't make any sense. What do we do?'

I made an executive decision. 'We ignore it. Maybe it's something to do with that thing.' I pointed at the oil rig. 'Or some kind of malfunction – let's turn around.'

As we did we watched the gauge in trepidation, which continued to fall and then rose again to normal levels. Gradually we allowed ourselves to relax as no awful disaster unfolded and to enjoy watching Trinidad growing ever closer. Later we learnt that the depth readings flew about whenever we passed over stretches that were too deep for the sounder to register.

Powerful currents now pushed us to the west, combining with winds and currents coming out of the Gulf of Paria and around the north coast of Trinidad to cause a confused, rough sea. We had to work hard to maintain our course towards the Boca de Monos, a narrow passage between Monos Island and the coast of Trinidad. We had been warned that currents could run as high as 8 knots through the Boca and we were feeling nervous as we approached. The chart showed shallow patches to the west and the sea rose up steeply as it crammed through the narrow waterway, land towering on either side. With our hearts in our mouths we aimed for the middle of the passage, praying that our engine wouldn't fail. But gradually our nerves were overtaken by awe, as a new and different coastal landscape began to unfold on either side of us. The boys clung to the lifelines, mouths hanging open as they stared up at the thick tropical jungle that tumbled down the steep slopes of Trinidad on our port side. To starboard elephant grey columns of guano-streaked rock rose starkly from the water topped with thick vegetation with strands of lianas hanging down towards the surging green water.

Within this sculpted confusion of growth there were dainty wooden houses, designed with a fastidious attention to detail that exceeded any architecture that we had seen in the islands thus far. Beautiful rounded corners and wide porches were set high so as to give the best view of the water and the most exposure to cooling winds. Winding stairways cut into the rock spiralled down to elegant private jetties, where children sat fishing amidst sleek motorboats. As we turned towards Chaguaramas Harbour we passed close to the island of Gaspar Grande where there were more exquisite houses, set in the midst of luxuriant gardens and painted in pastel shades of blue, pink, yellow and white. One house was shaped like a lighthouse with crenellated wooden eaves and arches, and inside I glimpsed wood lined rooms with filled bookcases and luxurious fans turning slowly on the ceilings. Flowers hung from the white-painted wooden porch and we could see people sitting at a breakfast table, barefoot and relaxed. This was our first sight of the moneyed side of Trinidad, where – unlike many of the other islands – the rich are local people who have been successful in business, not foreign tourists.

Our charmed impression of the island fast disappeared as we approached the mighty port of Chaguaramas where the boatyards were, progressing carefully as we had been warned about the classic Latin disregard here for the rules of the road. Oil tankers lay at anchor and large merchant naval ships were tied up beside sweltering quaysides lined with large industrial buildings. The thick jungle on the surrounding hillsides stopped abruptly at the fenced enclosures of the immense boatyards, where a new forest of white masts took over as hundreds of boats stood propped up on stilts. The water was slicked with diesel and we noticed rubbish floating in it as we motored slowly around, trying to get a grip on the confusing jumble of the place. At the waterfront we could see the odd bar or restaurant peeping out from the clutter of boats, pontoons and yacht businesses, but there was nothing picturesque about it. This place was about business, pure and simple – we were here solely to get a job done.

'So, this is going to be our home for a while,' I said. Juliet was silent, dreading the prospect of living in *Forever* on dry land whilst she stood above the dust on stilts. 'Don't worry – it'll be fine,' I said brightly, trying to convince myself as much as her. 'And it should only take a few weeks to get the decks done.'

'I hope so,' she said and I knew what she was thinking. 'Weeks' in a boatyard was a long time out of our precious journey coupled with the certainty that we would see a lot of our hard-earned savings frittered away on boat work. We couldn't really afford to be boat owners and now we were also facing looking after our two children in a hot, dusty, mosquito-infested boatyard, without the solace of life-saving sea breezes or swimming. 'Well I hope it isn't any longer than a few weeks,' she said. 'We'll be paying for every day we spend on the hard – and we're pretty tight for time to get back up north before hurricane season.'

But the news got worse. When I radioed Powerboats, one of the biggest boatyards and the one that we had opted to use for our haul-out, there was no response. And then, after my third attempt, an American voice cut in. '*Forever*, I think you'll find that Powerboats is closed for the Carnival. Yeah, the whole island is shut down for the carnival today – you won't get anyone until the week after next.'

This was a blow and we decided to leave the harbour in search of somewhere quieter where we could swim and relax while we waited for things to open up again. 'At least we can see some of the carnival,' Juliet said. We motored out of Chaguaramas Bay a few miles around a promontory called Point Gourde to Hart's Cut Bay, a quiet anchorage where a little yacht club was located. On the way we passed close to Carrera Island, the site of a maximum-security prison, clearly visible, its crumbling white buildings set high on the hillside above us.

'Hey Dad, I can see some prisoners,' Oscar said, passing the binoculars to me – and sure enough a line of men sat on the wall, staring down at the sea. Below a line of men wearing ankle chains walked wearily down the steps towards a waiting launch. It could have been a scene from *Papillon* – Henri Charrière had once passed this way on his last escape from the penal islands off French Guiana. We were all silent as our bubble of floating prosperity and freedom slipped past the incarcerated men.

Hart's Cut Bay was a protected anchorage surrounded by the usual covering of thick vegetation humming with insects and birds. As this was Carnival time the little bay was already full of boats, but we found a good place amongst some other live-aboard yachts close to the shore. We were also right next to the Trinidad coastguard base, which we found reassuring, until we realised that we would be continually woken in the night by the noise of the boats coming in and out. Oscar and Luke wanted to swim and though we were dubious about the quality of the thick, greenly turgid water, we let them. Later we went ashore and met some other live-aboard sailors, who shrieked with horror when they heard the boys had swum there. 'Don't you do that again boys,' a sweetly concerned American woman said. 'We've seen some pretty brazen sharks cruising about in there. There's a real good swimming pool, right here.' The boys quickly joined a clutch of local and visiting children, excited to be amongst other kids. Juliet and I left them jumping and splashing in the pool and settled down at the bar. 'Hi!' the American woman joined us at our table. 'You just come in? I'm Kate – those are my kids playing with your two and that's my husband Jim.' She pointed at a man with a long ponytail locked in earnest conversation with a couple of other men at the bar. 'It's real nice for my two to meet some new kids – it's one of the downsides of this way of life that they miss out on making friends.'

'How long have you been sailing for?' Juliet asked.

'Two years now. We came down the US coast and have been all around the Caribbean – this is our fourth time down here. Hoping to make it across the Pacific one day.' She smiled.

'What about the kids and school?'

'We do a couple hours every day – it's no problem really. Hey Jim,' she called her husband over. 'Come and meet Juliet and Guy!'

Jim had the cynical expression of a third-rate academic and his look was immediately critical – I felt as he shook my hand as if he was assessing me and wasn't all that impressed. He didn't seem to like *Forever* much either. 'That your boat there?' he asked, pointing to where she lay serenely on her anchor. 'I haven't got much time for those heavy boats – they're too slow and all that woodwork . . .' He shook his head. 'What are you getting done down here?'

I resisted the urge to defend *Forever*'s honour and explained about getting our decks replaced and the other work we planned to do. 'It seems a lot of people come down here to get their work done.'

He laughed. 'Yeah, and a lot of them never leave. They just sit on the quay and do trips and tours, pot luck suppers and all that – they have no intention of ever going sailing. It's like a floating retirement home.' His tone became sneering: 'We call it the assisted living facility.'

I shifted in my seat. 'Well, I suppose people get old and maybe it beats a retirement home?'

He looked at me with an expression that read simply: 'I refuse to even consider a response to that.' There was a pause, during which Kate looked nervously towards him as if she was worried how he might handle the experience of a different opinion. He pulled at his beer, then turned away to lean on the bar, and she asked brightly, 'Anyway, while you guys are here, do you plan to see some of the carnival?'

'I guess so,' Juliet said. 'We didn't even know it was happening until today.'

Trinidad has a reputation as a party island and during the carnival everybody dropped everything to have a great time. The next day we headed into Port of Spain to have a look around. After three months at sea, the crowds and chaos and most of all the noise were joyfully overwhelming. The costumes were fantastic – carnival kings and queens, dressed in elaborate, fan-like outfits in jewel-like reds, blues and gold, adorned with feathers and sequins and spread out like the tails of birds of paradise, with followers dressed in more modest versions of the same costume. The parties were followed by flatbed trucks bearing huge sound systems moving slowly along the streets, all playing excruciatingly loud soca music that conflicted noisily when two or more of them got snarled up in traffic jams. People staggered along behind them, dancing and circling as if sent into a trance by the rhythm and reverberations of the music, and I noticed several elderly men and women sitting on the trucks right beside the speakers, looking completely unperturbed.

After a time the atmosphere on the streets felt more manic than celebratory, and I held onto the boys' hands tightly, until we'd had enough of being pushed and jostled, the boys a little scared as they were repeatedly trodden on in the crowd. I glanced at Juliet, wishing for a moment that we could have done this alone without little hands in our own. As it grew dark we caught a taxi back to the boat, hoping for some peace and quiet, only to find that there was a party going on there too. Across the road from the anchorage a makeshift venue had been rigged up and the revelry continued right through the night and into the next morning. The boys were spellbound by the sight of adult life in full 24-hour party mode and we ran the gauntlet of difficult questions as we sat in the cockpit having breakfast to the sound-track of bottles clattering and smashing on the rocks and the sight of couples emerging happily from the bushes.

'Dad, why is that lady pulling her undies on if she has already got a dress on?' Oscar asked with great seriousness. I glanced at Juliet as she stifled a grin and shrugged her shoulders before looking over and seeing the girl pulling a pair of red knickers up her legs before patting down her dress whilst behind her a well-built man emerged from their hide behind some boulders.

'Not sure Oscar – now, some orange juice boys?' They both jangled their heads up and down in excitement and I breathed a sigh of relief that they were not quite old enough to have followed up on their question.

The next week was a frustrating period of waiting. We spent our days hanging out at the yacht club and trying to get Oscar into a routine of school. It was hard, when the weather was hot and there was no quiet place to work. Try as he might, his eyes would soon glaze over and he would begin to stare into space, his mind clearly drifting off somewhere far away. Meanwhile Luke would continue his breezy, distracting approach, torturing Oscar by stopping and starting whenever he felt like it, doing work that mostly involved drawing and colouring in and looked much more fun. As Juliet struggled to explain division and fractions I marvelled at the patience of teachers, watching as she explained and re-explained the same sum and wondering how on earth people could elect to do this when it wasn't even their own child. On the other hand, the pupil being one's own child undoubtedly made things harder, as I found when I offered to help Oscar learn to tell the time.

'OK Oscar, sit down.' I was using my cheery, determinedly positive tone of voice and held up a drawing I'd made of a clock face. 'Look at this.'

'It's upside down Dad.'

'Oh.' I hastily turned it up the other way. 'Well look at it now. What time is it?' Before we had even got there I knew I had failed already.

Silence for a long time as Oscar screwed up his eyes and stared at it, clearly trying to rein in his mind from whatever far-off fantasy it was engaged in. 'One past six?'

'No, it's half past one. You see, the small hand tells you the hour and the big hand tells you the minutes. When the big hand is at the six it means it's half past something. Let's try again.' I drew another picture. 'What time is it now?'

'Three past six?'

He was getting nervous and I knew from my own childhood that this would make it even harder for him to think clearly. His brows knitted with tension. 'Six past three?'

'No. Let's try again,' and so I drew another clock, and then another clock, and then another and each time the young cub climbed even deeper into his mental block and I sank yet further into the cliché of bad-Dad. 'What time now Oscar? Remember what I told you!' I held up the clock and waited. He got it wrong. I slammed the paper down on the saloon table and looked at Juliet. 'Is this normal? I'm sure I could tell the time at seven.' I began again in an exaggeratedly patient driving instructor-type voice. 'OK Oscar, what time is it now?'

He was red in the face now and I could see either rage or tears weren't far away, but I was sure I could crack it if I just persisted a bit longer. He studied it for a moment and then his face lit up. At last, he's got it, I thought and sat back to enjoy the moment of triumph.

'Quarter to six!'

'No! It's half past nine!' I dropped my head into my hands, struggling to get back into patient, good-Dad mode. I decided to use harsh tactics. 'Right Oscar, if you don't get the next one right you aren't going swimming this afternoon.'

'What?' Oscar looked at Juliet. 'Mum, that's not fair!'

'No, it isn't. You've done enough for today Guy, thank you,' she said sarcastically. 'Now let me take over.' That was my last engagement with our shipboard school, apart from knot lessons.

At last the carnival was over and we were able to make contact with Powerboats. 'Sure thing,' a languid woman's voice purred over the radio when I asked if we could be hauled out. 'How does tomorrow morning sound, ten o'clock?' The next morning saw us back in Chaguaramas Harbour, circling round in the maritime equivalent of a doctor's waiting room. Shabby boats like ours from all over the world were being lifted in slings in readiness for their surgery; whilst sparkling clean ones, fresh from their refits, were being returned to the water under the watchful eyes of owners who looked so relieved that one might imagine they had just been freed from a period of penal hard labour.

'Hey *Forever*! Guy!' I turned and saw a spry man in his fifties and an equally vital looking woman standing in the cockpit of a neatly kept yacht. They held up their hands and waved, full of smiles and sunshine. 'Remember, we spoke on the way down?'

I read the boat's name, *Marni*, on the bow. 'Oh yes, of course – how're you doing?' I shouted.

'Doing great! Are you being hauled out as well?'

I nodded. 'Yes – Powerboats, this morning.'

'Us too – not for too long we hope. See you there!'

All was activity in the harbour. Sounds of hammering and cutting metal drifted across from great covered sheds and every-where people were busy hosing down, scraping, painting and varnishing, climbing up and down ladders and zipping around in pickups and forklift trucks. I ran my eye over *Forever*'s deck: she looked unkempt and unloved, and I felt happy that she would soon be having some much-needed attention, resolving to catch up on some minor maintenance myself. 'Forever, this is Powerboats,' the receptionist's honeyed voice drifted out from the radio. 'Can you make your way over to the travel-lift? Fenders on the starboard side please.'

Juliet put out the fenders and then got the warps ready on the bow while I steered Forever into the lifting dock. It felt as if she were being laid out on a hospital trolley and three men dressed in blue overalls, the nautical equivalent of hospital porters, buzzed around tying her off on either side. Then the anaesthetist approached, seated high above us at the controls of the travel hoist. Suitably for a man in his station everyone stood back respectfully as he stepped down, lighting a cigarette and looking Forever over coolly as he did so. He was wearing sunglasses and a baseball cap and bore more than a passing resemblance to Morgan Freeman.

'Hi, my name's Guy,' I said, holding out a hand.

He leant over and shook it. 'Michael. I'm gonna get you lifted up and put in place.' His accent was pure, deep rich Trinidad and his voice made even richer by tobacco.

'Where are you putting us?'

'Up behind the office, right next to the showers and toilets.' He looked over his sunglasses at the boys, who were sitting together on the deck. 'Hey kids – lookin' forward to spending some time on dry land?'

'Yes,' Oscar replied uncertainly. 'Are you going to lift us out of the water?'

He lifted his sunglasses and smiled and I saw deep smile lines gather around his eyes. 'Yes I am – do you trust me?'

'Um, not sure,' Oscar replied.

He laughed. 'Well at least you're honest. Don't worry buddy, I been doin' this job for many years. Where y'all from?'

'Scotland,' Oscar said proudly. 'We're going back home soon, when *Forever* is fixed.'

'You gonna sail back home in dis boat?' He sucked his teeth and looked *Forever* up and down. 'Got to be real careful with these two young boys in your care,' Michael wagged his finger at me sternly. 'Atlantic Ocean ain't no joke and I like these guys too much already.' He glanced at his watch and called round to his men. 'OK boys, let's get on with it.'

A flurry of activity began as they passed great canvas straps under *Forever*'s hull, guided by a man wearing a mask and snorkel who swam in the dirty water beneath the boat. He held up a thumb when they were in place and snorkelled away looking like a piece of driftwood. Then the machine began to hoist us up, belching great clouds of black smoke as it strained to lift *Forever*'s sixteen tonnes. Juliet and the boys stood on the quayside looking up anxiously as water sluiced off her and she was raised. It was strange to see her undersides revealed for the first time, looking surprisingly clean, free of weed and barnacles. I stood in the cockpit looking around nervously, not enjoying the sensation of floating in the air as the machine backed up and drove us slowly through the yard. The machine's engine strained as it climbed a slight hill past the Powerboats office, and then we rounded a corner and headed for a gap within a line of boats. As we were lowered into our allotted spot men quickly placed some stands at various strategic points on *Forever*'s hull and then the crane backed off, leaving us propped up high and dry between two boats that had rather ominously been abandoned half way through their repairs.

I climbed down the ladder to Juliet and the boys, and we stood looking around us, adjusting to this new world. I narrowed my eyes as a little zephyr of dust rose and curled its way along the road. 'Close your eyes boys,' I said. 'You don't want to get dust in them.' We peered out from between our eyelashes at resigned-looking yachties wandering in and out of the toilet block, clutching towels and bars of soap, the swing doors whumping backwards and forwards. And all the while the heat sat heavily on our shoulders. I felt as if we'd entered a Japanese prisoner-of-war camp and I half expected Alec Guinness to march past with a column of men whistling a hopeful tune.

By contrast, the staff were positively buoyant. One of the team returned driving a little truck and efficiently manoeuvred the pressure-washer into place beneath us, whistling along to his music all the time.

'Hey I'm Brian!' He raised a hand to Luke, who slapped it hard. 'I gonna wash your boat's bottom now – wanna watch?'

He turned on the machine and began scrubbing energetically at any sticky patches and singing to himself as he did so. He looked truly happy in his work and I wondered what he and his colleagues thought of us sailors, spending so much time and money on something that was essentially all about leisure. Oscar broke into my reverie. 'Dad, is it safe to go onboard?'

'I certainly hope so, because we're going to be climbing up and down that ladder every time we need to use the toilet for the next six weeks – we won't be able to use the heads on *Forever*.'

Oscar began climbing up the ladder, closely followed by Luke, who took hold of the sides and placed one foot carefully on the bottom rung. 'Not so fast Luke,' I reached out and stopped him. 'Only one on the ladder at a time – otherwise you could get knocked off by the person above you.'

One by one we all climbed up the ladder, negotiating the tricky job of stepping over the top of it onto the deck, which was now 20 feet above the ground. It felt so wrong to look around and see land in place of the sea, the beauty of our watery surroundings replaced by the grimy chaos of the boatyard. Besides that Juliet and I were both realising the enormity of what we were taking on – watching the children climb up the ladder had been hair-raising and falling off the boat here presented perhaps a greater hazard than doing so at sea. A whole new set of rules had to be devised: just when we'd begun to get the hang of living at sea, now we had to take up a life like the old woman who lived in a shoe.

The heat was oppressive and we slumped in the saloon, not enjoying the sudden stillness of everything. I pushed open a hatch and a column of mosquitoes descended.

'Quick, close it!' Juliet had a phobia of all biting insects. 'We'll have to put the mosquito screens on. Oh God.' She dropped her head in despair, 'This is going to be awful – I can't believe we've got to be here . . .'

'I'm going over to the office to get the names of some tradesmen – the sooner we get on with our jobs the sooner we can get back in the water. And maybe it won't be as long as we think. Want to come with me boys?'

I helped the boys onto the top of the ladder, showing them how to hold onto the lifelines for support as they did so. At the bottom I walked slowly round *Forever*, examining her homely rounded curves and sturdy keel and feeling proud to own such a strong, seaworthy boat. She deserves this attention, I thought: we've come a long way together and she hasn't let us down. The boys stopped and stood with their hands on her comely sides. They splayed their fingers and pushed at her bulk looking like bright little fish against the dark sides of a whale.

In the office I asked the receptionist if there was anyone I could talk to about the work we needed to get done and she pointed me to Brent's office. I sent the boys down to play in the yard with dire warnings about being careful and not talking to strangers, and then knocked tentatively before going through the open door. Brent swung round on his chair, welcoming me to Trinidad. A semi-naked woman adorned his screen saver and he was perfectly groomed, with hair combed back and sunglasses hanging on the V of his shirt. He lost no time in getting down to business. 'So Guy, what work you plannin' on getting done here?'

'Well, the biggest job is going to be getting our decks replaced I suppose.'

'OK. You gonna do it in gel coat?'

I nodded: Juliet and I had agreed not to replace the teak, which was expensive and difficult to maintain. 'I can recommend a real good guy for that – Brian, his name is. I'll call him up and get him to come round and see you. Anything else?'

'The varnishing needs to be done, I could do it myself, but since we're getting the decks done . . .'

He waved a hand. 'No, you don't want to be doin' that. I contact Anthony – he's the best varnish man around here. What else?'

'We need to get the rigging checked and I've got a problem with the freezer compressor . . .' I frowned. 'We need an electrician too – we've got some kind of electrical leakage. Oh and we need to get the fuel tanks cleaned and of course the engine will need looking at . . .'

The list continued and he asked a few questions and made notes busily on a pad. When I'd finished he lifted his head. 'That's a lot of work Guy – looks like you're gonna be with us for a while.'

'I know,' I nodded glumly, 'a few weeks I imagine.'

'A few weeks?' He laughed, reached over and tapped a cigarette from a pack and offered me one. I took it feeling like a man about to be given bad news.

A zippo clinked open and he sat back expelling a funnel of blue smoke. 'There's no way you're gonna get all this work done in that time. I say two months if you're lucky.' He gave me a sympathetic grimace. 'That's a lot of work you're talking about and all specialist stuff too. Prices are fair here, but still . . . do you need to get it all done now?'

'Well we're going to be sailing across the Atlantic in a couple of months . . .'

'Then you do. You need to know your boat is in tip-top condition if you're doing an ocean crossing – don't want to take no chances. Only thing you could maybe skip is the varnishing, but if you spending all that money you don't want the boat letting you down by lookin' shabby . . .' He shrugged and I could see his logic: in for a penny, in for a pound. I sucked on the cigarette hard and made a mental note to take up secret smoking for as long as we were incarcerated.

He promised to send various tradesmen round to see me and as I made my way back down the steps into the fetid boatyard it felt as if I had been given a terminal diagnosis. How on earth was I going to break the news to Juliet that we would probably be here longer than three weeks? As I made my way towards our dusty parking space I remembered the line of broken prisoners in ankle chains. I looked down and noticed that I had begun to shuffle through the dust.

I thought briefly about not telling her, but then realised it would be impossible. I looked around but couldn't see the boys anywhere and felt a jolt of panic. 'Oscar, Luke!' I shouted. 'Boys, where are you?'

'Here Dad!' I heard Oscar's voice calling faintly and followed the sound to find them standing at the top of a ladder on the deck of a sturdy, battered fishing boat with several burly men working around them.

'Look Dad, these guys catch tuna!' Oscar said and the men grinned at me, showing glints of gold teeth. They were Venezuelan and looked tough and powerful and I greeted them in what scant Spanish words I knew before calling the boys down, who regretfully said their goodbyes before being lowered to me on a chain of strong arms.

Juliet was not happy to hear the news. 'Two months? God no!'

I held my hands out. 'Well what choice do we have?'

'We don't.' She lay slumped for a few moments and then sat up and pulled her hands away from her face. 'But still, we're better off than some people – I just met an English woman in the laundry room who has been here for eight years. She and her husband have been trying to get their boat sorted out, but they keep running out of money and he's had to get a job locally, trying to pay off their debts.'

'God, that's awful.' I shook my head, appalled at the thought. 'Oscar would be fifteen by the time we'd been here that long – just as well they don't have any kids.'

'But they do – they've got a four year old daughter who's lived in the boatyard all her life and they've sold up everything back in the UK, so they can't go back. The worst of it is, Sarah's never sailed in her life, so she doesn't even know if she'll like it. Crazy, huh? So we're not that badly off . . . we've just got to work hard and get out of here as soon as we can. And try to make our time here as comfortable as possible in the meantime,' she stopped to flap at a mosquito that was buzzing around her face. 'We can start by buying some mosquito coils and getting the insect screens up.'

That night we took the boys over to have a shower before bed and I waited outside listening to their shouts of joy as Juliet pushed them under the cold water. The sun was setting and I revelled in a rare moment of coolness as a breeze stole in across the boatyard from the sea. Work had stopped in the yard apart from the odd boat that was obviously on a tight schedule, where arc lights illuminated the continuing labour. Exhausted dust-caked workers filed past, heading to catch buses home to Port of Spain, and boat-owners sat high and dry in their cockpits staring out towards the horizon, no doubt dreaming about the day they'd get back to sea, and drowning their sorrows in booze meanwhile.

The family emerged from the shower room, Juliet chasing after the boys to towel-dry their heads and them playing their usual game of running away. As we walked back to the boat they scampered about ahead of us, laughing and chattering.

Juliet nodded towards them. 'They're going to be fine here – it's amazing how resilient kids can be, and even more so if your reality has just turned into a giant sand-pit.' We laughed and kicked the sand a little as we walked. 'I'm more worried about us: we have to make sure the bills don't get out of control. Sarah told me there's a saying around here, "no cash, no splash".'

She gave me a significant look. 'Let's just not get into that situation.'

FOURTEEN

BOATYARD LIFE

10.40N: 61.38W

I stared at Oscar: he'd been so badly bitten that he looked as though he had chickenpox. We'd been in the boatyard for a while and it was February – the dry-season heat and mosquitoes were even worse than we'd expected. *Forever* was now encased in a semi-circular plastic dome, so that work could continue on the decks without interruption from the fierce tropical rainstorms that were getting heavier and more frequent each day. The plastic cover cut out what little breeze there was and reduced the interior of the boat to virtual darkness, so that we were surprised anew every time we emerged into the harsh sunshine. It also seemed to act as a gathering point for the local mosquitoes, a particularly fierce variety with long, jauntily striped legs. We'd put mosquito screens on all the portholes and tried using coils, sprays, hideous plug-in chemicals or even a combination of all three, but nothing seemed to deter them and now constant scratching had been added to the purgatory of life in the yard.

Juliet was on the laptop – it was one of the small compensations of being ashore that we had constant internet access. 'Oh shit!' She put her hand to her mouth. 'Have you noticed that those mosquitoes bite during the day? Apparently, they're Asian tigers, the ones that carry dengue fever, and they breed in all that standing water everywhere in this yard. We'll need to make sure that we keep all the hatches shut as well as the companionway.'

'But we'll die of heat.' I couldn't bear this stifling humidity as it was.

She sighed. 'I think we need to get an air conditioning unit. You can rent them by the day from Powerboats.'

I closed my eyes briefly in what Juliet and I now called the 'cruiser's blink', which we had observed in other sailors. The long-term sailor has learnt that there is no point in shouting about yet another bill or snippet of bad news – it's a waste of energy. Rather he absorbs the blow and internalises it, a long slow blink the only external response he allows himself.

But it wasn't such a bad idea. Later that morning a technician came and fitted a unit over the hatch above our bunk and thirty minutes later the boat was transformed into a haven of coolness. Now there was a constant buzzing noise in the background and the mosquitoes still flooded in whenever we came in or out of the hatch but it was worth it. Oscar was able to get on with school now that the boat was cooler and he got into a routine of doing a couple of hours each morning while I worked on deck with the tradesmen. Luke drifted between us, hanging out with me on deck, colouring in beside his brother or playing alone in the dust beneath the boat. After a couple of weeks we were beginning to get used to this new life in the nautical equivalent of a trailer park and I began to understand how months, even years, could slip by almost unnoticed.

It had become our custom once or twice a week to eat lunch at the Roti hut, which was run by the wives of some of the Indian contractors. 'Together we aspire, together we achieve' is Trinidad's motto and Trinis aren't hung up about colour – in fact they are clearly proud of their country's mix of ethnic and cultural groups, which has resulted in, amongst other things, some great cooking and some of the world's most beautiful women (as I would teasingly keep telling Juliet). Today slightly over half the population is Indo-Trinidadian and the Roti hut was generally considered one of the best places to eat in the boatyard – many of the workmen ate there, as did the true gourmets of the boatyard, the French.

There was always a cheerful atmosphere at lunchtime as the rotund women served up rotis filled with their own versions of various curries, including goat. Among the sailors and contractors you could hear a hotchpotch of languages and accents, ranging from Guyanian dialects to downtown Miami. But the roti hut was essentially French turf and in a far corner an earnest group of Frenchmen would invariably be huddled in a circle around a chessboard, smoking profusely and discussing tactics in their dusky lugubrious voices. Dressed in improbably short shorts twinned with faded but obviously once good-quality shirts, they looked universally mournful. When Oscar and Luke waved at them they were met with Gallic looks of blank indifference, unlike with the other nationalities, who were almost all friendly, with the occasional exception of the British who still carried our islanders' cynicism everywhere like a bug carries its shell.

The Americans in particular would do anything for a chat and it was they who mostly ran the cruisers' net that was broadcast each morning on the VHF radio and listened to religiously by all boat-owners. Trades, information and gossip were all conveyed over the net and we appreciated it as never before now that we were in the market for bargains, advice and ideas for entertainment while we were captive in the yard. The boys had settled into boatyard life well and ran about like little scrap-yard dogs, getting to know every nook and cranny. They had formed a little tribe with some of the Trini workmen's children, and from time to time I would stop work and look up to see them shooting past, chasing a ball or gathered in an earnest observational knot beside a lizard-covered wall. Oscar and Luke were becoming notorious characters amongst the residents of the boatyard and made friends with everyone from the cats to the workmen. On almost every boat they passed a hand would raise in greeting and all my advice regarding going on strangers' boats became redundant as they set up a little network of visits that they would religiously follow each morning. Often they would come home clutching home-baked cookies, colouring books and various odd gifts in the form of redundant pieces of boat equipment. Once, in a real scoop, someone gave them a working set of walkie-talkies, which they played with for days, hiding from each other in and around the rows of boats. But mostly they made use of what they found lying around and spent days playing with a discarded shopping trolley, pushing each other around like a couple of little vagrants. If they felt threatened by other kids, they would unite to drive the offender from their patch, and once I saw a local boy shoot off with Oscar and Luke in hot pursuit. When they pulled up in a little cloud of their kicked up dust I heard Oscar shouting, 'And don't come back around here again!' followed by, 'Yeah don't come back!' from Luke, who stood with hands on hips and chest puffed out like a little fighting cockerel . . . just behind his brother.

I had now pulled all the old rotten teak from the deck and *Forever* lay naked and stained, waiting for her new gel coat. I walked over to the tradesmen's sheds to meet Brian, nicknamed 'The Professor' because of his in-depth knowledge of all things boat-surface related. I found him in a tiny cell of a space reeking of chemicals, peeling a banana with delicate fingers beside an immaculately organised desk. He was a native of Guyana, in his fifties, and had worked in the yard for years. 'Well that's her ready for you Brian,' I said. My input ended at the ripping-up stage and now it needed the hand of an expert to give our boat the pristine finish she deserved.

As the weeks passed, our world became ever more hellish as *Forever* filled with dust and the sound of sanding, and layers of itchy grit covered our bodies as we fell into our bunks each night. Then the smell of fibreglass started clearing out our noses and making our eyes smart. By now Anthony had started work on *Forever*'s beautiful woodwork, bringing it back to its former glory by sanding and then painting it lovingly with endless layers of varnish. Unlike Brian, who was a religious and cerebral man, Tony was a good-time guy; a Rastafarian with a wicked sense of humour, and soon a tacit war had set in between them regarding their entertainment while they worked. Brian liked to listen to religious radio programmes, a mixture of gospel music interspersed with hectoring sermons about Trinidad's problems with domestic violence, teenage pregnancy and single-parent families. Tony on the other hand liked to listen to music, played loud until Brian's delicate finger would attempt to lower the volume or change the channel only to be swatted away by Tony's gold ringed hand. To escape the fumes and the rising tension, Juliet and the boys more or less took up residence during the daytime at a nearby desolate hotel, whose huge swimming pool compensated for its Bates-Motel-like atmosphere. I spent my days running about doing errands, sourcing boat parts and tracking down contractors – no doubt looking like just another boat-weary, careworn sailor itching to get back out to sea.

To break the routine we tried to see something of the island and we got lifts to the local markets from an industrious and superbly gifted Indian named Jesse James. Beloved of the cruisers' net, he ran a little office beside the boatyard with his extended family and made his living by becoming a kind of life-support machine to the sailors who'd taken up residence on stilts, with little hope of ever getting further than the quay. He was always contactable, always had time for a chat and imbued everything with the warmth that we had come to expect from the people of Trinidad. We visited the windward beaches to watch immense female leatherback turtles emerge darkly from the sea looking like black Volkswagens and haul themselves up in the moonlight to lay their eggs, the boys as much entranced by being on the windswept beach at midnight as they were by the creatures themselves. Once a week we would wait outside the gates of the boatyard to catch a maxi-taxi to town to buy groceries. These were bright yellow mini-buses run as a kind of hybrid between a bus, a taxi and a friend's car. Wasp-like, they zipped all over the island hooting to people they passed at the roadside, slowing to see if a lift was required. They were always in a frantic hurry and terrorised us by overtaking on corners.

Saturday night was shark-bake night at a restaurant on the other side of the bay, a local delicacy of shark meat served with various relishes in soft white bread. It sounded appalling to me, particularly as I objected in principle to eating shark, but as there was such a cheerful atmosphere amongst the boatyard captives I was happy to go along. And it was here that we met David, a tall, shambling man with long white hair hanging from a baseball cap and a drooping moustache. Juliet and I both liked him immediately and he invited us on board *Rogue*, his once beautiful but now dilapidated sailing yacht, on which he was eternally working in the hope of getting back to sea.

Over time the boys, in their endless pursuit of snacks and tidbits, honoured David and Sandy with a place on their daily visiting schedule. We were full of respect for them, stuck as they were in the classic trap of the boatyard, having ploughed everything they had into *Rogue* but never quite reaching the point where she was seaworthy. But they refused to give up and their cheerfulness was inspiring. David was in his late sixties and had clearly been a towering physical specimen in his youth, but a long struggle with diabetes had taken its toll on his body and left him a little battered. He was a man after my own heart – always looking for the next adventure. Unlike me, perhaps, he greeted each new day with an unsinkable sense of optimism – and the only time I had seen David get angry was when somebody questioned the integrity of his hero, Barack Obama. He couldn't hear a thing against him.

'Hey, I've had a great time in life,' he told me one afternoon, as we sat enjoying a beer in *Rogue*'s chaotic cockpit. 'When I was young I was fighting the system and after the marines I became a hippie. I used to climb mountains with my friends, chase girls and then go fishing in Alaska to earn it all back again. I had a real successful life once: I had a good job, a wife and a big house in Sun Valley, California.' He leant back and laughed. 'I got real into it too, the whole suburban thing – I even got hooked on golf. It got so that once, after a bad game, I came home in a temper. My wife, she asked me what was wrong and I said' – he winced at the memory – 'I said, "Honey, I just played the worst game of golf in my life".'

He passed me another can of beer. 'Anyway, she tilted her head to one side and said "David, does that make you a bad man?" That's when I realised I was gettin' kinda obsessive.'

We laughed. 'But then we got divorced, she got the house and here I am. I wouldn't have believed that I could end up dead broke, but it happened . . . You never can be sure where life's gonna take you.' He paused and gazed out over the boatyard. 'But that's all part of the game, ain't it?'

He loved to hear of our plans to sail back to Scotland. Whenever it came up a misty look came into his eyes. 'My mother was born in Glasgow,' David said, 'I've always wanted to see the home isles.'

'That's not far from where we're heading. We'll be sailing back to the west coast, to the Isle of Mull where we live.'

'Some day we'll sail over to see you,' he said, 'I've always meant to get there – just never got a chance.' A little silence settled around us.

And then I had a rash moment and said half-jokingly, 'Well we might need some extra crew – perhaps you could come with us!'

'Oh my God!' He slammed down his can of beer. 'I would come with you in a flat-assed minute!' He bit his lip and shook his head. 'That would be something. Though I'm not as fit as I used to be . . . But hell, I'd give it a go! Are you serious?'

To my surprise, I found I was. 'Yes. We're not really sure yet how or when we're going to cross, but if we need crew I'll let you know.'

He looked at me in silence for a moment. 'You'll never know what that means to me Guy, whether it happens or not – just the fact of you offering.' The lines around his warm, friendly eyes creased into a smile.

By now it was the end of March and we had already exceeded our cut-off time of eight weeks. Brian had nearly completed his work on the decks and *Forever* was proudly sporting a shiny new white layer of gel coat, looking glossier and more businesslike than she ever had before. Her woodwork gleamed rich brown beneath its layers of varnish, and other problems, such as the electrical leakage, had mercifully been resolved. Now it just remained to tie up a few final jobs, such as servicing the engine and checking the life raft and rigging. Then we would face the grand reckoning, which we knew wasn't going to be pretty. In the meantime, we tried to enjoy our last days in the boatyard, in the knowledge that we would soon be moving on.

At last we reached the end of the refit and our credit cards took another hard hit as we settled what we owed. Cut-price or not, we were broke. But the work had been good quality and the pain was almost worth it when we looked at *Forever*, gleaming on her stilts above the dusty ground and looking like a doughty seabird, frozen for a moment before spreading her wings to take off.

A few days before we were due to leave I stopped to talk to Tom, a young Canadian who had been tirelessly working on his small steel-hulled sailing yacht. He lived alone with just a mongrel for company and I rarely saw him stop work, so driven was he to get back into the water. In the morning I'd pass by early and he'd already be hidden behind a shower of sparks, or buried within the bowels of his little universe, hammering away. His dog had scraped away the stones to make a nest in the dust in the cool shadow beneath his master's boat and would lie with his head propped on caramel-coloured legs, watching him work with that expression of incredulity mixed with resignation that dogs often have when they watch their owners doing things.

But on this particular afternoon he was doing something unusual: relaxing. He had pulled up a chock and was seated in the shade with a beer and a cigarette. Around the white area where his welding goggles had been his skin was covered with a thick layer of grime and he looked tired but happy. I waved and he raised a grease-smeared hand.

'Are you nearly off?' I stopped in the full glare of the white-hot sun.

'Yeah – can't wait', he replied. 'I'm leaving tomorrow morning. I won't be alone this time – found a girl who's going to crew me up north.'

'Well, good luck with everything.' I knew just how much Tom wanted to be back on the water, and hoped it would soon be us.

Listening to the net one morning over breakfast we heard an anxious caller asking if anyone had anything definite on a rumour about an incidence of piracy nearby in which a yacht had been 'shot up really badly'. We had all stopped eating and sat frozen in horror, the chill of this news spreading through *Forever* and no doubt every other boat in the boatyard. Normally there was a bit of enjoyment of these dramas, but this one was too close to home.

A boat named *Blue-Note* chipped in. 'Yes, we heard this too – happened yesterday morning, some guy got shot at by four men in a pirogue. He was twenty-four nautical miles north apparently, pretty close to the oil rigs. They tried to board but the sea was too rough – he was firing flares back at them and he had a dog on board which was being real fierce, that might have deterred them. He's lucky that his boat was steel or he might have been sunk.'

There was a pause as the news sank in, then the host's voice returned.

'Anyone else on board with him?'

'Yes, a female crew member – and that dog.'

Juliet and I stared at each in horror: it had to be Tom.

'Well this is very serious news indeed, exactly what we didn't want to hear. Did you hear if they got to Grenada safely?'

'Yes, we heard he got into Prickly Bay yesterday morning. Pretty shaken up but nobody was injured, thank goodness.'

The man then read out the GPS position of the attack.

I stood up and switched the radio off, then pulled out the chart to mark where the attack had occurred. It was right in the middle of the normal route from Trinidad back up to Grenada: right where we would be passing. I shook my head, feeling deeply worried.

'Dad, are we going to be killed by pirates?' Oscar asked, looking scared.

'Of course not Ozzy, we'll be fine, don't worry.' I flashed a glance at Juliet, who looked white with fear.

Later I went down to the bar and found a group of veteran American sailors taking a break from their morning's work. As I approached a few held up hands and gave me weary smiles, allowing me into their smoky circle. The talk was all about piracy.

'Well a month ago they killed one skipper and handicapped his crewman,' one said.

'Where was that?'

'Margarita.'

'That's not far from here, hey?' Heads shook and the men looked at the floor, pulling hard on the tobacco.

'What would you do about it – cross without navigation lights?'

'Or go in convoy perhaps.'

'What about the coastguard – they doin' anything about it?'

Bitter laughter broke out. 'No way – they're not interested. Apparently the guy called them on the radio, but they wouldn't come out.'

'But hell, don't they see this will stop boats coming down here? It ain't good for Trinidad if it gets a reputation for this kinda thing.'

'What about carrying a gun?' I asked, and they all turned to look at me.

A sage old campaigner shook his head. 'Only works if you have more than one armed boat travelling together – that way the fire can be focused and support given. If you're on your own it just becomes a one-on-one fight. That can be real bad if there are more than one of them shooting.'

'And firearms are illegal in most of the Caribbean,' another said. 'Most of the islands you have to hand them in, which becomes a real pain in the ass.'

By the end of the day it was confirmed that it was indeed Tom's boat and Chaguaramas was humming with a mixture of fear, excitement and anger as all those preparing to get back to the water grappled with this new concern. Attacks were not uncommon in Venezuela, which was after all very close by, but it was rare to hear of such an incident on the Grenada Passage, which was unavoidable if one wanted to get back north. I was all in favour of self-defence, but a firearm would be nigh on impossible to get hold of in the time we had left on land, so instead I bought a flare gun and a bucket of phosphorous flares in the vain hope that if anything happened I could at least hope to fill an approaching vessel with white hot fire.

The situation was fraught with dilemmas. Would firing flares just act like the piratical equivalent of poking a hornet's nest with a stick? Was there any point in fighting back if your means were so limited? A sailor had told me of the New Zealand sailor and environmentalist Sir Peter Blake, who'd been killed by Brazilian pirates on a remote river. His mistake was that he'd pulled a shotgun out, while the rest of his crew, who were unarmed, remained unhurt. Yet Juliet and I both instinctively agreed that we would have to at least make an attempt at self-defence – trusting our own and the children's lives to pirates was beyond contemplation. In Tom's case the pirates had come at him shooting, and they had got off scot-free – for all we knew might be planning another attack even now.

All this worry somewhat dented our excitement about getting back to sea. When the day of our 'splash' finally dawned I felt a mix of emotions – a hazy film of fear that seemed to lurk permanently in my mind as well as a sense of pride as we watched the workmen slipping the canvas straps over the rounded underbelly of *Forever*, who was gleaming and ready to go.

The crane puffed black smoke, roaring madly as it lifted us, and we drove slowly down through the yard, waving to all our newly made friends, the tradesmen and the Venezuelan fishermen as we inched our way towards the sea.

Eventually we reached the dock and as Michael gently lowered *Forever* into the water I was almost surprised to find that she still floated. We tied her off and then went round hugging and shaking hands with so many people that I felt a lump gather in my throat. As I hugged David he pressed something into my hand and I looked down and saw it was an old flare gun. 'You take this,' he said. 'You got real precious cargo. Hope you won't need to use it though.'

I thanked him, my heart lurching with dread at the thought. 'We'll be in touch. And maybe that Atlantic crossing might happen – who knows?'

I turned to see Luke clinging to Brian the deck man like a long-lost brother and Oscar giving his ragged but much-loved football to one of the dockyard children who had come to say goodbye. And then we climbed onboard and got back into our familiar positions: the boys knew the drill and tucked out of the way in the cockpit as Juliet untied the lines, while I stood ready at the helm. I switched on the engine, relieved to hear it start so well, and we went hard astern, pulling out into the grubby harbour and swinging around to head away. I hooted the foghorn and Juliet whistled and all the yachts around us joined in, hooting and waving and shouting good luck, the men at the yard shouting loudest of all. We motored out of the harbour, feeling the ties of friendship pulling us. Around the corner, we dropped our anchor in the auspiciously named Scotland Bay, a deep, mysterious inlet all set about with thick jungle. The water lapped gently at *Forever*'s sides, birdsong and the scent of woodland filled the air and it felt good to be at last back on the water, a cool breeze blowing through the boat. That night a heavy rain fell, washing the decks clean. The scuppers ran with dark water for several minutes before they ran clear, as if the Gods were purging *Forever* before her journey North. While the children slept we studied the chart, looking anxiously at the cross that marked the spot near the oil rigs where the attack had occurred. We planned to leave early the next morning, opting to make the passage in daylight rather than the usual practice of crossing overnight, so that we would at least be able to see any potential marauder approaching. If we arrived in Grenada too late to enter the harbour we would simply continue north, preferring that option to risking the Grenada Passage in darkness.

With Juliet watching closely, I picked up a pencil and carefully drew a course to steer around the spot where the attack had occurred, taking us well east of the normal route before turning northwest for Grenada. We hoped that by staying off the beaten track we would avoid trouble; it wasn't much comfort, but it was the best choice available to us.

FIFTEEN

THE REAL PIRATES
OF THE CARIBBEAN

10.42N: 61.39W

At four in the morning the woods around the bay filled with a deep throaty sound like the engines of a jet aircraft.

'What the hell is that?' Juliet said as she opened her eyes.

'Don't know.' I sat bolt upright. The sound rose to a crescendo, ebbed and died away for a few moments before building up again. It was so loud that the trees seemed almost to tremble.

'Dad, is it lions?' Oscar had climbed into our bunk next to Juliet. 'No Ozzy.' I dropped back down to the bunk. 'I think it must be the howler monkeys. Remember the monkeys we saw in the jungle near the boatyard? They're the loudest land animals on the planet. You can hear them from about three miles away! Go and see if you can spot them.'

He took the binoculars and climbed up to the cockpit. A moment later he returned. 'I can see them Dad – they're in the trees, all around us!'

We tried to get back to sleep but the eerie howl was far from reassuring for our already jangling nerves, and by dawn it sounded as if we were surrounded by hundreds of Tibetan monks lost in an ancient Buddhist incantation. At 5 a.m. we gave up, lifted the anchor and slipped out of the throbbing bay, the sinister figures of the monkeys moving like shadows amongst the trees.

As we cleared the Boca I went below to work out our course, calling up to Juliet who deftly turned *Forever* to point northeast. The sea was rough, as we had known it would be, but we winched her sails in tight to get as close to the wind as possible and soon found ourselves flying along at 7 knots. By 9 a.m. we were well out to sea and beginning to forget our fears as we lost ourselves in the delirium of movement; water, sunshine and wind combining to fill our sails and minds with happiness. Now our dread seemed exaggerated as I scanned 360 degrees around us for shipping. Nothing was visible, apart from the dim shape of the nearer of the two oil rigs a couple of miles away. I flipped on the autohelm and went below to check the chart.

The boys were playing quietly in their cabin and Juliet was in the galley making tea. 'I'm going to adjust our course to the west,' I said. 'We're pretty well past the oil rigs and if we turn west a bit the wind will come round onto the beam so we can make better time. We're doing well – at this rate we should reach Prickly Bay before dark.'

'We're not so far from the rigs as we planned though, are we?' she said. 'The current must have been taking us further west than we thought.'

'I know, but we're almost past them now – I think we can afford to relax.'

I went back up to the helm and Juliet came up with cups of tea. I adjusted our course and then slackened off the sails a little, which resulted in an instantly smoother motion and increase in speed. We settled back to drink our tea, staring out to the west.

A couple of moments later, Juliet stopped mid-sip and lowered the mug. 'What's that over there?' she put down her mug and pointed. 'Wait – it disappeared behind a wave. There, a boat. Can you see it?'

Sure enough, there was a small blue boat, half a mile away or so, barely discernible against the colour of the sea. I focused the binoculars on the horizon, losing sight of the little boat every few seconds as it disappeared behind the waves. But it was there all right: I could see the pointed shape of its bow and with sickening dread I realised it was a dark-blue pirogue. Small wooden fishing boats, pirogues are characteristic of the region, often powered by one or more powerful outboards. Frequently they are used to smuggle drugs or to intercept yachts.

My heart clamoured and took on an icy beat. The pirogue was well downwind of us but I knew that the power of their engine would far exceed ours and they could be alongside us in minutes. I couldn't see if the four men were armed but they did seem to be looking towards us – of course we were far more visible than they were, our sails announcing our presence from many miles away. Perhaps they were just fishermen, but it seemed unlikely that they would come so far from land to fish from a tiny pirogue. I was struggling with disbelief, but knew we couldn't take any chances: we had to take action now before they reached us.

As I watched, the bow of the boat turned towards us, plummeting up and down in the rough waves. 'Right, they're heading this way. Jules, get the boys under the saloon table and bring the flare guns and flares up here. Now!' I shouted as she froze momentarily before shepherding Oscar down below. I heard them crying with fear as she steered them beneath the table, our reasoning being that if they were below the water line they were safer from injury from gunshots. She frantically rummaged in the chart table and passed up the flare gun before returning to reassure them.

'Get the engine on!' I shouted down as I loaded the two flare guns. I gunned the throttle, adding engine power to the pull of the sails. The wind was on our beam, giving us its best possible angle and I trimmed the sheets a little to get us up to our maximum speed. Soon we were doing 10 knots and I switched on the autohelm so I could watch the pirogue through the binoculars. It was closer now, heading towards us at an angle as if to cut us off, but it was having trouble with the waves. To reach us it was having to steer directly into them and I saw the men baling as the pirogue rose up and then flipped down over the shoulders of the waves. I tightened the sheets again and headed further up to windward, making their approach more difficult still. I'd already made up my mind to ram them if they drew ahead of us, throwing all of our sixteen tonnes at them in the hope that I could smash their boat to pieces – if they didn't shoot me first. I wasn't going to go down without a fight.

Juliet had rejoined me in the cockpit and we watched the boat's struggle, praying that we could pull ahead. After a few minutes she lowered the binoculars and passed them to me, pale with relief. 'I think they're turning away.'

I looked through the binoculars myself and saw that she was right. They had half-turned and were lolling in the seaway, all the men sitting still and staring at us.

'Looks like the sea state was too much for them,' Juliet said.

'I hope so,' I said grimly, still not sure that they wouldn't resume their pursuit. 'Either way, let's keep going as fast as we can for a while – we don't want to lose the advantage.'

'We were lucky with the weather,' Juliet said. 'One of those rare occasions when we were better off in a sailing boat. Thank God we steered so far east when we left – if we'd taken the normal course we would have run right into them.'

At last we lost sight of the little boat and felt sufficiently confident to switch off the engine, still keeping a wary eye on the sea behind us. We sailed on, relieved but deeply shaken by the experience. Perhaps they had been innocent fishermen, but it seemed unlikely. It was hard to believe that we had actually had a close run with pirates, and I was haunted by thoughts of what might have happened. Unlike Tom's boat, whose steel sides had saved him from destruction, bullets would have passed through our glass fibre hull as easily as sparks through tissue, causing *Forever* to slowly fill with water and giving the pirates just enough time to loot us before we sank. Pirates don't make a habit of rescuing sailors and we would have been left to the mercy of the currents and sharks – a thought too horrible to contemplate.

It was with deep relief that we spotted the coastline of Grenada in the distance. I thought of the desperation that must drive men to these actions and felt a degree of pity. Yet overriding this was a deep-seated anger – their brutality and callousness knew no bounds. A primitive instinct rose up in me like bile, making me yearn to hear of pirates killed in the act, or hung from gibbets as a warning to all others who might choose to follow their example. Yachtsmen are generally easy targets and there has long been a spirit of trust and mutual support between people who are united in the face of the sea's challenges. But as long as this trust has existed, so people have exploited it, hunting their victims down as mercilessly as any shark, but with far more cunning and cruelty. We even heard of pirates using false distress calls to lure yachts.

'You know Jules,' I said suddenly, 'I'm glad we're leaving the Caribbean soon. I'm getting tired of all this menace – it's exhausting. I think we should head north as soon as we can.'

She sighed. 'I know, it's a pity. I love the Caribbean, but sometimes it just feels like too much of a struggle.' She looked out around the bay. 'We've got some big decisions ahead of us. We need to decide what route we're going to take across the Atlantic. And you know, I've been thinking . . .' She paused and looked at me searchingly. 'I'm not too sure about taking the boys across – I think it might be too long and scary for them.'

'I know, I've been thinking that too . . .' We gazed at each other for a moment and I knew that like me she'd been badly shaken up by the day's events. 'Well, let's sleep on it – we don't have to decide yet. Let's just enjoy our last few weeks in this place.'

Via a series of hops and skips, dropping anchor at dusk and weighing at dawn, we made swift progress up the islands. We aimed to fill in the gaps on our way north and visit some of the islands we had missed on our way down. One of these was Carriacou, an island surrounded by reefs. Oscar reminded us of 'Kick 'em Jenny', the active submarine volcano that rises 1,300 metres below the sea floor and last erupted in 2001. We had given a wide berth to it on the way down as advised by the chart. This time, however, we sailed right over it, feeling that after our brush with pirates a volcano was the least of our worries.

'What will happen if it erupts while we're going over it?' Oscar looked anxious as he watched a couple of other yachts that were steering a safe distance around it.

'We'll be blown 300 metres into the sky, then sucked down in a vortex of air to the bottom of the ocean. Nothing to worry about,' I replied casually.

We dropped anchor in Tyrell Bay towards the south of Carriacou, and the next morning went ashore, determined to see the island on our own, without resorting to a guide. Like a little troupe of penguins that had been blown badly off course, we hobbled along the sweltering sea front road to a threadbare settlement where we stopped at a run-down shop to ask if we could hire a car. The woman behind the counter stared at us as if we'd asked to hire one of her daughters.

I held my hands up, worried that perhaps I had offended her. 'Sorry – maybe there's some kind of misunderstanding. It said in our book to ask here if you wanted to hire a car?'

'You gonna drive it?' she said incredulously.

I looked about the shop and my eyes met the watery stare of an ancient toothless man. I smiled at him, but he kept on staring. Flummoxed by the total lack of humanity I turned back to the woman, 'We can drive.'

She sucked her teeth in disbelief and looked over to the old man, who appeared to have sunk into himself to such an extent that expression was no longer possible. I wondered what was going on: did this woman believe that all people from boats were so hopeless that they were incapable of driving? 'I guess we could call Rodney,' she ventured, as if she was about to let us into a life-changing secret.

The old man gave the barest perceptible nod and with infinite slowness she made her way over to the phone.

Shortly a harassed man arrived in a battered pickup. 'Get in, get in,' he said as if in a raging hurry. 'I am Rodney, I take you to the car.'

He was in his mid-fifties and dressed in an old army surplus shirt, a pair of canvas shorts and leather boots that finished halfway up his calves. He looked like a veteran gladiator, with grey chest hairs sprouting from his well muscled torso. Driving at a frenetic pace, he pulled up outside his house where a chubby teenager dripping in sweat and beneath a halo of flies was swinging a sledgehammer repeatedly down onto a pile of rocks. As we drew up he stopped and gazed at us with a sweet, bovine stare, his head still hanging after his last strike. His tongue hung out of his mouth in a comic book expression of exhaustion.

'Blake!' Rodney shouted. 'You don' get no job done stoppin' and talkin' to passers by. Get crackin' dem rocks boy!'

'Is he your slave?' Luke asked Rodney in a matter-of-fact tone.

Juliet gave me a horrified look. Clearly the subject of slavery had taken hold of Luke's ghoulish imagination and he was dying to see a real one in action. I turned to him. 'No he is not Luke – don't be so rude.'

'Sorry about that,' I said to Rodney and he shook his head.

'No matter.' He looked down at Luke as if in warning. 'That boy my son. He let himself get real fat and I will work it off him.' We all turned to watch the boy labouring in the pitiless heat.

'So,' I asked, swiftly changing the subject, 'do you have a car for us?'

'I am assumin' you can drive?' he said sceptically.

'Yes,' I said, though I was beginning to doubt it myself. What was so complicated about this car, I wondered, that it deserved all this fuss?

In fact it turned out to be a perfectly ordinary Ford. 'Make sure you back by sundown,' Rodney said. 'Lights ain't too reliable.'

We drove along a narrow road, passing through a desiccated landscape stippled with small concrete houses surrounded by chickens and little scrapings in the ground for vegetables. The road took us across the island, where we looked down on the windward coastline to see several large ships lying wrecked, the treacherous reefs clearly visible through the transparent water. We drove along close to the coast, the road gradually growing rougher and passing through a woebegone stretch of scrub trees, including twisted thickets of the highly poisonous manchineel, a tree so toxic that even standing beneath it is dangerous. We joked about the journey turning into the kind of road trip the Addams family might have enjoyed.

We drove to Hillsborough, the island's main town, which seemed to be asleep as barely anyone was visible on the streets. Although a bit run down, its spectacular setting along a long, white beach made up for it and between the simple buildings we caught glimpses of the azure sea. We discovered why the streets were deserted when we passed the town cricket pitch. A game was in progress and it was crowded with families. I was thrilled at last to see some local cricket at last. 'Boys, the West Indies have produced some of the greatest cricket teams in the world,' I announced. 'Let's go and watch.'

We walked into the walled cricket ground and there was a little hush as everyone stopped and stared at us as if we were visitors from another planet. The crackling vibe of racist hostility burned the air around our footsteps. 'God, this is awful,' I muttered as we settled down on the margins of the crowd, looking like a little huddle of pale, sickly animals. The boys too watched longingly as local children played mini games of cricket on the fringes of the pitch, under-standing instinctively that they were not invited. Nowhere that we'd gone had we had this reaction – we'd encountered the odd unfriendly person, but never had a whole community united in hostility against us. We sat uncomfortably for twenty minutes until we couldn't bear it any longer.

We drove back towards Tyrell bay in relative silence, each lost in our own thoughts. The chubby boy had completed his marathon task and a pile of pebbles that would have made a chain gang proud now lay in place of the rocks. We paid Rodney and declined his offer of a lift back to the boat, choosing to walk instead.

'Now I know how it feels,' Juliet said sadly as we trudged along the dusty road.

'What?' I asked, although I felt I already knew what she was going to say.

'Racism.'

At dawn the next day we headed north again and plotted our course for Union Island, the southernmost of the Grenadines. The trades had followed their usual pattern and swung round south of east, which now helped to push us strongly on. I concentrated on the chart of Clifton Harbour, which was so surrounded by hazards it felt as if we were about to thread our way into a minefield. To the east of the harbour lay Newlands Reef, a long shoal waiting to catch any boat coming from a northerly direction. To its south was Lagoon Reef, which encased most of the southern shore of the island and at the very centre of the harbour, waiting to catch any fortunate sailor who had managed to get that far, was a hidden mound of coral with the rather benign, municipal name of 'Roundabout Reef'. The pilot book went on to warn us that buoys and beacons were missing or out of position, which wasn't reassuring, particularly given Union Island's history as the haunt of pirates and shipwreckers.

'Hey Guy, come and look up here – it's so beautiful!' Juliet shouted and I shook the pilot book's gloom out of my head, reminding myself that this was the twenty-first century – not the 1790s.

'Look over there!' Juliet pointed, and I gazed round in awe yet again at the magical topography of the islands of the southern Grenadines. We had passed the high northern tip of Carriacou, and to our east lay the tiny islands of Petit Martinique and Petit St Vincent. Ahead of us we could see the eccentric profile of Union Island, with its distinctive peak, the Pinnacle, rising over two hundred metres into the sky. As we crossed the Martinique channel the seas built a little, but we weren't concerned as plenty of daylight stretched ahead. And then as we drew near to the island we got our first sight of Newlands Reef where white foaming waves were breaking repeatedly. When we got closer Juliet rounded into the wind and we dropped the sails, keeping our powerful jib ready to be quickly unleashed should we experience engine trouble. *Forever*'s steel heart now whirred away strongly and we listened to the notes of the beat with all our attention, knowing that if the engine failed, with this wind we would be wrecked in no time at all.

'You take over,' Juliet said, handing me the wheel. 'I haven't got the nerve for this. I'll just go and double-check the chart.'

I stepped into position at the helm. Juliet and I had become a good team, we trusted each other but still double-checked each other's every calculation, as we both knew how easy it was to overlook something or make a mistake. We slipped in behind the wind-strewn reef and pointed *Forever*'s bow towards the leeward side of the ferocious coral.

I handed the helm back to Juliet in preparation for anchoring. 'Tell me when we're at two fathoms and I'll drop the hook.'

She nodded. 'We won't need to pull astern – this wind will have us flying backwards. I just hope the anchor doesn't drag or we'll be sitting on that reef before we can blink.' She pointed behind her to the marker on Roundabout Reef.

I went forwards to ready the anchor. The water was crystal clear, growing shallower and shallower as we approached, and I could see the sinister brown and green coral breaking through the tops of the waves just a few metres away. Tight with tension, Juliet stared at the depth gauge. We both knew that we couldn't afford any kind of mishap, as what little financial safety net we'd had had been blown in Chaguaramas. 'Two fathoms!' she shouted, her voice drifting to me faintly over the roar of tearing wind and surf. 'Quick drop it now!'

I had just seconds to drop the anchor before we hurtled backwards and I watched as it fell into the clear water. The wind pushed us back and I let the anchor chain clatter and clank its way out and when enough had sunk to the bottom I made the chain fast and then placed my bare foot on the tightening chain, feeling for the jerk as it pulled us up short or alternatively that awful judder and vibration which meant that we were dragging. 'Be ready to push us forwards if need be!' I called back to Juliet. She raised her arm and nodded. Relief flooded through me as I felt the anchor bite hard and *Forever* swung up to put her nose into the wind. 'OK Jules, you can switch the engine off!' I shouted, and saw Luke rush to do it before she and the boys came forwards. Together we looked around at the most dramatic anchorage imaginable. Behind us lay the little Tintinesque-town with its brightly painted houses and high green hill rising dramatically behind. The houses stretched around the shoreline, and ended in an area of reefs and beaches, with a short runway behind.

We opened all the hatches and let the wind whip through, ridding the boat of the last of the boatyard dust. Mosquitoes would have to be jet-propelled to get out here, so we knew we were in for a comfortable night. That is unless our anchor dragged: 'Jules, I'm just going to check the anchor,' I called, pulling on my mask and snorkel. 'Come on Oscar.' We reached the end of the chain and he dived down and held onto the anchor, pointing to where it had dug completely into the white coral sand. The chain stretched out in a satisfying straight line behind it, and Oscar gave me the diver's sign for 'OK'.

Immediately ahead of us there was a tiny little hut perched on the reef itself. Standing just inches away from the line of surf, it was thatched with palm leaves and looked almost as if it had grown there. It was tightly shuttered with no sign of life, and we wondered if it was a fisherman's hut or a relic from another era. But then just before the sun began to go down I saw a stocky-looking man and two energetic young women busy tying back the shutters, sweeping and bringing out a few tables and chairs.

'What is that place Dad?' Luke asked.

'I think it's a bar,' I replied.

'Can we go over?'

I turned to Juliet. 'What do you think?'

'Yes let's – it's too cute to not visit, since we're so close.'

By the time we'd got the dinghy ready a few people were sitting outside, which made it quite crowded, as there was only space for ten people at most. The sun had almost sunk away as we approached the little hut, and as we tied up to the tiny dock we saw that the whole place was made entirely of conch shells and coral, stuck together with a bit of cement. We crossed the tiny area of sand and ducked inside the hut, where hammocks and bean bags were strewn around a shady circular room. The breeze blew through a glassless window that looked out over the reef, and beneath it a comfy window seat was made up with a quilt and multi-coloured cushions. The room echoed with the sound of the waves, giving the impression that we had entered a sea cave or even a giant conch shell.

'Y'all alright?' the burly man smiled in welcome as he stood behind a little counter made of driftwood, slowly stirring a jug full of lethal-looking liquid. He had long dreadlocks and a perfectly wicked, puckish smile. 'Can I fix you a rum punch?'

Behind us the two women lounged in the hammocks, their legs dangling provocatively over the sides as they rocked to and fro. I looked around and one gave me a cartoon-book wink, then let her head fall back with a silent laugh. I sensed there would be an opportunity for a single man, and the place had a distinctly sensual atmosphere with its dim lighting, jewel-like fabrics and soft seating that all seemed to have been arranged so as to encourage one to lie down. As the burly man, whose name turned out to be Zante, mixed us some drinks, Juliet went over and lay on the window seat, looking out over the darkening reef. 'What's this place all about?' she asked me as I carried our drinks over. 'It feels . . . well, a bit – adult – don't you think?'

'Hm, let's go outside,' I said, ushering the boys back into the light. We pulled up chairs and let them sink into the sand beneath us as we turned to watch the fast setting sun. As the boys played in the sand I looked over to Juliet.

'You know, this is a very sensuous zone we're travelling through, all sorts of excess is going on all around us, and here we are . . .'

Juliet finished my sentence for me. 'I know, here we are practising advanced parenting techniques!' She sighed. 'Still, we couldn't
afford to let our hair down anyway. All these people are on holiday,
whereas we . . .'

'Whereas we –' she took an exaggerated breath, 'we are on a
leviathan family odyssey.' I held up my hands in surrender. 'I know,
I know . . . I wouldn't want it any other way. Who would want to let
their hair down in this fabulously romantic setting when there are
bedtime stories to be read?' My tone was only mock-complaining,
and we smiled at each other.

Luke appeared by our side and said simply, 'Oscar's gone.'

I leapt to my feet, imagining a range of horrific scenarios
involving our older son. I drew breath to begin calling him, but then
heard some giggling coming from inside the hut. That has to involve
Oscar, I thought, and crept up to have a look. Concealed within a
patch of shadow I peered through the doorway and saw him lying
in a hammock, being rocked from side to side by the two girls. The
light of the rising moon shone through the windows, and the sound
of waves and wind filled the rich, seaweedy air. After a while the girls
came out with a tray of drinks, and we sacrificed more grocery money
as we accepted another round. Zante turned on some reggae, and the
boys began dancing. The girls gathered around them, laughing and
chanting, 'Go Oscar, go Luke!' as they whirled about. It felt wonderful
beyond words to see our boys dancing on a tropical reef beneath a full
moon, free from the constraints of Britain.

A launch was making its way over, and seeing it one of the girls
tapped her friend on the shoulder, looking serious for the first time.
Layers of life were shifting and the little period of snatched innocence
was over.

I nudged Juliet and we stood up to go, thanking the girls who
leant down to give the boys sisterly hugs before waving us off at the

dock. As we puttered back to *Forever* the launch sped past, setting us bouncing in its wake. It tied up and three white men climbed out.

'Mum, are those men friends with the girls?' Luke asked.

'Not sure, could be,' she said, looking at me.

Oscar studied our faces with an expression that revealed his growing perception that life existed on many more levels than he yet understood. 'Will they be OK?'

'Yes, they're fine Oscar, they've got Zante to look after them,' I replied.

Juliet shot me a dubious look. 'Look boys – the moon is up.'

We all tilted our heads to gaze at the moon that had risen high above our windy world, floating within the neutral stillness of space. Soon the boys were asking questions about the stars, most of which we didn't have the knowledge to answer, but at least they were no longer asking about the hut on the reef.

Early the next morning we weighed anchor and headed north, planning to stop off at Bequia or one of the islands nearby. This stepping-stone approach was pleasant, but it was taking too long. The wind was directly astern, which we had discovered was *Forever*'s worst direction and she was rolling biliously in the swell. Her sails wouldn't set properly on either tack and though I'd rigged a preventer to stop the boom from crashing across, it still tugged angrily as we rolled from side to side. Our progress was noisy, jagged and painfully slow and the thought of days on end like this was too much to bear.

'What was all that about being "blown back up north",' Juliet groaned. 'I'd rather be sailing to windward.'

I had an idea. 'Why don't we just bypass all these islands? We don't have time to see them properly anyway. Let's head directly for the Saints – the wind direction will be better and we'll make up some time so we'd be able to stay for a few days once we get there. It would only take three or four days. We've got lots of fuel, and we can run the water-maker to keep the tanks topped up. What have we got in the way of food?'

'Plenty. We might run out of bread, but I can make some I suppose. We've got enough fruit and veg to last a few days and plenty of canned food. But sailing all those nights, I'm not sure . . .'

'Well we're going to have to do it sooner or later – this can be a trial run. And if things get bad we can just head into one of the islands.' I was appealing to her adventurous spirit.

Over the next few days and nights we sailed north, keeping five miles or so to the west of the islands. It was reassuring to see the familiar high shapes of St Vincent, St Lucia and Martinique hazily in the distance, in the knowledge that we could go in somewhere if we had to. The wind direction was only marginally better, and we suffered intermittent bouts of seasickness as *Forever*'s lumpy motion continued, but we felt glad to be covering some ground.

My seasickness had been dramatically improved by a miraculous remedy that slow-releases a vast amount of hyoscine hydrobromide into your system via a skin patch. Available only on prescription, it was being sent out to me in batches by various sympathetic doctors, and it had transformed my debilitating experience of seasickness so much that I was confident I would be able to carry out in-depth engine work at sea. It was an enormous relief to know that I could be on duty at all times to look after the boat and my family no matter what the conditions. When Juliet tried it once though, she became practically comatose – clearly I needed a dose fit for an elephant.

On the way we talked about our plans for the Atlantic crossing. It was now mid-April, and if we were to cross by the conventional route, Antigua to Europe via Bermuda and the Azores, we would have to leave in around one month. Juliet was keen to join in the Atlantic Rally for Cruisers, a gathering of sailors who all crossed the Atlantic at the same time, meeting up at various points along the way. I very much did not want to, keen not to lose our independence. The alternative was to turn northwest instead of east, sailing from the Caribbean to the USA, travelling up the coast before crossing the north Atlantic to Britain by the Great Circle route via Nova Scotia. The appeal of this was the prospect of experiencing completely new territory and another two months' sailing, as the usual time to cross by this route was late June. It would, however, mean a much tougher crossing with the certainty of fog, storms and possibly even icebergs. It was a difficult decision to make.

'Crossing with the ARC would be the safest route,' Juliet said.

'But the boats are hundreds of miles apart,' I argued. 'You're alone out there if something goes wrong, whatever route you take.'

'I know, but at least someone is following your progress – it feels reassuring, even if it wouldn't make any difference in reality.' Juliet glanced at the boys, who were huddled miserably together in the cockpit, feeling sick. 'To be honest I'm not sure about doing the crossing with the kids, certainly not across the North Atlantic. I want to, but I don't think there's anything in it for them, and they can't really have any idea of what it would be like being at sea for a crossing lasting weeks – the longest we've ever done has been a few days, and that's been bad enough. And what if one of them was to get sick or injured? We'd be days if not weeks away from help. It just doesn't feel right.'

'But what's the alternative? Unless we were to send them home separately, and we do it by ourselves . . .'

The idea took hold for a moment until Juliet's characteristic common sense kicked in. 'That won't work – we can't ask family to look after the boys for weeks, it's too long. They'd be utterly miserable and worried, and if something did happen . . . well, they'd be orphans. Forget it.'

It was starting to look more and more likely that I might be crossing on my own.

Close to the south coast of Guadeloupe, the Saints, or Iles des Saintes, lie delicately scattered like a handful of precious stones cast across the turquoise cloth of the sea. Having been at sea for three days and nights, we sailed joyfully into their midst, feeling salt-worn but triumphant. As we approached the islands the boys jumped up and down, desperate to see land once again. We threaded our way in closer past treacherous-looking shoals and rocks until a wide bay opened up, and there before us lay the little town of Terre de Haut.

The town was stretched over a sweet set of low rounded hills, whose outline against the blue tropical sky might well have been drawn in crayon, such was the almost playful innocence of the settlement. We could see a clock tower, a church steeple, red roofed houses and a small airfield, its bright orange windsock blowing merrily in the wind. To the north a road stretched up an improbably steep hill to the well-preserved Fort Napoleon, which the pilot book told me had been yet another territory fought over by the French and British. We'd just made it in before darkness, and dropped our anchor, relieved to avoid another night at sea.

The next morning the boys woke up mad with advanced cabin fever. They jumped about with relief as we lowered the dinghy. The houses ran right down to the water and the little village was just waking up as we walked down its narrow streets, feeling for all the world as if we had been transported to France. The town clock chimed sweetly and the only giveaway that we were in the tropics was the rich plant growth: coconut palms and a cashew tree in rich flower, and some glamorous star fruits hanging like yellow lanterns from the branches of a spindly tree beside a whitewashed wall.

We sat at a little metal table in front of the boulangerie and devoured legions of pastries, several cups of coffee and orange juice, feeling as if we hadn't eaten properly for days. During the passage we had felt too queasy to eat much.

When our blood sugar had reached dangerous levels we wandered through the streets until we came to the little square, where we sat in the shade and watched the town come to life. Oscar and Luke were kicking a football around and before we knew it they were running about breathlessly in the midst of a gathering crowd of French-speaking children, communicating through the universal language of play.

As we'd intended, having made up time on our journey north we could afford to linger for a few days so we hung out at the square, swam from sandy beaches and explored the island. From the fort we gazed lovingly down on *Forever* as she lay contentedly on her anchor in the blue of the bay. On the other side of the island we found a long beach beset by dangerous, circular currents, surrounded by high red cliffs, and a mysterious lagoon-like bay with a palm tree forest at its head. On its shoreline we saw evidence of the island's last hurricane and Oscar and I snorkelled out to the half-sunk ships, looking down upon the disturbing sight of a boat consumed by the sea.

The island was a peculiar combination of cosiness and mystery, its red-sanded soil imbued by an atmosphere that we couldn't quite fathom. In comparison to the other islands the Saints felt safe – the fact was that, being maintained by France, the edge of desperation that we had experienced in the other islands had been removed. There was also a sense that the French islanders, who had been there since the seventeenth century, would not tolerate those who came with trouble in their hearts. We also couldn't help noticing the complete absence of black people, and one of the very few whom we did see was in the process of being arrested by two gendarmes – who looked more like hardened legionnaires than policemen.

Yet the Saints offered a temporary respite from the troubles of the other islands, and almost allowed us to forget the massive poverty that we had witnessed throughout the Caribbean. But we were realistic enough to know that the French islands suffered their problems too. There was something missing, as the relative affluence of the islands brought a consequent loss of the humour and warmth that we had experienced in the other islands. We felt that the Saints were a fitting end to our journey through the Caribbean and that we should begin the long road home.

On our last night we treated ourselves to a meal in a restaurant we had been circling with anticipation since our first day. 'You do realise we're going to have to cross the Anegada Passage again, don't you?' Juliet said over dinner. 'From what I've heard it's just as bad in the other direction.'

'No way,' I replied vehemently, 'I think we should go straight to the Virgin Islands. We can head north from there.'

'Does that mean we're not going to cross the Atlantic just yet then?' Things had been leaning that way, but we still hadn't made up our minds.

'I don't think so – I'm not ready to go home yet, are you?'

'No.' She twiddled her wine glass, 'I don't think I ever will be, to be honest, but it would be incredible to see America.'

This meant a long crossing through the turbulent waters of the south-west Atlantic, at a time when the weather was gearing up for hurricane season – and later the even grimmer spectre of the north Atlantic back to Scotland.

We took advantage of the French supermarkets to stock up for our journey, filling the dinghy with everything from packet soups to wine before motoring out with the children perched on top of the great mound. Then, after a few final checks, we pulled up our anchor, hoisted sail and pointed *Forever* onto her course. A good strong wind whipped us away from the beautiful islands, and Luke cupped his hand to his mouth and shouted, 'Bye-bye Saints! We love you!' and then he turned to Juliet. 'One day I'm going to live in the Saints. You can come too if you're not dead,' and with that reassuring thought we kept looking astern as the islands receded in our fizzing white wake.

We fell comfortably into our offshore routine, having now worked out simple strategies that helped us to deal with the rolling reality that the sea and wind imposed upon family life during passage-making. For cooking, we kept things ruthlessly simple, wedging ourselves into the small space of the galley and using the fiddles to hold boiling pots and pans in place on the stove. We did the washing up in a bucket of salt water in the cockpit to keep seasickness at bay, as an extended washing-up session down below in a rolling boat could leave one feeling a touch yellow. As before, I took most of the night watches to allow Juliet to concentrate on the boys and after supper I would sleep until midnight. Juliet would then take over at five or six in the morning, by which time I was longing to lie down. The boys had their own survival strategies, playing quiet, solitary games down below with toy soldiers or cars, emerging now and then to stare silently out at the ocean, at the endless vistas of sea and sky.

Gradually the pencil line on our chart inched north and we encountered no hazards bar Saba Bank, a submerged coral atoll that sent our depth gauge falling alarmingly. Although passing almost a hundred miles downwind of the Anegada Passage, its legacy followed us all the way to the Virgin Islands in the form of a rolling, lumpy swell. This time we were not so lucky as to arrive by daylight, and had to stand off overnight before we could approach the islands safely. We were all suffering from low-key nausea and it was frustrating to have to stay at sea in the knowledge that shelter was so close at hand. I hove to a few miles south of the coast of Salt Island, setting the sails in such a way that *Forever* stayed more or less motionless. I left Juliet on watch and was alarmed to find her a few hours later lying in the cockpit suffering from a rare bout of seasickness.

The continuousness of this leg of the journey had really got to her, and it was with great relief when after three days and nights at sea we rounded up and dropped the hook at Salt Island.

We spent a day or two sailing around the Virgin Islands, enjoying them more second time around in the knowledge that these were our last days in the Caribbean. They were quieter and less crowded at this time of year, anchorages that had been packed to bursting at Christmas were now deserted and we were able to appreciate the true beauty of the islands, unencumbered by tourists. But soon we had to face up to the great task that lay ahead of us, and begin preparing ourselves for the crossing. We constantly debated the best route to the east coast of America. We had to decide whether to go via the treacherously shallow Bahamas, a tempting but worrying prospect, particularly as we were beginning to hear warnings of tropical storms – and there could be no worse place to find oneself in the midst of a tropical storm than in shallow waters with few places of refuge. The second choice was to head west, via the US Virgin Islands, Cuba and Jamaica, island-hopping our way along to Florida. The downside of this was that we would have to pass through some dodgy territory, particularly Haiti, which had recently had some attacks on boats. Our third option was to strike out boldly across the ocean, heading straight for the US coast and bypassing all land en route.

Whichever course we took, we knew this would be our longest passage. For this we needed to stock the boat up with food, water and fuel and have a close look over all her systems to make sure they were in good working order. For some time *Forever*'s batteries had been overcharging so we decided to stop off in Tortola on the outskirts of Roadtown. As we were approaching the marina, Juliet noticed that the voltage in the batteries had gone sky high and a strange smell was coming from the boys' bunk. Checking the battery bank beneath she found them fizzing, smoking – they were overcharging to the extent that they were about to catch fire.

'Guy, you've got to slow the engine!' she shouted up. 'The batteries are about to catch fire!'

If a fire broke out on board we wouldn't stand a chance. I slowed the engine down as much as I could, but a certain amount of power was required to keep us on course in the strong wind.

'Shall we put down the dinghy? Just in case we have to abandon ship . . .'

'You do that,' I said, flicking on the autohelm. 'I'm going to put out a pan pan message – keep a close eye on all those boats!'

Down below I lifted the radio handset and issued a warning to all nearby shipping that we might be in trouble. It was an ignominious arrival to the marina and I knew that all the other boats would have heard it; nevertheless, at least they would know to stay out of our way if it all went wrong.

Thankfully the batteries held out for long enough for us to come alongside, despite an agonisingly long wait while a number of other boats cleared off. We tied up with a sigh of relief, feeling for the hundredth time that we'd narrowly escaped disaster. We couldn't afford any major repairs – we had thought the batteries just needed looking at – so I decided to sort it out myself. Thus began many hours of sweaty detective work, aided by a hopelessly optimistic book entitled *Electrics Made Easy*. I started work in the relative cool of the morning, the fetid heat of the marina gathering as the day went on until my entire body was slippery with sweat. Juliet tried to keep the children at the marina's pool for most of the day but even when they came back, tired and quiet, I found myself irritable and tense. I knew there was a strong possibility that if I continued to prod and pry my way around *Forever*'s complex systems I might suffer an immense electric shock.

I was drinking a beer in the cockpit the following afternoon, miserably near to calling for professional help when a spry looking man walked over. I instantly recognised him as one of those sixty-something capable American skippers blessed with a combination of physical endurance, clear intelligence and a complete lack of social hang-ups. He pushed his sunglasses up over his grey crew-cut hair and let his eyes pass over *Forever* before coming to rest on me.

'Excuse me, are you Guy? My name's Randy. I was in the pool and I met your son Oscar, and he was telling me that you're having some trouble with your electrics. I wonder if I might be able to help? See I have some experience in that line – in fact I used to teach electrics in college before I retired.'

'Oh, what a relief,' I said. 'Thanks so much. I'm completely out of my depth here. Come and have a beer.'

Despite the heat he looked cool and calm, and as he stepped onboard I felt I was in good hands. 'Now, what exactly seems to be the problem?'

I was in mid-explanation when I heard a discreet cough. We both turned to see another equally distinguished-looking white-haired gentleman on the quay. 'Hey, are you Guy? Your son Oscar sent me over, said you were having some trouble with your electrics . . .'

What was this, I wondered: was Oscar turning into some kind of electrical messiah, spreading the word of his technically challenged father far and wide?

'Hey Mike!' Randy said. 'You're probably more equipped to deal with this than I am. Now Guy's got a problem here . . .' Pretty soon the two of them had left me far behind, and within five minutes had exposed *Forever*'s insides and were systematically talking each other through her systems whilst prodding about with a hand-held meter. At one point they stopped and in a series of one-word statements discussed the solution to a conundrum. I leant down and made a suggestion, hoping to be helpful, and Randy smiled patiently whilst Mike leant on the side of the galley and fixed me with a puzzled expression. 'Son, that would be utterly illogical,' he said, sounding and looking like Mr Spock as he turned back to the complex mass of wiring. Their gentle hum of conversation continued as they opened up *Forever*'s nervous system, until eventually they wrapped up.

'Well Guy, it looks like your problem lies with the inverter,' Randy concluded. He held up the manual: 'If you look here, you'll see that . . .' and he continued to bamboozle me with diagrams and technical jargon so complex that pretty soon my brain was just hearing white noise. I tuned back in just in time to hear him say, '. . . So I'm afraid you're going to need new batteries, but at least we've identified what the problem was, so it won't happen again.'

Not for the first time, strangers had come aboard our boat and solved a problem for us for no other reason than just basic human kindness. The ethics were different afloat, and you knew that if you helped someone, the likelihood was that you in turn would be helped out in your hour of need.

'Did those guys help you?' Juliet asked when she came back.

'Yes – they were amazing. How did Oscar meet them?'

'Oh, he was talking to everyone in the pool about our problems – you're lucky you didn't have more visits, everyone wanted to help.'

'Well the upshot is that we need to replace the house batteries – both of them.'

'Damn!' She put her hand to her mouth. 'That sounds expensive.'

I grimaced. 'I know, but there's no way around it – they're completely fried. And all our electrics depend on them, it's not something we can do without.'

'Well we'd better find out how much we're in for I suppose. There's a chandlers at the end of the quay.'

'OK, I'll go now', I said reluctantly. 'I'll be back soon.'

I wandered down the quayside and was passing through the marina restaurant on the way to the chandlery when I heard someone say my name. 'Hey, that's Guy. Guy!'

I recognised the voice, but couldn't quite place it, though my gut told me it wasn't going to be good. I turned and looked around the restaurant, and saw two arms held high. To my horror I realised it was Henrik, whom I'd pranged in St Kitts, seated beside a glowering Myken. They were seated at a table in the midst of a group of people, and he waited until I'd made eye contact and then shouted loudly, obviously aiming to cause maximum embarrassment. 'Man of honour, hey? Man of honour!' He stood up and pointed a finger at me. 'You made me a promise, and I want my money back.' The whole restaurant went quiet for a perceptible and profoundly cringe-making moment.

My heart sank with each neatly accented syllable: the black tide of events in St Kitts came flooding back, and I knew that I was about to be hoisted on my own petard. In the period since we'd seen them, our insurance company had sent a surveyor to inspect *Forever* who'd concluded that the accident had indeed been the result of mechanical failure, and thus, under English law, neither they nor we were responsible to pay Myken and Henrik anything. We had been as surprised by this conclusion as they were, and had not yet replied to Henrik's angry email, which had demanded that I uphold my promise to pay him, whatever the conclusion of the insurers. Juliet and I had been caught in the grip of a moral dilemma – though we had wanted to pay them, we could no longer afford to as their email had arrived just as we'd finished our repairs at Chaguaramas, and so we had hoped to put off dealing with it until we got back to Britain. The bad luck of running into them now, just as we had received the news about the batteries, sent me reeling.

'Come and see me at the boat in a few minutes,' I said.

'Where are you? Don't want you disappearing again,' he said.

'Dock A, towards the end,' I said, feeling a loathing towards this man who, however justified his cause, took such pleasure in rubbing his point home.

He pointed his food-encrusted fork at me, 'I will be there, you can bet on that!'

I couldn't blame him – from his point of view it had been an extraordinary piece of luck, not just for the money, but also to have the satisfaction of publicly humiliating me, which must have made up for months of frustration. I walked fast back towards the boat, where I found Juliet watching happily over the boys, who were dangling fishing lines over the side. Her smile vanished as she read my expression.

'What's wrong – is it the batteries?'

'No, at least not yet. It's Henrik and Myken.'

'What about them?'

'They're here.'

'What?!' She raised a hand to her mouth. 'Oh shit, and we never got back to them. How did they find us?'

'They didn't – not on purpose.'

'Well what did they say?'

'They want us to pay them.'

She leant heavily against the companionway. 'If only you hadn't got so chummy with them we wouldn't be in this situation.'

'I know – but I gave them my word of honour.'

'Word of honour!' she said bitterly. 'What next – a duel? We're not living in the eighteenth century. And anyway, they're loaded – they don't need the money. They're chasing us because he's the type that always has to win.'

'I know all that, but he does have a point, and we'll have to find a way through this. If we had any money I would have paid him off straight away.'

'Well me too, but we don't.' She looked past me and stopped. 'Shit, here he comes.'

Sure enough, Henrik's portly frame was sweating its way down the quay, followed by Myken, who now looked positively Wagnerian such was her sheer size and menace.

I stepped onto the quay, and he squared up to me. 'You have broken your promise to us to pay, even if the insurers did not,' he barked in a staccato fashion, the smell of alcohol wafting over me.

I couldn't defend myself. 'I know.'

'Why didn't you answer our emails?' demanded Myken, her face bright red and almost spitting with rage.

'I'm sorry – it's just that we're pretty much broke.'

'Ha!' She gestured around *Forever*. 'You weren't broke when you got your boat fixed up – very nice job too!'

'I know, but that was before we got your message.'

'You already knew the outcome from your insurers – you're lying,' Henrik said, sweat dripping down his corpulent face. 'We thought we could trust you.'

Juliet was behind me. 'Wait a minute, just because we hadn't responded to your email yet didn't mean we weren't going to pay you – it's only been a month or so since we heard from the insurance company, and we were just as surprised as you were. We haven't had time to figure things out yet.'

Myken shook her head. 'I just don't believe you – you tried to run out on us.'

'We're not like that, we would have sorted it out when we got back home,' Juliet argued, but I could see they didn't believe her.

'Well whatever, fate has brought us together, and it's just as well because I was about to take further action,' Henrik said.

'Such as? We haven't done anything illegal.'

'No, but we know where you work, where you live . . . We could have taken steps.' I realised Juliet was right: this was a vengeful man. 'Well anyway', he continued, 'you will pay me now, yes?'

'We can't pay you in one,' Juliet answered. 'If you can wait, we'll do it over time.'

'That is fine, whatever you like. But I must have my money – it is the principle.'

'In "principle" we don't have to pay you, but we will,' Juliet said. 'Now I'm going to look after the boys.' She turned and stomped down into the boat.

Henrik turned to me. 'Anyway, let's let – what's that saying in English? – bygones be bygones. Is that it?'

I nodded stiffly, and he sat down heavily on the concrete quay and patted the ground beside him. 'Come on, let us be friends now we have sorted out this little "misunderstanding". Sit down.'

I did so reluctantly. Myken still stood above us, smouldering, and after a minute she said she was going back to the boat. The two of us were left alone on the quay.

'Don't worry about Myken – she will come round, but she takes these things harder than I do. You really disappointed us Guy, I hope you realise that. I thought of you as a friend.'

I stared down at my feet, uncertain of how I should be reacting.

'But no matter, it's all in the past now we've found you again. You know we bought a ranch in Argentina?'

'No,' I said stiffly.

'Yes, a beautiful horse ranch. We are going to move there and start a new life – we have done enough of the sailing for now. Would you like a cigarette?'

Reluctantly I found myself accepting one, finding myself drawn once more, against my better judgement, into the thrall of this oddly charismatic man. I fetched him a beer, and we carried on talking,

Juliet sending me daggers now and then out of the companionway. At last he struggled to his feet. 'Well, we must go – I don't suppose I can persuade you to join us for some drinks?'

I shook my head. I wasn't going to fall into that trap again. In my mind these two had become associated with the worst of my depression, and I did not want to revisit that territory when things were going so well, at least in all other senses but financially.

He wagged a finger at me. 'Well I will send you an email confirming our conversation, and you will return it, agreeing to our terms, yes?'

I nodded, and he gave a sinister laugh.

'If you let me down I will be coming to Scotland to find you – trust me Guy, I never give up.'

After buying two new batteries at a staggering price, we pressed on with preparing for our epic journey. Juliet staggered back several times from the supermarket with several trolley-loads of provisions, and then began the immense task of unpacking and repacking them in zip lock bags before stuffing them into every available drawer, locker and cubbyhole. The fridge had to be carefully layered so that the chilled food would be used in the right order – every time we opened it hard-earned cold air leaked away so, unlike with a household fridge, you couldn't afford to rummage at your leisure. I meanwhile did a thorough engine service, filled up tanks with fuel and water and re-organised the hellhole that was the cockpit locker. All safety items such as flares, lifejackets, torches, harnesses, cable-cutters, emergency tiller and washboards had to be dug out, checked and put in accessible places, and the faithful grab-bag stocked up with extra food and water. As Juliet and I sweated over these tasks, the boys had fun acquainting themselves with the marina and its occupants, running from boat to swimming pool and back again with breathless reports of each new discovery. Over the months we had seen inside some fantastic boats from super-yachts to tall ships, thanks to the boys' persuasiveness and charm, and we'd made some great friends too.

Finally, Juliet and I sat down to plan our journey. We spread the charts on the saloon table, and debated the options one final time. 'What about going west, through Puerto Rico and Cuba?' Juliet suggested, tracing her finger along the chart. 'I'd love to go to Cuba, and it's just a hop and a skip from there to Florida.'

'I know, but to see it properly would take weeks – won't it be frustrating to have to rush through? Also, they might make it difficult for us because we're going on to America.' American-registered boats weren't allowed into Cuba at all, but even for non-American boats the fact of just going there was enough to make the Cuban authorities suspicious of one's motives, and I'd heard of boats being impounded.

'Well, we don't want to get too close to Haiti either.' We stared at the chart as we considered the grim possibility of finding ourselves adrift off that supposedly lawless island – there had been some violent attacks on boats there and it was advised not to go anywhere near it.

'It'll take too long to go on the Caribbean side of the islands,' Juliet said. 'Look, it's much further. And the Atlantic coasts will be rough, even at this time of year – better to stay well away. What about this way?'

Her finger traced another route, northwest through the Turks and Caicos Islands and the Bahamas to the Florida coast.

'I don't know Jules, it's really shallow – look.' I opened up some large-scale charts of the Bahamas, which were almost solidly green and yellow, showing very shallow water. 'With the weather like it is . . . there aren't many places we could take shelter in, and the pilotage is really difficult. I can't think of anywhere worse to be in a storm. Anyway, is there any point in rushing through there either? I'd like to see it properly, and we don't have time.'

Juliet sighed and I knew she was facing the inevitable: the fastest, safest way of getting to America was to sail straight there.

But the grim reality was that it was a long passage, far off shore. Conditions were unpredictable and reports from people who had done the crossing varied widely from easy to appalling. The overwhelming point that everyone made was to avoid Cape Hatteras, which jutted out from America's eastern seaboard like a wounding elbow in a rugby scrum. Just the previous year, a much bigger yacht than *Forever*, and her very experienced crew, had completely disappeared with all hands in this region, and thousands of boats had been wrecked over the years along its treacherous coastline. Reports drifting back from participants in the ARC, which had left a week earlier, were of a horrendous passage to Bermuda. They had been overtaken by a scything low that had spun off from the American continent, bringing winds of up to 80 knots and some truly grim sea conditions that would have made the Anegada Passage look like a duck pond. But we could well come in for the same or worse, and the longer we left it the more likely we were to be hit by a tropical storm. Like everywhere else in the world, weather patterns were changing here, and the season of tropical storms was starting earlier each year.

We stared at the chart a little longer, until at last Juliet said, 'Well, where do we head to then?' I ran my finger up the US coastline. 'Not Florida – we'd still be too far south. Somewhere in the Carolinas ... Charlestown maybe. Or Savannah? We want to stay well south of Hatteras.'

Juliet laughed nervously and pointed at the chart. 'How about Cape Fear? May as well really let ourselves in for it.'

I opened the pilot book and quickly read the summary. 'Doesn't sound like there's anything too bad about the passage to it. OK, Cape Fear it is.'

'It's fourteen hundred miles.' She quickly did some calculations on a pad of paper and then stared at me. 'That's ten days, at least.'

We stared at each other as the gravity of this passage we were about to undertake came home to us. The most we'd ever been at sea was four days, and we'd been on our knees by the end.

'We can do it Jules, I know we can.' I stretched across the table and held her hand. 'We'll make a real project out of it – play games with the boys, read to them and all that . . .'

'That's all fine in theory, but what if the weather's bad?' She held her hands to the side of her face. 'Have we even got enough stuff to keep us going that long? I thought it would be a week at the most.'

'We're not going to run out of food – the boat's stuffed with it. As for water, we've got the water-maker, and fuel – the tanks are full, and we won't use much anyway, we'll be sailing all the way.'

We went to bed in a sober mood, each contemplating the great task that lay ahead. What I hadn't pointed out to Juliet was that we'd be passing through the infamous zone known as the Bermuda Triangle – it was no mystery to me why boats had disappeared in that turbulent corner of the Atlantic, where winds and currents ran in all directions. The Antilles Current ran towards the west, against the direction of the majority of lows that spun out from the continent of North America, spiralling their way east across the ocean. To cap it all, we would have to cross the Gulf Stream, one of the mightiest currents on earth. This ran powerfully in a northeasterly direction a hundred miles or so off the US coast, with various additional currents spinning off and forming leviathan eddies that were sometimes hundreds of miles wide. In anything other than a southerly wind the Gulf Stream could whip up ferocious seas and we had heard dark accounts of sailors whose boats had been literally shredded within just hours. In short, almost anything was possible in this area of the ocean.

SIXTEEN

AN INAUSPICIOUS DEPARTURE

18.26N: 64.45W

With a sense of history in the making, we weighed anchor and motored out of Great Harbour. Cries of 'Good luck!' and 'Safe journey!' rang out around the bay, and the boys leant over the side and shouted, 'Goodbye! Goodbye Caribbean! America here we come!'

As soon as we'd cleared the island we turned *Forever* into the wind, hoisted sail and switched our engine off, knowing that we had to be as economical as possible with our fuel. She caught the breeze, pointing towards the setting sun. A few minutes later we heard a distinct puff of air. 'Dolphins! Dolphins! Look!' Oscar shouted and we all rushed over to the side to see five dolphins, surfing and jumping and clicking around the boat. Dolphins swimming around a boat have always been considered a sign of good luck, and it felt as though they had come to see us off from the Caribbean, to wish us well and dispel our fears.

Later, as darkness fell and I took over at the helm, Juliet came up holding out a mug. 'Taste this,' she said.

I obediently took a sip of the tea and instantly spat it out again. 'Ugh – it's disgusting, it tastes salty. Where did it come from?'

'From the tap,' she said. 'I've been tasting salt for a while, but I hoped I was imagining it.'

Juliet was our canary when it came to water quality, her ability to detect the subtlest change of flavour in her cups of tea quite astonishing. I'd been running the water-maker to keep us topped up with fresh water and it obviously wasn't working.

We looked at each other as this devastating news sank in. 'What are we going to do?'

'Well it's still better than sea water – a bit. It'll be OK for showering and washing up, but we'll have to use bottled water for drinking. I would have got more if I'd known this was going to happen. We've got coke, ginger beer, a bit of juice . . . we'll just have to spin it out as best we can and hope we don't have too many delays.'

Later I dug my way into the bowels of the boat to unearth the water-maker, thanking my lucky stars for my seasickness patch. But no matter how much I adjusted the pressure and tightened up valves the water still came out brackish. Reluctantly we agreed not to use it any more as it would just pollute the water in the tanks even more. This was particularly annoying as we'd had it serviced in Trinidad at some expense – and before that it had worked perfectly.

We tried to subtly limit the children's intake of drinks without alerting them to the fact that anything was wrong. It was horrible to have to be stingy with drinks at sea, but we knew that it was better to conserve it now than run out later. As an added irritation, it meant that we had no fresh water to wash in and as the days wore on we grew increasingly itchy and salty, adding to our sense of confinement and discomfort.

Weather forecasts are crucial on a long offshore passage and this was our chance to hone our single sideband radio skills. We dug out the notes that we'd taken under Tessa's instruction, way back in Bonaire – at last the scrawled numbers and acronyms meant something – and each morning, as the boys sat hunched over their bowls of cereal, the inside of our floating home would resonate with clicks and bleeps as I tried to get a signal. After much fiddling with wires, an aged laptop and an outdated modem, we tuned into a frequency that allowed us to download a weather grid. Each morning we solemnly marked the progress of the various threatening weather systems on our chart, hoping that they would not swirl their way north across our track. I would also tune in to the broadcasts of various cranky radio hams, whose hobby was, oddly, assisting sailors in forecasting the weather while making ocean passages. These hams had god-like status for offshore sailors and went one step further than the standard forecaster, giving their opinion as to the best course to steer to take advantage of winds or run from storms. They could get quite irritated when their advice was ignored, and it had been known for sailors to be struck off their list if they acted contrary to directions.

Soon we were as hooked as everyone else, and listened in breathlessly as the well-known ham Herb Hildenburg passed on advice to sailors in our corner of the Atlantic.

'Herb,' I would hear a voice anxiously crackling – the sound was often poor with SSB, lending broadcasts a tense, wartime feel – 'Do you think I should keep steerin' north, or head west a little bit?'

I imagined him seated in an attic room, or garden shed perhaps, leaning a sage head to one side as he considered this particular person's dilemma. 'Oh, I would steer a little to the west if you can – avoid that system that's comin' down from Bermuda.' Sometimes I would try to fit in my own query, more just to make contact than anything else. His advice came from long experience of watching the weather in all its contortions and was always well judged – and at the mercy of the ocean, alone and inexperienced, it meant a lot to have somebody helping you figure out the best course.

Before we'd left, Juliet had made contact with Chris Parker, a professional ham broadcasting out of the Bahamas. He sent us daily forecasts by email, which we picked up via a laptop connected to the Iridium satellite phone. As well as the emails, we had also opted for the personalised forecast service and could talk to him by phone – all for a fee of course. It wasn't too long before we needed his advice as a series of lows combined to form a storm over the Pacific and there was much earnest discussion about which way they would track, and whether they would be upgraded to named tropical storms or even hurricanes. Even the mention of storms of this severity struck dread into our hearts.

For most of our journey the sea had been lumpy and confused, with fair-sized waves and unsettled winds, mostly dead astern. As we already knew to our cost this was *Forever*'s worst point of sailing, creating a rolling motion and lack of progress that was very frustrating. We all felt seasick intermittently, and once again fell into the pattern of barely eating. The one food that we never got sick of, strangely, was eggs and we ate them boiled, scrambled, fried and poached, usually on their own, as we'd run out of bread and didn't have the heart to make any.

Five days into the journey however, the wind dropped to nothing and the sea and sky became as still as a painting. After several hours of lolling about we discussed turning on the engine.

I was reluctant. 'What if we need it later on? I don't want to risk running low on fuel – we'll need the engine to get in.'

'I know,' Juliet replied, 'but the longer we're out here the more likely it is that we'll be hit by a storm. And we'll run out of water.'

I couldn't argue with her logic and so reluctantly turned it on, not enjoying the exhaust fumes that were blown through the boat by the following wind. We motored on all through the night and the following morning, as the day dawned overcast, I spotted the first great anvil-shaped thunderclouds glowering on the horizon. The waves rose up and fell away unsteadily, as if they too were nervous, and *Forever* began to labour in the awkward waters. I pointed to the north and predicted thunder.

Through the day the clouds grew bigger and bigger and more of them gathered until the whole horizon looked like a mountain range made up entirely of towering storm clouds. By late afternoon it was clear that we were not going to be able to avoid them and dark gusts of wind began to fly across the water towards us and patches of rain broke out. I tied everything down, leaving just the small staysail for stability. The tension was unbearable. Ominous rumbles broke out and forked lightning flashed on all sides. Between the storms I could see faint gaps and wondered in desperation if we could pass between them.

Juliet took the helm as I went to check the radar screen. The boys were settled in their berth now, and it felt snug and safe down below. I knew that it was anything but and that if we were hit by a lightning strike, which seemed almost inevitable with our great mast acting like a magnet, all our systems could go down in one fell swoop and we'd be left with nothing to navigate with. Worse still, the boat could catch fire. This was what could have happened to the lost boats in the Bermuda Triangle. I thought: it would be so easy to disappear out here.

The radar screen backed up what I'd seen with my own eyes, that we were indeed surrounded. The bright little white cross that represented our home and our lives glimmered in between the storm clouds, which showed ghostly green as if they'd been sent up from the graveyard of the Bermuda Triangle to hunt for fresh blood. There was no way out: we just had to await our fate and as if to underline that fact we suddenly lurched hard. I pulled on my oilskins and went back on watch, leaving Juliet to be with the boys, and I heard her soothing them, though I knew she was frightened herself. Heavy rain was now falling and *Forever* threw her bow into the growing sea. All at once it turned dark, with the sky stage-lit by the eerie light of flickering lightning, followed by the rumble and clap of thunder that was so loud I could feel the vibrations in my chest. Juliet put the weatherboards in the companionway, sealing herself and the boys inside the boat and I saw her pull the grab bag from its place beneath the steps.

I clipped on my harness and settled down to let it do its worst.

The wind and sea built over the next few hours, with periods of stillness on the black, lumpy ocean interspersed with gusts that reached 50 knots as cold air plummeted down from the storm clouds. From time to time I heard one of the boys cry out, and hated myself for doing this to them. At around two in the morning I decided to take the staysail down but it wouldn't budge and I realised something was jammed forwards. There was no alternative to going up on deck and taking the sail down by hand. I needed Juliet to take the helm.

Lightning crackled across an immense bank of cloud hanging above us and thunder ripped its way down so loudly that we ducked. 'Turn her into the wind!' I shouted as I crawled my way up the deck. Immediately we turned into the waves we felt their full size, and I clung to the Samson post as *Forever* lurched and pulled with a great weight of water on her bow flowing thickly around my legs. I worked as fast as I could to lower the sail as the boat climbed each wave. Although I was clipped on I didn't want to test out my harness or the jack lines which we had run down the deck on each side of the boat. Plenty of sailors are gravely injured hanging over the side of their boats.

At last the sail was in and I crawled my way back to the cockpit as Juliet bore away. Like me, she was completely soaked through and though she looked scared I knew she was nowhere near to her limits.

She was being sustained by a strength that seemed just as elementally powerful as any thunderstorm – her instinct to protect her children, her boat, her home and our lives. I motioned to her that she should go down below to be with the boys, she nodded, and without words I took the helm again.

By luck as much as design I seemed to be managing to keep *Forever* on the fringes of the storms, but just before dawn a giant mass of cloud hung over the horizon. This was the biggest storm yet, and I called down to Juliet to read the radar screen so I could try to steer a route past the menacing brute.

'Turn ten degrees to starboard,' she shouted. 'More: ninety degrees – three o'clock.' She paused as she watched our new direction take force. 'Try one-eighty!'

'But that's going back the way we came,' I shouted. 'The storm will catch us up!'

Another pause and then she emerged from the hatch. 'I'm sorry, nothing's working – this storm is so huge, we'll just have to go straight through it.'

I nodded like a man steadying himself before being read a death sentence. 'Can you mark our position on the chart and the time beside it? At least that way we'll know where we were if we get hit. Stay below with the boys and keep away from any metal.'

I looked around the cockpit to see what other precautions I could take, and was relieved that the wheel and deck of the cockpit had not been replaced in Trinidad and were wooden, and in addition I was wearing Crocs.

The sky seemed to be lit for disaster, orange-gold, with the great anvil-shaped thundercloud almost black ahead. As the storm moved to directly above us the wind dropped and for a while the seaway was as quiet as a library, until a single crack of thunder rang out directly overhead, followed by a shot of lightning and then heavy drumming rain. As we cut our way deeper beneath the storm cloud it felt as if we were entering the halls of some meteorological Valhalla, and I expected that any moment a bolt of lightning would sear down from the clouds and split our mast asunder. At one point I glanced down towards the boys' porthole and saw Oscar's face lit for a moment by the flickering light. He seemed to be in a trance, drained by the fear that surrounded him.

And then – like a miracle – we passed through the looming grey cathedral of menace, and immediately the sea grew choppier and a brisk wind caught our staysail and lifted our speed by a couple of knots. I turned to watch the vaults of thunder receding, and wondered at the sheer strangeness of the experience. How odd it felt in this crowded planet to be so alone with my family, days from land in any direction, utterly at the mercy of the elements in a small boat. Who would ever choose such a fate? Yet in a strange way it felt more natural than anything we had ever experienced as a family – as if we were facing up to and overcoming real fears. At home the adversity we faced was based around the virtual worlds of debt and repayment. Yet here no detachment was possible – we had gone back in time and were facing the same fears and challenges that families have faced since the dawn of it all. A journey, the elements, a hope for harbour.

At last dawn broke out across the eastern sky and as I hoisted a reefed mainsail, intense tiredness seeped through me. I looked ahead and saw that we had passed through the worst of it and the sky towards the northwest looked clear. I pushed open the heavy companionway hatch and climbed down the steps, zooming out on the radar screen to check there was no other shipping. Nothing was showing, so I stripped off my wet clothes and headed for our bunk. Juliet was lying half-asleep in the saloon, still in her wet gear, and sat up as I passed.

'Shall I go on watch?' she asked groggily.

'No – get some sleep. We're through the worst of the storms. I've switched on the radar alarm so it'll wake us if anything comes within 25 miles.'

I fell into a delicious sleep and a few hours later woke to the heavenly sound of the kettle going down on the stove. I peeped out and saw Juliet busy in the galley. The boys were drawing content-edly in the saloon as the boat rocked quietly on the waves. *Forever's* insides creaked lovingly and our world had become as snug as if we had moved into a nutshell.

'Everything OK Jules?' I called.

'Yes, I'm making pancakes.'

After breakfast I put the sails up and Juliet plotted our course for Cape Fear. The sky was bright, clear with white, fluffy clouds and a fresh happy drying wind blew in from the southwest. Juliet stared distractedly over the horizon: 'We're about halfway there now,' she said. 'I think we were lucky last night, don't you? Lightning is a completely random thing, there's nothing you can do to protect yourself.'

I nodded and waited: I knew she had something on her mind.

She took a deep breath and turned to me. 'Guy, I don't think we should take the boys across the Atlantic.'

'I know. I've been thinking the same thing.'

She sighed with relief. 'It's too far, and too dangerous. All that way too – we're guaranteed to have at least one bad storm on that route, and it'll be cold and wet and rough. There are too many risks. What if we were hit by lightning or one of them got injured, or we hit a container in the night? How would we live with ourselves? And it's not just their safety – it's also the boredom, and the seasickness. Weeks and weeks at sea is just too long at their age.'

'Jules, I agree. But what are we going to do then? We have to get the boat across.'

She took another breath. 'I'll fly home with them.'

'But what am I going to do?' I couldn't possibly bring the boat back alone. 'That's a massive sacrifice for you Jules. And I want us to be together – we're a good team.'

'I know Guy, but it's a sacrifice I'm prepared to make, for the sake of the boys. Get someone to go with you – how about David? He was keen. And you know it'll make the crossing far easier, not having the kids around. You'll be able to do proper watch systems, and not worry about cooking when the weather's rough. And you won't have that awful guilt when they're miserable and sick and scared – like they were last night. I think it's enough; we've done enough. I don't want to push them any more.'

I could see her mind was made up and I couldn't disagree. It would be vastly easier without the boys on board, yet it was a huge disappointment, having come so far, to separate at this stage. Juliet and I had just got the hang of running the boat, we were a good team, and now all that shared experience would be sacrificed at the time when I'd need it most. Would David really be prepared to come with me? And was he up to it, or would he just be someone else to look after? He'd run a fishing boat in Alaska for many years, so he must be used to rough sea conditions, and have some experience of engines, which would be useful. Yet it was a risk undertaking such a remote and testing journey with only one crewman, and at that a man whom I knew very little about.

I sailed on soberly, my thoughts full of worries and doubts and plans.

Days passed and as our pencil line extended up the chart we began to feel as though our journey would never end. One morning I saw Juliet raking through the lockers behind the saloon seat cushions. She was muttering to herself.

'How much do we have left?' I asked.

'Four two-litre bottles of water, that's . . .'

'Enough for four days, if we each have half a litre per day.'

Half a litre wasn't much in these hot conditions, and both of us knew it. Dehydration was one of the most common causes of problems at sea.

'And other drinks?'

'There are still a few cans . . . not much though. And we've got no fresh food left at all – and hardly any eggs. God I hope we get there soon! How much further?'

I looked at the chart. 'About five hundred miles, I'd say four days at least.'

'Still longer than the Caribbean crossing! Oh my god, I don't know how much longer I can deal with this. I feel horrible too – so salty. I wish that damn water-maker hadn't stopped working!'

The boys flopped about, doing surprisingly well at amusing themselves despite the confinement of the long passage that would have sent many adults crazy. Early on in the journey Oscar asked me, 'How much further Dad?' and I answered, 'Ten days, son.' He looked at me blankly, unable to comprehend it. They would move from drawing to reading to staring to reading to drawing again, interspersed with self-devised games using utensils from the gallery or lengths of string. A favourite toy was the corkscrew, which could be an aeroplane, a person, or – less popular with Juliet and me – a drill.

Admiring their manful efforts to keep themselves occupied, that afternoon I decided to treat them to a bit of fishing. They wanted to try trolling a lure over the side, which others seemed to do with great success, but we had never caught anything other than one barracuda, which nearly took my fingers off when I brought it on deck.

They were excited to see all the colourful lures, and it was wonderful to see them so happy and engaged with something. They attached them to the ends of their lines, and then rigged them on either side, beer cans with a few coins inside attached so that we'd hear if they caught anything.

The thought of trying to land, kill and gut a possibly quite big fish on deck in this rolly swell was not appealing, and I crossed my fingers that they wouldn't catch anything. Every few minutes one of them would call out, 'I've got something Dad!' and I would reel in yards and yards of the line, only to find the hook empty at the end. After a while they lost interest and drifted off to do other things. We forgot all about the lines and some time later we switched on the engine as we were making little progress and turned into the wind to furl the mainsail.

The engine suddenly choked and stopped. Juliet and I stared at each other in horrified realisation.

'It's those bloody fishing lines,' I said. 'They've fouled the prop! I'll have to go over the side.' I stood and lifted the helmsman's seat to fetch my mask and snorkel.

She stared down at the water, looking worried. 'Tie yourself on, the current's strong – about 2 knots – and you'll never keep up with the boat.'

I let myself slip out along the line and when I reached the stern ducked under the water to try to get down to the prop. But now that I was in the water I could feel the full speed that the boat was moving at – 2 knots didn't sound like a lot, but it was enough to make it difficult to get beneath the surface, as the current generated by our momentum kept sending me back up. In a series of short dashes I managed to slash at the fishing line, a task made much more difficult by the fact that it was impossible to see. Eventually it came free and the propeller began to turn again, and with relief I surfaced, giving a thumbs up to the family who were all peering anxiously over the stern.

I pulled my way along the line, realising that it was going to be very difficult to get back onto the boat. I tried putting my feet on *Forever*'s rounded sides to walk my way up, holding onto the line for support, but my feet kept slipping off. I tried reaching for the gunwale, but her sides were too high. This would be the moment for a shark to come along, I thought, as my legs hung down into the water, no doubt giving the appearance of a surfing fish. But then I had an idea.

'Jules! Pull me up on the winch!'

I flopped aboard like a stranded whale. 'Phew! I was beginning to wonder what the hell we were going to do there. No more fishing I'm afraid. I don't want to become the bait!'

At last the chart told us that we had only two hundred miles to go, and we began looking out for that great river in the Atlantic, the Gulf Stream. Running around one hundred miles off the coast, the Gulf Stream is around sixty miles wide in places and surges north at anything from 2 to 8 knots. We watched the weather carefully, hoping that the wind would not come round to the North as this would could make a crossing of the stream deadly. And then we were hit by another night of thunderstorms and squalls. This time we hove to immediately, not wanting to get anywhere near the stream in such turbulent conditions. The tactic worked and the weather passed over us to reveal a bright sunny morning and a good strong wind from the southeast.

Around mid-morning the next day we suddenly slowed down dramatically to half speed.

We had to be in an eddy coming off the stream and sure enough, ten minutes later we'd entered the stream proper, and could actually see it as we approached, the water a deeper, richer blue than the surrounding sea. For a moment *Forever*'s rudder felt loose, and then heavy as the vast current took hold of us. Great rolling waves surfed in a northerly direction, luckily we were now aided by the wind rather than struggling against it, and fluffy clouds scudded across a bright blue sky. All around us the world became full of euphoric movement, and soon *Forever*'s speed had increased to over 10 knots as the current and wind combined to push us on. I had to work hard to not let her be hit by the waves broadside, and steered her down the steep waves and then up again to skim along their tops before plummeting back down. The boys shrieked with delight and hanging onto the edge of the cockpit they spotted two fat, sleek dolphins, bigger than anything we had seen in the Caribbean, shoot out from the blue side of a wave. They called out with joy as they torpedoed into the curving valley beneath. This was far from the horrific meeting with the Gulf Stream that we had been warned of, and we knew we'd been lucky, as if nature had decided to give us a break.

The Gulf Stream was hurtling us in a northerly direction, and if she'd had her way we would have kept going till she dumped us at Cape Hatteras. Soon our problem was how to get off the oceanic conveyor belt, and we had to work quite hard to maintain our course to the west. After several hours our free ride was over, and as the colour of the water returned to normal and our speed slowed I knew we'd jumped off. I went below to check the chart, and then adjusted our course for the Cape Fear River in North Carolina.

Great caution was called for in our approach to this coastline, nicknamed 'the graveyard of the Atlantic'. The entrance to Cape Fear is bounded by the Frying Pan Shoals, a long, shifting area of shallows that juts out from the coast. It stretches some thirty miles south from Bald Head Island, which marks the entrance to Cape Fear, out into the ocean, and I could see from the chart that the area was littered with literally hundreds of shipwrecks.

'That's why they called it Cape Fear I suppose,' Juliet shuddered as she looked over my shoulder at the chart.

'Yes, that and the pirates – this was a piracy hotspot. Blackbeard lived for a time around here somewhere.' I pointed to the intricate offshore areas of sounds and sandbars shown on the chart that stretch towards the north, which must have made perfect hiding places for wanted men.

The fact that we were drawing close to land now turned from a joy to a concern, as we realised how dangerous a seaway this was. Although we were still some way off the coast, the shallows stretched a long way out and we were hurtling fast towards it on the shoulders of a 25-knot wind. Around dusk Juliet went down to check the chart, and came up looking worried. 'We're only fifty miles off,' she said. 'We're getting there too quickly now, after all that time when we were going so slowly. But I don't want to go any closer in darkness.'

'I agree – let's heave to overnight.'

I could see the light of the buoy that marks the edge of the Frying Pan Shoals flashing, and numerous other lights were now visible as great container ships ploughed up and down the coastline. From the chart I saw that we were just on the edge of the busy shipping channel that runs up the east coast of the US towards Newport, New York and other great harbours. The wind was still blowing strongly and even with the boat hove to we were drifting slightly into the channel. I wondered what to do: I didn't want to get closer inshore, or turn back east, yet I felt vulnerable with all this shipping around.

I decided to give the coastguard a call, and went below to the chart table. We all watched the radio in hope of a response, wondering if we were still too far out, and then it came, the beautiful confirmation that we were almost there.

'This is the United States Coastguard, North Carolina division. Go ahead *Forever*.'

'Thank you coastguard. We're a family boat at position 033°11'55"N; 077°40'48"W, we've just sailed up from the Virgin islands and are not keen to approach the coast in darkness. Hoping to remain hove to overnight in this position and will put out an hourly securité for shipping. Is this possible? Over.'

The radio crackled into action. '*Forever*, this is the US Coastguard North Carolina division, answer is affirmative, you may remain in that position. Welcome to the United States of America.'

As I thanked them and signed out, the boys jumped for joy on the saloon benches, grabbing expertly at handholds, like happy monkeys, as she rolled around. 'Mum! Dad! We're almost there!'

At midnight I sat in the cockpit looking all around in the darkness, clutching the hand-held VHF radio and calling out our position from time to time. In the early hours of the morning I saw the lights of a huge container ship to the south of us, and I called out my securité message. A richly accented southern voice crackled out in response.

'Sailing vessel *Forever*, this is *Fortuna*.'

'*Fortuna* this is *Forever*.'

'Go to channel 13.'

I switched channels.

'*Forever*, this is *Fortuna*, I'm gonna pass you on the port bow. I am aware of your position and will pass shortly. Over.'

The huge ship loomed out of the darkness and passed by, and then the leviathan radioed me again. '*Forever* this is *Fortuna*. Sure is good to see a boat hove to. Welcome to Cape Fear. Don't get no closer to that Frying Pan Shoal now.'

I radioed back our thanks and felt happier than I had been for a long time. I had a feeling that coastal America was going to be a good place, if this is how we were being treated offshore, and it was reassuring to have contact with the outside world at last.

At dawn Juliet took over on watch, and I grabbed a few hours of sleep before we pointed for land. Gradually the water grew shallower, and changed from deep blue to a bright green. We had been cruising over water 5,000 feet deep in places and now the depth gauge was showing less than five fathoms. For a long time we couldn't see land, and the children grew increasingly frustrated, as if it might be a trick.

And then at last we saw it, the faint outline of low-lying, sandy country.

'Land! Land!' the boys shouted, feeling the greatest excitement yet at making landfall.

Gradually, tantalisingly, we inched our way closer to the mouth of the Cape Fear River, followed by a boisterous swell. We were in tidal waters now, and the tide was flooding into the river mouth, bringing us hurtling in with it like a bath toy pulled towards the plug. After negotiating a choppy stretch of channel between ominously chiming buoys, we sailed past a golden sand bar to port and entered the river on sensuous curves that wound over to the dainty village of Southport.

As is the way with boats, just as we thought our difficulties were over, a whole new set of challenges was thrown at us in the form of tide, current and shallow water. Juliet had dug out the charts of the area, but they were in an unfamiliar format (we had relied mainly on Admiralty charts up until this point), and we had trouble reading them.

I gunned the throttle to keep *Forever* in the middle of the channel.

'I hope the engine doesn't give out on us.' She looked at the muddy banks, close on each side. 'We'd be literally up the creek.' We both laughed nervously and the boys joined in, chattering and squealing with delight, their noses in the air smelling the warm pine scented wind that came off the land.

'How's the fuel?'

'Probably pretty low actually. Take the wheel – I'm going to get the anchor ready to drop, just in case.'

But the fuel held out, and the anchor wasn't needed as we called the Southport Marina office, and then made our way towards the dock as instructed.

'Are you sure there's enough water in here?' Juliet agonised as she hung out the fenders.

'Well they said so – and I told them our draught.'

We approached the dock and peered down into the brown, muddy water, which revealed nothing, unlike the crystal clarity of the Caribbean. But the depth held good, and Juliet leapt ashore as we gently came alongside, almost collapsing as her legs hit the relative solidity of the quay. We tied up, and two men on a local yacht nearby looked on with good-natured disbelief as first Juliet and then the boys lay face down on the wooden boards and kissed the dock.

'We've made it, we've made it, I can't believe it!' exclaimed Juliet, turning over onto her back and staring up at the sky. Her eyes filled with tears, and in that moment I could see the toll that the journey had taken on her and the deep worries she had had to suppress for the boys' sake. A lump too caught in my throat as relief flooded through me. The boys staggered around on wobbly legs, lurching from side to side in exaggerated fashion like the pirates who had once roamed this region. We had crossed 1,400 miles of open ocean, not as a crew of professional seamen or a group of hardy men, but as a small family of four, and the simple sense of achievement was enormous. We had got there, we had found safe harbour.

As we carried out our standard post-passage routine, tidying up, collecting laundry and opening hatches, Juliet held up a half-empty two-litre bottle of water. 'That's our last one,' she said. 'And there are just a few cans left. A close-run thing, huh?'

We walked along the dock to the small marina office, where a man confirmed that the local customs officer would visit us the next morning. We realised how hungry we were and set off in search of food, wandering through the small town of Southport, where delicate painted wooden houses with cool, bare-footed porches were set within richly planted gardens. We revelled in the sight of green after so much blue, white and grey. To our scent-starved noses the aroma of magnolia and gardenia filled the air with a perfume that was intoxicating. Fireflies dotted beneath the bushes waiting for night, and cicadas chirped loudly. It all felt exotic and familiar at the same time.

We headed for the old fishing port, and walked into a waterside restaurant with the single aim of letting rip. Budget or no budget, cash or no cash, this was going to be a celebration of Romanesque proportions – with a few obvious adjustments given the presence of children, such as not getting blind drunk. I made a mental note never to forget this moment. The waiter came over, a bouncy young man with the kind of enthusiasm for service that you only get in America.

'Howdy guys, where've y'all come from?' he asked as he passed out menus.

Luke said enigmatically, 'From the sea.'

'That sounds nice buddy,' the waiter said. 'Been out far today, have you?'

'One thousand four hundred miles,' Luke muttered in the style of Russell Crowe.

The waiter looked at me, bemused, and I nodded. 'We just got in from the Caribbean.'

'How long did that take?'

'Ten days and ten nights!' Luke announced proudly sitting bolt upright. His older brother sighed and rolled his eyes to heaven.

The waiter looked at him. 'Hold on a moment.' He walked over to the counter and talked to a large man, who bent his head to listen and looked over to us, then raised a hand and smiled as the waiter walked back.

'Your dinner's on us,' he said to the boys, 'Congratulations – and welcome to America.'

We relished the joy of sitting at a table that didn't move, eating off plates that didn't slide and food that didn't try to escape from our plates. Sleep was going to feel better than ever before, in a still boat, with nothing to worry about and nothing banging or crashing.

Our boat lay lightly on her lines waiting for us, like a horse grazing on her tether and building strength for the journey still to come.

SEVENTEEN

AMERICA'S BACKYARD

33.55N: 78.1W

After a couple of days in Southport we continued north via the Intra-Coastal Waterway, a system of rivers, lagoons and channels that runs all the way up America's east coast. This route allowed us to avoid the dangerous shoals and currents around Cape Hatteras, and would take us two hundred miles through the 'backyard' of America. The navigational issues now changed and where once we had sailed over water so deep that our depth gauge couldn't register it, now we found ourselves edging our way along impossibly shallow stretches, as *Forever* turned from offshore passage-maker to canal boat. The route took us through varied country, from sandy to wooded, from built up to deserted, often running close to the ocean, so that now and then we still caught a familiar waft of the sea drifting across the low, scrubby dunes. Sometimes we passed through affluent neighbourhoods, the American Dream-style landscape of speedboats, wooden houses, immaculate lawns, launches and sailing boats tied up at their jetties. Other times we passed rough settlements, where houses stood on stilts and bunches of kids sat fishing from broken-down piers or simply stood staring at us as we passed. There was a slow, timeless feeling to this meandering and in one place we saw men treading through the shallows, feeling for clams with their feet in the mud in a style of fishing that was aboriginal in its simplicity.

With her six-foot draught, *Forever* was at the very top end of the kind of boat that it was possible to take through these narrow channels, so it was essential to follow the markers religiously. Occasionally the markers were in the wrong place, as the shifting sands had changed the geography of the channels, and we would find ourselves softly aground on yielding mud. Thanks to *Forever*'s powerful engine we always managed to reverse out of these situations, crossing our fingers in case she sucked up sand that could clog the engine. Then we would edge around nervously, trying to work out where the safe water was, more often than not running aground again. Sweat would gather with the searing heat of another windless day, and we would flail about like a hippo trapped in a drought-stricken river, before by luck or design we would find the channel and continue on our way, leaving a billowing cloud of silt and mud in the water behind us.

At night we anchored in narrow side channels that ran to and from the sea, the boat turning on its anchor in response to the tide and the fierce currents that ran through them. We sat for hours watching the wind playing across the dried tips of marram grass, turning them silver as the gusts passed over. One morning anchored off Belhaven we woke to what we thought was dense fog, until we realised from our smarting eyes and the scent of burning that it was smoke from fires. The wind had changed and brought the acrid smoke from the pine-clad wilderness inland in our direction, and for a couple of days we found ourselves navigating blind, unable to see anything beyond the bow. During these days we were completely dependent on our chart plotter and radar, and issuing a securité every so often to let other craft know that we were coming. Now and then we saw a commercial barge or fishing boat emerge from the gloom, and we sank back as far as we dared to the channel's edges, in the knowledge that we had only a few feet of water on either side.

The forest fires bought clouds of flying insects and as we left Belhaven we were hit by a plague of tiny flying beetles that had fled from the woods nearby. Never an insect lover, Juliet rushed round closing hatches, but in the space of just a few minutes they had filled every space, showing a particular preference for the watery solace of the heads, sinks and bilges. For days afterwards they'd turn up in the sugar, cereal, icebox, engine compartment and even our bunks, until we gave up screaming and just learnt to live with it.

After a day or two we cleared the forest fires, emerging from the gloom into the sunlight. Then we snaked our way along intriguingly named waterways – the Pungo, Alligator River – passing through long stretches of untended woodland thick with tangled lianas. Here the air filled our lungs with the thick scent of the herbaceous tangle, and we could smell the delectable hot resin from the pine trees. The cries of birds rang out into the stillness and amongst the trees we glimpsed deer, and even on one occasion a black bear. It was an affirmation of the many zones of near wilderness that still exist within America.

Ranged across the waterway were numerous bridges of every shape and size, some high and fixed, and we got into a habit of checking and rechecking their height, looking up nervously as *Forever*'s mast approached them. Our eyes told us that it must surely hit them, though we knew it couldn't. Sometimes we joined a queue of boats to circle impatiently and wait for a bridge to open, other times the bridge operator would see us coming, and we waved our thanks as we passed through. One late afternoon we were approaching Beaufort, where a long, sinuous channel wiggled its way towards a bridge that would let us through to the town. We'd left it late and were worried about finding somewhere to spend the night so I called the bridge operator to ask if we could get through. While we waited I turned in a circle within the pool that lay just south of the bridge, and after a moment the radio crackled.

'Sailing vessel heading south,' a voice said, 'this is the bridge. You might want to know that you're heading for shallow water.'

I checked the depth gauge and looked around: it looked perfectly innocent.

'Bridge, this is *Forever*. Thanks for the warning – I will be turning shortly.'

'Turn Guy,' Juliet said. 'He must know what he's talking about.'

'I repeat,' the voice said, 'you will run aground if you continue on that course.' And, as he ended the broadcast I clearly heard him say the word 'idiot' to the person beside him in his little cubbyhole.

'Bridge, we are not idiots,' I responded pettily.

Juliet looked at me incredulously. 'Do it Guy. Now!'

'I'm just about ...' and with a giant thud *Forever* stopped dead in her tracks. Everything went flying, including Luke, who came perilously close to falling off the bow.

'You are a fucking idiot!' shouted Juliet.

'Dad!' shouted the kids.

'Astern dummy!' shouted the voice from the bridge.

From the sudden and complete lack of motion I knew that this was no mud bank – we were stuck fast. I put the engine astern, and after staying put for a few seconds *Forever* came free of whatever obstruction she had caught on. I ran down to check the bilges and luckily *Forever*'s solid construction saved our bacon, and it seemed there was no serious damage. To do him credit the bridge operator refrained from making any further comments as we motored through, though if he'd called me an idiot again, this time I would have agreed. The incident was a warning: never be smug. No matter how many miles of experience you accumulate there is always space for stupid mistakes.

Soon enough our passage through the backwaters of America was nearly over and we weren't far from rejoining the ocean in the wide, gracious waters of the Chesapeake Bay. Just before we passed out of North Carolina and into Virginia, we stopped in Coinjock, which made me think of a particularly uncomfortable species of underwear. This tiny settlement had a scattering of houses, a motel-cum-marina and shop. We needed to stop for a few hours to do some work on the engine and as we came into the ragged dock we threw our lines to a man wearing a large straw hat. He had long hair, a majestic beard and moustache and was covered in colourful tattoos.

'Hey, my name is Earl. Can I help you guys with anything?'

'No, we're fine thanks. Just stopping off to have a look at the engine.'

'Sure, you guys just take your time.' He smiled widely at us.

As I began dismantling the saloon to get at the engine, Juliet made yet another attempt to sweep out the bugs. The boys ran off to explore returning within a couple of minutes.

'Mum! Dad! Can we go fishing? There's a boy along there that's going to give us some tips.'

They disappeared and we didn't hear anything for a while. Now and then Juliet popped her head out of the companionway to check and saw them standing on the quayside outside the store, happily trying out their new casting skills. Meanwhile I continued working at the engine. In doing some routine maintenance I must have dislodged something, and now, for some reason it wouldn't start. Eventually after much sweating, swearing and consulting of various books and manuals, the engine fired into life.

'Jules! I've done it!' I shouted triumphantly.

'Great, well done!'

'Come on, let's have a drink. I'll just turn off the engine . . .' I pressed the button, but nothing happened – the engine ran on unabated. 'Oh great. Now I can't stop it.'

I was puzzling over this new conundrum when I heard two loud retorts from a small calibre rifle. I jumped off the boat and ran towards the store, readying myself for the kind of encounter that I've only ever seen on film. The boys were jumping up and down on the quayside, shouting, 'Snake! Snake!' and pointing down into the water, while the locals laughed along with good-natured indulgence. A huge man stood beside them holding an automatic .22 pistol. 'Goddamn cotton mouth – where'd it go boys?' he drawled.

Luke pointed again. 'There!' and we all saw the long black snake, its sinister white mouth opening as it swam through the water. The man aimed and shot, but the snake swirled out of the way, heading across the river. He whistled loudly, and an equally large man with a handsome handlebar moustache emerged from a shack on the other side of the river, wearing nothing but a pair of underpants. 'Coinjocks' I thought to myself. He cupped his hands, and called across: 'What's bothering ya'all?'

'Cotton mouth coming your way!'

The man on the other side held up a hand and walked back into his house. He emerged moments later bearing an immense pump shotgun, and wandered down to the water's edge and cast about a bit before he spotted the snake, which he proceeded to blast into eternity, creating explosions as if he were depth-charging a submarine.

The big man on our side walked towards me, smiling warmly as if nothing out of the ordinary had taken place. 'You got some real good boys here, I gotta tell ya.'

'Thanks.' I held out a hand, which disappeared within his great leathery mitt. He looked over across the water. 'Them snakes get kinda aggressive from time to time.'

From what I'd seen the snake wasn't the one with the anger management problem, but I just smiled.

'Now Oscar here tells me you gotta problem with your engine?'

'Yes, there's something going on with the wiring that I can't seem to figure out. First it wouldn't start, and now it won't stop. Can you believe it?'

He grinned. 'Sure can. Be happy to take a look for ya – got some experience of these things. No charge now!' He clapped me on the back and walked beside me to the boat.

'Really?' Once again I was flummoxed by the kindness of Americans, who time and time again had come to our rescue. 'Well that would be great, if you don't mind . . .'

For the next hour he showed me how to manually stop the engine by reaching for a fuel shut-off switch but finally, after long diatribes about the state of American politics, namely 'that homo Obama', he admitted I would need a new part in order to fix it properly. Tolerant or not, he had been kind to help us.

Undeterred by the snake or the shooting, Oscar and Luke fished most of the afternoon and evening, as it became obvious that, with the engine unfixed, we would have to stay overnight. I'd given them advice about which lures to use, which they'd ignored, and been dragged out repeatedly to untangle lines and free snagged hooks from trees, ropes, the side of the dock and pilings. I decided to leave them to it and was just settling down for a nap in the cockpit when I heard shouting. Another false alarm I thought and sat up with a sigh. But then I saw that Oscar's rod was bent hard over in a great arc of excitement. I jumped off the boat and handed Luke the landing net. 'OK! Let's see if you've got supper!'

To my genuine amazement, Oscar pulled a beautiful big flounder into the net. The boys jumped and cheered and – thanks entirely to them – we sat down to a perfect meal of breaded flounder, caught from the muddy river beneath our floating home.

EIGHTEEN

THROUGH THE HEART
OF A NAVY TOWN

36.52N: 76.19W

'**S**ir, please step away from the dock.'

I froze as the officious, slow-moving lock keeper, covered in a dazzling array of buoyancy aids, whistles and radios, walked towards the quayside. We were tying up to the side of a massive lock, that would lower us from the ICW into the Elizabeth River, which in turn would lead us into the heart of Norfolk, Virginia, one of the world's biggest naval towns.

I wanted to get tied up as swiftly as possible before the immense lock gates began to open, and had been about to step ashore with our lines, when he stopped me. I waited in the cockpit impatiently as he walked across, making it clear with every step that he wasn't going to hurry on my behalf. He held a hand out for my stern line. 'Sir, do not embarrass me by attempting to step ashore without a life preserver. I control all the lines here; you do not step ashore at any time without my express permission.'

'I was just going to step ashore for a moment to tie up my boat . . .'

He held a hand up to silence me and turned to Juliet, who was waiting with the bow line, and sighed heavily. 'Perhaps my English isn't very good, can you understand me OK?' He shook his head in faux despair, he knelt down and looked at me squarely. 'Let me say it one more time. At no time are you able to step ashore here, understood?' He stood with a sigh, sounding like a punctured inflatable as he coiled our line around a cleat. 'OK, are you ready to pass through? You'll need to lengthen these lines as you go down.'

I thought how perfectly Dan Ackroyd would have played this officious character, who was deploying his municipal powers to their maximum potential. 'Yes Sir!' I raised my arm in a salute, trying to bring a little light to the proceedings and he froze for just a second as if he suspected, rightly, that I might be being facetious. For a moment I thought he must be reviewing his powers of arrest. Then he gave me a final scathing look to ensure that I registered his complete contempt for sailing boats and all who rode on them. As the water flooded out of the lock Juliet and I stood bow and stern, hastily paying out the lines, yet keeping them taut enough for *Forever* not to swirl too far out from the dock.

And then we were out, and sailing along the languid river, moving *Forever* gently downstream on our way to Norfolk, our first big river city. Gradually the wild growth on the banks of the Elizabeth River gave way to industrial sprawl. The boys stood on the foredeck, enthralled by the prospect of floating into the midst of a city as great steel bridges, blackened by time, Victorian in their solidity, rose to allow us through. As the river widened out towards the harbour we saw great shipyards stretching back on either side. Further into the harbour we passed more and more ships, feeling dwarfed by their immensity, staying just outside the channel for fear of being run down. The boys called and waved up to the ships, often getting salutes and smiles in return from sailors and airmen who stood on the decks. Watching their excitement I reflected on the amazing freedom of a sailing boat: that in the space of a one day, you could find yourself alone in a deserted anchorage, then drifting through the heart of the world's greatest armada.

By sea is the most wonderful way to enter a city, as you arrive right in the heart of it. The radio crackled into life and a stern voice issued a warning to all shipping. 'Any vessel coming beyond the one hundred foot exclusion zone around US Naval shipping and property will be stopped using lethal force, I repeat, lethal force.'

Up ahead of us the city of Norfolk began to open up, its pleasant-looking harbour front, with rows of masts showing the location of a marina. Yet we found ourselves in the midst of the seagoing equivalent of Spaghetti Junction and concentrated hard on following the markers as boats of all shapes and sizes moved all around us. We tied up in the marina and with a ticklish sense of novelty ventured into the city, finding it odd to be amongst traffic and crowds after many months at sea. We must have looked oddly bemused and out of time, staring at everything and everyone as we walked slowly amidst the crowds. We took the boys to the spectacular Nauticus museum and onboard the historic battleship USS *Wisconsin*, then sat on a bench and ate a takeaway, experiencing mixed feelings at finding ourselves once more in the modern world.

Back at the boat we talked again about the Atlantic crossing. It was now late June and we were officially in hurricane season, which began on the first of the month. We'd been hearing reports of bad weather in the Caribbean, including tropical storm Arthur, which kicked the season off two days early. Weather patterns were becoming increasingly unpredictable, and as sea temperatures grew warmer, many believed as a result of global warming, the incidence of tropical storms and hurricanes was increasing. Although we were no longer in the Caribbean, hurricanes often tracked right up the whole east coast of America, and the thought of being caught out by one was chilling.

'Are you sure about not doing the crossing Jules?' I asked, as we sat on deck watching the boys sweetly fishing from the dock. They had formed a little production line as Luke was lying on his stomach, sweeping a net along the bottom to catch shrimp that he then passed onto Oscar, who put them on his hook as bait.

She looked down. 'Yes. I think so. I know I'll have regrets, but those regrets would be a whole lot worse if we took the boys and something went wrong.'

'When do you want to leave?'

'New York. I think that would be a fitting end for our journey, don't you? Let's start looking into flights – meanwhile you'd better call David and see if he's still up for it.'

David was still up for it, very much so. Crossing the Atlantic would fulfil a lifelong dream at a stage in his life when such opportunities were closing down. I was happy for him, and glad to have the company, but as I put down the phone I felt worried. I didn't know him very well, and what I did know wasn't particularly reassuring. He was in his late sixties and his health wasn't good: he'd suffered from long-term diabetes and had to inject himself daily with insulin, as well as keeping a close eye on his diet. He was hardly what you'd describe as nimble, being permanently lame thanks to his missing toes, and thus could be a danger on deck in rough conditions. His eyesight was poor, also a consequence of diabetes, which was not a reassuring quality in a watch-keeper. I didn't know how good a sailor he was, never having been on a boat with him, and, more importantly, had no real idea of how we would get along together, confined in such a small space, possibly in very rough conditions and for a long time.

All in all, he was far from the ideal choice of crewmate when facing crossing the North Atlantic, one of the most notoriously rough passages on earth. Part of me wondered whether I'd be better off alone. But I liked him, and that fact was something to hold on to as I faced being separated from my family and venturing out into one of the greatest wildernesses on earth.

But we still had a few family weeks left, and I tried hard to free my mind of worries as we slipped out of the Elizabeth River into the wide waters of the Chesapeake Bay. With a coastline that stretches for over two thousand miles, richly indented with all manner of creeks and inlets as well as innumerable islands, the Chesapeake Bay is the largest estuary in America, famous for its wonderful sailing. Several major rivers run into it, including the Patapsco in Baltimore, and the Potomac, which runs through Washington DC. I had lived in the city as a child from the age of seven to eleven, and the wild edges of the Chesapeake sank deeply into my soul in that period, when my beloved stepfather Nicholas took me there to escape the city. We fished for the famed blue crab and wandered together along dusty red trails through woods and along the edges of little creeks. I would while away days with my best friend Matthew beside me, lying on the hot boards of a rickety wooden pier waiting for the crabs to gather in an underwater feeding frenzy on the chicken necks that we had lowered to the bottom on lengths of string. With the sun beating hard on our backs we'd catch enough to fill a basket before trooping back proudly to the ramshackle house where we stayed, deep in thick woods that surrounded a weedy little inlet. And then, as the sun settled and the woods filled with fireflies and the sound of chorusing frogs, we'd sit on the porch behind the rusted insect screens, around a basket filled with the autumn red shells of the boiled crabs, feeling privileged to be in the company of a man who spoke to us like adults.

Who could have guessed the passage of my life from then to now: an odd little South African boy with buckteeth and too much imagination, now approaching the Chesapeake under sail with two young sons of my own? After his posting in Washington DC we moved to London where my stepfather worked as Deputy Foreign Editor at the *Independent* newspaper. When I was sixteen Nick was diagnosed with a virulent cancer which killed him quickly. He was only forty-seven years old. This visit to the Chesapeake would act as a kind of homage to a man that turned my life around, in the hope that I could pass on some of those sacred experiences to my own children. Perhaps I wouldn't find that same creek that he and I visited together, but we could find another one, our own one, where Oscar and Luke could form memories that would one day be as precious as mine.

The beauty of the Chesapeake is its rivers and inlets, where it's possible to tuck oneself into a deserted anchorage and not see anyone for days. We zigzagged our way up the bay in the fresh balmy wind and at the end of each day felt our way up a shallow creek or inlet where we'd drop anchor and settle down for a night of blissful solitude. Three days in we turned into the Wicomico River, threading our way past innumerable shoals and sandbars until we saw the impossibly dainty entrance to a creek. Juliet checked the chart, 'Mill Creek. Looks like we can go some way up, but follow the channel markers – it's very shallow on either side.' The river looked more like glass than water, and stretched ahead like a bar of silver, growing shallower all the time, but we couldn't resist going on round just one more bend and then another, lured on by the need to find the perfect spot. The creek was narrow now and we felt like the children in *Swallows and Amazons*, except that we had a great big heavy boat that, if we grounded, might lodge itself irretrievably in the mud. This was where the phrase 'touch and go' really came into its own, connecting back to the days when ships would navigate their way up rivers by allowing themselves to gently touch the shallows at one side, before altering course for the other.

At last we reached a pool beyond which progress clearly wasn't possible, and we contentedly let our anchor sink into mud that must have been as thick as molasses, aided by a helpful little zephyr that pushed *Forever* gently astern. We turned the engine off, and as the perfect hush of still water and woodland descended upon us we took in our surroundings, through which we glimpsed a green hill of herby grazing rising up towards a farmhouse.

We edged our way up the Chesapeake to the almost too-pretty town of Oxford, passing through lush farmland and thick woods, interspersed with endless marshes and wild islands that teemed with bird life. In Oxford we stopped at an immaculate boatyard where we finally fixed our water-maker. More soberly, we also had some stout battens made for *Forever*'s butterfly hatch, as I worried that the glass hatch could make the boat vulnerable in a severe storm. In the unthinkable scenario that *Forever* capsized, that hatch would shatter, and the resulting weight from the inflow of water might make it impossible for her to right herself.

As we left Oxford we were pursued by a number of towering thunderstorms that whipped the shallow waters into a frenzy. We spent a night anchored off a desolate scattering of houses near the top of the bay, buffeted all night by strong winds. The next day we carried on, aiming to pass from the Chesapeake into Delaware Bay through the local canal. We timed our entrance carefully so as to have the tide on our side, squeezing past the commercial traffic on its way to Philadelphia and other cities. By the time we reached the Delaware end it was late afternoon and we were anxious about finding a place to spend the night.

A local man had told me about an inlet towards the top of the bay where one could safely anchor. 'It's about the only choice with your draught,' he'd said. 'It's good once you get in but the entrance is scary. There's a little pool behind Reedy Island, well protected and plenty of swinging room, but you gotta pass through an opening in an old stone dyke to get there. You've got to hit this opening exactly right, there's no depth on either side. There's a strong current, so you gotta get up some speed. Takes some guts . . .' His eyes twinkled, 'But I'm sure you got plenty.'

It was beginning to get dark as we drifted down, scanning the ethereal, low-lying edges of the bay looking for the marker that would denote the entrance. Unlike the Chesapeake, the Delaware felt imbued with a kind of lurking menace: the landscape was flat and drab and the shipping channel surrounded by malevolent shallows. To starboard we identified Reedy Island, and saw a decrepit marker poking out just above the water level beside a gap in a long line of coal black stones that looked just like the jutting spine of a starving black dog.

'Is that it?' Juliet said incredulously. 'It doesn't look as if we can possibly get through there.'

But the chart confirmed that it was the anchorage and taking a deep breath I brought *Forever* round to begin our approach. It took a leap of faith to head for the dyke without knowing for sure that there was enough water. As I headed for the gap in the dyke I felt the boat sluice sideways in the current and realised I'd have to increase our speed or risk running into the wall. I increased the throttle, praying that the engine would not conk out and pointed *Forever*'s bow well upstream to keep her from drifting off course.

'I don't like this, Guy,' Juliet muttered. 'If it's too dodgy just turn round.'

'I can't turn around . . .' I mumbled, realising that we had committed to our approach and there was no space to turn back. On either side of the tiny channel we would run aground on rock.

This was one approach that could not be fudged. The current was so strong that to run aground would spell disaster and as the depth fell steadily we watched the gauge and I now regretted attempting to anchor in such a crazy place. We were now approaching virtually side-on. I realised with a heart-stopping sureness that we would not fit through at this angle, and I had to increase speed to straighten up, though all my instincts were screaming at me to slow down.

'Guy! We're not going to make it!' Juliet shouted. 'Turn round!'

But it was too late for indecision. 'Hold on, just hold on!' I shouted and saw the boys drop into effective-looking protective rolls. At the last moment I swung the wheel to port and gunned the throttle, mustering all of *Forever*'s power to make the gap. As she lurched forwards her bow slipped in, the rest of her straightening up on the way through. With bated breath we watched as for one hideous second the depth gauge told us that there was less than half a foot of clearance beneath us as we passed over the remains of the dyke.

And then – miraculously – we were through and *Forever* was gliding into a good-sized pool. As the depth climbed, we began to breathe again. The current was still strong, so we quickly dropped the hook, felt it dig into the muddy bottom and give a reassuring tug as the chain pulled us up short. We turned the engine off and looked around the rather woebegone marshland, the mournful cries of wetland birds echoing over flat, swampy ground.

The sky turned deep purple as a rainstorm blew in, the weather was changing.

The clock was ticking: it was time to go.

NINETEEN

NEW YORK HARBOUR

40.47N: 73.59W

The next morning we rose early, impatient to get started. I was anxious to prepare for the Atlantic crossing; Juliet and the children were just excited to be going to New York.

We lifted anchor, shot back through the crazy gap in the dyke and turned onto the ocean freeway. As we'd sensed the day before Delaware Bay was a sinister piece of water, with swirling currents and hidden shoals beneath its inscrutable surface. The wind was flukey and we kept tweaking the sails to make the best of it, eventually taking them down altogether as we rolled on the lumpy brown swell. Huge boats passed us, sending us scuttling to the edges of the shipping lane, and though our pilot book told us that it was possible to take various short cuts, we'd learnt our lessons and stuck within the marked channel.

In the late afternoon we slipped out of the Delaware's spooky reaches and rounded Cape May into the wide Atlantic. After the relative claustrophobia of the many twisted inland waterways it felt as if we were at last able to breathe freely again. We hoisted sail and flew up the flat, sandy New Jersey coastline in a good offshore breeze, enjoying watching the great eastern shore unfold while to our east the Atlantic stretched seemingly towards eternity. As darkness fell we switched on *Forever*'s navigation and steaming lights. The weather forecast confirmed that the weather was expected to remain stable for at least twenty-four hours.

After supper the boys fell into contented sleep, lulled by *Forever*'s gentle rise and fall in the settled seaway, and Juliet and I relaxed in the darkness of the cockpit. The steady wind that came off the land was warm, softened by the land compared to the usual sharp sea breeze. On our last night passage together we talked quietly about how far we had come, taking care not to congratulate ourselves, as we knew King Neptune would be listening. I dozed dreamily on the cockpit bench while Juliet steered. We felt happy and safe held in the arms of our strong boat that we now knew so well. *Forever* surged powerfully on in the good wind, and the night filled with the familiar symphony of creaking wood and the sigh and fizz of water as we cut through it.

'Guy, you have to see this.' She shook my shoulder and I sat up. 'It's Atlantic City – look!'

She pointed to a brightly lit town that stretched out along the low coastline, its high-rise buildings looking like the set of a futuristic film. Yet we we might as well have been a million miles from that world of electricity and consumption. That night, as for so many nights before, our world was made of water and wind and our home was on the ocean again.

I went below feeling content and happy, took a glance at the chart one last time then sank deep within our berth and fell into a deep sleep, whilst Juliet sailed us on through the night towards New York.

Just before dawn she woke me. 'Can you take over? I need to get some sleep. I almost fell overboard!' I bounded up and set the kettle on the stove for coffee.

'What happened?'

We stood together speaking in whispers in the galley whilst *Forever* surged on. She told me how she had stepped onto the side to drop a teabag into the water, without lifejacket or harness, lulled into a false sense of security by the agreeable conditions. The boat had lurched a little and she had almost slipped off the wet caprail. 'Imagine that – one slip and I would have been in and the boat would have sailed on without me! Not only would I have died, but you would all have been sleeping while *Forever* sailed on towards God knows what!'

It was a sobering reminder, on our last night passage, that you could never drop your guard. One could be seduced and entranced and enveloped in sea love but still, despite all of it, one could never take anything for granted. The helmsman's job was a serious one, carrying responsibility for the lives of the crew and passengers, and it took a lot to entrust one's life to someone as you slept. I thought of David and wondered afresh about the logic of taking on a crewmate whom I barely knew. And as if to confirm my uncertainty, at five-thirty in the morning the radio burst into life with an urgent dialogue between the coastguard and the panicky skipper of a vessel that was rapidly filling with water.

The day was full of a hazy sunshine giving everything an indistinct edge that made it difficult to discern the line between sand and sea. Taking careful note of the chart, depth gauge and lots of peering through binoculars, we rounded Sandy Spit, a curling arm of tawny coastline that encloses the lower reaches of New York Bay. Standard practice on entering New York harbour is to anchor there and wait for the tide, but our timing was lucky, and we were able to steer straight in towards the Narrows, the fiercely tidal strait that marks the entrance to New York harbour.

'Watch the markers Jules!' I shouted, feeling frazzled as I tried to remember my careful planning from the night before.

'Dad, watch out!' Oscar cried and I glanced over my shoulder to see a mountain of steel bearing down towards us astern.

I hastily adjusted our course to stay just outside the shipping lane as the monster slowly drew past. Boats were coming down three massive shipping lanes, which all converged to pass through the same narrow stretch of water beneath the Verrazano-Narrows bridge. These ships were restricted by their draught and slow to stop, and all rules of the road fell by the wayside as we gave way to these goliaths who we knew could run us down without even noticing. A rhyme ran through my head:

Here lies the body of Mike O'Dea
He died defending the right of way
He was right, dead right, as he sailed along
But he's just as dead as if he'd been wrong.

We powered through the swirling water and under the great bridge, the sound of engines and water echoing against the concrete sides that towered over 200 feet above us. Juliet and the boys looked up in awe at the complicated struts and metalwork of the longest suspension bridge in the USA. I steered *Forever* to the edge of the channel and motored on, looking around in awe as the harbour of one of the world's greatest cities opened up around us. The Staten Island ferry rushed past, refusing to concede to anyone as it followed its hectic schedule. Tugs chugged to and fro, the terriers of the boat world, seeming to announce, 'I may be small but I'm strong!' Heavily laden barges plied up and down the Hudson, loaded with logs or steel girders. And in between it all were yachts like ours, looking distinctly frail in comparison to their rusted, noisy cousins. *Forever*'s insides filled with the unmistakable drawl of New York and New Jersey accents, as the radio relayed messages. Ahead, on our starboard bow, the skyscrapers of Manhattan Island loomed up beyond the low-lying Governor's Island, concealing the entrance to the East River, with its vicious currents, leading up towards Harlem and the Brooklyn Bridge. On our starboard side we could see the docks and industrial sprawl of Brooklyn, while to port were great areas of navy and commercial docks. Opening up ahead of us were the first reaches of the stately Hudson River. We were heading for the 79th Street Boat Basin, a municipal marina right in the heart of Manhattan.

Luke was sitting on the bow, enthralled by the scene that was unfolding around us. 'Look at that green lady Mum!' He pointed ahead.

'It's the Statue of Liberty,' Juliet called. 'She's welcoming us to New York City!'

My skin prickled as we passed one of the world's most famous landmarks, her bright gold-leaf flame sparkling at the end of her coppery-green outstretched arm. I thought of all the hopeful people who had sailed this route before us. Beyond was Ellis Island, for many years the main port of entry for immigrants and I experienced a flash of the hope and optimism that they must have felt as they began their new lives in this great country. This was the first time that I'd ever seen the Statue of Liberty up close, and she seemed to encapsulate a sense of maternal pride and love, mixed with a joyous kind of optimism.

'Oscar, Luke: you must never forget this moment,' I said pointing to Ellis Island. 'Over the years millions of people have travelled thousands of miles, some of them in really unsafe boats just to get here, for a chance to improve their lives. Some of them got sick on the way and they weren't even allowed in and were sent back home. Can you imagine that boys? All that way not to be allowed in. Ozzy, come and see what it feels like to enter New York. You take the wheel.'

His eyes widened in disbelief. 'But there are so many boats around!'

I waved his worries away. 'You steer and I'll keep watch.'

He stood on the helmsman's seat so he could see ahead and took the wheel, casting a glance at his mother that said, 'If I crash the boat it's not my fault.' *Forever* was drifting in the strong currents, and he did well to counteract them, keeping us on course towards the mouth of the Hudson River. Juliet said, 'Well done you. Can I steer for a bit now? I want to be able to say that I steered into New York City too!'

Soon we were steering up the Hudson, just a stone's throw from Manhattan. We passed the great space where the twin towers used to be, a conspicuous gap amidst the congestion of the city. We heard the buzz and hoot of New York City traffic and the air was thick with the universal scent of urban rivers, a not unpleasant mixture of brine, metal and weed. Oscar and Luke sat on the starboard side, staring up at the huge buildings. We passed the ends of jagged piers and boardwalks, some ruined and others spruced up and restored. The boys waved and shouted to people on the quaysides and many greeted them in return.

On our port side I noticed an immense length of timber floating by on its way downriver, spiked with rusty pieces of metal that protruded from its sides.

'Look at that!' I pointed.

Juliet peered over the rail. 'That's bad – if we get hit by one of those we've had it.'

We looked around and noticed many other pieces of detritus in the water, floating down from the upper reaches of the river. Juliet went up to the bow to keep watch, pointing now and then to alert me to other dangers.

But nothing could take away from our sense of achievement as we sailed up the river, still struggling to believe that we were actually sailing into New York harbour, something that we would never have thought possible. All the painful lessons were worthwhile, all the frustration, expense and fear, for this experience that would surely stand as one of the greatest of our lives.

We readied our lines in preparation for entering the marina, which lay just a few blocks away from Central Park. The inner part of it was lined by some live-aboard yachts and houseboats, and on its outer edge a few visiting yachts were tied up alongside a lethal-looking wooden dock, along which the Hudson sucked and swirled with the impatience of a hungry lion. It was not going to be an easy approach, as a fiendishly strong current was trying all the time to wash us downstream, while a strong wind blew from the other direction.

'We need the bow line on first, to hold us against the current while I get the stern in,' I shouted to Juliet, who was standing with the lines ready on the bow.

I approached the wooden quayside, heading for a space between two boats, and was just about to swing *Forever* in when I felt a hugely powerful eddy push against us so hard that I had to retreat back out into the river.

'There's a major eddy Jules, stand by!' I shouted, feeling the familiar coils of worry settle upon me once more. I approached again, gunning the throttle against the current, and got close enough for Juliet to step ashore and secure the bowline as I threw the stern line out to the docks man, who neatly dropped it around a cleat. Then I winched the stern in until at last we lay neatly against the dock.

The gnarly-looking dock man looked unfriendly, but soon opened up in a manner that we'd learn was typical of this city.

'Come from far?' he asked.

Luke said, 'From Trinidad!' and his eyes widened with surprise.

'Hey little guy, sounds like you done good. Welcome to New York,' he said in his rich accent. He reached into his pocket and brought out a packet of cigars, offering me one before he walked off in a wreath of pungent blue smoke. 'I guess you guys will need sometin' to eat after all that travelling,' he said over his shoulder. 'You should try out the café up there – get yourselves some hot-dogs for lunch.'

We sat in the café, enjoying the hustle of a New York lunch hour, before wandering further into the city. With no particular agenda we wandered from block to block, stopping for ice creams and cappuccinos, wandering through parks and busy streets and staring at people and traffic and advertising hoardings, all of us lost in the joy of contrast after spending so much time drifting through endless lonely reaches.

That night we returned to 79th Street and walked past the marina office, where a middle-aged Chinese lady sat outside, looking out over the river and smoking. As I passed she looked up, her eyes quickly scanning over Juliet and me with the kind of professional scrutiny that I associated with airport security. The boys said hello politely and she leant forward with a wide smile, long lines of smoke wreathing out from her nostrils like a dragon in an ancient wood-cut.

She gathered Luke towards her, hands glittering with gold. 'Oh, you a very beautiful boy,' she said gazing into his eyes.

He sunk his chin into his chest, gamely keeping a fixed smile in place. 'How old are you, young man?'

'Errm, five.' He looked nervously towards us, and she followed his look and let him go, smiling as she did so.

'You got one very beautiful boy there, very beautiful . . .' She took a deep drag on her cigarette. 'Where your boat?'

I pointed out *Forever*, and she nodded thoughtfully. 'Very good looking boat.' Then she looked at Oscar and opened her eyes wide with faux surprise. 'And you have a handsome brother too!' She grabbed his cheek and squeezed it and Oscar smiled sheepishly.

'Well, thank you,' I said, and we walked along the pontoons that rolled to and fro on the coppery shoulders of the great river. 'Spooky' muttered Juliet under her breath.

Forever had dropped dramatically with the tide. 'Thank goodness we left her lines so long!' Juliet said, peering over the edge to where *Forever* lay far below, her lines stretched taut.

I shimmied my way down the pilings, Juliet passed the boys down and half-climbed, half-leapt down herself.

Later, as Juliet and I were getting ready for bed, she said 'Guy – I forgot to pick up the washing. It's in the laundry room. I don't want to wait 'til the morning in case someone takes it. Can you go and get it?'

I laughed at the thought that anyone would want our tattered sailing clothes.

'No seriously, there are a few nice things there – please go and get it.'

I pulled on some shorts and wandered out along the creaking pontoons, lit here and there with lamps, soft circles of luminescence shining on the dark river. I walked past a few dark, abandoned boats and then one that looked like a studio, with artwork and materials stacked against the walls, plant pots ranged haphazardly on the deck. I could see a group of people sitting around a table groaning with booze, light music tinkling from the bow.

I headed for the mothy umbrella of light around the laundry shack, and pulled the clothes from the dryer into a plastic bag. As I walked back along the dock, a movement caught my eye on the muddy riverbank and I saw a raccoon digging furtively, looking around every so often with its robber's mask face. I stood and watched it, fascinated by the opportunism of animals that make their homes amid the hustle and bustle of the city. And then three scantily clad women came through the security gates accompanied by a nervous-looking man. They walked towards a large, teetering motor yacht that would have been quite flash in the 1980s, but now looked wonderfully seedy. Night-time was clearly not as quiet as it had first seemed.

'Oh hello there, father of the beautiful boys!' It was the Chinese woman standing with two girls who looked like Ukrainian javelin throwers. 'How are you finding New York? Fun city hey?' she said, her eyes roaming over me unnervingly.

'It's great, we love it,' I said, and the girls glanced at her and giggled.

'You having plenty of fun, yes?' She put a little more weight on the word 'fun' than I would have expected.

'Have you seen the raccoon?' I asked them, pointing. 'Over there on the bank.'

She bent to look and then laughed maternally as the two girls lost all of their professional poise and chattered together, watching it trot about on its nocturnal errands. Now the mood had changed and they were like two gawky teenagers in the countryside for the first time. A few minutes later the raccoon slunk out of sight, and they waved sweetly to me as I said goodnight, passing by the throbbing motorboat and back into the cooler darkness beside the houseboats. I glanced back and saw the Chinese lady counting from a bundle of notes, some more girls standing around her in the hazy lamplight. Here real dock life was on display, not hidden behind the gleaming sides of the super yachts or the corporate expressions of 'paradise' that were scattered throughout the Caribbean. The 79th Street Boat Basin was a municipal marina, run by the city for the city, set on a river that had long been one of the main arteries into a heart that beat as much with delicious sin as with glamour and sophistication.

TWENTY

JULY STANDBY

June, too soon
July, stand by
August, look out you must
September, remember

As enjoyable as 79th Street was turning out to be, conditions at the boat basin were far from secure with the huge tides hoisting *Forever* up and down against the end of the dock. There was also a large amount of menacing flotsam, heavy pilings that the river had pulled from the old and derelict docks upstream that hurtled down the river like battering rams, many of them studded with pieces of steel. And so we headed over to the more salubrious surroundings of Newport Marina on the other side of the Hudson, happily tying up to one of its floating pontoons where we were treated to a thrilling, film-set view of Manhattan.

Ricky and Jack ran the dock. Ricky was classic old-school New Jersey, tough ex-navy, covered in tattoos and straight out of the *Sopranos*. Jack was originally from Antigua but had lived in New York for most of his adult life. He was still nostalgic about his home island, and lit up when he heard where we had come from. Although both men were in their fifties they exuded a youthful air, into which was woven their own gentle, rather philosophical take on life. It felt good to be around them and I knew that Newport would be the ideal spot for *Forever* and me to get ready for our sternest test yet, the crossing back to Scotland. Emotionally it was going to be important for us too, as this would be where, in just a few days' time, I would say goodbye to Juliet and the children.

The plan had been to head straight across from New York, just below latitude 040°, heading for the Azores, and from there to the south-west coast of England from where we could hop up to Scotland. Yet already at this time of year, early July, there was a possibility of running into a hurricane, the risk of which increased with every day we stayed tied up in New York harbour. Hurricanes can spin in a northwesterly arc up the eastern seaboard of North America and then out into the Atlantic. The further north they go the slower they become, due to the braking effect of cold water. Nevertheless, they often form into a storm and then a severe gale, creating horrendous sea conditions in the North Atlantic, especially over the shallow banks.

So while Juliet and the boys celebrated the end of their journey I was contemplating the beginning of another testing passage, and this time the journey would span continents.. I studied the charts, hunching over the laptop studying weather patterns, and each day the picture grew worse as the waters to the south were boiling up with the most hurricane activity there had been for years.

On the Fourth of July, with the city in full holiday mode, I sat making notes on the chart table as a terse-sounding man relayed more bad news over the radio. The National Hurricane Centre had been following a long line of thunderstorms that was crackling its way west with increasing intensity from the coast of Africa. This 'tropical wave' was showing no signs of abating, and its status had now been upgraded to named tropical storm Bertha. I looked about the empty boat, imagining this tranquil space transformed into the chaos of a hurricane. I felt suddenly very lonely at the thought of being without my family. I thought of Juliet's steadfast bravery during the storms, and knew I'd never seen her even close to her limits. In the past few months we had really found our feet as a team, working together to keep the family and boat going, and I didn't relish the prospect of the crossing without her. We had found a way of propping up each other's morale, so that when one felt low the other took over, and vice versa, so that we were always able to keep going. I knew that Juliet had wanted to do the crossing, and it was some sacrifice to give it up, yet she had done so unquestioningly when the happiness and safety of our boys was at stake. But we had to get the boat home somehow.

Our last days together were spent as tourists in the city, but increasingly we all felt that we were spinning out time. It was impossible for me to relax when such a huge task hung over me and with each day's delay I was putting myself in further danger. I began combining our forays into the city with buying bits and pieces of equipment, ordering charts and extra pilot books. I read about the various alternative routes concluding that the best way might be by the Great Circle route, which led up the east coast to Halifax, Nova Scotia and then from there to Scotland. On this route I would be less likely to encounter a hurricane, with the added bonus that I would arrive further north, closer to Mull. The threats of certain thick fog, strong winds and big seas – even possibly of the odd iceberg, remained.

On our last night together we took the boys out for pizza as a treat.

'Are we going home tomorrow?' Oscar asked.

'Yes,' Juliet answered.

'Without Dad?' Luke asked.

'Dad's sailing *Forever* home.'

'Are you going to die Dad?' asked Oscar, his brow furrowing with concern but clearly quite prepared to face the possibility.

I laughed uncomfortably. 'No. At least I hope not.'

'Will he Mum?'

'No!' She ruffled his hair. 'You know how good *Forever* is in storms.'

'Will it be like the Anegada Passage?' Luke asked.

'Worse maybe! Are you glad you're not going?'

'Yes!' He paused, 'But what about Dad? He'll be all alone.'

He looked genuinely worried, and my heart melted as I looked at my younger son, already so sensitive and caring.

'He won't, he'll have David with him, remember?' Juliet paused, and I could see she was searching for a way to change the subject. 'By the way Guy, did you see the email from David earlier? He and Sandy have borrowed a car from his cousin and are driving up. They should be here in a few days.'

I was finding it hard to take in; suddenly everything was going too fast. I wanted to stop the whole project.

'You know, that man has a wonderful heart. I think he'll be great company too.' I nodded, hoping she was right.

The next morning, with a sense of total disbelief, I helped everyone pack. My heart ached as I saw the boys carefully packing away their treasures, hoarded pieces of stone and coral that represented so many experiences, so many places and new friends. Tears that could not be shown numbed my throat and made it hard to talk, and I could see that Juliet was just barely holding on too, though she kept her tone cheery for the boys' sake. I knew how much she was going to miss *Forever*, as she of all of us had adapted best to life afloat, and had grown to love every minute that she'd spent within this floating world.

As we stepped across *Forever*'s decks the boys stopped to kiss her glossy wooden cap-rail. She had looked after us all so well, and had become so much more than just a boat, a real member of the family. We walked to the waiting taxi, pushing a trolley with all of their bags piled high along the jetty, and I held Juliet's hand.

'I'm going to miss you, but I'm so glad you're not coming – it's going to be rough, I just feel it.'

She squeezed my hand. 'Be careful. If it looks impossible, don't do it. I wish I was coming with you.'

'Me too, you don't know how much.'

Under the impatient eye of the taxi-driver I hugged each boy, covering them in kisses before placing them in their seats and pulling their safety belts on. The boot closed, the doors were slammed shut and we all started to cry as the driver turned the car around. I saw Luke's face, wet with tears as he raised his hand to wave from behind the closed window. The driver looked bemused: to him it must have seemed the most hysterical of partings. He might have thought the boys were spoilt rich kids, leaving their yacht in the marina, but how could he know that the little boys crying behind him had put up with conditions that would have beaten many an adult?

I stood alone for a while as the car drove out of sight, taking with it everything that mattered to me on earth. It was a gentle, balmy day in New York but hundreds of miles to the south hurricane Bertha was building.

TWENTY-ONE

THE GREAT
RECKONING BEGINS

As Bertha moved on over warmer water she became stronger and by 6 July an eye-like feature had been identified, making her the first hurricane of the season, one of the earliest on record. Classified as category three, the winds she generated would be between 110 and 130 miles per hour.

As I waited for David I started going through *Forever*'s inventory, checking and re-checking everything. She was in good shape, thanks to having been solidly at sea for eleven months with a refit in the middle. Boats like to be lived on and she was positively purring with the love and attention she'd had from us.

Then on 12 July, the day David was due to arrive, Bertha sent her calling card in the form of strong waves and rip currents all along the east coast of the United States. Three people were drowned along the New Jersey coast as a result. The Great Circle route was looking more and more appealing as I learnt of the devastation that Bertha left in her path, in the knowledge that there might very likely even be stronger hurricanes still to come. I was plunged further in despair by reading my new pilot book, which confirmed the dangers that I was increasingly dreading. On the plus side, it was the shortest route, and the winds and current would be in the right direction to take us across, albeit more strongly than we might want.

As I sat in my silent boat contemplating the days ahead, I heard a knock.

'Hey Skip! It's your old buddy reporting for duty!' I looked over to the pontoon, and there, beaming widely beneath his moustache, was David Pettigrew. He carried a duffle bag over his shoulder, and as we were no longer in the Caribbean he had replaced the flip-flops with socks and sandals. Before I knew it I was enveloped in a bear hug.

'God damn it Guy, I am so looking forward to this I can't tell you!'

'Me too David.' There was time enough to tell him the bad news. I looked over his shoulder and saw Sandy.

'Hey Guy, nice to see you,' she said.

'You too Sandy, come aboard and have a drink!'

Once we had loaded David's mercifully small amount of gear we settled in the cockpit to have a beer.

'She's so damn beautiful and some sea-boat!' David said, looking up at the rigging. 'She's going to take us to Scotland, can you believe it?' He turned to me with sparkling eyes. 'Now, we got some news Guy . . .' He put his arm around Sandy and looked at her with eyes full of love. 'We just got married!'

'Wow, that's great news! Congratulations Sandy and David Pettigrew!' I remembered the boys asking David when we were in Trinidad why he and Sandy weren't married, and he had replied, 'Well hell, I keep asking her but she keeps turning me down!'

'Doing this trip made the decision for us,' David said. 'We just thought . . .'

Sandy cut in. 'We just thought, why not?'

'Wait a minute.' I wagged a finger at him. 'You're not planning to die out there are you?'

He laughed. 'Hell no ... but you know how it is, when you're setting out on something like this ... Well, you just don't know what's going to happen, do you?'

The next morning as we said goodbye to Sandy David embraced her, saying, 'Baby, this ain't much of a honeymoon but when I get back we can have a real party.'

Tears were falling down her cheeks as she held him tightly. 'I love you David. Please be careful, remember you're not a young man anymore.'

Ricky and Jack walked past. 'Hey there!' David called, raising a hand in the air. 'I'm David – Guy's crew for the crossing.'

I saw a look of concern flash across Jack's face before he smiled and shook David's hand. But being with David again had reassured me. Even if his body let him down, his spirit was more than up to it, and I believed that his good humour and positive outlook would see him through. And anyway, here was I, about to attempt my first Atlantic crossing, shorthanded and on the hardest possible route. I didn't really have much offshore experience either and David might be feeling just as vulnerable in my hands. He was being pretty brave – or foolish – setting out to sea with an untested skipper whom he barely knew.

'I've been thinking David, it might be best to take the Great Circle route.' I traced my finger along the chart from New York to Halifax and on to Scotland.

'I been thinking that too – better to get out of the way of that hurricane.'

'But it will be rough – you know that. And foggy around the Grand Banks. Pretty cold too.'

'Don't you worry Guy, I'm up for it! Brought plenty sweaters and stuff. I can't wait to see Scotland, that's gonna keep me going the whole way across.'

I'd already stocked up on dry stores and tins, and on our final day in New York David and I set off to the supermarket to buy a last load of fresh food: bread, fruit, vegetables, milk, eggs and bacon. I knew from our past experience that the fresh stuff would last around two weeks before we had to resort to dried food and cans.

We discussed *Forever*'s readiness as we went. Paranoid about running out of water following our last long passage, I had already loaded enough emergency bottled water for two men to drink two litres of water each per day for one month. Added to that we had one hundred and twenty gallons of water inboard. The water-maker was working well too, and this time I would watch it much more closely to make sure it didn't pollute our precious tanks. We also had one hundred and ten gallons of diesel tankage, and forty extra gallons stored in cans on deck. All told this fuel would give us approximately one thousand miles' range under power alone. I had spares for everything and a major first-aid kit that included morphine, IV lines and antibiotics for every occasion.

As we pushed the trolley around the supermarket David was astonished: 'We really don't need all this stuff Skip!' I knew he was concerned about all the money I was spending, but what I didn't want to say was that I was provisioning *Forever* for disaster, wanting to be sure that even if we drifted without a mast for three months we would be OK.

We pushed the yawing trolley back along the busy road to Newport Marina, looking completely out of place amongst the well-dressed commuters: David in his late sixties, bearded and limping; and me dressed in threadbare shorts, ancient Crocs and a torn T-shirt. To passers-by we must have looked like a homeless father and his son. We certainly weren't anyone's idea of a dynamic trans-Atlantic sailing duo.

David read my mind. Smile lines crinkled around his eyes: 'Maybe if we held out a hat people might give us some cash? God knows we need it!'

'Well I'm glad you find it funny David,' but before I knew it I was laughing too.

We were going to be OK.

ZERO HOUR

40.33N: 74.01W

At 9 a.m. on 17 July as we cast off from the dock, I saw Jack emerging from the harbour office with a fog horn, which he held up and started blowing as I spun the wheel and turned *Forever* in the basin before aiming her bow for the opening out onto the Hudson.

'Hey Guy – good luck!' cried George, one of the Italo-American firemen who manned the New Jersey fireboat based at the dock. 'I'll be seein' you again sometime!' He and his girlfriend dreamt about fixing their old sailing boat and travelling together, and as I waved back, I knew he would switch places with me at the drop of a hat.

I motored slowly towards the opening, and then saw Ricky careering round a corner, driving hell for leather on the Newport marina golf-cart to get to the long protective outer dock. As we passed out onto the river he stood at the end of the pier and blew his fog horn.

'Come back to New York Guy! Come back to New York!'

'I love your city Ricky!' I shouted back. 'Good luck to you in everything!'

'Good luck! Good luck!' The cries followed us down the river, and I had to concentrate hard on getting my head back into pilot mode.

As we passed Ellis Island David put a hand on my shoulder. 'That's where my mother came in from Glasgow,' he said.

'And now you are going to see Scotland,' I replied. I looked about. 'The wind is good – let's start saving fuel right now and hoist sail. You take the helm David – put her into the wind.'

'You got it Skip!' and as he swung her round I went forward and hoisted the mainsail.

Back on course, *Forever* leant happily into the breeze and I pulled out the staysail and headsail, then turned off the engine.

'I just can't believe that this is happening to me,' David said, standing by my side. 'I'm going to see the land that my mother came from – at last. I just can't believe it!' He smiled and looked at his watch. 'Insulin time,' he said. 'If ever I start getting a bit weird remind me to take my shots will you?' This was the first time he had mentioned his diabetes, and it occurred to me that I knew next to nothing about the condition.

We sailed out through the Lower Harbour, turning northeast along the grey, low-lying coast. Ahead lay a passage of over five hundred miles before we reached Halifax, Nova Scotia.

19 July
40.20N: 68.45W

At just after two in the morning, forty-one hours after we'd left New York and 60 miles south of Nantucket, we sailed into a great bank of fog that showed no sign of thinning. It was as if the cloudy sky had grown tired and decided to rest itself upon the sea. I had never seen anything like it before. The wind had dropped and *Forever* began to wallow in the turgid swell. The contents of her insides began their mournful dance: mugs rattling on their hooks, doors creaking and cans rolling to and fro in lockers. Our speed dropped to 3 knots, and it felt as if *Forever* was losing the will to carry on. For the hundredth time I thanked the stars of luck for my seasickness patch, as I would have been suffering badly in this weather without it. David had just come out on watch, and he sat behind the helm, looking out glumly as the fog thickened all around us. Dainty little drops of moisture gathered on his clothing as the damp settled upon him. 'This fog sure is thick – never seen it quite as bad.'

As if in reply the thick, damp air vibrated with the deep cry of a ship's fog horn. Fear rippled through us as we struggled with the very real possibility of being run down by some steel giant. 'Sounds like we're not alone,' David said. 'What's the plan Skip?'

'I'll just get down below and do some figuring on the chart – and I'll put out a message on the VHF.' I looked up to see if the sails were doing anything useful but saw that they were barely filling. 'Let's drop sail and get the engine on and take her up to 5 knots – at least then the radar won't suck our batteries dry.'

He nodded. 'Get me up a box of flares too – and that flare gun.' He gave a dry laugh, 'Course if it gets to the stage of shooting flares we'll be in deep shit with this amount of fog.'

At the chart table I did a quick assessment of our situation. We were three hundred and sixty miles from Halifax, and nowhere near anywhere that we could go to sit it out. I remembered my coastal-skipper navigation course, and our teacher telling us that the best thing to do in fog was to find a safe spot to drop the anchor. I laughed to myself as I looked at the depth gauge, which showed sixty-five fathoms.

I flipped on the radar and waited for the green circles to show, and then saw that two miles to the south of us a ship was moving our way.

'There's a ship at six o'clock', I called up. 'I'm just going to try and raise them on the radio to be sure that they've seen us.'

'OK, I'll keep an eye out. Any chance of some coffee up here?'

I shook my head and smiled at his spirit. He was showing himself already to be a gutsy companion.

It was a worrying feeling, knowing that we wouldn't be able to see the lights of other shipping. In normal conditions you can actually see boats better at night than during the day and from the colour and arrangement of their lights can work out more clearly what type of boats they are, how big and which way they're going. This time we had no such comfort, and at regular intervals I lifted the radio handset and called out our name and position, in the hope that it would alert any vessel within twenty-five miles. On the radar I programmed a guard zone around *Forever*, so that it would sound an alarm if a ship or object came within five miles. It was all we could do.

I made David a cup of coffee and went up on deck. 'Are you going to be OK up here? I'm going to catch a few hours' sleep.'

'Take four hours, I'm fine up here. See you around six.'

'Are you OK for food?' And insulin, I wanted to ask.

He raised a thumb. 'Fine Skip, feelin' great. You just get some rest.'

Down below, I pulled off my damp oilskins and stood staring at the stove as it swung about on its gimbals, cleverly keeping the kettle perfectly level on its surface. I lost myself in a little reverie on the subject of objects of pure domesticity that find themselves a million miles away from the suburban calm that they were intended for. Around me all was quiet apart from the sound of the sea thudding along *Forever*'s bow and gurgling past her sides, and I felt a tingle of loneliness. Pulling myself into the high-sided sea berth I looked over to the butterfly hatch and could almost see the happy orange-juice light of the Caribbean days, hear my two boys laughing and splashing in bright, warm water beside the boat, feel Juliet's warm presence. I missed them with a deep longing.

I dreamed that Oscar and Luke were telling me stories from deep below the ocean, their voices clear, their smiles radiant, but on waking I felt shivery and cold. A ghastly dampness permeated the boat and when I peered through the portholes the fog seemed thicker than ever.

A real pea souper I thought, looking up to the cockpit to see David behind the helm. He had the classic leathery look of someone finishing a night watch, his eyes glassy but determinedly focused ahead.

'Breakfast's on its way David,' I called up. 'How does bacon and eggs sound?'

He rubbed his hands together. 'Can't wait!'

As I cooked up bacon and eggs and boiled water for the coffee, I knew the homely aroma of a fried breakfast – the most reassuring scent in the world – would be wafting up to my tired companion.

I wedged myself in against the galley sides, put the plates on the swinging stove and ground pepper over each one, then carried them up to the damp and now very uncomfortable cockpit.

David ate with gusto and I watched him with a growing affection. I could see that he had been cold, and his wounded foot had bled a little through his sock, as he'd no doubt knocked it on something as you do all the time on boats. Yet he gave no sign of any pain or discomfort and chatted away cheerfully. I thought: I could learn from him, all the times I have wallowed in self-pity. But just as I opened my mouth to say so, he wiped a large smear of egg yolk from his moustache by sucking the entire grey hairy thatch in beneath his lower lip. As he mopped his plate with his fingers I reflected that having to watch him eat for the next month might just be my sternest test yet, no matter how much I was also starting to love the man.

TWENTY-THREE

THE GRAVEYARD
OF GEORGE'S BANK

42.02N: 66.11W

Listening to the coastguard's weather report on the radio, I learnt with relief that Bertha had been downgraded to a severe storm, having been the longest-running July hurricane on record. We continued towards Halifax, hoisting more sail within daylight hours to add a knot or two to our speed. My logic was that at night I would keep enough sail up to make decent progress, but would sacrifice speed for safety and a rig that could be quickly shortened should the wind get up. I did not want either David or me messing around on the foredeck in the middle of the night, so we erred on the side of caution, mainly powered by a reefed mainsail and full staysail with just a tiny crack of headsail.

With David tucked up in his berth for a well-deserved sleep, I stood my watch and looked out into the murk. The wind was causing the sea to get up a little, but didn't seem to be clearing the fog at all. This was a classic advection fog, created by warm wind blowing over a sea made frigid by the Labrador Current.

I nipped below to check our position, and as I marked 42.02N: 66.11W down in the log book, a shiver of fear ran through me.

We were sailing over George's Bank, a stretch of water where thousands of fishermen had drowned over the ages. The bank had shifting areas of shoal waters which dropped as low as one fathom in places, and were the cause of both the fishermen's fortunes, as they attracted great stocks of fish, and their downfall, as they created some of the most dangerous sea conditions on earth. The convoluted contours of the seabed combined with the shallowness of the bank could lead to awful conditions in bad weather.

The nearby fishing port of Gloucester, just north of Boston, had lost thousands of men on the bank as they chased cod in traditionally built schooners. The Gloucester men would sail out and anchor their ships on the bank, before rowing out to windward from their mother ships on little boats called dories, which are typified by a high stern and bow and the ability to carry great weight whilst also remaining seaworthy. Usefully the dories could be stacked, and generally each schooner held a 'nest' of around six of them. Two men at a time would work these doughty boats, letting out a long line of baited hooks, and when they'd pulled in their fill they would row back to the mother ship, hopefully with the wind now at their backs, and load the fish up before stacking the dories and heading for home. A neat little system, with one serious drawback: that the storms, fog, current and cold water would be doing their best to kill them the whole time. A storm would quickly kick up mast-high waves in these shallows, combining with huge currents to wreak havoc with the anchored ships, throwing them hard onto the shoal ground and killing fishermen with the same efficiency with which they'd killed the fish. In the late 1800s, when the fishing schooners had huge areas of sail built on for extra speed, they became more vulnerable than ever to being knocked down. In the space of eight years, from 1870 to 1878, seventy-one vessels went down and six hundred and sixty-six Gloucester men were drowned, right where we were now sailing.

Tension coiled around me as I strained to see ahead through the thick fog. I felt relieved that the family was not with me now. We had taken the right choice; this was no place for children, where so many men had died with mouths full of water and lungs stinging with salt.

Through the day we took it in turns to keep watch or potter around down below, preparing food, reading or dozing. Our only soundtrack was the sound of wind and water and so we existed simply within our one room afloat on the sea. While one kept watch the other prepared food, washed up, read or dozed, in preparation for the night when our world seemed to fill with ghosts.

I took first watch that night, and David came up at midnight. I noticed that the barometer had fallen slightly but felt happy that *Forever* was snugged up for the night, with two reefs in the main and the self-tacking staysail. This meant that the wind could reach up to 30 knots and we would still be able to sail in complete control, and if it increased further we could reduce sail with reasonable safety. The price of this caution was that we would not be travelling as fast as we might, which was frustrating. Nevertheless I reasoned that the danger of breakages from an over-strained rig were too great, especially as we were short-handed, and that our priority was to remain in control of *Forever* at all times. We couldn't risk problems this far from land, in these dangerous waters, in the knowledge that there were no teams of brawny men to salvage the situation if things went awry.

I slept that night in the Pullman berth – our luxury sleeping option, only useable if we were anchored or sailing in calm seas – but at around 3 a.m. I woke, alerted by a change in *Forever*'s rhythm. Where her motion had been slow and steady, she now seemed to be whooshing along with hair-raising speed. I lay still, wondering what was going on, feeling her bow lift alarmingly and then seem to hover, as if she were planing above the waves. David must have hoisted more sail and I felt angry that he'd gone against my wishes. I pulled myself along the dark insides of the surging boat, stopping on the way to take a fix on our position. With a sickening sense of past disasters, I saw that we were passing right over George's Bank. Then I looked out of the companionway at David, who was sitting serenely at the helm, chin resting on his hand, one leg crossed over the other – looking as if he hadn't a care in the world – while the auto-helm whirred and stopped, whirred and stopped as it tried to keep *Forever* on course on the growing sea.

I didn't shout, 'What the fuck are you doing?' – I took a deep breath and tried to sound calm. 'David, we need to reduce sail immediately. We're going far too fast, and we're pushing her too much.'

We were doing 9 knots in 25 knots of a wind that looked set to increase. Glancing forwards I saw that, as I'd suspected, the entire headsail was out. Our biggest and most powerful sail, which Juliet and I had long ago nicknamed 'the monster', was in control and had possessed *Forever* like some kind of demon bent on a course of destruction. There was another strong gust and I felt the strain in the rigging as *Forever* heeled hard over in 35 knots.

'We have to reduce sail now!' I shouted again over the wind and spray and David, as if rising from a dream, stood up and held the binnacle.

'Pull in the sheet!' I yelled, but it was too late. The boat had come round into the wind and as the sheet flailed in and out of the sea, lent power by the wind-demented headsail, it slipped beneath *Forever*'s rounded keel. Moments later it had wrapped around the propeller, and with a sudden inevitability the engine cut out. We now had no power.

I felt murderous. All my instincts were to start yelling, 'This is why I didn't want to have too much sail up at night. Thanks to you we are adrift without an engine in deadly waters!' But I knew that that was not the behaviour of a good skipper, and I had to take some of the blame myself for not controlling the sheet better. Besides, there was no time for shouting: we were now in a very dangerous situation, with our huge sail pulled out tight, inextricably wound round the propeller. Not only were we unable to use the engine, we were greatly overpowered in the growing wind. Right on cue a large gust ripped across the sea and stung our faces with spray as *Forever* heeled hard over. I had to get the sail in, but how?

I thought: this is it. This is what it feels like to stand on the brink of disaster. We were fifty miles abeam of shoal water, without engine and with a giant jammed sail. The wind and weather would drive us to destruction pretty quickly if I didn't take action. 'David, we're going to have to cut the sheet so we can get the jib in. Then I'll go down and try to clear the prop at first light, so hopefully we can get the engine going again. Take the wheel and do the best you can – I'll inch ahead and cut it.'

'You got it!' he shouted.

I undid my harness and clipped it onto the port side jack line then edged my way along the deck, dropping to my knees as the water sluiced powerfully over the leeward rail and surged along the deck, bubbling and frothing from the scuppers. At last I reached the straining sheet, which thrummed with many tons of pressure from the strong wind. Even though *Forever* was a heavily built boat, all the pressure that was now wrapped around our prop shaft could easily lead to disaster if the shaft was twisted out of place and water came through the stern gland. I slipped my knife from its sheath and sawed at the thick sheet, feeling the fibres pop away as the knife cut soundly through them. With a withering twang the sail shot away and *Forever* immediately slowed from her roller-coaster hell-ride as the great sail now flew out, flapping like an immense white flag of surrender. I crawled back and hauled the trouble-maker in, before letting out the full staysail.

'OK, David put her back on course. When it's light, I'll try and cut the prop free, tie on the spare sheet and get going again.' I was wrung out with relief and tension. Our speed had reduced to 4 knots – slow, maybe, but safe.

I had half an hour before I was back on watch. David smiled tentatively at me, gauging my mood and in that moment my anger dissipated and I felt for him, knowing that he was still getting used to an unfamiliar boat that I had been sailing for months and months. 'That was kinda scary Guy – I can see why you call that sail "the monster"!' I thought about embarking on a sermon about less canvas at night but thought better of it. David knew the score well enough, and I could see that behind the laughs he had learnt for himself one of *Forever*'s quirks that, if misunderstood, could be deadly.

The next morning, in the half-light of another dirty dawn, we hove to as we had time and the boat was relatively still. I tied a bowline around my waist and David winched me down into the sea. I gasped as the cold water gripped me, so different from the balmy temperatures of the Caribbean. We were in northern climes now, and it reminded me of the frigid waters around Mull, where in the best of weather the children would brace themselves to swim from time to time. I spat my snorkel out and gasped, 'We're definitely getting closer to Scotland!'

I took four deep breaths and then swam hard against the sucking current, into the dark green water along the length of the jammed sheet until I reached its tight coils around the prop-shaft forwards of the propeller. I sawed away at the sheet, being careful not to cut myself – one mistake could lead to another, events spiral out of control. The stern of the boat was bucking up and down above me in the swell and I had to keep telling myself, like a mantra, to stay low, stay low. After a series of dives the prop was free, and I bobbed to the surface. David winched me back onboard, and then, not daring to articulate our mutual fear that the engine might not start, we turned the key.

Forever's hot oily heart exploded into life and patting each other on the back, smiling inanely, we motor sailed on.

As we had a huge amount of water on board I had a fresh-water shower with water heated by the engine. It felt beyond luxurious as the soap and sweet water calmed me down. I dressed in clean clothes and made coffee, fortified by a very large slug of whisky in each mug. David and I sat together in the cockpit, savouring our alcohol-fuelled coffee even though five in the morning was not, strictly speaking, the ideal time for whisky.

'What about your diabetes? Is booze bad?'

He nodded. 'Sure is.'

'I don't suppose your doctor would approve of you doing this journey?'

'I'm supposed to be dead already! I've long surpassed the life span given to me, so I figure what the hell – may as well keep doin' what makes me happy, instead of sitting around being careful.'

'Let's hope we make it hey?'

'We will Guy, we will,' he said, his voice full of good-hearted warmth and infectious optimism.

I patted him on the arm. 'Insulin?'

'Yeah. I might have got a little low last night. It's just kinda hard to inject when the sea is so rough. I've bent a few needles trying . . .' He shrugged his shoulders. David was not one for self-pity.

We sat for a while longer, each lost in thought about our narrow escape, and what other tests lay in waiting in the great fog-strewn wilderness. I peered up towards the wind indicator on the top of the mast and could just about make out where it was pointing. It had come around to a good angle, and galvanised us into action. We replaced the sheet, hoisted extra sail and headed on, with just 158 miles to go until we reached Halifax.

SEA SCROUNGERS

44.35N: 63.32W

On 21 July we began our approach to Halifax harbour, still in thick fog, with a steep running sea of 15 to 20 feet. I flipped through the pilot book and charts, trying to figure out where we should go once inside the harbour.

'Let's head for the Royal Nova Scotia Yacht Squadron,' I called up to David.

'Sounds great – but isn't it a little Ivy league for us?'

'I don't know, maybe I can play on the old Scotland, new Scotland thing.' Juliet had warned me to spend as little money as possible as our financial situation was now getting desperate. 'I've got a little flag here from the Western Isles Yacht Club in Tobermory – maybe I can give them that in exchange for a free berth or something. Like a goodwill thing, you know?'

As we drew closer to the land the fog lifted enough to give us a quarter-mile or so of visibility, and we caught our first sight of the Nova Scotia coast. A dark, rocky shoreline loomed out of the murk, looking distinctly unfriendly, more so because of the big waves which were crashing against it. We were surfing at great speed towards the harbour entrance and I began to enjoy the sensation as the waves hurtled beneath *Forever*.

On the radio, a Canadian woman relayed shipping positions as boats came in and out of the harbour. Ahead, through the gloom, I glimpsed a long line of grey tankers on their way out of the harbour before the fog settled heavily again. Then the air began to fill with the funereal calls of foghorns and I kept *Forever* just outside of the shipping lane, knowing that these massive ships would be unable to stop or alter course should we get in their way.

David sat below at the chart table, watching the radar screen and calling out the bearings of various ships and navigational buoys as we made our way into the harbour. Inside, the sea was much calmer so we dropped our sails and motored. I looked ahead hoping to find a navigational light that would help me fix our position but the fog had closed in again and was now so thick that I couldn't see past our bow. We were relying on instruments alone and I felt deeply vulnerable, bringing a boat into an unfamiliar harbour, with almost zero visibility, surrounded by shipping and a jagged coastline.

Yet the brisk positive voice of the traffic-control lady sounded out from our radio with all the clarity of a bell, and we followed her siren call for a while until we were sure that we had reached the opening of the little creek. Like blind men feeling their way along the sides of an underground tunnel we edged on, sometimes putting *Forever* into neutral so we could glide at very low speed, all the time trying to make out the banks of the creek, our ears straining for sounds of danger. It was a huge relief when I could make out the pontoons of the Royal Nova Scotia Yacht Squadron looming out from the murk.

I circled as we called them on the radio, and a rather courteous man gave us directions to a berth. We eased *Forever* in, tied up and went straight to sleep, not caring that our berths were damp and we were hungry, dirty and covered in salt. The blessed feeling of still water and safety was enough for us, the sheer relief of arrival overriding every other sensation or need. We had just sailed over six hundred miles from the thrum of one of the world's greatest cities, negotiating fog, shipping and our first near-disaster, and now found ourselves in a very different world.

Halifax felt sombre and where once I had seen blue there was now only an enervating greyness. A loud drumming sound woke me and I lay in the gloom staring up as large raindrops splattered on the glass. David was oblivious, snoring gently and I felt happy to be there with him.

A few polite knocks on *Forever*'s side pulled me into the present, and I darted up to the cockpit to see a man looking up at me with a welcoming smile: 'Welcome to Halifax!' he said. 'My name is John. If you guys need showers or laundry or anything you'll find it all on the dock. When you're ready come on over and we can figure things out for your stay. Where are you heading from here?'

I felt a little embarrassed as I told him, 'Scotland.'

He raised an eyebrow. 'That's quite a crossing. Ever done it before?' I shook my head.

'I know a few of our boat owners here have been across – I can put you in touch if you'd like to talk to them.' He shrugged his shoulders. 'Might pick up a few extra tricks.'

'I don't think I have any tricks.'

He laughed. 'Well let's get some for you then! I'll try and send one or two people your way.'

I creaked down the companionway past David, who was now awake. 'Hey he sounded kinda nice. Is he the harbour-master? Think he might let us stay for free?'

'I'll try but I hate to even ask for such a thing.' Even though I only had two hundred dollars to my name and knew that our credit cards were up to the hilt, I knew I would feel uncomfortable asking for a free stay in exchange for my burgee from The Western Isles Yacht Club.

We were keen to explore our new surroundings, take a shower and clean ourselves up. We found John's office – a picture of boaty efficiency and thrift.

'You guys OK?'

I nodded. 'Thanks for being so welcoming, we really are grateful to you . . .' I put my wash things on the floor by my feet, along with the smelly bag of laundry.

I sensed that he knew what was coming. I shifted from foot to foot, trying to think how best to raise the shameful subject that we couldn't afford to pay our dock fees, but hoped to stay for a couple of days anyway.

'John . . .' I began, and then paused, searching for the right words.

He raised his eyebrows expectantly. 'Yup?'

'. . . I was wondering if we might be able to do a little deal which would go some way towards honouring the timeless connection between the old country of Scotland and the new one, Nova Scotia. You see I've got a little exchange that I would like to do with you guys.' I felt about in my jacket pocket for the burgee.

'Here Guy, you looking for this?' David pulled the crumpled Western Isles Burgee from his pocket, and I took it quickly, feeling like a second rate magician trying to maintain a faltering sense of drama.

'Thanks David. Yes, now, the plan is . . .'

'The plan?' said John, looking openly amused.

'I would like to present the Burgee of the Western Isles Yacht Club to you, the Royal Nova Scotia Yacht Squadron!' I said, passing it to him with a flourish.

He leant forward and politely took the little flag, before folding it and passing it back to me with the most natural, good-natured tact.

'Guy, I don't make the decisions on these things – you need to speak to the Commodore of the Squadron. Of course if it was up to me I'd love you to stay for free, but I just run the dock.'

At the mention of the word 'free' David and I both perked up, and he laughed and held up a finger. 'Unfortunately it's not in my power. Head on up to the clubhouse later – there's a do going on up there and that's where you'll find him.' He looked us up and down, 'One word of advice though: get a shower and shave before you go – and lose the laundry . . .'

We scrubbed up well. After a long, invigorating shower I put on my finest leather sailing shoes and slung on some crumpled, but clean, jeans and a long-sleeved shirt, and walked with a reasonably less scruffy David up to the clubhouse. The car park was full and there was an air of activity and excitement, a marquee on the lawn beside the clubhouse and waiting staff scurrying about with trays and drinks. Like two schoolboys making their way to the headmaster's office we rehearsed our lines and ran through possible scenarios and responses as we neared the ivy-clad building. I stopped at a little office and asked if I could meet the Commodore and the receptionist looked me over with a non-committal look.

'You should find him somewhere around inside,' she said. 'He's busy dealing with some of our young sailors who are joining the Canadian Olympic team.'

And so we made our way into the heart of the place, the opulence hitting us like a gale-force wind. Healthy young men stood around making conversation, tanned and fit and wearing club ties and blazers, with well-dressed young women at their sides. They looked at us curiously as we passed through, heading towards the door that opened out onto the lawn. I spotted a pompous looking man that I instantly knew must be the Commodore and in that one glance I knew our mission would be hopeless.

David pushed me forward. 'Go on Guy – slip him the burgee! I'll hang back – I think I might be able to score a free drink from one of these lovely waitresses.' He shuffled off and I saw the cream of Halifax society part to let him through. His long grey hair wafted out a little as he limped towards a waitress. I turned and with a deep breath moved towards the Commodore.

'Good afternoon – seems like you're having quite a day!' I said brightly, and he turned and looked me over with a faintly bemused expression. He was wearing a blue blazer with gold buttons and a handkerchief neatly tucked into his breast pocket.

'Thank you. We're giving our young sailors a proper send off. Can I help you with anything?' He exchanged a glance with his assistant, who had the tweedy look of some stalwart of the Women's Institute. I smiled at her and she smiled back coldly, her eyes telling me simply to go away. I should have made my excuses and left then, but instead I cleared my throat in readiness for delivering my speech.

'Would it be possible to present you with the burgee of the Western Isles Yacht Club?' I pulled the shabby flag from my pocket and held it up.

He looked at the flag, and then at me, clearly uncertain what response was called for.

'My hope was that you might perhaps reciprocate.'

His lower jaw dropped open, but I continued undaunted.

'Just a couple of free days on your dock, and then if anyone from your club came over to Mull we would return the hospitality. Well, what I mean is, I don't have a pontoon personally, but we – and here I refer to my wife and me – could certainly welcome people.'

I was digging a very deep hole for myself, but there was no going back. 'You see, we're sailing back to Scotland – *old* Scotland that is – and I'm hoping that maybe if you gave us a free stay I could offer hospitality to any of your members if they ever came over to the Isle of Mull. I live not far from Tobermory and would happily offer a spare room, free baths or a washing machine . . .'

I was holding the burgee out towards him, but he resisted taking it, as if its touch alone was enough to send him spiralling down the social layers.

'I am afraid I cannot help you,' he said. 'You see we are not a . . . a . . .' he tilted his head to one side as he searched for the word, '. . . ah, a club if you will.' He said 'club' as if it was a dirty word. 'The Royal Nova Scotia Yacht Squadron has links already with other outfits in Britain, such as the Royal Yacht Squadron in the Solent.'

I nodded, feeling silly now. It was as if I had sauntered up to the Prince Charles and said, 'I hear you like playing polo – if you're ever around the Isle of Mull you're welcome to come and ride some of our donkeys.'

Just then, right on cue, David stood next to me holding a plate loaded with canapés. 'Hey, how are ya? I'm David Pettigrew.' He held out a bony hand and the Commodore dutifully shook it then looked at his watch.

'I'm so sorry I can't help, but I've got to get to work here. Good luck with your journey.'

'So I take it that the answer's no to the free berths?' I asked, giving it one last try.

He nodded briskly. 'I'm afraid it is. Enjoy your stay in Halifax.'

'Oh we will, thank you,' David called after him defiantly and I gestured towards the door.

'Let's go,' I muttered, 'I've had enough of this place.' I had visions of further embarrassment if we were asked to leave. We walked back to the dock, depressed and wondering why the goodwill that I'd always found around sailing ran out at the Royal Nova Scotia Yacht Squadron.

Down at the dock we bumped into John and thanked him for his heartfelt help and hospitality. He waved our kind words away. 'Hey, you just get yourself ready for the crossing. I suggest you head into

Halifax and tie up at Queen's Wharf or somewhere around there. And before you go – I got a guy coming over in half an hour or so that you should talk to. I'll send him across.'

Shortly I heard a voice calling from the dock.

I pulled myself up the companionway to find a fit man in his late fifties standing on the dock.

'John tells me you're heading across to Scotland. My name is Harold O'Shaughnessy, good to meet you.'

'I'm Guy, thanks for coming round. Yes, we're sailing to the Isle of Mull. Have you done that route?'

He smiled shyly. 'Yes, I've been across four times solo.'

'Wow, that's something. How big was your boat?'

'She was 35 feet.'

'Goodness. Any tips?! Have you time for a coffee?'

He nodded and leapt onto the deck with the agility of a mountain goat.

'This boat is solid', he said, looking around. 'These Hans Christians will never let you down.'

He followed me down below, where we sat in the saloon looking at the chart. It turned out that Harold had done the crossings to visit his family in Northern Ireland and had, astonishingly, crossed without autohelm. He ran his finger across the Grand Banks towards the Flemish Cap. 'It will most likely be foggy until well past the Cap.'

I looked at David, who grimaced and raised his eyebrows. We had both hated our days in the fog, the most depressing of all weather conditions, causing day and night to merge until your whole body-clock felt confused.

'You must get an ice report before you go – ice can be a real showstopper. It breaks up further north and comes floating down on the Labrador Current.' His calloused finger traced the route of the current, down the Newfoundland coast and then along past Nova Scotia. 'And this current is no friend. It brings ice and then fog when the warm south west wind blows across it.'

'How about weather?'

He sighed. 'Listen to the forecast and go when you think it sounds good for a few days, but beyond that . . .' He shrugged his shoulders, 'You'll have to just wait and see. In the first part of the passage there are places you can shelter if necessary, but once you're out here . . .' He pointed to the immensity of the mid-Atlantic. 'Then you'll have to deal with what comes. There's nowhere to run to.'

I was listening carefully, aware that his insight and advice were crucial. 'Now you'll almost always run into a gale on this route, as all the weather is heading over the same way you are.'

We waited as he took a sip of coffee, and then placed the mug down before him, turning it between his fingers as if lost in thought. I could almost see the powerful images that were obviously replaying in his mind. David and I looked at each other apprehensively as we envisaged being at sea in the teeth of a gale.

'Now my strategy is, when the wind gets above 35 knots I lie ahull. I take all sail down, tie everything down hard, lock the wheel to leeward and batten the hatches. Then I sit it out till the storm is over. Well, it's always worked for me, at any rate. Feels pretty scary to hand yourself over to fate, but a boat like this should sit it out. Do you have battens for her?'

I nodded.

'And for that?' he pointed up at the butterfly hatch. I nodded again.

'Good, because if that gets stove in I don't like to think what might happen. Hey, I don't want to scare you but I have to be blunt. Preparation is everything in this game.' He took another sip of coffee and looked about, clearly sensing our worry. 'She's a stout boat though – you'll be fine. Is this your first time across the Atlantic?' We both said yes. 'Well you haven't chosen the easiest route, but you'll do fine. Just be careful, take your time and never stop second-guessing yourselves. This northern crossing is always pretty rough and you will get knocked about a bit from time to time, so just get your head around that fact and be ready for anything.'

With that he stood up and drained his cup, looking down at us and making me feel inexperienced and foolish. 'Beyond that I can't tell you any more. Every crossing is unique. You'll make your own mistakes and find your own solutions no doubt.'

After he left David looked over to me. 'Hell Guy, let's get out of here. I like the sound of that city dock – at least we'll find a bar there. I need a drink!'

We started the engine and slipped away from the pontoon, motoring slowly into the deep fog and relying once again on instruments and eyeballing to creep up further into the harbour. Gradually Halifax began to reveal itself to us – an eerie ghost town behind the banks of fog, which had begun to separate like cotton being pulled apart. We made for a space on the pontoon and came in very gently. As David deftly tied off lines I could see above us on the high side of the old wharf that people were going about their normal business – walking together, emerging from shops and loading shopping into their cars. I felt envious of the ordinariness of their lives: as they returned to their cozy domesticity here was I contemplating steep seas, calculations about fuel and water, complex navigational challenges, weather forecasts and various points of vulnerability on the boat that might lead to our doom. Every now and then someone would stop and wave down at us, and so starved were we of human company that we waved back, inviting anyone who showed interest to come down for coffee. Before we knew it *Forever* had become a minor tourist attraction, and we were shepherding crowds of people onboard.

After a while we'd had enough of the visitors. 'OK everyone,' called David like a professional tour guide, 'thanks for coming on board but the skipper and the first mate need to go get a drink!'

The next morning I stepped out into the cockpit and saw that the fog was as thick as usual, and I thought that this might be what it would feel like to live through a nuclear winter. There, on the dock, was a boy in his late teens, looking expectantly me. 'Hey there, my name's Ed and I'm in charge of the dock here; I just wanted to say that I love your boat.' I invited him in and he stood in the cockpit, running his hand over *Forever*'s polished woodwork.

'Wow,' he said quietly. 'Are you going to sail this to Europe?'

'We're going to try. Have you done much sailing?'

'No, but I love boats and the sea and stuff.'

He reminded me a little of myself in my youth and I remembered how I'd rowed out from Tobermory harbour to an old restored Brixham Trawler called the *Lorne Leader* one morning as she lay sleeping at anchor. Like a boy running away to sea I had begged to join her crew, and the skipper had taken me on as an assistant cook, skivvy and all round dog's body. I thought about the fact that we were short-handed, and made a rash decision.

'Hey, Ed, I could do with one more on the crew – you want to come?'

His eyes opened wide. 'Oh my God, yes! I'd love to. I can learn fast, I promise, and I don't get seasick.'

'Well, why don't you come? You'd have to pay your flight back, but you could stay with us in Scotland and get a local job until you made enough to fly back if you wanted.'

'Are you really serious?'

'Yup.'

'I can't believe it!' He stopped short. 'I'll have to ask my dad though. When are you leaving?'

'Soon – maybe tomorrow.'

'Tomorrow!'

I laughed. 'Well, the weather is catching up with us as it is.'

'I'll be back,' he said and darted along the pontoon before jumping onto his bike and shooting off along the wharf towards the town. David looked up from the companionway.

'Hey, you getting more crew?'

I shrugged. 'Why not? He could be useful.'

He nodded sadly. 'Yeah, he could.'

'What?'

'Oh nothing. Just wish I was twenty again.'

'Meaning?'

'Oh forget it Guy.' He turned back into his cabin.

As night fell and the lights along the wharf glowered in the never-lifting fog, Ed returned. 'Dad won't let me go,' he said. 'Says I'm too young.' I clapped a hand on his strong and as yet untested shoulder. I thought fast. 'Hey, don't be angry with him – he probably just saved your life. It's our first time across – and I thought about my rash offer to you and how actually you should do it on a bigger boat with a more experienced crew. You'll get plenty of chances working here no doubt.'

He nodded, and then looked up with eyes that were overflowing with a longing for the sea. 'I really hope it goes well for you, and you get across safely.'

I wanted to hug him, but instead we shook hands before he turned and cycled off into the fog. I walked up onto the wharf and looked down on *Forever*, enjoying the sight of her rich, woody insides lit up so warmly in contrast to the clamminess of the gathering night. I wondered how long young men had been coming down to the docks in Halifax, propelled by dreams of going to sea. I strolled along the dockside, stopping to look at a beautiful old schooner whose golden-coloured wooden masts stood wrapped in fog. It was a poignant sight, like the last few trees left on a hillside that had once held a thick forest. I imagined the harbour as it would have been once, full of sailing boats of every size and type. In those days the pull of the sea must have been a million times stronger, but it was somehow comforting to find that there were still a few young people who were drawn by the romantic notion of maritime adventure.

TWENTY-FIVE

ON THE EDGE
OF THE ABYSS

Early the next morning we slipped our lines and headed out into the murk. I was steering totally by the chart plotter, as I couldn't see anything on either side. Halfway down, in the narrow channel between George's Island and the mainland, I called David who was at his station by the radar.

'Can you switch on the steaming light please?'

'Where is it?'

'On the panel in front of you.'

After an empty pause he called, 'Can't see it.'

I felt a flicker of irritation pass through me. 'It's on the panel in front of you David – it's marked!'

'Goddamn it, I'm looking, but I can't see it!' he shouted back.

Then I heard him methodically switching all the switches on the control panel.

'What are you doing?' I called down.

'I'm switching everything until I get the goddamn steaming light!'

And with that, the chart plotter screen went black as all the instruments were turned off.

I slowed our speed. 'David! You've turned off all the bloody instruments, you fucking idiot!'

There was a silence, and then he appeared at the companionway and pointed his finger at me. 'Don't you ever swear at me again Guy – I won't put up with it!'

We stared at each other in silence for a moment, and then I said, 'I'm sorry David. I shouldn't have lost my temper. But please turn the instruments back on now, or we're going to hit something.'

'I'll do that,' he said, descending the companionway. 'But just don't talk to me that way ever again.'

'I won't and I'm truly sorry.' I'd been out of order. And little did he know it but at that moment David taught me an important, if rather old-fashioned, lesson: that as a skipper it was my job also to remember my manners.

I knew it would take a few minutes for the instruments to come back on, so kept our speed as slow as possible, radioing Halifax control in the meantime to check no shipping was due to pass through the narrow channel. To my relief there was nothing, and soon the instruments were on again. We motored on in silence. We were now only hours away from a journey that could become one of our lives' defining moments, or just as easily put an end to our puny existence.

We pulled up to the Yacht Squadron fuel dock, waiting as a Norwegian-flagged sailing boat called *Royal Wings* filled up. I gave David a hug to say sorry for being rude and then climbed up onto the high dock, where the crew of the other boat were busy filling up tanks and jerry cans. They were around my age, with classic Scandinavian looks, blond and burly with the distinctive look of people who'd been travelling at sea. Like us they were clearly getting ready for a long passage. A heavily bearded man smiled at me. 'Hey, you waiting for fuel?'

'Yep. Where are you heading?'

'We're going home to Norway. And you?'

'Scotland. Where have you come from?'

'South America.'

'Me too!' I said.

He bent to fill a jerry can. 'Come over for a drink before you go, OK? My name's Kjetl, this is Lars and that is Andreas.' When they were finished they left the dock, and I watched as they pulled away and tied up to a nearby pontoon to load supplies. I passed David the fuel pump and stood by the machine, watching with dread as the numbers multiplied upon themselves beside the dollar sign. She kept filling and filling, interminably, like some kind of cruel trick. At last, at four hundred dollars, David called, 'She's full!'

I raised a hand wearily and walked slowly towards John's office to pay up. I still felt a little ashamed at my shabby attempt to negotiate a free berth, and was relieved to see that he wasn't there.

'Can I have your card, sir?' an open-faced kid asked and I handed him my shabby, worn-out bankcard. The card machine whirred away, and I stood staring at it and praying as the signal was relayed to our bank by some mysterious wizardry, and my request for money was weighed up against some hideous table of numbers. The machine bleeped once and REJECTED showed up against the sickly yellow backlight. I felt my heart plummet and my face tingle with the heat of embarrassment.

'Seems your card doesn't want to pay,' the boy said, regarding me with a face that registered no idea yet of the reality of the precarious-ness of money.

'Can we try again?' I said weakly, hoping that it had been a mistake, and wondering what would happen if not. David didn't have any money, and I had no other options. Would I be impounded, or taken to the police?

Right on cue as the machine whirred and beeped a second refusal the door swung open and in came John.

'Oh, hi Guy, how are you? Heading off today?' he asked brightly. He gave me a friendly look, and then his eyes wandered from me to the machine, and then the young boy, and back again. 'Problem?'

I gritted my teeth and nodded. 'My card seems to be on the blink – could be a problem with foreign banks maybe?'

He shook his head. 'Don't think so – the Norwegian guys used their card just a few minutes ago and it all worked fine.'

There was a silence, and I felt shame and embarrassment settling within me. 'John, can I just have a quick word with my crewman? I'm sorry about this.'

'No problem,' he said, frowning at the machine, in an attempt to protect my honour.

David took one look at my face and knew immediately what was up. 'Card rejected?'

I nodded. 'I've got a hundred dollars in cash – have you got anything?'

He laughed bitterly and shook his head. 'I'm the homeless man you met in a boatyard in Trinidad, remember?'

I slumped down on the quayside and looked across at the industrious Norwegians loading their boat up, feeling at a loss for what to do. It was time to call home. I went back to John's office, trying to seem effective and in control. 'It's no good John, my card seems to be faulty. Can I make a very quick international call?'

Without even a grumble he pushed the phone over. 'Sure, go ahead.'

I dialled Juliet's parents' number, where Juliet was staying as our house was still let out. We'd spoken a few times since we left New York, and I knew they'd all be following our progress closely. Audrey answered.

'Oh hi Audrey, I'm sorry to call early but is Juliet there?'

'No, she's gone out I'm afraid Guy.' She could hear that something was up and so spared the formalities. 'Have you got a problem?'

'Yes, a bit . . . is J there?'

'I'll get him now.'

I looked round and saw to my humiliation that the whole boatyard office was following the discussion. There was nowhere to hide.

J picked up the phone. 'Hello?'

'Hi J, I'm in Halifax . . . just about to leave but can't pay the fuel bill. Can I borrow four hundred dollars?'

With no hesitation at all he answered in his cool and wonderfully matter-of-fact way, 'Hang on, I'm going to give you my card number.' He read the number out, and as I repeated it the dockhand typed it into the machine.

'Thanks so much J – I'm so sorry to have to ask you for this.'

Without any hesitation he answered, 'Money comes and money goes – it doesn't matter. Just get yourself home in one piece.'

The machine accepted the payment and I signed off the call. John walked with me towards *Forever* and shook my hand. 'You be real careful out there,' he said with great kindness in his voice.

'Thanks John,' I replied. 'Hold on a minute.'

He waited as I went below and rifled through the stores until I found a bottle of wine that I'd been saving for a long time. I walked past David who gave me a panicky look, 'You're not givin' away the booze, are ya?'

'I have to David,' I said as I pushed past. I climbed the ladder and passed it to John.

'Sorry we've been such a bunch of hopeless scroungers. Thanks for all your help.'

He smiled. 'Any time Guy – good to meet you. Just be careful and get yourself home.'

I walked over to the Norwegians' boat to find Lars, Andreas and Kjetl sitting around their cockpit table, looking at an incredible machine that gave them radar and charts combined, as well as identifying the names and bearings of any shipping that came near to them. *Royal Wings* had all the latest technical gear, and as David and I sat staring at the screen we must have looked like a couple of tribesmen being shown a television for the first time. We knew that the chief danger we faced in the immediate future was being run down by a tanker in the murk, and this gadget would have made a welcome addition to our electronics. On the other hand, as a much lighter boat than *Forever*, *Royal Wings* was less well equipped to sit out very rough weather, and whereas we could use tactics like lying ahull they would have to try to outrun a storm, or avoid it altogether by clever weather prediction.

But we had no doubt that the crew would succeed, as their boat was the picture of efficiency. We promised to keep in touch with each other from time to time as we headed across and this comforted us to a degree, even though we knew we would be many hundreds of miles apart. When you venture out into the ocean, you do so alone. There was no getting away from it – nobody could help us.

David and I sat in silence within *Forever*'s dark, woody womb. We both knew that today was the day. We had filled *Forever*'s fuel tanks, done our repairs and stocked up on dry and fresh stores. The chart table was clear and ready, the ocean chart unfurled and in place.

'Breakfast?' I asked.

'Yeah, why not? Might be the last time for weeks that we can eat when everything is still,' he said.

I put the kettle on and slapped a few rashers of bacon in a pan. 'Tea or coffee?'

'As we're heading for the motherland I better get myself a taste for doing things right.' He winked and in a faux Scottish accent said, 'Let's have a wee pot of tea.'

It was a lame joke, but we both laughed. I felt faintly hysterical.

As the bacon cooked silence descended again, and I leant over the chart and walked my dividers across, counting the miles. 'Well don't worry David, we've only got two thousand one hundred and forty-seven miles of ocean to cross. We'll be there in a jiffy!'

He shook his head. 'Shit, that is one long trip ...' He pushed himself back, looked up through the butterfly hatch and said in a deep, beautifully gravelly voice, 'We are heading out into the realm of God.'

Neither David nor I were religious, but at this moment I wished I had faith in something beyond just luck and circumstance. Now more than ever it would have been good to pray, to light a candle, to read a holy book. Once we were more than six hundred miles from the coast we would be beyond rescue, and at the mercy of the whims of the sea. But there was no point in dwelling on it: it was time to go.

'David ...' I drew a breath, and he looked up with a dollop of egg yolk dangling on his moustache. The sight knocked me a little off my step and, feeling like the nautical equivalent of Jack Lemmon I reached over and passed him some paper towel.

'. . . It's time to go,' I said.

He brushed aside my paper towel, wiped his moustache with the back of his hand, winked at me gleefully and stood to clear the dishes. 'Yeah, let's get on with it.'

Outside everything was thick with fog, and I felt the familiar claustrophobia descend. I was working hard to swallow an instinct to panic, and when David came up and gazed into the murk I knew he felt the same. We looked at each other for a moment and then hugged.

'Good luck, good luck, good luck,' I muttered over his shoulder through gritted teeth.

He clapped me on the shoulder. 'We'll do it Skip, we'll do it.'

As we pulled away from the pontoon I thought of Juliet and the boys, and felt grateful beyond words that they were not with me now. If

I died, so be it, but my children had only begun their journey, and had no place out here. I looked back at the grey buildings of Halifax – there was no one to wave us off this time, no foghorns or cries of good luck.

David walked back along the deck from the bow, saying, 'Hey Skip, don't you know it's bad luck to look back at the harbour as you leave?' He patted me on the shoulder. 'I'll go and watch the radar. Wonder when we'll get outta this fog? Forgotten what a sunny day looks like.'

He climbed down the companionway, and then stopped halfway. 'Wait a minute Guy, today's Friday right? Shit! Friday is bad luck. You don't leave port on a Friday.'

I felt an ancient superstitious instinct rise up in me and then banished it, opening my arms wide. 'Hopefully the gods of luck will forgive us!'

He wasn't smiling, and I feared an early mutiny as he shook his finger. 'And another thing: I've heard you whistling a lot onboard. That's bad luck too – calls up a storm.'

'OK, whatever you say, no whistling,' I said hastily.

He went down below and switched on the radar. 'Can't see anything ahead Skip!'

I felt a sudden pull of deep love for the man. Whatever came I knew that he was brave, with the heart of a lion, and would never falter from the task in hand.

We hoisted sail, steering carefully as we cut across the steep seas in the entrance to the harbour. By the time we'd travelled 66 miles I had calculated that we would be far enough offshore to set us on a course to steer for Scotland. The wind blew at a useful 15 to 20 knots, and *Forever* threw herself into the job she did best: passage-making.

David was washing up below with great gusto, and I was starting to get over my nerves and enjoying the feel of being underway again. Suddenly I heard a crash down below, and then silence. A moment later David appeared at the companionway looking sheepish.

'Cafetière's gone,' he announced.

'What do you mean, "gone"?'

'I mean I dropped the fucking cafetière.'

I felt a surge of unreasonable anger, thinking of my carefully hoarded stash of Italian filter coffee. I'd bought it in New York with the sole purpose of keeping morale going across the miles that lay ahead. 'That's great David – you've consigned us to weeks of instant coffee!'

He looked down at the floor, shaking his head, and then looked back at me. 'Guy, I happen to be half-Scottish, and can't think of a better time to pick up the habit of drinking tea!' And with that he began brushing up the glass.

Soon the wind dropped and we motor-sailed, realising that the Labrador Current would be slowing us down. We had one thousand miles' range on engine alone, a little under half the journey, so whenever we could we had to sail. Whenever the engine was on, however, I made the best of it, and heated water, ran the fridge on full power and ran the water-maker as well. When the engine was off I would turn everything to its lowest setting, isolate the starter battery and get the wind generator on to keep the vital navigational systems and radar running.

We fell into a good rhythm as we worked our way east. Not once did David falter, despite having to contend with the constant pain and discomfort of trying to inject insulin as we crossed the lumpy seas over the myriad banks of the region. He kept his store of insulin in the fridge, and bravely joked that if the fridge broke down at least the lack of sunlight would help keep the stuff cool, yet it had me worried. If the engine stopped working for any reason and the wind was light there was no way that we could keep the fridge going: I made a fervent appeal to the gods that we would not have to start improvising with his medicine.

At 05.30 the next morning I was stepping down from my watch to make a note in the log when I noticed that the engine was overheating. I woke David.

'Are you any good with engines?' I asked hopefully, knowing that he had run his own fishing boat for years off the Alaskan coast.

He shook his head. 'Hell no, I had an engineer.'

I sighed. 'Well that leaves my piss-poor engine skills. You'd better get up and get ready for your watch while I take a look.'

I pulled up the engine cover to check it over and saw immediately that there was a leak in the coolant water pipe. I made a note in the log, and whilst David lurched about in the rolling ship getting his gear on, I turned the engine off and repaired the pipe, grateful that I had packed what on land had felt like a paranoid quantity of spares, but which now seemed threadbare when our lives depended on it. I topped up the coolant and started the engine, and with a jittery of sense relief saw that the temperature stayed within normal limits. Thankfully for now *Forever* had only needed minor heart surgery.

As David took over I took my gear off and stood poring over the chart in my underwear. We had made good time, and in three days had covered three hundred and sixty nautical miles, despite an adverse current, near zero visibility and a lumpy sea-state. I carefully entered our co-ordinates on the chart and log book, and stared at the thin pencil line that stretched out from Halifax into the Atlantic. After clearing Halifax, we had left Sable Island to starboard, a long, crescent-shaped sandbar whose nickname alone, 'the graveyard of the Atlantic' – and recorded 350 shipwrecks – was enough reason to give it a wide berth. Now I saw from the chart that we were heading directly for a zone of treacherous shallows over the Grand Banks of Newfoundland, and quickly plotted a course to avoid them.

'Steer 080 degrees David. I want to avoid the Virgin Rocks and some of that shoal water on the Grand Banks.'

'Steering 080 Skip,' he called down.

I closed my eyes and rubbed my face, feeling salt rub uncomfortably, and then fell exhausted into my berth, grateful to be off watch. I realised that I had learnt to trust David.

'Call me anytime David,' I shouted, and then fell into a deep sleep.

For days the fog continued to hold us captive on the sea, making us feel disorientated and out of touch with reality. I would sit at the helm staring up at the top of the mast swinging through the gloom, sometimes surrounded by strange birds that flitted about the navigation lights like great powdery moths. One night I sat at the chart table in the early hours of the morning, thinking about the Grand Banks beneath us, and all the lives that had been lost there. I thought about the ice that drifted down, carried on the shoulders of the Labrador Current – although the radio had given a favourable ice report for the region, one could never be sure that they had spotted everything. Sometimes, I had been told, great icebergs lay with only a foot or so above the water line, their keel-ripping jagged weight hidden beneath. If the ice report had been bad we would have had to stop *Forever* at night and drifted, to ensure that we did not hit anything at speed. We were passing not far from where the *Titanic* had gone down, the tragedy of that sinking being that if she had drifted at night, which was common practice, she might have been spared – she was doomed by her owner's plan to set a record time to New York.

I was sitting in the little circle of red light, trying to banish all morbid thoughts from my mind, when I heard a little fluttering sound and felt a breath of wind touch my face. There on the table was a delicate, sooty-coloured storm petrel standing on the chart, just off the coast of Ireland. It looked as if it had been created by the spare brush-strokes of an ancient Japanese artist, and a rather shocked look registered in its dark watery eyes. Its expression seemed to say, 'Just stay very still, and think of something quickly.' We stared at each other for a while, and then I reached down, gently cupped it in my hands and walked up to the cockpit. I wished it godspeed, opened my hands and it flew up towards the crosstrees on the mast, preening its wing before shaking insulating air into its feathers.

I went below again, my mind full of thoughts about omen and superstition. What would the ancient sailors have made of such a visit? I stared down at the chart trying to remember where the bird had stood and wondering if I should have circled the spot and avoided it later.

TWENTY-SIX

WE ENTER THE ARENA

46.20N: 52.48W

Finally, as we were nearing the Flemish Cap, the last of the shallow banks, the fog cleared. I yelled out to David.

'What is it?' he asked, clearly braced for the next disaster. But then he followed my gaze and looked ahead, and like a Zoroastrian sun worshipper, raised both arms and let out a throaty roar. 'It's the sky! Goddamn it the fog has ended!' We grabbed each other and jumped up and down. Scraps of blue sky appeared and the sea began to turn blue again as a dry wind blew across the boat. I shot down below and opened the hatches, and as the breeze blew in, the damp confines of our world began to dry. In an ecstasy of delight we hung our damp oilskins and hats up in the rigging and *Forever* seemed to laugh as she slung her shoulder down into the frothy water, carrying us ever further out into the endless wilderness.

'This calls for a celebration!' I went through the list of fresh stores in my head. 'How does a dainty cheese and onion omelette, wine and a fresh salad sound?'

'I love it Skip! Roll on Scotland!' roared David, steering *Forever* on into the depths of the Atlantic.

That night for the first time we could see the clear night sky, and we lay out in the cockpit staring up as *Forever* buffeted the water aside with a lusty zeal as if she too was relieved to see the way ahead. But then, as if the Flemish Cap had been offended by our happiness, the wind came at us from dead ahead and continued that way through the night and into the next day, when we found ourselves having to deal with 15-foot head seas. It was a bitter pill to swallow when we'd only so recently come out of the fog, and *Forever* was struggling. It became clear that we couldn't continue on this course and would have to steer either to the north or south. We opted to head north, but still the wind and sea battered us ceaselessly, and no matter what we tried nothing worked. The calm was banished and our world transformed into a rolling, pitching purgatory, from which there was no escape. Down below crockery, pots and pans and stores clattered about as the water thudded along *Forever*'s sides, often seeming to almost stop her in her tracks before forcing her down the sides of a nasty, broken sea. On watch there was no relief either, as we were surrounded by tumult, like a toy ship trying to get across a rumpled blanket. I thought of the endless distance still to travel, and thought that we would both die if this continued, out of sheer misery if nothing else.

When I was off watch I would prop myself up by the chart table, desperate to find a more comfortable course, but each time I called up a course to steer David would answer:

'No – can't do that one!'

Any kind of comfort had become impossible. Cooking, reading, washing, using the heads, navigating, steering – even just sitting down became stressful, yet we could do nothing but endure. We more or less gave up eating, and David had to suffer an additional layer of torture trying to inject his insulin. Sometimes I would pass his berth and see that he had wedged himself into a corner, desperate to create some kind of stillness. 'Shit!' I'd hear him mutter. 'Goddamn fuckin needles!'

After one endless day of pitching and yawing and thudding we sat huddled together in the cockpit. Dirty grey clouds were scudding across the darkening sky, and as if the prospect of another night of spray and dreary fatigue wasn't enough, it began to rain.

'Oh, great,' I sighed.

David shook his head and looked up at the sky. 'Yeah, if only this head wind would just give us a break – even just for one night.' We sat in silence for a while and then I had a moment of inspiration. We were simply wasting our energy in pointlessly battering on when the wind and weather were against us.

'Let's heave to for the night and carry on tomorrow,' I suggested. 'Who knows? Things might have changed by then, and at least we can get some sleep in the meantime.'

So with nothing but a mean scrap of sail up we hove to, and the world suddenly became a gentler place. After a boiled egg and some crackers we fell into our bunks and slept like tired riders, while *Forever* drifted uncertainly like a hobbled horse on some unknown expanse of barren and broken steppe land.

After ten days at sea, ten days of constant sail adjustments and attempts to deal with the adverse winds and water, everything suddenly changed. At dawn, as I watched the sun rising in the east, we entered a realm of profound and eerie calm. *Forever* began to flounder, her sails flapping and whumping and the boom jangling about. David was still asleep, and there was no need to wake him as we had nothing to do.

As the sun rose higher I lay back, and in between catnaps watched as the sky and water appeared to drift into one another. Soon the puffs of cloud began to reflect perfectly on the glassy water, and I revelled in the calm, at the same time knowing that it would cause us further problems as there wasn't enough wind to sail. I turned on the engine and set the auto-helm, and then went below to make my daily call to Juliet. I was calling in our position each day, so that somebody had some idea of where we were should something go wrong. At the same time she would pass on weather information as she charted our progress. I unfurled the antenna of the satellite phone until it poked out from the companionway, and dialled her parents' number on Mull.

I propped myself up on a step of the companionway so that I could keep an eye out ahead, enjoying the contrast between the suburban sound of a dial tone and my surroundings in the midst of the ocean.

'Hello?' it was Oscar's voice, clear as a bell. I felt the pain of separation sting my throat as I answered.

'Hey Oz – it's Dad!'

'I know that Dad! Who else would it be?'

It already felt like years since we had seen each other.

'How does it feel to be home at last big boy?'

'It's great Dad! Are you in the Atlantic now?'

'Yes.'

'What does it feel like?'

'Well at the moment we're in a calm – there's no wind at all. But we've been going through fog and then head seas, and it's been rough . . . I think you should be glad you're not here.'

'How far have you got to go?'

'Oh, about one thousand seven hundred miles.' I tried to sound breezy, as if it was just a hop and a skip, but he knew what that meant.

'Still further than our ten-day passage! That's ages.'

There was a silence and then I thought about the re-charging of the phone, and said quickly, 'Oscar, can you get Mum? Sorry we can't take longer – give Luke hugs and kisses from me, will you?'

'OK Dad.' He sounded muted, and I remembered when I was in Alaska, four years before, and he had cried whenever he spoke to me by satellite phone. I had cried too afterwards, feeling impotent and ashamed of not being there with him and for him.

'Guy?' It was Juliet.

'Hey Jules: here's our position.' I read out the co-ordinates.

'All OK?' she said briskly. 'Still got that headwind?'

'No, it's totally died on us, which is a relief in some ways. But now we're having to motor, so I hope we get a breeze again soon. In the right direction this time – and not too strong,' I said hastily, in case King Neptune was listening.

'Yeah, well, I don't think this calm will last too long Guy, I've been watching the forecast. You've got a bit of a blow coming your way, from a good direction, but it looks like it's going to get quite strong. Still a couple of days away, but . . . you'd better get ready.'

My heart sank: I'd known that the odds were that we'd get a storm at some point during the crossing, but had been hoping against hope that we'd be lucky. 'Well keep an eye on it for us, will you Jules? Not that you can do anything, but it's nice to get a bit of advance warning.'

We signed off and I sat staring at the great wide nothing. It felt as if we had been at sea for an eternity, yet I knew that we must have at least two, maybe three more weeks ahead of us before we got anywhere near land. In normal life this doesn't seem long, but on an ocean passage it feels like for ever. I pulled myself up into the cockpit and was scanning the horizon for shipping when I heard the distinct and joyful puff of a dolphin expelling air. I peered into the water, desperate to receive the sense of blessed good luck and wellbeing that always comes with dolphins. I looked around in a fever of hope, yet there was nothing but silken sea. I walked forwards and stood at *Forever*'s fizzing bow, holding onto the furled staysail and straining my eyes for a sight. Nothing. Disappointed, I turned to make my way back to the cockpit, and then spotted the first one, hurling itself up and flapping its powerful tail fin in the air as it plummeted back into the water with barely a splash. Then, like a javelin thrown at a wave, it flew up again and rushed along the surface, splitting the water along its dorsal fin like a salmon in a Highland stream.

I called and I sang and I whistled, forgetting all about David's superstitions, and it seemed to work, as the water broke all around *Forever*'s bow with scores of dolphins, jumping and spinning and spiralling along the white smile of our bow wave. I dropped down and lay on the bow quarter to watch, reaching down as far as I could into the water and the dolphin edged up as close as it could beneath the flashing mirror of the water as if it too wanted me to touch me. I strained but just could not reach far enough. Dark thoughts circled in my mind about the irony of falling overboard for this reason. David was fast asleep, and would have woken to find an empty ship long after I was gone. Suicide would probably have been the logical conclusion: nobody could guess that I could be stupid enough to fall into the sea in an ecstatic bout of dolphin spotting.

I shot back to the cockpit to get my camera, even though I knew that I could never capture this fantastic, unearthly moment. It was as if we had sailed into the midst of a fairy circle. The dolphins swam fast on their sides so that they could look up at me, and between us the water became a clear river of glass as we stretched towards each other's worlds. I heard more puffs of air, even smelled their fresh fishy breath as we were so close, and looked up to see another group hurtling and jumping and charging towards the boat. I yearned to touch one, and reached out as far as I could with my fingertips, holding on with one arm as a dolphin swam closer and closer to the surface, its body a speeding and pulsing natural bullet made of impossibly fast piscine muscle. Yet despite being framed in movement the creature's eye remained still and steady, focused only on me.

Later the wind came up enough to sail, and as I lay in the darkness in my berth, below the water level, I heard the glorious sound of the dolphins clicking and squeaking to one another. We had gained a cohort of angels, and I felt strongly that as long as they swam with us we would be safe.

HARD TIMES

48.17N: 41.37W

We were passing over another realm now, and where before the depth had been in the forty to sixty fathom range now the chart showed that there were two thousand fathoms of water beneath us. We continued on our heading just north of east, making fast progress in a good wind. As we watched the sun go down at night we reduced sail, hunkering down into the darkness and superstition of the night hours and then yearning for sunrise as our primitive ancestors must have. In the morning I was at the helm, staring east towards the lightening sky. It was heartening that our way home led towards the sun, and as each night closed down behind us at least there was comfort in the knowledge that we were a day closer to home.

A thousand miles from Newfoundland, I made my daily call to Juliet, and she carefully marked our position on the huge chart of the Atlantic that was permanently out on the kitchen table. It was comforting to know that she was keeping track of our day-to-day progress as we sailed through the great lonely wastes of the mid-Atlantic. I knew that she didn't regret her decision to take the boys home, yet there was a certain wistfulness in her voice and I knew she wished she could have been sharing the experience. Yet we kept our calls very brief as we both knew that we could not allow the floodgates to open. To dwell upon emotional issues or family matters would not do me or her any good as my job had to be just about one thing and one thing only: getting across the great wilderness alive. But this time she sounded worried.

'Guy, that depression is right behind you, and it looks bad. You'd better get prepared.'

I pictured the tight isobars on the weather chart. It was hard to take seriously at that moment, with the skies clear and the wind still light. We both knew that *Forever* wasn't fast enough to outrun it, and with the wind in this direction we couldn't radically alter course. There was no choice but to wait it out. There was a pause and she spoke again.

'Keep calling every day Guy, and be careful – wear your lifejacket and stay clipped on. And don't take any risks.'

Later that morning the wind completely died, and *Forever* slowed as we passed through a lumpy zone of water. I sat staring at a gaggle of seabirds that had rafted together for the night. I watched them stretch and flap their wings as they woke, and take tiny sips of salt water, bobbing their heads up and down as if greeting us curtly as we passed. I wondered where they were going to, a thousand miles out in mid-ocean. As the sun rose higher I brewed mint tea and sat staring out across the immense plains of water, lost in thought. A movement on our starboard side caught my eye, and I lifted the binoculars and saw the brown, sandpaper-coloured side of a large shark dawdling about on the swell. It detected us, and I watched in horrified fascination as it suddenly lost its purposelessness and shot over to us at great speed, scything through the water until it was only a few feet from where I was sitting. It was a large oceanic white tip, and as I watched it nose around our hull, looking for an opportunity, I sensed that we'd lost the good luck of the dolphins. There was a sailors' superstition that shark sightings were bad luck on boats, and I could see why, as it was distinctly sinister watching this ocean equivalent of a junk-yard dog sniffing around us. I sensed that things were about to take a turn for the worse.

David emerged from below and stood in the companionway. I decided not to share my gloomy predictions with him, and was instead just about to open debate on our favourite topic of the day – breakfast – when I realised something was up. He looked dishevelled and was unsteady on his feet.

'David? Are you OK?' I asked, and he smiled sweetly, then jerked his head up to look around. He hauled himself into the cockpit and nearly stumbled, just catching himself at the stern rail.

'Whoa, David!' Something was clearly very wrong.

'It's OK Guy, it's OK, I'm fine,' he said, and then tried to sit up on the rail as if it were a step on a porch or a low wall, rather than the only barrier between us and the sea.

I held his arm, and tried to pull him in. 'David, that's really dangerous. Please don't sit there, you'll go over the edge.'

He yanked his arm away from me and rushed over to the other side of the cockpit. I saw that his bad foot was bleeding, and knew that he must have bumped it and split the thin skin.

'David! Go below. Now!' I reached over to guide him to the top of the steps, but he resisted and stood rigid, holding tightly to the binnacle: it seemed as if he couldn't hear or understand me and I wondered if the worry and confinement had finally made him crack. I managed to get him down into his berth, but sensed that soon he would be wandering out again. I looked about and saw the rack of knives in the galley, and immediately grabbed them all, opened the galley hatch and threw them out. I hid the dividers and looked about for anything else that could possibly be used as weapon, such was my worry that David had lost his sanity. An unreasoning anger rose up in me that nobody had told me that David had suffered from mental problems, as I was suddenly convinced he must have. I rigged up the satellite phone and called Juliet.

She answered, and without any preamble I said in a fervent whisper. 'David's gone nuts – he's acting really strangely – he's not talking, and his movements are all jerky . . . He's not safe on the boat Jules, he's ill. I think I might have to try and find a way of getting him off the boat – how can we find out if there are any ships in the area?'

'Hang on Guy, you're panicking. Sounds to me like he's having a hypoglycaemic attack – you need to do something about it quickly.'

Suddenly it all made sense: how could I have been so stupid? The irregular meals, the broken hours, the difficulty of keeping a regular routine around his injections. All of that must have contributed to the situation we now found ourselves in. How could I have forgotten what he told me? I cursed myself. 'What the hell do I do?'

'I don't know, but I'll find out. Call back in ten minutes.'

I hung up, wishing she were with me, and cursing both David and myself for not discussing this eventuality. He'd begun to moan, and I found him in a state in his berth.

'What do you need David?'

He swung around and gripped my shoulders, and I stared into his eyes, which reflected a world of inner turmoil.

'Do you need insulin?' He widened them and began to howl and blabber, clearly unable to talk.

'Noooooooooaaaaaaahhhh', he seemed to be saying which I reasoned was definitely not a 'yeeeeeeeeeeaaaaaaaassssss' sound, and racked my brains for what to do.

I glanced at my watch: ten minutes was up. I called Juliet.

'Guy, call this number – it's Sandy, she's going to tell you what you need to do.'

I hung up without a word and dialled the number.

'Hi Guy,' she answered in her gentle voice.

'Sandy, David's really ill, and I'm pissed off that nobody told me about this!' I hated myself for being angry, but I couldn't hide it.

'He's having a hypo,' she said, ignoring my outburst. 'Get something sweet into him – orange juice, yoghurt, whatever.'

I hung up and poured some orange juice, stirred in a couple of tablespoons of sugar and took it into David's cabin. He was now slumped on the floor and I held my hands around his shivering hand and guided the tin mug to him, relieved that he didn't put up a fight. I watched as he drank, and then mixed him another, and then helped him into his berth.

I checked on him during the day, and he seemed to be sleeping peacefully enough as we sailed on. In the afternoon, as I stood at the chart table I heard him cough, and found him slumped again on the floor of his cabin, leaning his head on his arms. As I looked down at him I realised how much more of an achievement his journey across the Atlantic was going to be than mine.

'David? Are you OK now?' I asked, and he nodded his head.

'Yeah, I just screwed up in managing this thing for a bit. I'm sorry Guy.' He gave me a wobbly smile.

I was relieved, but at the same time, still angry. 'Thank God you were just able to keep me from giving you insulin.'

'That would have killed me,' he said wryly.

'Jesus Christ!' I muttered, contemplating burials at sea. 'David, I need to know this isn't going to happen again. You need to manage things better otherwise I'll be looking for ways to get you off the boat. All I need to do is issue a Pan Pan on the radio and I'll stop any boat going back to the US and put you on it. I've got enough on my plate here without you dying on me.'

I knew I sounded unsympathetic, yet I had to be brutal: it was his responsibility to keep himself a well and functioning member of the crew.

He nodded sadly, and I softened. 'Bring on the land, hey?' I put a hand on his shoulder.

He tried to smile, repeating gamely, 'Bring on the land!'

Later I found him in the galley making coffee. 'Hey, where did all the knives go?' he asked.

'I threw them over the side because I thought you were going to turn into Jack Nicholson.'

'Oh shit! The sailing yacht *Shining*.' He let out his signature set of giggles, and it felt good to have him back in fine kilter.

As evening sank over us, while David patched up his foot, I called the Norwegian sailors and chatted with Kjetl. He confirmed Juliet's warnings about the weather, and what I'd seen for myself on our weather grids. 'Guy, bad weather is coming – we're all going to be in the shit for a while I think.'

'What you going to do?' I asked.

'We're heading south – *Royal Wings* is fast, we hope to outrun it. And you?'

'I suppose we'll have to run with it – got no choice really.'

'Good luck my friend.'

'You too. Let's speak again soon.' If we survive it, I thought.

The next day I sat at the helm watching the sun rise ahead of us in the east. After the darkness of the long night hours the sunrise brought hope back again. Through the false dawn I had been lost in a kind of sea reverie. The wind and water and fizzing progress of our boat underway had entranced me. I looked about and saw that the day would be good. Fair weather clouds filled the sky. I heard David down below putting the kettle on before shouting up his morning greetings. The wind was in a perfect place, abaft the beam, and I let all our reefs out of the main and gradually eased out all of our sail. The sheets tightened and the winches creaked as *Forever* caught the wind and channelled the power. Gradually with all of our sail out she began to come alive. It felt like letting a horse break out into a gallop after hours of holding it back. The darkness of the night was gone and now our world was transformed into one of elemental movement and sound. The wind rose steadily to 30 knots and then held. *Forever* leant over powerfully into her tack, throwing her sixteen tonnes through the seaway, smacking waves out of the way and bursting through the swell, throwing glittering green water over her shoulders. I watched the shattered water catch the light of the rising sun and sparkle for a moment before thudding on the foredeck and running in an obedient stream down *Forever*'s sides and out through her wide scuppers. We were now flying along at 9 knots, yet I held it all lightly with just two fingers on the helm.

David came up and whooped, his face lit up and full of joy as he leant in the companionway looking ahead. *Forever* was doing what she was built to do, making way just as our ancestors did thousands of years ago, long before someone sat in a shed and built an engine. She had became a wild living creature seeming to be made more of the wind and the water and the elements around us than anything a man could make. David turned to look at me and I could see his eyes were full of tears. I realised that this is the moment that sailors live for – when nothing on earth matters but the direction of the wind and the state of the sea. We were alone riding on the tip of a waterborne comet thousands of miles from the claustrophobia of the land and all of its pettiness and meanness. I raised a hand and called out to David to take over and he smiled and took the wheel and sailed *Forever* on. We were united that day by our shared and soaring love for the sea. We tore through 140 miles of ocean, and as night settled we said goodbye to a very happy day.

Fate now had other plans for us – the wind and sea became more sinister by the hour. And the next day we realised that *Forever* was in the grip of a building storm. Gradually we reduced sail, and as the wind reached a steady 40 knots we sailed on under staysail alone. In the space of just a few hours our world had changed completely, and we could no longer do anything but work to keep *Forever* and ourselves safe. Behind us the waves formed with malicious certainty, their blue-grey floors rising and falling. Where once there had been silken distance, now there was nothing but a terrible broken terrain made up of great slipping weights of water. There was no point in looking at our course or position: all we could do was deal with the here and now, and hope against hope that one of these monsters didn't get the better of us.

As the hours went on the seas rose higher and higher until we found ourselves traversing turgid valleys and screaming wind-whipped mountains of water that were like nothing I had ever seen before. The dolphins had returned, and this time I felt envious, as it seemed that the more afraid we became the more they enjoyed it. Their world had been transformed into an amusement park, and they jumped and twirled and surfed with glee down the ever-steeper sides of the waves. The wind was now gusting to 50 knots, and howled around us, whipping the wave-tops into a fury. And then the clew of the staysail ripped clear off, and the sail flapped out wildly. I made a perilous journey forwards to take the sail down, and lashed the boom down hard as *Forever* surfed at over 8 knots down the sides of the 30-foot waves. We streamed warps behind us in a vain attempt to slow her progress, and I cursed myself for not buying a sea anchor in New York, instead having spent the money on a great night out with the family. We clipped on our harnesses, and I watched over my shoulder as the monsters loomed up on our starboard quarter, turning our stern towards the biggest of them and steering along their tops in an attempt to prevent us from being swamped.

But it was hopeless. We were little more than a cork on the surface of this mean, malevolent sea. David and I held on grimly, wet and cold and tired and frightened. The wind had now not dropped below 50 knots for some hours, and was continuing to rise, the seas responding gleefully and growing steeper all the time. And then I felt things ratchet up into something else, and I glanced at the wind speed indicator to see it read 60 knots as *Forever* sank into valleys of water that were at times almost higher than our 55-foot mast. The spray had become so intense that I could no longer see to steer *Forever* out of harm's way when the truly big, breaking waves reared up. My eyes stung with the salt, and I knew it was only a matter of time before one of us made a serious mistake. I remembered an article I had once read in a sailing magazine, where the writer had suggested wearing a mask to deal with spray. I reached into the locker below the helmsman's seat, grabbed my mask and put it on, but quickly realised that his advice was not based on experience, as looking through it was like driving without windscreen wipers in heavy rain.

Night was not far off now, and the wind was so powerful that we had to scream into each other's ears to be heard.

'This is equivalent to a category one hurricane,' David roared into my ear. 'I've never seen seas this size, and I fished in Alaska!'

'It's bad – I don't know how long we can keep going. One of these waves is going to break over us sooner or later.' I remembered Harold O'Shaughnessy's advice. 'I think we should lie ahull.'

It was a serious moment, as we hadn't had to resort to this before, and had no real idea whether it would work. The thought of going below and leaving the boat to her own devices was terrifying, but the alternative was worse. It was growing dark, and soon we would have even less visibility, and less chance of steering out of harm's way. The odds were that at some point a monster wave would break over us, and if we were out in the cockpit we'd stand no chance.

We put on our survival suits, and then I made a call to the coastguard in Falmouth on my satellite phone. They were too far away to help us, but I hoped to get a weather forecast, and establish contact in case things should go wrong.

'Sailing vessel *Forever*, your position please?' The clipped British voice was reassuring. I gave her our position and names, then asked if she could give any indication of the weather to come.

'Standby.'

I held onto the phone in the half-light and wedged myself against the ship's bucking sides.

'Sorry Mr Grieve, you have more to come I'm afraid. You are currently in a storm that is forecast to become a severe storm. Can you give me details of next of kin please?'

I gave her Juliet's details, thinking darkly: so this is how it works – we even fill out forms before we die. I told her that we were going to lie ahull, and that we were wearing survival suits, and would keep in touch as we approached Britain.

'Thank you Mr Grieve, please do that. We will keep your wife informed of what is going on.'

I replaced the radio handset and looked round at David. 'OK let's give it a try.'

LYING AHULL
51.47N: 26.04W

We were both dreading the moment of turning *Forever*'s bow to face the waves at an oblique angle, which for a time would make us very vulnerable by lying beam on to the sea. I took my place at the helm, then stood looking over my shoulder and waiting for my chance, which came after a wave had broken, leaving us on the floor of a white valley before the next one. I turned the wheel fully to port, and then quickly lashed it to the port winch, tying it down with a nylon rope that gave some elasticity, so that the jarring effect of falling down the waves would not damage our rudder.

We huddled in the companionway to see if it had worked. *Forever* felt steady, and as the wind and water pushed her eastwards I noticed that her deep keel was disrupting the water to windward, and that the waves seemed to falter on this broken water and break early, lifting us up on their white shoulders. Most of the time she seemed to be slipping out of danger, and was certainly safer than when I'd been steering. Down below, I flopped into my sea-berth in the semi-darkness, thanking the lords of luck again for my seasickness patch, as I might well have died in these conditions without it. The motion inside was incredible, and it seemed almost impossible that *Forever* could withstand this battering as she pitched and yawed, plunged and crashed, sometimes flat on her side.

Cooking was impossible, and crackers and bottled water were now our main source of nourishment – it was impossible to move around. It felt awful, lying inside our pitching box at the mercy of fate, with nothing that we could do to save ourselves. Not for the first time on this journey I felt reduced to the size of an ant, our survival or otherwise being utterly unimportant in the scheme of things.

The storm continued to rage around us for two full days. Every now and then I pulled the hatch back and popped my head out to see if there was any sign of things improving, but each time I got the same terrifying view of the apocalyptic world around us. As *Forever* rose to the top of a wave and teetered there for a moment I looked west, and all I could see was rank upon rank of foam-streaked, occasionally breaking waves marching towards us, like an army of Orcs advancing from Mordor.

Due to the lack of proper food I was worried about David having another attack, but he kept up with his injections and never once faltered despite the extra hardships that he had to endure. One night I lay in the darkness, fearfully feeling the sea surging all around, and then I heard what I can only describe as a great white roar coming towards us. I gripped the sides of my berth and shouted to David, 'Hold on! Something big is coming!'

'Don't I fuckin' know it!' he shouted back, just as, for the first time, a wave broke right over us. A curtain of water shot through the butterfly hatch and landed in my lap, forming a dark puddle. I looked down at the little pool of salty water and saw phosphorescence glittering like welder's sparks. My sombre imagination dredged up a half-remembered line from a poem by Shelley, which gave me no comfort: 'Some coffin'd in their cabins lie . . .' I was trying to remember more when we rolled so steeply that I thought we were going to capsize, and saw green on the portholes on the deck, which meant they were beneath the surface. This is it, I thought, imagining her mast reaching ever closer to the sea. But then we slowly righted ourselves, and I thanked God for *Forever*'s heavy keel as I heard the signature fizz that told me that the wave had passed.

I lay back and allowed myself a little grin, as I remembered the Norwegians saying that wearing green on boats was taboo in their country. I had thought it silly at the time, but now I understood the basis of that fear. It felt very strange to find myself locked within the dark insides of a sailing boat reeling in a violent storm hundreds and hundreds of miles from land. If *Forever* had rolled there was a good chance that she might have gone straight down, to say nothing of the injuries that David and I might have sustained. I crawled over to the hatch to check the wind speed, and saw that the anemometer had broken. Perhaps it was just as well, I thought – sometimes it was better not to know.

When the storm continued unabated into its third day I was in despair. I didn't think that we could take much more of it – it seemed only a matter of time before something broke, leading to disaster. The only good thing that could be said of it was that it was taking us in the right direction, and we were still roughly heading towards Mull. But we still had a long way to go, and on my daily call home I spoke to J.

'Any advice?' I asked. I knew he'd been following my progress with Juliet and monitoring the weather.

'Head for the south of Ireland. It's much closer, and you can sit out the storm there. Or carry on up the Irish Sea, which will be sheltered with the wind in this direction.'

It was good advice, and I called Kjetl shortly after. We could barely hear each other over the screaming of the wind and water, as they were in the storm too. 'Shit, you're right in the middle of it,' he said when I'd told him where we were. 'Are you OK?'

'Yes, just, but it's been fucking awful.'

'We've been worried – we heard a sailing boat was missing.'

'Maybe you have too much technology for your own good Kjetl!'

'What will you do next Guy?'

I told him of my plan to head for Crosshaven on the south coast of Ireland.

'Maybe we will do the same, but we're well south of you. Be careful and goodbye.'

As I hung up I thanked God for the millionth time that we had not brought the boys across with us.

TWENTY-EIGHT

THE SWEET, BEAUTIFUL
SCENT OF IRELAND

52.17N: 20.48W

At 4 p.m. on 12 August, I emerged from the companionway for the first time for three days. The worst of the storm had abated but the sea was still steep, with 15- to 20-foot waves that occasionally reared up higher. I pulled back the hatch and called down to David.

'Brother! It's time we carried on.'

A kind of apathy had set in between us, as if having handed ourselves over to fate we no longer had the will to carry on. It was a dangerous mindset to get into and we had to force ourselves onwards, as to linger was to risk another storm. We hoisted a scrap of sail and let *Forever* loose once more, surfing our way towards Ireland.

Three days later we glimpsed the severe cliffs and rocky shoreline of Mizen Head on the south west corner of Ireland and the lighthouse at Fastnet Rock. It was joyful to hear voices on the VHF radio and to know we were once more in contact with the outside world, and as we listened to the rich Irish voices we both agreed that there could be no better accent to welcome us back to land. We stared in wonder at a few houses perched high up on the cliffs, overlooking the immensity that we had just crossed. But we didn't have long to glory in our arrival, as the wind suddenly blew up, and we found ourselves caught in a violently tidal zone of steep, sharp waves.

The wind was blowing strongly onshore as we approached Cape Clear, and the current was also taking us fast towards the coast. On our port side was the Fastnet Rock, the site of the fateful race in 1979 that caused so many deaths.

'Hey Guy, don't try and sail this one will you?' David said, looking worriedly at the shoreline.

'Why not, we'll make it won't we?'

He looked towards the white surf smashing against the rocks and then turned back, angry this time. 'Please turn on the damn engine and get us outta here, this place is giving me the creeps!'

'OK, OK, let's do that.' I held up a hand in surrender, thinking to myself that it wouldn't do to leave it too late and then find that the engine wouldn't start.

We kept well off that unfamiliar coastline as we were buffeted by bad weather, and then had to stand off for the night as it turned into a full onshore gale. We were exhausted and sick of being bashed around, and it felt frustrating to be so close to land and yet unable to bring this torment to an end. At one point, off my watch, I vomited in the forward head – the first time in the Atlantic crossing that I had been sick, perhaps due to my tiredness coupled with desperation for it all to end. Being close to land was no guarantee of safety – quite the reverse in fact. The Fastnet Race played on my mind, as did the fact that we weren't far from where the *Lusitania* ocean liner had gone down in 1915 with over a thousand people on board, having been torpedoed by the Germans.

On Saturday 16 August we at last made our final run for Crosshaven, gradually drawing closer to the green hills of Ireland, that seemed to glow in an almost clichéd illustration of its nickname,

Emerald Isle. It felt ominous to think that now, having passed close to the place where the wreck of the *Titanic* lay rusting, we would enter the harbour that had been her last port of call. We steered into Cork Harbour, and then turned up the Owenboy river towards Crosshaven.

The sides of the Owenboy were, compared to the torrid wastes we had just crossed, a picture of domestic safety. The rich scent of grass and soil was intoxicating after the monotonous briny scent of the ocean, and we breathed deeply, feasting our eyes on the intimate, and at this moment beautiful, sight of houses and gardens and normality. Drake had famously hidden his fleet from the Spanish up the Owenboy in 1580, and it felt wonderful to find ourselves creeping up the same protected waters after all of the hardship of the crossing. We spotted the village of Crosshaven tucked into a bend in the river, and approached the boatyard. In neutral, and at a snail's pace, I came gently to a stop beside a pontoon.

Feeling almost dazed with relief, we switched off the engine and sat quietly together in the cockpit. The enormity of the moment was hard to take in: we had crossed over 2,000 miles of open ocean and we were safe. It was over.

I looked at my watch. We'd been at sea for twenty-two days straight, and what eventful days they had been. 'Well done David,' I said, feeling almost shy for some reason. 'Welcome to Europe. That truly was something.'

He clapped me on the back, rather awkwardly, and I could see he felt the same. 'You've done good Skip. We're almost home.' He shook his head, saying, 'Oh my God – I can't believe it. I'm finally in the Home Isles.'

We sat for a few more moments in silence, each struggling with so many thoughts and emotions that we couldn't begin to articulate. And then I heard the man who'd taken our lines on the pontoon clear his throat politely.

'Erm, hello.'

I stood, and he stretched out a hand. 'My name is Emmitt. Welcome to Crosshaven. Have you come far?'

David and I looked at each other and laughed, and Emmitt smiled, looking a little confused.

'There's a great pub over there when you get settled boys,' he said, pointing behind him. 'Come over and have a beer with us when you're ready.'

David's face lit up. 'Oh my God: booze!'

Without bothering to wash or change, still dressed in our overalls and boots and salty and greasy after many days at sea, with great ceremony we stepped off *Forever* and walked towards the pub very, very slowly on wobbly legs, savouring every step on solid land, and staring at ordinary things as if discovering them anew. Halfway there we stopped and hugged, still unable to believe that we'd made it and full of gratitude and relief that we were alive.

At Cronin's we walked into the public saloon and stood staring, everyone stopping their conversations to look round at these two oddballs that had washed up on their shores. It was a charming place, clearly owned by a hospitable magpie and festooned with random collectables from boxing gloves to old black and white pictures and stuffed animals. We walked over to the bar and smiled at the owner, who looked like an affable version of Alfred Hitchcock.

'And where have you two come from?' he asked.

I looked at David and then answered, 'Halifax.'

'Oh yes, came down the North Sea, did you?'

'Halifax Nova Scotia.'

He raised his eyebrows in surprise. 'You must have had a pretty bad time out there – we've had some very bad weather. In fact the highest waves ever recorded have been hitting the west coast of Ireland this past week.'

David and I smiled and nodded. It was too early to put our experience into words.

He leant forward. 'Now, what'll you be having?'

Feeling like a character from the nautical version of *Ice Cold in Alex*, I asked for a Carlsberg and said jokingly, 'But only if it's ice cold.'

'The cheek!' the owner said mock-disapprovingly, before turning to David, who pushed back his moustache in readiness and then ordered the same.

He poured the two delectable cold pints and passed them over, saying, 'This is on us – and lunch too. Welcome to Ireland.'

I felt a thrill of love for all mankind.

Then David held up his glass and said, in a voice rich with emotion and humour, 'The road to wisdom can only ever be found through the gates of excess. Cheers!'

He raised his glass, and everyone sitting at the bar did too, and instead of the endless barrage of wind and sea and the creaking of our beloved ship, we now heard a sweet sound: laughter, and the chorus of happy human voices.

The Norwegians came into harbour the day after us – their flag, like ours, was almost in shreds – and I saw on their faces the same disorientated looks that David and I must have had when we first stepped ashore. We all hugged one another as if we were old friends, rather than just people who'd spent a couple of hours together a few weeks before. We had been brought closer by our shared experience and we had survived the same appalling conditions at sea. Actually, our situation mirrored the tortoise and the hare fable, as the much faster *Royal Wings* had been forced to divert her course to outrun weather that we, in a heavier boat, had been able to withstand. It had been a hair-raising ride for them, running before that storm.

Shortly before leaving Crosshaven we passed by Cronin's on our way to the village shop. David gave me a friendly nudge.

'Hey, there's a yacht club here that might take the burgee – the *Royal* Cork Yacht Club,' he said with relish, pointing further up the river. 'It's the oldest yacht club in the world apparently.'

I waved him off. 'Forget it! I'm not going through that again.' Then I had a flash of inspiration. 'Wait a minute – I have the answer! I'm going to present the burgee to Cronin's. After all, a yacht in port needs repairs and good grub and beer more than anything else, doesn't it?'

So that evening with the crew of *Royal Wings* as my witnesses, I dropped to one knee before Sean Cronin and presented the travel-worn burgee to him to mark the place of our safe arrival.

'Mr Cronin, on behalf of mariners throughout the world, amateur and professional . . .' I looked about and saw that everyone looked a little bewildered. My eyes darted over to David, who muttered:

'Go on! You're on a roll!'

'Yes, errm, I present this burgee to you and your fine establishment, in appreciation of your kind hospitality and welcome.'

With an amused look Sean took the burgee, saying, 'You're welcome at Cronin's lads! Safe travel home.' I knew it would happily join the rest of the memorabilia that crowded the walls of the pub.

After a final celebration we made our way back to *Forever* and fell happily into our bunks. I felt a sense of victory, proud that we had come so far. Many times during those three weeks I had salved my feelings of fear or discomfort with a little mantra that I would find myself repeating in my head over and over again: 'The boys are safe, the boys are safe, the boys are safe . . .' Every time I'd looked into their little cabin I'd felt deep relief that they weren't inside it, suffering fear, seasickness or boredom, or most likely all three.

But our journey was not yet over, and the knowledge we'd gained in the north Atlantic would help us negotiate the testing waters of the British Isles. Shortly before we were due to leave I wandered up to Crosshaven boatyard, where I fell into pleasant conversation with the wonderfully urbane owner. Crosshaven has a very long association with sailing, and Francis Chichester's *Gypsy Moth V* had been built there, as well as Tim Severin's traditional leather-bound boat, which he bravely sailed across the North Atlantic in order to investigate whether St Brendan's journeys could have been possible. I had heard fearsome stories about the storms and currents in the Irish Sea, and was hoping to get some local knowledge to help us get through it as quickly as possible.

'You'll want to speak to the boys across the road there,' he said. 'They do yacht deliveries, and run boats up and down all the time.'

I wandered over to their Portakabin, with David and the Norwegians in tow. As none of us had had haircuts or been any too diligent about shaving, we must have looked like a bunch of Neanderthals out hunting. We crowded through the narrow doorway into the little office, in which two men were enjoying their morning coffee. They greeted us with the characteristic Crosshaven hospitality, and we crowded round the chart.

'How can we get up here quickly?' I pointed to the Sound of Jura, on the west coast of Scotland, which was not far from Mull.

'You'll have to play the tides and currents right,' said one of the men. 'That your boat down on the pontoon?' he asked, and I nodded. 'Some sea-boat – they're built sturdy, those double-enders.'

He leant over the chart. 'The trick is to slip through the banks here,' and he pointed to the southeasterly corner of Ireland, where the chart revealed a series of terrifying shallows and treacherous rocks and shoals. Feathered arrows indicated the great currents and tidal races around the area.

David drew in a breath and mumbled, 'I'm starting to miss the Caribbean,' and the room filled with laughter.

'Oh, if the weather stirs up you don't want to go close to these banks – they'd chew you up and spit you out fast.' He flashed a piratical grin. 'But if the weather's good you leave Coningbeg Light to starboard.' His work-roughened finger tapped the beacon on the chart. 'Then you slip through here, and here . . .'

As he drew lines with his pencil Kjetl read out the name of one of the many shoals. 'Lucifer Bank,' he said, and looked at me. 'That is the name of the devil, am I right?'

I grimaced. 'What about the tides?'

'Ah.' The man grinned again. 'We have a trick which we will happily share with you. It's very simple: leave here 21 hours before high water in Dublin. The tide will take you all the way up.'

We stopped in a little huddle outside the boatyard and hugged each other, and I wished the Norwegians good luck on their journey home. I suggested that they come to Mull on their way back, but knew that with the weather being so changeable as summer came to an end their priority would be to get home as fast as possible. Their plan was to pass through the Caledonian Canal to Inverness, where they would wait for the right time to cross the North Sea.

Later that day at 4.30 p.m., exactly 21 hours before high water in Dublin, we slipped our lines and motored out of Crosshaven, bound at last for home. The tides and wind whipped us along at a solid 7 knots, and the evening was perfumed with the scent of rich agricultural land. As the apple-sweet fragrance of silage drifted out across the cold sea it was a reminder of our true place on earth, and the gentle embrace of the land, which we had begun to yearn for.

At 2 a.m. I was down below making a note in the chart when I heard a Mayday message being relayed by the Holyhead coastguard. I turned the volume up and sat with a pencil, ready to mark any details onto the chart. A yacht named *Flagrancia* was sinking, and I felt a deep chill as I visualised what her crew were going through.

That night David and I stood watch with extra care, aware that we were soon going to try our luck in some very tricky waters that we would never have attempted without local knowledge.

The weather seemed OK, and so at 7 a.m. the next day we shot through the banks like an Olympic javelin, the currents speeding us on our way at 8 to 9 knots. We navigated our way through the banks, trying to not lose our calm as we saw waves breaking on the shallow water all around us. One wrong turn and we would have run aground. We said very little as we cut our way along; each of us was lost in the task at hand, which was to get home in one piece.

At 4 p.m. we slipped into Dublin Bay and, as we could no longer afford the luxury of a marina, dropped the hook in the first suitable spot that we could find. We laughed when we saw that the bay was named Scotsman's Bay. Clearly plenty of broke Scots had stopped off here on their way home before.

Our tails were up, and the next morning at first light we hoisted anchor and charged on. The radio crackled with endless gale warnings, which were sometimes then retracted in the turbulent and unpredictable weather that was typical of this time of year. After a while we began to ignore them, charging on in the grip of the tide which ripped us north at a dizzying pace. But by late afternoon the wind was howling in earnest from the south, and the seas got up quickly as we knew they would in these shallow waters. I had marked various anchorages on the chart where I had hoped to stop for safe shelter overnight, but in these conditions they all looked untenable. Another gale warning was issued, and we stared at each other with grim resignation.

'Can't we just have one easy-going fuckin' day?' David sighed. 'For God's sake – I'm starting to feel tense with all of this shit!'

The radio crackled again. 'Will these guys please just make up their minds?'

It was growing dark, and I realised that if conditions continued to deteriorate we would not be able to risk going in anywhere, as the growing southerly gale had turned the eastern shore of Ireland into a potential boat-wrecking ground. I looked over towards the Isle of Man on our starboard side, and remembered local advice to never go near the place, as it seemed to have its own unique ever-changing treacherous weather system. We had seen far worse in the Atlantic, but here we felt in even greater danger as we had no searoom and were never far from rocks and shoals. Compared to the wide Atlantic the Irish Sea felt almost like a river.

Before we knew it the gale had settled around us in earnest, and I thought of the irony of making it across the Atlantic unharmed only to be wrecked within spitting distance of home. I strained my eyes towards a light beacon that marked the entrance to an inlet where I'd thought we could anchor overnight, but saw that its rocky coastline was frothing with the white of endless breakers. The wind was blowing us fast onshore, and I felt panicky.

'David, we have to get more searoom,' I shouted. 'We're too close to the coast!'

I tried to sound calm though I knew that if our engine failed or we had any other problem we would fast find ourselves in a terrible situation. We altered course to try to steer further offshore, but soon found ourselves having to deal with very steep seas that were breaking far quicker than anything we had found in the North Atlantic. There the waves had only broken at 30 feet and over, but here, due to the shallowness of the inshore waters, waves were breaking at 15 to 20 feet. If we ran with the seas we would certainly be run aground, but turning away from them exposed our vulnerable beam to the hungry-looking waves. But this seemed the lesser of two evils, so we struggled on, making as much to the east as we safely could, and then whenever we saw a killer wave breaking we would quickly spin the wheel to kick *Forever*'s rounded stern into the side of it, helping her to slip away.

I went below to look at our options, and saw that our only safe course would have to be to head for Belfast Lough. I plotted our course and then went up to give David the news and he sighed and shook his head. 'I got a feeling I would take up some other kind of hobby if I lived here,' he said. 'This high latitude stuff is something else!'

Just then the radio informed us of what we already knew, that we were in a gale and that this gale was forecast to become a severe gale. Thankfully we cleared the wave-wracked coastline and flew north as night fell, keeping a keen eye out for shipping, landmarks and the steep waves. At last, we sighted the light of the Mew Island Lighthouse that marks the southern entrance to Belfast Lough, and just as quickly realised our dilemma. To get into the loch we would have to turn west, thus taking the full force of the gale on our port side. There was no choice but to attempt this, however, as any other course of action was more dangerous still, and the thought of a night in the infamous current strewn North Channel in these conditions was truly terrifying.

'OK David, are you ready?' I shouted from the helm.

I gradually brought *Forever* around until we pointed more or less west, with her bow up as close as I could safely get it to the weather to make our run for safety. I looked towards the giant seas charging in at us, then my compass, then the depth gauge and then the staysail, and called to David to keep an eye on our engine speed and temperature. As we drew nearer the great yellow-white beam of the huge lighthouse swung its arc across us, revealing the ferocious sight of waves breaking on every side, spray hurling across our decks. Every now and then *Forever* faltered, and I had to spin the wheel to point her bow even more sharply into the weather so that she could right herself and carry on. The wind was screaming, and despite our best efforts the lighthouse still seemed so far away. I longed for shelter, yearned for escape and prayed for refuge, until at last we drew abeam of the lighthouse where lights glowed from within the keeper's cottage. I wondered if he had been watching us all this time, as our masthead light grew gradually nearer through the tumult of the storm. As we approached, we caught the heavenly scent of wood smoke, carried to us by the gale winds that whipped over the slates of his roof.

'Hey David, can you smell that?' I shouted.

'Sure can!' he roared. 'What I wouldn't give to be curled up beside that fire now with a bottle of rum and Sandy beside me!'

And then suddenly we were out of it as we came into the lee of the land. The gale disappeared as if someone had simply just turned off a switch and the waves gradually died down to a pleasantly rolling swell. We dropped the hook in Ballygowan Bay opposite Bangor, and I stood watching the anchor chain rattling away into the dark water until I felt *Forever* pull up happily on her leash. I let out thirty fathoms of chain, erring on the side of caution, as only half that was needed. But there were no other boats near us, and I wanted to spoil myself with the excessive luxury of knowing that we had a huge amount of weight on the seabed to hold us safe. I heard David clang the kettle down onto the stove and knew that he was brewing up, and I dropped onto my knees and kissed *Forever*'s bow. I whispered as one might into the ear of a secret lover: 'I love you my boat, I love you for keeping us safe, for never letting me down.' And it was true: I had just then fallen in love with my boat. It had not happened in the sunny waters, or even across the Atlantic. It had come now, just two days from home, as the reality of what she had done for us was hitting home.

Many times people had referred to *Forever* admiringly as a stout, salty, solid or true blue-water boat, but only in these past few weeks had I fully appreciated just what that really meant. *Forever*'s weight, her heavy keel, rounded lines, conservative sail plan and short, sturdy mast all meant that when things got really bad, seriously bad at sea, we still had a chance. To a large extent, if one judged it right, one could leave her to her own devices, like I once trusted my dog team to take me home through whiteout blizzards in the depths of an Alaskan winter.

'Hey Skip – a brew?' David asked as I came below.

I shook my head. 'Screw the tea David – let's have that bottle of rum!'

We had hoarded our last bottle of rum all the way across the Atlantic, and without a second thought David poured the steaming mugs down the sink-hole. 'I really hoped you were going to say that Guy,' he laughed.

We poured out monster measures of rum and flopped back around the wooden table, just as the radio announced that the severe gale had officially begun. We raised our glasses to each other and drank to the inexpressible joy of safe harbour in a storm. Later we listened in on terse messages between the lifeboat and a number of craft in trouble, and thought how easily it could have been us.

TWENTY-NINE

TOBERMORY HARBOUR

56.37N: 6.3W

'**D**avid wake up! Today is an historic day!'
I shook my old crewman until he opened an angry eye and muttered, 'Now what?'

'I have a good-morning cup of tea for you.'

He sat up and pushed a hand through his bedraggled hair. 'Why the special treatment?'

'Because today, my beloved crewmate – today we will see Scotland at last.'

'Scotland.' He pulled himself up and looked at me, his eyes shining. 'Can you believe we're almost there? It feels so much longer than a month since we left New York.'

We lifted the anchor and slipped out of Belfast Lough, and skirted along the coast below the dramatic high ground of Antrim. Then, with the Mull of Kintyre in full sight, we steered *Forever* out across the North Channel. For a while we made good progress, until the tide held us in place, so we added the might of the engine to sail power, which took us to the grand speed of 3 knots. Impatiently we urged *Forever* on, waiting for the flood to help take us north.

Once into the Sound of Jura the sun broke through the cloud and the familiar landscape of the west coast of Scotland opened up around us. The sparsely inhabited Mull of Kintyre stretched out on our starboard side, and to port we saw the beautiful high islands of Islay and Jura.

David looked around, lost in wonder. 'It's so remote! Reminds me of Alaska or Canada, somehow I never thought it would be like this. Damn, I can't believe we're in Scotland. I'm just so happy!'

I felt ecstatic too. 'Hey David, you know your mother would have passed out of Glasgow just on the other side of that.' I pointed to the Mull of Kintyre peninsula.

He stared over. 'Yeah, my mother, I wish we could have seen this together.'

The radio crackled into life. 'Gale warning, gale warning, gale warning. This is Clyde coastguard. Gales are expected in the following areas: Malin . . .'

'That's us,' I said.

'Oh great, here we go again!' David said, slapping the caprail.

This time I didn't want to leave it so late to head for shelter, but the wind came up quickly, and once again we found ourselves in the teeth of another ferocious southwesterly gale as we anchored in Tarbert Bay on the tiny island of Gigha. The wild wind whipped the water around us into spray, and we felt as though the gods were throwing one obstacle after another at us in an attempt to prevent us from reaching home.

The next day we hoisted sail again and charged for Mull, determined that we would not stop until we reached Tobermory. I called home and Oscar answered.

'Ozzy! Tell Mummy that we will be in Tobermory tonight!' I shouted.

'Mummy! Daddy's going to be home tonight!' I heard yelps and whoops as celebrations broke out.

'Guy?' It was Juliet.

'We'll be home tonight!'

'We can't wait to see you!' She sounded a bit tearful. 'Is David in good shape?'

'Yes, he's ecstatic! I can't believe we're almost home!'

But still the gods had one more trick for us, and just opposite the Gulf of Corryvreckan, the sea alive with currents and eddies, pockmarked with innumerable rocks, we were hit by a squall of strong wind and rain that was so thick that visibility was reduced suddenly to zero. *Forever* heeled hard over and I called David. 'Get up here quick – I need to get some sail down!'

'And I need to get back to the Caribbean!' he shouted as I frantically pulled in the jib. And then the squall passed and we shot through the sound of Luing and pulled out into the Firth of Lorne, laughing at the steep waves as we knew from hard experience that *Forever* would effortlessly slip out of harm's way. The wind filled our sails and we flew on, battering aside the water and slipping glecfully down the sides of the swell. Ahead the magnificent high ground of our island home soared out from the wild blue-grey sea. Sea birds wheeled and called to each other and the sun picked out the myriad variations of colour and shade that can only be found in the Hebrides.

David stood by my side, marvelling at it all. 'This is such a beautiful island!' he said. He was right. Amongst all the islands I had seen, all the countries and regions and climates and continents, Mull stood out as one of the most dramatic, the most magnificent, and to my eyes – at this moment at least – the best. We whooped and hollered and called out, and as we passed beneath the shadow of Duart Castle at the south east corner of the island David looked up in awe.

I anticipated his question: 'Twelfth century I think.'

He shook his head with disbelief.

We charged on up the Sound of Mull, and I revelled in the sight of all the familiar landmarks as we passed the Grey Rocks, the

Green Isles and Aros Castle. At last we glimpsed the entrance to Tobermory, and rounded Calve Island to see the most beautiful harbour in Scotland. The harbour was quiet and the water was still as glass. I looked at the multi-coloured houses along the front and experienced a surge of the most incredible happiness. I pulled back the throttle to dead slow, and looked around for Juliet and the boys. Then I heard voices calling: 'Dad! Dad!' and heard car doors shutting, and Juliet was driving around to the pontoons, waving and hooting. I motored across the mirrored surface and gently came alongside, exchanging ecstatic shouts with the family as I came in past a bemused-looking visiting sailing yacht.

Juliet took the warp from David and held it on a cleat, and at last *Forever* was made fast, safe in her home harbour for the first time. I went below and turned the engine off, and then stepped off the boat and fell to my knees on the pontoon, holding the knot of my family in my arms. Behind me David stood shyly, and then we all stood and hugged him too.

Juliet looked over *Forever* lovingly, checking for damage. 'Good girl for keeping them safe,' she said, patting her caprail, 'I knew you would do it.' She stood back and stared at her. 'I can't believe that *Forever* is actually here, in Tobermory,' she said. 'She's come so far, and yet she looks perfectly at home.'

And she was right: *Forever* had settled down with the same equability that she had always shown – from uncharted coral islands off Venezuela to fog-strewn Nova Scotia, she had taken everything in her stride. Here she was in Tobermory, having travelled over 10,000 nautical miles in less than one year.

After fetching a few things we drove back to our house. Everything felt new: the car, the roads, the house, beds: normality had taken on the flavour of extreme novelty, and though I knew it wouldn't last long, I was enjoying the feeling. The next day we got together with friends and family on the pontoon to mark the end of our journey. *Forever* became a floating play park as everyone's kids crawled all over her. I had just overruled an instinct to lecture a boy who was hanging from the boom when I noticed a boat in full sail entering the bay. I narrowed my eyes. Surely it couldn't be – the timing would be too perfect. But then I saw a frayed Norwegian flag playing out in the stiff breeze and realised that, unbelievably, it was *Royal Wings*.

'It's the Norskies!' I shouted. David, who was carefully pouring an immense glass of champagne lethally mixed with brandy, looked up and followed my gaze towards *Royal Wings*, now expertly coming into the neighbouring berth.

'Well I'll be damned!' he exclaimed, and handing the bottles to a bewildered child, stepped over the guard rail to take their lines. Once tied up, the four young men bounded ashore, blond and ruddy faced and as full of energy and good health as ever. I introduced them to Juliet and the boys, and we exchanged the kind of embraces that can only come from those who have shared and understood what it means to have survived a great reckoning with the ocean.

It was just one more moment of camaraderie, one of many that we'd experienced. We had discovered the best of humanity amongst the world's small-boat sailing community, and that moment when the Norwegians arrived seemed to sum it all up. We had all been belittled by the sea, levelled and frightened out of our wits by it. But we had also been ennobled by the lessons we had learnt, and the values we had discovered on the water and its edges.

Yet already, not far behind the smiles, were the first seeds of sadness at having to let go of this way of life and return to normality. We had found true meaning in the great watery regions of the world, free of petty officialdom and the tinsel of modern life. We had been lucky to tap into an older, slower world, based on the enriching values of self-sufficiency and independence, living with minimal fuss and clutter whilst leaving a very small imprint upon the surface of this jewel-like planet. But our time was up, and reality had come home to roost as we were flat broke. We'd spent all our savings and taken on a huge amount of debt to make the year at sea work, and had little to show for it in terms of qualifications or wealth. But if life experience was our currency, we were now as rich as oil barons. As we walked from the harbour we stopped to look back at our boat, all movement and action over now, as she lay easily on her worn mooring warps. We stood in silence until Oscar said quietly; '*Forever* would like to just keep going . . .'

AFTERWORD

This journey, for an ordinary family like ours, would be much more difficult to make happen now. When we planned our adventure in 2007, the world was a different place. It was a time when easy credit was on offer everywhere and banks were only too happy to lend you money without knowing or much caring what you were going to spend it on, or whether you had the means to repay it.

Of course we were aware of the unfolding of the financial crisis, and had followed it from a distance, but occasional radio reports and glimpses of days-old newspaper headlines did nothing to prepare us for the Britain that we came home to. During the time we were away the entire atmosphere of the country had changed, and almost overnight we found ourselves transported from a world full of openness and sunshine into grey misery and depression.

Reluctantly, we settled back into life on land. The children were re-enrolled in school, and had once again to come to terms with spending their days indoors, sitting down, confined by the weather, timetables and routines. As our tans faded, so did our prospects. With my newspaper column finished we had no money coming in and few opportunities in these increasingly straitened times. Debts had to be cleared, and with a sense of grim inevitability we faced up to the fact that we would have to sell *Forever*. With deep sadness we parted with our precious boat, who had carried us safely well over 10,000 nautical miles. Nothing can ever replace *Forever*, who had been the centre of our universe for one whole year. She had become part of us and to walk away from her was gut-wrenching in the extreme.

And then – it was time to earn a living. In a twist of fate, the sea which had almost bankrupted us now offered a way ahead. Desperate for cash and short of options, I began diving for scallops with two seasoned local divers in the cold grey waters surrounding the Isle of Mull. And thus a new story began.

But no matter what the consequences, in the years since our return we have never for one second regretted the wild and irresponsible decision we made to risk everything we had, including our lives, to go and live at sea. Our hope is that one day we will be able to return to that way of life, which has been a benchmark for every experience since.

ACKNOWLEDGEMENTS

I am grateful to Richard Atkinson, Natalie Hunt, Xa Shaw Stewart and many others at Bloomsbury for being endlessly patient with me. This book took a long time to write, for the simple reason that when we got back to the Isle of Mull the world had completely changed, and we were flat broke and in trouble. I will never forget Richard's kindness and support during this rather difficult time. And thanks so much to Gillian Stern and Caroline Knight for being such good, patient editors – and thanks, as ever, to Euan Thorneycroft at A.M. Heath.

And now on to our journey: above all else there is Juliet, who proved the ballast of the whole adventure. Mother, wife, skipper, crewmate, navigator, nurse, cook and friend – and often all at once. By the end of the journey we'd proved what I had always suspected to be true, that there is no better wilderness team on earth than that of a man and a woman. Our sons, Oscar and Luke, aged just seven and four when we left, must be thanked for their unshakeable faith in us (not always justified) and for their resilience even when things were tough.

Juliet's father J had the unenviable task of teaching us to efficiently run a rather complicated sailing boat. His contribution was vital in the early days and may just have prevented me from running us all into maritime oblivion. Juliet's mother Audrey was a stalwart presence both on the boat and on the other end of the phone, and she made the great discovery of a remedy for my seasickness.

In the Caribbean, Bob Phillips at Doyle Caribbean in Tortola saved the day when our mainsail ripped. He generously fitted us a new, excellent mainsail which survived the worst the North Atlantic could throw at it. In Trinidad, we will never forget the kindness, humour and profound warmth of the people, who were among the most welcoming we came across. The men and women at the Powerboats yard were unceasingly efficient and cheerful, and amongst all the many tradesmen who helped us I'd particularly like to thank Brian for working miracles on *Forever*'s decks, and Tony who worked wonders on her woodwork. We met many new friends at the legendary shark-bake, amongst them Jan and David, who made our time spent living on the hard in the sweltering heat and dust of Chaguaramas much less painful.

Throughout the Caribbean and America we encountered so many good people: in creeks, up rivers, alongside docks or anchored beside remote coral cays – each of these deserve a chapter of their own, such was the endless display of kindness that one finds amidst the floating world. Jon at Coinjock looked out for us when we had engine trouble, and then lent us his car, refusing payment even though he had only known us for three hours. The team at Oxford Boatyard in the Chesapeake finally solved the mystery of our faulty water-maker, saving us from the briny water we'd been drinking for several weeks. When we arrived at the pinnacle of our journey in New York City, surely one of the most exciting harbours on earth for any small boat to sail into, the friendliness of the people was unequalled. With an incredible view of Manhattan, Newport Marina gave us free berthing whilst we prepared ourselves for the immense challenge of the Atlantic crossing. We met many friends there, including George from the New Jersey fire department who welcomed me into his family, insisting on treating me to dinner at his mother's restaurant and giving me the best of Italo-America – tough but full of heart.

In Halifax Nova Scotia, thanks are due to John at the Royal Nova Scotia Yacht Squadron for treating us with respect and decency even though he could see that we were clearly trying to scrounge a free berth (which he did not give us, such was his professionalism). In Ireland we were given a huge welcome by Sean, Thecla, Denis and Joleen who own and run the wonderful Cronin's in Crosshaven. They gave us succour as only the Irish can in the form of food, drink and friendship after David and I had endured the horror of a severe storm in the North Atlantic. Then there were our fellow wayfarers across the North Atlantic, the Norwegians or 'Norskies' as David titled them: Andreas Vik, Lars Henrik Sutterud and Kjetil Belbo, who should have been my brother.

Which brings me to one of the biggest characters in our journey, David Pettigrew. How can I ever forget or repay this man, who shared with me the highs and major lows of bringing *Forever* across the great merciless North Atlantic? I will never forget David's beautiful positive spirit of adventure, his sheer tenacity and strength in the face of every obstacle life and the ocean threw at him. He met every challenge with a smile, and to me represented the absolute best of what it is to be an American: positive, liberal, generous and brave.

And finally I think of all the people we met along the way. Individuals and families who had rejected the confines of life on land, electing instead to live humbly and simply afloat. These are true individuals, constantly tested by the sea, who counter the cliché that you need to be rich to live on a boat, often making it work with very few resources. Yet they are richer than most as they are citizens of a realm defined almost completely by the elements, peopled by the best kind of humanity on earth.